Vol. 4

Vol. 4

Published by NRM Books.

ISBN: 978-1-965179-07-9

CREDITS
Cover Art by: Nathan Reese Maher

COPYRIGHT

Table of Contents

The Mysterious Warnings

By Eliza Parsons

CHAPTER 1

No sooner had the struggling soul escaped from the clay-cold body of Count Renaud, than his eldest son, Count Rhodophil, hastened to the library, and opening the secret cabinet, where his late father usually deposited his papers of consequence, after a strict examination of the contents, returned to the anti-chamber, on the floor of which lay extended his brother, the deeply-afflicted Ferdinand, just recovering from a fainting fit, and overwhelmed with inexpressible anguish.

"Brother!" said Rhodophil, in an accent of grief and tenderness, "Brother! here is my father's will, and I have little doubt but that you will find he was your father also, and that, however severely his resentment was expressed in his life-time, he has not extended it beyond the grave, nor forgotten, in the disposal of his effects, that he had a younger son, and a grand-child."

Ferdinand, who had been lifted from the floor, turning his eyes on his brother with a look of fixed sorrow, exclaimed, "His will! Alas! what have I to do with that? He expired without seeing me, without granting me, all I ever wished for, or expected, his pardon, and his blessing! O, Rhodophil! my friend — my brother — why, why did you not urge him to pronounce me forgiven in his last moments, to revoke that curse, which now weighs me down to the earth with sorrow and remorse!"

"Did I not urge him," replied the Count, "Did I not supplicate him on my knees in your behalf? Did I not beseech him to consider your situation and his own? Unjust Ferdinand to reproach me — me, who have for three years wearied my father with tears, supplications and entreaties, to forgive and receive you to his paternal arms! What have I left unsaid, or undone, to convince you of my brotherly affection?"

"Pardon me," cried Ferdinand, extending his hand: "Forgive me, my dear brother, I know my inexpressible obligations to you; but grief, despair, and heart-rending retrospections, deprive me of my reason. O, my father! to the grave, even beyond this world, hast thou carried thy hatred and reprobation of thy wretched son! How great, how good, how benevolent, how forgiving to all, was Count Renaud! What then must my crimes have been, in what magnitude must they have appeared to him, thus to draw down everlasting resentment!"

He covered his face with his hands, and throwing his head upon the bosom of his brother, wept aloud; his whole frame was convulsed, and Rhodophil was obliged to call for assistance, that he might be conveyed to a bed, where it was some hours before the extreme violence of his feelings subsided into a melancholy silent sorrow. His brother and the steward of the late Count remained with him, and when they found the turbulence of grief had a little abated, the Count again mentioned the will.

"As it may be possible some particular orders may be given respecting the funeral, and more than probable that the contents of this packet may speak peace to your wounded mind, it is necessary, my dear brother (continued he) that we break the seals." — — —Ferdinand bowed an assent; speech was denied him at that moment, the principal domestics being summoned to the apartment, Rhodophil broke the seals, and delivered the packet to the steward.

"Do you read it," said he; "neither my eyes or my heart will permit me to do it." — The steward obeyed. There was a schedule of his estate and effects, which in a few words Count Renaud gave to the entire possession of his dear and dutiful son Rhodophil, 'a few legacies only excepted to his servants.'

"How!" cried the Count, "all, what all to me! Impossible! Is there no mention made of my brother?"

"No, my Lord," replied the old man, delivering the papers with a look of sorrow; "no, I have too truly read all the contents."

Not a word escaped from the lips of Ferdinand; at that moment riches or poverty was indifferent to him, nor could the wealth of nations have given him peace or comfort, when unaccompanied with the forgiveness of a parent.

"How cruel, how unjust!" cried Rhodophil; "but he knew my heart. Yes, my dear brother," added he, embracing Ferdinand, "our father well knew that in giving all to me, he had procured to me the inexpressible delight of voluntarily sharing it with my brother. Henceforth (looking round on the servants) know you have two masters; my brother is equal with me in fortune, power, and command."

The servants bowed and withdrew, all but the faithful and affectionate Ernest, who had been upwards of twenty years steward to the late Lord, and had ever fondly loved the unhappy, reprobated, Ferdinand.—Rhodophil reiterated his caresses, and tender expressions: "We will no longer be separated (said he;) your Claudina, your little Charles, shall be equally dear to me, as to yourself."

Ferdinand started up:—"Claudina! my Claudina!" repeated he, "Well, have you reminded me, I left her oppressed with sickness and sorrow."

"Hasten to her, then," said the Count; "let her be removed to the Castle immediately; accommodated here, she will soon be restored to health."

Rhodophil withdrew; his brother taking Ernest by the hand, "My worthy old man, your looks bespeak a sympathizing soul. —You read my heart: Oh! Ernest, it is not the loss of riches I deplore, my brother's kindness will relieve me there; but a father's curse, carried beyond the grave! there, there's the wound that never can be healed. My wife, poor, poor Claudina! how shall I return to tell her the sad event, already sinking under sorrows she thinks she has deserved—in her situation too!"

"Dear master, dear Sir," cried Ernest, "I beg you to take comfort, the worst is now past, I am sure, I know my late good master forgave you in his heart, his mind never, never, harboured eternal displeasure and resentment. Things are contrary to my expectation; but—I dare not say all I think, nor will it avail now; but I beseech you, Sir, to hasten home to your poor dwelling, from whence you shall quickly return with all that is dear to you; I will prepare every thing, and then follow you."—With a heavy sigh that seemed to burst his heart-strings, a look of inexpressible grief, Ferdinand wrung his hand, and with slow and trembling steps repaired to his humble habitation in the suburbs of Baden, about a mile from the Castle of Renaud.

When his footsteps reached the threshold, he stopped, and paused: "The truth will kill her (cried he:) Sure, if ever deception was pardonable, it may be now; yet how dearly have I already paid for the violation of truth! Heaven pardon me, for I must deceive her. Alas! one deviation from rectitude is productive of innumerable errors which spring from each other, and plunge us rapidly into guilt!" He entered the house at the very moment when his unfortunate wife had given birth to a daughter. The intelligence pierced his heart: "Another burden on the bounty of a brother!" exclaimed he, softly as he passed to the room where his Claudina lay. The sight of her instantly banished every idea, but anxiety for her safety.

He flew to her, "My love! my wife!" She fixed her feeble eyes upon him: "I am become a mother to another poor unfortunate. Ah! Ferdinand, have you found a father?" What a dagger to the heart of her husband was this question!

"All is well, my love," answered he, struggling to repress his emotions: "Compose your mind, and expect happier days; the moment you can be removed without danger, we shall reside at the Castle."—She uttered a faint exclamation of joy, and fainted. Ferdinand was terrified, and blamed himself for his abrupt communication; but happily she was soon restored, and capable of rejoicing at such unhoped-for intelligence.

"You are no longer reprobated then," said she, tenderly kissing his hand, "no longer consigned to misery, and our dear infants will not endure the pinching gripe of poverty. Blessed, blessed Count! you have at length relented, and I may think existence a blessing." This apostrophe was more than the unhappy Ferdinand could bear. Unable to speak, he hastily left the room; his poor deceived wife judging what he must feel from such a (supposed) revolution in his circumstances, imagined he had withdrawn, that their mutual transports might not too much agitate her spirits; a thousand pleasing visions floated in her brain, and to have her husband restored to a father's love, to have her dear children rescued from want and misery, were such delightful considerations, that she was not sorry she could indulge them freely, and repressed her curiosity for particulars, satisfied that the event was certain.

Mean time Ferdinand sat lost in thought, and overwhelmed in wretchedness, the kindness of his brother afforded no compensation for the unalterable displeasure of his father, nor could he reconcile to himself, that determined hatred which one error (in his eyes a venial one, and not deserving such everlasting resentment) had drawn upon him, as at all consistent with the benevolence which had always formed a distinguished feature in the character of the late Count Renaud. Tormented by these painful conjectures he was found by Ernest, who came to acquaint him, that he had given orders for apartments to be instantly prepared for him and his family, and was come to wait on his Lady to the Castle.

Ferdinand, roused by the entrance of his good old friend, soon informed him of the impossibility of their immediate removal, from his wife's situation, and also of the deception he had been compelled to give into. — "She does not as yet know of my father's death (continued he;) her too susceptible heart would sink under the knowledge of what my sufferings must be in such circumstances; by degrees, as her strength returns, I must reveal the dreadful truth: — But, oh! my friend, I cannot live a burden on the bounty of a brother, something I must resolve on, and if his kindness protects my wife and children, I will endeavour to support a separation from all that is dear to me, and carve out my own fortune by my sword.

Ernest had nothing to answer against this resolution but affectionate regrets, he had but too much cause to think the intention would be as necessary as it was becoming in a young man of spirit and honour; therefore he only hoped, "that his dear young master would do nothing rashly, but wait until his wife and children could have some certain independence secured to them."

"How! (replied Ferdinand) would you have me limit my brother's bounty, or seem to doubt his generosity and kindness? How contemptible should I appear in his eyes by a bare suggestion, by the remotest hint, that I wished for any certainty more than what I may rely on from his affection and generosity, so recently proved on an occasion, where not one out of a million would have conducted themselves with that nobleness of spirit, that true fraternal affection Count Rhodophil has manifested."

"I presume not, Sir," answered Ernest, respectfully, "to dictate, or even to advise you; but, nevertheless, as we are all mortal, subject every hour to be suddenly deprived of health and life, as we can no more answer for our own hearts than for our own lives, as it is possible Count Rhodophil may marry, and new engagements may give birth to new sentiments; all these natural occurrences may happen, and both for your children's sake, and for his honour, it would be better to place a circumstance, of so much consequence to your family, beyond the power of chance to injure them."

"I own (said Ferdinand, after pausing a few minutes) I own what you say is both wise and prudent; but such a proposition as relates to any settlement must originate with my brother.—No selfish proposals, no narrowness of heart, shall mark my conduct, or render me less generous than himself."

Ernest sighed, but was silent.—The other observing his dejection, added: "You know, my old friend, that Rhodophil's mother was a woman of very superior birth, with a much larger fortune than my mother could boast, who, though by no means despicable, yet owed her elevation to my father's rank, more to her beauty than hereditary claims, therefore my brother's generosity is the more estimable."

"You, Sir, are the best judge (replied the steward) and I hope you will forgive my presumption, which is directed by true affection to your interest."

"I know it well (answered Ferdinand) but now, my good Ernest, return, and acquaint my kind brother of the event, which must preclude us from removing for some time. In the evening, or to-morrow morning, you may expect me, for I have a melancholy duty to perform, from which nothing shall divert me."

The steward bowed, and was about to retire, but stepped a few paces very reluctantly; then suddenly turned—"Sir (said he) I hope you will not be offended if I presume to leave this purse; when you are settled at the Castle, you may return it." He laid the purse upon a chair, and hastened out of the house.

"Good creature! (exclaimed Ferdinand) I will not now mortify thee by a refusal of proffered kindness, because now I know I shall have it in my power to repay the money, and reward thee tenfold in thy estimation, by my attentions and marks of gratitude."—He strove to stifle his painful reflections by procuring several little necessaries and indulgences for his Claudina, which in her situation were wanted, and which the fear of not being able to supply had tormented him for many preceding days. She received and enjoyed them with delight, as the proofs of a parent's returning affection.—In the evening, when Ferdinand was sitting by her bedside, and she observed the deep gloom that every now and then pervaded his features, in spite of all his efforts to appear happy. She looked at him several moments in silence, then pressing his hand: "My dearest husband (said she) from whence proceeds that sorrow which clouds your features, and seems to fill your eyes with tears? Tell me, have you deceived me into hope, or is your father's forgiveness fettered with conditions that distress your feelings? Your looks correspond not with the joyful intelligence you communicated this morning. — Tell me, I beseech you, what there is behind which is a drawback upon such an event as I thought must have insured your happiness."

Ferdinand endeavoured to recover himself, and by a little evasion prepare her for future communications. — "Your penetration, my dear Claudina, cannot be eluded; know then that the state of my father is such as inclines me to think it is almost past a doubt, that you will see him no more. I see you are affected (added he) but you know he has long been ill, and therefore such an event may be expected; compose yourself, however, and do not let me be doubly afflicted; to-morrow I shall see him again; perhaps, at my return I shall be in better spirits." —

"Heaven grant it (returned she, sighing.) Ah! what a world is this, so chequered, that seldom any good arises without its concomitant share of evil!"

"True, my love (answered Ferdinand;) but then reverse the picture, and thank our bounteous Father that almost every evil to our imperfect view, brings with it some alleviating circumstances we cannot always foresee."

"Yes (returned she) perhaps we are indebted to his increased weakness, and expectancy of death, the very pardon, and favour he has accorded to us. Would to Heaven, however, that I may once more see, and thank him on my knees for his goodness to you and my dear infants!"

Ferdinand could not stand this, tears gushed from his eyes, and, throwing his arms round her, he freely indulged them. She also wept, but not with that poignancy of sorrow to injure her health, the mutual indulgence relieved, and after a time, afforded them a melancholy composure.

CHAPTER 2

The next morning, Claudina having past a tolerable night, and her spirits being much better, Ferdinand left her avowedly to visit his father. On his arrival at the Castle, he saw the solemn preparations for an event that filled him with horror. Send- ing for the steward, "My dear Ernest (said he) I must see my father, he shall not be committed to the earth without my tears bedewing his clay-cold form, without supplicating his hovering spirit to speak peace and pardon to his most wretched son! Let me not be interrupted in my last duties; I will not be long, but I must be alone."

Ernest bowed in silence, and conducted him to the chamber of death, calling from thence those whose duty it was to watch the sacred remains. All departed; Ferdinand shuddered involuntarily at the scene before him, day-light was excluded, the glimmering tapers, the solemn stillness, the black pall thrown over the bed which concealed a lifeless form, once so beloved and revered, accustomed to smile upon a then darling son, and hold him to his heart with unutterable fondness.

"Oh! (cried Ferdinand, agonized by the painful recollection) oh! just Heaven, how severe has been my punishment for one act of disobedience!"—He advanced hastily to the bed, withdrew the pall, and saw a face from which death had excluded no trait of mild benevolence; the features were placid and serene, yet Ferdinand thought, on a near investigation, that an air of sorrow was diffused over the countenance, and that the very serenity wore more the face of pious resignation than perfect content. He gazed with inexpressible sensations, threw himself on his knees in an agony of grief:—"O, father, ever revered and beloved! forgive your unhappy son, let not my offence be remembered against me in the land of spirits; for, oh! severe has been my punishment, misery has followed hard upon my disobedience!"

His head fell upon the bed, and he wept aloud; but his almost stagnated senses were instantly recalled by a deep and heavy groan that vibrated to his heart: He started up, and eagerly gazed on the lifeless body, all was still as death; he looked fearfully round the room, the gloom seemed increased, the tapers burnt more dimly, horror took possession of his soul; the groan was not a chimera, not the illusion of fancy; but from whence could it proceed, for it seemed very near to him? Again he turned his eyes to the bed, busy imagination, agitated spirits, and unsteady eyes, made him conceive the lips moved; overcome with every sensation that terror, panting expectation, and trembling apprehension, could inspire, he sunk again on his knees, attempted to speak, to look, but the words died on his lips, and involuntarily he hid his face by the side of the pall. Almost instantly a low and hollow voice pronounced the words "Pardon and peace!" He heard the words distinctly, attempted to rise, but with a faint shriek fell senseless on the floor!

On his recovery, he found himself supported in the anti-chamber by Ernest and a maid-servant; the voice still seemed to vibrate in his ears; he looked earnestly from one to the other: "How came I in this apartment?" demanded he.

"We heard a sudden scream," answered Ernest, "and entering the next room found you on the floor; we brought you here, and, thank Heaven, you are recovered."

"Recovered!" repeated Ferdinand, — "Good God! what have I— —."

"You may leave the room," said Ernest to the girl. — She obeyed. — "Dear master," continued he, "compose yourself, why, would you wound your heart by a sight?" —

"A sight!" repeated he again: "Ernest, dear Ernest, deem me not visionary or mad; but credit me, when I declare to you I have heard my father's voice pronouncing the blessed words 'Pardon and peace.'" — Yes, such were the words; it was not the effect of fancy but a reality; the voice still hangs upon my ear, and I will now believe, that the spirit of the good and just man may be permitted to convey happiness sometimes to the wretched. My bosom seems lightened, my heart beats more freely, and I already feel returning peace."

"Thank Heaven!" cried Ernest, "I have no doubt, Sir, of your veracity, for you were never given to indulge visionary or superstitious notions. Extraordinary things do happen sometimes to be sure, but, if what you have heard was to be related, it might injure weak and credulous minds, and cause many ridiculous stories; it will be best therefore, my dear master, to conceal the whole affair, and submit with resignation to the stroke that now afflicts you, comforting yourself with the remembrance of those words which were spoken to console your mind, and relieve you from the oppression of that imprecation which has so long and so cruelly disturbed you."

"I am relieved," answered Ferdinand, 'that painful stroke is removed, at least, I hope so: Alas! happy I can never be; yet, my good Ernest, had my lamented father sanctioned my marriage by his forgiveness, had I been considered as a child, few men would have known more true felicity, for my Claudina justifies my choice; she is the best of women, and of wives."

"Then, Sir, you have more happiness than falls to the lot of thousands, and therefore should be content; but pray walk down, your brother, my Lord, the Count, is expecting you." With a look of awful veneration and sorrow, Ferdinand threw his eyes on the opposite room, and without speaking descended to the saloon.

Rhodophil rose and embraced him, and, without reverting to the melancholy visit he had been paying, congratulated him on the safety of his wife, and the birth of his daughter. "I trust (said he) she will soon be in a state of health to be removed hither, and will consider this house as her own: — Mean time, I hope, I shall be admitted to pay my respects to her."

Ferdinand, whose mind was in a state of agitation, equally susceptible to joy, or grief, was painfully affected by his brother's kindness, his heart overflowed at his eyes; but a little abashed at such womanish weakness, which the other seemed superior to, he hastily dispersed the drops that forced their way down his cheeks, and, in a faltering voice, thanked the Count for his attention to his wife, and assured him she would rejoice to behold him. One thing, however, he must promise to him, previous to the visit.

He then explained to him the necessity he had been under to disguise the truth of the late events. "She believes (said he) my father has forgiven me; that he still exists, and that I may probably be included in his will. I dare not yet acquaint her with the extent of our obligations to you; the death of my father I shall announce to her, the rest must follow some time hence: I know so well her sensibility, and the delicacy of her affection for me, that, was she now informed I was unpardoned, portionless and dependent, she would accuse herself as the cause of my misfortunes, and her constitution, which has been impaired already by her regrets on this head, would be unable to sustain the shock. Will you then, my dear brother, vouchsafe to countenance the deceit, and excuse the omission of those grateful effusions you are so justly entitled to?"

"Mention it not (cried the Count) you owe me no obligations, I have merely performed a duty, and a sacred trust; I beg therefore neither you nor your wife will ever pain me by acknowledgments I am no ways entitled to; for had our situation been reversed, would you have done less for me?"

"No, by Heavens! (exclaimed Ferdinand, with fervor) that wealth would have been worthless to me without the participation of my beloved Rhodophil."

"I believe you (said the other) therefore here ends the chapter of obligations and thanks, for we are friends as well as brothers."

They then entered upon some consultations on domestic affairs, after which Ferdinand retired to break the death of his father to his wife; but not before the Count had pressed upon him a sum of money, that made Ernest's grateful service useless for the present, and which he repaid before he left the house.— On his way home, the recollection of the scene in his late father's apartment, a scene which, however strange and improbable it would appear on relation, he was perfectly convinced was not the illusion of his senses, and which seemed to him the voice of the dead speaking peace to his wounded mind.

The more he reflected on the circumstance, the more extraordinary it appeared. The refusal of Count Renaud to admit him to his presence in his last moments, to bestow one consoling word, nor yet even to recall the heavy curse that he had laid upon him when his union with Claudina was declared. Such stern, such unrelenting anger, seemed as inconsistent with his natural goodness of heart, as a pardon pronounced after death.— "All supernatural interpositions (thought he) I have ever discredited, but I cannot resist conviction; possibly my father did not think his dissolution so very near, strong resentments cling to the heart, and he thought I deserved to suffer. Perhaps, at the very moment when he felt the awful separation between the soul and body, he might wish to pronounce my pardon; and how that wish has been granted is a mystery incomprehensible to me, and possibly improper for me to desire a solution of." The agitation of his spirits was visible in his countenance, and when he entered his wife's humble apartment, the disorder of his air caught her attention.

"Ah! (cried she) my dear Ferdinand, I fear to ask.— Your father — — —!"

"You already anticipate the event (said he, throwing himself into a chair) your conjectures are but too just."

"Alas! (returned she, softening into tears) how painful the reflection, that we cannot now have the power to show our love and gratitude, and that the pardon he has accorded to us, was more, perhaps, an act of piety than the result of filial affection."

"We must not be too nice (answered he) in our search after the motives of our best actions, but be content to judge of them by their effects: If he condescended, in his own good time, to reconcile us to ourselves, and to forgive us in his last moments, it is our duty to be thankful, and to examine no farther."— Claudina, who saw his mind was disturbed, and knew how to allow for it, made no reply; but after she had indulged those tears she found it impossible to repress, held up her sweet infant to his view, and exulted in the resemblance she traced between its unformed features and himself. Melted by her tenderness, and gazing on the lovely child, he embraced both with ardour, and, in grateful acknowledgments for the blessings before him, forgot, for a short time, both recent afflictions, and puzzling conjectures.

The funeral obsequies of Count Renaud, being over, Claudina able to leave her bed, and her husband more composed, though far from being tranquillized as his brother seemed to be, they began to think of a removal to the Castle, where in truth Claudina was very anxious to reside; nor is it to be wondered at when she contrasted her miserable apartment with the noble and splendid rooms at the Castle. Her humble dwelling was in the suburbs of the city, a lowly roof, small circumference, and meanly furnished; there she had known the extreme of wretchedness; now she was invited to partake of grandeur, to consider herself as the mistress of that superb mansion, and to see her dear children clothed, and attended suitable to their father's birth: 'Tis not surprising therefore that she exerted unusual strength to bear the removal, nor that, when she was settled at the Castle, the satisfaction of her mind should communicate itself to her body, and render her recovery equally rapid and perfect.

Rhodophil treated them with the highest degree of tenderness and consideration; every wish was anticipated, and he doted on the children. Near a month was passed in a most delightful manner on the part of Claudina, but a deep and increased melancholy clouded the mind of Ferdinand; to live idle and inactive, dependent on the bounty of a brother, even the small allowance which his late father had afforded him, he could no longer call his own. The Count, indeed, was profuse in his presents of money and valuables to his wife; but was there not something mean and selfish in the acceptance? Could they last for ever? Might not his brother marry, and, if so, what then might be their fate? He recollected the advice of Ernest, but could he condescend to ask, what, if agreeable to his brother's inclinations, he would voluntarily offer—a settlement? No, he would die first. He was resolved to enter into the Emperor's service; but what could be done for his wife and children during his absence, and before he had the power to assist them?

Under these, and a thousand other painful reflections, he used to escape from the observation of his brother and his wife, and range from the gardens to the wilderness, and from thence into an adjoining forest, where he commonly spent hours every day, forming a thousand schemes, and rejecting them as quickly from their uselessness or impracticability. One morning, as he was taking his customary ramble, at the entrance of the forest he met Ernest. He started, "Pardon me, my dear master (said he) if I have broken upon you abruptly; I have long observed your solitary walks."

"You have watched me then (cried Ferdinand, rather haughtily) it is an unbecoming liberty."

"Pardon me, Sir (returned Ernest, in a tremulous voice, and with a look of humble sorrow) pardon your poor servant, if duty and affection — — —."

"My good old friend (exclaimed the other, instantly recollecting himself, and ashamed of his petulance) my faithful Ernest, pardon me; I know your attachment, and truly love you; but indeed I am altered, vexation and perplexity sour my disposition, I grow hateful to myself and to others." The old man, overcome by this condescension, could have humbled himself at his feet, but being pressed for time, and anxious to know if his "poor endeavours" could in any shape be useful, he earnestly besought Ferdinand to explain the cause of his melancholy.

He very readily acknowledged to him every feeling of his heart, and added, 'that he was come to a determination to quit the Castle, but was distracted on account of his wife and children."

"As you resolve not to speak to your brother about any partition of my late master's effects, or any settlement for your children, I beseech you, Sir, to suspend your resolution for a few days, and, perhaps, I may obtain some information that may be of consequence. Fear not, Sir (added he, seeing Ferdinand was going to speak) do not be apprehensive I mean to say any thing to the Count; I am not honoured with his notice sufficiently to authorise any freedom of speech on my part; but I have other designs, and the result you shall know in a day or two."

With a low bow the good man departed, leaving Ferdinand penetrated with gratitude for the affectionate concern this faithful follower of his broken fortunes had ever manifested towards him and his family.

CHAPTER III

When the over-charged heart vents itself in a friendly communication, it lightens the oppressive load, and admits a ray of hope to illumine the prospect of future hours. Ferdinand returned to the Castle with quicker steps, and a countenance less overcast than for many preceding days; in the garden he met his wife under the supporting arm of his brother; he joined them, and was composed enough to converse freely on several subjects. Among other things, the war with Prussia was mentioned, and he dropped a hint that he should like the service. Rhodophil applauded his spirit, and observed, 'that a young man, with his brother's address and vivacity, would be a great acquisition to the army."

"Vivacity! (repeated Claudina) alas! it is long since that any traces of pleasure or vivacity have been visible in my poor Ferdinand."

"Then (returned the Count) he must be the most insensible of men; with such a wife, and such lovely children, I think him uncommonly fortunate." — At that instant the nurse appeared with the infant; Claudina quitted them, and retired into the house with her child.

"I think, brother (said Rhodophil) you seemed to express yourself feelingly on the subject of the war; have you any wish to offer your services?"

"I have (replied Ferdinand, rejoiced at this opening) nor would I hesitate a moment but on account of my family. I hope my dear brother can have no doubts or fears concerning their happiness; I take upon me to ensure you every thing that affection or fortune can procure for their pleasure and comfort; and you may command whatever is necessary or proper for your appearance, with honour to yourself, and credit to your family. Surely we have no separate interests."

"I think not (replied Ferdinand) at least I know my heart participates in every enjoyment of yours, and if I feel any distress it is all my own."

"But why should you feel any (asked Rhodophil) when you have only to speak your wishes, and they will be gratified."

"Generous friend! (exclaimed the other) will you then endeavour to reconcile Claudina to my departure? Will you employ your interest to procure for me a commission and introduction to the Emperor?"

"I will do every thing you wish for (returned the Count) and this very day shall witness my affection for yourself and family."

This conversation restored Ferdinand to some degree of composure, and bid him look forward to a situation where he might at least be independent, and he still hoped his brother would make some fixed establishment for his family previous to his departure. — That evening the Count told him he had written to Vienna, "and as I entertain no doubts respecting the success of my applications, we will lose no time in procuring the necessary equipments for your campaign."

Ferdinand thanked his brother warmly at the moment; but after he had retired to rest, and began to reflect on every occurrence, there appeared, he thought, an indecent eagerness in Rhodophil to hasten his departure: At first he told me I should possess an equal share of my late father's fortune; the servants were told they had two masters, and equal power was to be lodged in my hands. 'Tis true I had no right to expect it, yet why make such liberal offers, when the tenor of his conduct, and the behaviour of the servants were told they had two masters, and equal power was to be lodged in my hands. 'Tis true I had no right to expect it, yet why make such liberal offers, when the tenor of his conduct, and the behaviour of the servants are contradictory, when every thing he does carries the air of a favour, and every attendance in the servants is ushered in with "my master ordered me to do this, or that?" yet, perhaps, I am capricious, my situation is delicate, and my mind, from a long habitude of discontent, may see things with a jaundiced eye, which in themselves bear a very different interpretation: Let me not be unjust in my surmises, for surely the Count has been ever warmly my friend, nor is it his fault that I am cut off from a participation of my father's fortune. How few half brothers would have acted like Rhodophil! — Ashamed of his first uneasy doubts, Ferdinand turned eagerly to the bright side of his brother's character, and did him more than justice from an apprehension that he had done him less.

The next morning, taking his accustomed walk, he met Ernest, anxious to ease the heart of his old friend, and do credit to his brother, he repeated the conversation on the preceding evening. Ernest heard him with attention, and made the following reply: — "You will, I am sure, Sir, do justice to my heart, and believe that I am neither prejudiced against my master, the Count, nor naturally suspicious. I speak from the best grounds, and it is with pain I destroy the opinion you entertain of his affection and honour; but I must develop the seeming generosity that captivates your mind. Count Rhodophil has learned the courtly art of professing much and meaning little, which gives consequence to himself, and sends the poor deluded expectant away to indulge visionary hopes, and be again deceived by smooth words that mean nothing.

"That well remembered day, which cut you off from all legal claims on your father's fortune, never shall I forget the consequential air, the parade with which the domestics were informed that they had two masters." — "Stop, Ernest (cried Ferdinand) do not sully the generosity of my brother, by imputing to him such despicable motives as pride and self-consequence; it ill becomes me to hear one of his family rob him of the merit due to so much frankness and brotherly love: I cannot suffer you to proceed in this strain."

"Were I base enough to be unjust, or speak from the prejudices of my own opinion, I should be deserving of your displeasure, Sir, but I entreat you to hear me without interruption, and then I will submit to your judgment."

"Well, well (returned he, rather a little displeased) you may go on."

"That day, Sir (proceeded Ernest) after you had received such proofs of his affection, and returned to your miserable abode with an intention to fetch your Lady, I withdrew to an apartment, which I gave orders to have fitted up for you. The good old house-keeper, Madam Lambert was with me: — You know, Sir, it adjoins to the old library, and was, I believe, the cause why the books have been since removed; but, however, not to be tedious (here Ferdinand smiled) there we were, when presently the Count entered the library with Peter; they were speaking as they shut the door; we heard your name mentioned, and I put my finger to my mouth; we were silent and listened. I see, Sir, you look displeased; it was a liberty and a meanness if I could not justify it to my own heart, but I had my reasons.

"Well, Sir, we heard Count Rhodophil say, 'the world has in general thought my father very cruel in his treatment of Ferdinand, his whole fortune being given to me, they would be apt to censure and suspect me of taking an advantage of his resentments; it is therefore to avoid any unpleasant reflections, to do away any prejudices that might be conceived against me, and to humble Ferdinand's spirit into a sense of obligation, added to another view I look forward to still more gratifying, that I have made him and his family an offer of my house, which perhaps he will presume from what I said just now, to think is to be his also; but I was before determined how to act: I shall, by degrees, change every servant but yourself; Ernest I shall be obliged to keep until all his accounts are made up, but no longer; then the succeeding domestics, ignorant of my present declaration, and taught to believe highly of my generosity in supporting a brother's family, will learn to estimate us properly, and treat him accordingly.'"

"This, Sir, was verbatim your brother's speech, which Peter applauded in very free words I thought for a servant, and we stole softly out of the room lest we should be discovered. You must have observed, Sir, the servants are all changed, on one pretence or other, and being done without consulting you, proves how little equality of power you have in the house. Madame Lambert went two days ago; my turn will soon come; in truth but for you I care not how soon; but I believe your intention of going into the army has greatly rejoiced him, as it procures your absence without any reflection being thrown on him. Peter has of late paid much court to me, but as I look upon him to be in the plot against you, I have taken very little notice of him. Two or three times he has remarked, 'how very melancholy Mr. Ferdinand looked!'—I thought something might be gathered from him of his master's intentions towards your family, so yesterday I threw myself in his way after I had left you; and your Lady passing into the garden, I observed how handsome she was, and what beautiful children Master and Miss were; adding, 'that it was a pity but some settlement was made for them, lest the Count should marry, and his Lady not happen to like his brother's family."—As to marriage (said he) I believe my master don't think of that, and I dare say he will always be kind to Madame Claudina, if she is civil to him, so it must be her own fault if she loses his favour. As to settlement, Mr. Ernest, master knows better than that, make folks independent, and you make them saucy and ungrateful, whilst they are obliged to you they will be humble, tho' I fancy my master would have no objection to put forth a little to send his brother in some place abroad, for to be sure it is a shame to see a young man idling at home, who has nothing of his own, and hanging upon a generous Gentleman, who is but a half-brother after all, and not obliged to maintain him." I was so provoked at his impudence that I could have throttled the rascal; but I curbed my passion, and saying, "Very true, Peter," I turned short from him, and retired to my room. "Now, Sir, putting all this together, what must you think of the Count?"

Ferdinand, who was walking rather before Ernest, and his head hanging on his breast, turned round suddenly, with a look that expressed a thousand contending passions, twice he opened his lips to speak, but the conflict in his mind precluded all powers of articulation, and he gladly availed himself of a seat which just then appeared in view, though only the root of a tree, to sit down, for his trembling limbs could no longer support him. Poor Ernest saw, with infinite concern, the effects of his intelligence; tears stood glistening in his aged eyes. — "My dear master (said he) resume your courage; let not the machinations of the wicked have power to wring your noble heart with sorrow, to shake your fortitude, which has already struggled through the bitterest troubles."

"Ernest (said Ferdinand, after a long pause) you have bereft me of my last and only hope; all the consolation I could look forward to in life must derive its source from my brother. My brother did I say? alas! if what you tell me is true, and surely you would not deceive me, I have no longer a brother. Count Rhodophil is my father's heir, and I am cast off for ever. O, what a blessing is ignorance! Yesterday I thought myself wretched, but it was a state of bliss to what I now feel; my head burns like fire. Oh! my old, and now my only friend, tell me where, where shall I fly to, now that all my visionary hopes of this morning are vanished into bubbles! My wife! my children! merciful Heaven! who will provide for them?"

"That Heaven you invoke (answered the steward;) fear not, Sir, Providence never deserts the virtuous man." "But what, what is now to become of my intended expedition to the army?"

"If I may be so bold as to offer my advice (replied Ernest) I would act as if I was still unacquainted with the Count's real character; I only wished, Sir, to put you on your guard against duplicity, and not to have you weighed down with an idea of obligations which proceed only from selfish considerations. Whatever advantages you receive from the Count, is your undoubted right, as children of the same father you have an equal claim to his property; nor could resentment be justifiable carried to such lengths, as to consign one child to misery, that the other might riot in luxury."

"Surely, Ernest (cried Ferdinand) my father had a right to make what distinctions he pleased."

"I cannot think so, Sir (returned the other) in sudden anger was that will made, and I am confident it was intended to be altered, unhappily it was delayed until too late. Think of the words 'Pardon and peace!' Believe me, Sir, my blessed master never died with hatred in his heart: Be not scrupulous therefore, but take, without hesitation, what the Count offers you, and boldly ask for some certain income for your Lady; he cannot, I think, refuse; if he does, he unmasks himself at once."

"What! (exclaimed Ferdinand) receive, nay, even ask favours from a man whom I suspect of the vilest duplicity; owe pecuniary obligations, the existence of my family to."

"Softly, Sir (said Ernest) it is a share of your father's property, as such receive it freely. I beseech you, Sir, to keep what I have told you in your mind; but do not let it influence your actions to the disadvantage of yourself and family."

The appearance of Rhodophil and Claudina at a distance interrupted their conversation. Ferdinand arose, and walked hastily into the forest, unable to meet them in the present perturbed state of his mind. He revolved every thing Ernest had told him; he recollected a thousand little inattentions he had received; the air of protection his brother often assumed, the change in the household, his readiness to lay hold of the little inclination he had shown for the army: In short, the more he reflected, the more he was convinced no real brotherly affection existed in the bosom of Rhodophil: "Yet, (exclaimed he) did he not show us a thousand acts of kindness, when sinking under the displeasure of my father? Did he not often relieve us from want, and labour incessantly to bring about a reconciliation? And is it possible that a sudden change of fortune, being possessed of all, should make such a revolution in his principles? If so, alas! how dangerous is prosperity? What a contractor of the heart is wealth!"

Distracted with the various conjectures that occupied his mind, he walked on regardless of time or distance, until faint and weary, he stopped, and looked round, that he might trace his way back; but he had bewildered himself among the trees, and observed no particular path, he therefore was at a loss how to regain the direct road; to complete his difficulties, the air grew dark, the clouds heavy, and in a short time it began to rain violently. Scarcely sensible of the torrents that poured upon him, Ferdinand sought to explore his way to the Castle, though he dreaded to encounter the looks of its master. It was some hours, however, before he saw the turrets rising above the trees, and when arrived at the garden, he was so exhausted with fatigue, so drenched with the rain, that it was with much difficulty he reached the saloon door before his senses fled, and he fell extended on the floor. Happily a servant was passing the room, and hearing a noise, opened the door, and beheld the lifeless body.

His exclamations soon brought every one to know the cause, and poor Claudina was nearly distracted with terror and anxiety. — He was soon restored to his senses, and immediately put into a warm bed, and through the attention of his wife and old Ernest (who was terrified to death at an accident, of which he thought himself in a great measure the cause) after some hours he grew better, and able to account for his indisposition, by mentioning the length of his walk through the rain. He endeavoured to assume a composure in his behaviour to his brother that surprised even Ernest, and having taken his resolution, he stifled his feelings, and conducted himself as usual. A violent cold and fever were the consequences of his ramble, and for several days he was quite an invalid, and in some danger; during this time Rhodophil behaved with the utmost tenderness, which made him doubt the communications of Ernest, and to suspect the justice of his own observations.

The first day that he left his bed, the Count came to him in a transport of joy: — "My dear Ferdinand, we are successful, I have this moment received an express, your commission is granted, and the Emperor wishes to see you without delay. I am happy, my dear brother, in being the messenger of such agreeable and wished-for intelligence."

The agitations of Ferdinand were inexpressible; he hesitated whether he should accept or refuse the commission procured for him. The Count seemed surprised: "You are silent, my dear brother, have your sentiments undergone any change that I am unacquainted with?"

"They have indeed, (answered Ferdinand, with a deep sigh;) the danger I was in a few days since has alarmed me for the future welfare of my family. I know well (added he, fixing his eyes steadily on Rhodophil, whose own fell under the penetrating glance) how much I may depend upon your brotherly kindness; but you may marry, little occurrences may arise at present unforeseen to interrupt the harmony that exists in your family, and the idea of a precarious and accidental provision, must ever give pain to a feeling heart."

"What is it you mean or expect?" asked the Count, in a quick tone.

"A small settlement on my wife, that I may depart with a certainty that, whether I live or die, she will not want the common necessaries of life; superfluities, such as she now enjoys, I neither expect or wish for."

"What then (cried Rhodophil) you will not trust to my honour, or affection for your family?"

"Be not offended (answered Ferdinand, calmly) and I will be explicit; for my own provision, my sword shall carve it out, and for my family I expect only a mediocrity of fortune. The grandeur and elegance that reigns here they are not entitled to, nor can they expect a continuance of; a more humble situation is most proper for them: If therefore you will settle a very moderate pension upon my wife and children, I will place them in some decent cottage suitable to their fortunes, and then I shall depart in peace."

The countenance of Rhodophil underwent many changes whilst his brother was speaking, nor was his answer quite ready when he stopped. At last, "I know not (replied he) whether I should be most grieved or offended at your unaccountable proposition. Is not Claudina my sister? Are not your children my heirs? I never intend to marry; but supposing I should, would not my honour and fraternal affection compel me to make a handsome provision for you and your family?"

"A handsome provision I neither expect nor am entitled to (answered Ferdinand.) In this commission, you have procured for me, lies the extent of my wishes for myself. My wife has no right to splendid expectations, and my children shall be taught by industry to provide for themselves. The greatest misery of life is to be accustomed in early youth to indulgences which enervate both the mind and body, and lead to hopes which may be blighted by a thousand accidents. — My children shall indulge no hopes independent of their own exertions, and that I am convinced is the surest road to competency and happiness."

"What, then (said the Count) you would bring them up to trade, to disgrace their family?"

"No (replied Ferdinand, warmly) I will, if I live, prevent them from disgracing their family, by teaching them a spirit of independence, and a mediocrity of expectations; their minds shall be noble, though their fortunes may be humble; they shall be superior to base actions from an integrity of heart; and capable of providing for their own maintenance, they never can disgrace their connexions, though they may mortify pride."

"Your language and sentiments are very strange (replied Rhodophil, in a tone of pique and vexation;) but methinks you promise too much for your children, whose ideas may not happen to coincide with your's." — — —

"At least," said Ferdinand, "I will endeavour to inculcate my sentiments, and form their young minds agreeable to my wishes; there is no dependence upon the human heart it is true: I may fail of success, but I will not abate of my endeavours; the rest I must leave to Providence."

"Well," returned Rhodophil, "since you have no reliance on me, and insist upon an independence, be so good to name your terms." The spirit of Ferdinand revolted against this demand, and he was on the point of refusing every assistance; but the recollection of his family timely interposed, and with evident reluctance he named four hundred crowns yearly.

"Four hundred crowns!" repeated the Count, with surprise, "why, such a sum will scarcely find them bread!" "It is double, however, to any advantages I have had for them for those last two years, and I should despise myself if I considered your fortune more than their real wants."

"You are much too moderate," said the Count; "but I will enter into a compromise with you; I will settle that sum upon them during their residence in this Castle, and double it should I marry; but then I expect that you will permit them to remain here in your absence, during your first campaign. Deprive me not of all my comforts at once; let me sooth the sorrows of my sister on your first separation; your children are too young to imbibe any prejudices against your intended frugal system, and I expect, as a proof of your brotherly affection, that those sweet pledges of your dearest love may be confided to me."

Ferdinand hesitated a little, but at length said, equivocally, "Your kindness is truly painful to me, but Claudina shall decide on this point; and now my wish, as to a small provision for them being generously acceded to, I have only to hasten preparations for my departure."

"A small provision, indeed!" repeated the Count, "however, it will be always in my power to augment it, for I shall ever consider we have equal claims to the fortune of our ancestors."

He now withdrew at Ferdinand's request to reveal every particular to Claudina, and left him variously affected by the preceding conversation. "If I have wronged him by giving credit to erroneous reports, or suspicious observations, I must appear as an ungrateful and most unworthy character; and ought I to believe the perhaps mistaken representation of Ernest against a series of kind actions, particularly within those last two years, when interest could have no share in directing them to me, then under my father's malediction? Good Heavens! if I have wronged him, how shall I detest myself!" For some time Ferdinand dwelt on every favourable side of his brother's character with self-indignation, but soon other ideas obtruded. If he really had been sincere in the equality he talked of, would he not have seized the first moment to ensure it to me? Would he not have hastened to relieve me from a sense of obligations by nobly making me independent, and rendering my separation from my family unnecessary? — Could he not have resigned over one of his estates to me as a residence I might have called my own? Does he seem to have a feeling heart, or regret the loss of a parent ever good and bountiful to him? Has he not discharged the old servants, grown grey in the service of the family, with only the small legacies (much less, indeed, than I expected the munificent spirit of my father would have bequeathed to them) so insufficient for the support of their old age? Are not these many proofs of a heart deficient in generosity, and a right way of thinking? Tormented by these and many other doubts, he exclaimed, "Would to Heaven I could read his heart, that I might do him justice!" A deep and hollow voice cried, "It is a corrupt one!!!"

Ferdinand sprung from his seat, looked wildly round the room: "Astonishing! (he cried) again that voice, sure it is, it must be, more than human!" He opened the door that led into the next apartment; the room was empty, and universal silence reigned: — Again he reseated himself, in trembling expectation of the same sounds, but he heard no more. Extremely agitated, though he endeavoured to assume a composed air, he feebly crept to the dressing room of Claudina, where he found the Count. His blood grew chill at the sight; both started, and exclaimed at his appearance; with difficulty he supported himself till assisted by his wife to a chair; she blamed him for attempting to leave his apartment: "You are too weak (said she) to walk as yet; I was coming to you."

"I shall soon recover (replied he) and gain strength by the change of air; I already feel better."

Indeed, the first shock being over, though the voice still vibrated on his ear, he viewed Rhodophil with a scrutinizing eye, and traced, as he thought, duplicity in every line of his countenance, so governed are our ideas by accidental circumstances! His love, his reverence for his brother, shrunk into nothing, and he believed the voice of the dead against all those superficial appearances which had hitherto lulled him into an unsuspecting confidence. After a short pause, "I have been complying with your wishes, my dear brother," said the Count, "and had just opened the business to your wife as you appeared."

"Ah! Ferdinand," cried Claudina, "can you think of leaving me, of exposing your life to the uncertain chance of war?"

"The hand of Providence is there, is here, and every where," answered Ferdinand. "Fear not for me, my dear Claudina, divest yourself of prejudice, consider my situation dispassionately, and you will be reconciled to an inevitable necessity." — "I leave you," said the Count, 'to discuss the subject between yourselves; my prayers and wishes have been unsuccessful; you, Madam, may have more influence." He bowed, and left the room.

CHAPTER IV

For a few moments they were silent; at length Ferdinand explained to her his motives without entering into any strictures on his brother's conduct; and by the arguments he adduced in support of his plan, brought her to be convinced, or at least to appear convinced, that he was perfectly right. He mentioned his intention to take a small cottage for her and his children, at the same time that he told her of the Count's wishes that she would remain at the Castle. — "On this head, my dear Claudina, your inclinations shall decide, for I wish to leave you perfectly contented with your situation in my absence, determine therefore as you feel most inclined."

"I own, then," answered she, 'that I prefer staying here; to remove into a strange house, among strange people, unaccustomed to manage for myself, would be altogether unpleasant. Here, as our good brother solicits our stay, I can at least be as comfortable as it is possible I can be in your absence, and make myself useful enough to do away any sense of obligation."

"As you please, so let it be," returned Ferdinand, rather hurt at her choice, but determined not to control her, "and I hope a few days will finish all our preparations, and give me strength to repair to Vienna." A further conversation took place relative to domestic matters; but he cautiously concealed the two extraordinary occurrences that had befallen him, because he had never yet undeceived her, with respect to the pardon which, she believed, the late Count had accorded to him before his death.

In the course of the evening Ferdinand saw Ernest, and related to him, not only what had past between his brother and himself, but the words which he had a second time heard in his apartment. "It was the same voice that I heard before in the room where my father's body lay. You, Ernest, will believe me, to no one else would I mention the circumstance, for from no one else should I gain credit; but it is wondrous strange!"

"True, Sir," answered the steward; "but nothing is impossible, and now forewarned, you may guard against any evil practices." — "Would to Heaven my wife had otherwise decided," cried Ferdinand.

"Do not be uneasy, Sir," replied Ernest, "whilst I have life and limbs I will be faithful to your family, nothing shall escape my observation." "But if you should be discharged?"

"I have some cause to think that cannot well take place, and should I quit the house, I have an infallible method of knowing what passes here; whilst I live, therefore, you need not fear."

This cheerful assurance calmed the tumult of Ferdinand's mind, and enabled him with alacrity to prepare for his journey. The following day Ernest waited on him by the Count's order with a handsome sum of money for his necessary expenses; the colour mounted to Ferdinand's cheeks, he hesitated, paced about the room, and seemed in violent agitations. — "Pray, dear Sir," cried Ernest, 'take the money, think of it less as your brother's present, than as a small part of your father's property, to which you have unquestionably a right."

"Not so," replied Ferdinand, "I can have no right to what he has bequeathed from me, and to receive pecuniary favours from a man I think capable of duplicity, lowers me in my own esteem."

"Be not so scrupulous, Sir, I beseech you," returned Ernest; 'take it, fortune may enable you to return it, and I'll pledge my life you will not hereafter regret accepting the money, or think much of the obligation as you call it."

"You persuade me," said Ferdinand, "and against my inclinations I comply; (then seeing the largeness of the sum,) good Heavens! can this man have a bad heart? Is there not munificence in this present? O, Rhodophil, if concurrent circumstances have led me into an error, if I injure you by doubt and suspicion, how severe will be my repentance!"—Ernest was silent, indeed he could not view the necessary arrangement for the departure of a man he loved and revered, without feeling the deepest sorrow; yet he thought the plan he had adopted was most suitable to his birth, his age and situation, and therefore only regretted the necessity for its execution, whilst Ferdinand painfully looking forward to the hour of separation from a wife and children that he doted on, sought, in the bustle of preparation, to blunt the severity of his feelings.

The day of parting at length arrived, and as such scenes can afford no gratification to minds of sensibility, we shall not dwell upon them: Sorrow was reciprocal on all sides, at least to appearance, and we cannot penetrate into the remotest corner of the heart, therefore give those appearances due credit. To follow Ferdinand would be unnecessary, we shall then take this opportunity to look back into the family history of his father, the late Count Renaud.

CHAPTER V

Descended from a noble and an opulent family, Count Renaud succeeded to the estates of his ancestors at the age of five-and-twenty: Two years previous to which he had, to please his family, married a Lady of noble birth and great riches, her only recommendations. Proud, fastidious, and violent, she sought, by the haughtiness of her demeanour, to exact that respect and servility as substitutes for veneration and esteem, to which her manners and conduct laid no claims. The Count, who had another attachment, conscious that he was deficient in tenderness to her, and afraid of irritating a spirit so ungovernable by any opposition to her plans, quietly permitted her to conduct his household as she pleased, nor ever interfered with her pursuits or expenses. Nearly at the same period, when he came into the possession of his father's fortune, his wife presented him with an heir in the person of Rhodophil. The birth of a son made him for some time more attentive to his Lady, but his affection for a dearer object soon drew him into his customary distant civilities. Happily the Countess had no violent susceptibilities, her heart had never been softened by love, and though she was often provoked at the neglect of her Lord, yet her feelings arose more from disappointed pride, than from any warmth of affection, consequently, though displeased, she was not grieved, and offended pride found a relief in the imperiousness of her manners to all those who were subjected to her caprice.

When her son was about a twelvemonth old, a young Lady, who was a near relation to the Countess, and had just been liberated from a convent where she had resided from childhood for education, came to pay them a visit: She was received with kindness by the Countess, with politeness by the Count; but in less than a fortnight the sentiments of both parties underwent a total alteration.

Caroline, the name of this young Lady, had one of the finest forms imagination could paint; her face was handsome, her air and manners captivating, from a certain kind of bashful naivete which joined to a natural elegance, was extremely fascinating. At first sight you admired her, on an acquaintance an unprejudiced mind must love her. By imperceptible degrees, even to himself, the Count grew enchanted with the charms of Caroline, he delighted in her society; she was sensible, gentle, and unassuming; she was to him a new character; his Lady proud of her birth and riches, with a natural violence of temper, and devoid of personal attractions, was more than indifferent; she was disgusting to him: His mistress, vain of her charms, conscious of the power she had long held over his affections, and which had received additional strength from the birth of a daughter, had for some time past relaxed in her endeavours to please, and by her little solicitude to amuse him in those hours which he devoted to her, had insensibly weakened her powers of attraction, and rendered the visits he paid her rather a retreat from the more disagreeable society at the Castle, than the effects of that violent passion he had once and for a long while felt for her, and which, perhaps, only her own folly and caprice caused an abatement of.

His passions were therefore in that dormant state which of all others is the most dangerous in a susceptible mind, because, if once roused into action, they blaze with more uncontrolled fury than when kept in constant agitation. Such was the Count's situation when first Caroline became an inmate in his house; nor did her person at first sight appear particularly charming; he sought her company and conversation more as a pleasing variety than from any expectation of delight; but a short time convinced him how dangerous an indulgence was the society of a young and beautiful girl, who, new to the world, was grateful for the attentions he paid her, pleased with his conversation, and desirous of profiting by the information his understanding daily unfolded to her. Every hour her attractions gained upon his heart, and he was sensible that he had conceived a passion more delicate and violent than any he had ever before admitted to his bosom.

Unhappily the young and inexperienced Caroline caught the infection, the contagion spread itself through her innocent mind, and she grew melancholy and unhappy; for a long time insensible of the nature of her disease, until one morning that some unguarded expressions, and too tender looks of the Count, too fully explained his sentiments, and taught her to develop the secret of her own. Extremely shocked at the discovery, when she withdrew to her apartment she took herself severely to task for her involuntary crime, and directly determined to quit the house, and fly the dangerous society of its master. Whilst she was forming this prudent resolution the Countess entered her apartment, her features deformed by passion, her eyes flashing fire: "Insolent, depraved, ungrateful girl!" exclaimed she, "so, you have formed a vile intrigue with my husband; under a pretence of visiting me you carry on your shameless connexion in my very house. Abandoned wretch! I have seen, I have heard enough; you shall quit it this day, base as you are, I will expose you to my servants, to your friends, and to the world."

She was stopped in the midst of her threats by seeing the unhappy girl fall senseless at her feet. She rang the bell for assistance, but on the entrance of the servants continued her exclamations and upbraidings. "Recover the infamous creature who has so basely injured me; pack up her rags, and the moment her senses return, turn her out of the house to her base paramour my husband, whom she has seduced from me. I have discovered their intrigue, nor shall she sleep again under this roof. Disobey me at your peril," said she to the servants, who stood aghast at her fury; "let her be thrust out from my house within this hour." She flew out of the room at the moment when returning life visited the cheeks of the much-injured Caroline.

She opened her eyes and beheld the servants; she looked with terror round the room, her ears still holding the dreadful words which had deprived her of her senses. Seeing only the two women who looked on her with compassion, though believing her guilty: "Am I a base, infamous wretch?" said she: "Is my character lost, my innocence blasted, by vile suspicions? O, Heavens! what is to become of me, injured and undone, whither can I fly? But no, I will not go, I will see the Countess, she must, she shall hear me. I am innocent, indeed I am," added she, bursting into a torrent of tears that greatly affected the women, who endeavoured to sooth her into a composure impossible to be obtained. One of them, more courageous than the other, offered to go in search of her Lady, and entreat an audience for the poor afflicted. — "No," said she, rising hastily from the bed, "I will not entreat, I will demand to be heard, and you shall accompany me." She rather flew than walked towards the Countess's dressing room, who was at that moment abusing her in the vilest terms to her own woman. Caroline burst into the room, surprise chained the Countess to her chair, and stopped her tongue.

"Hear me, Madam," said she; "it is a justice I demand; you have accused, condemned, and insulted me with the charge of crimes my soul abhors: You seek to murder my future happiness by destroying my reputation. You are deceived and abused. Neither my conduct or sentiments ever injured you, and the infamous accusation of an intrigue with your husband is as false as Heaven is true; to that Heaven I appeal for my innocence and integrity. I will leave your house, but not as a guilty wretch, nor until my uncle arrives to take me hence; confine me to this room if you please, I will only see the Count once more, and that shall be in your presence: He will do me justice; but you shall not drive me from hence until you have recalled your accusations, and that I can depart with a character unspotted, as my heart is unstained, with guilt."

That the Countess heard her so long without interruption proceeded not from patience, or a desire of hearing her in her own defence: On the contrary, surprise and increasing rage precluded speech for a few moments; but just as Caroline pronounced the last words, she sprang forwards, and struck her so violent a blow as laid her on the floor, and would have trampled upon her, had not the women with-held her by violence. The noise of the fall, her rage, and the screams of the servants, alarmed the whole household, and the Count, who had just entered from the garden, hearing and seeing the confusion, ran up stairs with them to learn the occasion. — What were his emotions on entering his wife's dressing-room, to behold Caroline on the floor weltering in her blood, and the Countess foaming, stamping with rage, and struggling with her servants.

He flew to the senseless Caroline: "My God! what — how is this? Is she killed?" he was going to say; but overpowered, he sunk into a chair, whilst those that had followed him raised the poor girl from the floor, and said, the blood proceeded from her nose. — The women, who held the Countess, now gave way to her ungovernable rage, and carried off the poor victim of it to another room. The shock actually suspended all powers in the Count, and he looked on his wife with an air of stupid wildness. She, mistaking the cause of his silence, vented her passion in such language, and spoke of Caroline in such infamous, opprobrious terms, that he was no longer at a loss to account for the scene he had witnessed. He started up like a mad-man, seizing her hands, he forced her into a chair: "Sit there, Madam," he cried, in a voice choked with rage and horror; "Stir not for your life till I have seen that angel you have so basely injured: Yes, she is an angel, innocent and spotless; dare not to quit this apartment. When I have seen the injured Caroline I shall know what treatment you deserve." He quitted the room, and on entering the apartment where the unhappy girl was carried, found her restored to her senses, and the blood stopped; but she had a violent bruise on the side of her head, and another on her shoulder; she was incapable of speaking, and whilst she was conveyed to bed, and a surgeon was sent for, the Count was nearly distracted. One of the women gave him complete information of the preceding scenes, which threw him into paroxysms of rage little short of madness. — He a thousand times protested the innocence of Caroline, and execrated her malicious accusers. Not a servant in the house but believed him, for her gentle, unoffending manners had gained her as much love and respect amongst them, as the Countess was beheld with hatred and dread.

But little respect or attachment can be expected from domestics, when their principals degrade themselves by the exercise of insolence and passion over those whose humble situation in life is perhaps the only circumstance in which they are inferior to their employers; for goodness of heart, and nobleness of principle, are by no means confined to the rich and titled, who derive their boasted superiority too often more from hereditary claims than from their own personal rights.

The Countess had servants, but she had no friends, and her ill humour and insolence was borne by them, because from habitude they had learned to despise it. Their master they loved, and a simple asseveration from him gained more credit than oaths, or the most plausible testimony could obtain for their Lady: No wonder, therefore, that every one was attentive to the unfortunate young Lady, and anxious for the arrival of the surgeon; he at length appeared, and to their great joy declared no material injury had been received, the bruises he hoped soon to remove, but the great loss of blood, and a tremor which he supposed was owing to the fall, rendered it necessary that the patient should be kept exceeding quiet. A little more composed by this report, the Count returned to his wife, whose rage had been succeeded by a fit of sullenness and reflections not very pleasant.

With very little ceremony he reproached her warmly for her inhuman treatment of Caroline, vindicated her innocence with energy and truth; insisted that she should publicly ask her pardon for the insults she had given her, or be assured that he would instantly separate himself from her for ever, and do justice to the character of a young Lady she had so wantonly injured, without the least provocation. Not deigning to make any reply, she drew from her pocket a letter, and gave it into his hand. How great was his astonishment to see, in spite of an endeavour to disguise it, the hand-writing of his mistress, who, as a friend to the Countess, accused her husband and Caroline of an intrigue, and repeated a number of bitter expressions, which had sometimes been drawn from him relative to his wife's person and disposition, as if spoken by him to Caroline, and by her repeated to her. — The whole information was calculated to inspire every diabolical idea that jealousy, personal resentment, and a sense of vile ingratitude, could animate a naturally irritable temper to indulge.

He put the paper into his pocket: — "I know your wicked informant," said he, "and she shall dearly repent the baseness of this attempt, to injure a character superior to the machinations of persons who hate the virtue they cannot copy. This letter,

Madam, in a small degree, might excuse your suspicions; but nothing can atone for your improper and cruel treatment of a young woman, who, as a relation and a guest, had a claim to your hospitality."

"What!" interrupted the Countess, indignantly, "when I was informed she had violated the rights you talk of, and injured me irreparably?"

"At least," answered the Count, "you ought to have shown this letter to her or to me, to have judged, from your own conviction, before you took the liberty of being your own avenger, and not blindly have permitted your passions to be guided by a vile incendiary, and proceed to such outrages as the lowest of your sex should be ashamed of: However, Madam, you have still the power to atone for your aspersions on the young Lady's fame before your servants by a public recantation. The personal injury, the degrading blow, it is possible she may forgive; but if you have any feeling, you can never forgive yourself."

Ending those words he left her, and went to the house of his mistress, where he had not been for several days: To his astonishment he found it shut up, and on inquiry learned, that the Lady, with her child and nurse, had gone from thence two days before; that the furniture had been privately disposed of, and that a Gentleman came in a carriage and took them from the house without any one's knowing to what place they were gone. This information hurt the Count much, not on account of the Lady, who had been some time indifferent to him, but he was fond of the infant, and to have it taken away, solely in the power of a woman whose principles were not virtuous, distressed him greatly; and he painfully felt that the errors he had committed might too probably be retaliated on his own child, and that he had given existence to a being who might fall a victim to the vices of another, with passions as ungovernable as his own!

The conviction struck him with shame and remorse; he returned to the Castle overwhelmed with dejection, and more than ever anxious that the character of Caroline should be justified, that she might not be a sufferer through his attachment, which, however carefully concealed, it was evident, the jealous curiosity of his mistress had penetrated into, and possibly others might have made the same observations, though not impelled by the same motives. In consequence of these reflections, he sought a conversation with his Lady; to her he confessed the nature of his long attachment to his late mistress, the birth of a daughter, his growing indifference, and little attention to her for some time past, which he supposed had induced her from pique and revenge, to give her the information contained in that letter she had delivered to him, in the hope of creating jealousies and disturbances to embitter their future days.

"You tell me nothing, Sir," answered she haughtily, "but what I have long since been informed of, except who was the writer of the letter; the conjecture is not wholly improbable, nor the motives which gave rise to it, at all unlikely. My passions carried me beyond the bounds of decency when I struck Caroline; but she intruded at an improper time, and was the sufferer. I have no objection to accede to your proposition, and declare her innocence as far as my own belief goes; but I expect that letter shall be produced as my justification. You see, Sir, to what meannesses you subject me by your attachments; I expect this to be the last folly of the kind; if you choose to make yourself ridiculous, I desire to be left out of the business."

She left the room with an air of disdain and superiority, that convinced him concessions on his part only served to make her more arrogant. In a few days Caroline was perfectly recovered; she sent for the Count and Countess to her apartment, the first time she had admitted either from the day of the quarrel.

"I expect my uncle," said she, 'tomorrow to take me from this house, which I hourly regret I ever visited! Your unjust suspicions and cruel accusations have wounded my character, have injured my health; but I take God to witness, that I would not be the guilty, ungrateful creature you supposed me for all the enjoyments this world can offer. From you, Madam, I have a right to expect more than an apology, an acknowledgment that you have wronged me: Your women heard me accused; it is fit also that they should hear me justified."

"I own it," replied the Countess, a little affected, and much confused, "I have used you ill, my dear Caroline, I entreat your forgiveness, and request you will hear the information which threw me into passions so injurious to you, and unbecoming in myself."—She drew the letter from her pocket; Caroline rejected it: "No, Madam, I am perfectly satisfied; if you believe yourself imposed upon, if you are convinced that I am incapable of being the wretched creature you supposed me to be; I am restored to your good opinion, and justified in the sight of others; self-approbation, thank Heaven, I have never forfeited."

The Countess withdrew soon after, the scene was disagreeable to her on many accounts; she had injured Caroline, and therefore could not love her, and it likewise gave her a conscious superiority which the Countess could not admit of in any other than herself. The Count was in a situation most deplorable, his love for Caroline exceeded all bounds, yet respecting her with equal fervor, he determined to confine his passion within his own bosom, and never to see her more after she had quitted his house. On the next day, this amiable and unfortunate young woman took leave of the family, carrying with her a barbed arrow which pierced her heart, and wrung it with sorrow, when the last adieus were pronounced between the Count and herself. She returned home, but for a long time her days were melancholy, and her nights restless.

The Count and his Lady were little less unhappy; there was nothing respectable or estimable in the Lady's character to conciliate esteem, nor any endeavours to render herself pleasing. No longer a favourite mistress to engross his hours, his reflections on the past were painful, and in prospect no less disagreeable: He grew reserved, solitary and unhappy; yet behaved with more attention and complacency to his Lady, and was extremely fond of his infant son. Nine months passed in a dull uniformity, when an accident happened that gave a new turn to his thoughts.

The Countess was again in the family way, and generally went out in the mornings to ride on horseback. One day, when attended only by two servants, she was riding through the forest not far from the Castle, by the sudden discharge of a gun her horse took fright, and flying between the trees, she was thrown off with great violence, and when the attendants came up, lay to all appearance dead. On a nearer inspection they found she still breathed; between them she was conveyed to the Castle, a surgeon was sent for, and the Count seemed greatly affected. She remained speechless, though sensible, and the surgeon apprehended some very dreadful inward bruises from the fall, which was really the case, for in spite of every medical assistance she expired before the next morning.

Having already described the Count's feelings, it is needless to say, that after the first shock was over, a thousand pleasing images floated on his brain, and every thought was full of Caroline. When decency authorised him to make known the situation of his heart, he applied to that young Lady's uncle for permission to address her; an offer so very advantageous could not be refused, and he was permitted to visit her; but, alas! how severely was he wounded when he first saw her, pale, emaciated, and dejected; she was no longer the blooming Caroline, whose animated charms had first inspired him with a real passion; but she was an object a thousand times more interesting, for all her sufferings were on his account, and that idea rendered her inexpressibly dear to him.

Conscious of the alteration in her person, the generous girl decided against her own wishes, and refused to marry him; but the Count was not so easily induced to give up a favourite point so essential to his happiness; her uncle seconded his wishes, and wearied out by his continued perseverance, and yielding as well to the tenderness of her own heart, she at length consented; they were united, and the happy Count thought his felicity was now complete.

Poor simple mortals as we are! that see not by every day's experience how often the accomplishment of our eager wishes proves the source of future misery!

The amiable Caroline was indeed the most desirable of women, the most engaging of wives; but unhappily her constitution had been too delicate to support her under a fatal passion which preyed upon her heart, and for which she had incessantly reproached herself; a slow but gentle decay imperceptibly weakened her lovely frame. She was sensible of her own situation before she gave her hand to the Count, but was persuaded by her friends that a happy union might restore her health. For a few weeks she appeared better, and being in the way of becoming a mother, a relapse into weakness, debility and languor, was attributed to that circumstance. She knew better, but she suffered them to mislead themselves, because she could not bear to see her friends unhappy. She struggled with her complaints until the hour arrived when nature made its last efforts, the same moment that gave birth to a son deprived the unhappy Count of its angelic mother, and the spirit of the amiable and too tender Caroline fled to Heaven!

It is impossible to paint the distraction of her miserable husband, who for many days was in that dreadful state, to give great cause for apprehension that he would quickly follow his beloved wife to the grave; but at length it pleased Heaven to restore his health, but his vivacity and cheerfulness were fled for ever. He devoted the remainder of his days to the education of his two sons, and the image of his lost Caroline was never absent from his thoughts. Sensible that his eldest boy, Rhodophil, would inherit his paternal estates, he determined to save a handsome fortune for his young Ferdinand, who was the perfect resemblance of his unfortunate mother. The Count retrenched every useless expense, and though he was benevolent and liberal to others, he denied himself every thing superfluous that he might benefit his darling son, who, as he grew up, discovered every trait of a good heart, and an excellent constitution.

Rhodophil was the counterpart of his mother, both in person and disposition. —Stern, haughty, insolent and unfeeling, no tenderness could move, no remonstrances avail, to make him unbend his temper, and grow more tractable in his juvenile days; but when advanced to manhood, he became all at once fond of and submissive to his father, and almost servilely attentive to his brother, who, open, generous and unsuspecting, really loved Rhodophil, and rejoiced at the alteration that appeared to have taken place in his disposition.

CHAPTER VI

Rhodophil was about one-and-twenty, and Ferdinand in his eighteenth year, when walking one evening in the suburbs of Baden, they met an elderly woman, plainly but cleanly dressed, with a young one by her side, whose uncommon beauty instantly attracted the eyes of both the brothers. By mutual consent they turned and followed her; they observed them enter a mean-looking house correspondent to their appearance: — Both were eager to make inquiries, and were informed by a neighbour that the woman's name was Dupree, and the young girl, who was her niece, was called Claudina; they had only resided a few months in the town, and appeared to have but a very slender income. With this intelligence they returned home, both thoughtful, and each suspecting the sentiments of the other, which was, a desire of seeing and knowing a little more of this lovely Claudina.

When they met next morning, Rhodophil began to talk of the "pretty girl" they had seen; but in a lively manner, and in a tone of indifference that surprised Ferdinand, whose young heart had received a first impression, and who could not mention her but in terms of rapture that drew upon him the pleasantry of his brother. Ferdinand, incapable of art or dissimulation, openly avowed his intention of going in search of another view of his charmer; his brother laughed at his folly, and said he should take a different route.

Not to dwell too long on this part of the story, we shall only say, that Ferdinand found means to get acquainted with this young woman, and very soon engaged his heart to her, and acquired no small share of her's. — Mean time overtures were made to the woman by a friend of her's to sell her niece, or in other words, she was offered a handsome sum for herself, and a settlement on Claudina by a young Nobleman. Dupree, mercenary and poor, could not withstand the temptation; she endeavoured, to the utmost of her skill, to seduce the mind of her niece, by a display of all the advantages such an attachment would secure to her; but Claudina had the best security for the preservation of her honor, which was her love for Ferdinand, and the hope that, though not an elder brother, he would have a handsome fortune, and that his affection for her was an honourable one. — Those splendid overtures were therefore firmly rejected, though often renewed, and her lover felt himself under additional ties of love and obligation to a young woman, whose affection and good principles had stood the test of every temptation.

Mean time his mind could not be easy; he had every reason to imagine his father never would approve of a connexion so mean and unsuitable to the future views he had for his establishment; he dared not mention his attachment, and hourly dreaded the discovery and its consequences. His brother often rallied him upon his passion, and at first persuaded him greatly against the indulgence of a love so improper; but finding Ferdinand inflexibly determined to persevere, he had for some time ceased to speak on the subject. This young man grew daily more enamoured, and every moment more vexed and mortified at her humble situation, and the dangers to which she was exposed by her residence with an unprincipled woman. He had her taught privately several branches of education, and was charmed with her docility and the progress she made in her studies; every hour his love increased, and he determined to marry her privately.

One day walking in the garden, in a very pensive mood, Rhodophil joined him, and affectionately inquired into the cause of his melancholy.—Ferdinand, whose love for Claudina had by no means lessened his affections towards his brother, after a little hesitation, confessed the cause of his embarrassment, his resolution to wed Claudina, and the dread he entertained of displeasing so good a father, whom he dearly loved and honoured.

"If your resolution is taken," replied Rhodophil, "it would be a waste of time to enter into any arguments with you on the subject; the disadvantages attending it must be as obvious to yourself as to me. Your father never will give his consent, and if you do marry her, you must keep the affair secret; your father cannot live for ever."

This last observation shocked Ferdinand extremely.—"Good God!" exclaimed he, "shall I enter into an union where my only chance of happiness must arise from the death of a parent so tender and respectable? Perish the thought! No, let me be miserable from the disappointment of my wishes, but never let me be criminal, detestable in my own eyes." Rhodophil observed, that he was more hurt than was necessary at the hint he had dropped, which meant nothing more than a natural conclusion: "However," added he, 'to prove the sincerity of my fraternal affection, marry Claudina; I will add to your allowance by a portion of mine; you will then be enabled to maintain her, and by removing her to a different quarter of the town may elude all suspicion and observation."

How unequal was the prudence and resolution of eighteen to withstand the incitements of passion, or decline the indulgence of it when sanctioned by a brother! Ferdinand embraced his generous brother with transport, and, blind to all the ill effects that might be dreaded from an union so rash and unsuitable, he no longer hesitated, but the following day he informed Claudina and her aunt of his resolution, and for the first time asked, "Who, and what were her parents?" The aunt answered, "That her father, in early life, had been in the army, an officer; but dying soon after her birth, her mother had only a small pension to live on, which poorly supported her for about three years, when she also died, leaving Claudina to her care; that she (Dupree) having only a hundred crowns a year to live on, had remained in the country until this last year, when she thought it best to remove near the city, in the hope that her niece's beauty would get her a good husband." With this account Ferdinand was satisfied, and not a little pleased to find his mistress owed her birth to an officer, though she was poor and friendless. In a very few days he was united to his Claudina, and removed her to another quarter in the suburbs, where she lived decently, if not elegantly, and having an affectionate heart, and a good understanding, she was grateful for the advantages Ferdinand's love procured for her, without extending her wishes beyond them.

He had been married about six months; his wife promised an increase to their family, when one morning his father, who had appeared uncommonly grave at breakfast, ordered Ferdinand to attend him to the library. He obeyed; the manner, more than the words, struck him, and with an agitated heart he appeared before him.

"Ferdinand," said the Count, in a tone of solemnity, "I ardently wish to see you settled in life, an opportunity now offers not to be rejected. Count Benhorff has offered to give you his daughter, the Lady Amelia, whose large fortune and personal charms render the alliance most truly desirable, and entirely unobjectionable." He stopped, Ferdinand was thunderstruck; this was an occurrence that he had never once dreamt of. He hesitated, faltered, at length muttered out something about 'the impropriety of being married before his brother."

"That is not your business, Sir," resumed the Count; "your brother has other views; Count Benhorff and his daughter have done you the honour of a distinguished preference, and it only remains for you to receive my orders, and I should suppose, to comply with them immediately with gratitude and transport, suitable to an offer so splendid, and so much superior to my expectations of settling you in life; as you well know you have only a share of my personal fortune to expect." "With whatever share you have the goodness to appropriate for me, Sir, I hope I shall be content and thankful, nor meanly wish to aggrandize myself by marriage without I could love and honour the Lady. Pardon me, Sir," added he, gathering a little more courage, "pardon me, therefore, if I do not so readily accord to your wishes as you may expect, but never will I marry a woman I cannot love."

"And what, Sir," said the Count, kindling into a rage, "should prevent you from loving the Lady Amelia, who has a hundred adorers, though she has condescended to single you out, undeserving as I fear you are of the distinction. Tell me, Sir, what are the obstacles to your being attached to so charming a young woman?" Never did Ferdinand experience equal perplexity to that moment; he trembled, and his emotions scarcely permitted him to speak.

"I have no knowledge of her temper; her — — —."

"Say no more," cried the Count, interrupting him; "no more equivocation, I see I have not been misinformed, you have formed another attachment; say, tell me, is it not so?"

"I am above uttering a falsehood," answered Ferdinand; "I own it, Sir, there is a young woman — — —."

"Foolish, imprudent boy!" exclaimed the Count, in a violent rage; "your youth hath been seduced into an intrigue with an artful wanton."

"By Heavens! No," cried Ferdinand, "I have not been seduced, nor is she a wanton."

"Hold, insolent!" returned the Count, "and hear me; if you have formed an imprudent connexion, break it off, I will enable you to give a handsome sum, and have done with it. Prepare to carry your addresses to the Lady Amelia; these are my absolute commands, which I expect you to obey, or you are no longer a son of mine."

"Oh! my father," cried Ferdinand, — "reverse that cruel sentence, command not impossibilities."

"I do not," answered the Count, a little softened; "an affair of gallantry has nothing to do with an engagement of honour, an union for life. You are young, and have been drawn away by your passions; but decency forbids you to continue your attachment whilst you are soliciting the Lady Amelia's hand: I therefore request you, Ferdinand, I will not command, I desire you to dissolve your present connexion, and let me have the happiness of seeing you established in my life-time. You are the only pledge left me of a too tender affection: Your angel mother died in giving you life; let not that life so dearly purchased render my latter days unhappy; let me meet her in the realms above with the conscious delight of having completed the happiness of her child."

The Count's voice faltered as he pronounced the last words. Ferdinand was in agonies; he threw himself at his father's feet: —"Spare me, spare your wretched son; oh! Sir, happiness and Lady Amelia cannot be joined with me; happiness consists not in titles, grandeur, or riches: I am moderate in my wishes; my brother will aggrandize your house."

"And you," said the Count, interrupting him with fury, "you resolve to disgrace it. Just Heaven! how am I punished for my errors in the person of my darling son! Yes, you are my punisher; you have chosen to be the instrument of vengeance, to retaliate upon your father, and hasten the few short days that are allotted to me, full of sorrow and despair: But hear me, once more I command you to promise me that you will give up your present infatuation, that you will quit the society of that woman who has seduced you from your duty. Speak, say you will obey me."

"I dare not deceive my father," replied Ferdinand, with grief and horror in his countenance; "I dare not forfeit my integrity."

"You persist then in your folly, in your crimes," exclaimed the other, in a rage little short of madness; 'then mark my words: The allowance I have given you, I shall resume as long as you resist my will; the creature who has bewitched you I will punish, and if you dare to form any legal sacred connexion with her, my everlasting curses attend you both!"

"Stop, oh! stop," cried the frantic Ferdinand, "she is my wife!" The Count dropped into a chair.

"Wretch! unnatural wretch! what hast thou done?" said he, in a tone of horror, "thou art now an alien to my blood. I recall not what I have denounced; my curses are registered above; go, leave me, see me no more; dare not to enter any mansion where I reside, for I solemnly protest this is the last time I will behold thee!"—He rose from his chair, withdrew to a closet, and rang the bell. Orders were given to carry every thing belonging to Ferdinand out of the Castle that instant, and never to admit him more within its gates.

CHAPTER VII

Mean time the unhappy youth had fainted on the floor, where he was found by his brother, who recovered and tried to sooth him into composure; but the dreadful curse still vibrated in his ears, distraction was in his looks, and his tongue refused utterance to the emotions of his heart. He was conveyed to Rhodophil's apartment, who assured him he would leave nothing undone to soften his father's displeasure. — "Comfort yourself, my brother," said he, "all violences must subside, time must be allowed, fear not, I will be your friend and advocate, and for means of subsistence you may rely on me." — Ferdinand could make no reply; he pressed his brother's hand, and, attended by the faithful Ernest, left the Castle, and returned to his wife. The moment she saw him she screamed. Never was a man so altered in so short a time. Ernest was obliged to explain to her the discovery which had been made, and she no longer wondered at the grief and despair visible in her husband; she blamed and execrated herself as the cause; and in the height of her agitations absolutely proposed to him to give her up, to renounce her society, and permit her to spend her days in sorrow and obscurity. But Ferdinand would not be outdone in affection and generosity. — "You are my wife," said he; "you have not offended, and it is both my incliation and my duty to protect you, my dearest consolation, under every affliction." Ernest endeavoured to calm the grief and agitations of both; he promised to assist the entreaties of Rhodophil, by every representation that could soften the Count towards Ferdinand, and induce him to think favourably of Claudina.

But in vain was every effort to mitigate the Count's resentment, until one day, long after Claudina had been brought to bed of a boy, (whom Ferdinand named Charles Rhodophil, after his father and brother) when she was walking with her child in her arms, in the skirts of the forest for air, the Count and Rhodophil, who had been on a hunting party, met her; the latter dropped back to speak to her; the Count eyed her attentively, and when his son came up, inquired who she was; with some hesitation he acknowledged she was the wife of Ferdinand. He started, and was silent for several minutes; at length, sighing deeply, "I own," said he, "she is extremely beautiful; she has a child too! — Ill-fated Ferdinand! thou hast undone thyself, and rendered me culpable and wretched; but the infant is at least innocent; I did not curse, not reprobate that, therefore I will allow something to keep it from want." — On his return Ernest was called, and directed to pay them quarterly twenty crowns. The old man was overjoyed, and tried to obtain a larger allowance, but his master was immovable: "To keep them from want is sufficient, it is the charity I would bestow on a stranger, they have no claims upon me."

Glad even to have gained this point, Ernest hastened to them with the intelligence, with a quarter's advance, and bid them look on it as a lucky omen of future reconciliation. Ferdinand was transported; he wrote to his father a letter full of acknowledgments, deep contrition for having offended him, and every possible submission his situation would allow of; but his letter was returned unopened, and Ernest forbidden to mention his name. — — — Rhodophil frequently visited them, and often made Claudina little presents, which were very acceptable, for they experienced a loss which made their little income very confined. One morning, on coming down stairs, there seemed a disorder in the room very unusual; no fire was made, no preparation for breakfast, and the door of the house left on the latch. Their aunt, who had always performed all the offices of a servant, assisted by Claudina whilst Ferdinand nursed his little boy. This aunt it was plain was gone out, but for what, or where to, they could form no conjecture; however, they exerted themselves to do the necessary offices, but when they came to prepare their breakfast, they could find no spoons, and in a short time after discovered the drawers in the room had been opened, and all Claudina's linen was taken away; they likewise missed Ferdinand's watch, which hung in the room.

Strangely alarmed, they made every possible search, which only served to discover more losses, and to convince them they had been robbed, and by this aunt. Their consternation cannot be expressed; but the cruel truth was unquestionable, and with the very little money they had, they were obliged to purchase necessaries for use, which was a heavy drawback. What could have induced this woman to injure and desert them they could not imagine; but the fact was certain, and the loss and inconvenience great. Claudina was again with child, and this event added to the continued displeasure of the Count, which affected her husband with a deep melancholy, threw her into a low nervous disorder, which rendered her but little capable of domestic business, and but for the kindness of Rhodophil and Ernest, they must have perished. Mean time it was very visible that a heavy dejection overwhelmed the Count, his constitution grew weak, his spirits sunk, his appetite lost. — Every one was alarmed; the physician gave it as his opinion that it was a constitution breaking up, but no immediate danger; at length he confined himself solely to his apartment, and saw only Rhodophil, the physician, and his valet.

Ferdinand was informed of his father's situation, and was nearly distracted. He entreated Rhodophil to intercede for him, 'that he might once more throw himself at the feet of his justly offended parent, and receive a last blessing." His entreaties were rejected—his presence forbidden. He then wrote a few lines, imploring his beloved father to revoke the heavy curse he had laid upon him and his wife.—His brother returned the letter, his father had refused it, and commanded him to mention his name no more. The truly wretched Ferdinand used to walk before the Castle gates for days together, imploring admittance, but all was fruitless; no servant dared to disobey orders, so positively given to the contrary.

One morning, whilst leaning his arms on the outside gate, Ernest came to him: "I will run the risque, follow me to my chamber, Sir, no time is to be lost." More dead than alive, he attended Ernest without speaking, when, at the very entrance of the house, they met his brother. He started back with amazement: "Good God! Ferdinand! how came you here?"

"Pardon me, Sir," said Ernest, much confused; "but from what I hear, my noble master is at the point of death; now, and now only, when he must solicit mercy from his heavenly father, is the time to try if he will extend that mercy, on his part, which he must supplicate from the Almighty."

"You are right," replied Rhodophil;—"Come with me to the anti-chamber, my dear brother, and I will procure you admittance, though all others are forbidden."—Ernest bowed and withdrew; with a beating heart and trembling limbs Ferdinand entered the anti-chamber, where Rhodophil's valet sat, who also started at seeing the unexpected guest his master brought in.

"Wait without," said Rhodophil, "nor at your peril permit any one to enter."—The servant quitted the room.

"Now," said the former, "I will go in and see the state our father is in, and administer a cordial to support his spirits."—Scarcely daring to breathe, Ferdinand waited near a quarter of an hour in all the agonies of suspense and terror.

Rhodophil at length appeared:—"He sleeps," said he, "every thing depends on rest, we must not disturb him, wait a little." Ferdinand bowed his head, he could not trust to his voice, his heart beat with increasing violence. Near half an hour elapsed, when his attention was suddenly roused by two or three deep groans. He started, and flew to the door; a short gallery communicated to the bed chamber of the Count, there he listened, a kind of bustle seemed to be in the room, but the groans were not repeated; his hand was on the lock, hardly sensible whether he intended to open it or not, when it was suddenly opened on the other side. The Count's valet appeared: "Be so good to return!" said he, "all is over, my master is no more!"

Ferdinand tottered back into the other room, and fell lifeless on the floor, where his brother found him on his return to the library, at which period this history began.

The subsequent circumstances have been fully related, and having sent Ferdinand to Vienna, we shall attend to Claudina and her children, who were for several days inconsolable for the departure of her husband.

CHAPTER VIII

Every attention that affection, and the duties of hospitality enjoined, was paid by Rhodophil to his sister-in-law, and no longer restrained by the prudence and pride of Ferdinand, he made her a number of considerable presents, increased the finery of her wardrobe, was assiduous to amuse her, and in short gained so highly on the esteem and gratitude of Claudina, that she insensibly felt her regret lessened for the loss of her husband, and although she sometimes felt and expressed a concern for his safety, yet the well-timed amusements Rhodophil prepared for her, left that occasional anxiety but as a passing cloud upon her memory, that was followed by brighter ideas. Ernest, who had engaged to pay every attention to his mistress, as he called her, found nothing was wanting from him to comfort her, and so captious is the human mind, that, though he would have been grieved to have seen her unhappy, yet he was very much displeased to see her so cheerful.

She commanded the house entirely, every servant was at her disposal, and the master of it seemed to have no will but her's, no laws but of her making. If we look back, and see the very humble state in which Claudina had lived before she knew Ferdinand, and even the humble mediocrity which she enjoyed with him before the death of Count Renaud; if we consider that, though Ferdinand had procured masters to teach her accomplishments before she married, and of course with the advantages of his conversation her mind must have been enlightened, and her understanding improved, yet still a number of improper ideas, habitual from early life, would at times recur, and render both her sentiments and behaviour very unequal. She had been always taught to expect that her beauty would make her fortune, therefore of course she thought highly of her charms, and when she sometimes listened to the extravagant praises of Rhodophil, she was ready to blame herself for so quickly accepting the offer of a younger, portionless brother, when, in all probability, had she waited, she might have been a Countess.

A too frequent repetition of those thoughts by degrees undermined the warmth of her affection for her husband, and one day, when walking in the garden with Rhodophil, that he was lavish in his encomiums on her person, she interrupted by asking, with a look of naivete, "How it happened, that, if he thought so well of her, he had not loved her like Ferdinand?"

"And did I not love you? — Yes, Claudina," replied he, "from the first moment I adored you; but could I see my brother wretched? — Or could I hope you would reserve the blessing of your hand for me until my father's death? Neither dared I think of marrying you to involve you in wretchedness. Had you suffered for me, what I have known you to bear with Ferdinand, I should have been distracted. No, Claudina, such was the delicacy of my passion, that I chose to be miserable myself, rather than make the woman I adored unhappy; to lay her under the interdiction of a father, the weight of a curse would have sunk me to the grave."

Not a word of this was lost on Claudina; every syllable sunk into her soul; she began to reflect on what she had forfeited by marrying Ferdinand, and blamed the ardour of that love which had sought its own gratification at her expense. Rhodophil saw the workings of her mind, and pursued his insidious tale.

"When my brother married you, how great was my misery — what sleepless nights, what days of anguish! yet how did I labour for your happiness? Now I may tell you: — Know then, my father never allowed you one shilling; I invented that tale to spare your delicacy, that you might not feel yourself too much obliged to me; but could I do too much for the woman I adored? During my father's illness I laboured with uncommon zeal to procure a settlement for you, to procure a pardon for my brother. I ventured to brave his utmost resentment by taking him into the next room (not thinking his death so very near) in the hope of having him revoke that dreadful curse he had laid upon him; but, alas! he died, and all my endeavours were fruitless."

"How!" exclaimed she, "Did he not see his father? Did he not forgive him on his death-bed?"

"No," he replied, "he never saw the Count after the day your marriage was discovered."

"Good Heavens!" said she, "what imposition, what falsities did Ferdinand tell me!" She then repeated to him what has been already mentioned, and the very circumstances which he had invented to calm her mind, and restore her peace, were now turned against him, as a piece of base duplicity, and the inference drawn was, 'that if he was capable of so much deceit in one thing, he might in another, and therefore she could have no confidence where there was room for doubts." — Rhodophil, who was perfectly acquainted with his brother's motives for the deception, pretended to be entirely ignorant of them, and, by the most artful finesse, gave a colouring to an action dictated by tenderness alone, that stamped an indelible impression on the mind of Claudina, to the injury of that love and truth she owed to the most affectionate of husbands.

Letters very soon arrived from the much injured Ferdinand, acquainting them of his arrival at Vienna, his introduction to the Emperor, and the desirable situation in which he found himself placed. His expressions to Claudina were replete with tenderness, and all his anxiety arose from a separation that he knew must be equally painful to her. The only consolation he could promise to himself were her letters, and he besought her to indulge him with hearing of herself and children by every opportunity. To his brother he was grateful and affectionate; to Ernest kind and friendly, requesting him to watch over the health and peace of his beloved wife, whose tender sensibility he was apprehensive would injure her constitution.

Poor Ferdinand! little did he conceive that his little bark of happiness was wrecked upon a fatal shore that blasted all his hopes for ever; much less could he have an idea to what hand he was indebted for conducting her to the port of destruction. Ernest, when he had perused his letter, sighed heavily:—"Alas!" said he, "how one fatal action has destroyed the peace of a whole family for ever! The mole that has long laboured to undermine the happiness of Ferdinand has now succeeded; his own rash hand first pointed the weapon that must wound his bosom beyond all possibility of a cure, for I too plainly see his wife is grown indifferent to him, and attached to the pleasures of the world!"

Days and weeks passed away, and saw Claudina gay and happy; they heard often from Ferdinand, who had been twice in an engagement, and had been promoted.—When the campaign was over he hoped to return and embrace all the treasures he possessed in one circle, a tender wife, a generous and affectionate brother, and his darling children.—This hope, so flattering to him, was little capable of giving pleasure to the inhabitants of the Castle; and Ernest observed all at once a deep thoughtfulness take possession of the Count, and a pensive melancholy steal over the features of Claudina, for neither of which was there apparently any cause.

One day, being in the room which had formerly been the library, and adjoining to Claudina's bed chamber, sitting at the window indulging his own reflections, he thought he heard the Count's voice in a whispering tone; there was nothing extraordinary or reprehensible in his being in her apartment, yet some how Ernest found his curiosity excited to know why the conversation should be in a whisper; he therefore listened, and though he could only make out indirect sentences and half words, he understood but too much, and retired overwhelmed with astonishment and horror; a scheme replete with the most unpardonable wickedness seemed to be in agitation, which it was his duty, if possible, to prevent.

The following day Ernest sought out the Count's valet, who had been always more civil to him than ever his master had, since the old Count's death, and which indeed arose from a circumstance Ernest had long since forgotten. In the juvenile days of Rhodophil and Ferdinand, when they were riding out one day, accompanied by Peter (then also a lad) and Ernest, the horse of Peter took fright: Ernest, who had an excellent one, as quickly followed, overtook the other, and by a dexterous manoeuvre stopped the horse in the very moment when he must have plunged over a precipice. This signal service Peter never had forgotten, and though he could boast but of little principle or integrity in any one point, yet he always looked up to Ernest as the preserver of his life; when the old man scarcely remembered a single circumstance of it, and had sometimes been at a loss to account for Peter's particular civilities to him. These attentions, however, encouraged Ernest to address him, and to endeavour, if possible, to gain his confidence, being well assured that his master's secrets were in his possession.

Meeting by chance in the gallery, the old steward invited him to his apartment in the evening, an honour Peter was proud of, and took care not to neglect: He found a good bottle of wine prepared for him, and a very friendly reception; both warmed his heart. After a little preparatory conversation the old Gentleman remarked, 'that he was fearful the Count, or his sister-in-law, was ill, as they appeared to be very dull and melancholy."

"As to illness, Mr. Ernest," answered Peter, 'there is not much of that I believe; but they have enough to make them melancholy, when it is likely Mr. Ferdinand may soon come home."

"How!" cried the other, 'that is strange indeed! I should rather think they would be overjoyed at that, though to be sure he won't stay long."

"Ah! bless you, Mr. Ernest, you know nothing of the business, and yet it is as plain as the nose in your face."

"Why, you know, Peter, I never pry into secrets, and am no tattler of other people's affairs."

"No, I'll be sworn, you ar'n't; you are a good man, Sir, and don't know what wickedness goes forward here." — "Why don't you drink, Peter?"

"I do, I do, thank your love." Two or three glasses opened his heart still more freely. "To tell you the truth, Mr. Ernest, my master, the Count, is but a bad man, for seeing he has got all the fortune, he might have let his brother keep his wife to himself."

"How! why, sure! why, you do not think he wants to separate them, do you?"

"Bless your soul, why they be leagued together, and to my mind Madame Claudina loves him more than ever she did her husband."

"Astonishing!" cried Ernest.

"Yes, 'tis astonishing to be sure, because Mr. Ferdinand is a much handsomer man; but I'll let you know the whole if you'll be secret."

"You know I am no talker, Peter."

"Nor more you ar'n't, for you never made mischief on any poor servant, so I'll tell you, then, as sure as you be alive, Madame is a breeding."

"Impossible!" exclaimed the other.

"No, no, 'tis not impossible, the truth is out, and master wants to persuade her to go away to some place in Hungary, as if she runned away, and then they think Mr. Ferdinand will kill himself, or break his heart, or something, and then they two are to be married. This was one scheme; then another was, to have Mr. Ferdinand way-laid and killed, for if he comes home all will come out, and then 'twill for a certainty be murder among them."

"Good Heavens! what treachery and infamy! How did you learn all this, Peter?"

"Why, because I am in master's secrets; he can't do without me."

"Then I conjure you, Peter, to let me know all your proceedings; I will amply reward you, and God will bless you if you serve the innocent."

"Why, as to that, Sir, I know I am not very innocent to be sure; but I love you, for you saved my life you know, when the horse was going to caper over the mountain with me, and so I think it my duty to serve you, and if you desire me I will tell you all, only don't speak a word of it to master or any body." This Ernest faithfully promised, and Peter engaged to step into his room, whenever he could gain any intelligence to communicate.

This information of Peter's corroborating the conversation he had overheard in the library, left Ernest no room for doubt of a connexion terrible to think of, yet what steps to take, whether to acquaint Ferdinand with the dreadful secret, or to let him still remain ignorant and happy, were measures he thought must depend on the result of their determinations, and for the knowledge of them he depended on Peter. Nothing particular transpired for two days. Claudina's dejection increased, and she seemed very ill, her appetite was lost, and frequent faintings alarmed the family; but she refused to have medical advice, and said it was only weakness from a violent cold. On the third night, however, she was seized with convulsions, only her maid and Rhodophil attended her, and for hours her life was in great danger; but towards the morning she grew better. Rhodophil seemed transported that the convulsions had left her, and observed among the servants that his sister-in-law had for many years been subject to those fits at times, and the approach of the disorder had occasioned the weakness and dejection of her spirits for some days before, he was glad the crisis was over.

This tale passed current with the servants; but Ernest had his suspicions, which a short time confirmed, for she soon recovered, and was as gay and as happy as usual. The arrival of Ferdinand, in about three weeks after, seemed to give general joy in the family. — Ernest alone was unhappy, because he knew too much, yet he resolved to be silent, rather than destroy the peace of his beloved master, (as he always called him) and render his future days miserable.

CHAPTER IX

Ferdinand had a month's leave of absence; he had been promoted to a higher rank than he could have hoped for, his prospects in the army were such as to inspire a hope of being in a short time able to provide for his family. He returned to them enlivened by expectation, and transported to embrace a darling wife, and a generous brother. In the evening, when retired to the apartment of his Claudina, when expressing his raptures at seeing her so well and happy, a deep and hollow groan made him start from his chair, and threw his wife into a trembling fit. —"What, or where does that groan come from?" cried she. He was about to answer, when a second, still more alarming, was followed by those words from the same voice Ferdinand had twice before heard:—Fly, fly from her arms, as you would avoid sin and death!"—Claudina shrieked and fainted. Her husband rang the bell for assistance. She relapsed from one fit into another for several hours; all was fright and confusion, for he did not choose to account for her disorder among the servants: One, however, observed these were worse fits than she had lately, because they lasted longer.

"What then," asked Ferdinand, "has she before now had such seizures as this?"

"Yes, Sir," answered the servant, "a short time ago, and my master told us, as to be sure you know, that Madame was often troubled with them."

This information surprised him, the conclusion in his own mind was, that she had before now been alarmed in a similar manner; but the words dwelt upon his memory:—What could be their import—"As you would avoid sin and death!" Good God! how shocking! He had not time, however for much reflection, the state his wife lay in chiefly engrossed his attention; he insisted upon medical advice, and a physician was sent for. Before he could make his appearance distraction had seized her brain; she talked wild and incoherent, of death, murder, Rhodophil and Ferdinand! When the Doctor came he declared her in a frenzy fever, and methods were taken to lower it so effectually, that in a few hours she lay quite in a torpid state, insensible to every thing round her.—Poor Ferdinand withdrew for a few moments at the request of Rhodophil.

"Alas!" cried he, "is this my welcome! Have I returned home with the dear delight of being happy in the bosom of my family, and must this dreadful prohibition cause me consummate wretchedness!"

"What prohibition?" asked Rhodophil, eagerly. Ferdinand was sensible that he had said too much, that he had excited a curiosity he knew not how to elude. After a little pause and consideration, he acquainted Rhodophil with the preceding circumstance, adding, 'that the voice seemed to be his father's." The other sunk back in his chair, pale and trembling, unable to utter a syllable, his eyes fixed on his brother with a wild inquiring look. — "I see," said Ferdinand, "you are extremely shocked; had not Claudina been present with me, I should hardly have ventured to relate to you so strange and improbable a circumstance, fearful lest you should have ridiculed my visionary ideas; but I am too well assured of the reality."

"Of what?" cried the Count, falteringly: "What did you hear else?"

"No more than the words I have repeated, words sufficient to harrow up my soul, to fill me with dreadful apprehensions, and terrifying images. What they mean, Heaven only knows, for I am not conscious of any crimes, and after having so long lived with my wife, why this alarming caution now? Why, I am forbidden to return to her arms by supernatural powers, is beyond my comprehension to define; I see only that there is, there must be, some dreadful cause, and that I am marked out for misery. O, Rhodophil! wretched are the days of those who fail in their first duties, obedience to a parent; and sure destruction follows a father's curse." No longer able to repress his emotions Ferdinand wept aloud.

Rhodophil, who was by this time a little recovered (though his eye was still wandering with an affrighted glance, and his limbs no longer boasted their usual steadiness) sought to speak comfort to his brother: "I will not (said he) tell you that it is possible your senses might be deceived; I am neither credulous, nor superstitious, yet I think you would do right to pay some observance to a warning from the dead, and all that we can infer is, that the union between you and your wife is displeasing to Heaven." — "Wherefore," cried Ferdinand, "the want of birth and riches is no crime in the sight of God; I married unknown to my father, that was a sin against his authority; but can it be a crime of that magnitude to draw down the displeasure of Heaven?"

"Oh! yes, if it provoked a father's malediction, it rendered both criminal, and I am the wretched victim; I am singled out from hundreds who have committed the same error, the same unpardonable act of disobedience, to be held up as a pharos to warn unthinking youth of the miseries attending a too hasty connexion unsanctioned by a parent's approbation. Oh! my father, I am indeed severely punished!"

This apostrophe drove Rhodophil from the room; he could not support the sight of his brother's distress. Ernest immediately entered; the afflicted heart clings for consolation to the first sympathizing friend; the old man was shocked to see him; he rested his head on the shoulder of Ernest, whilst he repeated what had happened in Claudina's apartment. "Dear unhappy creature!"—added he, "I have destroyed her peace, my fatal love has undone her; in humble obscurity she might have been happy, and I have dragged her into wretchedness."

"My dear master (said Ernest) do not reproach yourself on her account; your wife cannot, ought not to blame you, whatever the circumstances may be that renders your union improper; to her you have always done your duty. If she is unhappy, you are not to blame; the offence against your father was designed to promote her happiness as well as your own, why it has failed, we are not to inquire; but remember this, that the same voice which bid you 'fly' from your wife, pronounced the words 'Pardon and peace;' if there is credibility in one, there is in the other."

Ferdinand raised his head, and looking earnestly in his face, "There is an implication in your words that shock me, that would fill me with the most torturing apprehensions, but that I know the impossibility of there being any grounds for them. The 'pardon and peace' has never been one day absent from my memory, strange if it should, when it is the ground-work, the only hold I have to reconcile me to myself: But, alas! if I lay hold on that for consolation, if I look on those words as a sacred command, what must I now sacrifice to the same mandate? My wife, my dear innocent wife, the mother of my children, the sweet comforter under all my misfortunes, must I give up her society, fly her arms? Oh! stern and cruel!"

"Stop, Sir (said Ernest, interrupting him) reflect, who you are accusing, remember that, to us short-sighted mortals, the events which often appear most distressing, are intended for our greatest blessings."

"Ernest," replied Ferdinand, "you are a natural philosopher, you know not the difficulty of being a practical one, and at your age the passions have lost their turbulence. O, that I also was old, or laid peaceably in my grave! But I forget Claudina," (added he, rising briskly, and rushing to her apartment.) She had just began to show some signs of recollection, but the moment he appeared she shrieked and turned from him. His little boy Charles was in the room; he ran to his father: "My mamma will not speak to me, will not kiss me; indeed, papa, I have not been naughty." — The artless voice of innocence overcame Ferdinand; he struggled to repress his emotions, but the big drops rolled down his face. He embraced his child, then turning to her, "Claudina! my dear Claudina, will you not speak to us?" She turned her head, her eyes met his, she groaned, and averted them to the child. "My poor boy!" exclaimed she. He ran to her arms. She embraced him: "Go, go, my child, to your father." Ferdinand was deeply affected. He ordered the attendants to withdraw, then seating himself by her: "My best, my only love (said he) take comfort, you have been terrified, recover yourself, my Claudina." He would have taken her hand; she withdrew it. "Revere the voice of Heaven," cried she, greatly agitated, "obey its decrees, pollution is in my touch, and unless you wish me mad indeed approach me not. Poor unhappy man! well may you curse the hour you first saw me."

"Who, I!" cried he, "I curse; alas! too well I know the horrors of that rash impetuosity of the mind. No, but for your sake I have no regrets; I have drawn down the wrath of Heaven and you, innocent as you are, must suffer the sad effects."

"Innocent!" repeated she, "leave me, Ferdinand, I beseech you to leave me; once more, if you would preserve us both from everlasting perdition, reverence that sacred command, fly me as you would do a scorpion that might sting you to death." Inexpressibly shocked, and apprehensive that her senses were again wandering, he rang the bell, and on the entrance of the servants withdrew: Regardless of what constructions might be put on the orders she gave, she insisted that neither her husband or Rhodophil should be again admitted to her apartment.

The house was melancholy, for every one in it was gloomy and unhappy; they shunned each other; the two brothers met at meals, but those meals were short and unsociable; each feared to inquire into particulars they had reason to dread; yet they heard Claudina was better. The third day, when torturing suspense, and disappointed love, had worn Ferdinand almost to a shadow, Ernest entered the room: "I am come, Sir, from Madame Claudina."

"What (cried the other) have you been admitted?"

"I was sent for, Sir, and have had a long conversation."

"O, tell me, quickly tell, the result, my mind is in tumults."

"I know it, Sir, and therefore am I come. Pray, Heaven, that what I have to relate may compose it. I received an order to attend on your Lady; I obeyed, and my old heart ached to see the ravages grief had made. She ordered every one from the room; she was sitting on the side of the bed: Ernest (said she, with much solemnity) you are the faithful servant and friend of the family; on your fidelity I rely, and your assistance I solicit."

"Assistance! (repeated Ferdinand) of what nature, pray?"

"Have the goodness to hear me, Sir, without interruption," resumed Ernest: "I assured the Lady she might depend upon my readiness to serve her in every thing consistent with my duty." This was her answer.

"Some circumstances have arisen that render it absolutely necessary I should quit this house, and be separated from my husband; I wish to go away equally unknown to him or his brother: I am not destitute of money, and for this purpose shall use it without scruple. I intend to retire into a convent, will you assist me privately?" I assured her I would, and immediately took an oath never to reveal the place of her abode without her consent."

"How! (cried Ferdinand) is this your affection for me? And do you think I will herself in a convent, she to be the sacrifice for my errors? Do you think I will ever suffer this?"

"I do, Sir (answered he, calmly) I think you respect the will of Heaven, that you will consider, you must separate to be happy.—I shall this day set about an inquiry for a proper residence for her, and when I have found it, neither force nor persuasions shall oblige me to reveal the secret without her permission. What I say to you is in confidence which she allows of; but it is her earnest request you do not mention it to your brother."

Ernest withdrew, leaving Ferdinand overwhelmed with grief, astonishment, and irresolution. He resolved, however, to watch her apartment and Ernest also, that they might not elude his observation, and that he might at least have the satisfaction of knowing her place of residence.

The next day the old man was absent, and Ferdinand rightly conjectured he was about making preparations for her departure. He kept his eye on her apartment, his heart was in great agitations, he found the "awful voice" had effectually terrified Claudina, and that her resolution was taken; he could not but applaud her fortitude, though he was overwhelmed with anguish. Sometimes it occurred to him as very extraordinary, that having resided several months together after his father's death in that house, in that same apartment, without the least disturbance; why now, after so much time had elapsed, a supernatural being should command him to 'fly from her arms, as he would avoid sin and death." The more he reflected, the more he was puzzled, the whole was so very wonderful, so much exceeding credibility, that he was sometimes tempted to think it was all illusion; but then the proofs returned, Claudina heard the last fatal command as well as himself, there could be no doubt of it: If then he admitted the one, he could not be mistaken in the other: Had his brother then a 'corrupt heart?' His brother, who had ever been his friend, the protector of his wife and children, whose conduct had ever appeared so fair, so open? Then he recollected his information from Ernest, and other circumstances, as a counterbalance to those acts of generosity. Puzzled, lost in conjecture, and miserably unhappy, Ferdinand passed that day and night, having inquired, previous to his retiring, how his wife did, and heard that she was much better, but desired to be undisturbed; they will then proceed on their plan, thought he, in a day or two, and it behoves me to be attentive to their motions.

The morning came, weak and unrefreshed, he threw on his clothes, and proceeded to the gallery, which communicated with Claudina's apartment, there he met Ernest: — "Return, Sir (said he) if you please, to your apartment, I wish to speak to you."—Ferdinand complied; they entered, and shut the door. "Now, my dear master, collect your fortitude, be governed by reason; Claudina is gone."

"Gone!" exclaimed the other, "how — where — when?"

"She went from hence last night, and is already in a place of safety."

"Then she cannot be far off," cried Ferdinand.

"Pardon me, Sir, when I said she was in a place of safety; it did not imply that she was at the end of her journey; but, however, here, Sir, is a letter, which she ordered me to deliver to you."—He hastily tore it open, and read the following lines:

"Adieu, my amiable and too tender husband:—Husband! O Heavens! my tears blot out the name; adieu then best, and most injured of men—warned by a miraculous event, I fly from you, from guilt and misery. Forget me and be happy: I am dead to you and the world; on the verge of the grave, the prospect was dreadful: I devote the rest of my days to penitence and prayer. My infant I take with me; she may one day emerge into the world if she lives; should she die, her happiness is secured.

"You shall from time to time hear of me, but you will never see me more. I have darkened all your prospects of felicity; I have returned the tenderest attachment with ingratitude. I am now no more. You have my full and entire consent to marry again under more fortunate auspices, for I again repeat that I am dead to you, solemnly devoted to a solitary life. May you live and be happy. Let not my dear boy detest the memory of his mother, he is young, and may believe I am dead; I wish not to be remembered. Return to the army, let glory be your mistress; she will amuse your mind, and lead you in the road to happiness, by teaching you to forget Claudina. Heavens bless you, and my dear, dear boy, for ever. I have written to the Count; the letter is of little consequence. May my name never more pass your lips. Hasten from hence; confide in the faithful Ernest; forgive and forget the unworthy Claudina."

Ferdinand perused this letter with all the marks of the wildest astonishment. "What fatal mystery lurks beneath the expressions in this paper!" cried he, "Of what crimes has she been guilty, but her attachment to me, and wherefore does she accuse herself of ingratitude? Marry again! Oh! Claudina, you little know my heart. There is, there must be some secret with which I am unacquainted, every line in her letter discovers it, why else call me injured? Oh! Ernest, declare this secret, whatever it is, the knowledge cannot make me so miserable as this dreadful uncertainty, this painful imagination."

"From me, Sir," answered Ernest, "you can learn nothing, for I have nothing to reveal; reconcile your mind to this event, which must be for the advantage of both.—Nothing on earth shall make me betray my trust, nor, whilst I live, discover the place of her abode. Should I die, when you are from me, I will take care you shall then, through a particular channel, still hear from, or of her, if you desire it; but I hope time will have its usual effects to restore your tranquillity, and forget the object that now causes your distress."

"Impossible!" exclaimed Ferdinand,—"impossible that I should ever forget my wife, the mother of my children, the choice of my heart! O, why, wherefore am I marked out to be the veriest wretch that crawls the earth, cut off from every endearing tie, and from some fatal unknown cause interdicted from enjoying the only blessing my misfortunes had left me!"

"My dear master," answered the old man, tears in his eyes, "recollect you have still one tie, one blessing, your son; to the dispensations of Providence it is our duty to submit, it avails nothing to inquire into the causes of things beyond our comprehension.

"Had she died, I trust, I should have borne my sorrows like a man; but this strange, incomprehensible mystery — — —. My child too! a blessing! O, Ernest, may he not live to wring a father's heart with grief, to retaliate upon me! He may, and I deserve it should be so, but, he may make me wretched, he may shorten my days by disobedience and affliction; but never, never shall he experience a father's curse, nor struggle under a malediction registered in Heaven, and never to be expunged!" "Do not indulge that idea, Sir, Heaven hears not, confirms not, man's rash imprecations, uttered in a moment of frenzy; their confirmation must depend upon circumstances; Heaven heeds not the curses of disappointed ambition."

"I have no longer any business here," cried Ferdinand, starting from a reverie, and hardly attending to the words of Ernest; — "nor will I return to the army, I care not what becomes of me, but I will see my brother." — He flew out of the room to Rhodophil's apartment, which entering without ceremony, he found him gazing on a letter that he held in his hand, fixed like a statue. The entrance of Ferdinand startled him; he rose, crushed the paper into his pocket, — "Well, Sir!" was all he could say. — "O, my brother! O, Rhodophil! Claudina's gone, fled, I know not whither."

This address occasioned an alteration in the looks of the other, from a haughty fierceness, they softened into an appearance of compassion and curiosity. "Is it possible (asked he) that she has not acquainted you with her motives for withdrawing, nor where she intends to reside?"

"Neither (replied he;) she bids me adieu for ever, will never see me more, and desires me to forget her as unworthy of my affection; for Heaven's sake tell me if you can divine the cause of this cruel, unaccountable conduct."

"Indeed I cannot (answered Rhodophil.) Some weeks ago she was low spirited and melancholy, then she had fits one night, but in two or three days got better, and seemed more tranquil; it is certain her disposition has been very unequal, the cause of which I could never rightly comprehend."

"Good God! (exclaimed the other) it is very strange, her letter seems to imply as if she had behaved imprudently, yet surely it is impossible."

"Something certainly lay heavy upon her mind (said the Count;) women are inexplicable beings; she may have deceived you; I do not say she has, because I know nothing; but some cause there must be, and all that I can advise you is, to forget her."

"How easy to advise where the heart is not interested! To forget is a hard lesson, memory given to us for a blessing, but too often proves the source of the bitterest sorrow; and my hopes of happiness are clouded for ever. One only request I have now to make."

"What is it?" asked Rhodophil, with some emotion. "As the unfortunate Claudina has entirely secluded herself, tell me, has she the means for her support?" The other hesitated a moment, then taking the paper from his pocket, which he had been gazing on, he gave it into his hands, that will satisfy you," said he. These were the contents:

TO COUNT RHODOPHIL.

"When this reaches you, I shall have bid the world adieu for ever; my much injured husband never will incur the wrath of Heaven for his attachment to a worthless woman after this day—I shall see him no more.

"The settlement you made on me is in the hands of Ernest; half of that sum I shall send for quarterly, but no clue will be found by that means to trace me; I have taken my measures too securely for any possibility of a discovery: The other half of that settlement I have made over in trust to Ernest for the education of my son. May he never hear that he has a mother existing! Two persons only know the place of my retreat, they know all! They are sworn to secrecy, and never will be bribed to betray their trust; if provoked they may say too much.

"May Heaven comfort, bless, and preserve Ferdinand and my child! I would extend my blessings, but they may prove curses; from a wretch like me all good wishes may be reversed; yet Heaven will distinguish between the innocent and the guilty; the 'awful voice' convinced me of that truth, and bids me fly from the world for ever! May the warning be extended to others guilty as myself.

CLAUDINA"

"Strange mystery!" cried Ferdinand; those two persons that 'know all!' What is that dreadful all? O, how torturing is this doubt! Ernest is one (he has confessed it) that enjoys her confidence; but he has declared no force on earth shall induce him to betray her. Who the other is I know not; but no doubt she was well advised in her choice of confidants. Her own words pronounce her 'guilty,' but of what? What guilt can she have committed? Where had she the opportunity?"

"It is in vain to puzzle ourselves with conjectures," answered Rhodophil; "time only can develop the mystery, and we must endeavour to be content until that period arrives; some unexpected incident may bring all things to light. You see she will not be without a support, which I shall regularly pay. As for your son Charles, I take upon me the care of his fortune, and will send him to a school at my own expense; the moiety of his mother's settlement shall be paid to Ernest, and be left to accumulate for his expenses hereafter.

"This has been a melancholy visit to you, my dear Ferdinand; but I entreat you to endeavour, if possible, to overcome this shock, to think of Claudina as dead, and as one whom you ought not, from her own confession, to lament."

With a deep sigh Ferdinand replied, "I will endeavour; but the more I think, the more the mystery increases, and the more wretched I am. I thank you for my poor Charles; the little Claudina, I trust, her mother will not neglect. Within three days I shall leave you."

"How! (cried the Count) in three days? Surely my brother will not desert me: Let us comfort each other, resign your commission, partake an equal share with me, and let me have the satisfaction of contributing to your returning peace. We will take a tour into Hungary; I have an estate there I have never seen. You will be amused. Pray oblige me."

"I thank you most sincerely (answered Ferdinand;) but my resolution is taken, and I intend to ramble, I neither know nor care where, chance shall be my guide."

"That is a ridiculous, romantic idea (said the Count;) you may encounter a thousand accidents by such a scheme, with scarce a possibility of being amused without a companion, or any plan in view." Ferdinand made but a slight answer, yet sufficient to convey his determination, and the entrance of company drove him from the room.

Ernest only was admitted into his confidence, and with him he consulted about the disposal of his son Charles. As there was an excellent academy at Baden, they thought it best he should be there, because Ernest would have him under his eye. — "My years are great (said the good old man) between sixty and seventy, and my days may be few, but whilst I live, never will I remit my attention to him. I have a nephew, a young man of integrity, who is the third master in that very academy: I can depend upon his care there, and here I will watch over his interests. I am certain the Count will not discharge me now."

"Why now, more than before?" asked Ferdinand.

"Because, because (said he, a little confused, conscious that he had said too much) he does justice to my fidelity, and is certain of my attachment to his family." Satisfied with this answer, the other consulted with him on his projected ramble, and as Ernest found him determined, he made no efforts to oppose him in a pursuit that he thought would amuse him for a time, and, like all other novelties, soon subside; and what made him the more readily come into it was, that an account arrived of a truce being agreed upon between the Emperor and his opponent, and that the troops were ordered into winter quarters, consequently there was no necessity for resigning his commission, as he might have leave of absence for a few months.

Rhodophil appeared to regret his design, yet nevertheless furnished him with a handsome sum for his expenses, and requested he would draw freely upon him whenever it was necessary. Charles was informed his mother was gone a journey (and after a time Ernest was to acquaint him that she was dead.) — The same information was circulated in the family, though not as readily believed, for every one concluded she was run away from her husband unknown to them all: But Charles, who was only three years old, gave easy credit to any thing he was told, and in his new situation, where Mr. Dunloff, the nephew of Ernest, paid him the attention of a father, and he had a variety of young companions (a thing quite new to him) he soon ceased to lament the loss of his real parents, and was delighted with the change of residence.

CHAPTER X

Ferdinand was impatient to be gone from the Castle, and within ten days after Claudina had disappeared he saw his son fixed, heard from Ernest that his mother and the little Claudina were well, and having taken leave of his brother, who requested to hear often from him, one fine morning, equipped only with a change or two of linen, which he contrived to put in his pockets, a stout stick, and a small pair of pocket pistols, he set off on his intended pedestrian tour. — Ernest accompanied him to the entrance of the forest, and when Ferdinand embraced the good old man, tears rolled down his aged cheeks: "May Heaven preserve you, my dearest master, when there is only a choice of evils, we must endeavour to bear with that which appears the lightest; I therefore trust you to Providence rather than to the wicked and malignant. Take care of yourself, and depend upon my love and fidelity." His increasing emotions precluded farther words on either side. Ferdinand wrung his hand affectionately, and unable to repress his own tears, they, as if by mutual consent, turned and walked hastily from each other, the one to the Castle, the other pursued his way through the forest.

He walked leisurely on for some hours without feeling fatigue, for his mind was wholly occupied with revolving on all the extraordinary occurrences that had happened since the death of the late Count, and although he had never given credit to the improbable stories of ghosts, or believed in the old legends handed down to posterity by the slaves of fear and monkish superstition; yet there was such a conviction in his mind, that he could not be deceived in the voice which three times had startled him; and the last time was not only heard by Claudina, but appeared from her own letters to have struck her with a sense of conscious guilt, (though of what nature he could not divine) that it was impossible there could be any misapprehension, where there was no fear, or expectation of terror. All was strange and inexplicable, and he found himself involved in a labyrinth of perplexity, without any clue to guide him through it.

He at length came to a side of the forest which had a very steep hill, or rather mountain, rising from a narrow valley, which was watered by a small stream that seemed to meander slowly round the sides of the hill beyond the view; here Ferdinand stopped, and for the first moment recollected that he was tired and faint for want of refreshment, which, though a very natural occurrence, he had never apprehended; and Ferdinand concluded, without inquiring, that he would take the right-hand side of the forest, where two or three little hamlets

lay dispersed, and would afford him some accommodation. —
He viewed the mountain with a wearied eye, beyond the little
valley the forest was very thick, nor did he know its
termination; the other side he was acquainted with, but here he
was entirely at a loss: Whilst he deliberated, he seated himself
on a piece of the rock, where he had rested but a few moments
before he heard the tinkling of a bell, and presently several
sheep came to the opposite side of the rivulet; they stopped,
looking at him, as if afraid of a stranger: — "Poor, simple
animals! (exclaimed he) fear not a wretched, powerless man!
Alas! thy very looks claim pity, so void of guile, hard and
callous must that heart be grown, whose profession leads him to
put the murderous knife to a throat so unoffending!"

He had scarcely finished those words, when he saw a young
shepherdess descending from the mountain to attend the
watering of her flocks. He marked her as she came nearer; plain
and humble was her attire, simple and unfashioned her air; a
good height, and a clear brown skin, with a ruddy complexion,
were all her attractions. "Behold the child of nature! (thought
he;) innocence of heart, simplicity of manners!" She came down
to her sheep, the small rivulet only parted them. He saluted her.
She returned a rustic bow, looking earnestly on him: "I have lost
my way, shepherdess, and am faint and tired."

"Go round the hill (said she, pointing with her finger) there
is a little bridge, cross it, follow the path way, it will bring you
up to our cottage, my father is there, and you may rest
yourself."

"And you (said he) where do you dwell?"

"There also (answered she.) When I have watered and
housed my sheep, I shall come there too."

Ferdinand did not hesitate; he walked slowly to the bridge,
and with difficulty began to climb the winding ascent. After
much fatigue he reached a kind of platform in the middle of the
hill, where he saw a small cottage, a deep hanging brow of the
mountain seemed suspended over it, and appeared as if every
moment it would fall, and crush the humble dwelling into dust.
He shuddered as he beheld it; but advancing to the cottage, saw
a venerable looking man sitting to enjoy the breezes that played
over the hills.

The old man viewed him with evident surprise; Ferdinand
related the direction he had obtained from the shepherdess, and
appeared so very much spent with toil, that the shepherd

desired he would walk in, gave him his own stool as being the best, brought him some milk, and a cake, he said, of his Maria's baking. Never was repast more delicious than this milk, when almost choked with thirst; Ferdinand drank the wholesome beverage, looked at the simple shepherd, and his humble dwelling clean and comfortable, though unadorned, with delight. "My good father (said he) I thank your hospitality, you have revived my fainting spirits."

"You are truly welcome (replied the shepherd;) but may I inquire, son, where you are going to on foot, and alone, for it is too late to reach Baden now before the close of night?"

"I came from Baden (said Ferdinand) and am going I know not whither; going to travel."

"To travel?"

"Yes."

"What on foot—alone?"

"And why not, father? I go to see the country, to amuse myself, a horse would be sometimes inconvenient, for instance, a horse could not have brought me here."

"No (replied the old man;) but was there a necessity that you should come here?"

"Not a necessity to come here particularly; but I am on a tour of curiosity, and therefore the lowly valley, or the towering mountain, will equally attract me; I can never be out of my way."

"Strange (said the shepherd, eying him attentively) strange, that a young man, who seems formed for the world, should take a fancy to roam the forests on foot, without a companion or necessaries to refresh him!"

"The first I want not (said Ferdinand) and for the last I trust to benevolence and hospitality, such as I now experience."

"But suppose you had not met my daughter, your trust would have been a very feeble one, for I know not another hut for a great way off, and you would have been benighted in the forest. Think of your danger in that case."

"Could we always foresee (observed Ferdinand) we might possibly avoid many disagreeable accidents, many melancholy circumstances; but no such prescience is allowed to man, and if it was, and the evils of life unavoidable, we should be still more wretched than we are."

"True (answered the old man;) but had I guessed you was coming here, I might have been better prepared, for we eat up our eggs at dinner; bread and milk is all your fare."

"I desire no better, and if you will permit me to lay on that bench till the morning dawns, I shall be still more obliged to you."

"Thank Heaven (said the shepherd) I can treat you better; to lay on the floor, wrapped up in warm skins, is nothing new, nor uncomfortable to me, and my poor bed is at your service; it is clean, though homely." Ferdinand was going to refuse, when the shepherdess entered. — — — After some conversation on their simple way of life, which he found they had always been accustomed to, they overpowered all his refusals, and obliged him to take the old man's bed, which was in one corner of the room; the other room was the young woman's and those two rooms were all they had.

He asked "if they were not apprehensive of the rock breaking over their cottage?" They said, "Sometimes, when sudden thunderstorms broke over them they were alarmed; but they trusted in Heaven for protection." "I have only one fear, one care (said the shepherd;) it is some years now since I lost my wife; should I be taken suddenly too, what must become of my poor child?"

"Whenever that day arrives, father, which I hope is yet far off, I will sell my sheep, and go to service; all my fear is, lest I should be sick, and not able to help you; but then I hope good Mr. Ernest, our Lord's steward, will consider you."

"What! (cried Ferdinand) do you know Ernest? Are you tenants to Count Rhodophil?"

"To be sure, Sir (answered the girl;) we know Mr. Ernest, for he buys our sheep. — As to tenants, Sir, we pay no rent, because the mountain is free to live in; but we are vassals to the Count, his estate lies round the forest."

"Do you ever go to the Castle?" asked he again.

"I never did but once (replied the shepherdess) and the walk is too long for my father; but Mr. Ernest sends to us sometimes, and we meet him in the valley, and agree about our sheep. He is a good man, and never drives a hard bargain with the poor."

"Well (said Ferdinand) I know him too, and will take care that both you and your father shall be more safely provided for in future." Each looked at the other with wonder, but spoke not. They soon after retired to rest, contented and happy; not so their guest, he flung himself on the bed, a prey to the most melancholy reflections; and it was near morning when nature exhausted, gave him a temporary repose for about three hours, which seemed to refresh him, and after breakfasting on milk, he prepared to renew his ramble.

He was but very little acquainted with that side of the country which being rocky and mountainous, was unfavourable to excursions on horseback, and therefore had not fallen under his observation; but just as he was taking leave of his hospitable entertainers, he remembered to have heard there was a convent situated somewhere beyond this mountain; that certainly (thought he) is the retreat of Claudina: I will go to it, perhaps she will not see me, but it will be a satisfaction to know where she is. He inquired of the shepherdess if his conjecture was right respecting the convent? She told him it was, that about seven miles off there was a convent so remote and dreary, that it seemed shut out from the world, and was almost as much unknown as if in a desert.

"I have never been near it (said she) for, indeed, what I have heard about it is enough for me, and I have something else to do than to ramble into such places, where one may get nothing but a great fright for one's pains." "Ah! (concluded Ferdinand) this is the very place which seems to be designed for an entire seclusion from the world, there I will direct my steps." Having bid adieu to the good girl and her father, and taking a direction towards the convent, he began to descend the hill. The morning was fine, the dew drops still hung upon the under-wood, sparkling as the rising sun glittered among the trees, the birds were singing on the lofty branches, and the whole scene was calculated to inspire pleasure and serenity; even Ferdinand felt the enthusiasm of the moment; he looked round with delight: —"Ah! (said he) the face of nature shines on all its children; happy is the mind that can enjoy the pure pleasures that it so freely offers, free from corroding care, or guilty self-upbraidings! How much happier is the lowly peasant than his proud guilty Lord, who riots in unlawful pleasures, forgetful of the sting that follows in the voice of conscience; whilst the humble shepherd rises blithe and innocent, pursues his daily occupation, blessed with content, he gathers in his flock at night, thankfully partakes the healthful food his family provides, and sinks to rest undisturbed and happy!"

Full of these thoughts he pursued his way until he reached the foot of the mountain, and descended into a narrow, wild and obscure glen, where nothing relieved the eye but high and lofty hills covered with trees which threw a dark shade beneath, and entirely obscured the sun from penetrating through; he heard the sound of distant waters, but knew not from whence they came. He walked on a considerable way, until by a sudden turning he found himself at the foot of another mountain, from whence issued the most beautiful water-fall he had ever seen, descending into two or three natural basins, which fell from one to the other until they came to the bottom, and formed the lake, which winding itself around the mountain on the opposite side, divided into smaller streams of which the rivulet he had first seen was one. Here he sat down to rest, and to admire the course of the water. He had another hill to mount, and he observed there was something like a path-way in a gradual ascent round the side of it; he could see it was not much trodden upon by the weeds, but they were not so high as to impede his steps, and therefore, after resting about half an hour, he followed the direction, made his way through the weeds and under-wood, and, with infinite labour, arrived at the summit.

Here he stopped to look round him, another valley was beneath, which seemed to terminate in a thick wood on the right, and more hills to the left. Heartily tired of ascending and descending, he resolved to go into the woods from the vale beneath, rather than climb another mountain: Descending, however, to the valley, his attention was arrested by the beauty of the vines, which entirely covered the southern side of the hill; and several small streams, which had forced their way from the cascade on the other side, here crossed each other in the valley, and divided it into many parts like a cluster of small vales, which had a beautiful effect upon the eye, and agreeably amused Ferdinand till he came to the entrance of the wood, which he found uncommonly thick, and seemingly difficult to penetrate. He hesitated a moment, supposing that it might be the retreat of a troop of banditti, which had for some time past committed many outrages in the neighbourhood of Baden: "But what have I to fear? (exclaimed he) my life is not worth the taking; from a single man they can expect no booty, and the basest of cowards only would attack a defenceless being that cannot injure them."

Fortified by these considerations, he proceeded through the wood, in which there was no path-way, and in many places so difficult to pervade, that he more than once repented of his attempt, which he was fearful would at last prove fruitless; persevering, however, with infinite difficulty, he walked on. The trees were very lofty, and it appeared as if he descended gradually all the way. For three hours he kept on, till quite exhausted, he was obliged to rest himself at the foot of a tree, and eat a small cake the shepherdess had given him. "I have no doubt (thought he) but that I must be near the convent, as it certainly lies in this direction, though most probably there may be a less troublesome road to it. They informed me at the cottage it was about seven miles from the hill, surely I must have walked over more ground than that:" But he considered not how much time he had lost in forcing his way through the wood, which impeded his steps, and made him advance but very slowly.

Having a little refreshed himself he went on, and at length the wood opened into a deep and narrow valley, with lofty thick pines on each side, which threw a gloom over it sufficient to create horror in the mind of the boldest traveller.

Ferdinand felt its influence, but he was not easily intimidated, nor, indeed, could he now well retreat. Walking forward, he saw at the bottom another thick cluster of trees, which, when he came up to them, seemed to terminate the valley, and to be impervious to any human being. These were chestnut trees, so interwoven with each other, that he looked round in vain for an opening, for the under-wood formed a thick fence that was impassable. — Extremely disconcerted, and apprehensive lest he should have the same road through the valley to retrace, he turned a little to the left, forcing his way down by the side of the trees, and after persevering near a quarter of a mile with infinite difficulty, to his great joy he discovered a small stream of water, over which was an old wooden bridge that led the way to a narrow path made through the wood. This track he followed, and, after walking near an hour, came to another dark avenue, at the end of which stood an old building encompassed with very high walls.

"At last (thought he) I have reached the convent;" and exhausted as he was with toil and want of refreshment, the appearance of those mouldering walls, gave him more pleasure than he might at another time have received from a view of the most superb palace. A pair of iron gates, which seemed rusted on their hinges, with a bell on one side, flattered him with the hopes of obtaining an entrance: He rang the bell with some force, and heard its sound, though at some distance. After waiting a considerable time, he was about to repeat the pull, when a very small wicket was opened (for the inside of the gates were lined with wood) and the meagre face of an old man appeared, who demanded, in a deep, feeble voice, "Who was there?"

"A wearied and unfortunate traveller, (replied Ferdinand) who entreats rest and refreshment."

"I fear (replied the man) neither can be obtained here."

"Is not this a convent?" asked Ferdinand.

"No (answered the other) there is a convent about five miles to the right of the valley you have passed."

"What then is this place?"

"Once a castle, now a heap of ruins!"

"Yet it is inhabited it seems, and I am really so overcome with fatigue, that if you can procure me entrance, I shall be most truly thankful to rest an hour."

"I will inquire," said the man, and withdrew.

Ferdinand was extremely mortified to find he had taken a wrong direction, from the convent as it appeared, by keeping to the left; yet he was so very languid and tired, that he found it hardly possible to measure his steps back without some rest or sustenance; for, however grief may fill up the mind, or weaken the appetite, nature will assert her rights, and remind the woe-begone traveller that something is necessary for her support. He waited some minutes, not with the patience of a Socrates, when at length the same face appeared through the hole: "I will let you in for a short time to the huntsman's room, but no farther." He proceeded to unbar the gate, which from its creaking noise, and the difficulty attending its opening, gave evident proofs that the practice of hospitality was not customary in that ruinous building.

When the gate was opened Ferdinand absolutely started at the figure of his conductor; he even hesitated whether he should follow him; haggard, emaciated and tottering, was the man before him. A large court, overgrown with weeds, led to another wall, with a pair of gates similar to those he had passed, and discovered no more of the building than the lofty battlements and high turrets he had discerned on his first approach. On one side of the court was an old low building, to which the man conducted him. They entered a hall lined with the huntsman's trophies, covered with dust; through that they went into a smaller room, where a table, some benches, and a fire place, had the appearance of having been once inhabited. — — —"You may rest here (said the man) and I will bring you some food; but if you stir one step beyond, your death will be the consequence."

Ferdinand, instead of being intimidated found his curiosity greatly excited, and though he quietly acquiesced with the prohibition, yet his thoughts were employed in considering on means to obtain further knowledge of these ruins and its inhabitants. Some time elapsed before the man returned with bread, wine, and grapes, which, whilst Ferdinand gladly devoured, he was observed, with the most scrutinizing attention, by his entertainer; nor were the other's eyes unemployed. — When he put the flask of wine to his mouth, for no cup had been thought necessary, he drank to the other's health, which was returned with a bow of the head; but no persuasions could induce him to return the compliment. "I drink no wine," said he, in a mournful voice.

"Indeed, my good friend, I think you need it," said Ferdinand, "weak and feeble as you are, wine seems absolutely necessary for you."

"I have sworn to the contrary," replied the other, with an increased dejection.

"It appears to me," returned Ferdinand, "to have been a very cruel injunction, if forced upon you, and a very unwise one, if voluntarily made, for the good things of this life were given to us by a bounteous Creator to be our support and comfort; the abuse of them is only improper, and when advanced in age, as you appear to be, such things as nourish the body and enliven the spirits, are highly requisite."

"To some persons," answered the man, "it may be so; but not to a man to whom the hours that he drags here are a weary pilgrimage, such a one seeks not by stimulatives to prolong a life long since grown hateful to him."

"Alas!" cried Ferdinand, "few men can be more wretched than myself; recent afflictions have driven me from my home, and from my friends; yet do I hold it cowardly to desert my post, I have no power over that life I could not give myself; and to neglect the means of its preservation, is little less sinful than to destroy it at once. — But, pardon me one question, are you the owner of this Castle?"

"I am not," returned the other; "but do not be curious in matters that cannot concern you, nor by an idle curiosity which can receive no gratification, oblige me to repent of my charity."

"You must at least," said Ferdinand, "forgive me one observation; your first appearance, and manner of bringing me here, led me to suppose you a domestic; your language convinces me I was mistaken: Whoever, or whatever you are, if you are unfortunate, as your words seem to imply, I most sincerely pity you; unhappy myself, I can feel for every child of sorrow." The tone, in which those words were uttered, with the look that accompanied them, had a powerful effect upon his auditor. He turned from him, clasped his hands, tears ran in torrents down his furrowed cheeks, and, with a heart-breaking sigh, he flung himself upon a bench almost suffocated with the excess of his emotions.

Ferdinand approached him: — "If I have been, though involuntarily, the cause of exciting those tears, and of recalling ideas that perhaps were faded on the memory, I entreat you to forgive me; indebted to your hospitality and kindness, I am exceedingly concerned to have made a return so unworthy to create pain in the bosom of my benefactor."

"You stand acquitted in my opinion," answered he, endeavouring to recover from his first transports; "sympathy, perhaps, led you to observations you could not foresee would plunge me into sorrow. It is now twelve years since I have seen a human being to interest me; twice only during that period have those gates, by which you entered, been opened to admit any one within them: Society is hateful to me, and I thought this place sufficiently hidden from the world to preclude all possibility of intrusion; the sound of a bell is but seldom heard, and only at stated times: I was therefore alarmed at the circumstance, and when I opened the wicket had no thoughts of admitting you; but the expression of your countenance struck me, the mournful accents of your supplication vibrated to my heart, and in one moment overturned the scrupulous caution of twelve years."

"I feel (replied Ferdinand) that my obligations to you are infinite, nor will I abuse them by an expression of curiosity which is improper to be gratified; not one step beyond the boundaries of your injunctions will I attempt to stray.

May Heaven give you comfort, and sooth your mind to ease and tranquillity. I am rambling to forget myself, and those most dear to me. I have incurred the heaviest maledictions, and am a victim to the severity of them. A cruel mystery hangs over me, and has driven me from every prospect of happiness."

"Poor youth!" exclaimed the old man, "how many are the unfortunate beings compelled to exist in this world of cares, either from their own misconduct, or through the crimes of others? I can afford you no comfort, for within these walls misery, oppression, and despair, have fixed their seat for ever!"

"Then," cried Ferdinand, "I should be an inmate; for equally wretched and hopeless is the being before you: I know not why it is, but methinks I am driven by an irresistible impulse to open my heart to you, if you can allow me to intrude so long upon your patience."

"The communication of sorrow, it is said, relieves the mind; if such may be the effect, I will readily listen to you; but must premise before-hand that of whatsoever nature your sorrows may be, it is impossible that I can either comfort, or serve you."

"They will at least prove to you," answered Ferdinand, "that you are not alone unhappy, and though you cannot, indeed it is impossible you should, serve me, you may at least give me the benefit of your advice."

The old man shook his head, but with a deep sigh requested he would proceed. The other obeyed, and took up his story from the first time he had seen Claudina, as the epoch from which originated all his subsequent troubles, and from which he dated her misfortunes and his own. He related every event without palliation or exaggeration, and complained heavily of the mystery which hung over the interview with his wife on his return from the army, and the self-accusation contained in her letters, her flight, and his ignorance of her situation.

CHAPTER XI

The stranger heard him with much attention, and when the narrative was concluded made the following reply. "Your imprudent marriage with a stranger, unknown to your father, was the source from whence flowed all your misfortunes, consequently from that wrong step you may trace every ill in progression. I do not however exculpate him from blame in being so rash and unadvised, as to draw upon you the evils of life by a father's curses; the idea is horrible, it is usurping the power of the Most High, to whom only curses belongeth; yet I have rarely observed through life, that an union, contracted contrary to a parent's approbation, has been fortunate or happy; to a mind of sensibility there must ever be a drawback from felicity, when conscious of giving pain, and disappointing the best hopes of those so nearly interested for our happiness, and who have a right to more than a negative obedience, if I may so express myself, when a marriage is contracted without consulting the parents; but when completed, contrary to their wishes and commands, few, I am convinced, are the instances of matrimonial happiness: But I see I oppress you, therefore, to drop that point, permit me to observe, you did wrong in not seeking opportunities to soften your father. Was your brother a warm advocate, think you? I fear not; much less can I believe that a good man could have left the world without being in charity with it, and revoking, as far as he could, the imprecation his passion had dictated.

"As to the other circumstances, the voice at different times, so applicable to your situations, I shall only observe, that they were very extraordinary, but not impossible. — Respecting your wife, I fear much black treachery remains concealed, beyond your penetration; her flight, after hearing the prohibition of the voice, confirms my conjectures. O, you know not (said he, starting from his seat) you know not to what excesses a corrupted heart may be driven!"

He paced about the room for two or three minutes, then suddenly stopping: — "The leading features towards explaining the particular circumstances of your story are wanting; it is impossible I can give any advice that ought to influence you in your future conduct or sentiments. Your wife may be in the neighbouring convent, but I see not what you can promise yourself from the discovery, because it is not at all probable that she will see you: I sincerely wish you returning happiness, and am sorry I must remind you that your departure from hence is necessary before the day is too far advanced; you must return through the valley, and take the opposite direction towards the convent, which is nearly as much retired as this melancholy place."

Ferdinand arose: "I beg your pardon," said he, "for obliging you to remind me that I have trespassed too long on your kindness: I feel regret at leaving you in this solitary desolated mansion, and yet, such is the complexion of my mind, I could be contented to remain in it myself with such a companion."

"Leave me (replied the other) add not to the horrors of my situation by permitting me to taste the solace of a companion from which I am for ever excluded."

"How! (said Ferdinand) are you then here alone? Did you not say that you was not master here?"

"I told you that I was not the owner of this castle: I spoke truth; inquire no farther." As his brow grew contracted, his eyes wild, and his whole figure agitated, Ferdinand repressed his curiosity, and prepared to depart. The other attended him to the gate with a sort of sullen civility, and opened it without speaking. Ferdinand took his hand, "Heavens bless you," said he, "I thank your charity. Must we never meet again?" The supplicating tone melted the hardened heart of the stranger, his features relaxed: — "Why should you wish it?"

"Not from an unwarrantable curiosity," returned the other, "not from a wish to penetrate farther into your secrets, or your habitation, than you would choose to allow of; but from sympathy, from a desire of participating in sorrow, and a wish to render your situation less deplorable by the converse of a fellow sufferer."

The man paused, viewed Ferdinand from head to foot with a searching eye, opened his mouth to speak, again paused, and turned from him. The other seeing his emotions, was also affected: "I have afflicted you undesignedly; pardon me (added he) I will not be intrusive, I submit to your restrictions." He was turning from the gate, the stranger caught his hand: "You have overcome (said he) my hitherto invincible resolutions; you have awakened sensations long, very long strangers to my bosom: I will consider, I must have time to reflect, and to determine, I can promise nothing; go to the convent, satisfy your anxiety respecting your wife. — Return to this gate to-morrow, I shall by that time decide on your wishes, and either wholly repress my own rising inclination, or gratify it without reserve; but expect nothing, for I make no promises." He hastily shut the gate without waiting for an answer, and left Ferdinand under a great perturbation of spirits.

He had now to retrace his steps, through the gloomy valley, and force his way through the woodlands. The various conjectures that occupied his mind relative to the old man, and his ruinous solitary mansion, lessened the apparent difficulties, and tedious length of the road. He regained the foot of the mountain, and turned to the right, where he met with a chain of small rocky hills both painful and dangerous to climb, and to descend from, and which so far impeded his haste, that he saw the twilight drawing on fast, and the appearance of the heavy clouds portending rain or snow. He redoubled his speed, and on coming over a pretty high hill discovered a grove of chestnut trees before him, in the midst of which he saw something rising above them like a turret. "At last (cried he, almost exhausted with fatigue) at last I have found the convent." The object in view seemed to diminish the distance, and he walked for some time through the grove before he arrived at a large moat, which extended round the walls of the building. — He took a circular walk, in the hope, which was not disappointed, of finding a bridge. — On one side was a narrow stone causeway made on piles, but more resembling a path-way than a bridge; this he crossed to the gate that appeared in the wall, and rung the bell.

The door was almost instantly opened by the porteress, and to his great joy he found himself at the desired port. She seemed extremely surprised at seeing him, and demanded his business. "Was there not a young Lady brought here within this fortnight?" said he.

"There was (she replied) and what then?"

"I beseech you (said he) to tell her, her nearest relation wishes to speak with her."

"'Tis very improbable a relation should come here to see her. Young man, you have not spoken the truth; nor will you, whoever you are, be permitted to see her."

"Oh! (cried Ferdinand, off his guard, and agonized by vexation and fatigue) oh! tell her it is her husband, it is the father of her child; she has no right to withdraw herself from me, nor can you answer it, to detain a wife from her husband without his knowledge or consent."

The porteress seemed staggered. "What you assert (replied she) seems very strange and improbable; I will, however, report it to the Abbess, which is all I can do in the business."

She shut the grate, and left him overwhelmed with vexation. He was now convinced that Claudina was here, and could he see her, and obtain from her satisfaction relative to her self-accusation, and a confession of the real motives which had induced her to leave the Castle under such an appearance of mystery, he concluded that he should be much easier in his mind, and submit patiently to a separation which seemed to have been commanded, though why at that particular period he could not conceive, and was what he supposed a conversation with her would clear up. During the absence of the porteress, his mind dwelt on these circumstances; the grate was at length opened, and the old woman appeared.

"The young Lady refuses to see you; she denies that you have any authority over her; bids you remember the dreadful circumstances lately passed, and never presume to trouble her more. The letter she left for you sufficiently explained her sentiments: Her child is with her, but it has no longer a father, nor after this day will any messages from you be received or delivered here."

"Barbarous woman!" exclaimed Ferdinand, "ungrateful and unjust! Would she but explain herself with openness and candour, I could submit to the 'dreadful circumstances' she alludes to; but this silence, this mystery, and my child too! 'It has no longer a father!' Just Heaven, how am I punished!"

"I am sorry for you," said the porteress; "but I cannot help you. Night is drawing on; a short distance to the left is a convent of Friars, there you may be accommodated for the night; but return no more here, for it avails nothing to complain where you cannot be heard." She shut the grate, and left Ferdinand standing in an attitude of fixed despair.

He stood for some moments insensible to every thing around him, when the sound of a distant bell roused him from the torpor that had seized him, and instantly recollecting the convent mentioned by the old Nun, with reluctant steps, and an oppressed mind, he walked through the wood, keeping to the left as she had directed him; but overwhelmed by a thousand doubts and painful conjectures, he proceeded so slowly that night overtook him, and it was with much difficulty he espied through the trees a rising hill before him which terminated the wood, and on reaching to the foot of it, he perceived an old building on one side of the declivity, with large pieces of rock suspended over it, which seemed to threaten hourly danger: He recollected the shepherd's cottage; "strange (thought he) that people should choose such dangerous situations to erect dwellings on! It appears to me a daring presumption, or a total insensibility." He rang the bell, a small gate was opened by a Friar, Ferdinand announced himself as an unfortunate and wearied traveller seeking shelter from the inclemencies of the night.

"Enter, my son, and welcome," said the father. Seldom does the traveller find his way to our solitary mansion, so remote and distant from any great road; enter therefore freely, and partake of our homely fare, and humble lodging." Ferdinand followed his conductor to a large room, where several of the Fathers were assembled just returned from their evening vespers. All but one saluted him, and withdrew, that one advanced, and requested he would be seated. Some bread, salad, milk and fruit, were brought in, of which Ferdinand partook very sparingly, for the uneasiness of his mind had destroyed his appetite.

"You look fatigued, my son," said the Friar, "and I suppose must have wandered considerably out of your way to have arrived at this dwelling, seldom in the habit of receiving strangers."

"I have indeed been wandering about," replied the other, "and with very little satisfaction to myself. To this house I was directed from a neighbouring convent; both houses are so remote, so impervious, even to the eye of curiosity, from the woods and deep valleys, that only a wretched fugitive, like myself, could possibly have found it."

"If you are unhappy, my son, I am sorry for you, but yield not to despair; hope is implanted in the mind of man by our great Creator as the sweetener of life, and only one set of beings are excluded from that cordial drop in earthly pursuits."

"And who are those?" asked Ferdinand.

"Men and women devoted to a monastic life," answered the Father; "cut off from every worldly expectation, their hopes are founded in heavenly promises which can receive no disappointment but from themselves; they depend not on others; no earthly views can distract their attention from the one great object of their wishes: Happiness unalloyed by fears or doubts must inhabit the bosom of a religious man."

"Most true," replied Ferdinand; "but that man must be detached from worldly cares, must have no dear connexions that twine about the heart; no wife, no children; no agonizing apprehensions for those he loves; no distracting doubts he cannot comprehend. The man who secludes himself from society, who can devote his days to religious duties only, must have a heart and mind at ease, ere he can embrace such a life as you have chosen."

"Alas! my son, and does not religion hold out comfort to the afflicted?"

"Undoubtedly, that is the rock on which we must erect the foundation of all our hopes and expectations both here and hereafter; but a monastic life I still aver, should be sought for only by those free from the ties that nature binds about the heart, and who have ceased to be solicitous for worldly objects."

This conversation was interrupted by the entrance of another Friar, not so old as the one before him, in whose countenance Ferdinand discerned traits of benevolence and sensibility, his heart sprung to meet him, and involuntarily he arose as if to do him homage.

"Father Joseph," said the former one, with a supercilious air, "you will see this traveller comfortably lodged, and then attend your duty:" Turning to Ferdinand, "Son, I shall see you to-morrow, and hold some further conversation with you." He withdrew.

"You will follow me, my good brother," said Father Joseph, with an air of mildness, taking up the lamp. The other obeyed; he was conducted through an outer court into a very small chamber, about eight feet square, with a bed made in a niche of the wall, a table, on which stood a crucifix, and one stool. "May you rest in peace under the protection of Heaven!" said the Father, and was going to leave him.

"Ah!" exclaimed Ferdinand, "and must you go? I feel a rising wish to be indulged with your company; must I repress it?"—"For the present I am obliged to leave you; but if sleep is not more desirable than conversation, I will return to you in half an hour. Go to bed, rest if you can, for I see you are overcome with fatigue." He retired, and left his companion with the pleasing hope of seeing him again. The countenance of this man beamed with mild complacence, and Ferdinand hoped from him to gather full information respecting the other convent, and possibly of the ruinous building where he had been so oddly received. Not to offend the Friar, he got into the bed, which was pretty hard, and very unlikely to lull him presently to sleep, he therefore anxiously watched for the approach of Father Joseph, who came when he had began to despair of seeing him.

"I have complied with your wishes, son, and now tell me how I may serve you; I have one hour to spare." Ferdinand then briefly repeated the latter part of his story from the time his wife had left him, his reception at the old Castle, and his treatment at the convent. He concluded with saying, that all he wished for from his wife was, "an explanation of her letter, and a candid confession of her motives for withdrawing herself from the protection of her friends."

"If (said he) as I suppose, you have communication with the convent, I beseech you to see my wife, tell her I will not force myself into her presence, let her but write to free me from my present doubts and inquietude, and I will obey her orders, and never intrude myself into any place she inhabits without her permission."

"Your story is very strange (observed Father Joseph) and I fear you will obtain no satisfaction; I have no power to serve you: Our Superior, whom you have been with, is the only one that visits the convent; the order is one of the severest in all Germany: Ours is much more relaxed, yet we can derive little advantage from the indulgence allowed us, because our situation precludes all chance of society, and Father Ambrose only admitted to visit the convent, to which he is confessor. As your wife is in that retirement, be assured she is dead to you. Those that enter that house seldom return again to the world."

"Distraction!" cried Ferdinand; "but my child, they cannot keep my child from me!"—"At a certain age she may make her own election: Mean time you may represent the case to the Bishop, that is all you can do, having taken sanctuary in the bosom of the church, and the child being at this age more immediately under the care of its mother; at present, you cannot oblige her to resign it." Observing that Ferdinand appeared overwhelmed with vexation, he went on.

"The building you have mentioned, so buried from all observation, was once, I have heard, a most superb mansion, inhabited by one of the Bavarian family, who marrying an heiress of a Suabian Baron, came into the possession of that estate which has long fallen into decay, nor did I ever hear that it had been inhabited these twenty years. On the other side it joins with the black forest, and has been always understood, from its being desolated in one of the late wars, and never repaired, uninhabitable ever since; the house must be in ruins, and the grounds round it barren and uncultivated. Who the person or persons can be that reside there I have no idea, and indeed I should suppose it can afford no accommodations for any other than banditti."

"Or the sons of misery," cried Ferdinand, "such are neither delicate in their accommodations, nor fastidious in their choice of situations; all places are alike to the wretched, and I hope to-morrow I shall be admitted as an inmate."

"And I hope not," returned Father Joseph. "My son, you are very young, let not the first disappointment in your calculations of happiness induce you to renounce the world. You have been wrong, perhaps, in your first selection of the means to attain it. Man has but little prescience, and that little is often ill-directed. Consider your present troubles as a chastisement for some misconduct, some rash actions resulting from the impetuosity of youth; receive the correction with humility, but give not way to despair. Believe me, there is no merit in retiring from the world; society has its claims not incompatible with your sacred duties; on the contrary, duty towards God, and duty towards your brethren, is equally commanded and inculcated. A young man may have a thousand opportunities of doing active service to his fellow creatures, and of promoting the cause of religion and virtue. Retirement suits not with the ardour of youth; let me advise you therefore to resume your situation in life, whatever it may be, to scan over your past actions with discrimination and impartiality; you will then discover the errors that have impeded your expectations of happiness; you will chalk out for yourself a new path, and the end will be mental tranquillity, and the never-fading satisfaction of having been beneficial to the extent of your abilities towards the less fortunate and happy."

"And is this," cried Ferdinand, 'the language of a man detached from the world, this the advice of a holy Father, to expose a fluctuating disappointed heart to the allurements and dissipations that tempt, in a hundred pleasurable shapes, the mind of youth, and lead him into vice?"

"It is the language of truth and reason," answered Father Joseph, with energy, "it is the advice of dear-bought wisdom and experience. Man was not intended for a solitary being, and a young man, who flies from the world because he has indulged delusive hopes, and formed expectations that in the nature of them must at one time or other receive a severe check, who neglects the duties he has it in his power to perform, and by a rash and ill-judged misanthropy, shuns mankind to give up his mind to despair; believe me, such a man is a pusillanimous wretch, who deserts his post, and by his cowardice and impatient spirit, lays up for himself bitter repentance, and never-ending regret, that will mix itself in his most earnest devotions, render those acts of religion, which should communicate joy and cheerfulness to the mind, cold, gloomy, and mechanical; whilst the good, the active, the benevolent mind, performs his sacred duties with delight, from conviction and choice diffuses blessings to all around him, and by precept and example animates others to the practice of religion and virtue, which his conduct renders both easy and pleasant."

"If I may judge from the expression of your countenance," said Ferdinand, "your advice is not the declamation of an unimpassioned man, who has forsaken the world from choice, but the warnings of a feeling heart, desirous of saving others from equal regret and misery with himself."

"You have observed justly, I will not deny," answered the Father: "Many are the victims in this house to pride, impatience, and avarice, sacrificed by their friends, or driven by the impetuosity of their own passions. Some there are doubtless from choice and the purest motives, but these last are comparatively few; a monastery therefore I do not recommend, nor a residence with that solitary being, whoever he may be, that inhabits those stately ruins; even this desultory mode of gratifying your curiosity, rambling among uninhabited and almost impassable hills and valleys, can benefit neither yourself, nor others, may subject you to much inconvenience, perhaps to certain dangerous situations, you do not apprehend: Once more then I recommend you to seek an active life, and an occupation that may diversify your thoughts, and engage your attention. Good night, reflect on what I have said, and may Heaven direct you for the best; I will see you again after morning service."

The good father having withdrawn, left Ferdinand overwhelmed with a variety of contending emotions, whether to profit by, or disregard the advice he had received: — whether he should yield to the dictates of prudence and experience, or follow the lead of his own inclinations. Sleep at length overtook him before he had settled the point, and, hard as his bed was, fatigue threw him into a profound repose, from which he started on the entrance of Father Joseph. "I come only to inform you," said he, "that you are expected by Father Ambrose, breakfast is prepared for you, hasten therefore to attend him."

"How!" cried Ferdinand, "do you leave me? I thought to have had a further conversation with you."

"I am forbidden to indulge it, and have received a reprimand for being so long in your room last night: I may just whisper you, that the passions of mankind are the same in all places, and in all situations; jealousy, envy, and avarice, prevail as much in monasteries as in palaces, they pervade in the most profound retirements, and lead to the most despicable actions and sentiments. Adieu, may Heaven preserve you." Ending those words, he darted from the room, and left Ferdinand to follow.

On entering the apartment he had quitted the preceding evening, he found Father Ambrose alone, refreshments before him, and having inquired of the other his name and rank in life, he began to launch forth in the praise of a monastic life, as the only asylum from trouble and pain; that abstracted from the world, its hopes and fears, the holy Fathers fixed their thoughts on things above, where no cares or disappointments could attend their hopes or desires. He harangued so long, and so eloquently on the subject, that, had not the advice of Father Joseph guarded his mind from the fascination of the picture of contentment held to his view, it is more than probable that Ferdinand, under the impression of his present vexations, might have been induced to end his travels, and have fixed himself for life in that solitary mansion; but already pre-possessed, the avenues to his heart were closed, and the eloquence of the Superior was exerted in vain: He heard him, however, with complaisance, but alleged absolute necessity for his departure, as an excuse for not embracing that plan of life so calculated to insure happiness. He added, 'that it was by no means improbable, but that he should return, and have the pleasure of visiting the community for a longer time, if he might hope for admission."

The zealous Father, eager to make a proselyte of a young Nobleman, greatly approved of his design, and assured him of a hearty welcome. Ferdinand felt half inclined to have mentioned Claudina, but not much pre-possessed in his favour, nor desirous of being then detained from visiting the solitary, who had permitted his return, he repressed the sentiment of confidence half rising to his lips, and rose to take leave, with grateful thanks for his hospitality. When conducted to the grate, he saw Father Joseph in company with some others; a general salute only passed between them, but their eyes spoke much cordiality towards each other.

CHAPTER XII

Ferdinand now hastened to the Castle in the wood, and knowing the way, he pierced through its intricacies that to a stranger seemed impassable, and in much less time than he expected was at the gates. He hastily pulled the bell, which, to his infinite vexation, broke off in his hand; for having been so long useless, it had been eaten out with rust, moved with difficulty the preceding day, and now, by a second pull, snapped to pieces. Exceedingly disconcerted, he began to apprehend that he should gain no entrance; fortunately the solitary man, who had expected him, being walking in the court, heard the faint sound, which the jarring of the wires occasioned, and instantly appeared at the little wicket. Ferdinand was agreeably surprised at his sudden appearance. "You see me returned (said he) anxious to cultivate your acquaintance, and in your conversation blunt the keen edge of my own calamities."

"Enter (said the solitary) I have expected you, curiosity is so strongly implanted in the mind of man that I scarcely doubted of your return." They passed through the first court, and walked round the wall of the second to a small postern door; on advancing towards it, he added, "Having once permitted you a free entrance, my confidence shall not be a partial one." He then opened the door which led to a handsome colonnade fronting the great gates that were boarded up, and excluded it from being seen in the outer court. They entered a large hall, round which run a gallery supported by pillars that led to the apartments above stairs; but the painting was almost effaced by the damp, the pillars entirely discoloured, some of them decayed and crumbling to pieces, threatening the destruction of the gallery they supported, and indeed the whole bore the appearance of total neglect. The solitary opened a door at the farther end of the hall, and conducted his guest into what he called his library, for as such it seemed to have been intended; but the glasses in many places were broken, the books all tumbling in disorder, and so covered with dust, that they were scarcely discernible. A few old-fashioned velvet chairs, once of crimson, but changed by the damps, two tables, with a writing desk of a very particular old-fashioned construction; a large dog that lay before a great wood fire, and seemed by age rendered almost incapable of moving, though he growled at the stranger; a sword, and a pair of pistols, that hung against the wall, comprised the whole furniture of this room.

Being seated, the solitary inquired of his success at the Convent. Ferdinand related his reception there, and at the Friar's monastery; adding, "You see my wife will afford me no sort of satisfaction, and her message is as extraordinary and inexplicable as her whole conduct."

The old man sighed deeply: "I pity you (said he) not for your present disappointment, but because you are young, and must feel, poignantly feel, the stings of ingratitude, and the destruction of those sanguine hopes of happiness you had figured to yourself in an union with the object of your choice, and who, I have little doubt of pronouncing, has proved unworthy of your attachment."

"How! (exclaimed Ferdinand) do you believe my wife is criminal?"

"Hath she not confessed as much?" replied the other.

"Impossible!" said Ferdinand, "she had no acquaintance, no man visited her, in my absence she resided with my brother, who lived very retired; impossible she could wrong me."

"Cease to torment yourself with conjectures that cannot be elucidated; one day or other be assured every thing will be explained.—Yes (continued he, raising his voice) time and accident develops the darkest schemes, the machinations of the wicked will be detected, and, if to know the worst, your imagination can form, will afford any degree of ease, doubt not but that you will one day be satisfied; 'till then, try to repress your anxiety, and revere that command so extraordinarily delivered; try to forget that you have a wife existing, for she has declared 'she is dead to you.'"

Ending these words he stamped on the floor, and presently a man, old and feeble, entered the room.—"Bring some bread and wine."

"Strange! (thought Ferdinand) this man said he was not the master, yet he seems to command; he drinks no wine himself, yet keeps it here, for whom then, when he lives thus solitary? Or is there another person here who is the master?"

The old servant returned with bread and wine and a cup; he looked very attentively on Ferdinand, and then withdrew. The Recluse, who penetrated through the silence of his guest, said, "I read your surprise, and guess at the doubts which occupy your mind: I will satisfy them in part. I am not the owner of this once magnificent seat, yet I am the master here, and have resided in it above twelve years. In a clear moon-light night I walk, sometimes to the skirts of the Black Forest, but at other times I never exceed the courts of the Castle, for the gardens are now a wilderness of weeds. Once a week the provisions I want are brought from a village about five miles off, on the edge of the forest. Wine is sometimes drawn here, though not by me, I have that within me which supports my strength and spirits; my old attendant requires more substantial food. Bread, fruits and water, is all that my table affords, and as much as nature requires. I am not so old as you may suppose from my appearappearance, only fifty-two, twelve of which I have past in the manner I tell you."

"It would ill become me (said Ferdinand) to express a wish to penetrate into the cause which has led you to this extraordinary seclusion from the world, though you must allow that it sufficiently warrants the most curious conjectures; but I will deserve the favour you have bestowed on me by my discretion."

"You are wise and prudent (replied the other) qualities not often attached to youth, and perhaps acquired by sorrow and experience; on such terms you are welcome to remain here as long as you please."

"May I be permitted to make one observation?" asked Ferdinand.

"Certainly, speak freely, the answer depends upon myself."

"When I first came to your gate, you expressed it necessary to inquire if I could be admitted, now you confess yourself the master, and without society."

"Your curiosity in this point is so very natural that I will satisfy it without reserve. The discovery of this mansion through the impenetrable, as I thought, woods, hills and valleys, so out of the common road, and even an object of terror to the few inhabitants that dwell on the other side, the sound of a bell, which had been silent for above nine years, and your appearance when I opened the wicket, altogether astonished me! Callous, as I thought my heart was grown, it softened at the view of sorrow and weakness in so young a frame. To your request of admittance I said, "I would inquire." I came back, and consulted Francis; it was possible you might be what you seemed, then there was no danger in permitting you to enter the outer court, but to guard against surprise, Francis secured the

gate of the inner court, and was planted in a small room, within
the huntsman's, where I led you, armed with that brace of
pistols, which had you attacked me, or strove to force your way
beyond the bounds I allowed, he had orders to discharge, and
instantly to dispatch you."

Ferdinand heard him with some degree of terror, and "Who,
or what can this man be?" darted naturally into his mind, and
having taken some refreshment, he began to consider whether it
would be prudent to remain in a place that seemed to be the
abode of wretchedness, fear and distrust. Curiosity however
predominated, and as he also was armed with a brace of pistols,
he thought himself at least a match for two old men, should
they harbour any sinister designs against him. Having thus
made up his mind, he began to remark on the conversations
between Father Joseph and himself, and the different language
of Father Ambrose, the Superior. "I much fear (said he) that the
former has been an unhappy victim, and feels no satisfaction in
his situation; for I can conceive that even a good mind well
disposed towards religion and moral rectitude, if compelled to
forsake the world, and lead an inactive life, contrary to the
natural disposition, grow languid in the performance of those
duties, which free-will might have performed with pleasure and
alacrity: For my own part, all my prospects of happiness for
ever clouded, oppressed with the weight of a much-loved
father's denunciation, and which seems to be so literally fulfilled
in this life—a brother, a husband, a father; yet separated from
every endearing tie; what can I promise myself in this world,
that can counter-balance that tranquil, that serene life which
pervades in a convent, and which my misfortunes seem to point
out as my only place of rest; and if I can assure to myself such a
companion, such a friend, as Father Joseph, what can I desire
more?"

"Revenge!" cried the Solitary, with an eye darting fire
through his emaciated countenance: "Yes, revenge!" repeated
he, with a violence that startled Ferdinand; "Live to detect the
artful villainy of those that have wronged you, and to punish
them!"

"But I know no such persons," said Ferdinand; "I know of no
wrongs that I have met with that require revenge. If my wife
has been guilty, she is already punished; and for her
accomplice, if such there be, he will not escape with impunity;
and to drag on a wretched life, with the diabolical intention of
destroying another, would be only redoubling my own miseries
here, and assuring to myself punishment hereafter."

"So young a stoic!" exclaimed the old man, with a look of contempt, "either you are a hypocrite, or you were born without passions."

"The detestable character of the first," replied the other, "I utterly disclaim, and had I been created without passions, all the misfortunes of my life would have been avoided: No, I am not without passions, but adversity has taught me wisdom, has moderated the impetuosity of youth, and suffering as I do under the violence of momentary rage, which in an instant may be guilty of excesses never to be repaired, I have learned to bear and to forbear in points that are doubtful, and where my courage and honour are not questioned."

"You are a philosopher, Sir," answered the Solitary, apparently much agitated, "and fitter for the convent, perhaps, than the world, since you can so easily, so tamely, wait for time to elucidate your injuries; but I beg pardon, it cannot concern me; persons born with different sentiments will act differently, and as in this point we do not agree, we will change the subject."

He did so, and Ferdinand found him learned, intelligent, and communicative, yet on every subject he discoursed with a vehemence so little to be expected from the feebleness of his looks and manner when he first appeared at the wicket, discovered a temper so violent and so decided, that his manners rather repulsed than conciliated any growing esteem, and seemed to promise that little pleasure could be derived from cultivating his acquaintance. After some hours conversation the Solitary took him up to the gallery, which was extensive, and had once been magnificent. He opened the doors of several apartments that overlooked the gardens, and an extent of country; but the former was a confused mass of trees, shrubs and weeds, and the country beyond appeared an immense forest.

This was certainly an unpleasant situation to build a superb house on, observed Ferdinand. Our Castle is on a rocky ground, and adjoining to hills and mountains; but they are cultivated and inhabited: Here every thing has the appearance of a desert. Is there no town or village near, for I profess myself entirely unacquainted with this part of the country, from always thinking the woods both dangerous and impenetrable? — "There is a village a few miles distant, but I know not its name," was all the answer. — He then carried him across the gallery to another wing of the building, and opening a door, "Here you may sleep if you please; Francis can find linen for the bed, and shall light a fire, though possibly the chimney may not draw." This room had been handsomely furnished, but it was in a very decayed state, and the whole appearance was so cold and comfortless, that Ferdinand hesitated a moment whether he should accept the offer, and sleep there or not; but the day was shutting in, and he might even lose his way to the monastery, he thought he could be in no hazard of danger, and therefore it would be most prudent to pass that night there, tho' he felt no inclination to prolong his stay, especially as he could hope for no gratification to his curiosity, for the Solitary's heart seemed locked up and carefully guarded. Returning to the lower room they spent the evening together in conversation on various subjects. Ferdinand was pleased with the strong understanding and knowledge of the world which the other displayed; but he observed, on several occasions, that he was decided and peremptory in his opinions, and that he evaded every thing tending to his own situation, and gave not a single instance of that confidence he had at first led his guest to hope for.

At ten o'clock Francis appeared with a lamp, the Gentlemen wished each other a good night, Francis was ordered to attend the stranger to the door of his apartment, and then return to his master. Ferdinand judged this order was to preclude any conversation between him and the old man, and therefore he was silent; but as they parted at the door he thought Francis suppressed a rising sigh, and looking at him saw his face was clouded by a heavy expression of grief. He bowed, retired, and pulled the door after him. A cheerful fire was blazing in the chimney, and examining the door of his apartment, he perceived there was a lock and two strong bolts; these he secured, and having placed the lamp on the table, he threw off his clothes, and got into bed.

Here he lay some time revolving all past circumstances, and considering which road he should pursue in the morning, when suddenly he conceived that he heard some faint shrieks as if at a great distance, he sprung up in the bed and listened; he heard no more, all was a dead silence; yet still he could not be persuaded but that he heard the cries: — He lay some hours in a kind of fearful expectation of, he knew not what. No sort of noise however invaded his ears, and at length he dropped asleep, from which he was awakened by a voice at the door, telling him breakfast was ready. He was soon dressed, and found the Solitary waiting for him, coffee on the table: — "Did you sleep well?" demanded he.

"Perfectly well," replied Ferdinand, suddenly determined not to mention the cries; "indeed my bed was so very superior to what I have had those last two nights, that no wonder I indulged myself so long this morning."

"You are welcome to use the bed as long as you like," was all the reply. The day became gloomy, and in a short time the snow fell in great quantities; this the Gentleman of the house observed, saying, "you are now weather-bound, and must amuse yourself as well as you can."

Ferdinand found among the books the works of many excellent authors, and therefore was at no loss to beguile the time, and indeed had reason to be thankful for his situation, as before night the snow was at least two feet deep on the ground. About the time of retiring the snow ceased, the moon broke through the clouds, and a cold, sharp wind arose denoting a severe frost. When he came into his apartment, the reflection of that resplendent orb induced him to go to the window, and he sat down by it for some time admiring the appearance of the trees and under-wood, which being covered with the snow, exhibited a hundred fantastic shapes to engage the attention.

Lost in the recollection of past events, he sat a long time without thinking of the hour, until suddenly the same faint shrieks broke upon his ear, that he had heard the preceding night. He started up, and opened the window, the voice ceased; he listened attentively a long time, it was no more repeated. Convinced, however, that it was no illusion of a disordered imagination, he began to consider from whom, or from whence it could proceed. The sounds both nights were exactly similar, and he concluded must issue from some person distressed and confined. "There is some unaccountable mystery hangs about this forlorn place, and the Solitary who inhabits it dares not trust me with the secret: I will avail myself of his permission, and stay here a few days to see if I can penetrate through it."

Thus thought Ferdinand when he retired to bed; he slept undisturbed, and when he appeared below, the first question asked him was, "If he slept quiet?"

"Entirely so," answered he; 'this place is remote from all disturbance, and is calculated for the Court of Somnus by its stillness."

The Solitary seemed pleased, and observed, "That the depth of the snow must preclude him from an attempt at travelling in that obscure and unfrequented part of the country." The other raised no objections to remaining another day, and both were much entertained by a mutual communication of observations that seemed greatly to relax the unbending features of the solitary man; but yet he preserved a profound silence relative to his own concerns. Fruit, eggs and salad, were their only refreshments, with which Ferdinand was perfectly content.

When night came, and Ferdinand retired to his apartment, he met Francis on the stairs. The old man stopped; "Are you going to live here, Sir?" asked he.

"For a few days only," replied the other.

"I am sorry for it," said the old man. — "God knows we want company."

"I think so," answered Ferdinand, "for your master must have a horrid time of it here."

"Horrid indeed! You know all then, Sir."

"No, indeed, I know nothing; your master keeps his own secrets, and I do not presume to be inquisitive, though certainly every circumstance about this mansion and its master must raise strange conjectures, and inspire curiosity." The voice of the Solitary calling Francis, obliged the old man to hasten away, though by his earnest look and the motion of his lips he appeared about to say something interesting. Ferdinand was vexed at the interruption, and retired to his apartment, not to sleep, but fixed himself again to the window, that he might more distinctly hear the cries, should they be again repeated.

The more he reflected on this man's conversation and behaviour, the more extraordinary and inconsistent it appeared. On their first interview there seemed more of melancholy than ferocity in his manners, and he had blamed the late Count for his rashness. He had given traits of sensibility and humanity; yet in a late conversation he had advised revenge, and seemed animated by rage to a degree of fury in his looks. He had said, on his entering the Castle a second time, "that his confidence should not be a partial one;" yet his secrets were more guarded than ever, nor was there any probability that he would be more communicative.

"I thought," said Ferdinand, mentally, 'that if admitted to this house I could be content to remain here and spend my days in solitude, I supposed this mansion might be an asylum for the unfortunate, or the abode of undeserved misery, driven from a faithless world; but I fear there is more of guilt than suffering in this man; for affliction makes people plaintive, and if the mind is free from guilt, it naturally expands and grows communicative to a fellow sufferer. I know not what to conclude upon, more than a resolution not to make this my resting-place, should I be invited to do so, which seems not very likely to happen; yet I should be loath to depart without being better informed of the mystery that pervades here."

He sat ruminating on the occurrences that had befallen him some time, when again his ears were assailed by the same cries, though rather fainter, and being on the watch to catch the sound, he was convinced that it proceeded from the other side of the building, and from some place where the sound was suppressed. Excessively agitated, he began to consider in what manner there was a possibility of being satisfied, or of obtaining a solution of this unaccountable business. — He had every evil to apprehend from the resentment of the Solitary, should he be discovered in prying into his secrets, and yet to know some person was regularly ill-treated, which seemed to be the case, and to be incapable of assisting that person, or to leave the Castle without receiving any explanation, was what both his humanity and curiosity revolted against.

In the day he was never alone, or if alone, always in view of the Solitary; nor had he ever an opportunity of speaking to Francis, his master carefully watched him; it appeared impossible therefore to penetrate into this mystery, unless he could by any finesse elude his vigilance, and have an opportunity to ramble about the mansion alone.

CHAPTER XIII

In forming and rejecting a thousand plans to gratify his curiosity Ferdinand passed the night, and obtained but a very few hours sleep in the morning, though they were none of them early risers. His looks unrefreshed, were observed by his entertainer, who asked him, "If he had not rested well?"

"No," replied Ferdinand, "I did not."

"Did any thing particular disturb you?"

"No, only my own uneasy thoughts; you will allow I have sufficient vexations, which, if reflected on, must sometimes preclude rest."

"At your time of life," answered the other, 'the activity of the mind cannot be confined by particular circumstances, or local situations. Retirement will not do for you; travelling will amuse the eye, and give a diversity to your ideas; variety is absolutely necessary to keep the mind alive, and prevent it from dwelling on such circumstances as might, if indulged, overwhelm it with despair, and stagnate the senses: The snow growing firm will be no impediment to your travelling, and for the cold, a soldier should be accustomed to bear it."

"I am not apprehensive of fatigue, or incapable of bearing cold," answered Ferdinand; "but perfectly a stranger to this side of the country, there would be some danger of losing my way, as there are no tracts in the snow to guide me: I think, however, that if the weather continues fair, I will pursue my ramble to-morrow, if you will allow me to partake of your hospitality another day?"

"Certainly," returned the other; "but I think your scheme a very desultory and unsatisfactory one. As you are now acquainted with the residence of your wife, and her determination to see you no more, what is it you pursue? Why not return, and pass your winter at the Castle, look after your son, if you think him such, and prepare yourself for returning in the spring to the army?"

"The mansion of my brother is hateful to me on many accounts," replied Ferdinand, "it would continually remind me of every misfortune: No, there I cannot reside; and to live near my boy, for mine I am sure he is, could be no benefit to him, and having placed him in the hands of integrity, I am entirely easy on that head. I once thought that retirement would make me at least resigned; but I am now of your opinion, that a diversity of objects is more likely to amuse my mind, and that, where peace and contentment are for ever fled to procure a chance of temporary ease, variety of places and objects are absolutely necessary; yet will you pardon me for observing, that either your advice proceeds from a conviction that you have yourself chosen wrong in devoting yourself to solitude, or that you are weary of my company."

"You conclude wrong in the first instance," answered he: "I have never repented my residence here, on the contrary, it is the only circumstance that enables me to support the burden of existence; on the other point I will not deceive you; I long since thought every passion, every feeling, but one, was annihilated in my bosom.—Your appearance, your voice and manner, was unexpected, was touching; a few dormant embers of sensibility procured you entrance at first, and a particular consideration, in which I have been disappointed, induced me to receive you a second time. I now feel that I have been too long secluded from the world to find any satisfaction in a companion, and therefore I frankly confess I do not solicit your stay here. In the advice I have given you I am governed rather by what I think more agreeable to your own feelings than mine, for we differ on particular subjects, and I, in your case, should act otherwise than you do: But—I have no more to say. You may stay a week, or depart to-morrow; consult your own convenience, and do as you please." He left the room as he ended these words, without waiting for an answer.

Ferdinand stood some moments in astonishment; he would have given the world to have known who this extraordinary man was, and to have penetrated into the mystery that enveloped him; but he saw no prospect of gaining the smallest intelligence to gratify his curiosity by remaining there, and after the civil dismission he had received, he could feel no inclination to a longer residence—being left alone, a thing not usual since he had been in the house; he went into the next apartment, which had a door opening into, what had once been a very spacious garden, though now entirely overgrown with weeds; a very narrow path-way, where they seemed to be trodden down but not cleared, went by the side of the building, close under the windows, and here he walked on, observing the dreadful ruinous state the rooms were in, the glass broken, the floors had been long entirely exposed to the weather, and bore every mark of decay and desolation.

He proceeded till he came to the other wing, and immediately recollected that the feeble cries he had heard seemed to have issued from thence. He walked slowly round, and elevating his voice, "What cruel neglect has this once noble mansion endured: Surely whoever is, or was the master of it, must have met with uncommon misfortunes; and to what a wretched state must that mind be brought that can support existence in this desolated place." He had scarcely pronounced those last words, when he heard a heavy groan and an articulate voice, which appeared to be at no great distance from him. He stopped: "Did I not hear a voice?" said he aloud.

"The voice of misery!" was the answer, in a feeble voice, that sounded as if underneath him.

"Whoever you are, speak; I am a friend, can I come to you?"

"I fear not," was the reply, and at the same moment Ferdinand observed Francis at the steps of the glass doors, as if looking for him. "I am called," said he, softly, "what hour of the night is safe?"

"Not till after twelve," repeated the same voice, with a kind of groan. — Ferdinand turned short round, and met Francis advancing as quick as his feeble frame would permit.

"Oh! Sir, make haste, pray make haste."

"What is the matter?" demanded the other.

"My master, Sir, O! pray make haste." He turned back quickly, Ferdinand following him, and being more nimble got before, and run mechanically to the library, where lay extended on the floor the Solitary, apparently insensible. On advancing towards him, he perceived one side of his face distorted; he fixed his eyes on Ferdinand, and attempted to speak, but his words were inarticulate, and gave evident marks of a paralytic affection. On the entrance of Francis they attempted to raise him; but succeeded with infinite difficulty, as he had received a partial stroke which entirely disabled one side; with much trouble they got him upon the bed, and not knowing what else to do, they poured some wine down his throat, though he strove with one hand to prevent it.

"What can be done?" cried Ferdinand; "Is there any help to be procured?"

"I know of none," answered Francis: "I am unable to get to the village." Before the other could reply, a sort of convulsive motion seized on the unhappy man, and in a few moments he was no more!

"O, good Lord!" exclaimed Francis, "he is gone, he is dead, and all his cruelties unrepented of!"

"He is indeed no more!" said Ferdinand, struck with horror at the sudden event, "and may Heaven have mercy on him, whatever may have been his errors. Follow me down stairs," added he to the old man, who appeared to be planet struck, "I wish to talk with you." They each took a glass of wine, and then looking steadfastly on Francis, "Tell me," said he, "who is confined in this Castle, whose cries are those I have nightly heard?"

"How, Sir!" cried the other, "have you heard their cries? Who, or what they are, I know not, nor their place of confinement; but that there are some poor souls some where underground is sure enough."

"What," said Ferdinand, "were not you in your master's secrets? Have you not resided with him many years?"

"I have lived with him nine years; Sir; but I never knew his secrets, for he never conversed with me more than to ask for what he wanted, nor ever sent me out of the Castle. Whenever the man, who brings things from the village twice a week, rings at the bell, he always went himself, and so, Sir, I could speak to nobody."

"How came you to be with him?" asked Ferdinand.

"Why, Sir, it is now better than nine years ago since I had been reduced by sickness and the rheumatism, to be unable to work for my bread, and lived by the charity of the village, which was little enough; so one day a farmer, who now and then gave me milk, said to me, Francis, if you would like to have a good bed, plenty of milk and eggs, and neither labour or trouble, I can get it for you; so, Sir, my heart leaped for joy, for many a day I had nothing, because my rheumatism would not let me walk; so I said, I should be heartily obliged to him. He then told me the Gentleman in the Castle, whom we had often heard of, and all the village was afeared to come near the place; so he said, this Gentleman wanted an old man to be with him, whom he would treat kindly, if he could bear confinement. At first, Sir, I was dashed, and much afeared; but the farmer said he was a very quiet good sort of a Gentleman, and I might live very comfortable; so I thought again he could mean no harm to such a poor fellow as me, and besides, if I didn't like him, I could come away with the farmer again—but there I was out of my reckoning; so, Sir, persuaded, at last I ventured to come to the gates on the other side the house towards the village; so when the farmer told him, he opened the gate and let me in: God help me, I little thought I should not go out again; and so, Sir, to be sure he always behaved kindly to me, but it was so lonesome that I grew tired; but what could I do? every time the farmer came he went with me to the wicket. Once I did venture to say, I would rather go back; so says he, what have you to complain of? So I said 'twas so cruel dull. O, said the farmer, if that's all, Francis, an old man (like you) may be glad to be quiet, you can want nothing with the world; and so, Sir, I saw plain enough he was glad to be rid of me, and, as I thought I might not live long, and to be sure had good usage, I rested quiet, and have been here ever since."

"Well," said Ferdinand, a little impatiently, "but what do you know of the persons confined?"

"Nothing, Sir, but this: One day, after I had been here about a month, I walked down where you was this morning, and I thought I heard some groans, so deadly affrighted I hasted back, and told my master.—Ah! (said he) don't go that way again, Francis, I have heard the same noise sometimes; but 'tis no where else to be heard, so don't go again.

"I said no, I would take care of that; but I was terribly scared, because I believed it was ghosts, and I could not sleep all night, and in the middle of the night I thought I heard some cries, so, Lord help me, I was in a terrible fright; but taking courage I got out of bed to go towards master's room, t'other side of the gallery, when, just as I opened the door very softly, I saw master go into his room, with a lamp in his hand, and a little whip and a basket, which I had always seen on a shelf, in t'other hand; so he went in and shut the door without seeing me, being in the dark: I thought it was cruel strange, so next day I looks in the basket, and seed crumbs of bread, so then I looked at the loaf, and some of it was gone. Well, Sir, I said nothing, but I made a hole on one side of my chamber door, and when I went to bed I marked the loaf; so instead of going in to bed I watched at the hole, and at midnight I saw him come out with the same things in his hands, and go down stairs, and after a little time I heard the same cries.—Lord! how I was afrighted; so after a time back he came, and next morning I looked at the loaf—a good piece was gone; so when I carried it in to breakfast, I said I believes the fairies or ghosts eat our bread, for I am sure it goes faster than we eat it. That's nothing to you, said he, with such a terrible look as made me shake again; you don't pay for it, and no matter which way it goes; so, Sir, from that day I said no more. I was for a good while always afeared, but at last, as I may say, I grew used to it, and so I was content as well as I could.

"When he came and told me your honour was at t'other wicket, and made me fasten the outer gate, and ordered me into t'other room to shoot you, if you forced your way farther. Dear me, what a fright I was in, the pistol was of no use to me, and when you came again my heart rejoiced, in the hope that you was going to live with us; but after the first day master told me you must go again, which made me cruel sorrowful, and this, Sir, is all I know."

Ferdinand, heartily tired of this prolix account began to consider how he could find the way to this unhappy person, or persons, who were confined. He returned to the room where the deceased lay, and searching his pockets found only one crown and a key, which key Francis said belonged to the library bookcase, where he kept all the keys of the Castle; they again descended to the library, and opening the desk saw a bunch of keys, which for the present was all he sought for. They went towards the other wing through a long gallery, which terminated with a large door; here they tried their keys, and at length found the right; on opening it a dark staircase was before them; they now concluded a light would be necessary, and Francis was sent back to procure one.

On his return with a lamp, they descended the stairs into a long vaulted passage. On one side were three rooms that had once been inhabited as domestic offices; they proceeded until their progress was impeded by an iron door: Here also they tried their keys, and opened it, there was another descent of a few steps, and the bottom seemed a damp, cold dungeon. — Ferdinand stopped, and speaking aloud, "Is there any person confined in this place?"

A faint voice replied, "Yes, two wretched beings!" The sound appeared to be near them, but still deeper; they moved a little onward, and perceived another door, with two strong bolts drawn across; these were easily removed, and another descent of three steps brought them to a vaulted room, but cautious in advancing, for their lamp emitted but a very faint glimmer. — "Is this your prison, are we right?" asked Ferdinand.

"Yes," answered a voice, so close to him that he started, and extending the light perceived a figure that made him shudder, and Francis scream with terror.

It had the appearance of a man, from an immense long beard that reached almost to his knees as he sat upon a bench, with a small table before him, on which was a wooden plate, and a little wooden basin: He had a blanket wrapped round him, and his hair covered his shoulders down to the bottom of his back; his features they could make nothing of, but his eyes, from the meagre countenance, looked sunk, yet wild; they now perceived a glimmering lamp was fastened against the wall on one side.

"Gracious Heaven!" exclaimed Ferdinand, "can a human being have existed here?"

"Yes," replied the poor wretch; "many years I have struggled with life, but wonder not at me, look yonder;" he pointed to the other side, where on advancing they perceived another iron door, and a little on one side a small opening in it, through which another human face was visible, but more emaciated than the other. — "Have we a key for this door?" cried Ferdinand, inexpressibly shocked.

"That door," answered the man, "is seldom opened," in fact none of their keys were large enough.

"O," said Francis, "I recollect a large heavy key hangs on one side of the chimney piece."

"Will you venture to fetch it, or will you remain here whilst I go back?" asked Ferdinand.

"O Lord, Sir, I'll fetch it; stay here!" repeated he, looking fearfully round the place, and at the shocking figure before him, "No, no, I'll make what haste I can." He took the lamp and hastened off. The faint one that glimmered against the wall served only to make "darkness visible," and to throw additional horrors on the place.

"Good Heaven!" cried Ferdinand, "is it possible human nature could support a long confinement in this place!"

"Ah! Sir," replied the man, feebly, "we know not till put to the test what very severe trials nature can sustain. Death is not so ready to relieve the wretched. Our cruel persecutor found out a way to make us support, nay even wish for life. That dear, unhappy woman! think what must have been her sufferings;

upwards of twelve years, as the avenging monster told us a few days since, have we been here. Long, long ago, we lost all power of computing time. O, Eugenia, shall I live to see you free!" — "To be spared the misery of seeing you die," answered a faint but sweet voice, "is all the boon I ask of Heaven!"

Mutual sighs succeeded this tender expression, and Ferdinand, overcome with emotions at a scene so replete with horror, could not suppress audible proofs of his sensibility. — "O!" cried the wretched man, "how piercing, how inexpressibly sweet, to the heart, is the voice of compassion! Heaven only knows how you obtained entrance here; but should that cruel monster discover you? — — —"

"Fear not," said Ferdinand, hastily, "he is no more; death has stopped his career of wickedness at last."

The man was about to reply, when Francis entered with the key, for so strongly was his mind impressed with terror, that, though he dared not stay in the vault, he was almost equally afraid to go back, and return alone. Much quicker than he had attempted to move for many years did he exert himself on his errand, and heartily rejoiced to find he was once more safe by the side of Ferdinand, who eagerly snatching the key unlocked the other iron door, and entered a dungeon still more frightful, with only a few rays of light that served not even to distinguish objects, and proceeded from a small iron grating at the very top of the vault, which grating was almost covered by rust and weeds.

His own lamp guided him to the woman, for such he found she was, her hair almost covering her whole figure: She was also seated on a bench with a table, plate and basin, similar to the man's, a blanket round her also. — "For Heaven's sake!" exclaimed he, "let us remove you from this wretched place."

"I know not," said she, feebly, "how it can be done — we are chained."

"Chained!"

"Yes, each hand and foot is chained together, so as not to prevent our moving; but the Count will show you."

"The Count!" cried Ferdinand, returning again to the man, who opening the blanket, the other saw a stout chain was fastened to each leg, which went round the opposite arm, not preventing the movement, but yet confined them so as to preclude any exertions, by pulling them cross ways when they attempted to walk.

"Is there no way of getting off those chains?" said Ferdinand.

"Only by a key or a file," answered the man.

"Have patience, my good friends," returned Ferdinand; "I will return, and seek for something that may answer the purpose."

"Yes," added Francis, darting out first, lest he should be asked to stay there, "we will find something I warrant you."

Notwithstanding the extreme agitation of Ferdinand's mind, he could not choose, but observe the great alacrity with which Francis hastened his steps. When they had reached the library, they searched about for a file; nothing of that kind was to be seen, but they found two odd constructed keys, which they supposed might belong to the chains; having recruited the fire with wood, taking a bottle of wine, their keys, and two or three old knives, they soon returned to the wretched prisoners, and to their great joy found they could relieve them from their chains. Ferdinand supported the woman into the next dungeon, they rushed into each other's arms, and fell to the ground. With the assistance of Francis they were lifted up: Ferdinand prevailed on them to take some wine.

"We are not strangers to this liquor," said the man, gratefully pressing the hand of his preserver; "once a week we have had a half-pint each of us, not as a favour, but with a degree of refined cruelty, to support and enable us to bear the miseries inflicted on us."

Without shoes, only coarse flannel stockings, a kind of petticoat of the same, and the blanket round their shoulders, they had only been accustomed to struggle rather than walk to the end of their dungeons, where a small partition was contrived to afford a proper separation from the place they were to sit and lye on, for beds they had none. With infinite difficulty Ferdinand and Francis got them out of the dungeon, and up the steps into the vaulted passage: Here they rested for some time, and at length reached its termination; but no sooner did the light and air dart upon them, than the woman fainted, and the man was almost blinded. By proper applications they recovered the Lady, and Francis, by shutting some of the windows, rendered the light less offensive; yet so extremely feeble were the unhappy prisoners, that it was a considerable time before their deliverers could get them into the library, where placed in two old easy chairs at some distance from the fire, that it might not operate too powerfully upon them, and being refreshed with a little bread and wine, their spirits began to return, and the Lady burst into a torrent of tears, that flowed for some time with such violence as frightened Ferdinand; but the man thanked Heaven for the relief. "Be not uneasy, Sir," said he, "not one tear has fallen from those eyes for years; I thought those sources of relief to the overcharged mind were entirely dried up; the indulgence will, I trust, be attended with happy effects."

Indeed it proved so, for after the first turbulence was abated, she recovered sufficiently to thank her deliverer in the warmest terms. Ferdinand proposed her retiring to bed, the one he had slept in Francis had prepared for her; he lamented the impossibility of procuring her linen and necessaries for the present.

"It is not impossible," said the Gentleman suddenly, "but that our trunks and clothes are still here, though perhaps decayed by time."

"I'll be hanged," cried Francis, "if those trunks, in a room next to this Gentleman's, ben't the very ones, for there they have been locked up ever since I came here."

On this hint Ferdinand sallied forth with his bunch of keys to the room mentioned, where the trunks were deposited, and after trying several keys to no purpose, Francis was dispatched for an instrument of some kind to break them open, which with much difficulty they at last effected, and found them full of clothes and linen for both sexes; also some children's necessaries, which last rather surprised Ferdinand; they however selected some for both persons, which seemed less injured by time than might have been expected; these were carried down, and when aired, the Lady was helped to her apartment, and linen left for her, which, from the stiffness of her arms and general debility of her limbs, she was a considerable time before she could put on; and when covered, and she was laid down, the sudden transition from such extreme misery to hope and comfort, affected her so forcibly as to preclude sleep for many hours: At length, however, she fell into a refreshing slumber; such as she had very long been a stranger to.

Mean time Francis had prepared his bed for the Gentleman, for though there were many other beds in the house, it was thought improper to put him into a room without first airing it. Being accommodated with comfortable linen, he very readily accepted their assistance to retire; and, after having seen him into bed, Ferdinand and Francis returned to the library to talk over this extraordinary affair, which afforded much room for observation and conjecture.

"Lord have mercy on us!" cried Francis, "how could they two poor souls live so for twelve years, naked and starving? O, dear me, I used to think my lot hard, but to be sure, Sir, it was Paradise to what they had. What a shame for me to think of trouble!"

"True, Francis," replied Ferdinand, "if we could, when afflicted, but examine into many circumstances that tend to lighten our own calamities, and compare them with the more painful disadvantages which others labour under, we should learn patience and resignation under the evils we suffer; but the human mind is too apt to view their own situation, and that of others under the medium of error, make partial comparisons, and draw unjust conclusions to increase their own misery.

"It appears to me that the Gentleman and Lady are the owners of this Castle, and had their persecutor died before I came here, doubtless they must have been starved in that horrid dungeon, for it is not likely you would have discovered them."

"Me, Sir! O, no, I should have crept out of the Castle as fast as I could if he had died when I was alone with him, though the Lord knows how I should have managed, for I could not walk to the village I am sure, and he might have died many days before our market man came, and I should never have been able to stay in this place with a dead corpse by myself.—So Providence sent you here, Sir, to save them poor souls from starvation, and me from dying of fear or fatigue." During this time Ferdinand had opened the bookcase to replace the keys, and curiosity induced him to search if there were any papers or memorandums relative to the deceased. Opening one drawer he met with a manuscript, the pages being open as if lately written, his eye caught the words: "The stranger, who calls himself Ferdinand."—"Ah!" exclaimed he, "this is doubtless a kind of journal, and may develop the whole mystery." Turning to the back, he saw it was entitled, "Memoirs of the Baron S******." The writing was extremely bad, and many pages seemed hardly legible, evidently written with a weak and trembling hand. He ordered Francis to make a fire in another apartment, air more linen, and get refreshments for the Lady and Gentleman against they should awake; then kindling a fresh blaze for himself, he prepared with eager curiosity to peruse the manuscript before him, which contained the following Narrative.

CHAPTER XIV

MEMOIRS OF BARON S******.

"Should these memoirs ever fall into the hands of an intelligent being, let him mark the instability of expected happiness; let him learn to detest the fascinating charms of false, deceitful woman, and to beware of the insidious arts, the treacherous designs of base, perfidious man; let suspicion mark his eye, and caution guide his judgment; let him shun the syren woman, turn his ears from the delusive voice of pleasure, and lock his bosom close from professions of friendship, which tend only to deceive, and under a specious covering envelop the most treacherous designs. Should those cautions be read too late to preserve him from the machinations of the deceitful heart, then let him learn from me the triumph of Revenge!!!"

"My father was a Bavarian Baron, but supporting his rank with that splendour necessary to keep his vassals in awe, and give consequence to his dignity at Court, he diminished the value of those estates bequeathed to him by his ancestors, and left me possessed of equal pride, ambition, and desire of grandeur and magnificence, without a capability of gratifying either. Unable to appear at Court with the consequence attached to my title, I retired to my estate, and sought, in the submissive obedience of my vassals, and in the authoritative and sullen grandeur I assumed over them, a consolation for that retirement disappointed ambition had driven me to choose, as a smaller evil than supporting the arrogance of riches, where there could be no superiority of birth to my own. Five years I dragged on an inactive life without enjoying any advantages from my seclusion, but what arose from lording it over my tenantry, without knowing the blessings of society, for there were none I deigned to converse with. In a kind of gloomy magnificence that was confined to my own estate, which inspired awe, but which repressed love or reverence, I passed my days in riding over the same track of ground which had no variety, and my nights in constant regrets for the loss of that consequence I was born to assume, but which the prodigality of my ancestors had compelled me to resign.

"One day, attended by several of my vassals, I was riding round the skirts of a wood which bounded my estate, when I was suddenly alarmed by quick and repeated shrieks that seemed to issue from the wood: I instantly rode to the side from whence the voice proceeded, and in a few moments perceived a

carriage surrounded by four or five banditti, and two horsemen
laying dead in the road. The appearance of myself and servants,
who sped towards them, caused the villains to desist, and
provide for their own safety. It was in vain to attempt pursuing
them, as through the closeness of the wood they might elude
our observation, I therefore hastened to the carriage where a
young Lady sat, who had thrown herself upon the bosom of a
man to all appearance dead or dying. When she raised her head,
never shall I forget the moment that decided my future destiny,
and ruined my peace for ever! When she turned her eyes upon
me, Heavens! what were my sensations! until that luckless hour
a stranger to the captivating charms of beauty, a blaze of charms
dressed in the fascination of tears and sorrow, and which
conveyed a thousand tender ideas to a susceptible heart: She
held out one of her lovely hands, 'Save him, O, save my father!'
she cried in a voice of softest melody, 'or pierce my bosom
also!'—O, the remembrance of that moment of delight, pregnant
with years of ceaseless misery! O, beautiful, false, enchanting,
destructive charmer! Woman, vile abandoned woman! but I will
be calm, am I not revenged? Yes, and that exquisite satisfaction
shall attend me to my grave!

Let me proceed: Under a delirium of sudden rapture I
exerted myself with uncommon alacrity, having prevailed on
her to quit the chaise, I entered it, and found the Gentleman had
received a wound in his breast, whether dangerous or not I
could not know, I perceived he still lived, and having sent off a
servant to procure the attendance of a surgeon, I entreated the
Lady to go on to my Castle in the carriage, whilst my vassals
formed a kind of litter, to carry the wounded man much easier
than the motion of the wheels would admit of. She acquiesced
in every request with the warmest expressions of gratitude for
my attention to her parent; every tender look, every gentle
word, twined itself about my heart, and confirmed me a wretch
for ever!

"We arrived at my Castle, the surgeon soon made his
appearance, and, after examining the wound, gave us hopes
that it would not prove mortal. The Gentleman did not recover
his senses until the pain, which the probing of the wound
occasioned, roused him from the insensibility that had
overpowered his faculties, and enabled him to discover his
daughter kneeling at the side of the bed, and bathing his hand
with her tears. My child! he exclaimed—Gracious Heaven, I
thank thee, my child is safe!"—He was desired not to speak, and
after some inarticulate blessings on his deliverer, weakness
compelled him to give over the attempt.

The two servants that lay in the wood when I first discovered the carriage, we found to be entirely deprived of life, and the post-boy had fled thro' the trees: I knew not therefore the names or quality of my guests, but every thing in their appearance and manners seemed to denote that they were of no contemptible rank. During three days, I saw the young Lady only at the bed-side of her father; but in that time the subtle poison stole into my heart, and love, the most ardent and most impetuous, took possession of my whole soul, and engrossed every faculty of my mind. On the fourth day, the old Gentleman was declared to be out of danger, and allowed the privilege of speaking. He desired to see me; when I attended him his gratitude was boundless; he called me the preserver of his life, and the guardian-angel of his Eugenia.

He told me that he was a Nobleman of Suabia, his name Count Zimchaw. Having been on a visit to a relation at Munich, he was returning to Suabia through Mindelhiem, that he might call on another friend. Coming thro' the wood, which he took as the nearest route, he was attacked by four men. His servants, as well as himself, having fire arms, prepared to resist them; but his faithful attendants were shot dead, and the carriage surrounded. Finding then that resistance could have no avail, he was in the act of resigning his pistol, after having, in the beginning of the attack, discharged it without effect, when, as he reached his arm to deliver it, a cowardly assassin stabbed him in the breast, and he fell back senseless: The shrieks of his daughter on that event he supposed reached my ears, and providentially brought me to their assistance. This little account of himself was accompanied by the warmest sentiments of gratitude, in which the too lovely Eugenia joined.

He recovered fast, and had more than once mentioned his desire of renewing his journey, from an apprehension of intruding upon me: But far gone in a fatal passion that was to mark my future days with sorrow, I earnestly besought him to remain some time with me, and endeavoured, by every act of attention and complaisance, to gain the esteem of the father, and the heart of his daughter. My sentiments could not long be unnoticed by either. The Count viewed me with kindness and complacency; but Eugenia grew more reserved, and though always grateful and polite, there was a respectful coldness in her manners, repulsive to the warmth with which I always involuntarily addressed her.

Unaccustomed to meet with any opposition to my will, I was not prepared to expect a denial to my wishes, when I should think it a proper time to disclose them, and being one day alone with the Count, I seized a favourable opportunity, and without reserve opened my heart to him, solicited the hand of his daughter, and made the most liberal offers my circumstances would admit of. — The Count's character was propitious to my views; he was naturally proud and avaricious, the want of a male heir had disappointed the first passion, and increased the second. A nephew was to enjoy his estates by the marriage settlements after his death, and what he could save from his income was all he could dispose of in favour of his daughter. He had been desirous of uniting her with his nephew, but that Gentleman travelling into England, had there married a young Lady of rank and fortune, an account of which had reached Count Zimchaw a very few weeks previous to my meeting with them in the wood. Disappointed in his wishes, he felt a good deal of anxiety for the settlement of his child; when therefore I declared my love, and made my proposals, he could not disguise his satisfaction: — "To bestow my daughter on the preserver of my life and her honour (cried he) is the highest gratification I could picture to myself, and confers on me additional obligations. Yes, my dear Baron, Eugenia is your's, I pledge you my word, and answer for my child, that she will with joy ratify the gift I make you of her hand, and reward our deliverer from death and dishonour."

"Mistaken man! he knew not the heart of his degenerate daughter. Transported with the prospect of my expected happiness, yet wounded by the recollection of her coldness, I entreated the Count to be my friend, and speak his approbation of my wishes, before I ventured to disclose them to her."

"We will lose no time," answered he, "and it is sufficient for me to declare my pleasure, and for her to obey. After we retire from dinner, your desires shall be confirmed." I left him under perturbations difficult to describe; joy, hope and fear, assailed me at once. I had no doubt of her compliance with the commands of her father, but I feared her heart would have no share in her obedience."

"After dinner we retired to the saloon, my mind was so extremely agitated, that my emotions attracted the observation of Eugenia, nor did the uncommon spirits of the Count pass unnoticed: She viewed us alternately with a mixture of concern, and curiosity depicted in her countenance, which I well understood, and when we entered the saloon, as I led her to a seat, I felt her hand tremble in mine. The Count scarcely permitted us to be seated, and the servant to shut the door, before rising briskly, and taking his daughter's hand, "My dear Eugenia, (said he, abruptly) our worthy friend and preserver

Baron S— — —**, has done us the honour to solicit an alliance with us; yes, my child, he offers his hand to your acceptance. I have with joy accorded to his wishes, and here, my Lord, I ratify the gift," putting her hand into mine, as I bowed profoundly before her. She started up, trembled, and strove to disengage her hand as I pressed it to my lips: "My Father! my Lord!" cried she, extremely agitated, "spare me, O, spare me, I cannot, indeed I cannot!"— — —

"Cannot what?" exclaimed the Count, with a wrathful countenance: "Dare you resist my will? Can you refuse the hand of your benefactor, the hand that saved your father's life? Ungrateful girl! cold and insensible to the honour you ought to receive with transports! Teach your tongue a different language, learn to be grateful, and obey my commands." He had scarcely pronounced those last words, when she fell lifeless before us.

The Count was excessively enraged: I was wounded to my very soul, yet called for that assistance he would have denied to her. She was carried to her apartment. "Pardon a foolish wayward girl (said he;) perhaps the idea of marrying out of her own country has occasioned this apparent reluctance; a foolish local prejudice has got hold of her, which argument and reason will subdue. Be not disconcerted, my dear Baron (added he, embracing me) I swear to you that Eugenia shall be your wife." He left me at those words, and I remained overwhelmed with a thousand turbulent passions, disappointed love, wounded pride, jealousy and despair, by turns agitated me almost to madness. Her coldness, her repugnance, augmented my love and inflamed my pride; passion and resentment were raised to their utmost pitch; I accused her of ingratitude and insensibility, and in the workings of my rage, swore she should be mine, whatever might be the consequences!

"I walked into the gardens to calm, if possible, the agitations of my spirits, but after strolling about two hours returned as restless as before. I met a servant, who said the Lady Eugenia wished to see me in her apartment. I flew thither with indescribable emotions. She was sitting on a sofa, looking pale as death, but more beautiful, more interesting than ever. Trembling I advanced, and would have flung myself at her feet. —"Hold, my Lord (said she, in a faint but serious voice) this humiliation neither becomes you nor me; have the goodness to be seated, and hear me with compassion, and without displeasure." I took my seat. "My Lord (continued she, in a firmer voice) think me not ungrateful, or insensible to your merits, or my great obligations to your generosity and humanity; I feel, I acknowledge all: You have claims I never can reward, and to give you my hand, circumstanced as I am, would be a base return for favours so unbounded.—My Lord, I have no heart to give! that has long been in the possession of another; my father knows it well, but as his consent could not be obtained to an union he thought unworthy of his approbation, I have sworn never to marry without it—I never will; but neither can I, will I, ever give my hand to another; deign then, my Lord, to withdraw your generous intentions in my favour, save me from the displeasure of my father, and let me be still further indebted to your nobleness of mind; the favour I solicit is no common one; but you have a soul superior to self-consideration, and on that I rest my confidence."

She might have proceeded for some time without interruption from me, so astonished and mortified did I feel at her address; but when she had ceased speaking, I endeavoured to recover my spirits, and told her, 'that had there remained a possibility of her being united to the object of her attachment, I would have imposed silence upon my wishes for ever; but as it was evident such a connexion never could take place, as I flattered myself that my tenderness, and earnest endeavours to gain her heart, and promote her happiness, would in time have the desired effect; she must forgive me if I could not comply with her request, or forego a blessing her father had so kindly promised me."

"Blessing!" cried she, indignantly; "can you call a reluctant hand, a heart devoted to another, and a lifeless form that will shrink with horror from an union imposed upon her by a stern parent, who to an unjust prejudice would sacrifice his daughter; can you call such a sacrifice a blessing? See, see me at your feet (added she, endeavouring to prostrate herself, which I prevented:) I beseech, I implore you, not to persist in your addresses; respect your own happiness, if you cannot feel for mine, misery must follow a compulsion so repugnant to my soul."

At this moment her father entered the room: She threw herself at his feet in an agony, "Father, my dear father! by that tender name I conjure you to hear me! To your commands I have given up the dearest wishes of my heart; I have sworn never to marry the Count without your approbation; do not compel me to be miserable with another; never, never can I love the Baron as a husband: I esteem, I honour him as your preserver; I would lay down my life to rove my gratitude, but I have no heart to give."

The Count sternly bid her rise. "I have heard you with patience (said he) and now do you hear me; and not only hear but obey me. You have dared to single out my greatest enemy as the object of your love, and even yet avow your affection for him to my face: I ought not therefore to be surprised that this Nobleman, who has preserved my life and your honour, should be the object of your aversion! Your conduct sufficiently explains itself, and I know how to set a just value on your love and duty so much boasted of: Now I put it to the proof; this instant I command you to give your hand to the Baron, or my everlasting curses shall follow you to the grave!"

She started up, in a kind of wild horror: "Hold! O hold! behold your devoted daughter, though distraction and death must be the consequence, take, take my hand, you may bestow, I can never give it!" He snatched her offered hand, and put in into mine; "receive her, my Lord, as a pledge of gratitude from a father, who dares to boast the gift is worthy of your love; duty and obedience will make her all you can wish for. And you, Eugenia, remember what you owe for me, and for yourself, happiness is in your own power." She answered not a word, her tears had ceased to flow, I lifted her hand to my lips, she withdrew it not, but appeared senseless and inanimate, looked alternately at her father and myself, a wildness in her aspect, that seemed unconscious of the objects before her. I tried to recover her from this torpid state by the tenderest expressions: She heard me unmoved, and the Count having called her attendant, advised me to withdraw; I did so, and left them together."

END OF THE FIRST VOLUME

VOLUME 2, CHAPTER I

I retired to my own apartment overwhelmed with vexation and resentment. What, could I submit to marry a woman who avowed her love for another, who detested me, and in whose eyes my very perseverance must appear meanness? Where was my pride, my feeling, to accept a reluctant hand? Yet when her beauteous form swam before me, her fascinating charms, could I coldly resign her to another? Was she not ungrateful and disdainful, and must I be the sufferer for saving her father's life? No, I would teach her to love, or if not to love, to obey and please me; I would consult my own gratification, nor bear the insult of rejection from a preference to another! Thus determined, love, pride, and resentment, took full possession of my soul, and I resolved to urge a quick completion of the nuptial rites.

The Count joined me soon after, and congratulated himself and me on our success. — "Bear with her coldness, my dear Baron (said he) I know her principles, her integrity. In a very short time she will be sensible of her duties, and become every thing you can wish for; the sooner the marriage takes place the better." This met my wishes, and we settled it that the ceremony should be performed in three days. At supper, when sent for, she directly followed the servant; she spoke not, but tried to eat; it was an attempt only, for she could not swallow. The Count and myself addressed her with the kindest expressions. She only bowed; but being warmly urged by her father, she drank a glass of wine, and instantly burst into a torrent of tears, so violent that I was quite terrified. — For upwards of an hour she wept incessantly, till quite exhausted she was conveyed to her apartment, and in all probability the tears she shed preserved her intellects, as, after they had ceased to flow, she grew more composed, spoke to her attendant, but passed the night without rest, and sighed continually. — The next day the Count passed above two hours with her alone, and then led her into the saloon to me. Pale, trembling and dejected, she received my ardent addresses without manifesting any reluctance, yet, without the least mark of complacency, tortured to death by her cold disdain, I ventured to complain, to remonstrate. She turned her eyes full upon me: — "Of what, Sir, can you complain? I hear you, I obey my father, you know I can do no more, I cannot play the hypocrite; if I become your wife I shall do my duty, but love or affection I can never promise, and — she paused, then fixing her penetrating eye on mine — and, to a mind so little delicate as your's, the tender feelings of the soul can be but of trifling estimation: — Urge me then no more, you may deserve my esteem, but never can possess my heart."

"Eugenia!" cried the Count, in an angry tone, "is this treatment for you to offer, or my benefactor to endure?"

"Your pardon, Sir," (returned she;) "I simply speak the dictates of truth, and the Baron has no cause to be offended; I know my duties, and will perform them."—Provoked as I was, and vowing vengeance in my heart, I thought it best to diversify our subjects of conversation, and appear submissive to her will: I endeavoured to repress my feelings, and by silent assiduities obtain her attention; but a chilling reserve, and a studied politeness, was all the return I met with. I freely confess, rage and resentful pride had an equal share with love in my desire to obtain her hand. Unaccustomed to have my will disputed, I was hurt and mortified to see all my complaisance thrown away, and to feel humbled before the woman I considered as under obligations to me:—Stimulated therefore by every turbulent passion, I determined she should be mine, be the consequences what they might.

Preparations were made for the marriage; she heard, she saw all, without a single observation; and the day previous to that on which we were to be united, her father informed her, that at twelve the following morning the ceremony was to be performed.

"I shall obey your pleasure, Sir," was all her reply.

"The day came, ten thousand curses on it, and the false, dissembling, artful wretch! But I am revenged." Let me then proceed: "At the appointed hour we assembled in the Chapel adjoining to my Castle, there I received the perjured creature's hand in the moment when she was planning to deceive and destroy my peace for ever! After the ceremony was performed, and we retired to the saloon, she turned to me with an air of solemnity: "I have obeyed my father, Sir, and complied with your wishes, permit me to solicit a favour in my turn."

"Name it, my angel," cried I, in a foolish transport, kissing her hand.

"Suffer me to pass the remainder of this day alone, in my own apartment."

"How!" said the Count, "not dine with us, Eugenia? Impossible, you cannot expect your husband will accede to such an absurd request."

"You, Sir," answered she, with an expressive look, "have this day resigned over all your authority to this Gentleman, it is to him therefore I apply. A few hours to myself is no great boon; I again repeat my request not to be broken in upon till the supper hour."

Fool! blockhead as I was! fearful of irritating her, and in the hope I should please her by my compliance, "Dearest Eugenia! (I cried) be mistress of your own time, I submit to any mortification that can oblige you, and let me trust to your generosity to reward my self-denial." I kissed her hand, and led her to the door. She turned her eyes upon her father, tears gushed from them, which she strove to hide, and, bowing to me, hastily withdrew.

"You are wrong, my dear Baron," said the Count, "to indulge her."

"Pardon me," answered I, "reflection will be favourable to my wishes, her vows are now given and a consideration of the duties she has taken upon herself to perform, will probably operate in my favour, and produce a desirable change in her behaviour."

"You may possibly be right," replied he, "but some how I am neither pleased nor satisfied." — Ah! he had his reasons for distrusting the perfidious wretch, whilst I was lulled into a blind security! The woman that attended her had orders to carry some wine and biscuits to her apartment. The Count and myself eat our dinner, and the day being wet, seated ourselves quietly to piquet, though my emotions did not permit me to pay much attention to the game; I felt more than once inclined to have asked particulars respecting the man who had possessed the heart of my wife; but delicacy repressed my curiosity, as the Count had always evaded any explanation on that head.

"The hours passed tardily until the time arrived, when she had permitted an interruption. The moment the supper was prepared I flew to her apartment, and gently knocked at the door: No answer was made, when I repeated it louder: I looked through the key-hole, and saw the key was on the inside; yet no noise or the least bustle was made. — Extremely alarmed I called for her servant; she was no where to be found, nor had she been visible for some hours. The Count by this time had joined me, and ordered the door to be forced. The apartment was empty!

"Never, never shall I forget the anguish of that moment! The window which looked into the garden was open: She is gone — she is lost! (I cried) and I am undone!"

"My dear son," exclaimed the enraged Baron, "lose no time in fruitless grief, let us pursue her through different roads, we soon shall hear of the faithless wretch, whom I blush to call daughter." The servants were instantly summoned; it was a dark, stormy night, but I ordered them to prepare horses for me and for themselves; it was impossible in such weather they could travel fast. On examining we found her clothes were gone. Agnes, who had waited on her, said, "that when she carried the biscuits the Lady ordered her to retire." The Count, with some of my vassals, were to search all the neighbouring cottages, whilst we scoured the roads. Heedless of the weather, myself and four servants took one direction; two more, with some of the tenantry I had caused to be called together, took another, and large rewards were promised to the successful pursuer.

Two days and nights were spent in a vain pursuit round the country and through the woods, without obtaining the least intelligence to guide our search, and I began to be well convinced that she must be concealed somewhere in my own neighbourhood. I returned to the Castle, and found the Count had not been more successful than myself. — Rage, vexation and fatigue, threw me into a fever, which confined me to my bed for eight days; but though incapable of acting myself, I still sent persons to watch the roads night and day. The fourth day of my confinement, a woman servant entered the room with two letters; "having that morning been to Eugenia's apartment to clean the room, and take the linen from the bed, under the pillow she had found those papers." I hastily snatched them from her hand, and saw one was addressed to me, the other to the Count, the writing Eugenia's. I tore it open, and read the following words:

"All endeavours to discover my retreat will prove fruitless, nor will you ever see me more. Had not the prospect of a deliverance from your power been held out to me, my own hand would have terminated my life. To avoid the completion of a father's malediction, I obeyed and gave you my hand, but I secretly repeated other vows. — May Heaven forgive me, for I had no alternative. Had they been given to you I must have been perjured. Love, such as I have an idea of, had no share in your bosom, for you sought your own gratification at the expense of my happiness: On your account therefore I feel no regret; you have preserved the life of my parent to deprive me of his love and protection. You have made me miserable, may you render his future days happy! Adieu for ever!

EUGENIA."

THE LETTER TO THE COUNT WAS AS FOLLOWS:

"Humbly on her knees the lost, unhappy Eugenia implores a father's pardon, and invokes from Heaven every blessing on his head! Had any thing but her everlasting happiness been at stake, she would have sacrificed herself with transport. To a father's wishes she gave up an attachment founded on merit, truth and honour, she resigned her fondest hopes of felicity. — Ah! my Lord, was she not then entitled to a negative voice? Must she be compelled to violate every feeling of her heart, and devote herself to misery? Impossible! the most rigid duty cannot require such a sacrifice. — You commanded your wretched daughter under the penalty of your 'everlasting curses,' dreadful denunciation! to give 'her hand' to Baron S***. He cruelly availed himself of the dread command, and she obeyed: — But there your power ends. The Supreme Being never will sanction constrained or perjured vows, and in the very act of giving her hand, she mentally pronounced others than those dictated by force to her trembling lips: No ties therefore subsist between the Baron and Eugenia; may he make another and a more fortunate choice. For you, dear and ever honoured parent, whilst your unfortunate daughter exists, for you, her prayers will be offered to the Throne of Grace, that every blessing that Heaven can bestow may be yours, and that you may grant that forgiveness she solicits on her knees with a bleeding heart, for the pain and disappointment she is compelled to give you. Grant, Gracious Heaven, that Eugenia may one day kneel and obtain a father's blessing! The pangs of death can scarcely exceed those she feels when she resolves to fly from your paternal arms, and bury herself in solitude, perhaps for ever!

EUGENIA."

Such were the contents of two letters indelibly imprinted on my memory. The Count's rage was little inferior to mine; from him I learned that she had, almost from infancy, formed an attachment to the young Count M****, son to a man he had once esteemed, but now detested, from a discovery that his principles were inimical to the good of his country: He had therefore broken off the intended marriage. The grief and disappointment attending that event had driven the lover to quit his country in search of returning peace, far from the object of his wishes. This affair had preyed greatly on Eugenia's spirits, and it was to relieve her disquietudes, and by a diversity of objects engage her attention from dwelling on one set of painful ideas, that the Count undertook a journey to Munich, and by a cruel fatality was thrown in my way to complete my misery; we had little doubt but that her lover had been instrumental in her flight, and that a secret correspondence had been carried on between them, but how or which way they could have conducted her escape, so as to baffle all intelligence, has ever remained a mystery to this hour.

I had scarcely attained a state of convalescence, before the old Count fell ill; indignation had for a time supported him, whilst there remained any hopes of discovering her; but when all our different messengers returned unsuccessful, he began to droop, and in proportion as grief and reflection on the loss of an only child, took possession of his mind, his bodily strength decayed. After staying with me near three months, heavily oppressed both in mind and body, hopeless and languishing, he took leave of me to return into Suabia; at the moment of his departure, however, he solemnly protested, that should his daughter ever be recovered, he should consider her as my wife, honour, gratitude, and the rights of an injured parent confirmed her such, unless I chose to break the ties between us. "My dear Baron (said he, as he entered the carriage that was to convey him from me:) My dear Baron, depend upon my integrity, you are free, but I and my daughter are bound; whether she ever returns to her duty or not, you are the heir to all I can dispose of from my nephew, and I trust that I shall shortly see you in Suabia."

We parted to meet no more. I had refused to accompany him, in the faint hope that time might bring me some information respecting the fugitive; and he was desirous of returning that he might make an inquiry respecting Count M***. Some time past before I heard from Count Zimchaw, and of course I concluded he was as far as myself from obtaining the least degree of satisfaction. For my part, neither time nor disappointment had abated my passion; I still loved to a degree of fury; for rage, and a desire of revenge on her and her paramour, went hand in hand with my inclination for her person; and being at length convinced they could not remain so long undiscovered in my neighbourhood, I was on the point of setting off for Suabia when I received a letter from the Count. He informed me that a severe fit of illness had prevented him from writing, tho' he did not neglect every necessary inquiry that might tend to procure a development of the dark plot against our happiness. To his astonishment he learned that the young Count M***, having been recalled by the death of his father, had resided for some time past at his estate, still overwhelmed with a deep melancholy, which had appeared lately to be greatly increased, arising, as he supposed, from the report he had given out on his arrival to his own Castle, "That the Lady Eugenia was married to Baron S****, still desirous (added the Count) of preserving the reputation of an ungrateful wretch, whom I can never again acknowledge as a daughter, unless she is your wife."—He added, "that from every circumstance he had investigated, it was certain that Count M*** held no correspondence with her, and that in his opinion the most certain conclusion was, that she had escaped to some Convent. He earnestly pressed me to come and reside with him, leaving a trusty person on my own estate, who might still continue every proper inquiry, and that should it be possible for her to lie concealed in my neighbourhood, my absence would throw her off her guard, and when we least expected it, she might be discovered."

This letter at once determined me, and in a very few days after I set off on my journey to Suabia. The Count's Castle lay between Stutgard, the capital of Suabia, and Baden, and, after a fatiguing journey, I arrived on the very day on which he had expired, of the gout in his stomach. I found his domestics expected my arrival, in consequence of my answer to their master's letter, and was presently informed he had declared me his heir, and from me they were to take every direction. I was touched with this proof of the Count's gratitude and affection, and more than ever desirous of recovering his daughter, that she might share in that fortune her worthy father had bequeathed to me. Not entirely divested of hope, I accounted for her absence by saying, "that she was likely to produce an heir, and being in a delicate state of health, the physicians had forbidden her to undertake the journey." This passed with every body. I took upon me the management of the household, saw the remains of Count Zimchaw deposited in the family vault, and as his nephew was to have possession of the Castle and estate, I disposed of the furniture, dismissed the servants, and took a lodging at a farmer's for a few days previous to my return home.

The truth was, I had an invincible desire to see Count M***, whose residence was only a very few miles distance. Every day I rode round his grounds, and grew quite desperate that chance did not befriend me.—One morning, riding through a narrow valley, accompanied by one servant only, I met a Gentleman with a gun, and an English pointer running by his side. As he advanced I saw a young man, of a noble air, and an engaging countenance; struck with a presentiment that this must be the Count, I accosted him, and inquired to whom that mansion, whose turrets we saw through the trees, and the neighbouring grounds, belonged?

"To Count M***, Sir (replied he, eying me with a scrutinizing look:) Are you a stranger in this country that you ask the question?"

"I am (answered I) having resided in these parts only a fortnight."

"A fortnight! (repeated he, with some emotion) you are on a visit then I suppose?"

"No; I came here for that purpose, but found my good friend dead, the late Count Zimchaw."

"Count Zimchaw! (he exclaimed.) Great God! perhaps I see Baron S***?"

"You are right, Sir, that is my name."

In a moment he turned pale, trembled, and convinced me by his emotions that my conjectures were just, and that in him I beheld a detested rival. To an indifferent by-stander our appearance must have excited astonishment; we viewed each other for some moments in silent rage, but fortunately prudence predominated over passion, and I recollected that it was necessary to dissemble. I immediately added, as soon as I could speak. "And I have the happiness of being the husband of his daughter, the Lady Eugenia." He leaned against a tree unable to support himself. "O name for ever dear! (cried he) sacred be your peace, whatever becomes of mine!" — "Leave me, Sir, leave me to retrospections more painful than you can wish to your bitterest enemy." For a moment the thought crossed me to put a period to his existence; but whilst I deliberated, two of his servants appeared with dogs and guns. Looking at him with the most pointed contempt I could assume, I departed in silence; but with more heart-felt ease than I had experienced a long while, convinced now that Eugenia was not with him, nor of course in that part of the country. Having in a short time settled every thing with Count Zimchaw's heir, who was also led to believe his relation was my wife, and at my Castle; I left Suabia to return home, richer, but more wretched, than before I had known the Count and his daughter. On my arrival I learned that every search had been fruitless respecting the ungrateful woman, who had so shamefully and suddenly deserted us, I sought to amuse my mind by embellishing my Castle; but in vain I endeavoured to root out my ill-fated passion from my heart. — Eugenia, beautiful and engaging, was ever before my eyes, and threw me into a gloomy dejection, from whence nothing could rouse me. The little society that I had sometimes indulged in, grew hateful to me, love, and a desire of revenge, wholly occupied my mind, and the only idea that could communicate the least degree of satisfaction to my soul, was, that Count M*** was apparently as wretched as myself.

Four years I passed without a friend or a companion to harmonize my feelings, or without the least intelligence of the object that had caused all my misery: During that time I had changed my servants two or three times, for nothing pleased me, and the men preferred serving in the army rather than to support the capriciousness of my temper. One faithful fellow only remained, who had been invariably attached to me for some years, who had the command over the others, and had been generally hated by them for that reason. This man, Peter, who was in my confidence, I had twice dispatched into Suabia, to make private inquiries relative to Count M***, and was informed, that within three months after my departure he had quitted his palace overwhelmed with deep melancholy, and was gone to travel for the recovery of his health.

The last inquiry afforded no other information than that he was abroad. I had also set on foot a diligent search through all the neighbouring convents to procure intelligence of my wife, curse on the name! but all proved abortive; yet neither time, nor despair, caused any revolution in my sentiments; I loved and hated to excess."

CHAPTER II

Four years had just been completed when one night I was suddenly awakened by Peter, who conjured me to rise and save myself, for the Castle was in flames. Greatly alarmed, I threw myself out of bed, and found his information but too true, and the principal part of the building was consumed, and my furniture destroyed before assistance could be procured. This event gave a new turn to my thoughts, I resolved to dispose of the remainder of my effects, to leave my ruined Castle without rebuilding of it, and to travel from one principality to another, that by change of place and objects I might amuse my mind. I settled every thing with my vassals, and, accompanied only by Peter, quitted Bavaria. I passed through Italy, France, the Netherlands, Switzerland, and at length came into Suabia, on my return to Bavaria, without deriving much benefit from my tour, either to my mind or body, for I carried in my heart a barbed arrow, which no local circumstances could extract; insensible to pleasure, my eye wandered over every new object with indifference, and Eugenia, the faithless, ungrateful Eugenia, occupied every thought and desire. — Passing through this country, my good genius prompted me to pay some attention to its romantic and picturesque views. Riding about, I had not attended to the sun's decline, and the approach of a heavy storm, which came on suddenly, accompanied with thunder and hail. We were on the skirts of the Black Forest, and distant, as we thought, from any village; finding the storm grew more violent, I sought to get some shelter from the thickest part of a wood at the extremity of the road: I rode with great swiftness towards it, and soon forced my way through the trees, and obtained from their thick foliage a defence against the fury of the storm. In a short time the weather changed, the clouds dispersed, and the moon rose with additional splendour from the contrast of the black clouds rolling off behind the mountains.

Turning our horses to leave the wood, I observed, at some distance, the turrets of a Castle, which, had not the moon shone full upon them, might never have attracted the notice of any traveller, being enveloped in the thickest of the trees, and far from any public road: Curiosity, or a powerful presentiment, urged me to explore this dwelling; Peter sought to dissuade me, he conceived it to be some ruinous place, the residence of a banditti, which was known to infest the Black Forest and its environs. I allowed the probability of his suggestions, yet could not be persuaded to relinquish my design: It was with much reluctance that he followed me; we pushed through the wood, until we found it so close on every side as to impede the horses from advancing. Peter again urged me to return, as the night was far advanced, and the neighbourhood dangerous, still, an unaccountable propensity to see this retired dwelling made me disregard his solicitations, and despise the apprehension of danger. I dismounted, and fastened my horse to a tree, obliging him to do the same, though he declared we should never see them again, and I firmly believe, had he not been afraid to go back alone, unknowing of the road, that he would have left me; but he run an equal risk, and therefore attended me through almost impassable places, when all at once we came to a declivity, at the bottom of which was a small vale, from whence we saw two towers very plain among some trees at a small distance.

We soon arrived through those trees to a large old building moated all round. After going by the side of the moat, about a hundred yards, we saw a small bridge, which led across to a pair of iron gates, which looked into an outer court, within which was another high wall. Peter I observed trembled with apprehension, but I boldly pulled the bell: In a little time a boy appeared, and demanded "who and what we were?"

I replied, "A Gentleman and his servant, who travelling had lost their way, and begged shelter for the night."

The boy replied, "That his master having been ill, was retired to rest, his Lady also; that the servants were likewise going to bed, and he could not disturb them, or admit strangers into the house: If we returned through the wood, and kept to the right-hand of the Forest, we should reach a small village." Ending these words he disappeared abruptly, and, though I repeatedly called to him, did not return.

Peter rejoiced that we were not to enter this Castle, pressed our immediate return lest our horses should be stolen. Vexed and reluctant I found myself obliged to comply, as I saw no probability of getting entrance there. The next step was to find the village, from whence I hoped to gratify my curiosity respecting this obscure habitation. We soon recovered our horses, and by the light of the moon explored our way from this difficult and dangerous place. After a good deal of trouble and fatigue we reached a few scattered cottages just as the morning dawned, and the poor industrious peasants were coming forth to their daily labour (how did my soul sicken at the sight!) whose ruddy, cheerful countenances bespoke happiness and content; whilst I, possessed of wealth, titles, and what the world might judge perfect felicity, was a prey to every torment, that disappointed love, and a hopeless desire of revenge, could inspire!

We alighted at a miserable public-house, for this being an unfrequented road, no decent accommodation could be expected; we got, however, rest for ourselves, and food and shelter for our poor tired beasts. Peter went to bed, but I had no inclination for sleep, and after eating a couple of eggs, and drinking some small wine, I inquired of the mistress of the house the name of the dwelling I had seen, and the quality of its owner? — She said its name was "The Solitary Castle," because of its situation; that it belonged to a great Count, she did not know what he was called, and that for these three years past some great folks lived in it; but nobody in the village knew who they were, they were never seen, and only one man servant came now and then for things they wanted.

This unsatisfactory account, in which there appeared to be a mystery, only augmented my curiosity and desire of penetrating into the secret; impelled by an irresistible impulse, I resolved to stay a few days in that wretched place for the purpose of obtaining further information. Soon, too soon for my peace, was the mystery developed.

About the middle of the day I lay down for a few hours, during which time Peter had risen. When I returned to the room, he entered it after me, and shut the door: — — —"Sir (said he) as I was standing near the window, a man entered the house, whose face was very familiar to me; I was on the point of going out when I heard him bargaining with the woman for ducks; they agreed about the price, and he said he would fetch them to-morrow. He left the house, and again passed before the window, when seeing him again I instantly recollected who he was; then I asked the landlady where he lived?" She answered, "He was servant to the gentry that live in the Solitary Castle."

"Ah! (cried I, interrupting Peter) and who is this man?"

"One of your vassals, Sir, who courted our housekeeper Agnes; his father was a substantial man, and we all thought it would be a match; but you know, Sir, after you returned from Count Zimchaw's, Agnes left you to go home to her mother, and I heard the young man went soon after to Vienna to live with an uncle. What has happened since I don't know; but I'll take my oath, this man I have seen is Mr. Arnulph, though they say he is a servant."

"I hope you are right, Peter, then to-morrow I shall have my curiosity gratified."

The to-morrow came, and I was constantly on the watch for the arrival of Arnulph. At length we saw him, and Peter darting out upon him:—"Your servant, Mr. Arnulph, who should have thought of seeing you?" The fellow started, looked wild and motionless:—"Bless me, Peter (said he, falteringly) how, how came you here?"

"Why, I have been travelling round the country, and came here only a day or two ago; but pray do you live in this neighbourhood?"—The fellow, without making a reply, turned to the woman: "I must leave the ducks with you two or three days longer." I had been observing his motions, surprise, confusion, and fear, were marked in his features, and I saw he was retreating to the door as he spoke, a sudden emotion I could not account for, impelled me to spring forward, and seize him by the arm. The moment he saw me he shrieked, and fell on his knees speechless. Peter raised him: "Follow me instantly" (exclaimed I, in an agony of suspense, doubt, and hardly knowing what I had to fear or expect:) I led the way to my room. Terror had so evidently overcome his courage that he quietly obeyed. When the door was fastened, I demanded where he lived, and with whom?

After much irresolution, and many subterfuges, he said, he was married to Agnes; that she lived housekeeper, and himself steward, to a Gentleman a few miles off; there was nothing improbable, or likely to interest me in this account, and I was growing very calm, and about to ask some particulars relative to his master; when taking notice of his extreme agitation, the wildness of his looks, and the terror with which he surveyed me and Peter, it naturally engaged me to believe there was some secret which he was fearful of being discovered, and which he was desirous of concealing from me. Possessed with this idea I laid hold of his arm, and in a commanding tone of voice: "Hear me, Mr. Arnulph, I am not to be imposed upon, I am no stranger to the Solitary Castle; hide nothing from me therefore as you value your life."

"Ah! Good God! (cried he) and is all discovered?" Then falling again at my feet, "Forgive me, my Lord, I had no hand in the business, I knew nothing of the matter till Agnes sent for me after she had left your service; I had never seen the Gentleman or your Lady till I came to this Castle in the wood."

Struck with astonishment, unable to articulate a single word, I stood gazing upon him with such an air of wildness, as added to the poor fellow's terror. Embracing my knees, he again supplicated mercy and forgiveness. Recovering at length my disordered senses, I bid him rise, assured him I could not blame him; but to deserve the pardon he solicited, he must acquaint me with every particular that had happened, and how long he had lived with Count M***, for I doubted not but that he was the companion of my faithless wife. His information was without reserve: "He knew not the name of the Gentleman but as a Count; he received a letter from Agnes about three years and half ago, saying, that if his love for her continued, and he had no objection to quit his residence and be united to her, she could insure him the place of a steward where she was housekeeper, and in case he liked the proposal he must be at this village on such a particular day, where she would meet him. His father being dead (he said) all places were alike to him, and having a great love for Agnes he joyfully complied, and was here at the appointed time. She told him her residence was retired and lonely, but that she had the best master and mistress in the world, who, on account of some cruel relations, were obliged to live in obscurity and unknown. If he could resolve to live retired she would marry him, and they might live happy with a good and generous pair."

To this proposal he consented with joy, remained two days in the village, on the third they were married at the village church six miles off, and, without returning here, he accompanied her across the skirts of the Forest to the wood, where they sent back their horses, and he followed her into the Castle. He said, he did not half like such a dismal remote place, but it was too late to retreat, especially as he loved Agnes. When introduced, he was thunderstruck to see the Lady, whom he had frequently seen at my Castle, and who he had been told I was married to, but who had afterwards gone into a Convent (for such was the report I circulated, and indeed believed); the Gentleman he had never seen before. Agnes told him they had been privately married some years ago, before Count Zimchaw came to my Castle, but dared not to own it, therefore when she was obliged to marry me she had fled to avoid the consequences; that apprehensive of my revenge they lived retired from the world, and that he must take an oath never to let any one know who or where she was. This he readily promised, and from that day they have all lived very happy, and the Lady lay-in of a little girl about two years and half ago.

This was the substance of Arnulph's information, which inspired me with the most eager desire of revenge; my soul was in tumults: I inquired what domestics were with them? He said, only a poor ignorant peasant lad, whom they had hired some miles off, and from the parish, who had no parents living, and who never went out of the Castle. I observed, from Arnulph's manner of telling his story, and words that dropped from him, that he was tired of a life so solitary, and that it would not be difficult to bribe him to my purpose. Giving him some pieces of gold, I assured him I would make his fortune if he would follow my orders, otherwise I would certainly put him to death: The alternative admitted of no consideration, for cowardice was his predominant feeling, and to that I was indebted for the relation he had made; I therefore soon arranged my plan, and kept him with me until towards night, when we set off together for the wood, walking my horses as far as it was passable, and then alighting fastened them as before. — On leaving the poor alehouse I told the people I had found the gentry at the Castle were my relations, and that I was going to visit them; ignorant and inattentive they heard and were silent. — Peter and myself were armed with pistols, and I had my sword. — Neither him nor Arnulph were acquainted with my purpose, and I privately resolved they should never witness against me. I declared to them I would not injure the lives of the Count or my wife; that my sole intention was to bind them, oblige the former to renounce all right to the Lady, and carry her with me into Bavaria.

The simple fellows either did, or affected to believe all I asserted; every circumstance was favourable to my design: The Count had been indisposed, and was still weak and incapable of any exertions; the child had been ill in the measles, and Agnes confined herself with her, the mother divided between the two had suffered an anxiety very detrimental to her health and spirits. When we arrived at the gate, I turned to Arnulph with a sternness that terrified him: "Now mark me well, if you, by word or look, give the least alarm, that moment you are a dead man; you know your master cannot help you, therefore beware how you offend me." He assured me of his obedience, and rang the bell, the boy appeared, we stood on one side, hearing Arnulph's voice, he unbarred the gate, and we rushed in. I instantly seized him, and pulling him into a kind of lodge, I gagged and bound him. From thence, by Arnulph's direction, I proceeded to the Count's apartment, we listened at the door; and I heard Eugenia's voice, as if speaking to her child. Fury, almost to madness, seized me, and I burst in upon them with a pistol in each hand. He started from his bed, she shrieked, and looking at me, sunk on the floor.

The Count attempted to throw himself out of bed, he uttered some words I do not now recollect, and called upon his servant. I advanced furiously towards him: You call in vain for help, I am master of your destiny. I ordered Peter to throw himself upon him, and hold him down. In vain he struggled, for the efforts being too much for his strength, he was the more easily overpowered. With the pistol to his breast, whilst Peter secured his arms, I obliged Arnulph to cut the cords from the bed, and in spite of every resistance securely confined the Count, who now condescended to implore mercy for Eugenia; his first execrations were changed into supplications, and I enjoyed them.

Arnulph had been endeavouring to restore to life the deceitful Eugenia; her child was crying over her, and by its lamentations brought in Agnes. On seeing us, her first intention seemed to be flight, for she screamed and run to the door; but looking at her mistress she flew back to assist her, as she appeared returning to life; she besought me to spare her Lady.

"You have no cause for apprehension," I replied, exquisitely gratified at seeing them all in my power: "I swear to you that I will not destroy your Lady, or your Lord, I do not mean to murder them."

"What then is your intention?" asked the Count. "Why break in upon us like a midnight robber?"

"I have no leisure to answer questions," said I, interrupting him, 'therefore you may as well be silent; for you, ungrateful, perjured creature," added I, addressing Eugenia, who by this time was restored to a sense of her situation, and hid her face in the arms of Agnes, both violently agitated, "you, who at the altar gave me your hand and faith, and now live as an adulteress with the man you swore never to be joined with without your father's consent; know you are still my wife, and I will prove my right by my power of punishing you."

She uttered not a word, terror had deprived her of speech. I ordered the two men to carry her into the next apartment. She made no resistance: I drove Agnes and the child after her; there I had recourse to the same means, cut the cords from the bed, and bound both mistress and maid, telling Arnulph aside I would release his wife the following morning: I saw by his countenance that he repented of his confidence, and was much moved by the situation of the women, and the cries of the child, which I silenced by threats that drove her to the feet of her mother. I was convinced it would be necessary to get rid of him speedily; having therefore secured my prisoners, and locked them in separate rooms, I bid Arnulph conduct me over the Castle. I followed him through the apartments, and found one wing of it had been neglected, and was more out of repair than the rest, looking only towards a thick wood from the tower.

I examined carefully, and at the end of a gallery went down a stair-case, which had a vaulted passage. Opening one of the apartments, which received a glimmering light from the top of a broken window shutter, I bid the man see if he could pull it down.—He tremblingly obeyed me, and as he was making the trial I stabbed him in the back: He fell; I repeated the stroke in his heart; he ceased to live, and I hastened from the place. The ferocity that had taken possession of my soul precluded every sense of fear, and drove every humane feeling from my heart for ever: I could now revenge my injuries, and I felt a gloomy triumph that inspired more pleasing sensations than I had for four years enjoyed.

Leaving the wretched victim, I explored the passage until I came into two horrible dungeons, and by the staples in the walls, and chains hanging from them, was convinced those dungeons had been formerly used as prisons by the owners of the Castle. This place answered my purpose exactly. I returned to the Count's apartment, told Peter Arnulph was employed at the other part of the house, and bid him assist me in carrying the Count to a place I had provided for him. He obeyed, incapable of resistance he submitted in silence.

When we descended into the dungeon I observed Peter trembled, and threw a melancholy glance on the prisoner; he was obliged, however, to help me in fastening the chain in a secure manner round the Count's legs and arms: I then unbound him.

"Use me as you please (said he) but spare the unfortunate Eugenia, and an innocent child."—His voice faltered.

"I mean not to divide you (I replied.)—You shall have your family party here to share your felicity." Ordering Peter to accompany me, I went back to the women, and obliged him to drag Agnes to the same vault. Eugenia made not the least resistance, when told she was to have her child and the Count with her.

"Conduct me where you will (said she) with the dear objects of my heart, and I shall not complain:" But when she entered the dismal abode, and saw him chained, she sent forth a piercing shriek, and then descended to implore mercy and supplicate forgiveness. I felt a sensation of pity at the moment, but I had gone too far to recede. Agnes and the child uttered loud and dismal cries; Peter's tears ran down his cheeks, but I shut my ears and my eyes against being moved by their distress. We carried Eugenia into the inner dungeon, and chained her in a similar manner with the Count. Having thus secured them, I demanded of the faithless woman by what means she had escaped from me, who assisted her, and where she had been concealed?

"Those are particulars you shall never know (said she;) I have nothing now to fear, for death would be a relief; your savage nature may be gratified by my miseries, but never shall you learn from me the names of those who were my friends and deliverers."

"It is well (cried I, enraged at her perverseness) here is one however," seizing Agnes, "who has been an accomplice, and whom I will oblige to speak: Say, wretch, where didst thou hide that infamous perjured woman? Who were thy assistants? Instantly confess the whole, or certain death attends thee."

"I had no assistants (answered she, firmly) nor do I fear to die; be assured, my Lord, that whilst I am confined in this horrid place, whilst those unfortunate — — —." I interrupted her, with my poignard at her breast, and at her peril bid her conceal any thing from me.

"I will follow the example of my beloved mistress (said she;) from me you will learn nothing."

"Die then, audacious wretch," I exclaimed, and plunged the poignard into her breast!

"Hold! O hold! (cried Eugenia) and I will tell you all:" But seeing the woman fall expiring on the ground: — "Inhuman monster! (added she) to murder the innocent and helpless, well dost thou justify the aversion my soul conceived against thee, stern, cruel barbarian! O, my father! my dear father! thy peace and happiness sacrificed to gratitude, and thy daughter a miserable victim to an unjust prejudice! Fatal, fatal prepossessions! 'Tis you, unjust and cruel woman, 'tis you (cried I) who are the cause of all those murders, of that ferocity and cruelty thou upbraidest; 'tis love, 'tis hatred, that teaches me revenge; one passion shall at least be gratified."

I turned from her, heedless of her lamentations, or the cries of her child. On entering the other dungeon I saw the Count trembling, and speechless from the violence of his emotions, I left him with the triumphant satisfaction that he was now as wretched as myself. On my return to the habitable part of the house, I examined the looks of Peter, pale and agitated, I saw he was but half a villain, and enjoyed not the glorious revenge of his master. He asked for Arnulph, in a tone of voice that conveyed his suspicion that he also was no more.—Plunged so far into guilt, murder was familiar to my thoughts, and to secure myself, it was necessary I should permit no witnesses to exist against me.

Could I have confided in his secrecy, he would have been most useful to me, but I dared not risk the hazard; therefore, after a moment's recollection, I bid him follow me, and he would see what Arnulph was employed about. With a doubtful look and a trembling step, he descended with me to the offices below, and passing the kitchens at the end of a long colonnade, I opened a door which led into a room that appeared to have been a laundry, and being detached some way from the other offices (the thing I sought for) was designed to rid me of all apprehensions from Peter.—"Arnulph is not here," said he, in a tremulous voice. Seeing that I stopped:—"No, but you are," and in a moment I buried the poignard in his bosom.—He fell dead without uttering a word, only one dismal groan, which made me start.—Looking round, and then on the bleeding object before me, whose services had ever been faithful, and who I had sacrificed to fear only, a transitory remorse smote me to the heart: I flew hastily from the dreadful scene without recovering my weapon. I regained the chamber where I found the Count, and throwing myself upon the bed which lay on the floor, gave way to the most terrible reflections I had ever experienced; the horrors in which I spent that night will ever live in my remembrance.

I had committed three murders: The fury that had possessed me on my first entrance, now subsided into gloomy retrospections, and unsettled designs. If I destroyed the Count and Eugenia I had nothing to fear; but my revenge in that case would be incomplete; I wished to see them miserable, to endure a living death. Some times different ideas struck me, which my still violent passion suggested as a greater triumph over Eugenia, to assert my claim as a husband, and force her to submit to me even in preference of the object she had preferred to me. In short, the morning dawned before I had resolved on any plan, or without having rested a single hour.

When the day-light advanced I descended to the kitchens, there I found bread, butter and cheese, with a cold fowl; a wine cellar well stored, and a yard full of poultry; plenty of wood, and an outhouse full of old hay and stray, that was musty from age. I opened the windows to give it air; and going from thence to the gardens, saw one part was well cultivated with vegetables, and another with flowers and fruits.—"It will not be difficult to live here," I exclaimed, and from that moment determined on my plan, and from which I have never varied in the treatment of my prisoners: Every day to carry to them a certain portion of bread and water; once a week a half pint of wine, and once a month clean straw to rest upon. I resolved to preserve their lives that I might prolong their sufferings, and the gratification of my revenge was a much superior pleasure to any that I could promise myself from society, or an acquaintance with a world I had long since been disgusted with; for altho' the bequests of Count Zimchaw had done away my first objections, by enabling me to appear with more consequence, and more suitable to my rank, yet habit had so accustomed me to retirement, that I felt no inclination to mix with mankind, and to retaliate my wrongs upon an ungrateful woman, and a successful rival, afforded me the most pleasing contemplation, and a supreme delight.

CHAPTER III

I passed the morning in examining every part of the Castle, which was a good deal out of repair, except in the wing where they had taken up their residence. About noon I visited my prisoners, and carried to them the portion I had allotted for them. — They appeared to be differently affected, the Count was very weak, his pride, his spirits seemed subdued by the consideration of the distress his child and Eugenia had suffered. He condescended to supplicate for them; the child screamed on my approach, and flew to her mother, who with a look, and in a tone of mingled grief and haughtiness, thus addressed me:

"Whatever evils you have resolved to overwhelm me with, I can bear. You think I have deserved to suffer; but who, Sir, made you a judge in your own cause? I never deceived you, I told you I had no heart to give; you persisted, ungenerously laid a tax on the gratitude my dear father felt, and insisted that the hand of his daughter should be your reward for services, which common humanity would have dictated to the poorest peasant, had his power been equal to your's. Your claims, added to an unhappy, and I will say unjust, prejudice my father had conceived against the man I loved, proved destruction to my peace and happiness; commands which I had never disputed, and the impending horrors of a parent's curse drew from me an equivocal promise that I would give you my hand. Heaven has punished me for a duplicity I could not, according to my own feelings, avoid or evade. At the altar, neither my heart nor lips ratified the gift of my hand, for my vows were given to another. The consequence you know.

"You now, Sir, usurp an unjust power over us; but do not deceive yourself, neither peace nor pleasure can follow such unjustifiable, such cruel deeds; murder has many tongues, and your own conscience will avenge our wrongs."

Here she ceased; I had listened to her with pain and impatience; the music of her voice thrilled to my very soul, but her words drove every soft idea from my heart as instantly as they were conceived. — "There is bread and water (exclaimed I, my passions roused to a degree of frenzy) that, and a bed of straw is what you may expect from me." I returned to the offices, I brought two small tables and benches; I fixed a faint and glimmering lamp against the wall, which served only to throw a gloomy light, and additional horror, on the dismal dungeons. A small opening was between them, and the length of their chains permitted their approach near to each other; I fetched straw and a blanket for each; they observed all these preparations in sullen silence, I was as little disposed to talk. When I had completed the business, and was about to leave them, "You now see that I am in earnest (said I;) once a day I shall visit you, and gratify my feelings by a view of your miseries."

"O, my child! my dear child!" exclaimed Eugenia, passionately.—I made no reply, but a look of scornful exultation, and returned to the apartments I had fixed on for my residence.

I was now alone, condemned to solitude without a friend, or even an attendant: I regretted the loss of Peter; he had served me some years with fidelity, why then did I distrust him? Why suffer my cowardly apprehensions to deprive me of a companion so necessary? These were my reflections as I looked round on the gloomy woods which appeared from every window, and heard the hollow winds whistling through the trees.—Surely, thought I again, this Castle was built for deeds of darkness; murder has been familiar within these walls, and the Count's ancestors, perhaps, were not less criminal than myself.

A violent storm of hail and thunder confined me to the apartment for the remainder of the day. I employed myself in arranging matters for my own accommodation, when towards the evening, as I was musing over the recent events, it darted into my mind that the poor boy whom I had confined in the lodge, if not dead, might be useful to me; the situation of this boy had never occurred to me till that moment: I hastened to the place, and found him in a most pitiable state, almost without life. I released and assisted him into the house; I told him, the Count and his family had been obliged to fly to avoid being imprisoned by the Emperor, whose orders had been issued for that purpose; that being related to the Count's Lady, I remained in the Castle, at their request, to keep possession for them, and would be kind to him if he behaved well.

Young, extremely ignorant, and overjoyed to escape from the apprehensions of death, he implicitly believed every thing I asserted, and when, by a little bread and wine being cautiously administered, I had brought him to a small return of strength and courage, he bestowed a thousand blessings on me for preserving his life; so strangely had the sudden fright and terror overcome his senses when he was seized upon, that he described five or six great tall men armed breaking into the Castle, and swearing to murder every one in it. He rejoiced to hear that his master and Lady escaped from them, and never once expressed any surprise at my being there, or asked by what means I came to know of his confinement. From that day he served me faithfully; I was obliged to trust him once into the village for necessaries, but after that time I engaged a farmer to come himself once or twice a week, and as I paid him handsomely, he never expressed any curiosity, or a wish to penetrate into my motives for this recluse way of life, and having slightly hinted the same tale I had fabricated to the boy, he as readily believed it.

Three months passed away without the least alteration in the plan I had laid down and regularly pursued, only that I visited my prisoners at night, after the boy was retired to rest, and had nailed up the doors of those rooms where the wretches lay whom I had sacrificed to my own safety. I am apt to believe the Count and Eugenia sometimes flattered themselves that time would subdue my resentment, or that I should grow tired of living in that solitary mansion; but if such ideas occurred to them, they were mistaken; solitude nursed the ferocity of my disposition, and the patience and resignation they evinced in their horrid situation only increased my desire of continuing their punishment till despair and sorrow should more completely gratify my revenge. 'Tis true, I sometimes looked back with regret on the few weeks I had spent with the Count and his daughter at my own mansion, far the happiest days of my life, and for which I have dearly paid by subsequent miseries!

I some times felt a degree of envy rise in my bosom when I read of the pleasures enjoyed by a social converse with our fellow creatures; and there were moments when I was tormented with the idea, that even my prisoners experienced some satisfaction in being able to communicate their feelings to each other. It is certain that had there been a possibility of placing them separately I should have done it, but I was incapable of making a new arrangement myself, and dared not confide in the boy. A circumstance, however, soon took place, which rendered them as completely wretched as my vindictive heart could desire.

On one of my nocturnal visits, I found the Count overwhelmed with an unusual gloom, and the mother supporting her child on her bed of straw, almost drowned in tears. — When I approached her, "See, barbarian! (cried she) the work of thy cruel hands; — behold this dear innocent victim devoured by a fever occasioned by the damps of the dungeon, and want of proper food. O, if thy heart is not more callous than the fiercest beasts of prey, compassionate my child, save, oh! save its life, or be merciful and destroy us all at once!"

My heart fluttered at this address, and a something like pity rose for a moment to my soul; but instantly recollecting that she had pledged her vows to me at the altar with an intention to deceive, that the child was the offspring of a detested rival, and that now was my turn to triumph; those ideas in a moment chased the weakness from my heart, and gave place to very different sensations. Before I could reply, the Count addressed me, in a tremulous voice:

"I never thought to supplicate pity, or sue for any favours, but nature, all-powerful, subdues both pride and hatred. My child! Baron, save my child, spare its wretched mother this bitter climax of sorrow." He was interrupted, the child called for drink, the small portion I had brought was quickly gone. Again Eugenia exerted her eloquence, her tears. I heard her unmoved, and turning from them, "Now then, wretches, you can feel, now you know what it is to mourn as I have done; may the loss of your dearest hopes revenge my injuries."

I returned to my apartment exquisitely gratified. The following night I repeated my visit; there, on her bed of straw, lay the once captivating Eugenia, pale, dishevelled, her voice choked with sighs and tears, her late beautiful child consuming by a fever, and gasping for life, the Count stretched on the bare ground in silent agony, incapable of assisting those objects so dear to him! O, what a luxury of revenge!

When I drew near, before the mother could speak, the child extended its feeble hand, "Water, water, mamma!" Eugenia started, hastily reached to take the jug; her weak and tremulous hand, too eager to grasp the prize, dropped it between us! She shrieked, O misery! O, Baron! Water, for the love of Heaven some water!"

"You have had your allowance, you must suffer for your own heedlessness."

With an air of distraction she crawled to my feet: "If you wish that Heaven should pity you in your last moments, now, now show mercy to the wretch before you; save my child, procure me instant relief, see life quivering on its parched lips! Oh! God, for me it suffers! Baron, Baron, save the innocent!"

She sunk back on the damp ground; the Count groaned with anguish, and dashed his chains with rage. The child again feebly called for drink; she sprung up, "O, inhuman, merciless monster, worse than a savage beast! Thou wearest a human form, cannot our misery content thee? This agonizing sight!"

She turned her eyes on the child, it was that moment seized with convulsions; its struggles, and the wild screams of the mother, made me shudder. I quickly hastened from the scene, which however gratifying to my wished-for vengeance, gave a temporary shock to my soul, that I was obliged to shake off by recalling to my memory the wrongs I had endured from a faithless, ungrateful woman.

That night and the following day I passed in steeling my heart against all supplications, and acquiring fortitude to bear the wild reproaches of a frantic mother, I doubted not but that the child was dead, and I anticipated the pleasure I should feel in seeing her wretchedness complete.

At the accustomed hour I entered the dungeon. The Count fixed his stern and haggard eye upon me with a look that penetrated me with horror: He spoke not a word. I advanced, and beheld Eugenia seated by her child, which lay, as I expected, dead. She spoke not, nor raised her head at my approach. "There is your allowance, (said I) and I will remove this object from your view." She seized the body, and turning up her face with a significance of woe inexpressible, a wildness in her eye, though sunk deep in her head by sorrow.

"Prepare the bed (said she) and I will follow; but my arms only shall convey my child, it sleeps sweetly now. Yes, yes, my love, your grand sire now relents; your birth-day shall be kept with splendour. Pray let us have a soft pillow, let us have music, the soft notes shall waft us to Heaven;—come, give me some food, I can eat now under this glorious canopy."—I saw her reason was disturbed, that grief had distracted her. She took the bread, and eat with eagerness; it was the day on which I gave them an allowance of wine; she drank it freely, talking wildly all the time, yet not with any violence.

My heart smote me, I went back to the Count: "Barbarian! (exclaimed he) now triumph, my child! the poor lost Eugenia!" His voice faltered, large drops fell upon his face. He dried them up, then looking steadily on me: "Whilst that dear unfortunate angel lives, I must exist; I receive this wretched sustenance for her sake; in its own good time Heaven will release us from thee, cruel, merciless wretch!"—But why should I repeat the ravings of a man in his situation? It is sufficient to say, that his insults, his impotent threats, roused me from that lethargy of soul, into which the incoherent language of Eugenia had plunged me, and turned my momentary remorse into fury: In the bitterness of passion I swore, that if Eugenia died, I would inflict unheard of tortures on him; and should he escape my power, then his mistress should feel the severest vengeance that I could devise. Worked up to madness by the agitations of my mind, I scarce remember what passed between us, nor did I ever pass a night so replete with horror as the succeeding one.

The following night I found Eugenia still the same, cheerful and melancholy by turns, but all recollection of her situation entirely lost. Sometimes she talked of her father, her child, her dear Count, as if all were present with her; then looking on me she would scream, and call for help, "a ruffian was going to murder her!" But, as during those paroxysms she walked swiftly backward and forward to the extent of her chain, I seized a moment, when her back was turned to drag the dead object of her sorrows from the dungeon to an outer hole, where I had left the corpse of Agnes. She soon missed her child, and uttered the most piercing cries, cries which froze me with terror, and which I saw no way to silence but by rough measures: I seized her by the arm, and drawing a dagger, which I always carried by my side:

"Woman! (I exclaimed, in a voice and with an action equally menacing) woman, cease these screams, be composed and silent, or this weapon shall be buried in your bosom." She shrunk and trembled; she, who had heretofore braved death, and defied my power, now shuddered with affright, and threw her eyes wildly round, as if imploring succour. Having succeeded in terrifying her, I placed her on the bench, again threatening her with death if she repeated her cries. —She sat still as death, her eyes fixed, her limbs trembling. I turned from her to quit the dungeon: "Stop, miscreant (said the Count) stay and end our miseries, give us the death you threaten, destroy both, and I will thank you!"

"Death! (I replied) No, that would rob me of my vengeance; you shall live to curse the hour you ever saw my wife; now revel in her company, now enjoy a teté à teté at my expense, and boast your triumph over Baron S———."

Without waiting a reply I left him. It is now eight years since this event took place. Eugenia continues in the same hopeless state, yet blessed in some degree that she is very seldom sensible of her miserable situation, except when I appear before her, she then utters the wildest lamentations; but on threatening her with a whip or stick she shrinks down and is silent. The Count evidently struggles to preserve his life for her sake, for hope I think must long since have forsaken him; he perseveres in a sullen silence, and my treatment of them has been uniformly the same. Time has not extinguished my hatred, nor glutted my vengeance; my death must forerun theirs; then, and not till then, will their sufferings end. How strong is the passion of love, but how much stronger the desire of Revenge!!

MEMORANDUM,

"I have lost my boy in a consumption: I have, through the kindness of the farmer, procured an elderly man, whose poverty renders solitude preferable to want. I envy his happiness, for he has peace of mind!!"

A stranger, calling himself Ferdinand, has discovered this place; his society may be useful and comfortable.—No! he is a poor humane, pusillanimous wretch; he is fit for the world, he shall go.

THE END OF THE MEMOIR.

CHAPTER IV

Ferdinand perused the manuscript with eagerness, and an increasing curiosity that would not admit of an interruption until he had gone through the whole.—When the memoir was concluded, he sat for some time motionless, overcome with astonishment, and scarcely believing there could have existed a man who had for years cherished in his bosom such a diabolical passion for revenge, and such a persevering cruelty. He shuddered with horror when he reflected on the situation of those unhappy victims, and the fate they must have experienced, had not Providence conducted him to the Castle previous to the old Baron's death.—His own misfortunes appeared light in the balance, when weighed against the uncommon miseries the Count and his Eugenia had sustained; and the heart-felt delight at being the instrument to deliver them, at that moment seemed to overpay all the sorrows which had conducted him to that wretched habitation.

Francis, whose youth appeared to be renovated by the enjoyment of society, exerted himself to make all the accommodations in his power to afford ease and pleasure to Ferdinand and his guests, not having the least idea that they were the owners of the Castle; fortunately it was the day on which the farmer regularly came for orders, and to his great surprise he had a demand for such luxuries as had long been unasked for there. Francis mentioned the death of his old master, and that his heir was now arrived, and desired to see him.

It was not without some reluctance that the man ventured inside the gates, for a thousand ridiculous stories had been promulgated in the village sufficiently strange to terrify a weak and ignorant mind; but Francis, who knew the stimulative to a selfish disposition, held out such hopes of advantages to himself in being serviceable to his young master, that self-interest predominated over fear, and the man was at length persuaded to appear before Ferdinand. He was then informed that the old Gentleman being dead, it was necessary to have proper measures taken for his funeral, and the farmer was requested to send such persons as would be useful on the occasion. This he promised to do, and also to bring a young woman to attend the sick Lady.

After the farmer's departure, Ferdinand more closely examined the papers in the cabinet where he had found the manuscript, to see if the deceased had held any correspondence, or to find by what means he had acquired money for his support during the twelve years he had resided in that solitary mansion; but his search was attended with no gratification to his curiosity, farther than the discovery of near three hundred crowns in a private drawer, and the deeds and papers belonging to the estate Count Zimchaw had bequeathed to him, which appeared very extraordinary, and unlikely to be found there: The more he reflected on the memoir, and conduct of the Baron, the greater was his astonishment that any mind could indulge the horrid passion of revenge to such a degree, as to render him indifferent to every pleasure and convenience in life, to undergo the most painful of all situations, an outcast from society, dead to the world, to family, fortune, and friends, solely to inflict punishments upon others, which from habit must, he thought, have long since ceased to afford the smallest degree of gratification to his vindictive and cruel disposition. His sudden death, under such a frame of mind, made Ferdinand shudder, and was, he thought, a severe retribution for his uncommon cruelties.

Anxious to hear the story of the Count and Eugenia, he flattered himself sleep would restore them to a comparative degree of strength, and enable them to relate their "eventful history."

Frequently, during the course of the evening, Ferdinand went to the doors of their apartments to listen if they were awake, and at length he heard the Count moving, upon which he entered the room. The Count extending his hand, pressed his deliverer's to his lips: "The voluptuary in his highest enjoyments," said he, "never experienced the luxury I have felt this day. O, Sir! to conceive the misery I have endured is impossible, nor can language describe it. To the goodness of Heaven (who strengthened me to bear, what must appear almost incredible for a human creature to suffer) I owe the preservation of my senses, and the enjoyment, the exquisite delight of this blessed hour. To you — — — ."

"Not a word to me, my dear Sir," cried Ferdinand, interrupting him; "I have simply performed a duty the poorest and most ignorant of mankind would have done as well had they been in my place. I rejoice to see you thus refreshed, and I hope the Lady will feel equal benefit from a few hours sleep."

"The poor Eugenia!" exclaimed the Count, with a deep sigh, "great and unparalleled have been her woes; for years, Sir, she lost her reason, and all sense of her miseries, and to that state I doubtless owe her life, which must otherwise have sunk under the oppressive recollection of past scenes, and continued miseries. 'Tis not many months since that her dreadful malady took a sudden turn, and that was occasioned by an accident which I feared would have been her death.

Walking one day pretty quick, the sudden check of the chain threw her down with such force, that she struck her mouth and nose violently, and bled to an alarming degree. Unable to afford her any assistance, judge what were my feelings to behold her in that situation! She rolled towards the straw, and at length fainted; that temporary death, which I thought a conclusive stroke, by stagnating the powers of life, I believe caused the bleeding to stop, and in a short time, to my infinite surprise, for I could scarcely be said to feel joy, she showed signs of returning life, and what was still more unexpected, the first words she faintly uttered convinced me that her senses and reason were also wonderfully restored. She continued very weak, and now and then rambled a little for several days, and even to the day of our deliverance she never saw our tormentor enter the dungeon without a temporary deprivation of her reason, by shrieking most violently as he approached to lay down our food; nor do I believe the inhuman wretch ever had an idea of her being at all recovered from the melancholy situation she had fallen into through his barbarity.

I hope her present refreshing rest will be of equal service to tranquillize her mind, and restore her to some degree of strength."

"I hope the same," replied Ferdinand, "and have already spoken to a person to procure an attendant for her; mean time you must be content with our services."

The Count made the warmest acknowledgments, and entreated the assistance of Francis to dress him: "My arms," said he, "have so long been confined, that the muscles are stiffened, and will be some time, I fear, before they are relaxed so as to enable me to help myself." — Ferdinand withdrew to send Francis, who was but an awkward valet de chambre; however, he helped on his clothes, and assisted him to the parlour, which they were obliged to darken, the Count's eyes not being able to support the glare of light after having been so many years in a visible darkness.

The Gentlemen partaking of some refreshment, and having stationed Francis at the door of the Lady's apartment, the Count addressing Ferdinand, "Doubtless, Sir," said he, "your curiosity must be sufficiently excited to know our extraordinary story, and if you'll pardon the frequent pauses which weakness may oblige me to make, I will endeavour to gratify you."

Ferdinand then mentioned the manuscript, which, he said, "had already acquainted him with every thing subsequent to Count Zimchaw's arrival at the house of the late Baron, except the Lady Eugenia's escape from him, and her story until the Baron discovered them in the Castle."

"What a mind of determined cruelty must that man have possessed," exclaimed the Count, "who could sit calmly down and commit his diabolical deeds to paper! I hope, for the sake of human nature, there exists not such another monster; but I have always observed, that it is dangerous to let a single passion engross the mind, it generally tends to the most violent excesses; the love of such a man as Baron S— — — must be furious, and meeting with a disappointment which equally wounded his pride, produced that implacable hatred which settled in a stern and cruel revenge, the gratification of which, like Aaron's rod, swallowed up every sentiment of humanity. Poor wretch! I can pity him, for his death, in such a frame of mind, disarms resentment."

CHAPTER V

Iwill briefly relate to you those events with which you are unacquainted. My father and the late Count Zimchaw were neighbours, and once good friends. Eugenia and myself, at an early period in life, felt a mutual attachment, which death only can dissolve. There was nothing to impede the progress of our affections; age, circumstances, and the approbation of our parents, gave a sanction to our love, and we arrived at an age, when it was determined upon, that in a very few months our marriage should take place. Alas! what revolutions may occur in a short space of time to overthrow the best formed plans for happiness! One evening the two Gentlemen entered into a conversation on the war, on the conduct of the Ministers in the Imperial Court, and such other topics as frequently produce disputation from different opinions. My father had retired from Court in disgust; he thought himself ill-treated, and his services neglected; he spoke therefore with some acrimony, and much warmth against the measures adopted for carrying on the war; Count Zimchaw, formerly a moderate man, having, by his interest not long before, procured a handsome establishment for his nephew, felt himself called upon to be the champion in defence of his friends: Their dispute was carried on for some time without personal resentment; but unhappily growing animated on both sides, they forgot the ground of their first argument, and turned every thing into intended insults on each other; they lost sight of friendship, and even good manners, and had not some company unexpectedly entered the room, it is more than probable the sword would have terminated the dispute. Every effort was used by their mutual friends to bring about a reconciliation, but they had gone too far on both sides to make any concessions; they parted with an avowed hatred to each other, and in the same hour Eugenia and myself were commanded to avoid all future intercourse with the respective families, and never to converse or see the object of our dearest affections more.

"Eugenia, who held the commands of a parent in the utmost veneration, promised implicit obedience, though her heart and spirits sunk under the effort, and she fell dangerously ill. Almost distracted with her situation and my own, I exhausted myself in fruitless endeavours to restore harmony between our fathers: I left nothing unsaid or undone to soften their resentments; but the remembrance of their long friendship only served to increase their animosity to each other, and the asperity with which both the one and the other accused his opponent, could neither be forgiven or forgotten. I wrote to my dear Eugenia; I conjured her 'not to give me up a sacrifice to her father's resentments, to consider that we were not amenable for their unjust quarrels, nor could compulsatory obedience be any virtue, where the commands were cruel and unjustifiable.' In short, I omitted no arguments I could adduce to over-rule the resolution she had taken to obey her father. Her answer was short but decisive: 'She never would marry, much less encourage a clandestine correspondence, contrary to the commands of her father; and as there existed no hope that his consent would coincide with her wishes, she conjured me, if her peace was dear to me, from that hour to cease all further desire of an intercourse between us, which could only be productive of misery to both; that her promise was already given, and her fixed resolution taken at the same time, that if not permitted to be my wife, I might assure myself she would never be the wife of another."

This answer was conclusive, for I knew her too well to hope for any change in a plan she had once decided upon: As soon as I heard therefore she was in a convalescent state, I resolved to quit my father's mansion, and by travelling give some diversity to that load of anguish seated at my heart. My father did not oppose my design, conscious of the misery his intemperate conduct had produced, I believe it grew painful to him to see me, and that a separation was little less desired by him than by myself.

My journies were by no means interesting, for I sought not pleasure, and received but little amusement: I preserved that respect due to a parent, of sometimes writing to my father, who concealed the increasing weakness of a broken constitution from me, until the faculty had given up all hopes of his life. This intelligence, quite unexpected, recalled all that dormant affection and respect I had once so warmly entertained. I hastened my return, but came too late; the night preceding my arrival my father expired. I was deeply affected, and still more so when the steward, and an intimate friend of our family, informed me, that a day or two previous to my return, he accused himself as the destroyer of my happiness, and entreated his friend to exert his best endeavours to procure a reconciliation between Count Zimchaw and myself; acquainting the former, that he lamented the part he had acted, and besought him to spare himself a similar regret in his last stage of life, by consenting to the union so long projected by both families, and so hastily and unwarrantably broken off by passion and prejudice."

"But, alas! in the same moment that I had this pleasing acknowledgment on the part of my father, I was told Count

Zimchaw had taken his daughter into Bavaria, and that a report was current in the country that she was married to Baron S— —. Distracted at this intelligence, I sent to the Count's mansion to know the exact truth, and was shocked by a confirmation of the report. My hopes of happiness were now annihilated: I sunk into a gloomy despondency for a long time, from which no endeavours of my friends could rouse me.—I was dragged about a lifeless body without a soul, from one friend to another, till at length, tired with exerting unsuccessful kindness, they left me to myself.

"About this time Count Zimchaw returned into Suabia, and his daughter's marriage was beyond a doubt. No longer desirous of his returning friendship, I avoided all intercourse with himself or his friends.—He was soon afterwards taken ill, and I was informed his son-in-law was sent for, to whom he had secured all his personal fortune. This intelligence gave me indescribable sensations, I doubted not but that Eugenia would accompany her husband, and I had not resolution enough to leave the country, though sure of suffering extreme torture by seeing her in the arms of another. The Baron, however, arrived too late to see the Count, and came without Eugenia, whose particular situation was mentioned as an apology for her absence."

"Will you pardon me, Sir, for interrupting you?" said Ferdinand; "but in the Baron's memoirs your meeting is mentioned, and every circumstance until his return to Bavaria."

"I thank you," replied the Count.—"Well, then, the Baron had left Suabia, I believe, a fortnight, when one day I received a note in an unknown hand, 'requesting me to be at the end of my Park, next the village, about twilight, when I should meet an old friend.' I hesitated for some time whether I ought to comply with this singular request; but at length determined to go, and grew quite impatient for the hour.

"At the appointed time I hastened to the spot, and descried through the gloom two young men, in an ordinary garb, approaching towards me: Not being entirely devoid of suspicions, I had a pair of pocket pistols, one of which I held in my hand, and as they drew near, and their features were not distinguishable, I cried out, stop, and announce yourselves, whoever you are."

"Ah!" exclaimed a sweet but tremulous voice, "does not your heart inform you it is Eugenia?" I heard no more, but flew, and caught the trembling fugitive to my breast. Neither could speak, for words were inadequate to our feelings. O, the rapture of that moment never to be forgotten! "Lead the way to your house (said she) and every thing shall be explained." In an instant I recollected that I had embraced the wife of Baron S— — —: I withdrew my arms, but she retained one as her support, and with hasty steps, and mutual silence, we proceeded through the Park.

When we entered the saloon she sunk into a chair, and bursting into tears, "I see," exclaimed she, "that I am no longer the object of your love or esteem!"

"Not love you," I cried, dropping at her feet, "not love you, Eugenia!" I could say no more, for I was overpowered by a variety of emotions difficult to describe, and dared to entertain suspicions unfavourable to the purity of an angel. She saw the tumults the disorder of my soul: "Rise, Count," said she, assuming an air of dignity, "I forgot, that in your eyes I must appear as a runaway wife, as a degraded character; compose yourself, and listen to me without interruption.

She then entered into a detail of all the circumstances attending her meeting with the Baron to the conclusion of her marriage; with all which particulars I find you are acquainted, I shall therefore confine myself to a relation of the subsequent events. Soon after her arrival at the Baron's, she perceived that Agnes was warmly attached to her, and she did not conceal the strong aversion she had to an union with her master. The good woman attempted not to lessen the prejudice she had conceived against him, on the contrary she ingenuously confessed, that the severity of his manners, and harshness of his temper, were but little calculated to render a marriage life happy. Thus strengthened in her dislike, which grew more confirmed every day, she concerted with Agnes the plan of her elopement, which was first intended to have been previous to the ceremony; but her father having been in the act of denouncing his malediction against her, if she did not give her hand to Baron S— — —; she was so extremely shocked as to promise unreserved obedience, and in that moment determined to become a sacrifice to her duty.

She retired to her apartment overwhelmed with sorrow, and meeting Agnes, told her, "She now gave up all idea of quitting that house, which henceforth she considered as the tomb of her happiness." This faithful creature (whose untimely death we have never ceased to lament) heard with surprise a resolution, which gave her equal pain; in her zeal to serve Eugenia, she disclosed some particular circumstances relative to her master, displayed his odious character, and cruel disposition, in such strong colours, as again staggered the fortitude the former had endeavoured to acquire; and at length she was persuaded by Agnes to adhere to her former design, and, by a kind of sophistry, not perhaps altogether defensible, she was induced to keep the promise made to her father of giving her hand to the Baron, and afterwards to effect her escape. This plan you know was executed, and it only remains to mention the manner in which she was so effectually secreted from all discovery.

"The Castle in which the Baron resided was large, and some parts of it entirely out of repair. At the back of the building were some ruinous apartments on the ground floor, which served for no other purpose than as a temporary shelter for the poultry, and a depository for their grain. The farthest of those apartments had a door, which opened to a descent down a flight of steps to a long passage which led underneath to an old Chapel, long before shut up, and entirely disused. — Here it was resolved upon that Eugenia should reside, until the search naturally expected to be made for her should subside, that she might be enabled to get undiscovered to a convent; and to this place, in this passage, Agnes had already conveyed several necessaries. She had procured, from a long-neglected wardrobe of her master's, a complete suit of man's apparel, with several other precautions taken from time to time previous to that day they were now obliged to decide upon for the execution of their design.

"After the marriage ceremony, when Eugenia retired to her room, she lost no time in escaping to this passage. The window of her apartment was opened that it might be supposed she had escaped from thence into the wood adjoining the garden, and the door, which led through an anti-chamber to a gallery on the other side, was locked on the outside. Agnes accompanied her to the dark passage, where a lamp, a stool, and a piece of matting for her feet, were previously prepared. Eugenia has often mentioned the horror that took possession of her whole frame when she was left alone in this dismal place, she foresaw not how many tedious years she was to exist in one still more horrid! When the discovery of her flight took place, when the house and out-houses had undergone a strict search, and the Baron, with his servants, were sat off, Agnes stole to her with refreshments, and conducted her to the little room assigned for the priest's use, in the Chapel where she passed the night, and indeed both day and night when the Baron was not at home; but as he employed many persons to scour the roads, she was obliged to remain in this painful situation, particularly as he had set a watch on all the neighbouring convents. At length the

Baron set off on his journey to Suabia (Agnes concealed from
Eugenia the illness of her father) and when he had been gone
about three days, disguised in her masculine dress, her eye-
brows blacked, and, with a pretended lameness in her gait, she
repaired to the house of a peasant in the neighbouring village,
where she hired a miserable apartment, giving out that ill-
health had driven her to that situation for change of air; this
account, which her pale countenance and lameness confirmed,
evaded all curiosity among those ignorant people:—Agnes
never came to her, but they used to meet in the wood
frequently; the good creature being busy in finding out some
asylum, some convent, where she had not been described, and
where she might hope to rest concealed.

The sudden return of the Baron, with an account of the
Count's death, his succession to his fortune, with the
circumstance of his meeting me, which he related to Agnes
when he questioned her if any intelligence had been gained
relative to her mistress.—Those occurrences determined Agnes
to be ingenuous with Eugenia respecting her father, and
persuade her to accept of an asylum with me. Hitherto my
father's death, and my return, were unknown to Eugenia, and
therefore she had no idea of my being in Suabia, though
possibly if she had, whilst Count Zimchaw had lived, her vows
would have been a barrier to our meeting. The information of
Agnes caused her much sorrow, nor could she for a long time be
persuaded to adopt the plan of Agnes, and repair to my estate.
At length, however, when her grief for the death of her father
was a little subsided, she accorded with the wishes of the other.
Agnes pretended to be sent for by her parents, and applied for
her discharge from the Baron, which was granted. Among her
own clothes she conveyed Eugenia's, which had remained in the
dark passage till that time, and having procured another suit of
men's clothes, after she had left the Baron, she disguised herself,
and came as the brother of the lame man to fetch him home.

So thoroughly was Eugenia altered by her dress, and the
precautions she had taken, that there was little room for
apprehension that she would be discovered, and the Baron
having relaxed in his inquiries since his return from Suabia,
they contrived to have their clothes sent by a wagon to Stutgard,
only nine miles from my house, and then quitted the village
together on horseback, until they came to the next town, where
they took a chaise to the small Hamlet adjoining to my Park,
from whence they dispatched the note to me that I have already
mentioned. Thus, Sir, I have briefly repeated what Eugenia
related to me.

"You may judge of my transports in thus unexpectedly recovering the woman I adored, and to find she was not more than a nominal wife to the man I had detested. My raptures soon removed every doubt she had expressed of my affection, and brought her to confess, that the death of her father having released her from those vows, passion and prejudice had compelled her to make, she no longer scrupled to become my wife, as she could in no light think the ceremony binding which had passed between the Baron and herself. — All that now remained to be decided upon, was our future residence, for although I would not have hesitated a moment to have asserted and defended my rights in the face of the world, yet her timid mind shrunk from the idea of being the public theme, or of hazarding any revengeful machinations naturally dreaded from the Baron.

I proposed going to France or England to reside, unhappily she objected, unacquainted with the language, and dreading the eye of observation, knowing that the Baron talked of travelling, she was fearful some unlucky chance might throw him in our way, she therefore wished to reside for some time in a profound retirement. Although I was still of an opinion that we should be much safer in a foreign country, yet finding her repugnance to that plan was not easily to be overcome, and being naturally of a studious disposition myself, and fond of domestic comforts, certain that in the society of my loved Eugenia, I could feel no wish for the amusements and trifling conversations which engage the frivolous part of mankind, I consented without reluctance to her desire of retirement. In our solitude I determined to make her acquainted with the English language, as I perfectly understood it, and hoped, by effecting that, to obviate her objections in time to a residence in that country.

This estate had belonged to my mother's family, but being in a situation so remote from either pleasure or comfort, so little capable of cultivation; it had been entirely neglected by my father, and the Castle suffered gradually to decay. What grounds were tenantable had been let off on long leases, and an old man and his family were permitted to reside in the house without expense. Some little time before the death of my father, he received an account of the old man's death, and that the widow and family were going to live in Bohemia with her friends; from that time no one had lived in the house. My steward had mentioned it to me, but from inattention, or other thoughts, I had neglected to concern myself about it.

The anxiety Eugenia expressed to live, secluded from observation, recalled this Castle to my mind, and I resolved to send over a trusty person to see what state it was in.—This step was perfectly agreeable to her; she and Agnes were to retain their masculine dress, and remain as visitors with me until the affair was settled, which, as I was impatient to be united to Eugenia, you may suppose I lost no time in forwarding it. I was very soon informed, that part of the Castle was habitable, and that some of the furniture, though old and faded, was tolerable. —On this intelligence I told my steward I had bestowed it on an unfortunate couple of my acquaintance, who were so far reduced in circumstances as to think it a comfortable asylum, and that they were to take immediate possession. This account precluded him from any farther care or inquiry about the place.

I restrained my impatience more than a fortnight after this, for as I was not sure but the Baron might have spies upon me, I was resolved to be very circumspect. I gave out that I intended returning to England: I collected together a good deal of money, and also made remittances to England, from whence I could draw at any time. When every thing was completed, the trunks of Agnes were removed from Stutgard to the neighbouring village under a disguised name, and they took leave of me three days previous to my intended departure, as if going back to Bohemia, but were to wait for me at the village. After those precautions for their safety, I settled every thing with my steward, whose integrity I could rely on, and telling him that I might possibly travel a year or two before he would hear from me, bid him not be uneasy, but act with unlimited authority for my interest during my absence; that I should take no servant with me, as a German, unacquainted with the language would be useless, but intended to hire servants in England.

Having thus eluded both curiosity and discovery, I soon joined my beloved Eugenia, and we proceeded to the Castle. I believe we both felt similar emotions on entering this solitary mansion. We threw our eyes round, and then looked at each other, but both were silent: Agnes, however, made her observations without ceremony, at the same time qualifying her first exclamations by saying, that 'when she had been a few days in the place she would give things another sort of countenance.' I shall not trouble you with our proceedings, to render it a little comfortable, we all exerted our endeavours, and the fourth day after our arrival, I had the happiness of being united to my loved Eugenia in the village church, she dressed in the plainest garb belonging to Agnes, and myself in a great coat. I then ventured to the village, and procured a boy to assist Agnes in the domestic business, and she proposed sending for Arnulph: It was doubtless a presentiment that made me shudder when she mentioned it; but we were too much obliged to her, and indeed too much in her power to refuse her request, and had really a strong affection for her that would not admit of an objection to her being equally happy with ourselves; we therefore consented: Arnulph came, and we enjoyed so perfect a contentment, made our rooms so commodious, and our garden and poultry-yard so pleasant and profitable, that I grew entirely reconciled to a seclusion from the world.

Eugenia in due time brought to the world a little cherub, the image of herself; (here the Count's voice faltered at the recollection of its untimely and miserable death, but soon recovering himself, he went on) and as she advanced in infantile knowledge, we had a source of entertainment that engaged many of our hours, and enlivened our solitude. —We agreed that when this little darling should arrive at the age of five years, we would go to England, under the belief that before that period the Baron would cease to concern himself about Eugenia, and perhaps form another connexion. Thus in a deceitful calm, in the midst of future happy prospects, that dreadful storm burst upon us, so unexpected and terrible, as to overwhelm us with complete misery.

"As it appears you are perfectly well informed, Sir," said the Count, addressing Ferdinand, "of every step that revengeful monster took to gratify his malice, I shall not trouble you with a repetition, and as to our feelings and sufferings, they will not admit of a description, for the horrors of our situation were beyond all conception or credibility. I shall only observe, that whilst our dear child existed, we endeavoured to support our own strength for her sake; nor indeed did we imagine our persecutor would long submit to a situation so painful to himself merely to punish us. The cruel death of Agnes was a severe stroke; but when we saw our dear infant began to droop, a slow fever consuming her, from the close and humid air, which we received only through a few iron bars on the top of our prison, from whence fell all the inclemencies of the winter season, and so small a quantity of air and light, as only rendered our abode the more terrible. When we saw our beauteous babe in danger of sinking a victim to the malice of our cruel gaoler; we then forgot our wrongs and our pride. What supplications, what entreaties, did we not use! but all was vain, not a drop of water to wet its parched lips in the hour of death.

"O, my God! never, never shall I forget that hour, and the calamity which followed! Its wretched mother lost her reason for years, yet at times seemed sensible of our miserable fate, and always knew me when she heard my voice. In this situation she never refused her poor pittance of bread and water, but rather took it eagerly; and I, Sir, I strove to repress my feelings, strove to live for her sake, for to die and leave her was a distracting thought that harrowed up my soul. Thus the monster had found the means to prolong our misery, and make me dread that death which otherwise I should have devoutly prayed for.

"Such a refinement of cruelty could only have been practised by himself, who, far from being tired out, or satiated, appeared to receive fresh gratification every day. It was very remarkable, that from the hour in which Eugenia's intellects were deranged, and even after the accident which I mentioned to you had restored her, from the night of the child's death, she never saw him enter without screaming, until silenced by fear. Often have I dreaded that the villain would have been provoked to strike her; many times has he threatened it, but yet never could subdue the terror that vented itself in shrieks whenever he appeared. Thus, Sir, I have related to you this strange story, which almost exceeds probability; for never, I believe, was the diabolical passion of revenge carried to such extremes before, for a man to resign every comfort in life, and be a wretch himself to punish others."

Just as the Count had concluded his relation, and before Ferdinand could make any observations, Francis came in, and said the Lady was awake, and wished to see the Count. Ferdinand assisted him to ascend the stairs (his legs being too stiff to accomplish it alone) and then returned to enjoy his own reflections on the extraordinary occurrences of the day, and the story he had heard. — The Count and Eugenia being now restored to life and liberty by the death of their tormentor, the Castle their own, and free to enjoy their fortune in whatever situation they liked, were now likely to feel the happiness that awaited them to a much greater extent than if they had known more tranquil days, and had been exempt from their former sufferings.

In this perfect content, thought Ferdinand, I shall leave them, for their felicity will throw a comparative wretchedness upon me, by reminding me of what I have enjoyed, and what I have for ever lost. Overwhelmed by a retrospection on his misfortunes, he sat for some time lost in thought, until the return of the Count and Francis; the latter withdrew.

"I have seen Eugenia in such a state of comfort," said the former, 'that it has given transports to my heart, long, very long, a stranger there. I have persuaded her to continue in bed, the warmth of which must be of service to her limbs, and I trust by to-morrow she will be a new creature. O, Sir! next to Heaven,

you are entitled to our warmest gratitude. May you never know
sorrow, or, if such an exemption is not the lot of mortals, may
you always meet with minds good and sympathetic like your
own, ready to communicate happiness, and restore you to
peace!"

"I thank you, Sir," replied Ferdinand, "for your good wishes,
which, in my case, must, I fear, prove fruitless; however, let me
not sadden his hour of pleasure: I rejoice to hear your Lady is so
much recovered, and we must endeavour to procure for her
some refreshment."

"Wine and toast," said the Count, "will be sufficient this
night, and to-morrow we shall have assistance." — After taking
proper refreshments, the Count was helped to his apartment,
and Francis having made good fires in two other rooms, and
aired some necessaries, he and his master, as he called
Ferdinand, retired to rest, after the fatigues of this eventful day.

CHAPTER VI

The next morning the farmer arrived with a young woman, and necessary people to attend the dead: The Count was with Ferdinand, and appeared as the heir of the deceased, who from a long and habitual melancholy had secluded himself, until finding his end approaching he had sent for his relations, who on their arrival found he had expired that very morning. This account was given and believed, because Francis had been previously prepared to corroborate it. The Lady's weakness was accounted for from fatigue, and a very violent rheumatic cold; the young woman was to attend her, and another was ordered to officiate as a cook. — In short, in the course of the morning, every proper arrangement was made. Francis was informed that the Count was the owner of the Castle from the late Baron's memoirs, and he heartily rejoiced that he had made such a desirable change in the person he was to serve.

At noon the Lady Eugenia, assisted by her female attendant, made her appearance below: She appeared like a fine statue that had long been exposed to the injuries of time, and lost the beautiful polish that first adorned it; a most elegant form reduced to that delicate thinness which the slightest blast of air might dissolve; — a face, the contour of which was inexpressibly beautiful; but the roses and lilies that once adorned it were all fled; the eyes hollow and sunk in the head, a sickly hue over the countenance, and a solemnity in every feature, altogether gave her whole appearance such an image of a woe-worn mind, that it was impossible to behold her without being deeply affected.

She returned the civilities which Ferdinand involuntarily paid her with some hesitation, but much sweetness. "Pardon me, Sir," said she, "if I am deficient in expressing my obligations to you for liberty and life; I have almost forgotten the use of language, but to utter words of misery and despair."

"Words," cried the Count, kissing her hand, "words which, I trust, my dear Eugenia, will never have cause to utter again: We have no longer cause for sorrow, no longer an enemy to fear, we may emerge into the world, return to our country like long-absent friends, and elude curiosity by saying we have resided in a foreign state." — "But your estate," said she, "by this time may have passed into other hands, your steward may be dead, and much trouble and perplexity may still await you to prove, and to enjoy your rights."

"Fear nothing, my dear Eugenia," replied the Count, "all my friends cannot be dead; I shall find no difficulty in proving my identity, and in being acknowledged."—She sighed, but made no reply.

Ferdinand then mentioned having seen in the cabinet the will and papers relative to the estate of the late Count Zimchaw, which, said he, "I was surprised to find there."

"It is rather singular," answered the Count; "but I suppose he had them with him when he set off on his travels; with those, however, we have nothing to do. If he has any heirs, they may have possessed themselves of his fortune by this time, and in justice to them and ourselves I think a paper should be drawn up, briefly mentioning his residence here, your arrival, and his sudden death, which, with the testimony of Francis, will be sufficient, and preclude any necessity for our names being mentioned at all."

"I agree with you," said Ferdinand, 'that such a paper is absolutely proper; it awkward affair, and I think an express should be sent to the Baron's estate immediately of his demise."

In this opinion Eugenia coincided, and it was a matter concluded upon: Ferdinand resolved also to procure a messenger on his own account, to carry letters from him to his brother and his faithful Ernest. He was anxious to know what had passed in the Castle since his departure, and to hear of his little son; but how great was his surprise when questioning the farmer (who was now their oracle) of the distance to Baden on horseback, he was informed that it was five days journey. —"Five days!" repeated he, "impossible! Why, I came here in two days over the hills and through the woods."

"It may be so," replied the farmer;—"but I believe, Sir, no man but yourself would have made the attempt: I am sure I have never heard of any body that has penetrated the woods, or crossed those rugged hills, nor indeed did I think it could be done; but horses, Sir, can go no such places, and the road is a very troublesome one, because great part of the way, by the skirts of the Forest, has never yet been levelled."

"Well," cried Ferdinand, "be the distance what it may, I must have a messenger." This was promised him the next morning, and as he conceived the Count and his Lady would gladly be alone together, he retired into another apartment to write. Having given Ernest a brief recital of his travels through the woods and valleys until his arrival at the Castle, he mentioned nothing of his adventures there, though he confessed his visit to the convent, and the strange and unsatisfactory answer he had received from Claudina. He besought Ernest to be unreserved, to develop the mystery that hung over him, let the consequence be what it would, for that the most painful truths could not give him greater misery than the suspense he now endured. He recommended the old shepherd and his daughter to his care, and desired he would, if possible, procure for them a safer habitation than among those impending rocks, which seemed to threaten them with hourly destruction.

Having finished his letters he returned to the other apartment, and was surprised at his entrance to mark an increased air of trouble about the Count, and deep sorrow trembling in the eyes of Eugenia; he was too delicate to make any observations; they sat down to a slight repast, of which the others partook but very sparingly, and exchanged but a very few words.

Some time after, when they were alone, the Count addressing Ferdinand, "Your penetrating eye, my good friend, must observe the gloom that pervades my countenance, it is a transcript of my mind; from you I ought not to have any reserve, you are impartial, you shall judge fairly between us:— Now, when the heavy cloud that has so long involved us in night and wretchedness, seems to be withdrawn, and the prospects brighten to our view. Will you believe it possible that Eugenia, she who has a thousand times told me that I was dearer to her than life, who in a horrid prison felt her own woes but lightly, when she considered what her husband suffered— can you, will you believe, that this wife ever adored, and a million times dearer to me than ever from her unparallel'd sufferings, can, now that happiness is in our power, tell me, 'that on the most mature deliberation this past day and night, she has determined to retire to a convent for the remainder of her days; beseeches me to make no opposition to her choice, but rather strengthen a resolution founded on the purest principles of religion and virtue."

"I will not tell you what were my feelings, nor repeat to you the arguments I have used; as a husband I can command, and I can prevent the accomplishment of her strange unkind intention; but I disclaim all power, if her heart no longer acknowledges me, if the years of misery we have suffered together has worn out all traces of her former affection, I submit to be the victim; but let an unprejudiced person judge between us, and say whether I have deserved to lose the affection of my wife."

"Oh! Count," cried Eugenia, the tears no longer restrained from dropping on her face, "ever beloved of my heart, spare the unkind reproach: Hear me, Sir," added she to Ferdinand, "you have candour, you will judge me fairly. You know our story, you know I had vowed never to marry the Count without my father's consent: I did more, at his command I accompanied the Baron to the altar. Ah! was I not guilty of sacrilege, of profanation, when I uttered with my lips vows I rejected in my heart? Say they were compelled, could that excuse my subsequent conduct? Passion blinded me to the impropriety of my intentions; I ought never to have approached the altar, or when I had done so, I should have fulfilled my vows; my father's prejudice, or cruelty, could be no excuse for my depravity:—Heaven approved not of my broken vows, and Heaven was pleased to punish me; but was I the only sufferer? O, no! When I look back, how many innocent victims bled for my crimes! Arnulph, the faithful Agnes, Peter, and, O misery, my child! my dear innocent babe! let me not dwell on that;—even the wretch who was ordained to be my punisher, he lived, he died, miserable! And can I return to the world, can I talk of happiness, and trample on the memory of those unfortunates who suffered for me? No, it is impossible: Great have been my miseries, but great have been my faults; let me then expiate them as I ought; let me retire to peace, penitence and prayer; let me pray for the souls of those who fell by an untimely death on my account, and let me make my peace with Heaven by devoting my future days to retirement. You, who are, who ever will be dear to my heart, who will be a principal object in my orisons, you must strengthen my resolutions; you must approve of my conduct, and though the heart murmurs, the reason must be convinced. And now, Sir," concluded she, addressing Ferdinand, "now I have explained my motives, speak with candour; tell me, does not your judgment approve my determination? Do you not see that in the world my life would be embittered, by painful retrospections that must preclude happiness, and that in devoting myself to retirement, I pursue the only path that points to peace and tranquillity?"

Ferdinand was for a few moments silent, astonished at such a revolution, so little expected, from that plan of felicity he had so lately thought them possessed of, and which to him seemed an enviable situation. He paused a little, but seeing they both impatiently expected his reply:—"Forgive me, my dear Sir," said he to the Count, "if thus called upon, I confess that my esteem, my admiration for the Lady Eugenia, rises in equal proportion with my compassion for you; for the more I approve her exalted resolution, and admire her virtues, the more I feel must be your distress at the idea of being separated from an object so truly deserving your esteem; but I must be free to confess, that this Lady's reasons are unanswerable, and that however innocent she may be of any actual guilt, yet as the death of so many persons was in consequence of her flight from the Baron, a feeling mind like her's would constantly revert to the primary cause, and never cease to accuse herself;—therefore under such circumstances, her intention of retiring from a busy deceitful world, to devote her days to the duties of religion, is surely praise-worthy, and commands our approbation."

"It is well, Eugenia," said the Count, in a mournful tone, "you have found a champion to support your opinions, and I have no more to do than to acquiesce; but since you have chosen your path towards happiness, I may be allowed to chalk out one for myself. I shall take this night to consider of it, and to-morrow will acquaint you with my final resolution." "May Heaven, who knows the fervency of my affection, inspire you to choose that which may conduce both to your present and future happiness." Ending these words Eugenia desired to retire, for the weakness of her body, and the agitations of her mind, overpowered her fragile form, which could hardly support the transitions she had experienced, and was unequal to the sight of that melancholy, but too visible, in the Count's pale face, that seemed silently to reproach her of cruelty.

When she had left the room, Ferdinand observing the sorrow that seemed fixed in the features of the Count, strove to change the current of his thoughts by speaking more freely of his own affairs than he had yet done, and at length, encouraged by the interest the Count appeared to take in his concerns, he made an unreserved communication of his whole story.

"Indeed, my young friend," observed the Count, when Ferdinand had concluded his relation, "indeed, there are some very extraordinary and unaccountable circumstances in your story, that one cannot elucidate by any conjectures on the subject. I do not blame you for seeking to amuse your mind by travelling, but you are wrong in choosing this mode of doing it; wandering through woods, and over almost impassable hills, may be attended with more danger than you are aware of, and in an evil moment you may fall a sacrifice to some concealed ruffian, or a troop of banditti; besides the natural inconvenience of suffering both cold and hunger."

"What you observe is very just doubtless," answered the other; "but you should remember I am not a man of fortune, an independent man, and that it behoves me to avoid all unnecessary expenses in my rambles, for travelling, in the general sense of the word, is beyond my abilities to undertake; I wish to forget myself at present, and when the campaign opens, may possibly resume my station in the army, yet, that must depend upon circumstances.—With your leave I will remain here until my messenger returns, and then the world will be once more before me."

"This conversation," said the Count, "has given a different turn to my thoughts from what I entertained an hour ago; I already feel that interest and affection for you, that it shall not be my fault if we are separated; but more of that to-morrow."— Having sent off their different expresses, one to Baron S———'s estate, another to Count M———, and a third to Count Rhodophil's Castle, it was thought most advisable to delay the funeral of the Baron until the return of the messenger.

The following day, when they all assembled at table, the Lady Eugenia appeared less feeble, and with a more placid countenance, than on the preceding day. When the servants were withdrawn Ferdinand congratulated her on the visible amendment.

"I do indeed feel better both in mind and body," said she, 'the one is generally dependent on the other. Since I have determined on my plan, and my dear Count has given up his objections to it, I find a composure in my soul to which it has very long been a stranger. The dreadful malady which I laboured under for years, has certainly weakened my intellects, as I frequently experience a confusion in my ideas, and very odd sensations in my head; the world therefore would be a very unfit place for me, and the sooner I can find a retirement, such as I wish for, the better; the pang of separation must be felt, and I am anxious to have it over."

It instantly darted into Ferdinand's mind, that if Eugenia entered the Convent where Claudina resided, it might afford them mutual consolation, and possibly might, by mutual confidence, put it in the power of the former to develop to him that mystery so carefully and cruelly concealed from him by Ernest and Claudina. He hastily mentioned the adjoining Convent, as having been well spoken of by Father Joseph, and offered his services to make all the necessary inquiries. This offer was joyfully accepted by Eugenia, nor opposed by the Count. She said, 'that, to avoid impertinent questions, it was her intention to pass for a widow, who wished to retire into the bosom of the church for the remainder of her days. I must be a boarder, (said she) but I shall conform to all their rules, and subject myself to all their severities and self-denials. In calling myself a widow I am guilty of no deception, for from the moment I enter the gates of the Convent I am parted from the object of my affections for ever!"

The Count rose greatly agitated — "Eugenia," cried he, "you either deceive yourself when you talk of your affection for me, or you have more than female fortitude."

"Neither the one nor the other," answered she: "I know my own heart, and I feel that, in this separation, it must endure pangs worse than the stroke of death; but conscience, that all-powerful monitor, has spoken incontrovertible truths; her voice has taught me my duty, and pointed out the only way by which I can atone for my errors, and procure pardon for the death of those innocent persons that were sacrificed for me."

"I have no more to urge," replied the Count; "it is fit that I also should be a victim."

"By no means," exclaimed Eugenia; — "you have nothing to blame yourself for, you have committed no errors but pardonable ones, and I trust, my dear Count, that many, very many, happy years are in store for you: My tranquillity must, in some degree, be dependent on your's; return to the world, and to society, they have claims upon you: I hope you have here acquired a friend that may succeed in composing your mind; forget Eugenia, or if you remember her, think only that she is set off on a long, long journey, where you may at some distant period arrive also, and remember, that it is only her duty to Heaven, that she prefers to you."

Overpowered with her emotions, she rose, and with feeble steps she retired to another room.

"Exalted creature!" cried the Count, — "from this hour I will no more add to thy distress by my reflections, nor wound thee even by my looks; I will try to assume a composure, though my heart is torn with anguish." Ferdinand then mentioned his intention of going the following day to the Monastery adjoining to the Convent, and through Father Joseph get the Lady proposed as a boarder, desirous of conforming to all the rules of the house. This being agreeable to all parties, early on the next morning he went to visit Father Joseph; the Count pressed him to take a man with him through the gloomy and solitary road he had to pass; but Ferdinand chose to go alone, and after more than four hours tedious travel over the hills, and through the deep and woody valleys, he arrived in view of the Monastery. Having pulled the bell, and inquired for Father Joseph, the good man soon appeared. He uttered an exclamation of joy on seeing Ferdinand: "Heaven bless you, my young friend, this is an unexpected pleasure."

"It is a pleasure to me, my good Father, to see you in health; I have undertaken business of consequence to serve another, chiefly that I might once more behold you."

"Enter freely, my son, I will conduct you to Father Ambrose; he only is privileged to talk of worldly concerns, or transact business."

With hasty step he led the way to a private room: "Rest here," said the good Father, "and I will acquaint Father Ambrose of your visit to him; he is before this apprised of your entrance." He withdrew in a quick way, that reminded Ferdinand of his former observation relative to the envy and jealousy which pervaded through a Monastery. The Superior soon appeared, with a look so gracious, and so unbending from the natural haughtiness of his demeanour, that Ferdinand, whose soul knew no disguise, advanced to salute him with equal complacency. — "You are welcome, my son, I rejoice to see you; I trust that Heaven has directed you here as to the mansion of peace."

Ferdinand, without entering into any particular discussions, opened the business which brought him there: "A widow Lady, of family and independence, having lost all the ties which had bound her to the world, was desirous of retiring to the neighbouring Convent for the remainder of her days; but a stranger to the modes necessary to procure admittance, he had waited on Father Ambrose as the Confessor of the Convent, to acquire information on that head."

"Is the Lady related to you?" asked the Father..

"No," replied Ferdinand; "but she is nearly related to a dear friend of mine, and at their joint request I undertook this commission."

"Well, son," said the Father, with a more reserved air, "if the Lady is a woman of character, she need not fear admission: I will speak to the Abbess on the subject, and if she wishes it, and will apply to me, I will introduce her. She has no doubt sufficient to pay handsomely; the Convent admits none but such, as the expenses of the house are great, so many poor, sick and disabled, to maintain, their charity consumes a large revenue."

"The Lady will have no cause to fear a rejection on that head," answered the other; "she will readily contribute her share to enlarge their charitable beneficence." — "And you, my good son, what is your plan of life? May we hope for your society?"

"Not at present," replied Ferdinand; "I have yet some duties to perform which call me into the world; I know not how long indeed, but my mind is not now disposed to enjoy that monastic tranquillity that appears to reign here."

"I am sorry for it," returned Father Ambrose; "but believe me, son, if your mind is disturbed, this retirement is most suited to restore your peace: However, I hope you intend to pass this night here. From what distance did you come?" — Ferdinand named the village, and as he had previously disposed the Count not to be uneasy if he should be absent for the night, he very readily accepted the Father's invitation; for the walk being no small fatigue from the difficulties that impeded his passage, he was not sorry to have a place of rest.

The conversations that took place in the course of the day is not necessary to be related. Nothing was left unsaid that could give Ferdinand a favourable opinion of their society, or hold out inducements to fix a wavering mind in a situation so replete with tranquillity and comfort. He heard them with attention and complaisance, but longed earnestly for bed-time, in the hope of holding some converse with Father Joseph, to whom he had found an opportunity of conveying his wishes, which had been answered by a significant nod: Nor was this hope disappointed, in less than an hour after he had retired, the good Father softly opened the door, and appeared before him. Ferdinand took his hand with reverence: "My worthy friend, this is kind indeed!" — "My dear son, I thank your kindness in remembering me, and am glad my business has procured us the pleasure of seeing you."

"Ah!" said the former, "strange events have happened since I saw you last; but I feel too much interest for you to be prolix on other matters. Tell me, my good Father, have you connexions in the world, attachments of any kind in which I can serve you?"

"None," replied the other, "I stand a solitary being, not more cut off from the world than from connexions. I will tell you my story in a few words:

"My father was a man of family; my mother expired two years after my birth: I was, until six years of age, the darling of my surviving parent, and his chief amusement. About that time he conceived a strong affection for a haughty, dissipated woman, of high birth, but no fortune; this Lady he married: I was sent to a Jesuit's College for education; twice a year I came to see my father, but, alas! how changed, how cold the reception I experienced from the tender endearments I had been accustomed to!—Young as I was, I soon perceived the marked alteration. His Lady looked on me with an invidious eye, and the short periods I was permitted to spend at home, soon became irksome and disagreeable. When I was about fourteen, my tutor one day gave me to understand that it was my father's will that I should dedicate myself to the church.

"I was thunderstruck at this intelligence, for I had other views; my mind was active, my body strong and robust, for my age; I had long entertained a wish to be instructed in military exercises; I wished to go into the army; my father was a man of fortune; he had no children by his Lady; why then was I to be condemned to an unsocial sedentary life I had no propensities to? I reasoned with my tutor; he bid me talk to my father on the subject, and the first time, after this conversation, that I saw him, he soon afforded me the opportunity, by a communication that I little expected. My mother-in-law, after being married nine years, without having any children, was now pregnant. I was not then enough acquainted with the world to practise hypocrisy, or affect a pleasure I could not feel. He observed my silence and my countenance: 'This news does not please you, young man (said he) and you are selfish enough I see to grieve at an event likely to be productive of so much joy to me: I am glad I understand your disposition so well.'

"}Do not, Sir," I replied, "form a conclusion so unfavourable to me, Heaven knows I shall share in every joy of your's; but pardon me, my dear father (added I) if, when I reflect on the coldness which I have ever experienced from my Lady, and the information I have lately received from my tutor, pardon me if I fear the affection you once honoured me with is already greatly weakened, and that the event you allude to will, perhaps, entirely drive me from your heart; that consideration alone, not sordid interest, affects me.'

"Boy (cried he, interrupting me) 'you have at least learned to talk well; but you cannot command your features, those speak an unequivocal language, which I perfectly comprehend: however, you know my pleasure, I design you for the church, it is the proper situation for young men like you." He left me almost petrified with astonishment, there was a something altogether so strange and inexplicable in his words and looks, that I retired to my chamber overcome by a variety of painful emotions: I saw plainly that I had lost a father, and young as I was, I foresaw the consequences to myself. The few hours that I remained buried in reflection gave me months of understanding, but I resolved to make one effort more. I wrote a letter to my father in the most respectful terms, tending to remove every prejudice he had conceived against me, at the same time acknowledging my predilection for the army, and besought his permission to attend in future to military exercises."

The answer I received was short. — "Return to the College, attend to your duties there, and I shall hereafter consider on the propriety of your request." — I obeyed without hesitation; and to please my father paid the strictest attention to my tutor, not without observing, that all his lessons were calculated to inspire a dislike of the world, and to display the superior happiness of a monastic life. In due time my mother-in-law was brought to bed of a son, which was announced to me with great exultation: I heard it with a palpitating heart, as the downfall of all my hopes from parental affection.

"I continued two years longer at the College, during which time I saw my father only thrice, and had but little cause to value myself on his tenderness. I was now in my eighteenth year when I received a summons to attend him: I flew with eager expectation, his looks chilled me. "Tis high time, Louis (said he) that you should enter upon your professional duties; I have before now told you I intend you for the Church, my resolution still holds."

"Ah! Sir (I exclaimed) why must I be the sacrifice?"

"Stop (cried he) and learn who you are, and that you have no claims to sacrifice. I never was married to your mother: She was a Bourgeoise, I could not marry her, yet I loved and respected her; whilst she lived I resided in the country, to avoid disagreeable circumstances to her. This truth I was obliged to acknowledge to my wife before she would accept of my hand, having an idea that I had degraded myself; you cannot wonder therefore that she did not treat you with respect, although she has always behaved civilly. I have now a son who must inherit my fortunes. To spare you painful reflections, I wish you to choose the Church, all circumstances may then remain known only to ourselves, and you shall find I will not forget that you are the son of a woman I once loved. It becomes you to preserve her reputation by submitting to my orders." I heard this long development in a kind of stupid distraction. I replied not a word. He mistook the nature of my feelings for sullenness.

"Sir! (said he, raising his voice) I see my kindness is thrown away; hear then my commands, and my fixed determination: If you comply, and return to the Church, I will endeavour to get you a proper situation; if you refuse, and chalk out a path for yourself, I will give you five hundred Louis-d'ors; leave France, and see me no more." These last words roused me in an instant; pride, grief and indignation, took possession of my soul. —"Since I no longer have claims upon your affection, Sir, since I am to live an alien from you, I may at least be permitted to choose for myself; I will therefore accept of the money you offer me, and learn to forget that I have a father, since he disdains to acknowledge me; but have I no connexions in a humbler line of life? Had my unhappy mother no relations? Or was she too reprobated by all?"

"Your mother (answered my father) was an orphan when I first knew her; she resided with a brother, a shopkeeper; he died a short time before her, and I know not that you have any relations in the world. Had you chosen the Church, in me you would have found a parent; but as neither my wishes or commands are attended to, in giving you a sum sufficient, with prudence and economy, to settle you in a line of your own choice. I conceive I have done my duty as to every claim you can have upon me.

"There, Sir (added he, rising, and opening his cabinet) there are drafts for £500, Louis-d'ors, may they be successfully employed, and gratify your own expectations." I received the papers with such emotions of mingled pride, indignation and love, that I was incapable of speaking. At the door I turned to take a last look, tears gushed from my eyes: "Heaven's bless you!" was all I uttered, and I saw him turn with his handkerchief to his face.

"Thus was I thrown upon the world without any friends or connexions, a degraded, solitary being. I retired to an auberge in the skirts of the town, and began to consider on my situation. Without rank, fortune, or even a name, how could I think of entering into the army? My pride suggested a thousand insupportable slights I might encounter in a public line of life, and those very circumstances attending the late discovery, so humiliating, served only to render my temper more irritable and haughty. —Without being able to fix on any plan, I resolved immediately to quit France, which I did the following day, and travelled through Germany.

"Strange to say, in one so young as I was at that time, I grew morose and splenetic; I thought every man happier than myself, and I envied and hated all mankind! In this disposition I came into this neighbourhood; its wild romantic hills and valleys charmed me; in the adjacent village I resided some time, and spent my days in rambling in the woods. At length I met with a solitary hut, which seemed to have been not long uninhabited, on the side of a hill. In this spot I fixed my residence for near two years. It has been observed, 'That a person must be either a God, or a brute, who can be able to live alone.' Providence certainly designed us for a social state, and a misanthrope lives a burden to himself, and dead to every pleasure in life.

"A very severe cold, which I caught in one of my rambles, and which produced a fever that confined me near a week, and precluded me from getting even the necessaries to preserve my existence, first brought me to a sense of my extreme folly in living thus unknowing and unknown. Had my illness continued a few days longer I must have perished from actual want; but it pleased Heaven to restore me to some degree of strength; with difficulty I crawled to this Monastery, as it was much nearer than the village. A worthy Friar, long since dead, relieved my necessities, and by his kindness unlocked my heart. He sympathized with me when he heard my tale, and that sympathy gave an energy to every office of humanity that endeared him to me, and rendered his conversation a balm to heal those wounds long rankling within, and which had been productive of the most hateful passions.

"In a very short time I felt no happiness but in his society, and mistaking the nature of my emotions, I conceived that in this retirement, to which I had once such an insuperable aversion, I should find that peace and comfort the world had denied to me. — I made application here, and was soon admitted, for I had still upwards of three hundred Louis-d'ors, which spoke volumes in my favour in the most persuasive language that can be addressed to Monasteries. The novelty of every thing about me (for there is no judging of the interior management in those places by exterior appearances, even if educated in Convents) the kindness and attention I received from the Fathers, and the pomp and solemnity which accompanied our religious duties, for a time afforded me real transport, and I hourly condemned myself for resisting my father's will. In this frame of mind I wrote to him, but received no answer, and whether it reached his hands, or whether he was living or dead, I know not.

"Within six months after my entrance here my good friend died; we had a new Superieure, and things wore a different aspect. I had lost my friend and comforter, that loss could not be supplied. I had acquired a relish for society, and my heart felt a vacuity which I looked round in vain to have filled up; no one appeared interested for me, and I was permitted to wander about unheeded with the rest of the brethren. It was now that I felt how mistaken I had been in the nature of my emotions; without the converse of my friend, the performance of my duties grew cold, languid, and tiresome: I regretted my seclusion from the world, and languished to be at liberty, that I might again enjoy the blessings of society which I had so rashly renounced. In this frame of mind I continued some months, and the agitations I endured produced a long and tedious nervous fever. On the verge of the grave I was brought to a sense of my duty; a revolution took place in my heart; I soon recovered, and from that period have, with humble submission, conformed to my situation.

"Thus, my son, I have run over my short history, and from thence you may learn this important truth, 'Man was not intended for a solitary being,' and be warned never to let the disappointments of life prey upon your mind, so as to produce a temporary disgust to the world, that may, in a fit of despair, throw you into situations productive of repentance and unavailing regret."

CHAPTER VII

Father joseph, having concluded his story, was informed by Ferdinand of the motives which had brought him to the Monastery, and that having been successful in his commission he might possibly accompany the Lady, if within a short time she was capable of the undertaking: "After what I have said to you," returned the good Father, "I hope you will inform yourself thoroughly of the Lady's motives for secluding herself from the world, and advise her to commune with her own heart deliberately and seriously, and not from a temporary disgust seek to find peace and happiness in a Convent; the mind should have shaken off worldly considerations, and have no objects to regret before it is fitted to devote all its faculties to religious duties. For yourself, you have dear connexions, you are a father, you have no right to quit the station in which Providence has placed you, and I hope are determined by active duties to deserve, if you cannot obtain, happiness. The one is in your own power, and if you are disappointed in your wishes and expectations, be assured it is for wise and good reasons calculated for your real benefit, though short-sighted mortals judging only of the present, ungratefully repine in those moments when they ought to be most thankful."

"My good Father," said Ferdinand, with a sigh, "I bow to the justice of your observations; but the human heart is refractory, and often errs against reason and conviction: I promise you, however, that I will no longer indulge my wishes for retirement, and that if I ramble a short time in search of novelty to amuse my thoughts, I will endeavour so far to profit by your advice as to determine on reassuming my station in the army when the campaign opens; and in that field for action I may either obtain a comparative degree of peace, or lose the remembrance of my sorrows altogether." — He added, that the Father might depend upon his observance of the kind cautions he had given respecting the Lady. — They now parted with mutual blessings and good wishes, as they had no hope of holding any farther conversation in the morning.

At a very early hour Ferdinand arose, and appeared in the room where the Friars were assembled after their first matins. Father Ambrose received him with much complacency, and again renewed his promise of introducing the Lady to the neighbouring sisterhood, who he was certain "would make no objections, as she had sufficient property to answer the necessary expenses her admission would draw upon the house." Ferdinand took leave, and though he cast a longing, lingering look towards the Convent, yet, convinced that of himself he could obtain no satisfactory information, and that all his hopes must rest upon Eugenia, he vented a few anxious sighs, and proceeded with all haste to the Castle.

His arrival was welcomed with much pleasure by all parties, for the intermediate time of his absence had been spent in fruitless endeavours by the Count and Eugenia to suppress their own feelings, and to reconcile and console each other; but each saw the painful emotions neither could disguise, and Eugenia had occasion for abundant resolution and fortitude to withstand the silent grief of the Count, the tenderness of her own heart, and to exert that apparent firmness in her determination as might effectually annihilate every hope, that they could be weakened by affection or arguments; their situation was therefore so distressing, that the company of a third person, particularly Ferdinand's, was a most desirable relief. He entered upon the success of his commission, and failed not to repeat, in the strongest terms, the advice and admonitions of Father Joseph. The Count fixed his eyes on Eugenia with a look that penetrated to her soul. She was greatly agitated for a moment, but struggling for composure, "I thank the good Father, and you, my amiable friend; but I have no doubts of my own resolution, no fear of future regrets: Only one object can claim a share in my thoughts with the Deity, to whose service I mean to dedicate the remaining days of my existence; and every remembrance of that too dearly beloved object will more strongly enforce the necessity for pursuing my present plan, by reminding me of my errors, and pointing out the strict observance of my religious duties, as the only means of procuring pardon from Heaven, and of obtaining future tranquillity to myself."

"To a mind resolved like your's, Madam (replied Ferdinand) I have no more to urge, and shall most readily attend you to the destined place when it shall appear convenient to you."—She bowed, and looking on the Count with a tearful eye, rose and retired.

"Come, my friend (said Ferdinand to the Count, perceiving that he was fixed in a profound reverie, with all the marks of extreme sorrow on his features) come, assert that fortitude so becoming in a noble mind, and which for many years has supported you: How delighted would you have felt under the pressure of your sufferings had life and liberty been offered to you on the single condition of the Lady Eugenia's retiring from the world: Would the alternative have admitted of the least hesitation? Certainly not: And can you now repine that she has the power of her own election, and in her own words, 'only

prefers her duty to Heaven to her earthly happiness with you?'
Let us both unite as fellow sufferers to comfort each other."

"I accept your offer (said the Count, hastily interrupting
him.) From this hour you are my friend and brother; we will
together seek the path to glory, and in the din of arms forget our
private sorrows!"—His eyes sparkled as he spoke, and every
feature grew animated; he seemed as if suddenly informed by a
new soul, and from that moment struggled to subdue his grief,
and assume an appearance of resignation and content.

Several days passed with cheerfulness, tho" not entirely free
from anxiety by either party, for the return of their several
messengers:—The first that arrived was Ferdinand's, with a
letter from Count Rhodophil, and another from the good old
Ernest: Respect superseded affection and curiosity. He opened
the Count's letter first; it was not a long one.

"He was glad to hear from his brother, whose strange whim
of rambling among unfrequented paths on foot had exposed
him to so many dangers: He approved of his design of returning
to the army, and repeated his readiness to furnish him with
money upon all emergencies—congratulated him upon the
welfare of his son, without making a single observation on the
late occurrences at the Castle, or once mentioning Claudina. He
added, that his health not being very good he had some
thoughts of travelling, as the spring advanced, therefore might
possibly not be so regular in his correspondence, but earnestly
requested, that his brother would inform him when it was his
intention to join his quarters at Vienna."

This letter was so cold, so uncircumstantial, and in some
respects so inconsistent, that Ferdinand, after looking it twice
over, felt a dissatisfaction that he could hardly account for.
—"He does not press my return (said he) nor lament my
absence; it is true, had he done so, I should not have acceded to
his wishes; yet methinks he ought to have done it; but perhaps I
expect too much, for I have no absolute claims either upon his
affection or fortune; the first I can perceive is much weakened,
and I may have already intruded too far on the latter; yet why
should I think so, when he still makes me such liberal offers?
The stile in which those offers are made is what hurts me. Alas!
few men that confer obligations have the graceful art of making
the obliged person satisfied with the favours he receives; 'tis the
manner, more than the act, that strikes a mind of sensibility."

Musing in this manner, with the letter in his hand, he had
forgotten, for a few minutes, that there lay another, from which

he might hope to derive more information, and greater gratification. Turning his eyes from the letter to the table, he hastily caught up the one written by Ernest: "Ah! (cried he) here at least I shall read the dictates of the heart, of pure affection without reserve." — He broke it open with precipitation, and read what follows:

HONOURED SIR,

"How my heart rejoiced at the sight of your well-known hand! Ah! my dear young master, hard is your lot to wander about in search of peace; sad, sad doings to be sure: But your dear son, master Charles, is well, and my nephew dotes upon him, he is so good, and so clever; he will live, I hope, to be a blessing to you. — You ask, Sir, about Madam Claudina; she is as well as she can be, but desires to be forgotten by all the world. At a proper age your daughter will be restored to you, till then I beseech you, Sir, to make no farther inquiries. Madam Claudina is dead to you.

"The Count, my master, seems oppressed with melancholy: He has also received some unknown caution, advice, or reproof, from the same voice which astonished you; for a few days ago, after being about an hour in bed, the servants were alarmed by the ringing of his bell; all flew to his room, I among the rest; we found him in the anti-chamber in his shirt, terror in every feature. He asked wildly if any one had been in the chamber or closet? All replied, No. — Had any one heard any groans, or a voice? No, was the answer. He walked the room very fast, regardless of his situation. At length he dismissed all but his valet, who was ordered to stay by him the remainder of the night, and since that a bed has been put up in the anti-chamber for him to sleep close to the Count. These are strange things, my dear Master. I see and hear a great deal, but it does not become me to repeat more than is necessary. Yesterday Peter told me that his Master was courting the Lady once offered to you, the daughter of Count Benhorff. — You know, Sir, the Count died some time ago, and left the Lady a great fortune. Peter said, that after you had refused the Lady, your father offered Count Rhodophil, but the young Countess would not hear of him, and has continued unmarried ever since. — Your brother used to visit there sometimes, and since your departure has been to see the Lady every day, and Peter thinks that she likes him, and that it will be a match at last. So much the worse for the Lady.

"As to the Count's love for you, Sir, you know what I think; what he has done, and what he offers to do, is more for fear of the world's blame for his being unnatural, than from any affection: I am sure of it, and I must speak my mind, though I dare not speak all my mind; but I hope I shall live to see you happy, my dear Master; if I die, I have taken care to leave such things in my nephew's hands as will explain every thing. As you are in a friend's house I wish you would stay there, and not go to the wars; indeed I can't bear to think you should be driven to that, although any place is better, aye and safer too, than Renaud Castle. Do pray, Sir, write often to your old servant under cover to my nephew, and fear not for Master Charles or your interest, whilst I live I will watch over both. God bless you, Sir; may you be happy, and live to triumph over your enemies, prays,

Your faithful servant,

ERNEST."

This letter from the old steward occasioned various emotions in the mind of Ferdinand, several expressions were to him inexplicable, and infused suspicions, though unable to fix on the nature of them. That voice, which still continued its supernatural admonitions, filled him with equal terror and wonder. — Those secrets, which Ernest dared not to reveal, perplexed and astonished him, and his expressions concerning Claudina were equally extraordinary. The latter part of the letter seemed to imply a doubt of his being safe under his brother's roof: He then reverted back to the conversation Ernest had told him past between the Count and Peter; a conversation which his brother's subsequent conduct and seeming kindness had almost obliterated from his memory, though he had felt hurt at the indifference of his behaviour when they parted; those circumstances now returned with double force, and seemed strengthened by the coldness of the letter just received.

Distracted with doubt, curiosity and anxiety, he communicated his sentiments, and the letters to Count M— — —, who had been some days before acquainted with his story. The Count perused the letters, and heard his comments, and being pressed to give his judgment, replied, "There undoubtedly hangs a mystery over every circumstance relative to your brother, that without a clue it is impossible to unravel; but I have no doubt in my mind to pronounce that he is not the friend he would appear to be; and I am also convinced, that, however improbable it may appear to you, your wife has been unfaithful to you; whether your brother is acquainted with the circumstance cannot be known, I should rather think he is not, otherwise his affection, or delicacy, would not have prevented him from disclosing it: But since you have now given me a fair opening, I have two proposals to make, which I have been revolving in my mind to submit on the first opportunity to your consideration.

"To you, under Heaven, I am indebted for liberty and life, and for the preservation of Eugenia's, much dearer to me than my own: For some days past I have struggled with my affection and regret; reason, or perhaps despair, has, in some degree, tranquillized my mind to bear the idea of being separated for ever from the only object I ever did, or ever can love. I have no near or dear connexions, perhaps scarcely an acquaintance that may remember me. My fortune is not inconsiderable, and however my estates may be disposed of from a supposition of my death, they must be restored to me: Condescend then, my dear friend, to complete the work of your generous hand, restore my mind, my peace, as you have liberated my body. If I must live in the world, do you make that world estimable in my eyes, by the value of your company: Let us never be separated, mutually unfortunate, let us console each other, reject the paltry assistance offered by an ungenerous brother, and share the fortune of a faithful friend."

Seeing Ferdinand was going to speak, he continued, "Hear my proposals: If retirement is your choice, go with me to Suabia; if you prefer an active life, I will either accompany you to the army, or I will travel with you wherever you please; the instant I hear how my affairs stand, you shall be independent, and then your home shall be mine, and your choice of situation shall meet my approbation, whatever it may be: Thus you will make my life valuable if you consent; but your refusal will cloud my hopes and prospects for ever. I leave you to reflection; a single Yes, or No, is all I will hear on the subject, and on those two monosyllables rest my future happiness."

The Count rose to leave the room. — Ferdinand caught his hand: "Stop, generous friend, no consideration is necessary, I can distinguish between favours coldly offered, and the effusions of benevolence and friendship; the proud heart that would refuse the latter feels not a generous enthusiasm. — I accept with transport your offers, because I know you feel a delight, a gratification superior, even to mine, in the pleasure of bestowing favours. — Yes (added he, embracing the Count) we will indeed console each other; with such a companion I will travel through the painful journey of life with patience and resignation, and to you be indebted for every comfort without feeling myself degraded by the acceptance." The Count was delighted, and withdrew to acquaint Eugenia with the acquisition he had fortunately obtained of a friend and a companion for his future days; whilst Ferdinand retired to reflect on his letters, and the generosity of the friend, so infinitely superior to the obligations frigidly bestowed by a brother.

CHAPTER VIII

Two days passed away without any material occurrence, the third brought visitors to the Castle. Baron Reiberg and his son, the nearest relations and heirs to the late Baron S— — —, arrived about the middle of the day at this Solitary Mansion. The Baron had for some years enjoyed the revenues of the estate by the courtesy of the Emperor; every inquiry had been set on foot to discover the existence of the Baron, and all proving fruitless, it seemed so unaccountable, that a person of his rank and fortune should so suddenly disappear, and his fate be unknown, that at length some person in the neighbourhood, who had heard a vague report of his being married to a Lady who had run away the same day to a Convent, conjectured that he had gone a volunteer to the wars under a borrowed name, and had fallen undistinguished among the slain.

This idea soon got abroad, and was generally credited, so that the present Baron found but little difficulty in prevailing upon the Emperor to allow him the possession of the estates, to which he was the legal heir, on the demise of Baron S— — —. The express sent by Count M— — —, addressed to the steward, or possessor of the estate, had infinitely surprised him; but as it brought a confirmation of his relation's death, it relieved him from a doubt which had often given him pain, lest he should be dispossessed of his fortune. Curiosity induced him to take the journey, accompanied by his son, and no time was lost in putting his design into execution.

Count M— — — received them with politeness, and without reserve related every event which had taken place at the Castle. The astonishment of the two Gentlemen may be easily conceived; they detested the cruelty of the late Baron, and reprobated his conduct in the strongest terms: They could offer no reparation to the Count, who was superior to pecuniary favours; but Baron Reiberg earnestly entreated the Lady Eugenia would accept of that income to which she would have been entitled as the late Baron's widow by the marriage settlement, particularly as the Baron possessed her father's fortune. — This offer she strenuously refused; much generous altercation took place between them, at length a compromise was agreed on. As Eugenia could have no just expectations to any part of the Baron's fortune, neither had she power to claim any share of her father's property bequeathed unconditionally to him; yet, as the Baron, who now possessed all, was so extremely desirous of making some restitution to her, she reluctantly acquiesced with his wishes, to accept from him a sum of money sufficient to insure her a most welcome reception when she retired to the Convent.

This plan met with great opposition from Count M— — —, who could not support the idea that his Eugenia should owe any pecuniary favours to a stranger, and a relation of their cruel persecutor; but the urgent entreaties of the Baron, and the remonstrances of the Lady, who considered the obligation forced upon her, more as a generous resignation of a small part of that property to which she had once undoubted claims, than as a gift from an indifferent person not benefited by her family; as a very inconsiderable share of what she had a natural right to have expected, she consented to gratify the Baron's feelings by her acceptance of, and so greatly did he feel interested in her melancholy story, that her acquiescence was considered as a high obligation to himself.

One great difficulty equally affected all parties; it was essential to the Baron, that the death of his relation should be publicly announced, that all doubts should be removed, and his possession of the estates be unquestionably his right. How this matter could be elucidated, without involving the names and story of Count M— — — and Eugenia, puzzled them all. Several plans and stories were suggested, but all liable to objections, until Ferdinand being requested to give his opinion, proposed that the account should be as simple as possible, and that his name only should be brought forward, in the following manner: —"Having lost the road, he was conducted by chance to this Castle, where he was admitted by the late Baron, who acquainted him with his retirement from the world in consequence of his wife's leaving him on the day of marriage, and flying to a Convent; that unable to discover her retreat, and conscious of her utter dislike to him, he had grown weary and disgusted with mankind, and rented this Solitary Mansion of Count M— — —, having only one domestic with him. That a few days after Ferdinand's residence with him he was seized with an apoplectic fit, which deprived him of life, in consequence of which Ferdinand had sent off expresses to his estate, and to Count M— — —, whose abode he had been informed of by the Baron. This story, corroborated by Francis, he presumed to think, would effectually satisfy any curious persons, if such there were, who felt any concern about the deceased, and the Lady Eugenia might enter into the Convent as his widow, or not as she pleased."

This arrangement was immediately adopted, except that Eugenia utterly disclaimed an intention of assuming a name to which she had no right, and which indeed was odious to her, and as her marriage with Count M— — — was a secret to all but the present party, she had determined to take upon herself the name of Madam of Valse, which had been a name in her mother's family; "and carrying with me (added she) all such requisites as may ensure a welcome, and give me consequence in the eyes of the Nuns, I apprehend any investigation of my family must be a matter of indifference to them."

Those difficulties, which had perplexed the Baron and Count, being now got over, the Baron dispatched expresses to his family, conformable to the plan decided on, and ordered all things to be prepared for the funeral, as he thought it an incumbent duty upon him to have the body of his relation deposited in the vault with his ancestors; all requisite preparations were made for that purpose, and within two days the procession was to set off for Bavaria.

That day and the following passed agreeably to all; the Baron and his son were so exceedingly interested for the Count, and so delighted with the placid manners, the unassumed good sense, and good nature of Ferdinand, that the idea of a separation, even on so short an acquaintance, was painful to them; the Baron therefore seized an opportunity, in the course of the evening, to express his wishes that his new friends would accompany him to Bavaria. He urged a number of inducements, backed by so many persuasions, that, had not the Count thought it essential to his interest to visit his own estate, and settle all his long accounts there, he could not have resisted an invitation so warm and pressing: Both Ferdinand and himself promised to pay him a speedy visit when they had executed their present unavoidable business. With this promise the Gentlemen were obliged to be contented, and when the hour arrived for their departure, they took leave with many expressions of esteem and gratitude;—of the Lady Eugenia, with respect and consideration, such as her misfortunes, and present laudable resolution, had a claim to.

Those remaining in the Castle, though they were much pleased with the Gentlemen, could scarcely regret their absence, as it relieved them from all concerns relative to the late Baron, the removal of whose body seemed to take from them a heavy pressure, and a painful inquietude.

Count M——— began to feel some uneasiness, that the messenger he had dispatched to his estate did not return by the time expected, and blamed himself for sending him, as his own appearance would have answered every purpose: Eugenia was very desirous of entering on her new plan, but she could not take Ferdinand from the Count in his present frame of mind, nor did she wish that the latter should accompany her. The following day all their anxiety was done away by the arrival of the expected messenger, and with him the Count's faithful old steward, who had resisted every attempt, persuasion and temptation, of those persons who, being next in succession to the Count, had long since been desirous to profit by his absence, and, under a supposition of his death, to take possession of the estates.

This honest servant produced the orders of his Lord, to hold the management of his fortune until his return to Suabia. He was ready to submit his accounts to their inspection, but he would not resign a trust delegated to him by his master, until convinced that master no longer existed. Apprehensive at length that some sinister means would be used against him, he was compelled to appeal to the Duke of Wirtemberg, who, on hearing both sides of the question, decreed that the management of the estates should remain in the steward's hands for seven years longer, subject to the inspection of the heir; after which period, if the Count did not appear to claim his rights, the property should pass into the hands of his heirs.

Eight months only of this limited seven years remained unexpired, and Mr. Duclos, the steward, had given himself up to despair, when the arrival of the Count's messenger transported him with joy; his eager desire to behold his master would not permit him to wait his return; but sending for a relation, in whom he could confide to remain with the housekeeper, he accompanied the man to the Castle, and seemed ready to expire with delight when admitted to the Count's presence.

Eugenia was not in the room, nor would she be seen by this man, who knew her when she resided with her father. She considered not the alteration which time and affliction had wrought in her face and form, which was such that the steward never would have recollected her; but as this could not in delicacy be urged to her by the Count, he made no objections to her wish of being absent. Ferdinand leaving Mr. Duclos and his master together, repaired to the apartment of Eugenia, whom he found in a flood of tears. He apologized for his intrusion, and was about to withdraw, when she earnestly called on him to return.

"Dear Sir," said she, when she had prevailed upon him to be seated, "you come most opportunely to my relief; I must leave this house to-morrow, indeed I must; the arrival of that good old man has recalled to my mind past scenes that overwhelm me with distress; I shall relapse into sorrow or madness if haunted with recollections that pain me to my very soul; a fugitive daughter, whose conduct perhaps hastened a parent's death, who died without blessing or forgiving me; he might be arbitrary, prejudiced and cruel, but he was my father, to whose goodness I owed every comfort in life, and to whose tenderness, to whose parental care of me in my infancy, I was indebted for my very existence: What sacrifices had not such a parent a right to demand? And what has been the consequences of my resistance to his will?"

Here she wept aloud. This was a subject that wrung the heart of Ferdinand, every word had sunk into his soul, and painful retrospections darted into his mind—Observing his silence, Eugenia resumed her discourse:—"The state you see me in cannot surprise you, but you have the power to tranquillize my spirits: I cannot support a parting interview—I cannot take leave of the Count—I have endeavoured to acquire fortitude, but the heart in such a moment cannot be trusted; let us go then, Sir, to-morrow at an early hour, I will leave a letter, and my clothes can be sent after me. Do not hesitate (pursued she) consider my peace, my reason may depend upon your compliance."

"Then, Madam," replied Ferdinand—"assure yourself of my obedience to your wishes; to-morrow I will attend you: I only fear that you will find the way more fatiguing than you are aware of, and that arriving at such a place on foot may excite curiosity, and give rise to unfavourable conjectures."

"Well," answered she, hastily, "make what arrangements you please, but let me go to-morrow, and go without taking leave of the — — — Count," she would have said, but the word died on her tongue, her voice faltered, and she turned from Ferdinand as he arose to leave her. He was greatly affected, and withdrew to consider on the best manner of obliging her. After much deliberation he conceived that he could not accomplish his wishes without communicating their intention to the Count, whose good sense, he trusted, would enable him to coincide with Eugenia's plan, and spare both her feelings and his own.

In this he was not mistaken, for when he had repeated the late conversation he had held with that Lady, the Count, though evidently much distressed, made no objection: "Her resolution being fixed (said he) I own to you that I think the sooner every thing can be settled the better, for her peace and mine. It is a hard struggle, my friend, to resign the woman we love, for ever, yet, as it is to be, delay can only increase the difficulty, and prolong sorrow.—To-morrow morning I will take Duclos to the village, or, if I cannot walk so far, into the Forest. Let Francis accompany you, and take such things as he can carry; there are now two horses in the stables."

"That is sufficient," exclaimed Ferdinand; "I will walk by the side of Eugenia's, and you may depend upon my care to see her safe into the Convent. We may possibly not return for the night; should it be so, entertain no apprehensions for our safety."

"And must I see Eugenia no more?" asked the Count, with a melancholy air.

"If you wish it, and think it right to indulge yourself with another interview," answered Ferdinand, "an interview that, under the present circumstances, must be painful to both, you certainly may go to her apartment: I presume not to advise, you must be the best judge of the consequences."

"Well then," said the other, with a deep sigh, "I submit to reason, nor will I wound her feelings for the gratification of a moment, which must be equally afflictive to both.—May Heaven restore her peace, and then I cannot be wholly miserable!" He left Ferdinand at those words, whose sympathizing heart felt deeply for this unfortunate pair, and was not sorry they had resolution enough to avoid a last distressing interview. The following day every thing was arranged for the departure of Eugenia; she seemed to have collected all her fortitude for the occasion, and in the hurry of the moment to have forgotten the sacrifice she had made.

On their arrival at the Monastery, Ferdinand seized a moment to recommend Claudina and his child to her notice, and to request that, as she had promised to write one letter, under cover to him, a week after her residence in the Convent, she would afford him all the information she could gain relative to those dear objects. Father Ambrose being informed of the Lady's arrival soon made his appearance, and, at Eugenia's request, proceeded with her to the Convent, where she was expected. The parting between her and Ferdinand was very affecting: He bowed upon her hand; "Adieu, my amiable friend," was all he could utter.

"May Heaven bless you," replied she, "remember our common friend, and may peace and happiness be the portion of both!"

When the gates of the Convent opened, grating on their hinges, and the Porteress appeared, Ferdinand's heart beat tumultuously: "What (thought he) have I a wife, a child, within those walls, and cannot I be permitted to have one look?" At the instant, when he was about to speak, to supplicate the Porteress for permission to see his child, the gates closed, and he remained alone. Throwing a reproaching melancholy look at the building as the grave of his affections, he returned to the Monastery, and obtained an interview with Father Joseph: That good man sought to tranquillize his mind, and promised to enter into a correspondence with him when a place should be fixed on for the conveyance of their letters.

In less than an hour Father Ambrose returned, and said he left the Lady apparently much satisfied with her reception and situation. Ferdinand having nothing to detain him, and the time allowing of their return by day-light, he took leave of the Fathers, and to the no small joy of Francis returned to the Castle, where they arrived safely and unexpectedly to the Count, whose anxiety was greatly relieved by the presence of Ferdinand.

The letter which Eugenia left for the Count, it is unnecessary to repeat, as it was only expressive of those sentiments before mentioned, calculated to inspire him with resignation and fortitude.

Mr. Duclos was very urgent with his master to accompany him back, as it would be requisite that he should appear to silence the claims of his relations, and give a sanction to the future proceedings of Duclos, that he might remain unmolested. Ferdinand was of the same opinion, and, after various consultations, it was settled that the Solitary Castle and Estate should be let, if a tenant could be found for it; that the Count and Ferdinand should return with the steward, and after the former had surveyed his estate, and finished his business with Duclos and the tenants, the two Gentlemen should proceed to Vienna, and attend the opening of the campaign. Mean time workmen were hired to repair the Castle, and render it more habitable. They were under some difficulties respecting Francis; he was too far advanced in life to bear the fatigue of travelling, and if they sent him to the village with a comfortable provision, the natural garrulity of age would lead him to talk of the strange events he had seen and heard of, which, among illiterate and superstitious people, might occasion such fears, and such exaggerations, as would very possibly prove injurious to the disposal of the estate, and the reputation of its owner. Frequent consultations were held upon the subject, and at length Francis was admitted to counsel, and asked how he wished to dispose of himself for the remainder of his days, when secured from future want?

"Ah!" replied he, "I am old and helpless, I have no relations living that I know of, nor any place to go to, except to the village, and I don't care much for any body there. I wish, methinks, I could lie at your Lordship's house with that there Gentleman (pointing to Duclos) he looks so good-humoured, and speaks so kindly; but I must go where your Honours please."

This answer of Francis's pleased the Count. "Well, my friend (said he) you shall then go with us; we will go slowly on the journey to accommodate you; a day or two on the road makes no great difference." Francis was profuse in his thanks, and tears bespoke his gratitude. He assured them of his silence respecting the recent events at the Castle; and now that his own destination was determined on, he exerted all his strength and abilities to assist the persons employed in the repairs. — Within a few days after this, a respectable farmer offered to lease the estate; terms were soon concluded upon between them, and immediate possession was to be given; they only waited to hear from Eugenia, and at the promised time her letter came.

The contents gave pleasure, surprise and pain; it breathed a spirit of serenity and contentment. She had entered upon the strict observance of the Convent rules; they grew easy and delightful; her mind was more tranquil, her soul superior to earthly considerations, farther than her wishes for the happiness of her friends, of which the Count was the dearest. She had already met with two Ladies who had kindred souls, in whose society she looked forward to much comfort and pleasure. Her friend Ferdinand would not be surprised to hear that one of these Ladies was the person he had requested to see; but she believed he would be astonished to be told that Lady was not Claudina; a coincidence of circumstances had led to a false conjecture on both sides, for the Lady had also been deceived; but it was a certain fact this Lady's name was Theodosia; that she was a stranger to this country, under the most melancholy circumstances from unparalleled ill-treatment, and the child with her was only six months old. — This was all she was allowed to say on the subject, but Ferdinand might be assured, as a solemn truth, that Claudina was not in that Convent, nor ever had been. She then recommended to him an endeavour to banish from his memory a woman he must be assured was unworthy of his regard; nor to waste his time, and ruin his health, in a fruitless pursuit of developing a mystery which could afford him no pleasure: She besought him to attach himself to her dear Count, and in the reciprocal delights of mutual friendship, find that peace and happiness which she daily implored Heaven to bestow on them."

This was nearly the contents of her letter. The Count had generosity enough to rejoice in her tranquillity, though it cost him dear; but the surprise and anxiety of Ferdinand cannot be described. He had established it in his mind for a certainty, that Claudina resided in that Convent, and from thence adduced pleasure to himself when Eugenia had readily agreed to go there, from the expectation of obtaining some intelligence of the former through her; astonished indeed he was, and lost in conjecture. He knew Eugenia too well to believe she would attempt an imposition, or be capable of any duplicity under her present frame of mind; yet it was so extraordinary that the message he sent, and the answer returned, should coincide so exactly with his situation, that the more he reflected, the greater was his surprise, and the more severe his disappointment.

The Count found himself obliged to smother his own feelings, that he might administer consolation to his friend, who, although he could not hope to receive any pleasing intelligence, had Claudina actually been in the Convent, yet felt additional disquietude from being again in a state of ignorance as to her residence. He now determined to see Ernest, to visit his brother for a few days whilst the Count was settling his affairs at his Castle. This design he communicated to him, and could not be persuaded to relinquish.

Both Gentlemen having written to Eugenia, and the tenant being ready to take possession of the Solitary Castle, within a few days they took leave of a place where the Count had known so much misery. His heart felt comparatively light as he quitted it, and but for the painful separation from his dear and much-regretted companion, he would have left that part of the country with transport. Mr. Duclos, Old Francis, and one servant, attended them; they travelled slowly, for the Count was still weak, and Francis very infirm.

When they arrived at a part of the country where the road separated, one direction to the East towards Stutgard, and the other in a direct line to Renaud Castle, a little to the South West of Baden, the Gentlemen halted; the Count once more earnestly pressed his friend to accompany him: "For a few days only shall we be separated," said Ferdinand; "I am mortified that I cannot ask you to my brother's Castle, but an unexpected, perhaps an unwelcome guest, myself, I dare not run the hazard of your reception: If I find a welcome, I will immediately dispatch a messenger to you; if on the contrary I meet neither a brother or a friend, within eight days I will insure to myself the possession of the latter by joining you. Whatever may be my reception, you may depend upon me to accompany you on the earliest notice." Satisfied with this assurance, the Count only requested that the servant might attend him, as he would then have a proper person either to send to him, or to wait upon Ferdinand, when he gave him the pleasure of his company. This friendly desire being complied with, they parted reluctantly, both agitated and occupied by unpleasant reflections.

That same evening, at the close of day, Ferdinand reached his brother's mansion. — He rang at the gate, and when the servant appeared, asked, in the same moment as he dismounted, if Count Rhodophil was at home? The man instantly recollected his voice, and drew near to him: "Heavens bless you, Sir!" exclaimed he, in an accent of joy, "how glad I am to see you returned! No, Sir, my master is not at home, but Mr. Ernest is, and he will be joyful indeed." Ferdinand recommended the servant with him, whose name was Anthony, to his care, and took his way to the steward's apartment. Knocking at the door, the old Gentleman bid him "come in."

"An unexpected friend salutes you," said Ferdinand, as he opened the door. The voice announced him, and in a moment he caught the good Ernest in his arms. — Wonder and joy precluded speech, and the large drops run down his cheeks as he pressed the former to his breast. — "My dear, dear master!" he exclaimed.

"My worthy friend!" returned Ferdinand, "you are doubtless surprised to see me; but I seized a favourable opportunity to see my dear boy, and express my thanks to you." He had taken a seat as he spoke, and requested Ernest to resume his: "I have a thousand things to say, and many questions to ask; but tell me, I conjure you, how affairs stand in this Castle; I find my brother is away from home."

"Yes," replied Ernest, "I believe he is on his daily visit to the Lady Bonhorff."

"But," said Ferdinand, "he wrote to me that he was very low spirited, and had some thoughts of travelling; the former you confirmed."

"True," returned Ernest, "and he is still at times seemingly much oppressed, yet I have reason to believe his design of marrying is in a speedy way of being concluded, from the alterations and preparations ordered, and making in the house."

"Most cordially I wish him happiness," said Ferdinand, adding, with a sigh, "May his union prove a more fortunate one than mine has been; at least he will have no act of disobedience to reflect upon, nor be a weight upon his spirits."

"Ah! Sir," cried Ernest, 'there are more causes for being unhappy than one, every man has his share of troubles; but, my dear master, you told me you had found a friend, thank Heaven for that." Ferdinand then briefly mentioned his ramble to the Count's Castle, whom he described as a Gentleman retired from society on account of great misfortunes; but that his arrival had made a change in the Count's sentiments, and they were now going to Vienna to attend the opening of the campaign, and he hoped a friendly intercourse would tend to lighten their mutual misfortunes: "You, my good friend (added he) have it much in your power to alleviate mine, if you choose to do so." — "Pray, Sir," cried Ernest, "don't break my heart by such a reflection; what I have sworn to I must fulfil; and do your faithful servant the justice to believe, that, could I communicate one word of comfort or pleasure, I would not with-hold it a moment; for Heaven's sake therefore cease to think on what is past. Let me tell you that master Charles is all you can wish, and that a day will come when every thing concerning Madam Claudina will be cleared up, although you never will see her more."

"Good Heavens!" exclaimed Ferdinand, "what a torture is suspense! Tell me, however, is she in a Convent?"

"At present," replied he, "she is not; but in a situation equally dead to the world, and to you: But now, Sir, how do you mean to meet your brother?"

"That depends upon him," answered the other; "I come not to ask favours of him, I have a noble friend, who is more than a brother already; but the voice you mentioned as having alarmed him, that strange unaccountable circumstance, has it disturbed any other part of the family?"

"Never," replied Ernest. "Our master's questions, the night he was frightened, gave some strange suspicions to the servants, which were strengthened by a recollection of the odd occurrences about Madam Claudina; but I endeavoured to dispel their apprehensions by several arguments between jest and earnest, and if they still entertain any doubts or fears, they do not express them openly. Last week, my dear master, I gave a sealed packet into the hands of my nephew, directed for you, with a strict charge never to let it pass his hands until my death, without my consent should be first obtained.

"I mention this for your guide whenever the event takes place that closes all my earthly concerns, and I conjure you, Sir, not to let my nephew be ignorant of your residence wherever you go."

This request Ferdinand assured him he would observe. They then entered into a detail of family occurrences, until the bell at the gate announced his brother's return. Ferdinand hastened to the parlour, and there waited the Count's approach, as he supposed the servant would mention his arrival.

CHAPTER IX

In a few minutes Count Rhodophil entered the room, and with an exclamation of joy embraced his brother, which was as cordially returned. For a moment Ferdinand forgot all past events, and his brother's coolness on former occasions; the seeming since- rity, and warm reception he so little expected, vibrated to his heart, and he felt a true fraternal affection. The Count, after many expressions of joy to see his beloved Ferdinand returned, inquired what had happened to procure him a pleasure so little hoped, though so much wished for? Ferdinand, who had recovered from the momentary transport, was very limited in his confidence, nor gave the smallest hint relative to the story of Count M— — —; he avowed his intention of returning to the army accompanied by that Nobleman, and that the visit, which affection and gratitude demanded at Renaud Castle, was chiefly owing to the design his brother had intimated of travelling, in consequence of indifferent health and bad spirits; he was agreeably surprised (he added) to observe in the Count's appearance no traits of either the one or the other."

"I am indeed much better," answered the Count, "and (smiling) have some thoughts of making a different arrangement in my household, which will at least suspend, if not entirely supersede any necessity for a journey. In short (added he) I am going to be married, and what will perhaps surprise you, to the very Lady once offered to you, the Lady Amelia Bonhorff! What say you to this, brother?"

"That I most sincerely wish you happy," replied Ferdinand.

"Permit me to observe," said Rhodophil, hastily, 'that you shall not be injured by my marriage; I will still be your banker, and answer all your demands, as I know you are very moderate."

"I am much obliged to you," returned Ferdinand; "but one motive which brought me here is, to thank you for all past favours, and to acquaint you that henceforth I shall make no farther demands on your generosity."

"What do you mean?" asked the other.

"I mean that I have accepted an offer to share the fortune of a friend, not as a dependant, for his soul disdains the idea of conferring favours; but he has given me a title to an independence, that we may be on an equality, and considers himself as the obliged person by my acceptance."

"A rare instance of generosity indeed," cried the Count, much disconcerted; "you are wonderfully fortunate in acquiring such a friend: But, my dear brother, are you well acquainted with the character of Count M— — —, for I suppose he is the man? Are you sure no injurious or unworthy design lurks under the semblance of generosity? He binds you in chains by this free-will offering stronger and heavier far than a state of dependence, which you can at any time reject without reproach; know your man well therefore before you decline the kindness of a brother, and fix yourself the slave of a stranger."

"I thank you for your caution," answered Ferdinand, coolly; "but I do know the man, and can read his heart, where there is neither guile nor duplicity. There are some minds that are superior to falsehood or reserve, such are open to every intelligent person; his is enveloped by no dark schemes, he has no points to carry, no errors to disguise, under a semblance of friendship."

"Well, well," cried the Count, greatly confused, which he sought to hide by a haughty air of contempt, "enough of your faultless man, I wish he may prove a disinterested friend. How long pray may I flatter myself you propose to stay in the Castle?"

"Three days," answered Ferdinand, "if you will permit me to do so."

"Most certainly, if you can spare me so much of your company: I am sorry you will not remain here long enough to witness my nuptials, which will take place within three weeks."

"O, Rhodophil!"—cried Ferdinand, wounded to the soul by a painful recollection, "O, Rhodophil! may your marriage be fortunate and happy; blind, inconsiderate and rash, I have dearly suffered for the impetuosity of my passions. You speak not, you ask not after Claudina, yet surely her strange conduct, her sudden disappearance, must sometimes have a place in your thoughts.—Did you never in my absence make any inquiries concerning her?"

"Why should I?" answered he, in a quick tone, "What expectations could I form, that, if she absented herself from you, any information would be granted to me?—In short, brother, I wish you to forget an ungrateful woman, and therefore I never shall revive the subject." Supper being then announced precluded farther conversation, and Ferdinand retired early to his apartment.

He retired, but not to sleep; a thousand bitter thoughts obtruded to agonize his mind; he had carefully examined Rhodophil; he saw confusion, restlessness and perturbation, in every word and look; there was a mystery hung about him that he could not penetrate; yet he saw enough to convince him there existed no brotherly affection in the Count, and that he was not a little pleased to get rid of one he considered as a tax upon his honour and generosity. He next reverted to Claudina, then to the voice, which, though he was not credulous in the belief of supernatural missions, yet was it wholly unaccountable in any other light. He passed the night without rest, and when day-light appeared, gladly left his bed, and repaired to that part of the Castle inhabited by Ernest.

The good old man had just opened his window shutters, and was surprised to see Ferdinand thus early, who entered without ceremony, where he could insure to himself a welcome. They had a long conversation, as the Count was no early riser. Ernest mentioned the shepherdess and her father, with whom Ferdinand had passed a night in the cottage under the hanging rocks: The steward had provided them with a safer and a more comfortable habitation, and they blessed the day which brought the strange Gentleman to the side of the rivulet. Ferdinand declared his intention of going after breakfast to see his son, and of leaving the Castle the following day.

"Will not the Count be displeased that you shorten the time you first purposed to stay?" asked Ernest.

"I believe not," replied Ferdinand; "my preference can give neither pleasure nor information; if he is not sincere in his professions of affection, he will be glad to be relieved from the irksomeness of dissembling, and of beholding a man whose penetration he may fear; if on the contrary, I do him injustice, he can set no value on my company, when he knows I have preferred a stranger, by declining all pecuniary favours, and have consented to owe obligations to another;—thus, every way, he can derive no satisfaction from my being here, and he has sufficient employment in his new prospects to engross all his attention." Ernest subscribed to the justice of this opinion, and Ferdinand soon after attended his brother.

A very general and uninteresting conversation took place at table; both seemed equally desirous of avoiding particular subjects, and when breakfast was over Ferdinand ordered his horse, and set off to see his little boy. The meeting was truly affecting; poor Charles hung about his dear father, and repeatedly cried, "My poor mamma is dead, Yes, indeed, my poor mamma is dead!"—Stung to the heart by the infantile tone of sorrow which accompanied these words, and the reflection that his child was deprived of all those maternal cares so necessary at his early age. Ferdinand could not repress his emotions, but pressed his boy to his bosom, whilst the big drops fell on his face.

Mr. Dunloff, the nephew of Ernest, now entered the room, and relieved both. To him the anxious father recommended his little Charles in the most moving terms, beseeching him to be a father to his child, and to watch over the first dawning of reason, that, as his mind expanded, his ideas might be properly directed to the practice of truth, humanity, and a proper pride to disdain a mean or unworthy action. "Pardon me, my dear Sir (added he) for presuming to dictate to you, but I am well convinced, that were children accustomed from the earliest dawn of reason to a strict observance of truth, humanity, and generosity; if the virtues were inculcated with the same care, which is generally bestowed to teach them different languages before they are capable of understanding their own properly; if the morals of children were more attended to as the foundation for future improvements, we should see wiser and happier men than are generally met with; but unhappily, in most seminaries for education, the useful is neglected, because the shining, or rather superficial part, is supposed to reflect most credit on the master."

Mr. Dunloff received those remarks of Ferdinand with much complacency, and assured him, that whilst he presided over the child, it should be his unremitting study to do his duty in the strictest sense of the word, by forming the mind, as well as the manners, of his young pupil, as his reason appeared to expand. "I shall teach him to love me (added Mr. Dunloff) and when I have obtained his affection my work will be very easy, for he will fear to offend."

Ferdinand was perfectly satisfied with this Mr. Dunloff: "Ah! (thought he) here is the counterpart of our good Ernest; my boy, under his care, will prove a worthy man." After spending a few hours with little Charles and his master, Ferdinand tore himself from the caresses of the former, and returned, oppressed with melancholy, to his brother's house.

In the evening at supper Ferdinand announced his intention of pursuing his route to the Castle of his friend on the following day. Rhodophil made some faint efforts to detain him, but his manner wanted that cordiality which might have been expected from a brother, and therefore the other found no difficulty in persevering. He arose at a very early hour the next morning, that he might have an hour's conversation with Ernest. — The good old man deeply regretted the necessity which obliged him to leave the mansion of his forefathers, but in the present state of things he could not urge his stay. The conversation that ensued it is unnecessary to repeat, as it afforded no information to Ferdinand, and consisted chiefly of assurances on the part of Ernest to watch over his interests, and to pay a fatherly attention to his little son.

When the brothers met to take leave, Rhodophil assumed an air of affection and concern, which Ferdinand really felt. He had been for many years accustomed to consider Rhodophil as a brother and a generous friend. The late strange occurrences had deprived him of every comfort, the coldness of Rhodophil, and a suspicion of his duplicity, completed his misfortunes, and obliged him to turn his eyes towards a stranger for every future expectation of peace and support; but the natural and habitual affection he had so long indulged could not be eradicated entirely, and when Rhodophil embraced him his heart glowed with tenderness. "I leave you, Rhodophil, and perhaps for ever; if I die, remember my child; the prospect that now awaits you, may in a short time inform you, what the feelings of a parent are. May you never experience the agonizing pangs I have suffered; but when you become a husband and a father, think of, and pity me."

His emotions became too powerful to proceed; his brother was still more agitated; with difficulty he pronounced a "farewell," and turned quickly into another apartment. "What! (thought Ferdinand) is he really grieved? Then have I wronged my brother!" That moment Ernest, who had been a distant witness of this scene, observing the looks of Ferdinand, and guessing at his sentiments, drew near to him: "Heavens bless you, my honoured Sir, doubt not of its protection;" adding, in a low voice, "be not deceived by appearances, pursue your plan." — This roused Ferdinand from a momentary self-reproach, and shaking the friendly hand that was humbly extended: "I thank you, my good friend, and will endeavour to deserve your good wishes;" then lowering his voice, "I will remember your admonitions." No more passed; Ferdinand, attended by the servant who had accompanied him, pursued his route to the Castle of Count M— — —, which was about thirty miles to the East of Baden, between that and Stutgard, the capital of Suabia.

The wind was high, and the cold very piercing, which retarded his speed a good deal, and finding it would be impossible to reach the end of his journey that night, they hastened to a small village about twelve miles short of it, and arrived, just as the day closed in, at a mean looking inn, at the extremity of a few scattered houses, and, as they were informed, the only house of accommodation in the village. Here, to Ferdinand's great mortification, he found already accommodated Mr. D'Alenberg, a German Nobleman, his daughter, and several servants; in short, there were already many more persons than could be conveniently lodged in that place, and they were consulting in what manner to dispose of their company, when the arrival of Ferdinand and his servant threw them into fresh difficulties.

The master of the house came out to inform them they could have no room there. A violent drift of snow came suddenly on, the night was dark, and they had a wood to pass through; these circumstances made it impossible to proceed. — "At least (cried Ferdinand) permit me to sit by your kitchen fire; I can be contented without a bed, but to go on a journey of some miles now, you must see, cannot be thought of."

"I am sorry it cannot be thought about (answered the man) but I know it must be done; for, indeed master, neither in kitchen or cellar have I room for man or beast, be the weather what it will." The fall of snow increasing, Ferdinand again applied both to his humanity and interest, and to the latter he spoke so forcibly, that at length he cried, "Well, well, Gentlemen, you must come in, if you insist upon it, the house is too full already, some must turn out somewhere, and you may take your chance with the rest."

Ferdinand hardly attended to the end of this speech, for hastily dismounting he desired the man to take care of his servant and the horses, whilst he made his way to the kitchen, as they called a very miserable small room, already, as the landlord had declared, filled with servants, and two or three other passengers. He had suffered too much from the weather to be fastidious either as to the company or accommodations, and some of the servants observing his situation, and struck by his appearance, drew back, and made way for his advance to the fire.

"I beg," said Ferdinand, in a courteous manner, 'that I may displace no one, I only wish for a covering from this dreadful weather, and not to incommode any person." — This address procured him more room, every one seemed ready to give way to a Gentleman so considerate; so true it is, that gentle and complaisant manners, and a conduct free from pretensions and arrogance, are sure to be allowed much more consequence than they give up; for the mind of man, in every situation, naturally revolts against the demands of pride and insolence, but willingly show respect where the manners prove their claim to it, and not the look or tone of assumption.

One of the servants felt the rights of Ferdinand, and immediately went to the apartment occupied by his master and young Lady, with a report so much in favour of the Gentleman in the kitchen, that it procured him an invitation from Mr. D'Alenberg to "partake of his fire-side and ordinary supper."

Ferdinand saw by the pleasure with which this message was delivered to him, that he was indebted for it to the favourable report of the servant; he therefore accepted the invitation without hesitating, and requested that he would permit his servant to occupy some corner of the room with the present company. This desire was readily accorded to, and he was leaving the kitchen preceded by the servant, when he beheld the figure of an aged man in one corner, whose head was supported by a female, but whether old or young could not be discerned, as she was wrapped up in a large cloak, and her head dress was drawn quite over her face.

Ferdinand stopped: — "Is the man ill?" asked he.

"Very ill indeed," was answered in a low, tremulous voice; "but I believe all will soon be over."

"Good God!" returned he, "is he so reduced as to give room for such a supposition, and is there no bed he can be put into?" At that moment the landlord came up: — "You see (said he, addressing the woman) my rooms are so crowded, that I cannot possibly let you stay here; I have no room for sick folks." The woman raised her head: — "What would you have me do, he cannot move?"

"Do!" cried he, "why let somebody help to take him into the out-house, he can't die here."

Ferdinand turned full upon him, and was going to speak, when a sudden groan from the woman, who fell towards him senseless, and dropped the head she had supported, stopped him from speaking. He caught her in his arms, as the servant did the old man, who, to his great terror, proved to be lifeless. All present crowded round those moving objects; Ferdinand conveyed the woman to a seat, and supported her until, by the assistance of water thrown in her face, and forced into her mouth, she began to shew signs of life. In doing this they were obliged to remove her head dress, and open her cloak. — Greatly was every one astonished to behold a young and lovely female, whose complexion, hands and arms, exhibited a delicacy but little suited to her garb or situation.

There is something attractive in beauty, even to the most vulgar souls, and though I would hope the humanity of every man would be excited towards objects in so deplorable a state, yet it is most certain, that when the young woman's face was discovered, all eagerly flew to administer relief, and the buzz of pity was general through the room, except with the landlord, who was rubbing his face with vexation, and exclaimed — "A pretty piece of business this! Here is a dead man, no hole to put him in, nor any one to bury him: Come, come, carry him to the stable for the present."

The unfortunate girl, for she appeared to be not more than nineteen, had just recovered sufficient recollection to hear those words. — She sprang from the encircling arm of Ferdinand, threw herself on the body, and exclaimed, in a wild, piercing tone: — "To the stable! Great God! the stable! Never, never shall my father be so degraded. O! that I could but expire with him; for me, for me, he died!"

Her heart-wounding shrieks brought out Mr. D'Alenberg and his daughter, who stood shocked at the scene before them; she had sunk on the floor, and dragged the lifeless body on her lap. On their entrance she looked up with such an expression of woe and horror, that both involuntarily started back; but suddenly the young Lady exclaimed, — "Good Heavens! Do I not see Louisa Hautweitzer?"

"Yes," said the other, in a tone of voice which touched every one present, "Yes, I was called Louisa Hautweitzer, but now I am nobody; there (putting her hand to her father's cheek) there is the author of my being, he exists no more, and I am a wretch without a name, a home, or a parent. Pray, pray, afford us one small spot of earth, bury us together!" She threw her head down on the face of the deceased, with sighs that seemed to burst her heart-strings.

Miss D'Alenberg took her hand, and addressing her father, "My dear Sir, this young Lady is an old school-fellow of mine, good, amiable, and of genteel birth, save her, pray save her from despair and death!"

The old Gentleman wanted no persuasions to serve the unhappy; he ordered his attendants to carry her into his apartment, but she clung to the body, screaming, "No one should carry her father to a stable;" that he was compelled to have the body taken there also. Ferdinand attended, and Mr. D'Alenberg ordered the priest of the village to be sent for, that he might, through his means, procure a place for the deceased to be carried to, and give some assistance to the unfortunate young woman.

On their entrance into the room the body was placed on two chairs, and Miss D'Alenberg administered wine and drops, which fortunately she had in her pocket, with the most soothing expressions of tenderness to Louisa.

The poor afflicted at length shed a torrent of tears, which greatly relieved her; kissing the hand of the young Lady, "I feel your kindness, but I am undeserving of it; my imprudence, my credulity, has destroyed my father, and made me miserable for ever!" Before any reply could be made the priest appeared, and being informed of this strange event, and assured by Mr. D'Alenberg that he would be answerable for every expense, the priest readily consented to receive the body at his house, and to take care of the young woman for the present: Understanding also how greatly they were crowded, he offered to accommodate Miss D'Alenberg with a bed, and as his house was but a few yards distance, and the hostess could lend her cloaks, with the permission of her father, she readily accompanied the unhappy Louisa, who seemed mechanically to follow the body of her father without being at all curious, or even heeding the conversation that had passed. Ferdinand requested leave to attend them with the servants to the house, and taking leave of them at the door, returned, as desired, to Mr. D'Alenberg.

The old Gentleman saluted him with much complacency: "This is a melancholy business," said he; "my daughter seems much interested for her young acquaintance, and indeed the poor girl's situation is very pitiable. I am sorry that a particular engagement will oblige us to leave this place tomorrow: I know not what can be done for this young woman, as her circumstances are unknown to us."

"It is most probable, Sir," answered the other, 'that your daughter will gain every information that may be necessary; if she is distressed by pecuniary wants, I will most gladly contribute my share towards her relief; the heart-felt blow she has sustained, time and reason only can reconcile her to bear with patience and resignation."

Mr. D'Alenberg paid Ferdinand a compliment on his humanity, and having learned which road he was taking, seemed not a little pleased that they were going the same way. "My house (said he) is about twenty miles the other side of Stutgard; I have concluded a very advantageous marriage for my daughter, during a visit that I have been making to a friend, and am now hastening home to forward the necessary preparations: I shall, however, borrow a few hours in the morning to see what can be done for the peace and comfort of this poor orphan." Ferdinand had made the same resolution, and after partaking of a very poor supper, he retired to take possession of the bed intended for the young Lady.

He arose at an early hour, and was just drinking his coffee when he was joined by Mr. D'Alenberg. They quickly finished their breakfast, and proceeded to the priest's house, where they met the young Lady with every mark of sorrow on her countenance.

"Ah! Sir," cried she to her father, "poor Louisa is extremely ill: A physician was called in about an hour ago by the good father here, and he pronounces her to be in a violent and dangerous fever; I cannot leave her in this situation, without either a relation or a friend; I knew her, I esteemed her, in happier days, it would be inhuman to forsake her now."

"Indeed it would," answered the good Mr. D'Alenberg; "we will see what can be done to reduce this fever, and then get her removed to our house; if she is only unfortunate, we will protect her; if her conduct has been faulty, she shall be placed out of temptation, and means afforded her to atone for past errors."

"My dear, my generous father!" cried the young Lady, in a tone of exultation, "you know not how happy this kind intention of yours makes your Theresa!"

Ferdinand, who had scarcely looked at Miss D'Alenberg the preceding evening during his concern for Louisa, and who was on his entrance engaged in speaking to the priest, found his attention suddenly engaged by the animated voice behind him; he turned quick round, and met a countenance so interesting, so illumined by a glow of humanity and tenderness, that his eyes were fixed on the young Lady's face, until her blushes, and the confusion with which she turned aside from his eager gaze, made him sensible of his rudeness. It was the enthusiasm of the moment, for the sweet accents of pity and humanity vibrated to the heart of Ferdinand. Mr. D'Alenberg declared he would freely retard his journey for that day, until some information relative to the health and situation of the young woman could be rendered satisfactory to his daughter, and Ferdinand, who was not limited for a day or two, readily offered to remain there also, as he was equally desirous, to the utmost of his abilities, to share in the pleasure of assisting the unfortunate. The priest, who happily was a man of a good and humane heart, voluntarily made an offer of his humble accommodations to their utmost extent. His sister, an ancient maiden, resided with him, and was equally good and charitable as her brother. Mr. D'Alenberg desired to be at the expense of the burial of poor Louisa's father, and Ferdinand hastily requested the physician might attend at his expense. Miss D'Alenberg was permitted to remain there, and the two Gentlemen took a walk round the village until their return to the miserable inn, where they had ordered dinner. As the Castle of Count M— — — lay in the route of his companion, and the landlord was ill prepared to receive or entertain so many persons, Ferdinand sent off his servant with a cursory mention to the Count of the cause that detained him on the road for a day or two, when he should have the advantage of a large escort within a mile of his house.

Towards the evening a message from Miss D'Alenberg carried both Gentlemen to the priest's. They found her in extreme agitation; Louisa had been delirious for several hours, but by copious bleedings, and other applications, now lay more composed: "But, my dear father," added the young Lady, "you will not wonder at my emotions, when I inform you that in the height of her delirium she continually called on Count Wolfran, and in such terms as imply a degree of intimacy very incompatible with his professions to another."

"You indeed surprise me," answered the old Gentleman; "but be not too credulous, my dear Theresa, nor judge rashly on slight presumptions; I hope this young creature will get better, mean time I wish to be informed who she is, and what you know of her."

"My dear Sir," said she, "very soon after I was placed at Ausburgh, Louisa Hautweitzer came there as a boarder; her father was an officer in the Imperial service; she made a very genteel appearance, and was much esteemed throughout the Convent. — As I was her elder by at least three years, she paid me great respect and attention, which I returned by a very sincere attachment. — Four years we continued together. About that time her father came to fetch her from the Convent: I had understood her mother died when she was a child, and she appeared surprised and sorry to leave us, as she was not more than sixteen, and rather too young to conduct her father's family. We parted with regret, and she desired to correspond with me; but from that day I never heard of her, although many of the boarders made inquiries among their friends, which all proved fruitless, as we knew not where her father resided.

"I left the Convent about six months after, and frequently, when I wrote to my companions, inquired if any information had been gained of Louisa; but no one had obtained the least intelligence, and I have often thought it was a very singular circumstance. It is now near three years since I saw her, and it is certain some uncommon misfortunes must have reduced her father to that poverty which is apparent in the dress of Louisa, and the situation in which we met with them. Last night, when I accompanied her to her room, she kissed my hand with an energy that surprised me. — "Dear Miss D'Alenberg, I deserve not the honour of your attention; I am an unfortunate wretch, a victim to my own credulity, and the baseness of a perjured man; my follies, for sure they were not crimes, yet why should I seek to soften those errors that have eventually destroyed my dear unhappy father! There, there," cried she, in extreme agitation, "is the climax of my miseries!'

She fell into violent hysterics, and recovered only to experience a temporary madness which brought on a terrible fever for many hours. During this suspension of reason she raved on Count Wolfran, called him the "destroyer of her peace, and the murderer of her father." Then again she exclaimed, "Heaven was a witness of our union; I am, I am, your wife!" In short, Sir, I cannot repeat every expression, nor is it necessary, enough was said to convince me that she has been very ill treated, and to determine on being perfectly acquainted with every circumstance relative to her intimacy with the Count, previous to any preparations for an event, which possibly may never take place."

"I cannot blame your resolution," answered Mr. D'Alenberg; "I am equally anxious with yourself to have this affair elucidated; if, indeed, we are deceived in the Count's character, no prospects of rank, or fortune, shall induce me to entrust him with the happiness of my Theresa." The entrance of Mrs. Dolnitz, the priest's sister, changed the subject; the Gentlemen paid her many compliments on the humanity of her brother, and her kindness to Louisa. She was a woman of plain sense, with a very good heart, and appeared to be much gratified that she had the power of being useful to a fellow creature. "This poor village (said she) affords no accommodations but in our

house and the inn; you must experience great inconvenience
there I have no doubt, as very few persons lodge in it but from
necessity.—I am sorry we can only entertain Miss, and the sick
young woman; but our power is more limited than our wishes
and good-will, for my brother is one of the best men in the
world, he is truly the father of all his flock. I beg your pardon
for saying so much, but when I speak of my brother I could talk
for ever."

"I honour you, Madam, for your feelings," said Mr.
D'Alenberg; "a good man is a theme that must please every
honest mind, and you cannot give us a better eulogium on your
own character, than by your praises of a worthy brother.
Heaven has conducted us to this spot, I trust, for our mutual
advantage." — — — Ferdinand spoke little, but his eyes said a
great deal, and his heart sympathized in every word of Mr.
D'Alenberg's. Mr. Dolnitz and the physician soon after joined
them; the latter had found his patient more calm, and the
extreme violence of the fever abated. They consulted on proper
measures for the interment of the deceased, when Louisa was
more composed to speak on the subject. Mr. D'Alenberg drew
the physician aside, Miss Theresa returned to the sick chamber:
Ferdinand therefore entered into a conversation with Mr.
Dolnitz, whose modest and unreserved manners, charity
without ostentation, and beneficence without a hope of reward,
from a very moderate income, denoted real piety and goodness
of heart. When the others joined them, Theresa's father drawing
a purse from his pocket, put it into the hands of Mr. Dolnitz,
saying at the same time, "My worthy Sir, you must permit me to
share with you in your charitable attentions. Be not offended, if,
knowing that your income is very inadequate to the
benevolence of your disposition, I entreat you to disburse this
money in whatever manner you please for the advantage of
those persons now in your house, or any others deserving or
wanting your donations."

"I will not decline the office of your almoner, Sir," replied
Mr. Dolnitz, respectfully; "but you must permit me to be
accountable to you for the disbursements; on no other condition
can I receive the trust."

"It must be as you please," answered the other. The
physician, who lived about two miles from the village, finding
the strangers were persons of consequence, offered the two
Gentlemen beds at his house, but they declined the civility; for
although their accommodations were extremely indifferent, yet,
as they were permitted to consider themselves at home in the
house of Mr. Dolnitz, they were very well reconciled to sleep at

the inn.

Ferdinand, indeed, began to consider himself as a useless person; the generosity of Mr. D'Alenberg left but little for him to do, and having no other interests but those of humanity towards the unfortunate Louisa, and as it appeared very probable that the others would be personally concerned in the events of her story, he was fearful it would betray rather an unwarrantable curiosity, than a concern for the melancholy objects that had at first engaged his attention, if he remained at the village. He was revolving this in his mind, and consequently looked very thoughtful, which Mr. D'Alenberg observing, said, "Are you not well, Sir, or has any thing particularly occurred to give you pain?" The other recovering from his reverie by this address, frankly confessed what had been his ideas, and given him that momentary thoughtfulness.

Pleased with his ingenuousness, the old Gentleman said, "I know not the nature of your engagements, or whether you are at liberty to spare us your company. If a day or two will not break in upon other plans, I do assure you, Sir, that you will make me very particularly happy, by obliging me with your conversation and residence here for the short time I hope, that I shall find it requisite to remain."

"You do me honour, Sir," replied he, "by the request, which will be a gratification to myself I have not the resolution to decline, and must trust to the kindness of a friend to allow me." They refused an invitation to supper, and returned to the inn, where Ferdinand gave a slight account of himself, as the brother of Count Rhodophil, and an officer in the Imperial service, now going to a friend, who was also about to join the army.

"Mr. D'Alenberg said, he was a widower with this only daughter, and a fortune sufficient for all their moderate demands, with a surplus for the service of the unfortunate. —"My daughter (said he) has chiefly resided in a Convent, until I thought her age and understanding were mature enough to preside at my table with ease and dignity to herself, and satisfaction to me. I have reason to be perfectly satisfied, and I must think very highly of the man to whom I would entrust the happiness of such a daughter; you have heard enough to understand, that in Count Wolfran I thought such a man had met my wishes. I cannot easily relinquish my hope; his external appearance was decidedly in his favour. The friend, at whose house we met, gave him the highest character, and on his judgment and word, I think, I can place implicit confidence. The exclamations uttered by this young woman in her delirium certainly give rise to unfavourable conjectures, and if on an investigation I discover such circumstances as must impede his marriage with Theresa, I confess to you that it will give me an infinite deal of sorrow, not only because it is an advantageous settlement, but for the honour of human nature I shall regret, that such an exterior, so much understanding, and so many plausible, and apparently, so many good qualities should cover a depraved heart."

"Justice demands an impartial and an unprejudiced hearing on both sides," replied Ferdinand, "before we should venture to condemn any person. If Louisa recovers sufficiently to disclose her situation, you will then, in some measure, be enabled to judge what degree of credit may be allowed to her, and give the Count an opportunity to vindicate his own character, if unjustly accused. Miss D'Alenberg appears to be a treasure no common mind can deserve; her beauty, which I believe is superior to most of her sex, I have scarcely remarked, for the heavenly goodness, and animated compassion, she has displayed towards a distressed and unfortunate young woman proves the excellence of her disposition, and entitles her to equal admiration and respect. Heaven forbid that such a mind should not meet with its kindred heart when united for life!"

The old Gentleman, charmed with the energy of Ferdinand's expressions, and delighted with the delicate praise bestowed on his child, felt a lively interest in his behalf, and ventured to inquire more minutely into his situation and prospects. Among other things he said, with a smile, "I do not suppose you are married." Ferdinand started; his whole frame was agitated; he attempted to answer, but his faltering tongue was incapable of uttering a word. Mr. D'Alenberg was surprised and concerned: "I beg your pardon (said he) if my impertinent curiosity has given you pain; be assured that I meant no offence, you will therefore confer an obligation on me, by obliterating from your memory the question I incautiously asked."

Ferdinand sensibly felt the politeness of Mr. D'Alenberg, and gladly availed himself of it for the present. The supposition had recalled many painful ideas, which he endeavoured to repress, and with a half-smothered sigh, that did not pass unobserved, he bowed, saying, "You are very obliging, Sir; there are certain questions which sometimes cannot be answered satisfactorily, and particular situations which cannot be explained, without entering into details tedious and uninteresting to a stranger. As a parent of such a daughter you must doubtless be exceedingly uneasy, until the expressions that fell from Louisa are explained to your satisfaction. — A short time, I hope, will elucidate them, for, if she is an ingenuous character, the generous humanity of Miss D'Alenberg will unlock her heart to repose a confidence in that young Lady, otherwise my conjectures will be less favourable of her than they now are."

"My opinion coincides with yours," answered the other, "and to-morrow, I think, will put an end to a suspense that I own gives me an infinity of concern. The evening passed in conversing on a variety of subjects, and when they separated for the night, each Gentleman retired with an increased good opinion of the other, and each internally was desirous of a more intimate acquaintance."

The morning came, and they had scarcely exchanged the customary salutations before a message came from Miss D'Alenberg, requesting the presence of her father, and from the messenger they learned that Louisa was much recovered.

As Ferdinand was not, nor indeed expected to be, included in the invitation to Mr. D'Alenberg, he was preparing to leave the room, after desiring his respects to the young Lady.

"How!" said the old Gentleman, "will you not accompany me?"

"Undoubtedly, Sir, if you wish me to do so. I am only apprehensive of being an intruder."

"No, no," replied the other, "by no means, we have no secrets; if Count Wolfran is worthy of my daughter, it is for his honour that you should know it; if on the contrary he proves to be a worthless character, it is equally proper that he should be exposed; therefore I beg you will go with me." Ferdinand readily assented; they quickly dispatched their breakfast, and set off for the house of Mr. Dolnitz.

They were received by the good Lady of the house with kindness and complacency.—She gave a very favourable account of her patient, the violence of her disorder was abated, and there was less turbulence in her expressions of grief.—"The consolatory attentions of Miss your daughter," said Mrs. Dolnitz to the old Gentleman, "has greatly aided the doctor's prescriptions, perhaps has been of more real service, as it appears the disorder of the body was occasioned by the emotions of the mind."

The entrance of the young Lady interrupted Mrs. Dolnitz, and she immediately withdrew. Miss D'Alenberg seemed a little embarrassed at the presence of Ferdinand, which he observed, and politely rose to leave the room.—"Stay one moment," cried Mr. D'Alenberg. "Tell me, Theresa, in two words, what am I to think of Count Wolfran?"

"As of a man unworthy of your notice, whose crimes disgrace his rank and character. I speak on good grounds, my dear Sir (added she;) Providence has preserved your daughter from infamy and wretchedness."

"Good Heavens!" exclaimed the Father, "can such an exterior, such an apparently polished mind, cover a depraved heart!"

"Yes," replied she, with some emotion, "his person and accomplishments are the superficial covering to veil the blackest designs, the most abandoned and selfish passions. The poor Louisa is a melancholy victim to his baseness, nor is she the only one; but I am writing down her story, which may be perused at leisure. What I have now to request is, that you will send off a servant with a few lines to Count Wolfran, just to say, 'that your daughter, having thoroughly investigated his character, declines, in the most decided manner, the favour he intended her of a hand, without a heart, or a name, to bestow.' Do not add another word, my dear father, his conscience will speak all the rest that may be necessary."

"I will comply with your wishes," answered Mr. D'Alenberg; "my dear Theresa, you are a heroine."

"No," said she, with a faint smile, "it requires no heroism to give up a man one despises. Count Wolfran is not the man a sensible mind can regret. When once the object we had been taught to esteem through false lights, is proved to be a man capable of the vilest duplicity, and most atrocious wickedness, our detestation and contempt must rise in proportion to the deception of our senses, and the heart can endure but little pain in shutting out such an object for ever."

She instantly changed the subject, seeing both Gentlemen were preparing to speak in admiration of her sentiments. She understood the expression of their eyes, therefore assuming a supplicating air, "My dear Sir," said she, "as my obligations to the unfortunate Louisa are infinite, as she is deprived of every friend, and in want of every necessary, though legally entitled to rank and fortune, I trust, you will not refuse to permit your Theresa to be her comforter and friend, to offer her an asylum in your house from the machinations of a base enemy."

"Undoubtedly, my dear girl, you are at liberty to make what offers you please, both for me and yourself; I will confirm them all, and shall look up with gratitude to Heaven for this signal preservation of my child from dishonour and misery."

Mr. Dolnitz now joined them, and was happy to hear of the favourable change in Louisa's fever. "Violent attacks (said he) have generally a speedy termination, and I rejoice that the event has turned in her favour. "I flatter myself," said Miss D'Alenberg, "that our joint attentions will quickly restore her, and that in a day or two we shall be able to take her in a carriage by easy stages to my father's house." After spending three hours in the house of the good priest, the Gentlemen returned to the inn: Here Ferdinand appeared to be under some degree of inquietude, which the old Gentleman remarked, and asked the cause of."

"I confess to you, Sir," answered the other, "that I feel the warmest admiration at the conduct of your daughter, and I am greatly interested for the unhappy Louisa. I am sensible of the honour and pleasure of your conversation; but I am under engagements to meet a friend, whose mind, from some untoward incidents, is but little calculated to bear disappointment, or to be left to its own reflections: Mortified as I am for the necessity which obliges me to leave you, I should not, however, forgive myself if I gave pain to my friend."

"Then you must leave me?" asked Mr. D'Alenberg.

"Indeed I must," replied Ferdinand,—"because it appears you will unavoidably remain here two or three days, and as I dare not intrude so long on the kindness of a friend, the sooner I leave you the better, as my regret to part from you must hourly increase."

"You are a worthy young man," returned Mr. D'Alenberg, "and it is no compliment to say, that I shall part from you with very great reluctance.

"After the deception I have lately met with, you could not wonder if I shut the door of my heart, afraid of entertaining another delusive guest; but I trust that I have not lost my charity, though my confidence may be more guarded. A countenance like your's is a letter of recommendation, and I do assure you, that you will do me a very particular pleasure, if you continue in this country, by bringing your friend in your hand, and insure to him a welcome reception at my house, on your account."

Ferdinand was not backward in his acknowledgments for this kindness, and having now broken the ice, gave orders for his departure immediately after dinner. At Mr. D'Alenberg's request he promised to write to him before his departure for Vienna, if he could not pay him a visit; and the former assured Ferdinand, that if the story of Louisa was of a fit nature to be communicated, he should certainly receive a transcript of it from him. "My daughter (added he) will be surprised and disappointed, when informed of your departure without taking leave."

"Be so good, Sir," said Ferdinand, "to make my best respects to Miss D'Alenberg; I have had so little opportunity of recommending myself to her notice, that I am not vain enough to believe my departure can for a moment engage her attention; but of her I shall ever think, with pleasure, admiration and respect. My best wishes also attend the unfortunate young Lady, she so humanely protects; to offer any pecuniary assistance would be an insult to her goodness, and your benevolence; but if on any future occasion either my purse, or personal services, can be useful, command me as freely, Sir, as you would do your own son."

"By Heaven!" exclaimed Mr. D'Alenberg, "I wish you was my son; but — — —."

"You do me infinite honour, Sir," said Ferdinand, interrupting him; "I hope you will find a man deserving of the appellation, and whoever he is, his destiny will be enviable, because he will be the happiest of mankind;" then rising from his seat, he inquired if his horse was ready? and being informed it waited for him at the door, he took a hasty, but an affectionate, leave of Mr. D'Alenberg, and followed by his good wishes, set off full speed for the Castle of Count M— — —.

CHAPTER X

He arrived at the Castle without any accident, and was joyfully received by his friend. "I began to complain of you," said the Count; "I am a selfish mortal it is true, for, as I heard from the servant you kindly sent forward, that you were engaged in an affair of distress and sickness, knowing the benevolence and sympathy of your heart, I ought not to have desired to monopolize such a disposition to myself."

"Indeed," replied Ferdinand, "you do me more credit than I deserve: I was merely a spectator of the benevolence of others, without even presuming to offer my mite when I left the unfortunate young woman you have been told of. I left her, indeed, in much better hands, and feeling myself useless, when I understood she was out of danger, I hastened away; though I confess to you that I left hearts so congenial to my own, and I will say, to yours also, that I lamented the distance which seems placed between us."

At the Count's request he related the scenes already described, and mentioned the characters with esteem and respect. — "It is a singular affair," observed the Count, when he had finished his narration, "and a most providential meeting between the D'Alenberg family and Louisa. I have heard often of Count Wolfran before my seclusion from the world, he was then a very young and a very gay man, he can be but little turned of thirty now. I remember I once saw him, and thought him a most elegant figure."

"So much the worse," said Ferdinand, warmly, "since it is beyond a doubt that he is a villain, and would, most probably, but for this fortunate discovery, have ruined the happiness of a most lovely and amiable young Lady. I hope I shall never see him; but come, my dear Count (added he, in a quick tone) tell me in what manner you have been received coming from death to life, and in what way you found all your affairs?"

The Count told him he had found but little difficulty in being acknowledged by his friends, whom he had amused with an account that he had been travelling, under a borrowed name, to avoid trouble, and had resided both in London and Paris as a private man, until he was tired of the frolic."

This story, he said, had gained credit, and, as it was supposed he did not live without a companion, he had been rallied on his English and Parisian Ladies, which he bore tolerably well, and had therefore silenced curiosity by giving way to their own conjectures.

As to his estates, he found them in perfect good order, and was so well satisfied with his good old steward, Mr. Duclos, that he had presented him with a pretty little estate, and made him independent for life. "I have still enough (said he) I trust, to satisfy the demands of gratitude and friendship, and sufficient in my own power to make the man I esteem superior to receiving the narrow bounty of selfish, contracted hearts, who are incapable of doing justice to virtues they know not how to estimate, because no such inhabits their own bosoms.

"The variety of occupations in which I have been engaged," continued he, "since my arrival here, has given a diversity to my thoughts, very favourable towards recovering that tranquillized state of mind I wish for. Happiness is fled like a vision of the brain; but when I remember what I have been, and what I am now, I should be ungrateful to Providence if I was not thankful for the good, and submit to bear the evil with patience and resignation."

Ferdinand was delighted with the rationality of the Count's sentiments, and presaged much future contentment to a mind capable of such proper discrimination. His friend told him, "that having many accounts to settle, and leases to renew, he apprehended it would be at least a week or ten days before he could conveniently leave the country. Mean time (added he) command here as myself, the carriage, horses and servants, are your's. Do not confine yourself, but make a circuit round the environs of the Castle, you will find amusement and information. — Follow my example, engage your ideas in a continual variety that you may get out of yourself, and avoid a train of unpleasant reflections."

Ferdinand followed the Count's advice, and for three or four days, when the other was engaged with his steward and tenants, he was continually on horseback; but, alas! happiness is not dependant on exterior or local circumstances; whilst his eyes wandered over hills and dales, mountains and glens, his mind's eye had other objects in view, and he found it a vain attempt to turn his thoughts on the beauties of nature, whilst the barbed arrow still rankled in his bosom, and the remembrance of past events, of Claudina, his brother, and other recent occurrences, obtruded on his memory. On the contrary, without society, and at liberty to "indulge meditation even to madness," he returned always fatigued in body, and distressed in mind.

The fifth day the weather was bad, and he could not take his accustomed rides; the morning, his friend being busy, he passed in the library, but his temper took its colouring from the weather, and when he entered the dining parlour, the Count was extremely concerned to see his features clouded with melancholy, and all the marks of a deep dejection. "Are you not well," said he, hastily.

"I am certainly not ill," replied Ferdinand; "that is, I have no bodily complaints; but I feel a weight on my spirits which I cannot shake off."

"Ah! my friend," returned the Count, "this inactive life ill agrees with a discontented mind. I am sensible that the present composure of mine is but temporary: I can easily allow for your feelings, and am provoked that my haste to finish all my affairs here, compels me to leave you so much alone. In our present state of mind (added he, with a faint smile) we are not fit to be trusted alone; company and active employments suit us much better than solitude."

Ferdinand was about to reply, when a servant entered with a packet for him; being a stranger to the hand, he opened it hastily, and saw the name of D'Alenberg. "Ah! cried he, here is a large packet from Mr. D'Alenberg; from its bulk I dare say it contains the history of the poor Louisa."

"You will then have something to amuse, or at least to engage your attention (said the Count) and I am glad of it, as I am obliged to meet two persons for an hour or two after dinner." Ferdinand's impatience, and this friend's engagement, caused them to make a hasty meal, which, when finished, the former retired to the library, and perused the following letter:

MR. D'ALENBERG TO MR. FERDINAND RENAUD.

"I do not forget, my young friend, that you seemed to feel an interest in the late occurrences that fell under your eye; and you impressed me with too favourable an opinion of your heart to doubt of your being anxious for an explanation of such circumstances relative to Louisa, as materially concerned the peace of my Theresa and her father. I have full leave to acquaint you with every particular of the villainous treatment the much-injured young woman has experienced from the most abandoned of men: Crimes like his cannot go unpunished, and it shall not be my fault if the world does not brand him as a villain. I bow with reverence to that Being, whose benign hand conducted us to the spot where the late unfortunate Mr.

Hautweitzer breathed his last sigh; had it pleased Heaven to have prolonged his existence to this hour, that he might have seen his child under my protection, the last pang of nature had been stripped of half its terrors; but to regret is useless, it is our duty to think all is as it should be. To-morrow we propose to leave this place; our poor invalid thinks she is capable of taking the journey. This morning her worthy father was consigned to the grave; I trust he exists in happier regions.

"The good Dolnitz shall not be forgotten; he and his sister have hearts, and good ones too; it is the duty of those that have power to enable such persons to gratify their generous humane feelings. You know my address; I again repeat my wishes to see you and your friend; if this lays not in the chapter of possibilities at present, I request to hear from you.

"Remember, young man, that you have opened a fresh account; once more I feel an esteem, and place a confidence on a slender knowledge: Old age ought to be wary and circumspect, particularly when deception has so lately wounded an unsuspecting heart; but I have not learned the ungenerous maxims of the world, nor, because I have unfortunately been deceived by a worthless wretch, suspect each man to be a villain. — You, I hope, will justify my candour, and when I tell you that you possess my regards, will, by your subsequent conduct, give me credit with myself for my discernment.

"To see you will give me pleasure. To hear you are well and happy is the next best satisfaction you can convey to me; for well I see, and grieve to see, that you are now unhappy: But if the cause originates from no vice or folly of your own, take comfort, all may yet be well. My respects to your friend, I know him only by name, that speaks in his favour; I should be glad to know more of him. My daughter desires her compliments: Louisa scarcely remembers having seen you, but she is grateful for your attentions. Adieu, my young friend, remember my claims upon you.

C. D'ALENBERG."

This letter was very gratifying to Ferdinand; but he looked it hastily over, being impatient to read the story of Louisa, which was thus prefaced:

"By permission of her friend, and at the request of her father, Miss D'Alenberg sends this transcript of Louisa's misfortunes, in her own words, to Mr. Ferdinand Renaud."

END OF VOL II.

VOLUME 3, CHAPTER 1

My father was descended from a younger branch of a Noble family: He lost his parents before he attained the age of manhood, and found his commission all his patrimony, and his sword his only friend. He conducted himself so properly in the management of both, that a Captain's commission was his reward at the age of two and twenty.

During the suspension of the next campaign, he went to Strasburg to visit a very distant relation, who had thought proper to recognize him when he was in a situation to provide for himself. With this old gentleman he staid some time, and unfortunately lost his heart to a very amiable young woman, who had every claim to admiration but one. That trifling deficiency in my father's eye, though of great magnitude in the estimation of wiser and more prudent men, was the want of fortune. My father, who had been bred up in the school of liberality, who had no selfish considerations, and paid but little attention to prudential maxims, no sooner discovered that his heart was irrevocably fixed, and that the lady's character justified his pretensions, than he openly avowed his partiality, and sought to gain her favour. In vain his relation remonstrated, soothed, allured, and threatened. He was master of himself — of his own affections — despised such paltry objections as the want of money; persisted in his endeavours to gain the lady — was successful — was transported at his promised eternal happiness, and laid up for himself a "load of cares."

Reprobated by his mercenary relation, he married, and carried his wife to the quarters where his duty called him. For a time, he was as happy as a man could be, who, in possessing a darling object, hourly expected to be torn from her. It happened, before that dreaded period arrived, peace was concluded on between the contending powers; and he had the supreme delight of remaining with the object of his affections — of looking forward to an increase of family, but had forgot, in the hour of exultation, that he was now reduced to half-pay.

The first moment this blow struck on his heart, was when some preparations were thought necessary for the accommodation of his wife. Alas! then, and not 'till then, did it occur to him, how insufficient the poor pittance he possessed would be to support the unavoidable expenses coming upon him. What he could retrench from his own little accustomed indulgences, he did, and provided, as well as it was possible, for the hour which brought me into the world, and eventually proved the death of a parent I have ever revered, though I never beheld her.

From the day which gave me birth, although she seemed to recover as well as most women do in the like situation, and at the expiration of a proper time, resumed her family employments: whether she caught cold, had any inward complaints or uneasiness of mind; whatever was the cause, I know not, but she fell into a rapid decline, and her pure spirit fled to Heaven five months after she had given me life.

"'Tis needless to repeat my father's sufferings; a feeling heart may conceive them; when time and necessity compelled him to struggle with his grief, and remember the pledge his darling wife had left him, he resolved to retire into a distant part of the country, that he might devote his whole time to the care of his child. With this dear father I past my life, until near twelve years of age; and to his unwearied care, I owe more than life, in the good and virtuous principles he instilled into my mind. Unhappily he was but little acquainted with mankind;—bred up in the school of adversity, with a narrow income, and few connexions, his spirit had kept him from engaging in habits of company and expense, which he knew his small income could not support; and therefore he had avoided society, and mixed but very seldom among young men of his age and rank, consequently knew but little of their vices, or general profligacy.

I had nearly completed my twelfth year, when my father one day told me, that tho' it would be almost death to him to part with me; yet it was his duty to prefer my interest to his own satisfaction. He had lived in obscurity, and, with the most rigid economy, that he might save a sum sufficient to pay for my pension in a convent for two or three years, that my education might be completed. "The time is now come," said he, "when my intention must take place; I am again called upon in the service of my country; I have inquired for a situation where I can entrust the only treasure Heaven has given me; and where you will acquire such accomplishments and female knowledge, as must be necessary for your future provision."

"I shall not dwell on the sorrow which pervaded our bosoms, when the hour came that annihilated all my happiness for ever.—Our little humble dwelling was disposed of; my good old nurse, who had been our only domestic, my father got received into a hospital; and I accompanied him to that convent, where I most fortunately was distinguished by the friendship of Miss D'Alenberg.

"I pass over the years I resided in the convent, as nothing material took place in my affairs, until I was one day suddenly called from the refectory, and informed my father waited for me in the parlour. Surprise and joy almost overcame my senses; I flew to my dear parent, and shed tears of unbounded transport; his eyes also overflowed. After the first expressions of joy were a little abated, he told me, he had quitted the army, was arrived to take me from the convent, and desired I would be prepared to quit it the following morning, when he should call and settle for my pension.

"I cannot even now forget, nor yet account for, the universal tremor which seized me when I heard of my father's intention: I had many agreeable companions; I loved Miss D'Alenberg, and was honoured with her friendship, except which, I had nothing to regret: And surely my affection for her bore no proportion to the duty and love I owed to my father: Strange, therefore, that I should be shocked—should feel a repugnance, and even horror, at the thoughts of quitting the convent with a parent so dear to me. Alas! it was too sure a presentiment of all the evils that awaited me, and the moment when I left that peaceful abode, was the last of my tranquillity. When I gave my last embrace to my loved Theresa, and the gates closed between us, I gave a faint shriek, and threw myself back in the chaise more than half dead.

"My kind, my considerate father, gave way to the first emotions of my grief, and soothed me with so much tenderness, praising the sensibility of my heart. (Ah! he knew not then how dearly we should pay for, how bitterly we should deplore, that fatal sensibility) that I grew ashamed of indulging a sorrow that reproached me with ingratitude to so good a parent. This consideration assisted me in the recovery of more composure, and at length enabled me to recollect our situation, and to ask, where we were going to reside? My dear father heaved a deep sigh.

"I will not attempt to deceive you, my dear Louisa; I can no longer afford to pay for your pension; an unfortunate circumstance has compelled me to leave the service of the Emperor, and obliges me to seek a situation in the army of another Prince; I might have left you ignorant of this compulsatory arrangement; I might have suffered your pension to have run on for another year; but my dear girl, your father cannot stoop to even a negative imposition, and in the incertitude of the success my present plan may lead to, I could not subject you to receive obligations, to be indebted for your support, whilst I had a doubt upon my mind that I might possibly fail in the power of making the just returns due for your maintenance.

"I grieve only for you, my child; but I trust Heaven will give you strength of mind to encounter with the evils of poverty, when unaccompanied with guilt or remorse. I have sought for a retirement where you may not be absolutely excluded from society, but where you may live unknown, and free from observation, without the danger of being subjected to the triumph of insolent prosperity over indigent merit. Louisa, you was nursed in obscurity; to that obscurity you must return. I had flattered myself with far better hopes for you; but those are no more, and we must submit to the fate that controls us: All that remains is, to bear adverse fortune with patience and fortitude, than we are superior to the evils that befall us.

"You are young, my child, to hear and profit by a lesson so painful to practise as adversity; but you have good sense; you are the daughter of a soldier, and a man of honour." My father pronounced these last words with a peculiar emphasis, and with an animated countenance, that surprised and interested me; but I expressed no curiosity, and contented myself with assuring him, that "my mind should be directed by his precepts, and my conduct deserve his approbation." My answer pleased him, and he endeavoured to rally his spirits, by giving a cheerful turn to our conversation.

"We arrived at length to our place of destination, a very small village in the vicinity of Heilbron, romantically and beautifully situated. At the extremity of a few scattered houses, was the residence of a good priest, inhabited by himself, his mother, and a peasant girl as a servant: We were expected, and therefore received with kindness. To one accustomed from childhood to retirement, this solitude had nothing in it so frightful as to create terror or disgust. I was charmed with the mildness, the placid content that pervaded the countenance of my new friends, and not only strove to appear pleased, but really felt a degree of pleasure in my mind, that I might hope to have cheerful companions. My father watched my looks with visible anxiety; and when he saw me enter into conversation with a lively unembarrassed air, I observed the instantaneous effect it had upon him: Every feature was illumined with satisfaction; he seemed as if a weight had been removed, which had before heavily oppressed his spirits, and from which he had scarcely an expectation of being freed.

"In the evening, when we were for a few minutes alone, he asked me, "if I could reconcile myself to reside with the Abbe Bouville and his mother?" I answered in the affirmative, without the least hesitation. He affectionately embraced me:—"Then, my dearest girl, more than half of my sorrows are done away, and I will no longer conceal my situation from you. A general officer, whose arrogance far exceeded his rank, and whose fortune enabled him to support an appearance, that threw every one else at a distance from him by the superiority he assumed. This meanly proud man affected to treat his inferiors in rank and fortune with a supercilious contempt that was insupportable. It happened, that on a particular service, I was subjected to his command; I did my duty, but scorned to flatter his pride by mean flatteries or condescensions unbecoming my character. Provoked, I believe, by my conduct, yet unable to complain of any deficiencies in the services he commanded, he one day gave me three contradictory orders, before I had time to perform either, and consequently I was obliged to apply to him in person, for an explanation of the orders delivered to me.

"The moment I appealed to him, he flew into a violent rage, and accused me of disobeying command. Irritated as I was, I yet suppressed my feelings, and respectfully, though firmly, represented the impossibility of obeying orders which had been in the same instant contradicted by others entirely opposite. He threw himself into a paroxysm of rage, and insulted me in a manner beyond all endurance: My indignation, hardly repressed, now burst forth—I defended my conduct, as became a man of spirit, and retorted upon him for his frivolous and indeterminate proceedings. In short, he bore hard upon me— threw me off my guard—and I vented some menacing expressions, which were instantly caught hold of. I was ordered into custody; shortly afterwards brought to a court-martial, and dismissed from the service for "disobedience of orders, and insulting my commanding officer."

"I heard the sentence with a disdainful silence. But as soon as I had obtained my liberty, I sent a challenge to my ungenerous enemy. I have no doubt but that he expected it; for on the breaking up of the court, he had set off to other quarters, to "confer," as he gave out with other general officers respecting a secret expedition. I was persuaded, by the whole corps, to present a petition to the Emperor; but my spirit rose repugnant to the idea of a petition. I therefore wrote a plain narrative of facts, which I sent to my royal master, and quitted the army immediately.

"Alas! my child, when the hurry of tumultuous and indignant passions had subsisted, your image swam across my sight; and how was my Louisa to be supported? The first idea that occurred to my reason. What my feelings were, I will not describe. Providence graciously recalled to my mind the Abbe Bouville, whom I had known in early days, and on whose benevolence and wisdom I thought I might repose confidence. I knew his residence, although I had not visited him in his retirement; nor indeed was then certain of his existence, but to seek him, was my only resource; most fortunately I found him; the man my heart could be laid open to, and from whose piety and goodness I could derive comfort. The result of our conference was my journey to the convent; the rest you know; and now, my dear child, here you may reside in safety, whilst I seek in another service that fame, and that recompense, of which I have been unjustly deprived."

CHAPTER II

Thus my father finished the painful recital of his injuries, and I assured him of my perfect sensibility of his affectionate cares for me, and my resolution to improve my small talents, that I might be enabled to provide for my own maintenance, without being a burden on so good a father. It would be tiresome to repeat our conversations that evening when he gave me to the care of his good friends. As he had not determined what Prince he should apply to, his journey was undertaken without being able to point out for us any channel of information, until we could hear from himself. The hour of separation was dreadful; but I sought to acquire fortitude, that my father might not have my sufferings to contend with, added to his own.

The next day he left us. It was three weeks before we heard from him, and learnt, he was in the service of the King of Poland. Four months past in a quiet uniform manner, that had tranquillized my mind; and as we had heard several times from my father, whose spirits appeared to return with a ray of hope, from the nature of his employment, my mind naturally partook of the complexion of his, and I grew cheerful and easy, in proportion as his letters breathed content and returning vivacity.

It was about this period when I had been near five months with the good Bouvilles, when we heard that a small hunting seat, situated in a most beautiful park about two miles from the village, was repairing for the reception of a young nobleman, just returning from his travels. This information seemed perfectly immaterial to me; nor had I the least curiosity respecting our neighbour, when told of his arrival.

One morning, coming out of my little apartment, which was in the garden, and entering the parlour, I saw a very genteel young man talking to the Abbe with earnestness; I retired in confusion, muttering some trifling apology; but before I had got three steps from the door, the stranger was at my side; taking my hand respectfully, he entreated my return, protesting he would leave the house instantly, if his presence had driven me from the room. I was so extremely confused, that unable to utter a word, I suffered him to lead me quietly back, and seat me in a chair, before I could recollect myself to make any return to a hundred polite things, that he addressed to me with an astonishing rapidity. After some time, however, I recovered, and on the entrance of Madame Bouville, ventured to join in the conversation. I was soon informed this gentleman was the young Count Wolfran, our neighbour. He made an extreme long visit, and departed with visible reluctance.

The effect that his figure, his compliments, and extreme attention, had upon a young and susceptible heart like mine, need not to be described. A thousand new ideas broke in upon my mind; I passed the night sleepless, and arose without that cheerfulness natural to my disposition. When we met at breakfast, the conversation turned upon our neighbour. The Abbe informed me, that in a hunting party the day before the Count's visit, some of his domestics had greatly injured a small enclosure belonging to the good father, of which he had sent notice to the Count, and which had brought him the preceding day to the house, with a view of persuading the Abbe to part with this field, as it lay contiguous to his grounds. This requisition the other had resisted, and they were growing warm in the argument, when I unhappily broke in upon them, and not another word was said on the subject.

I apologized for interrupting them; my friend said he was much obliged to me; for, added he, smiling, as I had just given my negative in a very decided manner, and he neither renewed the proposition, nor appeared to be displeased when he took leave. I hope I shall hear no more of it. The second day after this, the Count made his appearance, attended by a servant with some game, which he entreated Madame Bouville's acceptance of in terms so friendly and persuasive, that she was obliged, however reluctantly, to receive his presents, and of course to pay him attention and respect.

From that day, he never neglected a single one of making us a visit; and his extreme politeness to me grew so very marked, that the good Abbe thought it requisite to have some conversation with me relative to his attentions. And here let me, with confusion, acknowledge my own weakness and folly. I had suffered my eye to forerun my judgment; was already greatly prejudiced in favour of the Count; and I believe had but too plainly discovered these favourable sentiments towards him, by my unguarded looks and behaviour. The good Abbe soon discovered the secret of my heart, which afforded him no satisfaction, because he was apprehensive of the consequences. He explained the nature of his sentiments to me very freely, but with great delicacy. Alas! how unequal was the dictates of prudence, or the cautious advice of age, to combat with a growing partiality in a young mind, a stranger to the world, and entangled by the dangerous superficial advantages of person, and that softness, that insinuating tenderness, which so easily makes its way into an unsuspecting bosom.

I heard my friend, indeed, with respect, but not with conviction, and the first moment that I saw the Count again, one look, one tender expression, overthrew all the poor Abbe's arguments, and confirmed the seducer's power over my heart. My prudent guardians saw too plainly the danger of my situation, and despairing of gaining any ascendancy over me, they one day took an opportunity of an early visit, when I was not in the way to talk to him, in a manner they conceived to be their duty, and to request that he would refrain from any future visits.

He was too closely pressed to allow of any disguise or subterfuge, and was at length driven to own his attachment to me in very unequivocal terms. He said, "that he had a small independency from his father securely settled. He had also great expectations from a relation, exceeding old, whose death might daily be expected, besides what he must enjoy hereafter as his paternal fortune; but that he was sensible his father must, and would, disapprove of his marriage with so young a person as Miss Hautweitzer, who, however beautiful and accomplished, was deficient in those requisites which parents too generally looked upon as absolutely essential in a union for life. His own sentiments were far more liberal: Convinced that he should possess a very handsome fortune in his own right, he was perfectly indifferent to the want of it in a person from whom he was to derive his future happiness, which could not be dependent on money. He besought the Abbe's interest with me; said, that he would immediately write to his father of his intentions, and ask his consent, a compliment certainly due to him, but from which he frankly owned he expected nothing agreeable to his wishes, knowing too well the disposition of his father in such matters. However, be the event what it might, it should make no alteration in his sentiments; his present income would be sufficient for competency and happiness; his paternal fortune could not be alienated from him."

All this, and much more, he urged to the Abbe and Madam Bouville; and though their judgment disapproved of a further intimacy, without the sanction of our parents, yet so seductive were his persuasions, so irresistible his solicitations, that if not convinced, they were at least overborne by his eloquence, and at length gave a tacit permission to his visits, because they had not resolution to deny him.

This great point gained: He forgot not to make his advantages with me on the open and candid declarations he had made to my friends; whilst I, young and unsuspecting, gloried in the affection of a man so amiable and so disinterested, and gave up my heart without reserve, to the indulgence of passion, for an object so worthy. The Abbe, however, was not quite easy; he felt himself responsible to his friend for the honour and happiness of the child committed to his care; and although the prospect was fascinating, and such as he conceived must be for my interest; yet knowing my father's high notions of honour, he was very doubtful that his approbation to our union would not be obtained, if the Count's father refused his consent. He therefore wrote to my beloved parent on the subject; unhappily this letter never reached him, as he had been ordered on duty to a different part of the country.

Mean time, the Count continued his assiduities to me, and daily insinuated himself more into the favourable opinion of my friends. At this period, the good Madame Bouville caught a violent cold, by being out too late one evening in her garden, when the damps arose imperceptibly round her; the consequence was, a violent rheumatic and inflammatory fever, which in nine days terminated a life that had been uniformly good, pious and charitable.

The poor Abbe felt this stroke most severely; he had lost a parent and a friend, — his own health had been always delicate, and subject to frequent asthmatic spasms; he was of a remarkable studious and retired disposition, but ill calculated to struggle with the common affairs of life in a domestic way, in which he was as unknowing as a child. — My situation with him was another subject of distress, without a companion or an adviser, no female acquaintance to countenance me, alone in the house with him, visited by a young man of fashion avowedly my lover. — What an improper, a dangerous situation! — When the last duties were paid to the respectable woman we had lost, he wrote again to my father, and ventured to hint to me before the Count, that as there certainly was an impropriety in my residence there, he conceived it would be most for my advantage in every sense of the word, to retire into a convent, until some arrangement should be concluded upon by my father.

This opinion was a thunder stroke to us both; so infatuated was I by my fatal passion, that it superseded every sense of decorum and propriety, and I considered only the pangs I must feel in being separated from my lover. After a few moments silence, the Count requested the Abbe to walk with him into the garden: They were absent near an hour: I was almost sick with suspense and apprehension what this conference could mean. At length they returned: Joy shone in the eyes of the Count: he flew towards me; and kissing my hand with transport, — "My love—my Louisa!" exclaimed he, "the dear Abbe has consented to our union."—"Conditionally, only," said the latter, with an embarrassed air; "and I expect you do not interrupt me, Sir, whilst I speak my whole mind to my dear ward."

He then told me, that the Count had urged him to unite us immediately, as the only way to secure my happiness and reputation: That, should his father refuse to gratify his wishes, all he would desire was, that our marriage might be concealed until he had either softened him, or obtained the sanction of his relation, whose fortune would amply support us; whose tender regard for him he had little doubt would incline him to use his influence with his father. In short, every argument love and ingenuity could suggest, he had assailed the Abbe with, and he fairly repeated them all. "Now, added he, "attend, Louisa, to my objections; let reason and dispassionate judgment direct you. I have, I own, very reluctantly, been compelled by an eloquence I could neither silence nor resist, to promise an acquiescence with your determination. Consider well, therefore, before you give your final answer, in which my peace and your own is so deeply involved."

He then represented the disgrace and attendant disagreeable consequences to me, which must inevitably wait on a private marriage; the pain which must follow the disapprobation of our friends—the possible repentance and coldness of my husband, when passion subsided; and he found himself an alien from his family, and reflected on the sacrifices he had made to love. In fine, the Abbe said enough to have convinced the reason of a prudent young woman, and to make even a thoughtless one deliberate on the rash step suggested to her by the impetuous passion of a very young man. But alas! with the most painful conviction of my imprudence, I candidly own, I heard him only with impatience, and attended to nothing but the flattering idea of being married to the Count, and being inseparably united to a man, who, I was persuaded, would love me for life with unabating affection. Childish, romantic expectation! how bitterly have I been convinced of its fallacy, since the very concession I made in his favour, and submitting to the humiliation of a private marriage, must of itself lessen his esteem, when he reflected on my want both of prudence and delicacy. Rarely, indeed, I believe are such marriages happy, as need concealment, or are unsanctioned by the approbation of our parents; but I was to be convinced of this truth by experience; for I refused to listen to the voice of prudence.

When, therefore, the Abbe had exhausted himself, and borne hard upon the patience of the Count, without, to my shame be it confessed, having made the least impression upon me, by all the arguments he adduced against a private marriage. I replied to him with a courage that I saw surprised and hurt him; "that I was very sensible of his regard for my interest and happiness; but that, as the Count had honoured me with an offer of his hand, situated as I was, and with the esteem I felt for him, I could neither be so ungrateful to him, nor so much an enemy to my own happiness, as to decline the offer, which it was impossible my father could disapprove, when declared publicly; and when that time arrived, all apprehensions of the old Count's disapprobation must be done away." My lover threw himself in raptures at my feet, to thank me, and in the same breath, claimed the Abbe's promise. He heaved a deep sigh. "I own," said he, "that I am disappointed, and thought I might trust to the gentle and delicate mind of Louisa for a more proper regard to circumstances: But since my own confidence in her has misled me, and I see that you have acquired an unbounded influence over her heart, I shall no longer oppose your union, because I am now convinced all opposition would be fruitless. Heaven grant that I may have no cause to regret the hour that you first saw each other, and that your marriage may be productive of mutual happiness." We were both too happy to attend much to the evident chagrin of the good Abbe; the Count only replied to what was pleasing to himself, and entered into a consultation in what manner we should live together, without betraying our secret to the world, until it was convenient for our interest to make it known."

After much deliberation, and several schemes formed, and rejected as inexpedient, it was concluded upon, that, as I was scarce known in that neighbourhood, and the Count still less; that he should give up his hunting seat, discharge his servants, all but his valet, in whose secrecy he could depend, and take a small house in a neighbouring hamlet, where, as Mr. and Mrs. Sultsbach, we might live unknown and unobserved, until the Count had softened his family into a compliance with his wishes. His letters to be all addressed to and from the Abbe's house, which, being only four miles from the house proposed for our residence, would quickly afford us every intelligence.

This scheme being adopted, the Count lost no time in putting it into execution; his valet took the house, which, belonging to an officer in the army, whose wife had died in his absence, was let ready furnished, and was very suitable for us. Two maid servants were hired in the hamlet, which, with the valet, was to be all our domestics. Every arrangement was completed in about ten days; and on the morning when we were to take possession of our house, the good Abbe joined our hands before Heaven in his parish church. After the ceremony, when returned to his house, the servant of the Count being the only witness to our union, he seized an opportunity to draw me, for a few moments, into his little study. Taking my hand, the large drops falling from his eyes — "My amiable friend," said he, "I have this day done an act my better judgment condemns; but such are the existing circumstances, that I saw evidently there was no alternative to pursue. The great error I have committed, was admitting the Count as a visitor into my house. All other subsequent events was the result of my weakness in that point; Heaven grant that you may, as now, ever consider it as a fortunate hour for your happiness; and that I may never upbraid myself for my conduct, I hope soon to hear from your father; and if he does not disapprove of your union, as you hope, I shall then be better reconciled to myself than I now am. Here is a paper I have drawn up, and signed as a certificate of your marriage, and I entreat you carefully to preserve it." He embraced me with great tenderness, and blessed me with much fervency, promising to be a frequent visitor.

Elated with my marriage, anticipating future scenes of happiness and independence, and enjoying the pleasure my father must feel, when acquainted with a settlement so advantageous to me, not one gloomy idea presented itself in the chapter of possibilities that could for a moment cloud my prospects of felicity. Poor, wretched deluded creature; how soon was thy vain and high raised expectations tumbled into the dust! A month past away on eagle's wings; for every moment brought with it fresh instances of my husband's affection. No letters had as yet arrived from either of our fathers; but both being in the army, though in the service of different princes, we knew they could not always command their time, or be in the route to receive letters; therefore we patiently waited, without feeling any disappointment, as the days past by us.

I had been married nearly five weeks, when one morning, at breakfast, we were surprised by seeing a man on horseback ring at the gate, and presently a message was delivered from the Abbe, who then lay in his bed hopeless of recovery, from the return of his dreadful spasms. He requested to see us without delay. This moment was the first since I had left him that I felt pain, and I prepared instantly to attend him, the Count equally desirous with myself to see our mutual friend. We were not long before we arrived at his house, and beheld him upraised in his bed, struggling for breath, and so amazingly changed in the course of a week's illness, that I was more shocked than ever I had been in my whole life. He ordered the servant to withdraw, and then with extreme difficulty, agonized by the spasms in his side, he addressed us in these words: — "I believe my days, I may say hours of existence, now draw towards a period. I have little to regret but my neglect of duties, which, however, I hope I have not violated, and trust in a merciful God to pardon all my omissions.

"My dear children, you are now happy in each other; let me entreat you to attend to the duties of your situations, and you will continue so. Count, remember I joined you to my dear charge; her happiness, her honour, are a deposit in your hands, which you are accountable for to the Supreme Being, and to her respectable father. To your honour and generosity I bequeath her. And you, my once dear Louisa, now the wife of a noble gentleman, who has proved his affection for you by disregarding all selfish considerations: Do you give him credit for his judgment, and prove, by your amiable conduct through life, how much superior virtue and native goodness are to the boasted advantages of riches and titles. — May the Almighty bless you both, and may your union often occasion you to recollect a man to whom, in his last moments, your happiness was his only concern."

With a faltering voice, and infinite labour, the poor Abbe pronounced this affectionate farewell. A relation of his had been sent for, the heir to his small possessions, who entered the house just as he became speechless, and our attendance was no longer necessary.

We returned home oppressed with melancholy: The Count was thoughtful; and I felt more poignant sorrow than I had ever before experienced. My spirits sunk, and a heavy gloom seemed to hang over me, which I could not shake off — too sure a presage that my happiest days were flown to return no more. At supper, I tried to appear cheerful; 'twas an attempt only; for sighs surcharged my bosom in spite of my endeavours to repress them. The Count saw my emotions, and made an effort to be talkative: — At length he said, "We both feel sorrow for our good father, but you know, my love, he often suffered such misery, as his real friends cannot be sorry that he is released from — — — Most fortunately for us, he lived long enough to give you a husband and a protector. Had he died before that period, how much more cause would you have had for sorrow, without a friend in the world near you." There was something in this speech that displeased me, and I was considering what answer to make, when he added; "except our Frank, there remains no witness now of our union."

"Yes," I replied with some earnestness; "I have one material one, a certificate drawn up, and signed by the good Abbe."—"Have you, indeed?" answered he with surprise, strongly marked in his countenance,—"I am rejoiced to hear it; I hope you take great care of it." "Most certainly," I returned, "I keep it in my little ivory cabinet, presented to me at the convent, and lock that safely in my escritoire."—"That's right, my love, we may one day find it necessary to produce so unequivocal a proof of our marriage." He then changed the subject, and sought to amuse me by repeating some entertaining anecdotes, that he remarked in his travels. Two days after this event, a messenger came from the late Abbe's, with a letter to the Count, which he had left orders should be forwarded to him for his friend the Count; as we still retained the name of Sultsbach.

I trembled at the sight of this letter, and absolutely gasped for breath whilst he perused it. I watched the turn of his countenance, and saw it promised no good to me.—"Tell me," I cried, "what answer has your father given to your request?"—"One that surprises me as much as it hurts me," he replied. "He refuses his consent to our marriage, not merely because you are portionless, but because you are the daughter of a man he hates; one whose insolence obliged him to complain against him, and to have dismissed from the army."—"Good Heavens!" I exclaimed; "is it possible Count Wolfran was that destroyer of my father's happiness! Oh! my dear father, why, why did you not name your cruel enemy to me!" "You mistake the matter," said my husband, very coolly: "It appears that the insolence of Mr. Hautweitzer drew upon himself the just indignation of Count Wolfran."

The tone in which he pronounced these words, had more in it than the words themselves: It pierced my heart, and I burst into tears. He seemed affected—besought me not to be uneasy; time might do much for us.—The mutual hatred between our fathers was certainly an unlucky business; but as he found that the Count his father would soon return to his estate, no endeavours on his side should be wanting to do away the prejudice conceived against me. I endeavoured to be content with this assurance; but from that fatal hour, thought I could perceive a change in his disposition; he grew thoughtful, capricious, and often left me for hours alone, without apologizing or accounting for his frequent absences. No letters arrived from my father, nor did I know where to direct to him. The house of the late Abbe was now occupied by a stranger, and it was a million to one if any letters would ever reach us. This reflection gave me great pain, and I often requested the Count to set an inquiry on foot relative to the Polish army, that I might obtain some intelligence of my father's destination. This, he assured me, he had done without effect.

One day he told me, that as his father might soon return, he thought it would be most expedient for him to visit the relation on whose fortune he had such great expectancies, and prevail on him to interest himself in his behalf. "He also," said he, "will doubtless be displeased with me; but I know my influence over him; his anger will be but momentary, and I shall easily persuade him to coincide with my wishes." This proposal from my husband appeared wise and plausible; I had nothing to object to it, but being left alone. This fear and reluctance of being separated for a week or two, he treated as childish, until, ashamed of my folly, I gave into the plan, and a short day was fixed on to begin his journey, which I learnt was at least a hundred and fifty miles distance; but he promised me a letter from every post town.

The day came; I saw him depart with a sad foreboding that some untoward circumstance would intervene between us. I suffered unutterable anguish, and retired to my apartment overwhelmed with grief. After giving way to my sorrow for some time, I tried to shake off the despondency that oppressed me; and having begun some time before to embroider a sword knot for him, I drew out my work to employ myself. I wanted some silver thread, and recollected a parcel of it was in a drawer of my small ivory cabinet, which had been presented to me by my dear Miss D'Alenberg.

I opened the escritoire, where this cabinet was deposited, and easily found the thread. — A sudden inclination seized me to peruse the certificate of my marriage. I opened the private drawer, and found it empty. Astonishment, for a moment, overpowered me; but recollecting myself, I conceived I had mistaken the drawer. I hastily explored every part of it; but the object of my search could not be found. What my feelings were, I cannot describe; nor can I recollect the anguish of that moment without horror. — What was become of my treasure, or on whom could my suspicions fall? was the first questions that presented themselves to my mind, and caused an universal trembling through my whole frame.

I had some little ornaments of value, — those were all safe; the locks of the trunk and cabinet I found in good order, yet it was a fatal truth that the certificate, which not many days previous to this I had seen in the drawer, was lost, and must have been taken by some one who knew of its importance to me. "Good Heavens!" I exclaimed — "Surely the Count — —

—."—The words died on my tongue; the idea was horrible; the extent of misery which that thought might lead to, overcame my senses, and for a moment rendered me insensible. When my reason returned, in a state little short of distraction, I again renewed my search, but in vain; the fatal certainty of my loss was confirmed, and a thousand dreadful images rushed upon my mind at the same time.

With difficulty I descended to my apartment: I had never entrusted my keys with either of the servants; nor could it be probable they would have taken a paper of no consequence to them, and have left several valuable baubles, which, as I did not wear them, might not have been presently missed. There was but one person that I could suspect; and what his motives could have been, to rob me of a paper he had allowed to be very essential to me, after the death of the good Abbe, was a doubt, the solution of which tortured me almost to madness. Yet so fervent was my affection—so perfect my confidence in the love and honour of my husband, that I strove even against conviction to believe I wronged him by my suspicions, and endeavoured to support my spirits until the following day, when, as I expected to hear from him, so I intended to write, and inform him of this extraordinary event.

CHAPTER III

The next day came, and my agitations every hour in the hope of a letter, cannot be expressed. Alas! every succeeding hour, both on that day and the next, brought with it disappointment and sorrow. I grew almost frantic; my servants were astonished at my emotions, which, however, I sought to suppress, were but too visible, as I could neither eat nor sleep. In this state of wretchedness and suspense, I past five days; the sixth put an end to the last, and completed the first. I had scarcely left my pillow, where my wearied head had in vain sought repose, before I was informed a man on horseback at the door had brought a packet for me. I snatched it with trembling eagerness. It was the Count's writing: Even now I sicken at the recollection of what my feelings were, when I perused the contents. Indeed, I could not get through the whole, before I lost my senses, having just time to pull the bell, as I found myself sinking from my chair.

Let me briefly hurry over this part of my story, so dreadful even at this distance of time, that I wonder my life or reason had not been the sacrifice to such inhuman baseness. The letter informed me —

"That his father, having in the most peremptory manner forbidden our marriage, in consequence of an engagement he had entered into with another family, and also because of the insuperable aversion he entertained for Mr. Hautweitzer; he (the Count) was inexpressibly grieved to acquaint me, that in obedience to the author of his being, he was compelled, though with extreme reluctance, to relinquish the hopes he had indulged of passing his life with a lady he so truly loved and esteemed; but the sacred commands he had received, with the insurmountable difficulties that impeded such a union from ever taking place, obliged him to take this method of conveying to me the information, in compassion to both our feelings. As he must ever be interested in my happiness, he had taken care to leave four hundred crowns in his writing desk, which he hoped would be a sum sufficient to convey me to my father, or support me in the hamlet until his arrival."

Such were the cruel contents of this horrid letter, so deeply imprinted in my memory, never to be erased. The moment I regained my senses, I called for the messenger. No such person was to be found. — While the servant came to me, he had taken the opportunity to disappear. My cruel destiny now unfolded itself at once. I had no witness to my marriage; my certificate had been basely stolen by the most inhuman of mankind: I had assumed a fictitious name, which, when known, must at best give me a questionable and doubtful character, and I had no one being interested enough for me to assert my rights, or chastise the author of my wrongs.

Continual faintings brought me into such a state of weakness by the following day, that my servants thought it necessary to call in a physician, with which I was much displeased; for I most earnestly wished for death; but it pleased Heaven to restore me to health, or at least a comparative health, that I might endure yet greater miseries, if possible, the consequences of my credulity and folly. What bitter self-reproach have I not suffered, and must ever feel to the end of my existence.

As soon as I was able to leave my bed, I determined to pursue my cruel husband, and try, by gentleness, to restore him to a sense of his duty to me; but that, if he still persisted in refusing to acknowledge me as his wife, I would then boldly assert my claims upon him, and publish his baseness to all the world. I knew not where to find my father; but even if I had known, I shrunk from the idea of meeting him under my present humiliating circumstances. When I grew collected enough to form my plan, passion and resentment contributed to give me unusual courage; and from the timid love-sick Louisa, I became the haughty injured wife of Count Wolfran, and assumed a character very unlike my former self.

As he had, in the early days of our marriage, mentioned the residence of his relation, I did not hesitate a moment in forming a resolution to follow him there. I therefore hired a carriage for my journey, dismissed my servants, gave up the house, and prevailed on the relation of my late worthy friend, the Abbe, who resided in the village to take charge of my trunks and other effects. Despair gave me spirits, fortitude, and perseverance, astonishing even to myself, and enabled me, within a very few days, to set off for Ulm, the residence of Baron Nolker, the worthy uncle of a most unworthy man. — Happily, I met with no interruptions or accidents, but arrived safe at a capital inn in the city of Ulm.

It was not difficult to gain information of the Baron's house, or his character; the first was not far from the city, and the landlady of the inn spoke warmly in praise of the latter. I was now to reflect on a proper mode of introducing myself, whether to send for the Count, or go boldly to the house. — Whilst I was deliberating, turning my eyes involuntarily towards the street, I saw him pass with a lady and a gentleman. My whole soul seemed in tumults, racked by love and indignation. I hastily rung the bell, and sent a servant after him, to say that a gentleman, an old friend, wished to speak with him immediately: He, knowing the natural timidity of my character, had not, at the moment, the smallest suspicion of my having undertaken such a journey. He turned back, and was in an instant before me.

Never shall I forget the guilt and confusion portrayed in his countenance; he started, and was about to retire without uttering a word, scarcely, I believe, knowing his own intentions; but I was too quick, for laying hold of his arm. — "Stop, Count," I cried, endeavouring to repress my emotions. — "Stop, my dear Count, do you not know your Louisa. — Be not offended; I am here unknown, without you choose to acknowledge me." More astonished, if possible, by this address, than even by my presence, he led me in silence to a chair, doubtless considering in what manner to impose on my credulity, or bring me over to his wishes. — "Louisa," said he at length, in a voice soft and agitated, "Louisa, I am surprised and concerned to see you here. You have taken a very wrong step, which may materially injure me and yourself." "I hope not," I replied with quickness; "for certainly what affects you must concern me. Man and wife can have but one interest; but I felt a necessity for coming here, that you might disavow a vile forgery in your name, calculated, no doubt, to make me miserable. I have too firm a reliance on your love, honour, and integrity, to be for a moment imposed upon by an attempt so impudent and so improbable. Here, my love," added I, drawing out the letter I had received; "read this horrid scroll, and then you will not be surprised that your Louisa determined to afford you an opportunity to vindicate your honour, and trace the infamous hand which sought to destroy our happiness."

He took the letter; his hand trembled, and every feature in his face betrayed the agitation of his mind. — "You ought," said he, falteringly, "to have written to me, if there was a necessity for so doing: You must be sensible, that, in the present state of things, your journey here was highly impolitic, to say no worse of it. — "Ah!" cried I, "could you think it possible for me to be composed, when thus convinced that we have some unknown enemy, who, having gone such lengths as to assume your name, and imitate your hand, will surely hesitate at nothing to make us wretched, and may possibly try to practise on your judgment, as he designed to do on my credulity."

At the moment, when tracing this scene, I am astonished at the fortitude and dissimulation I had the power to acquire over my feelings, and never, I believe, was a man so truly perplexed and confused as the Count. My behaviour was so unexpected, that he was entirely at a loss what answer to frame; whether to own or deny the letter, which he still held without opening it. I saw the workings of his mind, and exulted in the propriety of my plan.—"Why do you not read that detestable scroll?" I asked.—"My dear Louisa," said he, "I have not time now to attend to that or to you; a particular engagement obliges me to leave you, but I will return in the evening, and explain every thing to your satisfaction."—"Well, my love," I replied, "I wish not to intrude on your time or engagements: You will find me perfectly obedient to all your wishes;—now that I see you forgive this apparent rash step, and are convinced that the necessity justified my proceeding." He made me some vague and trifling answer; again promised to see me in the evening, and requested I would keep myself concealed.

CHAPTER IV

When he had left me, I gave a free indulgence to my tears, and those emotions I had so hardly repressed. I saw too plainly the duplicity of his character, and that I was to be the most unfortunate of women. Yet the conduct I had adopted appeared to be the only mode I could pursue. Reproaches would avail nothing, and only harden a depraved mind; whilst, by discrediting the authenticity of the letter, I gave him time for reflection, and an opportunity to disavow it, should honour or tenderness soften him to do me justice.

In a thousand reflections of this kind, I passed the intervening time of his absence; and when I heard his voice at the door speaking to a servant, my heart fluttered almost from its enclosure. He entered the room with an air of haughtiness, mixed with complacency, rather assumed than natural, and bespoke different feelings from those I had observed when he left me. I had time for those remarks, as he deliberately shut the door, took off his hat, and drew a chair close to mine.

"Louisa," said he, in a firm tone, "I come not now to indulge in foolish expressions of a romantic passion, which your own understanding must inform you cannot long exist. I do not pretend to exculpate myself from blame, by pleading the violence of love as an excuse for duplicity; now that the veil is withdrawn, when passion has subsided, I can see and acknowledge my errors. I have misled you. I have imposed upon your reason, and for my own gratification, have sacrificed your peace; yet I hope it will prove only a temporary suspension." He stopped.—I felt almost choked with indignation:—However, I commanded myself, and said, "Go on, Sir, as yet I do not comprehend you."

"To be brief, then," resumed he hastily, "for the subject cannot be expatiated upon; My father commands me to marry a young lady of fortune and connexions, to whom my uncle is guardian. I dare not refuse him." Here I started and exclaimed, "How! dare not?" "No," answered he, "I dare not: I deceived you as to my fortune; I have a very small independence;—my father can dispose of his property as he pleases: My uncle assures me his, only on condition that I comply with my father's commands. Thus I am compelled to obey; for I have no possibility of maintaining you or myself, if I brave their requisitions, and must be for ever reprobated, if I indulge my own desires by a further connexion with a lady, who, however dear to me, is the daughter of a man hateful to my father, and obnoxious to my family.

"The compulsatory acquiescence I have been drawn into, has given me an infinite deal of pain; the letter you have given to me I must acknowledge (at this moment I was absolutely speechless). Let me add, that on yourself depends your future happiness.—Your father is unacquainted with what has past between us. I have not had the temerity to mention any particulars to mine.—You must know, that you can produce no claims upon me, if I choose to disavow them. Therefore, both for your honour and interest, you must relinquish all idea of making such claims as you cannot justify: By so doing, you will retain my friendship, and a handsome allowance, which I will settle on you for life. If, on the contrary, you persist in your present plan, to expose yourself, and compel me publicly to throw you off, you will make an irreconcilable enemy of me. Your father will hear the reputation of his daughter for ever destroyed, and the hatred of my father will find gratification in the dishonour attached to a family he dislikes.—Consider deliberately on all the arguments I have adduced, for the preservation of your character and future independence."

Here the base deceiver stopped, after having completely unmasked his character, and developed his dark designs. The latter part of this long speech had driven all foolish tenderness from my heart. Conscious innocence, pride, and indignation, raised me to a spirit above all fond complainings.—I viewed the man before me with a contempt that superseded affection: For when once an ingenuous mind feels the object of its tenderness in a despicable point of view, as void of integrity or honour, it is not difficult to change the nature of its sentiments, since true love must be founded upon esteem; and when that is annihilated, the other ceases to exist in a well informed mind. The errors, the imprudence I had been guilty of, in forming this too hasty connexion, perhaps deserved a punishment, but not from him. His behaviour had lifted me above myself, and conveyed more knowledge to my understanding in one hour, than from my little experience I had acquired in years. But to return.

I saw he impatiently and anxiously waited for my answer, as he took a turn or two about the room; whilst I was endeavouring to acquire composure, and some degree of dignity, which might cover him with confusion.—This at length was my reply, with as much calmness as I could assume.

"When I undertook this journey, Sir, it was with a faint hope that some one spark of virtue might inhabit your bosom, and that recollection had before now been my friend, to give you a just sense of your duty to me. I therefore gave you an opportunity to recall yourself to honour, and to do me justice. — No such spark of virtue lay dormant: I see all is treachery, deceit, and sordid interest. — Unhappily my weak mind and unguarded heart was captivated by an exterior too fascinating, and a semblance of honour I had not the penetration to discover from a reality. — But those days of weakness are no more. — I will preserve the honour of my father, whatever is the consequence to myself. I have been weak and imprudent, but never will I consent to appear a guilty creature in his eyes, for any worldly advantages offered as a compensation for lost innocence. — No, Sir — my fame, my character, shall be justified."

"And pray," said he, interrupting me, "who is to justify it? Have you any witnesses to prove it; any testimonies to produce?" "The last, Sir, you know, you have basely robbed me of; my best friend is indeed no more: — But your servant" — — — "is a stranger to every thing between us," answered he with a sneer. — "More than that, you left the Abbe, and resided with me under a false name. You will find, upon inquiry, his knowledge extends no farther." — "'Tis well, Sir," said I, rising. — "I comprehend all your schemes perfectly; I have no more to say to you: Leave me, Sir, and see me no more."

"Louisa," cried he, much agitated, "consider well what you are about; I will not have my future happiness destroyed by a rash unthinking girl; do not therefore oblige me to take such measures as must inevitably hurt your peace, and make your father miserable." "Do what you please," I returned; "as your wife, I must obey you: And though I utterly despise you, I never will forego my claims." He looked at me with a contemptuous smile. "And pray what is the plan you intend to pursue?" "That I shall deliberate upon, and you will doubtless know the result soon." He took up his hat — "You have decided your own fate, Louisa, and must abide the consequence." I made no reply, and he left the room.

No sooner was the door shut, than my spirits sunk; and though I no longer loved the base betrayer, yet the difficulties, the prejudices I had to encounter with; the malevolence of the world, and above all, the hatred of the old Count, who would doubtless shut his ears against conviction, to gratify his malice. All these considerations arose to my view; overpowered the little resolution I had laboured to support, and threw me into the most pitiable state of distress. I determined, however, to see the Baron the following morning, and disclose every circumstance that had passed between his nephew and myself.

I was now alone at an inn, a stranger, without a companion or a servant. The kind of doubtful appearance that I must make to the people, now first occurred; and when I desired to be conducted to my bed-room, I thought the hostess threw a scornful and scrutinizing look at me. Confused and mortified, I hastened to the apartment alloted for me, which was through a short enclosed gallery or passage, that served for a dressing-room, the inner apartment being small. I sent away the servant, locked the bed-room door, and threw myself down in my clothes, so truly miserable, that I had neither inclination or power to take them off.

Towards the morning, I fell into a short slumber, from which I was awakened by a knocking at the door. I hastily opened it. The servant said, a gentleman waited for me below: I could not mistake the person, and my first intention was to refuse seeing him; but presently I conceived the idea that it was possible he might repent of his unjust behaviour, and wished to acknowledge it. After a moment's hesitation, therefore, I said, I would attend him, and very soon followed her down stairs. When I entered the room, the Count met me, and seizing my reluctant hand—"Louisa, you have conquered: I have ventured to hazard my best hopes for your happiness.—Success, beyond my expectations, has attended me. My uncle forgives me, and has promised to be my advocate with my father. He even consents to receive you, and his carriage will soon be here to fetch you. Forgive my past conduct, which has wrung my heart as much as it has wounded your's.

This address, so unexpected, penetrated to my heart. Joy, hope, fear, and doubt, by turns assailed me.—Love had but a small share in my emotions; for that had received too rude a shock; but my fame, my character, was of far too much consequence to reject the possibility of its being established.—Yet still I involuntarily hesitated. He saw the conflict in my mind.—"I do not blame your want of confidence," said he; "I have deserved it; but respect yourself, if you no longer esteem me." Those words were like a talisman. My dear father recurred to my mind, softened my heart, and I burst into tears, yielding up my, 'till then, repulsive hand to him, with a look, that I saw covered him with confusion, and which I then thought was the effusion of a self-convicted mind.—He desired to breakfast with me. I readily complied, but very little conversation ensued. I was afraid of saying too much on my present prospects, lest it should be a tacit reproach on past transactions. His silence, doubtless, proceeded from other ideas, but he was extremely attentive and tender in his manners.

A carriage at length was announced:—"'Tis my uncle's," said he in a quick tone. "Hasten, my dear Louisa, to be received as you may wish for." My preparations were few, as I had brought but a small trunk with me. He discharged the expenses at the house, and with trembling limbs, and a beating heart, I seated myself in the carriage. As it drove off, he asked me, for the first time, to whom I had entrusted the management of my house, and who were acquainted with my journey. The first I told him, was given up; my effects in the house of our old friend, and the cause of my journey, a secret to every one. He praised my conduct and prudence; adding, that he hoped that day would see a termination to all my doubts and fears. I thanked him with fervor, and began to make a thousand excuses in my mind for his past unjustifiable behaviour, trying to restore to him my love and confidence.

When suddenly awaking from a deep reverie, I remarked, we were in a narrow gloomy road.—"I thought," said I, 'that your uncle's house was not a mile from the town?" "His town house is not," replied he, "but another house to which he set off this morning, is about two miles further on." A sudden chill seized on my heart; but checking a rising apprehension, I remained silent, until we entered a narrow road through a thick wood, and I saw the spires of a large building through the trees. —"Is that the house?" asked I.—"No; my uncle's is about half a mile further; but he talked of calling here, to take up a young lady, a relation, as a companion for you." I, blind and credulous, ready to believe what I wished for to be a truth, simply congratulated myself on his uncle's kind consideration. We soon stopped at the outside of a large building with a pair of iron gates.—"Bless me!" said I, "surely this is a convent."—"Yes, you are right; it is in this convent your future companion resides. I will step out and inquire if my uncle has been, or is here." He jumped out of the carriage; was wanting about ten minutes, which I thought an age, when coming up to the door of the chaise, with a smiling countenance—"Step out into the parlour, my dear Louisa; Miss Nolker will attend you instantly. We are before my uncle."

Where was my reason and prudence at that moment, when a duplicity so obvious, a scheme so ill contrived, never struck me as a fallacy. I readily gave my hand to the base betrayer; entered the gates, and in a moment was in the great Court, surrounded by eight or ten nuns, and my companion gone. For the instant I put my foot inside the outer gate, and turned towards the parlour. He dropped my hand; the other gate opened, and the nuns appeared. The whole was so quick, that I scarcely missed his hand before I lost sight of his person.

I looked on the nuns.—"Where am I going, and where is Miss Nolker?" I turned, as if going back to the parlour.—"This way, Miss," said one of the mothers; 'this way, if you please." Surrounding me, and urging me forwards—"What is it you mean?" I exclaimed, turning on every side. "What is become of the Count? Where is Miss Nolker?" One of the nuns took my hand.—"Do not distress yourself, by inquiries which cannot be answered to your satisfaction. Accompany us to the Abbess; you will there have every thing explained." I no longer resisted their entreaties. Conviction struck me at once of the vile treachery that had made me it's victim. I saw I was trepanned into a convent to be confined. It was useless to complain to the sisterhood.—I followed them in silence to the apartment where the Abbess was seated in state.

"My dear child," said she, in a soothing voice; "my dear child, you are welcome.—I hope you will find here every thing that can contribute to your peace and tranquillity." Without taking any notice of this "hope," I requested to speak with her alone. She nodded her head, and the nuns retired. I then briefly told her who, and what I was; related the cruelty and imposition of my husband; the crime he meditated of marrying another; and warned her to beware how she became a partner in an action so atrocious, as she might assure herself I had friends who would move Heaven and earth to trace me out, and bring my persecutors to justice.

When I stopt—"Bless me," said she, "This is a very extraordinary story, and totally foreign to the representation I have from Baron Nolker."—"How, Madam!" cried I: "From Baron Nolker?" "Yes, my child," replied she; "'tis by his orders I receive you here. He is a good man, and he will pay your pension here to preserve you from evil, and the deceits of the world." "If this be true," I exclaimed, "then is he imposed upon by the basest of mankind; but I rather think his name has been used without his permission. What, Madam is the information you have received concerning me?" "Excuse me, my dear child, I am not at liberty to answer your question.—Make yourself easy; here you will find friends, and meet with good treatment. If your own story is true, time will elucidate every thing to your advantage. At present, opposition will be in vain. I am amenable for your safety, and if you behave with prudence, in me you shall find a friend."

This speech of her's convinced me at once, that indeed all "opposition would be in vain," and that the plot was laid too deeply, though hastily conceived, for me to countermine at that time. I therefore contented myself with again warning her of the consequences, when my confinement should be known to my friends, and hastily left her presence. I came so quick into the outer room, that I discovered some of the nuns in the act of listening through the cracks of the wainscot. How erroneous is the opinion generally entertained, that those persons detached from the world, and shut up in cloisters, are dead to all the passions which agitate the human frame. On the contrary, all the little mean passions, such as envy, malice, curiosity, and selfishness, are to be found inhabiting the bosoms of too many who have apparently retired from all worldly concerns. The good mothers were confused; but as I addressed them civilly, they soon recovered, and paid me much attention.

When I had been about three weeks in the convent, I was one day much surprised by the information, that my trunks of clothes had been brought that morning, and left without any message or inquiries. On examining them, I found all was perfectly right; my ivory cabinet was also in one of the trunks; but not a single paper of any kind remained. Convinced now that I was to be confined for life, without some miracles should effect my deliverance, my spirits no longer supported me. I fell into a low nervous fever, that reduced me extremely, both in body and mind. One of the lay sisters, who occasionally attended me, appeared to compassionate my situation. She shrugged her shoulders, shook her head, and calling me poor child, gave such indications of pity, that I ventured one day to complain of the cruel deception that had brought me there.

"Have you any friends," asked she, in a low voice, as if fearful of being heard. — "I believe," I replied, 'that I have a father, but I know not in what place he resides." — "That's bad, indeed," said she. — "If, however, you can write to any friend, I will find means to get your letter conveyed; the porteress is my aunt; she will not refuse to pass a letter of mine to a relation in the city, and she shall forward one for you." It instantly occurred to me to write to the relation of the Abbe, give her an account of my being forced into a convent, and enclose a letter of information to my father. As it was most probable he would either write or come there, when he had the power of being absent from his duty. I eagerly accepted her good offices, and promised to have my letter ready the following day. In the small trunk that I had brought with me to Ulm, I had packed up my writing box; and most fortunately, when the nuns, as is customary, examined the trunk, they had not deprived me of this treasure; whether from complaisance, or because they were fearful of doing it, I know not, but now this box was to me of inestimable value.

I lost no time in writing, and anxious to exculpate myself from the charge of guilt in the eyes of my father, I gave him a very circumstantial account of every occurrence that had befallen me since our separation, without, at that time, considering what might be the consequences of such information to a man of honour and a parent. The lay sister performed her promise; my spirits revived, and gay hope once more shed her illusive smiles over my mind. But this temporary ease was of short duration. Week after week rolled away, and brought no change in my situation: Continual expectations wore me to a shadow; 'till months passing by, and no letters or intelligence respecting my father, I all at once entertained an idea of his death.

Despondency then took fast hold of me. — I was a prisoner for life, sacrificed by the basest and most avaricious of mankind. Madness and despair worked me to a kind of frenzy; and one day, after a fit of gloomy recollection, I rose in a hurry, flew to the apartment of the Abbess, and insisted, in very peremptory terms, upon being liberated; — bid her, at her peril, detain a wife forced into confinement, and the daughter of an officer who would soon demand me from her hands. She appeared terrified at the state of my mind, tried to sooth, to reason with me; but finding I grew quite outrageous, she called for assistance: I fought like a tiger with three of the nuns; but being overpowered by numbers, I was carried speechless and senseless to an apartment used as a prison, when any of the boarders deserved punishment.

Here I was left alone upon a miserable bed, with some bread and water for my support. Being exhausted by the violence of my passions, and the resistance I had made to the nuns, the turbulence of my emotions subsided, and I fell into a paroxysm of tears, that in all probability preserved me from a state of insanity, so much apprehended by the nuns. After this relief to the oppression of my heart, I dropped asleep, and having some hours rest, waked to a more composed state both of body and mind. I remained alone the remainder of the day, and all night. I was terrified at my situation; the melancholy place where I lay was indeed sufficiently gloomy to inspire terror. Convinced that I should gain nothing by menaces or force, I resolved to adopt a different line of conduct, to subdue my resentment and impatience, if possible, and try the effects of a more conciliatory manner, as if I grew reconciled to what I could not overcome.

Never was the approach of day more welcome than it appeared to me. I had passed such a night of weak, and indeed foolish apprehension, that I am confident the fear of continuing

there would have deranged my intellects. When the nuns came
to me, and observed the alteration in my temper, they retired, to
make, as they said, a favourable report, and obtain my liberty,
which, through their interposition, was effected by the dinner
hour, when I appeared vexed and mortified, and with a heart
throbbing with grief and disappointment. I endured a short
lecture from the Abbess (who persisted always in calling me
Miss) with a sort of restrained pride, that sat very ill, I believe
on my features; as she gently cautioned me against indulging
improper notions or visionary expectations. I made no reply,
but from that hour, gave myself up as a lost creature, disclaimed
or forgotten by all my connexions.

Once or twice after this, when I was upon tolerable terms
with the Abbess, I ventured to question her, whether Baron
Nolker, or his nephew the Count, was still at Ulm. — She assured
me they were not; that they had quitted the country within a
month after my residence in the convent. She knew not where
they were gone to, as she had received a twelvemonth's pension
in advance for me. Indeed, I have no doubt but that she had
received a handsome douceur besides. This information gave
the finish to all my hopes of a release, unless some very
unforeseen event should take place. I had forgot to mention,
that in my cabinet, among my trinkets, I found the money
which the Count mentioned in his letter; for which, indeed, I
could have no use, unless hereafter to purchase necessaries.

CHAPTER V

And now, my dear Miss D'Alenberg, I am coming to the most melancholy part of my story, which indeed I dread to enter upon. Excuse the prolixity of my recital; the conclusion I shall endeavour to hasten over, as too painful to dwell upon.

I had resided in the convent near eighteen months, without any alteration having taken place in my circumstances. Twice, during that time, I had again written to my father, almost without hope, and as I thought, without effect. One day, about noon, a paper was delivered to the Abbess, brought by a stranger at the grate. She opened and read it, with surprise and confusion strongly marked in her countenance. She withdrew immediately. Very soon after she had left the room, I was desired to attend her. My heart fluttered strangely. Good Heavens! thought I, can that paper relate to me. What now is to become of me? I flew, rather than walked, to her apartment. She still held the paper in her hand. — "Miss," said she, "I have here an order to deliver you up to a gentleman, who calls himself Hautweitzer and — — — "My father," I exclaimed, and sunk to the ground.

By the assistance of an attending nun, I was soon recovered. — "Oh! let me fly; let me go to my father," I cried, the moment speech was lent me. — "Stop, Miss," said the Abbess, "you shall be properly conducted: your emotions convince me the claim is just, and that I have been imposed upon." By the bye, I never gave credit to that assertion, because she was deaf and callous to every thing I had urged, tending to convince her of the duplicity practised against me. This was no time, however, for words; I was requested to hasten in packing my trunks, as a person waited for me in the parlour. I had no doubt but that this was my father, and my agitations scarcely permitted me to waste a moment. One of the mothers assisted me; I took a hasty and incoherent leave of the community; slid a remembrance into the hand of the lay sister, and, with trembling impatience, run to the parlour, where I beheld — not my father, but a stranger.

I gave a scream, and sunk back in a chair, gasping with terror at my disappointment, uttering something about my father. — — — "Here, Madam," said the stranger, giving me a slip of paper: 'this will satisfy you as to my commission." I snatched the paper, and glancing my eyes over it, saw it was the writing of my father, with only these words: "Come to me, my dearest Louisa, I am at Ulm. My friend will conduct you to the arms of your father."

I no longer hesitated, but giving my hand to the stranger, incapable then of speaking, was by him placed in a carriage. Recovering, in a short time, from my first agitations, I asked some questions relative to my father's situation, and why he had not come for me himself. The gentleman viewed me with an air of compassion, I thought, and seemed embarrassed what answer to give me; but at length said, "he was sorry it fell to his lot to give an explanation of circumstances that must distress me, but that my father had requested him to prepare me for the disagreeable intelligence which must be communicated. Let me, however, assure you," said he, 'that Mr. Hautweitzer is entirely out of danger, in a state of convalescence that will soon restore him to perfect health."

Without attending to an exclamation I uttered, he went on — "Your father, Madam, some time since, fought a duel; he was dangerously wounded, but happily not mortally so. He lay long in a doubtful state. I have the pleasure to assure you, all apprehensions of his life are done away. Do not therefore alarm yourself," added he, observing my terror, and the emotions which affected my mind. "My friend wished you to be a little prepared, that the surprise might not too greatly distress you." "Ah! Sir," I exclaimed, "if indeed my father is out of danger, I return thanks to Heaven: But who, pray tell me, was his opponent? My heart already divines."

"It was Count Wolfran." — "The father or the son?" asked I, gasping for breath. — "The father," replied he, "who was the aggressor in every sense of the word." — — — "And does he live," said I. — "No, he survived but three days." This answer was like a bolt of ice; it threw me into a fit of trembling. Cold damps bedewed my limbs, and I thought my last hour was at hand. — My companion was extremely shocked; — but being a medical man, he had luckily some drops in his pocket, which revived me. He besought me to be composed. The event had turned out favourably for my father, who had been exculpated by the Count's own confession. This, indeed, was some ease to my mind; but the reflection that my folly and imprudent marriage had brought on such shocking events, wounded my very soul, and I was scarcely able to support myself when the carriage stopped at the gentleman's house.

He gave me drops and wine to restore my spirits, and I accompanied him to the apartment, where I found my dear parent supported by pillows in his bed. Our meeting cannot be described; it was most truly distressing to both. He neither blamed or upbraided me, but soothed me by his kindness, which was a thousand times more painful to a self-convicted mind, than the most bitter reproaches could have been. He saw what I felt. "Forgive yourself, my Louisa, for you are exculpated in my eyes. An ingenuous unsuspecting heart was no match for the dark designing arts of an accomplished villain. You erred, 'tis true, but you was young, in love, and a stranger to the world.—Your faults were venial ones, even in the eyes of prudence; for you preserved your virtue, and knew not that the man in whom you confided would prove a monster, a disgrace to human nature."

He then told me, that the army in Poland, being sent into winter quarters, he had repaired with all diligence to the house of the good Abbe, not having received either of his letters, or any intimation of his death. He was therefore excessively shocked at the news that awaited him, and my letters were put into his hands. 'Tis not possible to conceive the rage, indignation, and sorrow, which he experienced on reading them; he took his measures instantly, and departed for the house of Count Wolfran. On his arrival, he was informed that the old Count was gone on a visit to his son and daughter, at their estate near Ulm. Boiling with increased rage at this information, he pursued his journey, and came there when the whole family was rejoicing at the christening of an heir to the estate and title, the young Countess Theodosia having been brought to bed near six weeks.

My father requested to see the old Count on particular business, and was shown into an apartment to wait for him. In a few moments he appeared, and started on seeing the person before him, who, endeavouring to calm his passions, desired he would wave all former animosity, and hear him on an affair which concerned their mutual honour. The other, with a mixture of surprise and haughtiness, requested he would be seated, and hasten what he had to say, as he was particularly engaged with company. My father then drew out my first circumstantial letter, and gave it to him, saying, "read that, Sir, with candour, and give no answer until you have gone through it.—Although we are not friends, yet I trust you are a man of honour."

The Count looked hastily over the letter, several times smiling with an air of disdain and triumph, which the other could ill brook. At length, returning it to my father—"I am sorry the wild chimeras of your daughter should have engaged you in such a fruitless journey. Be assured, she never was the wife of my son, although it is very natural a young lady should wish to throw a veil over her own frailty." My father instantly took fire. —"How dare you," cried he, "insinuate the smallest reflection on the character of my child; her only act of frailty was in supposing truth or honour could inhabit the bosom of a son of your's; but her honour is unblemished, without any stain, but what must follow in being the wife of a villain."

He had raised his voice to a pitch of fury. The other, equally exasperated, exclaimed, "Your daughter was preserved from want and infamy, by my son. Yes," added he, "after having prostituted herself to him, he placed her in a convent, to preserve her from the vilest degradation." My unhappy father, raised almost to a state of madness, forgot every thing at that moment, sprung forwards, and struck the Count. — "Slanderous villain," he cried, "I will choke those words in their birth." That instant the young Count, the Countess, and some others, burst into the room. My father was seized, foaming with rage, whilst some ran to the old Count, whose nose and mouth bled profusely. The son demanded the cause of this outrage, little suspecting who the person was before him. My father exclaimed, "I came here to demand justice, to oblige the son of that man to acknowledge his legal wife. Yes, my daughter is the wife of Count Wolfran."

A faint shriek from the Countess caught the attention of her husband. He attempted to lead her from the room. "Stop," she cried; "if this man asserts a falsity, let it be proved such. I will abide the decision; I will not leave the room, when an assertion of such consequence to my fame and happiness has been publicly declared." The old Count now advanced. — "You have dared to degrade me; you have calumniated my son. — Though you are inferior in birth, in rank to me; yet, as having borne arms, I wave my privileges, and challenge you to meet me to-morrow at eight o'clock, in a field at the west end of the city. Your blood only can atone for this outrage." — "I accept the offer," replied my father. Then turning to the Countess — "I feel for you, Madam; — and nothing less than the justice I owe to my child could compel me to give you pain. — Read that letter, Madam, and judge for yourself." He gave my letter into her hands: — The Count exclaimed, "an impudent forgery," and attempted to take it from her. — "No, my Lord," said she — "no, I will read it; but strong indeed must be the proofs, e'er I can credit any thing to the disadvantage of your honour."

"Go," cried the old Count arrogantly — "go, Sir, after having interrupted the happiness of this family, to preserve the fame of a worthless daughter; leave it, whilst I can command myself; to-morrow, at eight, I shall expect you." Without deigning any other reply, but "I shall attend you, Sir," my father quitted the house.

He employed the intermediate time in writing to me; lamented his inability to provide for me, and advised me, rather than submit to be confined as a pensioner of the Count's, "to take the veil, if it might be allowed to me under my own name, or the one I bore in the convent." This letter he carried in his pocket to the field of action the next morning, and was very soon joined by the Count and a surgeon, the gentleman who had kindly taken me from the place of my confinement. This gentleman he was astonished to see. He had formerly been a surgeon to a regiment in which my father had a company. On recognizing my father, he advanced, and expressed his regret at being called to attend in such an affair between two gentlemen he respected, and inquired, with some earnestness, if the dispute could not be amicably settled.

"My father replied in the negative — "His own honour, and the peace and honour of his daughter, had been irreparably injured." "One favour, Sir," added he, "I will request, because in your power to serve me in. If I fall, in my pocket you will find a letter addressed to my child, under the name of Miss Sultsbach; promise me to convey that letter into her hands, under whatsoever name she may now bear. She is in the convent a few miles from the city; — but until I can do her character justice, I wish not to see her. Perhaps that blessing may be for ever denied to me." The friendly surgeon engaged to observe his request, and the two gentlemen presently engaged.

They fought desperately; several wounds were given and received on both sides, 'till at length each sheathed his sword in the body of his antagonist; both fell, to all appearance, lifeless. Two servants of the Count's had attended at some distance; to those the surgeon made a signal; and as they advanced, two peasants happened to pass through the field, and were likewise called upon to lend their assistance. My father the surgeon most humanely ordered to his own house, and the Count was conveyed to his son's. The blood had been stanched before their removal, and another skillful man was called in to attend upon my father, the surgeon being previously engaged by the Count.

The wounds of both were apprehended at first to be mortal. The Count's verified their fears; for on the third day, all hopes were over. Being informed of his situation, he sent for both surgeons, and the two servants who had carried him home; before them all, he declared he had wronged Mr. Hautweitzer, and had provoked his fate. — He was then sensible that he had injured him in his fame and in his fortune; and he bitterly regretted that his son's marriage put it out of his power to do Miss Hautweitzer justice.

After this, he had some serious conversation with his son; but there is every reason to believe, that son, so devoid of truth and honour, even in that awful hour, persisted in denying his marriage with me, to his father.

The Count's death was concealed from my father; and though he anxiously wished to see me, yet he would not consent that I should be acquainted with his situation. — The young Count and his family left Ulm on the same day the father died. It was above ten days after this event, before an application was made to the Bishop, for an order to the Abbess to liberate me, which was easily obtained; for the Bishop was nearly related to the Wolfran family, and wished to have the affair as little known or talked of as possible. Therefore the duel was generally supposed to have originated from a military quarrel, and the son's name not mentioned in the business."

This was the information that I received from my beloved parent. Alas! bitter were my self-reproaches; he was wounded both in mind and body; his situation afforded him no means of providing for himself or me; I could adduce no proofs of my marriage, and my assertions would but little avail against the power of an opulent family, who were all interested in preserving the character and honour of their worthless relation. The surgeon, to whom my father related my whole story, sympathized in our distresses. He saw no prospect of good to us in prosecuting my claims. The Count was married in the face of the world; had now a son and heir; no inducements, therefore, of honour or justice, would have any probability of success, where every thing militated against us. "My dear friends," added he, "to Heaven you must leave this unworthy man: Doubt not, but in it's own good time, providence will revenge your wrongs, and punish him. At this moment his feelings are not to be envied. — He must be callous, indeed, if the crimes he has committed, and the death of his father, who fell a victim to his deceptions, does not fill him with horror and hourly regret.

My dear father recovered very slowly; — and we held frequent consultations in what manner we should provide for our mutual support. I believe the anxiety of his mind retarded his recovery, and certainly undermined his constitution, which had long been delicate, from the difficulties and misfortunes he had to struggle with. For myself, a retrospection on the past, and the prospect of the future, was so dark, so afflictive, and so humiliating, that 'tis a miracle how I supported my health, or preserved my reason.

I had resided with my father near a month; he was yet unable to leave his bed, when I was one day informed a lady requested to see me. The message surprised me; but I went down to the apartment, and saw a very elegant woman in deep mourning, who rose at my approach. "Do I see Miss Hautweitzer?" said she, in a very plaintive voice. I answered in the affirmative, and requested she would be seated. She took a letter from her pocket—"Forgive me, Madam, for thus recalling to you such distressing events, but permit me to ask if this letter is of your writing?" I saw it was the letter I had written to my father, and immediately judged the lady before me was the Count's wife. I trembled excessively, and replied, in a faltering voice, "Yes, Madam, it was written by me, and the contents are a solemn truth."

"I do not doubt it," said she, tenderly; "your appearance sufficiently convinces me of it. I am, Madam, equally unfortunate, and equally innocent with yourself; but never will I stand between you and justice.—The cruelty of an unprincipled man cannot annihilate your rights. I have none— nor have I parents or relations. Fortunately I have still a large income in my own possession sufficient for my ill-star'd child, without any claims on his worthless father. I have quitted the Count, Madam, for ever.—Wretch as he is, he knows we cannot expose him without entailing disgrace on ourselves. You, for want of proofs, and myself on account of my child. To the justice of Heaven, therefore, we must leave him.

"My visit to you was to a sister in affliction; permit me the privileges of one.—I have made very minute inquiries into your character and circumstances; pardon the liberty. Fortune, I hear, has dealt unkindly by Mr. Hautweitzer, and unjust to his merit. From Count Wolfran, I am sure, you will accept no assistance, unless by repentance he restores you to your rights. Deign, then, to make me happy, by permitting me the inexpressible pleasure of preserving you from further distress. Accept an annuity that will place you above want, without having the weight of an obligation to cold unfeeling minds." She rose, embraced me, and burst into tears.

I was so astonished, so penetrated with wonder and admiration, at a generosity and greatness of mind so uncommon, that unable to move or speak, I mingled my tears with her's, and pressed her to my bosom with an ardor that spoke my whole soul. She understood the expression of my heart. "Compose yourself," said she, "my amiable friend. Tell me how your worthy father does?"—When speech was lent me, I was not backward in delineating the feelings of admiration with which she had inspired me, and related to her, without reserve, my dear father's situation. She desired to see him; I flew to acquaint him of the dear lady's visit, and the scene that ensued between us, beggars all description. Long my father resisted her generous offers; but at length her irresistible tenderness conquered. She then proposed our living at Stutgard. She had a small estate on the skirts of the city, with a neat house on it: That, and a moderate income, for my father would only accept a very moderate one, she declared should be ours, for our joint lives; and whenever I should have the misfortune to lose my father, she would claim me as a sister, and as an inmate of her dwelling, wheresoever it was. — At present, added she, I design to retire into the convent you have quitted, until I have deliberately fixed on my future plan of life. I am sorry to say, Baron Nolker, who is a worthy man, is yet so prepossessed in favour of his nephew, that your story is entirely discredited, and I am accused of injustice and caprice in separating myself from the Count. 'Tis impossible to argue against prejudice, or to open the eyes of the blind. I submit, therefore to the censures and opinions I cannot controvert; but I will judge for myself; and if I had ever entertained any doubts, your appearance, Madam, must instantly remove them."

I cannot repeat to you a tenth part of the kind and polite attentions we received from this noble-minded lady. My father was affected even to tears, and besought her to add additional value to her favours, by residing with us. She expressed herself obliged to our wishes, but said, the convent was for the present her preferable choice; that it was not unlikely but that hereafter she might pay us a visit; but even that depended on circumstances. "You are not the only one unhappy," said she, taking my hand kindly; "and you have a blessing I never enjoyed, a worthy father." Then rising and taking leave, she said, I should hear from her the following week, and she promised to herself much pleasure in my correspondence. When this dear generous lady had left me, I felt ready to have resigned my claims, to have submitted to bear the ignominy the Count wished to throw on me, rather than be the cause of distressing such a mind as her's. — Yet, on a retrospection of every thing, I could not perceive that sorrow or affection had any share in her regrets for the necessity she conceived that had obliged her to leave the Count, I was thoroughly persuaded her love for him never could have equalled mine, from the composure with which she mentioned him; and that idea afforded me no small consolation.

The next week, a gentleman came to us from our generous benefactress, and settled every thing relative to our taking possession of her gift at Stutgard, with a handsome sum for our present wants. This last I declined; for having still by me the money which the Count had left to me, and which was sent with my clothes; I resolved to make use of that without any scruple. My dear father had been so extremely reduced by loss of blood, and anxiety of mind, that his recovery was long, tedious, and fluctuating. Near three months we remained at the surgeon's, during which, I received three letters from the Countess. She had altered her intention of fixing in the convent near Ulm, by the persuasions of an old friend, who had professed in a convent not many miles from Baden; and from that situation, I had last the pleasure of hearing from her.

At length my father thought himself able to bear the fatigue of travelling. We took leave of the friendly gentleman to whose care and skill we had been so much indebted, and set off on our journey; but on the second day, it proved more than his strength could support; he was taken ill on the road, and was confined six weeks at an inn before we could proceed. Once more we continued our route, and by easy stages, had reached the skirts of the wood within two miles of this village, when suddenly we were attacked by five or six banditti, who rifled the carriage, took from us our portmanteau and money, cut the traces of the horses, and then bid us walk to the place of our destination, as we had now no baggage to encumber us.

There was no alternative; night was drawing on; and we were compelled to walk; for the horses being loosened, they run away through the wood, and the post boy went in pursuit of them. With infinite difficulty, my poor father crept to the inn, where his troubles in this life were to have an end. A very miserable bed was allowed for him, and I watched by the side of it in inexpressible agonies. The next morning the landlord told us, "we must turn out; he had no bed to spare for sick folkes." I sought to reason with him, and assured him I should soon have money amply to reward him, if he would accommodate my dying father: But in vain I tried to reason with a selfish brute. He insisted upon our departure before night; and though he assisted me in getting him down from the hovel which he called a bed-chamber, and saw that he was too weak even to stand alone, nothing could soften his obduracy. The rest you know. My dear, my suffering father, whose life had been a series of misery, was at length, by the folly and fond credulity of his imprudent daughter, cruelly destroyed. That fatal duel, the effects falling on a broken constitution and a wounded spirit, with fatigue and anxiety, at last terminated a life marked out with continual sorrows, from the day of his marriage.

Those sorrows, my misconduct, and the baseness of another, greatly aggravated, and must entail remorse upon my mind to the last day of my existence."

Thus concludes the narrative of the unfortunate Louisa, which she communicated at different periods, as her weakness permitted, and which Miss D'Alenberg was allowed to commit to paper, for the perusal of her father and his friend.

CHAPTER VI

When Ferdinand had gone through this long story with an indignation and pity natural to a feeling and well-disposed mind, there were some circumstances that struck him in the perusal of it, which led him to believe the lady in the convent where Eugenia was, whom he had supposed to be Claudina, was the Countess of Wolfran, and that she had mistaken him from a coincidence in particular points, for the Count. He was charmed with the character of this lady, and lamented her destiny little less than he grieved for the ill-treated Louisa. Yet it appeared very unaccountable to him that the Count should think of paying his address to another lady, when his recent marriage at Ulm could not be forgotten; and when his uncle was so well acquainted with all those circumstances, was it not natural to suppose that Mr. D'Alenberg would take care to be well informed of the character and connexions of a man with whom he entrusted the happiness of his daughter, previous to the marriage; and if he had made any investigation, by what means had the Count escaped detection, or how could any man expect that he should go unpunished, or not be exposed by those he had already deceived?

In short, the conduct and character of the Count was strange and inexplicable to him; the more he sought to penetrate into either, the more he was puzzled to account for his baseness and folly. Reflecting deliberately on the story of Louisa, he traced the misfortunes of her father to an imprudent marriage in early life, and the subsequent distress of his daughter to the same source. Reverting then to his own perplexities, he could not but acknowledge, that, in forming a union for life with prudence, on the approbation of friends, as well as the mutual affection of the parties concerned, eventually depended the happiness of themselves and all their connexions.

"Yes," said he, with a sigh; "I am now sensible, that out of a thousand instances of wretchedness in a marriage state, there is scarcely one that does not originate from the imprudence of youth, in forming connexions contrary to the advice and inclination of their parents and friends. Parents may sometimes be selfish, arbitrary, and unfeeling; but youth is too generally impetuous, obstinate, and inconsiderate. They permit their passions to lord it over their reason, and are only convinced, by sad experience and painful consequences, of their own too hasty determinations in such points, as must decide their future happiness or misery."

Whilst he sat ruminating on past occurrences, the Count, having finished his business, entered the library, and roused him from his reverie. "Happily," said he, "I have now concluded all my engagements with my tenantry, and in two days shall be at liberty to attend you wherever you please." — "Indeed," cried Ferdinand, "it will be necessary to enter upon some field of action that may change the present current of my thoughts; for an indulgence of them would, in a short time, I believe, turn me into a complete misanthrope." "Nay," returned the Count, "if you are inclined to turn hermit, I am ready to concur in the design. I promise you the world holds forth no allurements to me; and it is only with a wish to forget myself, that I propose going into a public situation, if therefore you incline to solitude."

"No, no," said Ferdinand, rising hastily. "Solitude is only the nurse of discontent. — I am equally desirous with yourself to forget that "such things have been;" and in the busy din of arms, to seek that diversity of thought which may tend to lessen my present vexations. That you may not wonder at the captious manner in which I spoke just now, I entreat you to look over that manuscript I have just finished reading of, whilst I take a walk in the park, and harmonize my mind by a view of the sun, now breaking through the clouds, and shining on the verdant lawn, which refreshed by the passing showers; by its additional enlivening verdure, captivates the eye, and tranquillizes the human breast."

Quitting the library, he strolled through the gardens and park, until the first dinner-bell warned him to return and adjust his dress. At table, he met the Count, who, with an honest energy, and a warmth of heart, which did him honour, expressed his indignation against the villainy of Count Wolfran, and equal astonishment, that in so short a period, in the same country, and in the hazard of continual detection, he should have the effrontery to pay his addresses to Miss D'Alenberg. "'Tis a temerity, indeed a mystery," cried Ferdinand, "which I cannot develop. He is neither a madman nor a fool, and yet his rashness would tempt one to believe his senses must have deserted him, or his strong attachment to the sex has thrown him into situations he has not the fortitude, I may say honesty, to decline making an advantage of." "He is a worthless wretch," replied the Count, "and will doubtless meet with a severe retribution; but I am enchanted with the unfortunate lady who bears his name. — Her conduct is so generous, so noble, and so becoming a truly great mind, that I cannot enough admire her. How few women in her situation would have sought out the unhappy Louisa, after having her happiness broken in upon, her own claims let aside, and her child stigmatized, by her connexion with an infamous seducer."

"But what is still more admirable," returned Ferdinand, "is her voluntary secession from the Count, when her rights were indisputable; her marriage witnessed—allowed of; and when, by so doing, she threw up her child's claim to his inheritance, which Louisa never could have contested, from want of proof. Such heroism, such delicacy and disinterestedness, is certainly very uncommon." "True," answered the Count, "her whole conduct evinces a greatness of soul superior to any woman I ever heard of. A mind like her's never could be contented with a doubtful title, or respect a man whose honour was at least equivocal. And what a wretch must he be, who, losing such an angel, could so soon pay court to another."

"Miss D'Alenberg," said Ferdinand, "by the little I have seen of her, is both in person and mind beautiful and captivating; such as might well warrant the warmest passion; and he must be a thousand times a villain that would seek to entangle such a woman in the black catalogue of those who have suffered by his artifices. But," added he, "you see what are the wishes of Mr. D'Alenberg. Have you any curiosity; do you feel interest enough for those worthy persons, to step out of the way, and pay them a visit?" "With all my soul," replied his friend;—"we are not circumscribed as to time, and I shall be happy to see such characters as may put one in good humour with human nature."—This point settled, on the second day after, the Count, having taken leave of his tenantry, and recommended them to the kind offices of his steward, whose integrity was beyond all doubt, and whose attachment to his interest had stood the test of time and temptation. He readily accorded with what he saw was the inclination of Ferdinand, and they took the route towards the mansion of Mr. D'Alenberg.

Their presence was equally welcome as unexpected; they were no sooner announced, than the good old gentleman hastened to meet them with a cordiality that was truly gratifying to his visitors. "You have agreeably surprised me," said he to Ferdinand, after saluting the Count.—"My wishes were stronger than my hopes, and I am pleased to find that you gave due credit to my sincerity. You have enhanced the obligation of this visit, by affording me an opportunity of paying my respects to Count M———." Neither of the gentlemen were deficient in proper acknowledgments for the kindness of this reception, and, after a little desultory conversation, Mr. D'Alenberg introduced them to the ladies. Surprise and pleasure were strongly blended in the features of his daughter; nor did the melancholy Louisa appear less gratified, though the languor which hung over her whole frame, gave her less animation. Mr. D'Allenberg, in a cheerful voice, bid them "rally their spirits; and now that he had been fortunate enough to take two gallant knights prisoners, he expected the ladies of the Castle would do their best to make their chains easy, and their captivity light."

Theresa answered her father in his own style; and in a short time, the conversation became animated and entertaining. Even Louisa sometimes joined in it when applied to, though it was pretty evident that the effort was painful, and that she had a mind but ill at ease.

In the evening, after the ladies had retired, Mr. d'Allenberg of himself reverted to Louisa's story, and observed that he had to congratulate himself on the discovery of Count Wolfran's baseness, and also, that the heart of his daughter was much less attached to him than might have been expected from his handsome person and insinuating manners. "She has even told me," said he, "that her predilection was never decidedly strong in his favour; but that, having no attachment to another, no reasonable objection could be made against him. On the contrary, all appearances being to his advantage, and seeing that his addresses met with my approbation, she thought herself happy in complying with my wishes, where there was every prospect of future happiness to herself. — What a fortunate escape has my dear child experienced," added he.

"But my dear Sir," cried Ferdinand, "will you pardon me for observing, that it appears rather extraordinary you should not have well informed yourself of the Count's character and circumstances, previous to your consent for addressing Miss d'Allenberg." "You cannot suppose, my young friend," answered he, 'that I neglected a duty so important to a parent. I actually did make inquiries, the gentleman at whose house we met with him, told me, that he was a widower; that he had married some time ago a ward of his uncle's, who died soon after she was brought to bed. His father, he said, had been killed in a duel by an officer, on account of an old regimental quarrel; — and that he had the misfortune to lose his worthy uncle very shortly after, for whom he then wore mourning. In short, my friend represented him as a worthy young man, who had met with great distresses from the premature death of his connexions, and congratulated me on the power of restoring him to happiness, by giving him the hand of my daughter."

I have not the smallest doubt but that my friend implicitly believed every syllable he told me. Louisa's story was known to none but such whose interest it was to keep it secret. The Countess, or more properly speaking, the lady he had married, withdrawing herself and child, declaredly to him, for ever. The death of his uncle soon after that of his father, to whom only he was accountable for his actions, left him at liberty to promulgate what stories he pleased. None were interested either to doubt or to investigate them. — From our earliest acquaintance, I had understood he was going to make a tour to England; and when he had obtained my permission to address Theresa, he warmly solicited us both to join in his intended plan, which coinciding with our inclinations. — When you met with me at the village, I was returning to this house, with the double purpose of making preparations for the wedding, and at least a twelvemonth's absence. The Count and my friend were to join us in a week, when the marriage was to be completed, and we were directly to have set off on our tour. Thus you see he run no risk of an immediate detection, and doubtless would have remained abroad some time, or have changed his usual residence.

But providence often defeats the deep-laid schemes of villainy, and unmasks the contriver to the world. I have written a circumstantial account to my friend, and besought him to treat the base betrayer with the contempt and ignominy he deserves, nor as he values my friendship to engage in any personal resentment with a wretch so unworthy of his sword, but to let disgrace mark his steps, and his character fly before him. To the Count I disdained to write. Louisa and my daughter have both written to the Countess; the former, at our request, gratefully declining the generous settlement designed for her father and herself; my daughter, in terms of the warmest admiration of her noble conduct, relating to her the late occurrences, and earnestly entreating her to pay us a visit. Should she do us that favour, there will be a singular trio, two wives, and one intended to make a third.

"Upon my word," said Count M———, "I know not which to admire most, the temerity, or the villainy of the man. Such unprecedented baseness in the same province, among his own acquaintance, where so many doubtful circumstances must have appeared against him, had any particular inquiry been set on foot, is truly astonishing." "It would have been more so," observed Ferdinand, "had not many points coincided in his favour. Mr. Hautweitzer's assertions before the old Count and the company, bore no proofs of the marriage which the young one disclaimed. He represented Louisa as his mistress; his father and uncle doubtless believed her to be such. She could adduce no evidence to prove the contrary. Therefore, though his connexion with her was reprehensible, even from his own acknowledgment, yet it bore not the marks of guilt attending a double marriage; nor had his lady sufficient conviction to authorize her withdrawing herself and child from him, had he persisted in his claims. But her honour and delicacy could not be satisfied with a disputed title; and from the Count's subsequent conduct, there is but too much reason to believe, that in possession of her fortune, and weary of being confined to one object, and to a dissembled regularity of life, inconsistent with his libertine principles, he made use of no endeavours to reconcile her doubts, or establish her claims, but left her to her own painful conjectures, the termination of which was in all probability little less satisfactory to him than to herself, as it left him at liberty to form fresh projects, and seek for new objects."

"Upon my word," returned Mr. D'Alenberg, "I believe you have represented the affair in its true point of view; and as a man, without honour or principle, governed by the most sensual and selfish passions, his conduct wants no further explanation; nor can we wonder he should succeed with the ladies, when setting aside his personal attractions, he certainly has the most insinuating address, the most plausible manners I ever beheld; so much so, that you would scarce feel an inclination to make inquiries that you must consider as equally an insult to him, and to your own discernment. But enough of this disgrace to society; let him no more be remembered among us."

Two days past away in this hospitable mansion with such celerity, from the delightful suavity and uncommon cheerfulness which Mr. D'Alenberg exerted to entertain his guests, and the more refined and elegant conversation of the ladies; that, on the third day, which the gentlemen had fixed upon for their departure, they felt infinite reluctance to give up the charms of such society, and relinquish domestic happiness for the clangor of arms, and destructive war. A sigh of heart-felt regret, and painful retrospection, escaped from both, when they met at the breakfast table, prepared for their journey.

"How," said Mr. D'Alenberg; "do you mean to throw a cloud over our little party, by deserting us? Did you come here with the ill-natured purpose of engaging our esteem, of giving us a relish for those pleasures arising from entertaining and improving conversation, and then suddenly leave us to regret and disappointment? In truth, my good friends, this is not well done of you;—and I expect you will give up your intention and your boots together, unless you will escort the ladies in an airing this morning."—"I hope, Sir," replied Ferdinand, with a look of earnestness, and in a tone of dejection; "I hope, Sir, you will believe there needs no persuasion to induce us to comply with your kind wishes, which so well accords with our own inclinations; but there are particular circumstances—motives of honour and delicacy—feelings which impel us to give up the happiness we have found in this society, and to follow that plan we have chalked out for ourselves, from whence we expect to derive neither profit nor pleasure, but, in the tumult of a camp, to lose the remembrance of ourselves."

"Far be it from me, to pry impertinently into your motives," returned Mr. D'Alenberg, "or urge you to favour us with your company one moment longer than is consistent with your inclinations and engagements. I must regret that both will not allow you to oblige me, but you must be masters of your own time and actions." The Count made suitable acknowledgments to the old gentleman, and lamented the necessity which forced them to relinquish their present happiness.

The ladies spoke not a word; a general dejection pervaded at the table with a silence of some minutes. Mr. D'Alenberg was the first to recover. "Plague on it," said he, affecting a gay tone, 'that we cannot always command our wishes, though perhaps they may be sometimes extravagant, and militate against the interests of our friends. Aye, aye, we are not the best judges of the fit, and the unfit, I believe, and so must try to reconcile ourselves to present mortifications, looking forward to more pleasing expectations hereafter; and this hope, my friends, I will not relinquish, that we shall one day meet again, when the joy of meeting will amply recompense us for this temporary separation." They all joined cordially in "this hope;" and the moment breakfast was ended, Miss d'Allenberg arose. "I have an utter aversion," said she, with a faint smile, 'to formal taking leave. You have my best wishes, gentlemen, for your health and happiness. I flatter myself you will sometimes remember us." With those words hastily pronounced, she quitted the room, followed by Louisa, who made them a similar compliment, without waiting for an answer.

"The girls are sorry to lose their beaus," said the old gentleman: "Their pleasure has been very transient; and if I have any skill in physiognomy, this parting accords as little with your feelings as with ours; and yet it must be, I suppose?"

"Dear Sir," cried Ferdinand, "how kindly is that question put, and what justice do you allow to our sentiments. Yes, we must go," added he, rising. "May every good angel guard you and your family, and uninterrupted happiness attend your lovely daughter and her suffering friend."

"I thank you most cordially—I thank you," replied Mr. D'Alenberg; "health and success will, I hope, be your's. We may one day meet again."

No more was said; they proceeded down the avenue which led to a gate, where their horses and servants were in waiting. The Count shook the old gentleman's hand, and vaulted into the saddle. As Ferdinand prepared to do the same, he whispered in the other's ear,

"Pity two unfortunate men, both married, and unhappy. You will do justice to the motives which hastens our departure."

He sprung upon the horse, and waving his hand, they were out of sight in a moment.—Mr. d'Allenberg stood all astonishment, looking after them, his lips half unclosed—words trembling on his tongue; but they were gone; he turned towards the house, deeply musing on Ferdinand's last words, and with a sigh of pity that two such men should be "married and unhappy."

Count M———— and his friend pursued their route for some miles without stopping or speaking, absorbed each in his own painful reflections; the other was unheeded; until, coming out of a wood, and ascending a rising ground a little to the left, Ferdinand saw the hills on which the city of Baden was situated, and instantly recollected his little Charles. Ah! thought he, shall I not once more fold him in my arms; the dear, unhappy, forsaken boy, perhaps soon to be an orphan, without a father or a friend. He stopped his horse, and turning, saw the Count galloping towards him, who, observing his agitation, eagerly inquired if any accident had befallen him.

"No," replied Ferdinand, "but do you not see those distant hills? A little beyond, you know, stands Baden: I have a son."———

"I understand you," said the Count;—and guess what passes in your heart. But my good friend, you have lately seen him; you know he is in safe and honourable hands.—Why then would you seek a renewal of sorrow to yourself, without conveying a single benefit to him?"

"Enough," returned Ferdinand, pulling his hat over his eyes. "You have convinced me I ought not to seek a selfish gratification, which can only tend to harrow up my soul, and unman my resolutions; no, I will not go."

He spurred on his horse, and was again silent, until they arrived at a small village, where they were obliged to halt, and refresh the poor animals, almost dead with fatigue.

Each being desirous of amusing the other, they soon fell into a cheerful conversation, and sought to forget the past, by talking of their future plans. The war, which was now to be carried on with great vigour against the Turks; the marriage which the Emperor had projected for his daughter, afterwards so famous in history, as Queen of Hungary; and many other common topics, that carried them out of themselves.

Thus they spent some hours, until they resumed their journey, purposing to sleep at a small town about twelve miles further; but the roads were so bad, and they were so much impeded in their progress, that they were constrained to halt at a wretched inn on the skirts of a small hamlet, and pass a sleepless night, without any tolerable accommodations; but they were going to the army, and therefore disdained to complain of hardships, though they paid the price of luxuries.

The dawn of the morning saw them on horseback; and as they rode on, new scenes, and brighter prospects, gave a relief to their minds, and cheered their conversation. The remainder of their journey grew more pleasant; was passed without any accidents, and in due time they arrived in safety at Vienna.

CHAPTER VII

Here the busy preparations for the recruiting of the army, the Court of the Emperor, and the multitude of strangers resident there at that time, could not fail of attracting attention, and inspiring ardor in the bosoms of two brave men who wished to distinguish themselves in a cause against their common enemy. Count M. was introduced to the Emperor, Charles the Sixth, who, having just received an account of the death of that brave and successful General, Prince Eugene, without knowing any one deserving, or capable of undertaking the command of his army, was at that time greatly perplexed, and gratefully acknowledged the volunteer services offered by the Count. — Ferdinand had heretofore been honoured with his approbation, and both gentlemen had abundant cause to be satisfied with their reception.

They passed some weeks at Vienna, in the usual amusements of the city, before the army was ready to take the field; during which time, they had received letters from their friends that had helped to tranquillize their minds. Ferdinand heard from Mr. Dunloff, that his son, and the good old Ernest, were in health; and he had also a letter from his brother, informing him, 'that he was married to the Lady Amelia Bonhorff; but at the same time assuring him, that his present engagements did not weaken his regard for Ferdinand, who, whenever he was disposed to prefer services from a brother, to pecuniary obligations from a stranger, would always find his arms and purse open to his wishes."

This letter, the tenor of which seemed so affectionate, was nevertheless worded with a stiffness and a sort of haughty upbraiding, an air of superiority that alarmed the pride of Ferdinand, and again recalled to his mind the scene which passed immediately following the death of his father, when he was told, "that he was to be an equal sharer" in that fortune, solely bequeathed to Count Rhodophil, and the servants were ordered to remember they had two masters." — — — Ah! thought Ferdinand, in that moment, sorrow had softened his heart to the ties of nature, and a resolution to make me some reparation for the disappointment he supposed I must feel; but power and prosperity soon changed his sentiments, and chased the tender affections from his heart. He soon exulted in his superiority, and found gratification in ostentatiously bestowing as favors, those attentions, and that assistance, which at first he had taught me to expect as my right. Alas! how difficult is it for us to know our own hearts. Poor Rhodophil! that brother disposed to love and honour you. You have, by an ill-judged pride, by a duplicity unworthy of yourself and me—you have alienated from those ties that bound us, and compelled him to prefer that "stranger," whose generosity and spirit disdains the idea of an obligation, where his own nobleness of heart is abundantly gratified in making another happy. A stranger! No—Count M. is my brother; we have congenial souls, superior to the ties of blood.

This idea instantly cheered the mind of Ferdinand, and Count Rhodophil, with all his wealth and boasted happiness, neither excited his envy nor regret. His son and old Ernest were the only objects entitled to share his heart in Baden; not a word was mentioned relative to Claudina; and although a tender and sorrowful remembrance of a woman he once adored, frequently obtruded, yet he had ceased to think of her with those pangs, and that agonized affection, that had wholly occupied his mind previous to his connexion with the Count; and the silence observed by all parties concerning her, was sufficient evidence, that she wished to be forgotten: A sigh followed the conviction, but he endeavoured to divert his attention, by throwing his thoughts on other subjects.

Count M. had also received a letter from Eugenia: The contents breathed a spirit of piety and cheerfulness; her situation grew daily more pleasant and desirable; peace had once more returned to her bosom, and the performance of religious duties had composed her mind, and she trusted, would atone for her errors. One only regret had power to give her a moment's pain, the union between the Count and herself, which precluded his happiness in that state with a more deserving object: But even this only interruption to her perfect content, she did not despair of removing at some future period. Her health, she added, was perfectly restored, and she had acquired a friend whose nobleness of mind was a pattern for her constant imitation.

The Count, who had, from the moment of their separation, exerted all his fortitude and resolution, to bear the decided plan Eugenia had fixed upon, who well knew her perseverance and courage, and saw all future expectations of enjoying her society would be equally vain and fruitless; whose passions, by sufferings, had been weakened and brought under control; though he was wounded to the soul by her determination to forsake him, no sooner found the event had taken place, and that no power or persuasion would avail to make any change in her plan, than he sought to call reason and resolution to his aid, to seek in an active life, and in a diversity of occupation, that variety of ideas which might preclude them from dwelling on one object; and this, with the friendship of Ferdinand, whose similarity of misfortunes, gentleness of manners, and goodness of heart, had gained his warm esteem, assisted him in subduing his sorrows, and restoring his mind to a comparative degree of ease.

The two friends having made a mutual communication of their letters, found, in a reciprocity of sentiment, mutual consolation; they had little doubt but that the lady mentioned in such high terms by Eugenia, was the Countess of Wolfran; nor could they forbear execrating the wretch who had poisoned the happiness of such a woman, by degrading her to a connexion with himself.

In a short time, the Emperor was ready to take the field; the friends were in one Regiment, and determined to share one fate: —They proceeded on their march, and soon came within view of the enemy's lines. —Here the Emperor halted; a council was convened, and the plan of attack settled, which was to take place the following day at sun-rise. The intermediate time the Count and Ferdinand employed in sealing their papers, writing to their friends; and the former generously erased all anxiety from the mind of the latter respecting his little Charles, by a bequest of a handsome provision for him, and constituting Mr. D'Alenberg the protector of his fortune and person; to which trust Ferdinand gladly added his acquiescence and signature; embracing his noble friend in a silent transport, much more expressive than a flow of words.

This necessary arrangement being completed, the Count wrote a tender adieu to his beloved Eugenia. —He had, from her first entrance into the convent, secured her future establishment. —Nothing, therefore, remained upon his mind to be performed. —She was already as dead to him; and he left no relatives to mourn his loss, should the chance of war deprive him of life. Their letters and papers were all deposited with the Emperor's private secretary, who was not unknown to the Count, and then they retired each to themselves for a few hours preparatory to the dreadful business of the following day.

At the first dawn of day, the drums and shrill sounding trumpets gave the alarm, and called them to the field. —The friends embraced, and hastened to their posts. The Turkish army was a numerous host; ashamed and enraged at their former defeats, they seemed now resolved to conquer or die on the spot; to retrieve their former blasted laurels, or return no more to meet the fury of their monarch, or bend the neck to the fatal and ignominious bow-string. Their opponents, equally emulous of glory, and desirous to rid themselves of a troublesome enemy, advanced to meet them with eagerness and resolution. A hard fought battle ensued; dreadful was the carnage on both sides; but the multitude prevailed. The Turks poured in on all the ranks of the Imperialists with such velocity, that they were unable to sustain their posts; were compelled to retreat; were pursued, and a horrid slaughter marked their sanguinary fury.

The Count and Ferdinand did all that men could do; they fought like lions; they were beat back several times: Again they rallied and returned to the charge; but though well supported, all availed not; the numbers were too powerful, and the friends fell desperately wounded among the dying and the dead. — The Imperialists were obliged to fly, and the honour of the day rested with the Turks. — By a piece of singular good fortune, the two wounded friends were discovered by a Turkish commander, who perceived they still breathed, though life seemed hovering on their lips, and their wounds pouring forth torrents of blood. The officer who observed their situation, was not deficient in the feelings of humanity; he exerted himself, and called in assistance to stop the bleeding, and bind up their wounds. They were carried to his tent, and properly attended. Insensible alike to his cares or their own danger, they remained for several days with very little signs of life, and with still less hopes of recovery.

During this period, a truce had been agreed upon between the two armies, and the Emperor appeared to be very much inclined to make peace on the terms he had before rejected. The face of things was now changed; Prince Eugene, whose name alone carried with it terror to his enemies, no longer existed. — The Turks had recovered from their panic; their courage returned with their numbers: Charles had many interior enemies, whom it behoved him to guard against. The first wish of his heart was the establishment of the pragmatic sanction, in favour of his daughter Maria Theresa, afterwards Queen of Hungary. To carry this favourite point into execution, he was willing to give up some secondary ones, and finding the Turks were at that time too powerful for him to subdue, he readily was persuaded to make overtures for a truce preparatory to proposals for a peace.

The Turks, though now victorious, had been so harassed, and exhausted in their treasures by former wars, that they made but a show of objections to the Emperor's advances; a truce was therefore speedily agreed upon for six months, and both armies withdrew from the field to their own homes. An exchange of prisoners was also settled, but unfortunately an officer, who had fought by the side of Ferdinand and the Count; seeing them both fall, to all appearance lifeless, reported their death in the army, and the bodies not being found, did not seem extraordinary, as few persons could be distinguished among the slain. The Turkish cavalry, in their pursuit of the vanquished, had rode over, and defaced most of the unhappy victims who lay in heaps upon the plain.

So great was the slaughter on that day, and so many brave men and officers had the Emperor lost, that the news of Count M— — — and Ferdinand being fallen with the rest, was only included in the general regret. The gentlemen entrusted with their letters to Mr. d'Allenberg, the Count's steward, and Mr. Dunloff, the good Ernest's nephew, sent them off with the melancholy account that those brave men no longer existed.

Whilst those letters were on their way to cause a mortal affliction to their friends, the Count and Ferdinand were carried in a litter to the house of their preserver in Adrianople. This Turkish commander, as we have observed, had some traits of humanity in his composition, and following the impulse of the moment, had administered relief to the dying friends from compassion alone; but after they had been conveyed to his tent, the blood washed from their persons; the contents of their pockets examined, in which were memorandums that denoted their being men of some condition, the predominant passion of self-interest was a greater stimulative than tenderness towards affording them that unremitted attention which most certainly conduced to the preservation of their lives.

Ferdinand was the first restored to his senses, and a recollection of past events. He saw only Turks around him, and an elderly woman who officiated as a nurse. His reason returned for two or three days before he had strength to speak. He therefore made his silent observations, and was very soon sensible that he was a prisoner. His regret was greatly lessened, when he saw that his friend the Count was also alive, and in a similar situation, from which he derived a hope that they might be companions, and useful to each other. Within a very few days, both gentlemen were enabled faintly to express their gratitude to their preserver, and rejoice in the safety of each other.

To their being together in one room, and capable of conversing now and then with each other, may doubtless be attributed their speedy recovery from a state so very dangerous, and even after the return of their senses, so very often fluctuating from the extreme weakness and debility occasioned by the great loss of blood.

One morning, when Ismael, the Turkish commander, paid them a visit, after they had enjoyed a good night's rest, and found their spirits greatly revived, they entered into a conversation with him relative to the truce which he had informed them was agreed upon between the two powers. He spoke both the German and French languages tolerable well, and they found no difficulty in making him comprehend they were men of family and fortune, and were desirous of returning into Germany as soon as possible.—They besought him, therefore, to let letters be conveyed to their friends, and to let information of their existence be expedited to the Emperor, that they might hope soon to be included in an exchange of prisoners.

This Ismael promised with much seeming sincerity, to undertake for; and assured them, he would exhibit his power and influence to procure for them a speedy release from captivity; giving them to understand, that their rank was known, and that he was answerable for their persons. Far different was the truth; their death had been generally credited in the Imperial army; the little inquiry that had been made relative to their bodies, had been unsatisfactory, and 'twas supposed they had been trampled upon undistinguished in the day of battle, and had been thrown with the multitude of dead bodies beyond all power of discrimination.

When carried to his tent, he perceived, from their military uniform, that they were of some rank in the army; he had therefore craftily destroyed their clothes, and from their wounds, their persons had but few traits left that could answer any description given of them. He had taken care to place no one near them that understood their language;—and by these artful manoeuvres, had them securely in his power.

As they advanced in a state of convalescence, he began to reflect, that in Adrianople, it would be impossible to retain them from the hazard of being known, or of finding an opportunity to give information of their existence, if they were permitted to be at liberty, which he could not well refuse when they had recovered strength sufficient to walk.

To perfect his schemes, it was necessary to take them further into the country, where their dependence must rest solely on him, nor any knowledge of affairs reach them but through his hands. This determined on, he came to their apartment one morning with an air of haste and distraction. He told them, a commotion had begun in the city; that the troops, dissatisfied with the commanders for agreeing to a truce, instead of pursuing their victories, had risen in large bodies, both in Constantinople and in that city also; and, as it was impossible to judge of the event, or how far the rage of the soldiery might proceed, their only safety depended on flight. Fortunately he had a country house in the neighbourhood of Philippo, where they would be secure against violence or disaffection. To this house they should be immediately conveyed in a litter, to preserve them from the fury of the mob, which might possibly know no bounds, if they were discovered to be Germans.

This plausible tale, fabricated to impose on the unsuspicious friends, were by them credited without reserve, and they felt the warmest gratitude towards Ismael for his kind solicitude to save and serve them. — Within a few hours, every thing was arranged and they were on the road to Philippo, Ismael assuring them of his attention to their interests, and that he would either quickly join them, or if the insurrection was subdued, send orders for their speedy return.

Their state of health would not admit of travelling fast; therefore the slow proceeding of the litter was to them a convenience; and in the open roads they were permitted to be uncovered, and have the benefit of the air. The small villages they stopped at afforded but indifferent accommodations; nor did they meet with a single being who understood their language.

On the second day, they halted at a tolerable large hamlet, at one end of which were the remains of a miserable fort, inhabited by a few soldiers. The person who commanded them held some conversation with their conductors; presently after which, they made signs for them to alight. Two of them took hold of the Count to assist him. Ferdinand was preparing to follow, when instantly two men with drawn scimitars jumped into the litter, seized his arms. The curtains were closed, and they moved forwards, regardless of the struggles and exclamations of Ferdinand, and the cries of the Count, which died away upon his ear as they proceeded.

Too late convinced that some treachery was intended, distracted at being separated from his friend, and equally incapable of making any resistance, or obtaining any compassion from his guards, without money to bribe, or language to persuade, he resigned himself to despair; and the most heartfelt sighs, and pathetic gestures, portrayed the anguish of his mind. Totally insensible to his distress, and mindful only of their charge, they conversed with the utmost insensibility, eying him continually with glances of disdain and suspicion.

It was the third day before they arrived at the end of their journey. For some miles they had travelled through a barren and mountainous country: At length they descended into a plain, which was extensive, and terminated with a view of another mountain, on which stood a castle, with several small fortresses on the declivities, all of which were surrounded with high walls, that reached a considerable way on the plain. At some distances from each other, thinly scattered on the skirts of the plain, and a rising hill on one side, stood a few houses; but the general appearance of the country seemed desolate and uncultivated.

Ferdinand was permitted to take a view of this cheerless prospect, as they crossed the plain towards a large pair of gates fixed in the wall at the foot of a scraggy part of the mountain, and at one end of the wide extended plain. Here a paper was delivered to the sentinel at the gates, which, having read, they were opened, and proceeding round the mountain, they came to a similar pair of gates, where the same ceremony was observed, and on their entrance, an easy winding path-way led them to the Castle, passing several small forts, guarded by savage and half-starved looking men, who scowled under their bushy eye-brows, and, by their haggard ferocious countenance, inspired terror and despair.

At the Castle, Ferdinand was assisted to alight. He was so far exhausted by weakness, fatigue, and distress of mind, that they were obliged to carry him into an apartment, and give him some sherbet to prevent him from fainting. He laid himself down on a sofa, indifferent to life, and overwhelmed with misery. He was now a prisoner in a dreary and uncomfortable place, deprived of society, lost to his child, his friends, and his dear Count. This last stroke of being separated from him, was the completion of his misfortunes; and in the bitterness of his grief, he cursed the barbarians, whose callous hearts had divided them.

At night, he was shown into a small room about eight feet square, with a couch to sleep on, the only furniture it contained. Some cakes made of rice, a few grapes and sherbet had been put ready for him, of which he partook very sparingly, and retired to rest upon a mattress, covering himself with a quilt, as is the custom of the Turks in all places.

For several hours, Ferdinand lay a prey to the utmost inquietude, and the most distressing recollections. Why Ismael had deceived them, what purpose it was to answer, or wherefore he had cruelly separated him from the Count, were the questions that agitated his mind, and precluded sleep.

Wearied out at length with uncertain conjectures, and his spirits fatigued for want of rest, towards morning, he dropped into an unrefreshing slumber, from which he was awakened by a Turk, who stood beside him with a basin of coffee. He started up, and receiving the basin with an inclination of his head, and a few words in thanks, which, though not understood by the man, yet the tone and courteous look that accompanied them seemed to please him, and a little relaxed the unbending severity of his countenance. He stayed until the coffee was drank, then making a sign for the other to follow, he led him into a larger apartment, that overlooked the opposite side of the Castle from that which he had entered at, and appeared to terminate in a wood or grove at some distance beyond the walls. At the right, he observed the ruins of several noble edifices, and farther off a building in a circular form, resembling an amphitheatre. — To the left, were some extensive fields, but uncultivated, there he saw some goats bounding about from thence to the sides of the hills, at the foot of which run a small rivulet of water, clear as crystal.

Such was the prospect that presented itself on all sides, dreary and uncomfortable, without a hope of any thing more animating to gratify the eye, or indulge the search of curiosity; for he judged most rightly, that the walls which enclosed the Castle would be the boundary of his liberty.

For the rest, he had not much to complain of; he was served with fruits generally dried, milk, sherbet, and rice, and with some little show of civility; but he had no one to converse with; no books to amuse him; no friend to partake either of his distresses or comforts; and his own recollections of the past, any more than his expectations of the future, were not calculated to afford him any amusement, or even to indulge a visionary hope of relief.

Yet strange to say, under all this anxiety, with little rest, and less appetite, his weakness decreased: he found himself in three or four days considerably better in health, and with amended strength, which he attributed solely to the salubrity of the air. His solicitude for the safety and health of the Count contributed not a little to augment his uneasiness; and the incertitude whether his letters from Adrianople had been sent to his friends, which, from subsequent transactions, he entertained some doubts of, gave him the most poignant concern.

Entirely precluded from conversation, by his ignorance of the Turkish language, he resolved, if possible, to attain some knowledge of it. The person who commanded at the Castle, now and then visited him. — Policy, as well as good breeding, induced him to behave with politeness. To the man who attended him, he showed a complacency and thankfulness, which appeared to be gratifying. He began, therefore, to make both understand, by his signs, that he wished to comprehend them. He repeated their words, and retained the names of things brought to him, and of such as he pointed out from the windows.

The Turks appeared pleased with his attentions, and desire of knowledge; and in about a week after his residence there, the commander was constant in his visits; delighted in making him understand the names of every thing he wanted; taught him several common and useful expressions; and, as their language is much more comprehensive than our's; as Ferdinand had nothing to divert his thoughts, and was determined to profit by his master's instructions, it is not at all extraordinary, that, in the space of two months, he had acquired as much knowledge, if not more, than in the ordinary course of things he might have learnt in six or eight.

During his progression in the language, he had obtained information, that Ismael was nearly related to this gentleman who commanded the Castle; that he had received instructions to be extremely careful of Ferdinand, as a prisoner of his, for whom he expected a considerable ransom. By no means to permit him to emigrate beyond the Castle walls; but at the same time to treat him with civility, that his captivity might not injure his health, and deprive him of the sums he expected for him, and also another prisoner, whom he had ordered to be confined elsewhere.

This intelligence unravelled the whole plot to Ferdinand. He saw that liberty was not to be hoped for in the usual way of an exchange, and doubted not but that their letters had been suppressed to prevent the application of their friends. Though he detested the duplicity and avarice of Ismael, yet he was rejoiced to find a clue to account for his conduct, which held out a remote hope, that the Count and himself might be liberated, since he was well assured that any demand he should think proper to make, their friends would readily comply with, however undeserving he might be of their generosity.

This information, in a great degree, contributed to restore both his health and spirits; he made many attempts to find out the name of the place where the Count and he were separated; but Heli, which was the name of the commander, protested his entire ignorance. Whether he was sincere or not, could not be known, and Ferdinand was obliged to be contented with the limited confidence he had obtained, and amuse the tediousness of his captivity, by studying the language with unremitted diligence, and conciliating the esteem of Heli.

He made no attempts to subvert the fidelity which the commander had pledged to Ismael; for in the first place, he held a trust committed and engaged for in a sacred light: And could he have satisfied his scruples in that point, he risked every thing; the loss of every indulgence, if he attempted, and was repulsed. By this prudent conduct, he engaged the regard of Heli, who begun to unbend from that frigid reserve and taciturnity which characterize the Turks, and to be pleased with the diligence and progress of his pupil. One morning, when the weather was uncommonly fine, he entered Ferdinand's apartment, who was standing at the window, just then in a very pensive mood.

"Are you not well?" demanded he.

"I cannot say I am ill," answered Ferdinand; "but I am weak enough to be affected by a dream, which I have had, and have risen quite unrefreshed from my couch, with a great depression of spirits."

The Turks are extremely superstitious. — Heli viewed him for a few minutes in silence; at length — "I am sorry you are afflicted," said he; "and it shall not be my fault if you do not shake off this dejection. I am come to a resolution to enlarge your liberty. This morning I have heard from my kinsman Ismael; he is gone to Constantinople. He charges me to be careful of you; but hopes soon to ease me of the trouble, as he expects daily to hear from your friends. Believe me, Christian, I shall rejoice at your enlargement from your captivity, though I shall lose a companion, which, in this solitary place, must be a cause of regret. I come, however, to prove my regard and confidence, to invite you to a walk. Have you no curiosity to stroll beyond these walls?"

"Doubt it not," replied Ferdinand, agreeably surprised. — "I have frequently wished to view those buildings, and that amphitheatre which appears to be mouldering into ruins; but I had too much respect for you to ask any thing you did not seem inclined to offer, or to express a desire to pass beyond the bounds limited for my residence."

"I am not insensible of your moderation," returned he; "and 'tis in that consideration, I am tempted to extend your liberty. Come then, if you can walk. The morning is truly inviting." Ferdinand wanted no further invitation, but with much pleasure, followed his gentle jailer to the gates, which, having passed, they walked on down the declivities into the plain.

They crossed a considerable extent of ground before they came to the ruins of several noble buildings.

"Here," said Heli, "once stood the superb edifices of many Roman senators. In those adjoining fields was fought the memorable battle between Marc Anthony, Augustus Caesar, Brutus, and Cassius. By tradition, every step you take here is sacred, either from the battles of heroes, or the residence of noble Romans, with whose names or actions I am but little acquainted; but you Christians, who possess an insatiable curiosity, to you every object here must be of consequence."

"Of consequence, indeed," cried Ferdinand, whose heart glowed with the idea that he had the power of contemplating the ground so renowned in story, and reviving the remembrance of those heroes, once law-givers to the world; but how quick the transition from admiration to wonder and regret. "Where now was that mighty universal empire, which delegated her authority over all the known nations of the world? Whose heroes were as invincible in war as they were superior in peace: Whose principles were incorruptible; whose integrity was unquestionable. Are these mouldering ruins; these decayed mansions, all that remain here to mark the conquerors of the world? Melancholy idea.

"Whilst brave, great, and virtuous, Rome was invincible; but when luxury and corruption crept into the state; when senators became venal, and heroes selfish and ambitious, Rome fell from her ancient glory:—Degenerated from her great forefathers— plunged into licentiousness; sunk into a supine weakness.—She turned her arms against herself; destroyed her own powers, and no longer revered as the virtuous republic, giving laws to mankind. Her glory gradually diminished, 'till she fell, to rise no more.

"What a warning to nations! what a lesson to the princes of the present day!—Rome fell by corruption and licentiousness; by civil wars, and internal commotions;—by ambitious and self

interested statesmen; — by the tribunes; by the men of the
people, who, loudly crying for liberty, and, by factious
intrigues, distracting the state, and interrupting the course of
justice; by pretending patriotism, and by sowing sedition
among the lower classes of men, ever ripe to trample upon all
order, and assemble in tumultuous meetings. By such wicked
and imprudent measures was Rome destroyed.

"Whilst virtuous and united, she was invulnerable; but "a
kingdom divided against itself cannot stand," and in the general
decay, all share the common ruin: There can be no
discrimination; for who shall say to a misguided tumultuous
people, Thus far shalt thou go, and no farther." Alas! a turbulent
spirit, once raised, it is difficult to subdue; and measures never
once intended, are often times pursued to the confusion and
ruin of its first projectors.

CHAPTER VIII

Lost in these, and such like reflections, Ferdinand wandered over the broken monuments of ancient glory, every pillar of which raised an enthusiastic spirit, and a concomitant sorrow. Heli, unmoved, walked among the ruins without either reflection or reverence; but observing that his companion looked fatigued, as well as thoughtful, "I think," said he, "your walk has been sufficiently extensive for the present.—To-morrow you shall take a view of the amphitheatre and the grove. Yet, if it has no other effect than to increase your dejection, we might as well remain in the Castle."

"Do not mistake the nature of my feelings," replied Ferdinand.—"'Tis impossible to view these fragments of ancient grandeur, without ruminating on the causes which tumbled them into ruin. But I assure you, that I am much obliged and gratified by your indulgence; and could the mind of man divest itself from the selfishness inherent to our nature, we should have but little reason to murmur at our own losses and misfortunes, when we reflect on the entire downfall of a nation once so great and mighty as the Romans."

"I cannot say," returned Heli, "that looking on these ruinous palaces, at all lessens my regret for the want of fortune, or comforts me for being doomed to live in this solitary place."

"I am not more abstracted than yourself," said Ferdinand, "since I do not scruple to confess, that I am at this moment not the less sensible of my own unpleasant situation, less unmindful of local attachments, nor less anxious for the fate of my friend, when contemplating the fall of empires; but it proves to a thinking mind, that sorrow is the lot of man, in some stage or other of his life: And if he loves his country, he must dread, that the same vices, luxury, ambition, licentiousness, and discontent, too prevalent in most countries, must at length terminate in the destruction of that nation, where their growth is encouraged by faction, and nursed by the countenance of superior abilities."

Heli nodded his head, but whether in approbation of the justice of those observations, or because he did not comprehend them, and could make no reply, cannot be determined; but he had received so little pleasure from the walk, that he stretched his inclination to make the utmost speed back, that the gravity of the Turkish movements would allow of.

Ferdinand, whose mind had found much relief from the novelty of the morning's ramble, after his return, seemed to have recruited both his strength and spirits, and conversed with more cheerfulness than usual.

"I have frequently," said he to Heli, "had an inclination to ask you one question, but I was fearful you would be displeased at my curiosity."

"And what is that," returned the other. "Speak freely; the answer depends upon myself."

"Have you no women in this Castle? — Near two months that I have been here, I have seen nor heard of any: Yet can hardly persuade myself that you reside in this solitary place without some companions to soften your melancholy hours."

"And have you not made this inquiry before of the man who attends you?" asked Heli.

"Never," replied Ferdinand. — "I have always forborne the meanness of interrogating a servant relative to his master's concerns."

"I admire your discretion," returned he. "You deserve confidence. I have women here, in a distant part of the Castle from this, where they are shut up, and have only a garden to amuse themselves in, which is as much liberty as the laws of our prophet, and the custom of the country, allows them. — You Christians make your women infamous by toleration of their vices, and giving the reins to their natural depraved inclinations."

"As I make it an invariable rule," answered Ferdinand, "never to enter into any controversies against declared and established prejudices, I shall make no other reply to your observation, than to assure you, that in the European countries, we generally find an undue restraint, a severity of conduct, either from a parent or a husband, almost always is productive of those errors and vices we are so sedulous to guard them from.

"The English repose an unlimited confidence in their women; and though doubtless there may be, and I dare say are, very many who disgrace themselves and their families, yet both, from reading and information, I am led to believe that the number of vicious women bears a much less proportion than in Spain, in some parts of Italy, or even in Turkey, where their whole study, and all their ingenuity, is employed to deceive and betray their husbands, whom they look upon rather as severe masters or jailers, than as the partners of their hearts.

"However, as I before observed, I never interfere in established customs; I am obliged to you for your confidence, and am glad to find that you have such objects with you, as may sooth your solitary hours in a place which appears so distant from all social converse."

"I thank you," returned Heli; "but I have at least as much plague as pleasure with them; and had our prophet exterminated them from the world, mankind would have been no losers."

"And yet," replied Ferdinand, "your prophet has made your chief happiness in paradise to consist of beautiful virgins."

"Yes," said Heli; "but those virgins will be always beautiful, always young, and never unfaithful."

"Then," returned the other, "you may well bear with their follies and decay here, since their comparative defects must enhance the delights of your promised happiness hereafter."

"Fine talking," cried Heli; "if you had two or three hundred women to rule, who, shut up together, are perpetually quarrelling, envious, jealous, and revengeful; all of whom you must reconcile, please, and caress. I believe you would scarcely think expected pleasures a sufficient recompense to make you patiently endure such a slavery. Thank Heaven, I have but eight, and trouble enough they give me."

Ferdinand smiled.—"And is not the trouble of your own making. Why increase your plagues; why have eight women?—Can you not select one from the number to make you happy, and dismiss the others?"

"One!" exclaimed Heli; "be confined to one woman! Great happiness indeed I should find then. And that one, what would become of her, without companions.—Shut up from all social converse—nothing to amuse her—nothing to animate or agitate her mind; what a dull insipid mass of clay should I meet, when I condescend to unbend and divert myself."

"I had indeed forgotten her situation," returned Ferdinand, "and must acknowledge, if the severity of your customs oblige women to solitude and confinement, one could not exist long without a companion; but she might have slaves, attendants to converse with."

"It would never do," said Heli.—"Too much consequence and power thrown into the hands of one woman, would make her insolent and rebellious. By dividing our attentions, we reduce them to an equality that prevents intrigues, discontents, and insolence; makes them emulous to please, and cautious to offend. But they are so capricious and so envious, that among themselves they are perpetually disagreeing, and I am often called upon to decide quarrels, and to compel them to keep good order: Yet, were it not for the variety and spirit this diffuses among them, they could neither entertain me, nor amuse themselves. Therefore, though sometimes I am fatigued and angry at their disputes, upon the whole it is less disagreeable than a stupid sameness, which would be disgusting."

"You have accounted very well," said Ferdinand, "for the necessity that compels you to have many women; and whilst your customs respecting the sex subject them so much to your power, and deny them those rights which our divine legislator bestowed on all mankind without discrimination, that of liberty and free will. Whilst both their minds and bodies are in captivity, one unfortunate female, as you observed, can neither be happy in herself, or make another so."—Heli grew thoughtful, and made no reply.—The subject dropped; and for the remainder of the day, Ferdinand applied himself closely to his studies.

The following day, Heli waited not to be asked, but voluntarily offered to accompany Ferdinand in a walk to the amphitheatre.—The other gladly accepted the civility, and they directed their steps to this noble building. Great part of the circular wall remained entire. Many superb pillars supported different parts of the structure. Nearly one half of the inside was in ruins; but in some places there were regular seats rising over one another to an immense height.

The whole exhibited a sullen state of grandeur sinking to decay. Half broken pillars of marble, of granite, lay scattered in large fragments on a kind of Mosaic pavement. Several fine pieces of sculpture, maimed statues, and decayed paintings, that at the touch crumbled into dust, lay in heaps at different parts of the building. In fine, all was great, admirable, and gratifying;—but at the same time mortifying, depressive, and humiliating, to the pride of human nature.

For who that beheld those stupendous buildings, those superb monuments of antiquity, once adorned by the most virtuous and bravest of mankind, now trampled under foot, decayed, mutilated, and sinking into ruin; but must shrink into nothing, on a comparative view of his own littleness, of the modern architecture of the present day, and feel, that soon the one will be no more, lost and forgotten; levelled to the earth, without a stone remaining to engage either veneration or regret: Whilst on this hallowed ground ages hence, mankind will tread with reverence, and recall to their minds those heroes who once were the saviours of their country, and to the latest posterity will be the envy and admiration of mankind.

Ferdinand eagerly gazed on every part of this immense building. His enthusiastic spirit seemed raised above himself. He glowed with delightful recollections, and traced in his mind's eye, those mighty armies commanded by the first of men, now marching to the adjoining fields, to decide, in one day, the fate of Rome, then mistress of the world.

But his feelings cannot be described; nor can this weak pen delineate a hundredth part of the admirable remains of this once incomparable structure; in the examining of which, he had spent more than four hours, without going half over the buildings. Heli, whose complaisance was at its utmost stretch, and who had exhibited several marks of impatience; for what was statues or pillars to him, broken and destroyed by time, and the depredations of vulgar uninformed souls. Fragments like these were to him contemptuous ruins; and he admired, at the ignorance and superstition of Ferdinand, in making them objects of such consequence.

"Well," said he, he a tone of fretfulness, "do you design to pass the day here; or are you inclined to walk in the grove?"

The other perfectly comprehended the spirit of the question, and replied very complaisantly, "that he was ready to attend him." — To the grove they turned, which, though thick and impervious to the eye, was by no means so extensive as Ferdinand had expected, and seemed to have been the work of modern times; for the trees bore not the marks of centuries. This he remarked.

"I believe you are right," returned Heli. "I have heard this plantation was made by some hermits, who chose this spot to build their cells in, one of which only now remains, and is inhabited by Father Abdalla."

"How!" cried Ferdinand, "does any one reside here?"

"Yes," replied Heli; "one holy man has here devoted his life to serve Allah and his prophet."

They now penetrated through a thick underwood, darkened by some lofty trees, and descending a slope, came to a small rivulet, on the opposite side of which he saw among the trees the moss covered cell of the hermit, who was reclining on a little bank, raised about a foot above the earth, reading the alcoran. They had crossed a small wooden bridge, and, as they approached, he raised his head, and viewed them steadily, but without any marks of surprise; then threw his eyes down towards his book.

Heli saluted him, by laying his right hand on his breast. "Abdalla," said he, "holy man, thou art a true servant to the Most High. Praise be to him, and his prophet Mahomet."

The old man arose, and saluted them courteously. He invited them into his cell, where he set before them some dried fruits, and water clear as crystal.

Ferdinand was charmed with the sweet and placid countenance of this hermit—so different from the frigid austere looks of the Turks in general. His voice was mild, his eye soft, though penetrating; and he invited them to the simple repast, with a cordiality that denoted a beneficent mind.

"'Tis long since I have seen thee brother," said he to Heli.

"True," replied he, "I have had a companion, whom thou seest, a Christian captive, under my care; who has acquired our language tolerably, and deported himself so as to deserve my favour."

"As a captive, I pity him," said Abdalla. "As a Christian, I will pray for him, that our holy prophet may convert him from his errors, as he has enlightened his understanding."

"I thank you, holy father," answered Ferdinand.—"Though a Christian, I reverence true piety, and honour good men of every religion. The prayers of an upright heart I shall ever be grateful for. But pardon me if I ask how long you have resided in this grove?"

"Upwards of fifty years," replied he. — "I was near thirty when I first came here.

"When young I was bred to arms. I fought under our last great Sultan. He thought I deserved well; he promoted me. This raised me many enemies; I fell under the displeasure of the Grand Vizier; that was sufficient to mark my ruin. My death was resolved on; a faithful slave gave me notice of my danger, at the hazard of his own life. We fled together, and after encountering a thousand perils, we arrived at this grove, by a different road than the one to the Castle. — In this cell dwelt a holy man; he received and cherished us. In a few moons after, I lost my faithful Sadi. My grief was unspeakable. That event, and the unjust treatment I had met with, gave me a disgust to the world.

"Here I found a friend, a protector, and an instructive monitor. Our holy prophet sanctified his labours. I renounced the world and all its deadly passions, love, hatred, ambition, and envy. Twenty years I possessed a friend, who was the chosen of Allah, and a true son of the prophet. He purified my heart, and fashioned it like his own. — His translation to paradise is the only cloud that has, for a moment, shadowed my content since the death of Sadi.

"I possess health, and every wish of my heart. I expect soon to enjoy the blessings of Mahomet, the joys of paradise: My days are numbered, and draw to an end: I always keep a week's provision in my cell, lest, for a short time, I should be unable to quit it. Allah be praised; I wait his appointed time, which cannot be far off."

This simple recital inspired Ferdinand with admiration and respect. He bowed involuntarily before the good man, whose animated countenance corresponded with the purity of his heart. "Holy father," said he, "let me entreat your blessing. I am a man of sorrows: Captivity is the least of them: Let me have your prayers, that my latter days may be as tranquil as yours."

"Hope, my son — hope," replied Abdalla. "Trust in the Most High; so shall thy troubles fly from thee like a passing cloud: Thine enemies be cut down, and thy latter days be peace."

Heli, who grew impatient at this scene, abruptly reminded Ferdinand it was time to return. He turned to the good father. — — — "You have cheered my spirits," said he. "You have communicated to my heart faith and hope. — If I am permitted, I will see you again. Holy father, remember me in your prayers."

The hermit, with a look of dignified complaisance, bowed his head. — "The blessing of Allah be upon thee, my son, and upon you, my brother."

Heli and Ferdinand left the grove, and returned to the Castle, the former thoughtful and fatigued; for the Turks are extremely indolent; seldom walk for pleasure; and it was no small effort he had made to emerge from the supine indulgence so habitual to him, as to walk two following days. The other, delighted by new scenes, charmed with what he had seen, and looking with admiration and reverence on every spot so celebrated and so sacred, felt an uncommon flow of spirits, and as well as he could, in a language but new to him, expressed to Heli a thousand obligations for his kindness, and spoke of the pleasure he received in the most lively, and, to the other, enthusiastic terms; which was heard with a frigid coldness, and a more than usual reserve.

Ferdinand, at length struck with the silence of Heli, apologized for his loquacity, and restrained his raptures. On arriving at their apartments, Heli threw himself on the sofa, and complained of immense fatigue, though the whole of their walk had not exceeded three miles; but that was a journey to the Turk, who sometimes had been accustomed to visit the hermit, but through a different road; for on the other side of the Castle was a very short way to it; but then they must pass a few scattered houses, which, being inhabited, Heli did not choose to take Ferdinand near them; nor was he informed that any such places were in the neighbourhood. On the contrary, he supposed Heli's family, and the few soldiers who guarded the small fortresses, he saw on coming to the Castle, were all the people that dwelt in that neglected and deserted spot.

All that day, Heli persevered in an unusual silence. Not that indolent taciturnity natural to the Turks, but a thoughtful gloom seemed to hang upon him, as if revolving, in his mind, some affair of importance.

Ferdinand observed and trembled. — "Some event, productive, I fear, of no good to me, is in contemplation." He passed a night of painful inquietude. The following morning afforded no relief to his anxiety. Heli did not appear at the usual hour. — The noon came, but no Heli. Unable any longer to restrain his impatience, when the slave attended with his coffee — "Is not the governor well?" demanded he.

The man bowed his head, put his finger to his lips, and withdrew. The day passed heavily: He endeavoured to recollect if he had given any offence to Heli; his memory charged him with no fault or imprudence in their several conversations. To what then was owing this sudden and unaccountable revolution in his behaviour?

A second night, and the first part of the second day, passed in the same uneasy conjectures. Towards the close of the day, the door of his apartment opened; Heli appeared, followed by — — —Judge the transports of Ferdinand—followed by the Count! Yes, his friend Count M— — —. They flew to embrace each other, regardless of all but the joy of this unexpected meeting; as unlooked for by the Count, as unhoped for by Ferdinand, whose mind, having been wound up to expect some horrid design against him, was so overcome by a rush of sudden joy, that unable to speak, he sunk almost motionless on the sofa.

The effect was momentary; for he soon exclaimed, "My friend! my dear Count.—Dear—generous Heli."

The Count was not less transported, nor less grateful in his expressions to their benefactor. Heli approached them—"I leave you together; an hour hence I shall return, and communicate important news."

He withdrew. The friends had a thousand things to say—a thousand questions to ask. It appeared, that after they had been separated, the Count was carefully guarded. He met with no ill treatment, but he obtained no companion like Heli. His days past heavily, without any employment, and his mind oppressed with sorrow and despair; a situation, he observed, which must very shortly have overpowered his constitution.

The preceding day, Heli accompanied his guard into his miserable apartment. He made him a sign to follow Heli; he knew resistance would be in vain, and was indifferent as to consequences. He was placed in a covered carriage; they travelled all night, and for some hours on this morning.— — —"When we arrived at this Castle," proceeded the Count, "I supposed I had only changed one prison for another still more dreadful; and when, by signs, I was ordered to accompany Heli to the door of this apartment, I prepared to enter it as the grave of all my hopes, and the closing scene of my life.

"Good Heavens! what a transition from absolute despair to exquisite joy. How little did I hope ever to see my friend again. Yet let me not be too sanguine; perhaps we are prisoners for life;

yet if they will permit us to be together, I am careless of future circumstances."

"What is intended by bringing us together," said Ferdinand, "I am as ignorant of as yourself: For when I once questioned Heli as to the place of your confinement, he protested he was ignorant of it. In this, 'tis plain, he practised deception: Therefore I cannot pretend to judge what may be his future views.

"I have experienced civilities from him which call for confidence; and if I am deceived, I would rather suffer for my candor, than wrong him by unjust suspicions."

The Count seemed to derive hope from Ferdinand's account of Heli. They both execrated the treachery of Ismael; judging that, from such a man, they had every thing to dread, should his expectations, or demands of a large ransom, by any unforeseen means, be fruitless.

By the time appointed, Heli entered, and carefully shutting the door, seated himself by Ferdinand. — "I am now going to prove my confidence in you," said he. — "Five days ago, I received intelligence, that my kinsman Ismael was imprisoned, by the machinations of his enemies. This event nearly concerned me; yet I hoped his relations and interest at Constantinople would preserve him. The contrary has happened; the last morning that I walked out with you to the grove, I was informed of his death, the confiscation of his effects, and the determined ruin of all his family.

"I debated in my mind, whether I should fly the approaching storm, and leave you to preserve yourself as you could. — Other thoughts suggested themselves: This government, not being very important, might not be immediately thought of. If I left you, you might indeed regain your liberty, but you might run a thousand hazards. — Your friend would have but little chance of an escape for a long time to come, if ever, as he could not give information to his friends, and the persons who had the care of him, were of an inferior order of people.

"Considering all this, I fixed my plan immediately. I set off for the confinement of this gentleman, and demanded him in the Grand Seigneur's name; I was well known; and though I produced no signet, they presumed not to disobey me: By this step I have obliged you both; and if you will solemnly subscribe to the conditions I propose, I will not only give you your liberty, but open to you a way of returning to your own country, without ransom or difficulty. You may possibly entertain some doubts of my sincerity, because I denied the knowledge of your friend's residence, but it was a trust reposed in me, and I think myself entitled to the more credit, for preserving my faith; you may judge as you please."

"I assure you," replied Ferdinand, who had listened to him very attentively, that he might perfectly understand him, "I honour you for your integrity; name your conditions, therefore, without reserve; they must be hard ones indeed, if we hesitate a moment to fulfil them."

"This then is my plan," returned Heli. "I now acknowledge to you, that within this last moon, peace has been concluded upon between our great Sultan and your Emperor. All officers remaining in Turkey are declared free, and may return to their homes. Nevertheless, many of them, secured as you have been, will find great difficulties. It must be in every governor's power to retard their freedom, without he is interested to liberate them. You understand me. — And in the next place, the natural aversion the Turks have to you Christians, might subject them to many insults, without they have a proper guard.

"Now, if you will swear to take me with you, and to protect me, and one person more, in your country; I will attend you through the country to the first sea port, as the safest way of going in the habit of a Janissary, and as a guard deputed to see you on your way to the port. The other person I speak of is a woman, once a Christian, but now a true disciple of Mahomet — I cannot leave her behind. She must travel as your wife; but she must be sacred from your touch; for I swear by Allah, if in any one point you disappoint or deceive me, both shall instantly suffer death, though I were sure to die a thousand times."

"I will answer both for my friend and for myself," replied Ferdinand; 'that we will sacredly keep our faith with you; that we will amply provide both for you and the woman, and enable you to spend the remainder of your days in comfort."

"Enough," replied Heli; "in two days we will be on the road; but fear not that I shall be a burden to you; I am not destitute of riches, though hitherto they have been useless to me, because I dared not spend beyond my income. Subject to so many jealous eyes, we must have the "wisdom of the serpent" to escape our enemies."

Heli departed with a countenance so changed from the gloom and anxiety which had for some time pervaded his features, that even Ferdinand was surprised at the alteration, and the Count viewed him with wonder and curiosity. When he had left the apartment, Ferdinand quickly informed his friend of their agreeable prospects, from the proposals of Heli. The Count was not less pleased than himself, but could not help observing, that they were more indebted to the selfish gratifications of the proposer, than to his generosity.

"This man's conduct," said he, "confirms the opinion I have early been taught to hold of the Turks, that in their dealings with us, they are selfish, deceitful, and avaricious. Was it not Heli's interest to escape from this country, I believe we should owe him no obligations, either for our liberty or lives, if the sacrifice of either, or both, were essential to his own views."

"We must not search too nicely into the motives which influences men's actions," returned Ferdinand. — "There are so many hidden springs, so many latent causes. — — —Sometimes scarcely known to ourselves, from which originate our best purposes, and guide our designs, that I fear few could stand the scrutiny, without the imputation of selfishness."

"I shall not now dispute that point with you," answered the Count, 'though I am inclined to think more favourably of human nature than you do."

"Do not mistake my general observation for an invariable rule," said Ferdinand hastily. "There are minds of a superior mould, doubtless; but they are comparatively few. And as for this Turk, as we could have no right to expect his services, I am willing to accept them upon his own terms."

In the afternoon Heli attended them, and after a long conversation, their plan and route was settled, and he bid them prepare to set off by the eleventh hour next day, when he and the woman would join them.

"The lady, I suppose," said Ferdinand, "must be silent, otherwise her language will betray her."

"Not so," returned he. — "I told you she had been a Christian; nay, more, she is your countrywoman, a German."

"And you can be contented with one woman?" asked he, smiling.

"I cannot be contented without this woman," replied Heli.
— "That's all I can answer for at present."

The friends passed a night of impatience, and not entirely free from apprehension. — Should any discovery of Heli take place, they might, as accomplices, be involved in very disagreeable situations. If they discovered themselves as German officers, entitled to their liberty, he might, in revenge, accuse them of some crimes which would draw on them unpleasant consequences. — And to irritate, displease, or disappoint a Turk, is seldom done with impunity, they are in general so furious and revengeful.

Therefore, after much consultation, and revolving all circumstances together, they thought it best to submit with a good grace, and trust to the ingenuity and diligence of Heli to extricate them from impending difficulties.

The hour at length came, appointed for their departure. Heli appeared in his usual garb alone; their hearts misgave them. — "Follow me," said he, "and fear nothing."

He led them across a court, and through a small postern door, which opened upon a ragged and unfrequented part of the hill; — and it was with some difficulty they kept their feet steady in going down the declivity. At the bottom was a thick underwood, through which they easily penetrated to a small decayed building: Entering a few steps, they perceived a soldier with a drawn scimitar. — They started back, and supposed themselves betrayed, casting a look of reproach on Heli. — He saw their thoughts in that look. — "This is a friend," said he; — and going forward, he returned with a bundle, that contained the dress of a soldier, and in which he quickly arrayed himself, throwing his other clothes under some large stones and rubbish.

"We have now the day before us," said he, "and no time to lose before we reach a place of safety. I have given out in the Castle, that I shall pass the day with you at the hermit's. No suspicion, therefore, will be entertained 'till night, nor any thoughts of a pursuit 'till morning, because no one has a right to command or leave his post, consequently much time will elapse before that is determined upon."

"But the woman," said Ferdinand.

"Will be safe with us," answered Heli, smiling, and pointing to the soldier, who was so perfectly disguised by her dress and mustaches, that they had not the least suspicion of her sex.

"Will she not be missed?" asked the Count.

"No," replied Heli. — "Yesterday she was impertinent — we quarrelled — I ordered her into confinement, and, in a feigned passion, swore she should remain there three days, sending to her room some dried figs and water. I locked the door, and secured the key.

"This morning I pretended to regret my oath, and said, I would go and consult the holy hermit, how far I dared to remit her punishment. Thus you see neither will be sought after, as I had forbidden any one to approach the door of her apartment; and I am so well beloved by the men, and so little suspected of having any cause to absent myself, as they are ignorant of Ismael's fate, which involves his kindred, that unless an order should arrive to arrest me, I dare say they will not think of my flight, or pursue me 'till after tomorrow, if then; and before that, I trust we shall be in safety."

They could not but acknowledge that he had taken every prudent precaution to preserve them from danger; and without any further conversation, they pursued their way across the plain to the next town, which was a few miles distance. Here they easily procured a carriage, under the pretence that the Count and Ferdinand were prisoners, whom the soldiers had in custody.

The Turkish soldiers are in general so formidable to the common ignorant people, that few would presume to dispute their commands. The same pretence carried them through several small towns and villages without interruption or accident, tho' not without much fatigue, as they proceeded with great speed.

It is not necessary to trace them through their journey, as they had neither time or inclination to make observations. Therefore I shall only say, that they reached the river Danube in safety, which they crossed, and after several days travelling, arrived at Belgrade. Here they rested, and were enabled to breathe, after their fatigues, both of body and mind.

Having stayed two days, they proceeded on to Vienna, and, to the great joy of the whole party, at length entered that Imperial city in perfect safety, just sixteen weeks from the day when the battle took place, and they were carried off by Ismael.

CHAPTER IX

The Count and Ferdinand soon made themselves known to some of their acquaintance, and were received with as much surprise as if they had risen from the dead; so firmly was it credited, that they had perished in battle. Proper clothes were soon procured for themselves, Heli and the wo- man both readily conforming to wear the German dress, though both persevered in their own tenets of religion, and the worship of the prophet Mahomet.

Heli now displayed a great many valuable jewels, worth five or six thousand pounds at least. How he had acquired them, he never thought proper to divulge; nor had they any right to inquire. He had sufficient to live on, in a moderate independence, and proposed retiring into the country, to reside free from observation. The gentlemen sent off letters to their friends immediately on their arrival, as they were very doubtful that their former ones had never gone forward from Adrianople. They purposed waiting on the Emperor, and as there was now no occasion for their active services, to obtain his permission for returning into Suabia.

The morning following, after all their clothes were brought home, Heli entered their apartment, and asked leave to introduce his Fatima in her proper habit. They readily accorded to his request, being desious of seeing a woman whom he had preferred to all others, and who had changed her own form of worship for that of the man she loved.

He quickly returned, leading in a very beautiful woman, whom he no sooner introduced to Ferdinand, than the latter recoiled a few paces back, with all the marks of strong surprise, and even terror, in his countenance. Heli, observing his emotions, was instantly seized with a jealous fit. He changed colour, and pulled down her veil, drawing her on one side, as if to leave the room.

"Be not offended or hurt, my friend," said Ferdinand, recovering himself, "nor leave the room, I beseech you. — To account for my emotions, I must tell you that this lady bears the strongest resemblance to my late dear and honoured father, that ever I beheld in two persons of different ages and sex. Very striking it must be, to have such an effect on my mind. Let me entreat you, Heli, to uncloud that face, and permit me to ask your lady a few questions."

Heli complied, but it was with an ill grace, his looks betraying suspicion and vexation.

"You say, Madam," said Ferdinand, "that you are a German. — Have the goodness to inform me who, and what you are; — for I am strongly persuaded you are somehow connected with my father's family. — Do not hesitate," added he, seeing she appeared in great confusion. — "Whoever you are, in me you will find a friend ready to promote your happiness with Heli, since he is the man of your choice."

Those words he repeated in the Turkish language to him, to quiet a little the turbulence of his agitations. After some little hesitation, Fatima began the following little narrative: —

"I have heard my mother say, that I was born in Baden; that my father was a nobleman, who had an estate near that city, and seduced her, at an early part of her life, under a promise of being faithful to her, and never marrying, as the difference in their rank precluded him from giving his hand to her."

"Did she never mention his name to you?" asked Ferdinand eagerly.

"She did," resumed Fatima; "it was Count Renaud."

Ferdinand struck his breast, greatly agitated, but requested she would proceed without attending to him.

"My mother informed me, that after my birth, he grew fonder of her every hour; but at length his father compelled him to marry a lady of rank and fortune, under the penalty of being disinherited, if he refused. This caused equal grief to both; and it was long before my mother could be reconciled to see him, or receive his visits; but her dependence on him, and affection for me, at length prevailed, and she had every reason to be convinced that all his real love was confined to her. Under this conviction, she submitted to her situation.

"After some time, she perceived a coldness in his attentions, and a profound melancholy in his looks, for which he assigned no cause, and pretended it was her fancy only; but being convinced, she said, that his dejection must spring from a new attachment, as he was daily more negligent towards her. — She had him carefully watched, and at length discovered that he was passionately in love with a young lady, on a visit to his wife, who, being of family, and virtuous, repulsed him, though it was believed she was equally attached.

"My mother, made desperate by this discovery, gave his wife information of the attachment, and driven to despair, in a fit of madness and jealousy, she accepted the protection of a German officer, who had long persecuted her with his addresses, and accompanied by me and my nurse, quitted Baden for ever, without deigning to see or to reproach him.

"With this officer she resided some years; and although she had a daughter by him, she loved me most affectionately, and has often said I was a perfect resemblance of her once beloved Count. We lived very happily, until I was about twelve years old, my sister only ten, when my mother's protector died, leaving his property divided between her and his daughter, with a small legacy to me. My sister and her fortune was left in the care of my mother, and the latter always assured me, her share should be mine at her death; which unfortunately happened in less than a twelvemonth after, and so suddenly, that she had not time to make a will; and as she had lived very retired, and her situation had prevented her from having proper acquaintance, whose honour and integrity might have been useful to us, we were left solely in the care of my old nurse, and a man who had been a kind of humble friend and dependant on the Colonel.

"How they managed I know not; but in less than four years we were informed our fortunes were spent, and that we must seek some employment for our support. Within the last twelvemonth, I had been noticed and followed by a nobleman, who was very amiable, and held high rank in the army. — Want of birth was an invincible obstacle to our marriage, and I had rejected, with disdain, every other overture; but when my nurse explained our situation, I confess, with shame, I no longer kept him at that distance which I ought to have done, and gave him but too much encouragement.

"One morning my nurse came into my room; said she, "we will sell the furniture, turn everything into money, and leave this place. I have been making inquiries; your father still lives; we will go to Baden; I will find some way of making you known to him, without alarming his family, and oblige him to provide for you, which either fear or affection will make him do. Your sister has also an uncle in Suabia — I will find him out; 'tis fit those relations should maintain you."

"This proposal of Dupree's. — "

"Dupree!" exclaimed Ferdinand;— — —"Great God! what do I hear—but go on."

"This proposal," resumed Fatima, "did not please me. I was not willing to run the risk of being rejected as a burden, or treated with contempt, when I had the alternative of independence, pleasure, and an agreeable lover. I therefore accepted the nobleman's proposals, put myself under his protection, and one evening quitted the house to reside in a more elegant one. In a few days, Dupree found me out, and made such an uproar, and behaved so clamorous, that my protector was compelled to give her a handsome sum to hold her tongue, which perfectly contented her.

"My lover was obliged to join the army. I accompanied him. The General was compelled to give battle; he was victorious, and the Turks defeated; but unhappily a party of them, headed by Heli, had, in the mean time, surrounded the tents, where the women and officers" baggage remained, pillaged them, beat off the guards, and carried me and several other women off in triumph.

"At first I was in despair, and expected death. We were put into a covered wagon, and carried to Adrianople, where I remained in close confinement upwards of two months, and had well nigh fretted myself to death; but the arrival of Heli saved my life; his generosity and affection won my heart;—'tis true, the recluse life I was compelled to lead suited very little with my inclinations; but there was no remedy; and after giving myself up some time to sorrow and regret, which availed nothing, I got the better of my trouble, and resigned myself to my fate.

"When Heli was appointed to the government of Philippo, I gladly accompanied him.—I have had no reason to repent; and thank Heaven, I am once more unexpectedly restored to my own country. What is become of my sister, Dupree, and Keilheim, her friend, I know not. Thus, Sir, I have related my story, and now you know whether I am any ways related to your family or not."

When Fatima ceased speaking, Ferdinand was for a few moments silent, he found but little cause to congratulate himself on the discovery of a relation so nearly connected by blood; whose conduct, even by her own acknowledgment, had been so faulty and reprehensible; but when he viewed that face, whose every look reminded him of his dear and much regretted father, a rush of tenderness sprung to his heart, that obliterated her errors, and rising hastily, he was about to embrace her, forgetful of Heli's presence and uneasy conjectures; he who had needfully observed his emotions during Fatima's relation, and had watched him with an eye of suspicion, furiously rushed between them, darting a look of vengeance at Ferdinand, and muttering curses on her, roughly pulling her from her seat.

"Stop, Heli," cried Ferdinand; "judge not rashly from appearances. — — —Fatima is—my sister!"

The last word seemed unwillingly pronounced, and to Heli rather the effect of a sudden duplicity, than a serious truth; but Fatima sunk back, evidently shocked and confused repeating the word sister, sister.—"Oh! if that is true, you must despise and hate me."

She burst into tears, and drew down her veil. Heli stood suspended between passion and curiosity. Ferdinand took his hand.

"My friend, compose yourself; I will relate every circumstance to you that indisputably proves your Fatima to be my half sister. Strange, indeed, are the events which have brought us to the knowledge of each other; but her features stamp the credibility of her story; and though the situation in which I find her must be wounding to the feelings of a brother, yet, as I can claim no right to control her inclinations, you have nothing to fear from me; she is free to act as she pleases."

Those words, in some degree, calmed the turbulent passions of Heli; he reseated himself without speaking, visibly impatient for the promised explanation. This Ferdinand entered upon; and at the conclusion, addressing Fatima, he said—"If necessity, and not choice, is now the tie that binds you to Heli, I think it my duty to offer to you a more eligible situation; from preceding circumstances, delicacy, and honour, equally militate against a hope of an honourable connexion with any other man; but I have the power to procure for you either a residence in the country with some worthy retired family, or to place you in a convent, where I will pay for your pension.

"In providing thus for you, I secure to you the liberty of choosing your own destiny. I pretend to no rights over you beyond what you are willing to allow me. If you voluntarily throw yourself on my protection, your interest shall be as dear to me as my own.—Decide, therefore, for yourself."

"I am very sensible of your kindness," replied Fatima, "but my choice is made. — In Turkey, perhaps the desire of liberty might have guided me to embrace your offers with transport; but I am now free; and whilst Heli behaves well, gratitude for his preference of me to all my companions, and for the affection he has displayed towards me during our late dangerous undertaking, induces me to declare, that I will partake of his destiny."

"Yes" Heli, added she in the Turkish language, giving him her hand, "with you I will remain, and trust that I shall never repent refusing my brother's offers to live with you."

The Turk appeared to be transported; — his doubts and suspicions were instantly dispelled, and he thanked her with an air of tenderness and gratitude. Ferdinand was concerned, but not surprised; the libertine life in which she had been engaged by her own confession, gave but small hopes that she could be reconciled to a retired and regular mode of conduct; and from several little traits that escaped her unguardedly, he conceived she had much natural levity that would ill brook restraint: What he could not control, therefore, he was resigned to; but assuming some degree of freedom, from his connexion with Fatima, he asked Heli in what manner he intended to regulate his future conduct.

"I design," answered he, 'to live quietly in the country, not ostentatiously, to avoid observation: To regard Fatima as my wife, and mistress of the other women. I pretend not to have a seraglio here; but as I am unknown, I shall have no visitors, nor will Fatima be exposed to the eyes of men."

Ferdinand accidentally turned his eyes on Fatima at those words, and observed a suppressed smile playing on her lips, and an archness in her looks, that but ill accorded with the plan Heli had designed, nor at all correspondent to the mortified and afflicted air she had assumed, when he first discovered himself to her as a brother. This observation tended to confirm his first suspicions, that she had a light mind, and was capable of much duplicity.

He was mortified, by the conviction from the affinity between them, but he had no power to control her inclinations, nor influence to effect a change in habits she had long since ceased to think vicious or blamable: Therefore, after a long conversation, in which she avowed her partiality for Heli, and a decided preference for his tenets of religion, Ferdinand left them to their own determinations, recommending to both constancy in their attachment, and the practise of good actions towards others. He added a few words of advice to Fatima in German, and concluded with assuring her, that if she should ever want a friend, the daughter of a respected father should always claim his attention and assistance.

When retired to his apartment, he was painfully affected by the recollection of such circumstances in the story of Fatima, as convinced him that his wife Claudina must have been that sister she mentioned, and the daughter of the officer by a woman his father had once been connected with. He shuddered at the idea. Yet surely, he thought, there cannot be that degree of consanguinity between us, which should raise the dead;—to bid me "fly from her arms as I would avoid sin and death." Or why, if our union was sinful, why was the warning so late.

"Ah!" cried he, "if my father knew her, ought he not to have discovered the secret? But no, it was impossible; had he known she was the child of a woman he once fondly loved, surely he would have made inquiries after her and his own child, nor have left even Claudina in indigence; no, he could not have known this painful mystery, and my fatal impetuous passion blindly led me to credit any tale that the wretch Dupree might invent, and to unite myself to the daughter of an infamous woman, who has blighted all my prospects of happiness for ever. Yes, that woman, that mother, if from the grave she can behold the misery that has developed on me, will rejoice, perhaps, that her wrongs from the father are retaliated with bitterness on the son, and that her own offspring has revenged her injuries." This idea led him into a train of unpleasant reflections, that concluded with lamenting his youthful rashness, and an ungovernable passion, of which he was the victim; nor could he help reverting to his father's connexion with the mother of Fatima and Claudina.

Could the libertine, or to speak in the softened term which fashion has established, could the man of gallantry look forward to the consequences of his errors; did he see the unfortunate innocents born of vicious parents; brought into the world under the stigma of criminality; subject to the eye of scorn;—nourished in vice; corrupted by example;—grow up lovely to the eye, but with minds depraved.—Subject to temptations, they have neither fortitude nor inclination to resist;—sink into a vortex of misery, guilty, hardened, despised, forsaken; and to close the climax, see those unfortunate children of guilty parents abandoned by the world; and when youth and beauty is no more, left to die in wretchedness, without relief, without pity, and without a friend to close their eyes, or speak one word of consolation in that awful moment, when the retrospection of a misspent life, fills them with unutterable sorrow and despair.

"Surely," thought Ferdinand, on reviewing this melancholy picture, which his misfortunes delineated to his mind's eye in the most gloomy colouring; "surely, if the sins of the fathers are visited upon their children, I am marked out as an object for retribution and vengeance. How far my marriage with Claudina may be criminal, I know not. — — —That union, so rashly entered into, and followed by a father's curses, wants not the aggravation of criminality to add to my wretchedness; and if she is a lost, a guilty creature, the sins of the mother have fallen upon us both."

These, and such like reflections, threw him into a profound reverie, from which he was roused by the entrance of the Count.

"I left you, for a few moments, my dear Ferdinand," said he, "because I thought you would wish to recover from the surprise and vexation that visibly affected you during the relation Fatima gave of herself; her subsequent choice of attaching herself to Heli, I think ought not to afflict you; for perhaps had she given him up, you would have found it a very unpleasant task to regulate a young woman like her, accustomed to a gay desultory kind of life."

"Your observation is undoubtedly just," replied he. — "I am convinced she is a stranger to all principles of decorum, and would ill brook that regularity I should naturally have expected. I am mortified, I confess, to find a person who owes her existence to my father, under such reprehensible circumstances; but that is not the only cause of the surprise and concern you remarked; I am still more nearly concerned in her story." He then acquainted the Count with every particular relative to Claudina, and severely condemned his own impetuous passion, which wildly pursued its object, regardless of such information as is generally found essential to confidence, if not absolutely necessary to happiness, that of knowing the family, character, and connexions of those with whom we form a union for life."

"Unquestionably," said the Count; "a prudent man would consider such knowledge highly requisite: But my dear friend, I fear, whilst all-powerful love had such an absolute dominion in your breast — had you really been informed that Claudina was born of worthless or vicious parents, passion would have suggested a thousand alleviating circumstances in her favour, and under the flattering guise of compassion for an unfortunate and innocent young woman, you would have deemed it a meritorious act to rescue her from ruin."

"Perhaps so," answered Ferdinand; — "for the heart, by its pleadings for a beloved object, is generally too hard for the frigid lessons of prudence; and I have given sufficient proofs of my weakness to warrant the severest conclusions against my understanding."

"We will drop the subject, if you please," said the Count, "as it can lead to no pleasurable reflections; and as we propose taking leave of this city in a few days, let us make some visits to diversify our ideas."

Ferdinand very readily consented to a proposal, calculated to draw him from a train of painful retrospections.

In the course of a week, no material incidents happened to the friends. They accompanied Heli in several little excursions round the environs of Vienna, to discover some pleasant retirement that might coincide with his wishes of living unknown and unobserved.

One morning, taking their usual ride, they passed a carriage, which was driving very quick; two gentlemen were in it; and from the transient view they had, Ferdinand thought he had some knowledge of them, but could not ascertain who, or what they were. Presently, however, a servant overtook them, and requested to know if Count M— — — was one of the company? The Count, though surprised, readily announced himself, when the man respectfully presented the compliments of Baron Reiberg and his son, who, he said, were waiting in their carriage, to know if their conjectures were right, and hoped the gentlemen would return, if fortunately he was not mistaken.

The Count and Ferdinand readily accompanied the servant back, and were recognized with great pleasure by the Baron, who congratulated himself upon this desired and little expected meeting.

He, with many others, had heard the report of their deaths; but struck with their appearance, as they passed on the road, had stopped his carriage, and dispatched a servant to know whether the resemblance that surprised him was the illusion of his senses or not.

He told them he had a house at Vienna, to which he hoped they would accompany him and his son, and give them the pleasure of considering it as their own, whilst business or amusement induced them to remain in that city. They made proper acknowledgments for this politeness; told him, their stay would be short, and that they had friends with them.

"If your friends will accept of the same accommodations I can offer you, gentlemen," said the Baron, "they are heartily at their service; and I feel so much interest and curiosity to know by what means you preserved your lives, when your death was generally credited, that I really cannot relinquish my earnest wish to have you inmates of my mansion. Come, come," added he, seeing they hesitated, and looked at each other, you know I am in possession of your promise to pay me a visit, and I now claim the performance of it."

This obliging earnestness was irresistible, and they readily accorded with the request, assuring him, that they would wait of him in the evening. Taking the Baron's address with his invitation to their friends, they parted with him for the present, and returned with speed to Heli. Before they rejoined him, Ferdinand observed, "that he could not think of introducing Fatima to the Baron's house, nor did he suppose it would be at all agreeable to Heli. I hope, therefore, said he, the little estate he is now in view of will answer his wishes."

As he spoke, they saw Heli slowly returning back to meet them.

The Count told him of their meeting with a friend, and took notice the other seemed very thoughtful, which, on demanding the cause, he said he longed for retirement; that the increase of their acquaintance was painful to him, and their self-denial, in giving up so much of their time to his accommodation, was too great a tax upon their kindness. — He had therefore come to a resolution to take the small solitary cottage they had seen the day before; and as it was furnished, he could have immediate possession.

To this plan no objection was made. — They called on the owner of the cottage, and presently concluded the bargain. The house, and a small farm belonging to it, lay extremely retired, on the side of a rising wood, which afforded shelter from the sharp air of the north; and on the south was a delightful garden, with grounds attached to it for their cattle, and other necessaries of life, whilst a small but beautiful rivulet run almost round the house, and fertilized the earth.

Heli, having made the purchase, was impatient to take possession; and on their return to Fatima, bid her prepare for her removal the following morning. It was easy to see she received this mandate with dissatisfaction; nor did a description of her future residence at all tend to lessen her chagrin. — The gay multitudes, which she saw from her windows, were far more gratifying to her than woods or gardens, where she was not likely to see the "human face divine."

Ferdinand easily penetrated into the workings of her mind, and saw but little prospect of happiness to Heli, if it was dependant on the constancy of Fatima. For the present she was silent, because the alternative he had offered to her was also retirement; and therefore, of the two evils, she submitted to accompany Heli, but without ever pretending to a satisfaction she did not feel.

In the evening, the Count and his friend took leave of Heli and his lady. To the latter, Ferdinand ventured a few serious admonitions, but they were heard with a look of careless contempt, and a silent bow. — Heli requested they would sometimes visit him, as themselves would be the only persons he should receive. This they readily promised, and parted with mutual good wishes.

The Baron welcomed them with much cordiality; the young Baron with equal attention; but he had not that pleasant frankness of manners which seemed to characterize his father. On the contrary, it was obvious to both gentlemen, that something oppressive lay upon his spirits, and that tho" he behaved with much complacency and politeness; yet it appeared an effort upon his natural disposition, more inclined to reserve and taciturnity.

The father, who was a man of the world, had travelled a good deal, and profited by his observations on men and manners, exerted himself to entertain his guests; and, by his endeavours, they passed a very pleasant evening.

When the Count and Ferdinand met in the morning, the former took notice of the young Baron's want of spirits, and a disposition so entirely opposite to his father's.

"I made the same observation at the time they passed with us in the solitary Castle," replied Ferdinand — "He then spoke little, and rather avoided than courted society. — But as some characters do not open themselves at once, as we were strangers, and every circumstance there unpleasant, and indeed melancholy, I allowed much for his reserve, and supposed it might be rather accidental than habitual; but I was mistaken I see now; for certainly he has a natural tendency towards an unsocial disposition, and 'tis on the father we must draw for our entertainment here."

They were soon after joined by the Baron. He introduced them to several of his friends; was sedulous to show his esteem, by every gratification he could procure to them.—Sought every possible mode of entertainment, and delicately avoided any reference to the former unhappy situation of the Count, or his irreparable loss of the lady Eugenia.

Once only that day they saw the young Baron; but they found by the conversation, when he appeared at the dinner table, that he spent his hours chiefly in the library. They remarked his father's extreme solicitude to draw him out, and to amuse him; but the few marks of cheerfulness, which now and then broke off, were evidently forced, and the effects of complaisance only.—After the dinner hour, they saw no more of him.

On the second day of their residence with the Baron, when his son had withdrawn from the table, turning to his guests with a suppressed sigh—"Although you are too polite my friends, to express any curiosity, yet 'tis impossible but that you must observe the peculiar disposition of my son; that unsociability, that dejection of spirits so very visible to every eye, is the only thing that disturbs the tranquillity of my life. Poor unfortunate boy, an early and a strong attachment has embittered every hour of his life for upwards of two years past. Hopeless as it is, he cannot drive the fatal passion from his heart.—All my efforts to restore his spirits are fruitless.

"I flattered myself your conversation would tend to lighten the anguish of his mind, and your example animate him to rise superior over unavoidable and irremediable evils; but I see no change, and therefore feel it necessary to apologize to you for his conduct, by explaining the cause of it."

"I feel deeply interested for the unfortunate young gentleman," replied Ferdinand; "and being a fellow-sufferer, can sympathize with him. As I am nearly of his own age, and know his situation, if you will allow me, I shall use all my endeavours to obtain his notice; and if I succeed, I may, by sharing his confidence, divert the current of his thoughts from dwelling always on one object. That a communication of grief, which hangs heavy on the heart, certainly tends to lighten it, I know by experience."

"You kindly anticipate my wishes," said the Baron. — "If you will condescend to fall in with his humour, and attach yourself to him, 'tis the only chance I can see likely to succeed in drawing him from himself."

This plan being agreed upon, the Baron and Count ordered their horses to ride; and after their departure, Ferdinand ventured to dispatch a servant with his compliments to the young Baron, requesting the honour of his company to take a walk. — Or if that was disagreeable to him, would he permit him to join him in the library. He had waited but a few moments for the return of his message before Reiberg appeared. He politely, tho" distantly, apologized for not making a tender of his services, as he thought his father had taken that office upon himself.

"I have indeed a hundred obligations to the Baron for his attentions," replied Ferdinand; "but my spirits are not always calculated to give or receive pleasure from a mixed society: I often prefer a solitary ramble, or the company of a serious rational companion, to mixing with the great world."

"An uncommon turn of mind in so young a man," observed Reiberg, eying him with a more complacent look; "and what is altogether as singular, I am very much of your opinion: Therefore, Sir, I am at your command, either for a walk, or for the library."

"At present," said Ferdinand, "I prefer the former; let us visit some of the gardens in the suburbs."

The other readily complied. They took a long walk, being absent near three hours; and, on coming back, met the Baron and Count just returned.

"Ah!" said the former, "like minds will mingle. — How natural for youth to court the society of each other."

"And yet I have my doubts," replied Reiberg, "whether the entertainments of these youths have not been of a much graver cast than what you may have engaged in."

"Not unlikely," answered the Count — "My friend is of a sedentary turn, and the amusements he seeks are generally of that complexion."

Reiberg viewed his companion with an air of graciousness, that seldom had pervaded his features, and, in the course of the evening, attached himself to Ferdinand with evident satisfaction.

From that day, the young friends were much together; and in the course of conversation, had both thrown out hints of mutual unhappiness, but each was too delicate to express a desire of prying into the secrets of the other. One morning it had been agreed upon between the Count and Ferdinand, that they would visit Heli and Fatima. They set off at an early hour, and soon reached the cottage.

At the door, reclining on a kind of sofa, lay Heli; the noise of the horses made him start: Discerning who they were, he hastened to meet them.

"Ah!" cried he, "never more wished for, nor more welcome. The prophet has sent you to my wishes, or this night I should have sent for you."

"Have you then particularly wanted us?" asked Ferdinand.

"Yes," replied Heli. — "Strange things have happened; but come into this little room, and I will unfold the whole to you."

As they dismounted and entered, the Count asked for Fatima.

"Ah! the ingrate," cried he; "she is but too well, I believe."

This reply induced them to suppose she had behaved ill, if not deserted him; but they waited a farther explanation from him; and when they were seated, he thus began, addressing Ferdinand, as the Count was not so well acquainted with the language.

"From the first day that we came here, the ungrateful Fatima was sullen and discontented. — I did my best to amuse her; we had only two women slaves, or servants; they attended the business of the house, and to please her, I took no notice of them."

"Two nights ago, at midnight, I was alarmed by a loud knocking at the door; I opened the window, and demanded the cause. I was not understood; but hearing a voice, a woman spoke in a tone of terror and supplication. Without disturbing Fatima in the next room, I took my lamp, and went down, opening the door: A young woman rushed in, and directly swooned at my feet.

"I was then obliged to call for assistance; the women soon came about me; the poor creature was helped, and recovered. — I saw she was very pretty, though pale and thin. — Fatima did her best to revive and console her.

"When she was able to speak, she said she had escaped from a small house in the wood, where she had reason to fear it was intended to murder her. We did not ask many questions; but she was put to bed, and yesterday morning I was told she appeared to be a good deal revived; that she earnestly requested, should any person make inquiry after her, we would deny our knowledge of her. I began to think the prophet had thrown this young woman in my way, to be a solace to me, and a companion for Fatima, so I let them be together.

"About noon, two horsemen, like a gentleman and his servant, appeared at the door. — They asked me had I seen a young woman; I kept her secret. — Whilst they were talking, Fatima came out. — I was very much displeased, and commanded her, pretty roughly, to retire. — She refused, and said some words to the stranger I did not understand. — He smiled, and answered her with great quickness. Highly provoked, I pushed her in, and shut the door. — The traitress opened the window above, and talked again. Enraged to madness, I flew in, dragged her from the window, and gave her a little chastisement, though not what she deserved.

"Her cries brought in the men, who, forcing the door, came up, and snatched her from my hands. — She directly run down stairs. — One of the horsemen took her before him, and they galloped off, regardless of my cries or imprecations. — 'Twas in vain to pursue them; I had no horse, and was unacquainted with the turnings in the roads, if I had.

"Whilst I was tearing my beard, and cursing the vile ungrateful wretch, one of the servants came in, and said the young woman was in fits; so here was another plague upon me. — However, I had not lost my charity, so I ascended to help her, but she did not recover 'till night, and has continued very ill ever since; hardly speaks at all, but sighs from the bottom of her heart. — It seems 'twas the voices and bustle those vile Christians made, which occasioned her fits. — This is the state of things here; I am almost mad, and your treacherous wicked sister has basely deserted me; me who preserved her life, and gave her liberty at the hazard of my own!"

"I am more concerned than surprised," said Ferdinand; "for I had no dependence upon her constancy, as she evidently wanted principle. — Retirement suited not with her disposition, and I think you have little cause to regret the loss of such a woman. The young person you speak of may want friends and assistance; if we can be of use to her, I am sure the Count will readily join in offering his services."

"You Christians," answered Heli, "are like the knights in romance, in your wishes to serve women. — Was you more discreet, and less complaisant, they would behave better; but women, having no souls, can practise no virtues, and only subjection and confinement can keep them within bounds."

"Why then accuse Fatima of ingratitude or levity?" said Ferdinand. — "If she has no soul, she may give unbounded loose to her inclinations; and where there exists no virtues, vice and folly only can be expected. — Gratitude is a virtue that flourishes in a noble mind; the produce of the soul, that feels a conscious sense of benefits concerned. If the freedom you procured for Fatima was solely to gratify yourself, she owes you no obligation; nor can you claim any merit from the deed."

"'Tis well," returned Heli, with a lowering brow; "I see what kindness I may expect from you; I have been a tool to all. — Oh! prophet," cried he, with a furious menacing air — —

"Stop, Heli," said Ferdinand. — "Spare your appeal to Mahomet; I am more your friend that you are willing to believe; I despise and detest Fatima; she is a worthless woman; you may rejoice to get rid of one who would have proved a constant source of trouble to you; I vindicate her not; nor do I desire ever to hear of her more, because I am convinced she is incorrigible; but any services we can render you, command us, and you shall see that Christians know how to be grateful and hospitable to strangers."

Heli was affected by the earnest tone in which the other addressed him. — He unbent his angry brow, and lowering his voice —

"I believe I may judge too rashly; if so, may our holy prophet, and you, forgive me. I feel that I loved Fatima, but I will try to despise her: If this young woman lives — but I fear she will not; we cannot understand each other. — The few things I know in your language I have said to comfort her; but either she does not, or will not understand me."

"I would ask to see her," said Ferdinand, "and learn who and what she is, if it is agreeable to you."

"Yes," answered Heli, after a little hesitation — "Yes, you shall see her; but remember I already design her to supply the place of Fatima."

"Fear me not," replied Ferdinand; "I will deserve your confidence."

Heli then preceded them, to announce to her a visit from two of her countrymen. — Ferdinand followed him. — The sick person, who lay fronting the door, at his entrance gave a sudden shriek, and fainted. They advanced hastily to assist her, and in the same moment both recognized the unfortunate young woman, notwithstanding the alteration of her person, and the improbability of her being near Vienna, and both exclaimed, "Louisa! Good Heavens! Louisa!"

"How," said Heli, "do you know her too?"

They were too busy in getting water and other things to restore her, immediately to attend to him; but when she began to show signs of returning life, Ferdinand turned to him — "We do indeed know this lady, one of the most unfortunate of her sex. We left her a few months back under the protection of a worthy family, far from hence. How, or by whom she was brought here, is very extraordinary."

Louisa, for her it was, opened her eyes. — "The shadows are gone," said she, faintly, "or was it the phantom of my brain?"

The Count instantly recollected that it was possible she might have heard of their deaths. Therefore, without advancing, he said, "fear nothing, Madam; two friends of your's are yet alive, and eager to serve you."

"This is happiness indeed!" she exclaimed. — "Where are you?"

Both drew near the sofa, and bowed before her. — Pleasure danced in her eyes, but for a moment she had not the power of speech.

"Take comfort, Madam," said Ferdinand, "you are in safe hands — Mr. and Miss D'Alenberg — — —."

"Ah!" cried she, much affected, "I have been torn from them; they are on the road."

"What! to Vienna?" asked he.

"I believe so—I left them at Ens; there I was discovered—That villain the Count—he—he got me into his power to destroy me."

She had not strength to proceed, and they requested she would not exhaust herself by the attempt; and turning to Heli, (who was pacing the room, and cursing his malicious stars, and his own folly, for introducing them into the room) "it will be necessary to send a physician to this lady."

The Count offered to fetch one, and immediately set off for that purpose, though Louisa tried to oppose the design. Ferdinand, who was eagerly desirous of hearing some intelligence of the D'Alenberg family, remained with Heli in the apartment.

The latter, greatly agitated, had thrown himself upon a sofa. Louisa looked at him with evident terror, and appeared to shrink from his menacing aspect.

"My evil genius seems to predominate," said he to Ferdinand.—"I am to be robbed of this young woman too by Christian artifices."

"Heli," replied the latter, "do not repine that you are made the instrument to rescue an unfortunate lady from villainy. She is of birth and character; has powerful friends, and is married.—She is under the protection of a family I respect, and who will feel the warmest gratitude for her preservation, and can be nothing more to me, or any man, than an object of reverence and admiration.

"You cannot suppose, my good Heli, that every lady, who may eventually be thrown in your way, must be subservient to you; a thousand causes may impede any attentions of your's in a particular light; but for your humanity and kindness, you will ever experience a grateful return."

Heli heard him, but answered not.—A sullen silence denoted a mind but ill satisfied. The remembrance of Fatima's charms, and her elopement, sat heavy at his heart; for he had now no companion that he could converse with, or who even understood his language.

The Count was not long before he returned with a physician, who confirmed Louisa's own judgment, that terror and surprise had caused the great agitation of her spirits, and a shock to her constitution, which was extremely delicate and languid, but that no immediate danger need be apprehended. — He ordered her some light cordials, and had no doubt but that she would soon be better.

This opinion of the doctor's was gratifying to all parties; but Ferdinand felt some perplexity on the score of leaving Louisa under the care of Heli. — He asked, could she be removed? the physician thought there would be no danger in a proper conveyance. — — — Where she could be carried to, was the next question. The medical gentleman, finding that they were strangers on a visit in the city, and that the lady was a person of fashion, and had powerful friends, very humanely offered an apartment in his own house, an offer most readily accepted, and he hastened off to send a carriage, and an aunt, who resided with him, to attend on the lady, whilst he prepared for her reception.

No sooner was this plan communicated to Heli, than he grew quite furious; upbraided the gentlemen in the most opprobrious words passion could suggest; but finding that they were resolute, and not to be intimidated, his fury fell upon himself; he cursed his own folly, in preserving two Christian wretches, whose acquaintance had been the ruin of his peace; ungenerously ascribing Fatima's desertion from him as originating from the offers Ferdinand had made of providing for her.

The Count, who was apprehensive of some revengeful stroke from the mad passion of Heli, kept a steady eye upon all his actions; while Ferdinand endeavoured, by reason, to calm his transports; and among other things observed to him, that as there were many Turks in Vienna, he might easily find such as would be useful to him in his domestic arrangements, and plenty of women who would accept of his protection.

This last argument seemed to have some weight with him; he grew less agitated; and before the carriage came for Louisa, told them he would take their advice; and having now nobody to guard, he would come into the city the next day, to seek out some of his countrymen, and purchase two or three beautiful women, that he might no longer think of the unfaithful woman who had abandoned him.

This resolved on, he assisted in carrying Louisa to the carriage. — A middle aged respectable lady waited to receive her; cushions were placed for her to recline on; and moving very slowly, she was safely conveyed to the physician's house, under whose care the gentlemen left her for the remainder of the day, that quiet might help to restore her; — and although both were dying with curiosity, yet they suppressed all appearance of it, in consideration of her weakness.

CHAPTER X

On their return to the Baron's house, they found him under a good deal of surprise at their long absence; for so much had their minds been occupied, that they had entirely forgotten the necessary compliment of accounting to the Baron. They apologized for their neglect, by a relation of the cause, and described Louisa as a much injured deserving young woman.

Young Reiberg appeared greatly interested; there was a novelty in the case, which, added to his natural humanity, roused him from the apathy that generally predominated over his conduct, and induced him to be particularly anxious in his inquiries, and offers of assisting them to discover, and punish, if possible, the offenders.

Ferdinand was pleased with the warmth he expressed, but not conceiving himself at liberty to disclose the story of Louisa, he only observed, that until she was in a state to elucidate facts, and give them full information, no steps could be taken to do her justice. — "I have my suspicions," added he, "as to the person, but do not think it fair to communicate them, lest I should be wrong."

Reiberg seemed pleased with the discretion of Ferdinand, and attached himself to him with an appearance of regard, very flattering to the other, and highly pleasing to the Baron, who presaged the happiest consequences to the peace of his son, should he conceive a friendly regard for Ferdinand, and unlock his bosom to the sympathizing attentions, and disinterested advice of a friend.

Early the following morning, they sent to inquire into the state of Louisa's health, and had the satisfaction to hear she had rested tolerably, was better, and would be happy to see her preservers in the course of the day. This pleasing account diffused general content to the gentlemen, and gave promise that their curiosity might be gratified.

Mean time, Ferdinand felt a good deal of vexation at Fatima's conduct. His reverence to the memory of his father would have led him any lengths to have preserved his child from infamy; but it was too evident that her heart was debased by the way of life she had chosen for herself, and that the loose principles of the parent had descended to the children. Again he sighed at the truth painful experience had taught him, "that the principles and character of parents is an essential consideration, when about to form a union with a young person for life; since example, as well as precept, must influence the disposition and actions of young and ductile minds, and lay the foundation for progressive virtue or vice."

At a proper hour, the two gentlemen repaired to the house of Dr. Renau, and were introduced to Louisa.—She was seated in an arm chair, and accompanied by Madam Blomfielde, the physician's aunt, who rose at their entrance, and after a few compliments, left the room. They congratulated the invalid on her appearance, so much for the better.

"I am indeed," said she, "under infinite obligations to you, gentlemen, and to the good Doctor; and feeling myself in safety from the power and machinations of the most profligate of men, has restored a comparative peace to my mind, which has its influence on my general state of health. Permit me also to felicitate myself and you, on your preservation from death, an event so unquestionably believed by all your friends, that seeing you, Sir (addressing Ferdinand) follow the Turk into the room, occasioned the faintings I was seized with, the weakened state of my head at that moment leading me to suppose it was your spirit emerged from the grave. Forgive me, therefore, if I am desirous of knowing why the report of your death was circulated, and why you have concealed yourselves from your friends."

Ferdinand, without entering into a particular detail, briefly mentioned their captivity, and recent return into Germany; adding, that they had sent off letters to all those whom they supposed might be interested in their fate, and hourly expected letters. — — —"You may be certain," said he, "we did not omit writing to Mr. D'Alenberg."

"Ah!" cried Louisa, "had those letters reached him before we quitted Suabia, 'tis more than probable we should not have undertaken this journey, and my dear friends would have been spared much sorrow and anxiety. If you will allow for the pauses my weakness may occasion, I will give you a short account of the events which have thus, fortunately for me, procured us a meeting.

"For some time after your departure, my friend Theresa exerted herself to heal the wounds of my mind, and administer to the recovery of my health. I was grateful for her kindness, though it had not its deserved success. Unhappily she caught the contagion of melancholy, and from a disposition of the most enchanting vivacity, changed to a despondency, a kind of habitual gloom in every word and action, that alarmed us inexpressibly. The distress and despair of Mr. D'Alenberg cannot be expressed. She resisted every persuasion, even prayers and tears, to draw from her the cause of such an alarming change, always protesting she could not account for it; that she had no disquietudes, nor any thing that afflicted her mind, but that she had taken an inclination for a monastic life. This inclination her worthy father opposed, and besought her, in the most moving terms, not to desert him, and render his future days wretched.

With some difficulty she was brought to relinquish her design, and promised she would struggle against the malady that oppressed her.

"I reproached myself incessantly as the cause of her disorder; I would have left the house which I had infected with melancholy, but she protested violently against my design, and I was compelled to submit. Mr. D'Alenberg could assign no other probable idea for her distress of mind, than that she had deceived herself, and was actually warmly attached to the unworthy Count Wolfran."

"Impossible," exclaimed Ferdinand, warmly.—"A mind pure and exalted as her's, could not, for a moment, entertain a preference for such a wretch."

"The event," resumed Louisa, "justifies your assertion. As I felt conscious that her unhappiness, from whatever cause it proceeded, must originate from me, I tried to assume a new character, to stifle my own feelings, and to cover a breaking heart under the mask of cheerfulness. Every effort of mine was exerted to amuse her. We went to Stutgard, compelled her to go into company, to mix sometimes in the entertainments of the city. She refused no request of her father's, but no change appeared in her disposition.

"One day Mr. D'Alenberg received a letter from his friend, who had introduced Count Wolfran to his notice. He lamented that he had not the power to punish a villain who had so basely deceived him, but that, after the most minute inquiries, he had reason to believe the Count had left the kingdom, to avoid the disgrace and shame attendant on a conviction of such vile actions as he had been guilty of.

This letter the good gentleman read to his daughter in my presence, both of us carefully watching its effects on her. No change appeared in her countenance.—"Poor wretch," said she, "what a mind must he possess, conscious of his base duplicity!"

"How, my dear!" exclaimed Mr. D'Alenberg, "do you pity him?"

"I do, Sir," answered she. — "When we can despise the man, and know he has failed in his pursuits, that he has had no power to injure us, and must be covered with confusion and guilt, charity may induce us to pity one so completely mean and detestable."

Those words, delivered without any emotion either in her person or voice, convinced us that Count Wolfran had no share in the disorder of her mind. A thousand different conjectures we then hazarded to each other, but in three days after, the whole was elucidated at once. Mr. d'Allenberg received some intelligence that grieved him, and too hastily communicated it to his daughter: — Its effects were instantaneous; she fell into violent and repeated fits, that ended in a delirium, and discovered the secret so tenaciously observed, so strictly guarded, that I was equally surprised with her father.

"Ah!" said Ferdinand, "may we presume to ask — — —?"

"Pardon me for interrupting you," returned Louisa; "I would not hear a question that should make me doubt of your delicacy or prudence; all that I can, in honour confide, you, gentlemen, have an undoubted claim to be informed of; but a secret retained with so much perseverance by my friend, can never be at my discretion to reveal."

"Amiable Louisa," exclaimed Ferdinand, "I stand corrected, and take shame to myself, but do justice to the purity of my motives."

"I do," replied she; "I know they were friendly ones, and I saw the same question trembling on the lips of the Count."

"I own it," said he; "and you must allow it was a natural question, if not a discreet one, and the impulse of the moment; but, pardon our impatience and interruption."

"This secret discovered," resumed she, "gave the severest affliction to Mr. D'Alenberg. — He had not the power to relieve her distress, or procure happiness to his child. — There were certain circumstances that impeded every hope of restoring her to a cheerful turn of mind, and his despair on the conviction was little less terrifying than the dreadful state in which my charming friend continued for six days.

"At the expiration of that period, Heaven heard the prayers of this worthy father, and restored her to reason. It was near a fortnight before she could leave her bed; and then how affecting was the figure she presented! A delicate skin thrown over a skeleton, a look of dignified sorrow, that wounded every eye, and a struggle for that composure so necessary to her father's peace, which now seemed the only object she had in view. So shadowy was her frame, that we almost feared to breathe, lest it should dissolve into air; and when she spoke, so faint, so sweet was her voice, that it penetrated to the very soul.

"Judge what a father must feel; for I see you are affected. Not to dwell, therefore, on a situation so painful, the fortitude she sought to acquire, and her consideration for her father, which still rendered life valuable to a duteous mind like her's, uniting with youth and a good constitution, restored her to comparative health. — The physicians advised travelling, that change of air, and a variety of objects, might dispel that gloom which seemed to impede her natural cheerfulness, and undermine her strength.

"In compliance with this advice, for near two months past we have lived a desultory kind of life, without any fixed plan, but moving from place to place, as fancy or inclination directed. By this management, we have succeeded in amusing Miss D'Alenberg; and though that playful gaiety, and animating vivacity she once possessed, appears to be entirely lost, yet there is a soft complacency, an earnest desire to look contented in every word and action, that highly gratifies her father, and inspires hope, that time and effort may restore her tranquillity.

"About ten days ago, we arrived at Ens, in which city lived a relation of Mr. D'Alenberg, who received us with great kindness. The next evening I accompanied my friend in a walk by the side of the river, not far from our residence. We strolled sometime on the banks; the evening was delightful. — Several boats were passing; the moon was rising in majestic splendor; its beams playing on the smooth surface, and conveying unspeakable tranquillity to the mind. We stood for some time in fixed admiration of the scene, forgetful of the hour, 'till a servant came to remind us of the time we had been absent.

"We were so enchanted with our evening's walk, that we resolved to repeat it the following night, and declined having a servant to attend us, because we apprehended no danger, and wished to be unobserved.

"Unfortunately we were indulged in our request, and we extended our walk, thoughtless of the distance, until no more boats passing, we recollected that it grew late; we turned to quicken our pace home, when suddenly a boat drew towards the shore, and three ordinary looking men jumped out and followed us. Fear lent us wings, though we knew not that they meant any ill. Miss D'Alenberg was more nimble than myself; hastening, and I fell. Two men instantly seized me; I screamed.

"Stop her mouth," cried one of them, "and bear her off; the other has got the start of us."

"I heard no more, but found myself carried to a boat, which rowed off with great swiftness. A large cloak was thrown over me, and between terror and affright, I was scarcely in my senses.

"How long we continued on the water, I know not; I was carried out still wrapped up, and incapable of making any resistance. At length I was uncovered; some bread and wine was given to me, which I refused. I saw only strange faces, and demanded to know why I was thus dragged from my friends?

"No answer was given; and in a short time after, a handkerchief was tied across my mouth. I was again tight wrapped in a cloak, and put into a carriage. — When in the high road, I was uncovered — and high time it was, for I was nearly suffocated, and had suffered great agony. We came within sight of a town; I was then obliged to undergo the same misery again, until we had stopped, changed post horses, and were once more on the road.

Not to tire you with more particulars, in this manner we proceeded, without stopping to sleep on the road, and only taking some bread and wine from the post-houses. At length we entered a wood: No longer able to preserve silence, I cried out, "Ah! my God, what is now to become of me!"

Being so frequently muffled up, and having only once taken any refreshment, both my spirits and strength were exhausted, which, with the terror I felt on entering a thick wood at the close of day, entirely overcame me, and I fainted. How long I continued in this situation, I know not; but on my recovery, I found myself in a very decent apartment, with two men and an elderly woman.

The former perceiving that my senses were returned, ordered the woman to retire; she obeyed, and after a short whisper, one of the men followed her.

The other having shut the door, advanced close to me, and, to my infinite astonishment, taking off a false covering of hair, and removing a pair of black eye-brows, discovered to me the features of Count Wolfran. I shrieked with the wildest affright.

"Once more," said he, "I have you in my power. — You, who have destroyed my happiest prospects, and blasted all my hopes; who have injured my character, and procured for yourself protectors at my expense. What have you to offer as an atonement for the mischief you have done; what reparation can you make for the ruin and disgrace you have brought upon me?"

I was speechless at this address: The effrontery, and the well-known villainy of the man, filled me with the most dreadful apprehensions, and impeded any attempt at articulation; he saw, and enjoyed my terror.

"I see," said the wretch, "conscious guilt ties your tongue: Know then, that I have taken my measures too securely for you to entertain any hope of an escape from my power. I have two proposals to make, one of which you must choose — Death or marriage. I should suppose the alternative will not be difficult to decide on.

"Indignation restored my speech. — "Marriage," I exclaimed. — 'You well know that I am your wife."

"Aye," said he, "there is the point on which we differ: That is the assertion which I deny. — You were once indeed a kind obliging girl, and chose to patch up your reputation at the expense of mine. But to have done with this foolery,' said he with a stern look, observing my agitation, 'know, that you are either to marry my servant, your old acquaintance, or this house is your grave.

"Understand me — I do not want your murder to hang upon my spirits, but I am determined to secure you from doing me further mischief. My valet shall marry you, and in justice to him, I shall indulge him with a few days to amuse his pretty wife; — after which, by his authority, you will be placed in a situation that will effectually secure me from any more discoveries of your's.

"I now leave you. — To-morrow, at an early hour, we shall conclude the business."

He then opened the door, and retired. — I heard it locked and bolted on the other side.

For some moments, I remained fixed in astonishment and terror. I knew him too well to doubt of his resolution, and I saw no means of escaping from his power. — Furious and malignant, he was capable of the most atrocious actions, and I had every evil to apprehend.

The alternative of death would have been my preferable choice, but that was only thrown out to alarm me. — Murder was not his choice. — For some hours I sat almost stupefied with horror: I found, that during the deprivation of my senses, my pockets had been emptied of their contents. I looked round the apartment; it was a decent room, but without a bed; a sofa, a few chairs, and a table, composed all the furniture.

One window very high from the ground, with a chintz window curtain: No light was left with me, but fortunately the moon shone sufficiently through the window for me to discriminate every object.

Rousing at length from the stupor of terror, I placed a chair on the table, and looked through the window; a large garden was under it, and beyond the wood. The distance from the ground was so great, that to reach it, appeared almost impossible; but what will not despair attempt, and ingenuity contrive.

With some difficulty I got off the window curtain, and with my teeth affected different breaks, by which means I tore it into six parts; but the fear of being heard, obliged me to be long and cautious in doing it. — At length I effected my design; I tied each part together in repeated strong knots; I opened the window softly, and letting it down, saw that it reached the ground.

There was a chance indeed that it might break, or that my hands might slip; yet as death was far preferable to the evils that impended over me, I was not terrified by the apparent danger. I fastened the end of the curtain to the iron across the window, and with a courage desperation only could inspire, ventured from it, holding firmly by the kind of rope I had made.

My weight carried me quick down to the first knot: Here my hands were stopped, and it was with the utmost hazard I freed them;—but, by the time I reached the second knot, they were too feeble to support me, and I fell from a great height, but most providentially on a bed of earth, fresh turned up;—and though stunned with the fall, I soon found I had broken no limbs, and in a short time got on my feet, and made towards a door that led into the wood. I had here another difficulty to encounter, to get over the wall, but it was not very high, and I accomplished it, though not without some injury to my person.

I was now in the wood, unacquainted with any path-way, and exposed to a thousand dangers; but all weighed light in comparison of those I had escaped from: I therefore pierced through the trees, and walked with all the swiftness my strength would permit, though often obliged to sit a few minutes and rest.

I believe I must have walked upwards of four hours, when I observed a path to the right, which I entered upon, and in a short time came to a descent, from whence I thought I could discern the top of a house.—The idea gave me spirits; I hastened down the declivity, and arrived at that house where most fortunately I met with you.

That it was the Count who came next morning, I have no doubt: Nor am I surprised that he should take the lady; but as doubtless she betrayed me, I am greatly astonished that he did not return, and force me from thence.

Thus, gentlemen, I have accounted to you for my appearance.—Heaven, doubtless, sent you for my preservation; but I feel most poignantly for the affliction I know my amiable friend and her benevolent father must suffer, from the incertitude of my fate."

Louisa having concluded her story, Ferdinand proposed setting off immediately for Ens, to relieve the inquietude of her friends. She gratefully thanked him, but said, she had many reasons to prefer sending a messenger, as it was not unlikely that Mr. d'Allenberg might have left Ens, and the journey prove fruitless; but if he would have the goodness to procure a courier, she would endeavour to write both to him and the gentleman they had visited, and by that means should certainly gain intelligence of their route, if they had quitted the city. This method was adopted, and a proper person soon obtained, who was dispatched with the letter.

Mean time, Ferdinand and the Count expressed a good deal of anxiety that they had no return to the letters they had written. — For five or six days past, they had daily expected them, and the disappointment grew very painful.

To divert their attention, they asked the young Count Reiberg to ride with them to the Turk's cottage, as they wished to know if he had gained any information relative to Fatima.

On arriving at the house, they were surprised to see all the window shutters fastened. The Count advanced to the door, and knocking with his whip, found the door was on a jar. They alighted, and repeated the knock; but no one appearing, and fancying they heard a noise something like the moan of a person in pain, they pushed open the door, and ventured in. There was no one below, but an appearance of disorder in the room, the closet open, and things scattered about, that gave them an idea some ruffians had broken in and plundered the house.

They had no fire arms with them, and therefore went cautiously up stairs. — The same disorder was apparent in the first room they entered; but on going through to an inner apartment, how greatly were they astonished and shocked, to behold a gentleman on the floor dead or dying, and Heli also on the floor, with very little appearance of life, though he feebly moved one of his hands, as they hastened towards him.

The blood was running from a wound in his neck; this they quickly staunched with their handkerchiefs, bound up the wound, and raised him upon the sofa; whilst the Count and Baron were attending to him. — Ferdinand had examined the gentleman, who seemed to be dangerously wounded, and scarcely alive. His wound was in the side, and, as they supposed, proceeded from a pistol; therefore, not knowing where the bullet might be lodged they could form no judgment of his danger; however, they stopped the blood, washed his face with cold water, and, by the help of drops, he soon began to show signs of life. He opened his eyes, and making a great effort to speak,

"Your help is in vain — I am dying."

"Do not despair, Sir," said Reiberg." — And pouring some drops into water, he got a little down his throat. — Again trying to speak, he said, "'Tis in vain!" — Not, however, discouraged, they raised him upon a sofa likewise, and Reiberg got upon his horse, and flew towards the city for a surgeon.

On his return with one in a very short space of time, he found they were both alive, Heli in a much better state than the other;—but he preserved a sullen silence; the gentleman was incapable of speaking. The surgeon having examined their wounds, pronounced Heli's not dangerous, but the other's very doubtful, as he could not then extract the ball. After he had dressed them, and given them some cordials to restore their spirits, the gentleman seemed to acquire some strength.

"I must die," said he to the surgeon; "I know I must; flatter me not."

"I fear indeed," answered he; "if you have friends, or any thing to do, no time should be lost."

"This then is the end," exclaimed the other feebly, and paused for a few moments; then turning to the gentlemen, "this is the conclusion of a life short as to years—but an eternity in vice and wickedness.

"I am Count Wolfran—Louisa Hautweitzer is my lawful wife—she must inherit. I die by the hand of a vile Turk, cut off when projecting the death of others. This is retribution.— Women—passion, vile principles, have destroyed me.—I have a house, servants, wretches in the — — —."

Here his articulation failed; he struggled violently to speak, which occasioned his wounds to bleed afresh, and carried him off in a few moments.

Heli viewed this scene with a gloomy ferocity, but spoke not. Ferdinand and his friends were equally shocked and surprised.

"Unhappy man," cried the Count, 'this is indeed a terrible conclusion of an ill-spent life."

"Do you then know the gentleman?" asked the surgeon; "I understood he was a stranger."

"Personally so," returned Count M— — —, "his name, I know, has too often been disgraced by bad actions—but here they rest."

Turning to Heli—"Perhaps he can give some solution of this strange business.—My friend," said he to Ferdinand, "will you inquire."

The surgeon here interposed. — "I think, gentlemen, you had best defer 'till to-morrow any examination; the sudden and fatal effects which attend the agitation of the spirits, we have just seen; and if I can translate that man's looks, he is not likely to be very placid."

They subscribed to this opinion; and therefore Ferdinand addressed him in very soothing terms, to which the other made no reply.

The body was removed to another room, and the surgeon undertook to send a proper person to attend on Heli.

"But what," cried the Count, "is become of the women servants?"

This question was again asked of Heli.

"The devil has them," answered he, sulkily.

They then proceeded to search the house. No person was to be found; the trunks and closets were all open and stripped.

"The house is robbed," said Ferdinand to Heli.

"By your cursed sister," returned he in German.

The surgeon and Reiberg stared. — Ferdinand was extremely confused; but recovering himself — "If the woman you call my sister," answered he in the same language, "has robbed you, you can blame only yourself; I disclaim all knowledge or affinity to her."

Heli did not perfectly understand him, but again furiously and maliciously repeated, "your sister, the cursed Fatima."

Provoked and much hurt, he said to the surgeon, "I entreat of you, Sir, to inquire out for an interpreter for this man; he knows not what he means; let him have a proper person to explain what he says, that he may not be misunderstood."

The surgeon, whose curiosity was evidently much excited, promised instantly to comply with his request; upon which they left him there with one of Count Reiberg's servants, another having been sent away for the surgeon's assistant, on whose arrival he promised to set off and procure an interpreter.

The gentlemen, particularly Ferdinand, left the house under much perturbation. The latter bitterly lamented his folly, in making himself known to Fatima; for as he supposed her capable of any excesses, should the Turk promulgate the report of his consanguinity to her, it would reflect infinite disgrace on his name, and render him an object of curiosity to the inhabitants of the city.

Perplexed and uneasy, he returned to the Baron's, and saw no method to do away the prejudice with which Heli's story and malicious expressions might possibly fill young Reiberg's mind to his disadvantage, than by a brief recital of the adventure which had brought him to the knowledge of Fatima, to the truth of which his friend the Count could bear testimony.

He therefore seized the first opportunity, when the dinner was over, and the servants withdrawn, candidly to repeat every circumstance; and concluded with saying, that from Fatima's elopement, and the presence of Count Wolfran at Heli's, he had little doubt but that they had contrived some dark plot, in the execution of which the Count had fallen a victim; but by whom the house was robbed, or the preceding circumstances, could only be learnt from Heli, whose sullen taciturnity for the present afforded no lights to guide their search.

When Ferdinand had concluded the little narrative, which he thought requisite to do himself justice, he could not avoid remarking an uncommon spirit and animation in the appearance of Reiberg; his looks, his voice, his whole form, seemed to possess a new soul; involved in perplexity on his own affairs, 'till this moment the alteration had escaped his notice.

The other, observing that both the Count and Ferdinand looked at him with surprise, caught the hand of the latter—"My dear Sir, I can translate your thoughts; know then, the events of this morning nearly concern me; they hold out a dawn of hope, a possibility of happiness, which I thought for ever extinguished: Count Wolfran was my mortal enemy; he robbed me of the woman I adored; his relations were her guardians, they compelled her to give him her hand;—he is dead, and she is free.—Heaven is just—and I may hope."

The Count and Ferdinand were astonished at this development, and more so to find that he was unacquainted with the circumstances that had occasioned a separation between the Count and his lady.

"Where does the Countess reside?" asked Ferdinand.

"I believe in a convent," answered Reiberg. — "I have only once heard from her since her fatal marriage. She wrote to me, that, by mutual consent, she was separated from her husband, and intended to retire from the world; conjured me, as I valued her future happiness, if chance should ever throw me in the way of Count Wolfran, whatever reports might reach my ears, as probably many false stories might be promulgated, never to lift my hand against his, or embitter her days, by hazarding my own life: Entreated me to consider her as dead to the world, and to form another connexion, which she knew was most anxiously wished for by my friends."

The first part of her request I resolved strictly to observe: I sought not Count Wolfran — I desired not to meet him, since his death, by my hands, would have placed an insuperable bar to any hopes from Theodosia; but the passion she had inspired was interwoven with my existence, impossible to be eradicated, and being hopeless, produced an entire change in my disposition. I found myself insensibly growing morose, unsociable, and unpleasant to my friends; my temper seemed to be utterly ruined; but the events of this morning has occasioned an entire revolution in my feelings; the possibility of hope has restored me to myself.

A few words the Count uttered, as he was dying, surprises and confounds me. — He said, "Louisa:" The tumult of my spirits, at the moment, has lost the recollection of the other name; but he said, "Louisa is my wife — she must inherit."

What could be meant; had he two wives, or is my Theodosia dead? The idea chills me; for I know not the name of the convent she retired to. — 'Till this doubt is removed, I cannot give myself up to joy, tho' my heart feels light, and presages happiness. The Count, I know, has an estate near Ulm, and I believe relations there: We must dispatch a courier to them, and then my destiny will be decided."

Count M— — — and Ferdinand, having listened with much satisfaction to the volubility of Reiberg, who had spoken more words in a few moments than he had uttered in several days, felt infinite pleasure that they could do away some part of his apprehensions, by assuring him that Theodosia still existed, and even named to him the convent she resided at; but their confidence was limited; for her situation, in respect to the Count, being very delicate, they held themselves bound to conceal that part of her story, and even prevailed with the Baron to delay sending off a messenger until the next morning, under the pretence of gaining further information from Heli; but in reality they wanted to inform Louisa of this event, and consult with her the proper steps necessary to assert her rights.

By advice of the Count, Ferdinand set out to see her, whilst the former, with Reiberg, went to visit Heli.

CHAPTER XI

When Ferdinand arrived at Dr. Renau's, he heard that Louisa was very much recovered, and on being introduced to her, was charmed to see her more easy, and apparently in better health than he could have expected. After a few compliments, and a little preparatory chat, he bid her prepare to hear news interesting and pleasing, and then entered upon the scenes which they had witnessed at Heli's cottage.

Louisa was both surprised and affected. — She shed many tears for the dreadful fate of a man she once tenderly loved; thus cut off in the high career of vice, when he was planning new schemes of mischief. After she grew a little composed, he repeated the story of Count Reiberg, and concluded with asking what directions she would give him or her friends to prosecute her claims to a share of the late Count's property, as his widow; his last words before witnesses would corroborate the circumstances she could bring forth. — After pausing for some time, she delivered her sentiments in these words:

"There was a time, when, to be acknowledged the wife of Count Wolfran, would have been my pride, my happiness; that time is no more. To be justified in the opinion of my generous friends and protectors, is now the only gratification his confession can afford me.

"I never will make any public claims; — my story is unknown, but among my few friends; there let it rest. — The generous, noble-minded Theodosia, was married in the face of the world; she has a child; that child is his lawful heir; nor for millions would I deprive it of its rights, or occasion confusion to its amiable mother, by the ill natured observations of little minds, who will judge superficially of the deception practised against her.

"This then is my determination: I will not appear in the business; Theodosia is Countess of Wolfran; send an express to her; let her emerge from her solitude, and act for her child, as heir to the Count; her claims are incontestable — mine, were I inclined to assert them, might subject me to trouble from his relations; but I have no such inclinations; a thousand reasons of delicacy, honour, and gratitude, determine me to resign all my pretensions."

"But," said Ferdinand, "how shall we account for the last words of the Count, spoken before Reiberg and the surgeon? of which the former has taken notice."

"As the delirium of the moment," answered she. — "The surgeon cannot be interested to investigate it: The Countess will be recognized by all his friends and her's, and Reiberg may be led to believe it was some transient attachment he had lately formed. The words of a dying man, situated as he was, may easily be overlooked."

"Well," said Ferdinand, "I admire your resolution exceedingly; I trust we shall, in a few hours, have the benefit of Mr. d'Allenberg's advice; for I think they will not delay their journey, when they know your situation."

"I believe so," replied Louisa, "and shall rejoice to see them; but my determination is fixed, as to resigning all claims on the deceased or his property. — On that head, I have made up my mind; nor will any advice or persuasions prevail upon me to alter it; and indeed there is less generosity than justice in this resolve, because I have no one that can be benefited by the Count's fortune; and his child is, and ought to be, his heir; therefore, dear Sir, have no doubts on the business; send off to the Countess without delay; I will prepare a letter to go by the same courier."

As Ferdinand observed that she appeared fatigued with talking, and saw she was truly decided, he forebore intruding on her by farther conversation, and retired to procure a messenger; also to fabricate some plausible story to account for the last words of Count Wolfran.

When he returned, he found his friend the Count, and young Reiberg, were still absent; he waited on the Baron, and consulted him about the disposal of the Count's body, until the pleasure of his lady should be made known. The Baron readily undertook to manage that business, and to send a proper person with a shell to remove it from Heli's.

They began to be extremely surprised at the long absence of the others; night came on, and they did not appear, when suddenly a loud knocking revived their spirits; presently they heard a bustle, when four armed men rushed in, and produced their authority to arrest Ferdinand for robbery and murder!

Inconceivably astonished, the Baron and he gazed on each other for a few seconds in silence; but the former first recovering, cried out, "This is a false and malicious charge; I know this gentleman; I can answer for his honour and innocence."

"Very possibly, Sir," replied the principal of them; "but that must be proved; we can do nothing about it; we must obey the warrant; and if the gentleman is innocent, he will soon be at liberty; he must, however, go with us." Ferdinand had by this time recovered from his surprise; turning to the Baron—"Be not disconcerted, Sir, the business will soon take another turn; the man is right; I must comply with the mandate, and appeal elsewhere." At that moment entered the Count and young Reiberg.

"How! What is the meaning of all this?" cried the latter."

His father briefly informed him of the charge and arrest.

"That cursed revengeful Turk," exclaimed the Count; "but he shall not be carried to a prison."

"I beseech you, my good friends," said Ferdinand, "not to oppose the authority issued against me. Innocence is best proved by a quiet submission to the laws, and a proper appeal to higher powers. I am ready to attend you, said he, turning to the man."

"Sir," returned the man, who had spoken before, "you are a gentleman and an honourable one too.—I am certain—I am sorry I am ordered on such an affair; but I hope you will soon have your liberty."

"I thank you, my good fellow," replied he.

Then embracing his friends, after they had inquired where he was to be carried to, they parted.

No sooner had Ferdinand been taken off, than young Reiberg gave the following relation to his father:

"When we arrived at the cottage, we were extremely surprised to be seized upon by five or six men, on our entrance into Heli's apartment. My first idea was, that they were banditti, but I was soon convinced of my mistake. Heli was reclined on the sofa, as we had left him; a man, who we found was an interpreter, standing by his side.

"On seeing us, he spoke with an appearance of chagrin to the other: He asked where the other gentleman was that had been there in the morning? I replied we had left him in the city, and demanded to know the reason we were thus seized upon. The interpreter made the following reply:

"I was sent here this morning by a surgeon; just as I arrived, came these men also, with orders to arrest this Turk for the murder of Count Wolfran, information of which had been given to a magistrate. — I explained to Heli their business; he grew outrageous, and denied the fact: Meantime, two of the men had searched the house, had found the dead body, and some empty pistols.

"This corroborated the charge, and they were on the point of dragging him away wounded as he is. — When he understood this, he declared, that a gentleman, who called himself Count Ferdinand, but who he believed to be a rogue and a sharper, with his sister, calling herself Fatima, had concerted with the late Count to enter his house, and plunder him of some jewels, which the two former knew he had with him.

"That the Count, Fatima, and a strange man, assaulted him; he made resistance; — upon which the woman had stabbed him in the neck, and he directly caught up a pistol, and fired on the Count: That seeing him fall, and Heli faint with the blood that flowed from his wound, also falling, they had proceeded to plunder the house, had carried off his casket of jewels, and fled, leaving him and the Count to all appearance dying; and then the former confessed Ferdinand had persuaded his sister to get possession of those jewels.

"In the morning, he said Ferdinand, with two gentlemen, came to the house, the former, no doubt, expecting to find him dead, and seemed much surprised and confused when he saw both alive. The Count dying soon after, Ferdinand went into the rooms, and then returned, crying out, the house was plundered; upon which he (Heli) accused his infamous sister: That Ferdinand spoke to him in the Turkish language, desiring he would not expose him, by calling Fatima his sister; but he disdained any other reply than the same accusation in German; upon which the other, greatly confounded, pretended to show much compassion for him, but made off as soon as he could; and he supposed some of his confederates had charged him with the murder of the Count, to get rid of him; but he now charged Ferdinand, his sister, and other accomplices, with an intent to murder and rob him."

"This," continued the interpreter, "was the account delivered to the men. Some circumstances seemed improbable; yet there were others not unlikely, because it was plain he had been robbed, by the disorder in the house. Two men were left to guard him, whilst three went away to repeat this story to the magistrate.

"They soon returned; we were ordered to wait here, and seize who ever should come to Heli. Mean time, an order was given to arrest this Ferdinand at the house of Baron Reiberg, according to Heli's directions;—and now, gentlemen, this is all I know of the business; the Turk persists in his story, and the affair must be investigated by those in power."

"When the man concluded his account," said Reiberg, "I asked to speak with Heli, but I was refused; we then demanded to be conducted to the magistrate, which was complied with; and on coming before him, and declaring our names, he permitted us to depart at liberty, as no particular charge had appeared against the Count or myself. All this business occasioned our late return, but we little thought the order for Ferdinand's arrest had been so speedily issued and executed; and now, dear Sir, what can be done?"

"Nothing can be done this night," replied the Baron.—"Early in the morning I will attend the magistrate myself.—At any rate, the Count's testimony and mine will procure his liberty, on our parole of honour, I should suppose."

"That villainous Turk can only be actuated by malice," said the Count; "for he well knows the innocence of my friend.— What share Fatima had in the business, I know not; but I believe that Count Wolfran came there to seek for the lady, and not to rob the house.—I only fear it will be difficult to investigate the truth, for want of evidence; but to-morrow I shall most certainly apply to the Emperor himself to prove the rank of Ferdinand, and then I hope we shall soon confound his accusers."

Ferdinand was conducted to a prison; but he was treated with gentleness, and had (for a prison) tolerable accommodations. He was not without very unpleasant reflections; no letters had arrived from his friends, which involved him in doubts and anxiety for his son, Claudina, and his brother.—By his imprudence, in acknowledging his connexion with the worthless Fatima, he had brought on himself his present disagreeable situation: Then he considered, that if the affair was prosecuted on Heli's testimony against him, he should be compelled to make his father's weakness known, and the attendant circumstances.

He then reverted to the story of Louisa. Miss d'Allenberg's situation gave him the most poignant concern; a young woman so respectable, so charming, a victim to a hopeless passion; who could the object be? that her heart was free, when she consented to marry Count Wolfran, was a certainty avowed by herself. He then recollected every little circumstance of her behaviour, when Count M— — — and himself were on a visit to her father. Her politeness and attention then appeared to be equally divided, but now, on a review of every thing, Ferdinand remembered the Count had much the greater share of her notice. She talked mostly to him; she leant on his arm in the garden;—and on the day of their departure, he had observed in taking leave, she fixed her eyes on the Count as she spoke.

"Yes," said he, on recapitulating those trifling circumstances. —"Yes, I am convinced the Count has been so happy to touch that heart so good, so amiable; he is unconscious of the distress he has given birth to, and his situation will, from honour and delicacy, ever preclude him the unspeakable delight of restoring her mind to peace."

What a fatality, thought he, that so lovely a woman should have placed her affections so unhappily; never shall I forgive myself for that unfortunate introduction to her acquaintance. The more he reflected, the more he was convinced the Count was the object that had produced the lamentable change in this amiable young lady.

Our confession at parting, that we were "married, and unfortunate," her father doubtless repeated, and from thence originated the melancholy that oppressed the daughter. He sighed heavily for her disappointment, and scarcely thought life worth preserving, when subject to such various events, productive of certain misery.

"Did not my child exist," exclaimed he in a fit of despondency; "did I not feel, that I owe to him a duty I cannot delegate to another, that of superintending his conduct, and directing his mind as he advances in years; instructing him to guard against the impetuosity of youthful passions; a too easy confidence in the seeming integrity of plausible appearances, and from the example of his unhappy father, see those precepts illustrated; example, which speaks more forcibly to an inexperienced mind than the most elaborate reasoning adduced from theory only. Yes, for his sake, I must endeavour to retain my existence, that my follies may not spread wider in the conduct of my child."

"Under the oppressive recollection of former scenes, and doubtful anxiety for the future, poor Ferdinand passed a wretched night; nor were his friends much easier.—Count M— — —, whose affection for him was truly fraternal, lamented, that it was in consequence of his advice they had remained in

Vienna 'till the return of their letters. — — —Whatever
unpleasant consequences might have attended their sudden
appearance, they could not have been productive of such
vexatious circumstances as had now happened, he thought. Yet,
then, what might have become of the poor Louisa? How would
young Reiberg have acquired that promise of returning
tranquillity, if the events that had taken place at Heli's had
remained unknown? Those questions again reconciled him to a
degree of comparative ease, to think less of the blame he had
attached to himself, and to trust in Heaven for the protection of
his friend, and their deliverance from the malicious accusations
of Heli.

The next morning, at the instant when the Count, Baron
Reiberg and his son, were preparing to wait on the magistrate,
and from thence, if they found it necessary, to address the
Emperor; the long-expected letters arrived from Suabia. The
Count received one from his steward, very much to his
satisfaction; the good Duclos being overjoyed at the restoration
of his master from death to life, particularly as he had applied to
the Duke of Wirtemberg, and obtained leave to keep possession
of the estates for six months, or until a certainty of his master's
fate within that period should arrive. This prudent proceeding
had saved much trouble.

The next letter was from Eugenia, and written in a style of
such content, and calm resignation, that although she expressed
an infinity of satisfaction from the receipt of his letter, yet that
satisfaction seemed more like the affectionate joy of a sister,
than the transports of a wife: Her expressions were kind, but
guarded; her congratulations were warm, but not rapturous; in
short, it was such a letter as a sister might write to a beloved
brother; not one word reverted to past scenes; not a line of
regret for their separation. She told him, "she was more than
tranquil; she was happy: That the tender interest she must ever
feel for the state of his mind, was the only cloud that hung over
her, otherwise, perfect content; and as she had but little doubt of
the good effects of time, of the cares of friendship, and of the
advantages resulting from employment and amusements, she
hoped that cloud would soon be brushed away to their mutual
satisfaction."

The perusal of this letter at first rather displeased Count M—
— —; but at the second reading, he was more just; it was selfish
to feel discontent, because religion and good sense had
tranquillized her mind, and that the situation she had chosen
from the purest motives should have realized her expectations
and wishes: Did he not wish her happy, after the years of

misery she had struggled with; and was not her conduct truly laudable and praise-worthy? Those reflections recalled him from his temporary displeasure, and rendered the sentiment she expressed more estimable in his eyes, from the very circumstances that first offended him.

She did not mention the Countess in her letter, and therefore it was uncertain if she remained in that convent, or had changed her residence.

The Count, having examined the contents of his own letters, saw there were two also for Ferdinand, one with a black seal. As he was not acquainted with the writing, he could not have an idea from what quarter it came. At first he proposed taking the letters to him; but after a little deliberation, it was settled that young Reiberg should visit him with the letters, whilst the Count and the Baron pursued their first intention of exerting all their joint interest to procure an order for the release of Ferdinand.

END OF VOL. III.

VOLUME 4, CHAPTER !

he young Baron Reiberg was admitted without any difficulty to see Ferdinand, but he was excessively shocked on entering the wretched hole of his confinement, though informed it was one of the best rooms in the prison. "One of the best" could not reconcile it to his feelings, and when he embraced the prisoner, his emotions were very visible.

"I thank you most cordially (said the latter) for this kindness; but, my good friend, do not throw your eyes around thus, with such a revolting kind of horror in your features. A prison is not a desirable place I grant ye, but is disarmed of all its terrors when conscious innocence brightens the gloom. You know I have no cause for apprehension, this temporary confinement, therefore, is only a little variety in the chequered work of life."

"I am rejoiced (said Reiberg) to find your mind is cheerful in this horrid place; in similar circumstances I am sensible that I should possess neither your resignation or fortitude: However, I think your confinement will be of short duration. My father and the Count are gone earnestly to work, and I am certain will not give over until they have obtained your enlargement. I came here, I hope, to bring you some consolation, to bring you letters from your friends, that you have so much wished for."

Ferdinand eagerly took the letters, looking on the superscription, and then on the seal. "This black herald (said he) forebodes no good news I fear; but the worst must be known, and no place so proper as a prison to bear sorrow, or teach patience under unavoidable evils."

He had turned the letter two or three times whilst speaking, irresolute how to open it. — Reiberg observed his embarrassment: "Do you wish to be alone? (said he.) Speak, I will retire, and come to you by and bye."

"No (replied Ferdinand) for my own sake I do not wish it; but perhaps — — —."

"Say no more (interrupted Reiberg) peruse your letters, I have a book in my pocket." The other obeyed, and with a trembling hand broke the seal.

"It is from Mr. Dunloff (exclaimed he) the guardian of my son! Ah! what am I to hear? Thank Heaven, my child is well." — Reading further on, he again cried out, — "How, Claudina dead! Poor, poor Claudina! then I have indeed lost thee for ever!" He continued to read, his emotions increased, the big drops fell on his face, he turned from the Baron, and leaning against the wall, —"Excuse me (said he, falteringly) I have lost a wife, once dear to my heart!"

Attempting to read on, but being too greatly affected at the moment, "My dear Baron (said he) I avail myself of your considerate kindness. An hour or two hence I shall be better enabled to thank you for this visit."—Reiberg immediately withdrew, trusting on his return to bring an order for his enlargement. Ferdinand, at liberty to indulge the sorrow that oppressed him, read the following letter from Mr. Dunloff:

"Let not the black wax too much alarm you, Sir, your son, my amiable pupil, is well: My good old uncle is also well as a man can be, who is ready to expire with joy, on receiving intelligence so little hoped for and unexpected; but — — — your Lady, Madam Claudina, who had retired from the world, who was before dead to her friends, is now released from all her cares, and is happy, I trust, in Heaven!

"This event ought not, Sir, to afflict you. My uncle and myself attended her; with him she was some time alone, but before both she confessed herself unworthy of your affection, that she had deceived and injured you. She lamented most bitterly your supposed death, the report of which I believe accelerated her's, because she accused herself as the primary cause of all your misfortunes. Not to dwell on this melancholy subject, she died a true penitent, entreating mercy for her offences, and imploring blessings on her dear child, who had long before mourned the loss of his mamma, and was therefore spared any further concern.

"My uncle, who is confined to his bed with the gout, orders me to express his transports of joy for your health and safety.— The letters which conveyed the intelligence of your death had nearly deprived him of life, and brought on that disorder which has hung upon him ever since. He hopes you will condescend to write to him once more before your return, that he may know where to attend you. He has not seen the Count, his master, since your letters arrived, but hears they have caused more surprise than pleasure; of that you will have a circumstantial account hereafter."

Mr. Dunloff concluded his letters with "praises of his young pupil, whose docility and good disposition gave promise of much future satisfaction to his father. His little daughter, whose delicate health would be most considerately attended to by his uncle and himself, was placed with a very worthy woman within a few doors of his own residence, and was visited by him daily. He conjured Ferdinand to divest himself of all anxiety for the health and safety of his children, and rely on his watchful care for the preservation of both."

When Ferdinand had recovered from the first shock naturally felt on hearing a woman he once adored was no more, when he had acquired composure sufficient to peruse the letter through, indignation kept pace with sorrow.

Claudina's last confession had confirmed the implied guilt frequently insinuated, but of which he never could have thought her capable; he resolved in his mind the whole tenor of her conduct; he saw nothing wrong, nothing reprehensible, in word or action, before their removal to Renaud Castle: There then she must have met with the object that seduced her from her duty to him and herself; but among all his brother's visitors, there was no particular man to whose artifices he could attribute the misfortune that so deeply wounded him. Lost in conjecture, he saw only that the fact was certain, and from Ernest only he could hope to have the mystery elucidated. He grieved for the unhappy Claudina, and from his soul forgave a crime which her subsequent conduct proved she deeply and sincerely repented of.

"This then (said he) is the termination of an union formed in disobedience, pursued with rashness, which entailed upon me the curses of a parent, brought misery and guilt on her, sorrow, shame, and unavailing repentance, on the wretched Ferdinand!"

He remained for near three hours overwhelmed with the most painful reflections, and entirely forgetful of the other letter which he had put into his pocket. At length the remembrance of his brother made him start from his reverie, recollect the letter, and hastily search for it. The superscription was Count Rhodophil's. He tore it open; it was not a long one.

The Count expressed more surprise than Ferdinand thought needful; the joy was more reserved: He said, "that he was delighted to lay aside his mourning, and rejoice in the restoration of a brother;" but he wrote it as if he did not feel it; there was an air of constraint; the expressions seemed not the genuine feelings of the heart, but the laboured sentiments of a man fearful he should not say enough, and therefore ran into the contrary extreme, and said too much; at least so it appeared to Ferdinand.

"Ah! (thought he) all this eloquence breathes not the air of sincerity, which glows in the simple words of nature, uttered by Ernest through his nephew's pen." The farther he read the more he was dissatisfied, and when he had finished the letter he was thoroughly disgusted, and yet knew not well of what to complain.

"Whether it is ill-humour, prejudice, or the effects of a distempered mind, I know not (said he) but certainly this letter does not please me. He mentions the death of Claudina too so slightly, and with such little concern, that it is not decent, and of his own Lady he is entirely silent."

Revolving on those things which appeared so strange and unnatural, he had fallen into a deep dejection, from which he was roused by the entrance of the Baron, and his friend Count M— — —, who warmly embraced and congratulated him on his liberty.

"Liberty!" repeated Ferdinand, surprised.

"Yes," said the Baron, "we have succeeded in obtaining your freedom on our parole of honour. The accusation of an insignificant person like Heli, without he can adduce proofs to substantiate his charge, is not sufficient to weigh against a man of your birth and merit; but as all accusations claim attention from justice, though your innocence is not questioned, yet, for the due observance of form, we were obliged to be answerable for your appearance."

Ferdinand warmly thanked his generous friends, and preparing to leave the prison, asked after the young Baron.

"He is gone to Heli's (answered the Count) as we wish to know what is transacting there, and whether he still persists in the false story he has promulgated."

They saw the dejection that clouded the countenance of Ferdinand, but avoided appearing to notice it, and exerted themselves to amuse his mind in the way to the Baron's house, where, on their arrival, he was left alone with the Count, who gave him an account of their proceedings, and also the contents of the two letters he had received. Ferdinand was equally as communicative, and in the Count's friendly sympathy found some alleviation to his sorrows.

The late occurrences had rendered them forgetful of Louisa, and they proposed calling on her in the evening. Young Reiberg was not yet returned, and they began to grow uneasy at his absence, when the Baron was informed a Gentleman requested to speak with him; his name D'Alenberg.

They started with joy, the Baron hastened to the library where the servant had conducted him, and very soon returned, introducing him to the Count and Ferdinand. — They flew to welcome him.

"I am at a loss for words (said the friendly Gentleman) to express the unexpected pleasure of this meeting: I came here under the most painful inquietude; two words from this Gentleman (pointing to the Baron) has almost intoxicated me with joy."

The two friends congratulated themselves on this agreeable meeting; the Count eagerly inquired after Miss D'Alenberg.

"Poor Theresa (answered he) has suffered much, a disorder on her spirits, a nervous affection the doctors term it. The strange adventures which befell Louisa did not tend to lessen it; but the letters we received from her and you gave a sudden and uncommon turn, a flow of spirits, such as I could scarcely have expected.

"We lost no time in setting off for Vienna, and arrived safely this morning; but had hardly time to embrace our young friend, when the doctor entered with a story that threw my poor invalids into a very terrible situation, no other than that Count M— — — and Count Ferdinand had been accused of robbery and murder, were taken up, and confined in a prison. This relation, of which the doctor could not foresee the sad effects, gave me more exquisite pain than any I had ever experienced: The anxiety I have felt for some hours cannot be described; I came here under the apprehension of hearing the fatal certainty of the doctor's report. How little did I expect to see you both!"

"Indeed, Sir (said Ferdinand) we are much indebted to you for the kind solicitude you express, but there has been but too much truth in the story you heard."

"Well, well (cried Mr. D'Alenberg) I have not time to hear the explanation at present; it is sufficient that I see you safe; I must fly back to remove the anxiety of my daughter and Louisa."

"May we not be permitted to wait upon the Ladies?" asked the Count.

"Not this evening (answered he;) the journey has fatigued Theresa, and she has been thrown into great agitations on your account. Early in the morning I will see you again. The Baron invited him to breakfast, and he promised to attend them."

The friends were exceedingly pleased at the arrival of Mr. D'Alenberg, and promised to themselves a speedy termination of an affair so injurious to Ferdinand, from the concurrent testimony of him and Louisa, in his favour; as her account would develop the design of Count Wolfran in forcing his way into Heli's house, and the elopement of Fatima the preceding day with the Count, naturally accounted for the fatal effects that followed his intrusion; for the rest, conceiving that he had lost Louisa through her knowledge of Ferdinand, and feeling himself deceived and abandoned by the person he had acknowledged as a sister, Heli had, from mere malice and revenge, accused Ferdinand of crimes he could not for a moment think him really guilty of. As to the robbery, their suspicions fell on the attendants of the Count, as the two Barons could prove Ferdinand was in their house during the whole transaction.

On a review of these circumstances they concluded the false accusations would be unquestionably proved, and Heli, if he lived, meet the punishment his baseness truly deserved. The Baron was just beginning to express some anxiety for the safety of his son, when he entered the room.

"Your looks are full of importance," said the Baron.

"They are a transcript of my mind then (answered he) for I promise you that I have not been idle since my departure from you this morning; I shall therefore wave my congratulations to Ferdinand, and relate to you my proceedings.

I repaired without delay to Heli's cottage, most fortunately I met one of our servants, and took him with me. When arrived there I was admitted by one of the men who guarded Heli, who told me that he was so much better, they intended to remove him to the prison.

I went up to him; he preserved the same sullen silence, and as I could not make him understand me, I desired the interpreter to inform him, "that his malice had proved ineffectual to hurt Ferdinand, whose innocence of his charges

had been satisfactorily proved by my father and his friends; but
that the murder of the Count would bear hard upon him, as not
a single person knew him, or could he adduce any
circumstances in his favour that would tend to invalidate the
proofs against him, for no one would credit a story so absurd, as
that Count Wolfran intended to rob his house, whatever were
the motives that brought him there."—The interpreter repeated
my words; he answered him with fury in his looks, and a kind
of desperation in his air that shocked me. The answer was
explained to me thus: "That he cursed Ferdinand, Fatima, and
the Count, and to the former attributed all his misfortunes; for
Fatima would have been faithful, had she never known him as a
brother, and the other woman (meaning Louisa) might have
consoled him for her loss, had not that "Christian dog" forced
himself into her company, and contrived to get her away; for all
which he never would forgive him, nor cease to pray that his
prophet Mahomet might destroy him.

As for himself, he despised all threats, and laughed at their
menaces, for they could not hurt him.

He was then told, "that he was to be conveyed to a prison,
and that his trial would prove the innocence of Ferdinand, as
Louisa could declare in his favour by an account of the
circumstances of the preceding day, when he had insulted
Count Wolfran, and Fatima voluntarily eloped with him."

This intelligence threw him into a violent rage: "I have lost
my jewels, lost the woman I loved, another torn from me, am
wounded, and insulted; to serve those Christian dogs I have
suffered all this! and shall I have no revenge? Great Prophet,
avenge thy servant! Shall I prove the innocence of Ferdinand?
No, he and his sister have been my ruin!"

"He gnashed his teeth with fury, and doubtless had any
weapon been at hand he would have destroyed himself; but at
this instant was heard a knocking at the door; it was opened; a
man entered, who seemed confused at seeing so many persons,
and inclined to retreat; but Heli immediately exclaimed, "That is
one of the villains," and the interpreter seized him.

My servant exclaimed, "How, Sancho!"

"Sir (said he to me) this man I well remember; he was
discharged from my late master's service for some dishonest
practices, and enlisted himself in the army; It is now four years
since he left Vienna as a soldier."

"What is your business here?" demanded I, pretty sternly.

"Sir (said he) I will to you make a free confession of some very particular circumstances, if you will pledge your honour to save me from punishment; without that assurance I am dumb for ever."

"Being dumb, as you term it, will but little avail when this man proves you entered his house to rob and murder him; but if you are just in your confession, and repent of your crimes, by giving up your accomplices, I will exert my interest to procure you pardon, and you may depend upon my protection."

He was then freed, and entered on the following detail. "After the last battle with the Turks, the regiment he belonged to being disbanded, he sought to enter again into the service of some Nobleman, but his character was too well known at Vienna; he went therefore to Ratisbon, as he was related to a man who kept an inn there, and who, he thought, might possibly procure him a place.

At this inn he met with, and was hired by, Count Wolfran, who had only a confidential valet with him. The Count was very fond of the Ladies, and had two or three mistresses in the city. They lived there for some weeks, when the valet one day told him, they should soon go to a small hunting seat, which his master had near Vienna, and as the summer advanced they should travel.

A few days after this information the valet received a letter, which, he said, would be joyful news to his master. They had several private conferences, and one evening he received orders to pack up the baggage, as they were to leave Ratisbon the following morning. They did so, and arrived at a small village about two miles from the city of Ens; here he was told on no account to mention the name of his master, as they had some private business to transact.

The same evening the Count sent for him, and, after some conversation, promised him a handsome reward if he would assist in securing and carrying off two Ladies who had greatly injured him. The bribe was too considerable to be refused, and he was ordered to watch in a particular part of the city for the arrival of some company at a Gentleman's house.

In less than a week, a Gentleman, two Ladies and servants, were seen to alight at the house, which information he conveyed to the Count. He believed the first intention was to attend to

their motions, to follow them, and if they could not secure the
Ladies whilst they remained in the city, to surround and seize
upon them in their road to Vienna.

The Count never walked in the city, only sailed about the
river. The day after the arrival of Mr. D'Alenberg, as he was in a
boat, he saw the Ladies alone walking on the banks. This
suggested to him a possibility of carrying them off by water. He
immediately ordered his carriage to be in waiting every evening
at a certain distance; the valet, himself and the Count, disguised,
were in a boat with two men he had also bribed for his purpose.

He little expected to succeed so soon, as the whole scheme
depended on seeing the Ladies alone, and no boats on the river
to observe him, which might possibly be some time before such
an opportunity happened; but, contrary to his expectations, the
very next evening they appeared on the banks alone, and
walked a considerable way; it grew late, the air was rather cool,
and the boats drew off sooner than was customary.

He lost no time, but made towards the shore and landed; the
Ladies seemed frightened, and ran back; they pursued them;
one had considerably the start of the other; the one behind fell;
she was secured; in that moment, when they could soon have
overtaken the other, a boat appeared at a distance coming down
the river; they were compelled to retreat with only half of their
expected prize.

She was carried to the boat, and soon conveyed to the
carriage, after which, by cross roads, they arrived at the Count's
hunting seat. He understood this Lady was an old mistress of
the Count's, who had injured him with another whom he loved.
He was highly provoked at not getting the other, but swore to
be revenged on this.

What the design was he could not say; the Lady was
confined for that night, and they were ordered to be in readiness
to travel again: But the next morning all was confusion, the
Lady had escaped out of window by a very extraordinary
contrivance; the Count was almost raving mad; he ordered the
valet and himself to take horses, and attend him through the
wood and adjacent villages, and promised a hundred crowns to
the person who discovered her.

They stopped at a small house, at the end of the wood, to
make inquiries. A Turk came out; it was with difficulty they
understood each other. Whilst they were speaking a very
beautiful woman came out, and asked, "If they were gallant

Gentlemen, who would release a Lady from Turks and Infidels?"—The Count told her, he would die in her service.—The Turk compelled her to go in, and presently they heard her scream, upon which they burst into the house, gave the Turk a drubbing, the Lady ran out, the Count took her on his horse, and they rode with her to his house in the wood.

This Lady pleased him so much that he staid at home with her, only sending the others to make inquiries after the run-away Lady, and he believed might have forgot her, had he not been desirous of revenge, and fearful she would get to her friends.

He understood from the valet, that when the Lady with them found it was not love that induced the Count to seek her, she owned that the person he sought for, was in the Turk's house, and very ill; upon which it was resolved that they should break into his house, confine him and the women servants, and carry off the Lady.

Before this scheme was to be executed, they had prepared every thing for leaving the house in the wood, to embark as soon as possible for Turkey, where they intended to leave the Lady in a strange country, without money or friends, to make her way as she could, and all this trouble was taken to satisfy the Count's revenge.—"He believed (he said) there was more plots intended than he was informed of, because the Count and the valet were always conferring together."

However, they all set out two nights after for Heli's, the Turk's Lady waiting at some little distance in the carriage. On breaking into the house, the two women escaped by a back door into the wood. Heli told them the Lady was taken away, but they would not believe him, and proceeded to search the house; he taking up pistols foolishly, threatened them, upon which the valet fired and wounded him; in the same moment he fired, and the Count fell, crying he was a dead man.

The valet then said both would die, and they must provide for their own escape; but first he would have some of the Turk's riches. They opened the drawers and closets. He saw the valet take a small box, which he said belonged to the Lady, and he secured it for her. They found gold and many valuables, which they took, and then hastened to the Lady, telling her what had happened.

She seemed to be much frightened, and asked what they could do? He whispered to her, and then said, "It would be better to return to the house for that night, and dismiss the carriage." — The other thought this very strange; but presently the valet told the post-boy to bring the carriage next morning, as his master had met with a friend, and would not go on his journey that night. They entered the house, only one woman servant was there, who supposed them gone, and was surprised at their return. The valet told her the same story he had before said to the post-boy, and then proposed to the other going immediately into the city, hiring a carriage, and to bring it at the first dawning of day to a place in the wood, where they would join him, make the best of their way to the water, get on board a trading vessel, and sail into Turkey.

He, frightened with apprehensions of being discovered, staid not to consider about this strange wild plan; but instantly left them, though on the road his heart misgave him that some way they intended to deceive him; but he went on, called up the people at an inn, and ordered a carriage directly to be ready, resolved to go back in it to the house.

It was some time, however, before he could execute his purpose, and the day began to appear as they drove through the wood. — He went to the appointed spot, no one was there, and he proceeded to the house. The doors were fastened, he knocked, and at length the servant came down and let him in. He asked if the Lady and Mr. Bissot were ready? — She had not seen them. — He went up stairs, knocked at the Lady's door, no one answered, he opened it, and found the Lady was gone.

"He searched the other apartments, neither of them were in the house, the back door was on the latch, and he supposed they had gone that way. He directly got into the carriage, and returned into the wood, every part of it he searched; where the horses could not penetrate he alighted, and explored every recess, but all was fruitless; he wasted the whole day in examining the wood and its environs, and at length was compelled to dismiss the carriage, and return to the house.

"He now thought they had contrived to escape, and leave him to suffer; yet where they could be hid was very extraordinary. — He resolved to go the next morning to all the post-houses, and, describing their persons, find if they had, by any means, got a carriage. This he had done all that morning; and at length it came into his head to call at the Turk's, and by some pretence learn whether the Count and the master of the house were dead or not."

CHAPTER 2

"Such was the relation," continued the young Baron, "which the fellow gave me. Providence, doubtless, conducted him to the house to clear up the strange mystery of the Count's death, otherwise one would have thought the man mad to come there."

This account certainly tended to exculpate Heli from the murder, as it was evident he had been wounded first by persons who broke into his house, and every man, in a situation like his, had an indubitable right to defend himself. I ordered the interpreter to explain the man's confession to him, and told him, that, as he could now clearly understand Ferdinand was entirely unacquainted and unconnected with the persons who had injured him; he must be convinced that he ought to make the humblest concessions to that gentleman and his friends for the insult offered to him, by imprisoning his person, and aspersing his character; that if he was disposed to behave properly, I would very readily exert my interest to serve him.

At first, I believe, from the looks that accompanied his words, he was stubborn and very ungracious; but after some conversation, the interpreter told me, he was very sensible of my kindness, and sorry for the injury and trouble he had brought on Mr. Ferdinand. The man who had so fortunately dropped in upon us, I left in custody, assuring him that his confinement should be short, and that I would perform all my promises in his favour.

I left the house at length, and went to the prison; there I had the pleasure to hear our friend had just been liberated; from thence I proceeded to the magistrate's, related to him the odd story I have been repeating to you, and requested the man might be brought before him to-morrow. Also, that some inquiry might be set on foot through the city, to discover, if possible, the wretches who have robbed Heli.

"Ah! my dear Baron," exclaimed Ferdinand, "in that point I cannot wish you success; consider one of them is but too nearly connected with me by blood. Would to Heaven I could recompense Heli for what he has lost."

"That would be a Quixote generosity," said the Count, "which his malice to you can by no means deserve: If, however, he is stripped, I have no objection to join in securing to him a support, that may enable him to spend his days with comfort; this our own feelings may be gratified in doing; at the same time that I am persuaded, had he not conceived our company and connexions were necessary for his own convenience, we might have remained in Philippo, and got free how we could."

"I believe you are right in your conclusion," replied Ferdinand; "but through him we did obtain our liberty — and I also owe him obligations for civil treatment and many indulgences; he therefore shall not want in a strange country, while I have the means of preventing it.

"Count Wolfran's character and proceedings is, I think, the strangest medley of follies and inconsistencies I ever heard of; for he was open to detection in every scheme he pursued; and that he carried any plan into execution, appears to me the effect of chance and accident; for there was neither regularity nor decision in any thing he undertook. He is said to have been a very handsome and plausible young man; but surely the most inconsiderate that ever existed, and at an early age, has fallen a sacrifice to his own vices and follies."

"Thank Heaven!" said the Count, "that Miss D'Alenberg escaped his villainous designs, and that Louisa was saved from the destruction he threatened to her."

"Again," thought Ferdinand, "I see how it is. — With what earnestness did he inquire of Mr. D'Alenberg for his daughter, and now, with what animation he thanks Heaven in her behalf: The Count is most certainly the object of her attachment; and without much penetration, I can see that she has superseded Eugenia in his heart. Yet surely, if I am not greatly mistaken in my judgment, her delicacy will always impede a union with him in his present circumstances. — How unfortunate for both, that such an obstacle should intervene, where both honour and justice must revolt against a single wish to remove it."

As Ferdinand appeared lost in thought, his friends endeavoured to rouse his attention, by talking of the pleasure Louisa must experience in being restored to her friends; and Reiberg naturally reverted to the ill-treatment his adored Countess had experienced from a man of such loose principles and absurd conduct.

"Do not think me selfish and ungenerous," said he, "if I bless the hand of Providence that has recalled from the world a man whose exterior advantages were made the passport to the vilest profligacy, and whose heart was so depraved, that a union with an angel could not ensure his constancy."

The Count and Ferdinand looked at each other, and read their reciprocal sentiments.

"Little does he think of the base duplicity to which his admired Theodosia was the sacrifice, and the unfortunate Louisa a willing victim."

Fatigued with the various occurrences of the day, they all retired early to their apartments, and Ferdinand was at liberty to indulge that sorrow which pressed heavily upon his spirits.

Claudina returned to his mind's eye with all that innocence, beauty, and tenderness, which adorned her, when struggling under poverty and affliction. How difficult to believe, that she who had borne every evil with fortitude, who had preserved her honour, when poor and subject to temptation, should, when fortune smiled, when every want and wish was supplied, should fail in the trial, when blessed with ease and affluence.

"My absence," said he, "was her ruin; some artful wretch took the advantage of an unguarded moment to destroy her honour and happiness, and to plant thorns in my bosom, which must rankle there for ever."

He more earnestly than ever wished to return into Suabia, and meet with Ernest, Claudina now no more. Surely there could no longer exist reasons for concealing those secrets, known only to that faithful old man, and which had so long tortured him. These uneasy reflections were not the only ones that tormented him: He dreaded the discovery of Fatima, whose association and flight with the late Count's valet, too plainly spoke her guilt, and laid her open to punishment, should they be found; the consequence of which must give him the most painful concern, both as relative to herself, and the disgrace that an illiberal world might attach to his father's memory, and his own name.

"A too hasty discovery of our connexion, by my imprudence," thought he, "has involved me in this additional labyrinth of vexation: Would to Heaven I could leave Vienna; but I cannot separate from the Count, and I fear he will not be prevailed upon to quit the city, now that Mr. D'Alenberg and his charming daughter reside in it."

Under this variety of inquietude, Ferdinand past the night; and when morning dawned, quitted his bed, languid and unrefreshed: He went down and amused himself in the garden, until the servants were up, and then strolled away towards the suburbs, which were infinitely more pleasant than the city itself. Heedless of time or distance, unmindful of his friends, who would naturally feel anxiety at his absence, he proceeded on 'till the connexion of the houses were broken, and a few scattered ones of mean appearance, first led him to recollect the extent of ground he had gone over: He looked at his watch, and, to his surprise, saw that he had exceeded the breakfast hour already, of course could not return in any time for that refreshment, which, until that moment, he had never thought of.

He drew near to the last house; a woman appeared; he asked could he have any thing to eat; she told him bread and milk he was welcome to; this he accepted, and entered a poor little room to rest. Throwing himself upon a window seat, he accidentally cast his eyes upon the floor, and under a small stool opposite to him, thought there lay something like a seal; he rose, and picked it up: To his infinite astonishment, he beheld a gold seal, with a device upon a white cornelian, which he well remembered Heli had purchased for Fatima a day or two after their arrival at Vienna. — He called to the mistress of the house, and asked if that trinket was her's.

"No, indeed, Sir," said she; "I have no such fine things belongs to me, or Anthony either."

"I found it here," returned Ferdinand.

"Dear me, then it surely must have fell out of the pocket of the lady or gentleman that was here yesterday."

"Very possibly," said Ferdinand. — "Pray who were they?"

"I don't know, indeed, Sir, — it was a very tall lady and a short gentleman, that came here, as you have done. Yesterday morning they had some milk, as you be going to have — then they walked away, and in the afternoon came again — stayed here some time eating bread and fruit; then payed me well — and I have seed no more of them."

The "very tall lady" did not answer the figure of Fatima, who, though elegantly formed, was not above the middle size; yet he was confident the seal had been her's. — He asked several questions of the good woman, but could obtain no satisfactory answers.

"Do you think," said he, 'that they are in this neighbourhood; for then this trinket might be returned to them?"

"No, indeed," replied she," eying the seal with a look that implied a wish to retain such a pretty bauble; "but perhaps they may come again; for I heard something about "Pratt's-Grove;" and so likely they be going there to-day, and will call here again, when I shall be sure to give it to them."

"As you please," said Ferdinand, delivering it to her: "'Tis certainly your property, without you see them, or they send for it. — But pray where is "Pratt's-Grove?"

"Why, in the Little Island, Sir, where all the gentry goes to make merry, and walk about."

"And can I go to it from hence?"

"O yes, a little below, to the river's side. You will see a boat, that will take you over."

"Then I will go," resolved Ferdinand, swallowing his milk in haste.

With many courtesies and blessings from the good woman, who was well satisfied with his liberality and her golden toy, he left the house, and followed her direction, which brought him to the banks of the river, where a boat lay conveniently for his purpose. He was soon carried over to the Island, which was indeed a little paradise; the most enchanting walks among groves of fine tall spreading trees, that in some places were almost impervious; then suddenly breaking through small openings, long narrow vistas terminated with some beautiful romantic views, that astonished and delighted the observer.

He wandered about here a considerable time, before he began to reflect that this was the most unlikely place in the world for persons to come who wished to be unnoticed, because it was the resort of much company in fine weather. He began likewise to feel himself fatigued, and incapable of making a tour through all the walks that were cut in this beautiful grove. What then shall I do, thought he; go into one of the buildings to rest myself, or return back? He felt ashamed of the impulse that had brought him to the Island, without considering that its situation, and the number of persons who made it a place of entertainment, must effectually preclude any concealment.

"Well then," said he, "I will walk to the next building, repose myself for half an hour, and then return. — Some future day, when my mind is more calculated to admire and enjoy the beauties of this delightful spot, I shall be glad to devote more time to it."

He was now close to the building, and about to enter it, when he thought he heard voices as if disputing; he stopped.

"If you can find the means to get off undiscovered, and will go to England, I will accompany you; but I hate the thoughts of going into Turkey—nor will I go. To remain here many days longer, cannot be done. Had you taken my advice, we had been safe."

"What! to murder the man:—"No—I'll have no murder on my conscience.—As to robbing the Turk, I hold it no sin; for they are all a parcel of freebooters and unbelievers; yet I may be hanged for it;—therefore I say, no place so safe as Turkey, where we may live in some snug place like a King and a Queen."

"How ridiculous you are! I tell you again, that there you will be plundered by the Turks.—If you are seen to live without employment, they will suppose you rich;—you will be informed against; your head will be off, and your house destroyed in an hour. I have heard enough of their tricks and rogueries— therefore to England I will go: If you don't choose it, let us divide, and do each as we like."

"No, I shan't part with you so; but I am afraid to leave Vienna, because I dare say there's an information against us before now."

"Against us! Pray what have I to do with it—I stole nothing; this casket of jewels is my own property."

"The devil it is: Pray how would you have come at it, after running away with the Count?"

At this moment, two gentlemen were seen coming down a vista; a man and a woman darted out from the building, so close upon Ferdinand, that they almost threw him backwards. They were staggered, and retreated; for he stood in a narrow path way; the gentlemen were advancing in front; he stepped in after them, and instantly saw that Fatima was in a man's dress, and the man wrapped in a loose robe of her's, with a long cloak and woman's head dress.

She as quickly knew him, and gave a violent scream.

"Be silent," said Ferdinand, "or you are undone; you are traced and discovered; if you attend to me, I will preserve you from punishment; but first return to me the casket of jewels which belongs to Heli, who is alive, and out of danger. — The man you seduced to join in the theft, and then deceived, is in my custody; he had discovered all the Count's designs, and your baseness."

The valet, with the weakness that generally attends little minds, when convicted of guilt, fell at Ferdinand's feet.

"Preserve my life, Sir, and I will give up every — — —."

"Poor despicable wretch!" exclaimed Fatima, "thy life is not worth saving! You may do with me, Sir, as you please; you are my brother; it will be honourable for you to deliver your sister into the hands of justice; but be assured, whilst I have life, I will retain my jewels; jewels which Heli plundered me of, when he basely broke into the women's tents, rifled our baggage, and carried me off; these jewels were my property, and I will swear to it."

Ferdinand stood thunder-struck at her unparalleled effrontery; she saw her advantage, and pursued it.

"There are persons coming," said she; — take your choice: Suffer me to leave you instantly, without discovery or pursuit; or if you insult, detain, or give me up, I will immediately declare my affinity to you, claim the late Count Renaud as my father, protest he was married to my mother, commence a process against you for his fortune, and accuse you as an accomplice in urging me to regain my own diamonds."

The gentlemen were now pretty near to them; she turned to Ferdinand — "One word of discovery, and you are ruined." — She walked out; the gentlemen past, and she followed them pretty closely. The valet was silent, though dreadfully agitated. Ferdinand kept his eyes fixed on her as long as she remained in sight, with so much mute surprise, such horror and astonishment, that it took from him all power of speech or motion for some minutes.

Recovering at length, when she was lost to his view — "Good Heavens!" he exclaimed, "is it possible that woman, so soft, so lovely, so interesting in her gentleness, can, by vice and profligacy of manners, attain to such a degree of boldness and impudent bravery, as would shame the most hardened of mankind!

"For you," said he, turning to the trembling valet — "you who have profited nothing by your crimes, I know not that your conviction could afford any satisfaction to Heli, without the recovery of his property; tho' guilty of many base actions, you scrupled at murder, which I heard that wretch who has left us upbraid you for; and I am even tempted to think the robbery was more the impulse of the moment, from the existing circumstances, which you could not foresee, than a premeditated design.

"If you can repent, perhaps you may find friends; follow me, however, I must dodge that woman."

The man obeyed, and gathering up his robes, looked with conscious shame on his dress, now that he was discovered: They walked quick, and soon came in sight of Fatima, who was then walking with her two beaus towards one part of the Island, where lay a small pleasure-boat; — to Ferdinand's infinite astonishment, one of the gentlemen handed her in.

"How," cried he, "has she confessed her sex; or have they penetrated through the disguise?"

The boat put off, and he remained fixed to the spot.

"Well," said he, resuming his recollection, "had this woman's conduct been represented to me by another, I should either have believed it fabulous, or very greatly exaggerated: What a strange adventure have I made of my morning's ramble?"

He then turned, deeply musing, and so entirely forgetful of the valet, that had the man been possessed of a weapon, or any evil designs, he might have had cause to have repented of his carelessness.

But fortunately weapon he had none, and therefore had no temptation to commit an injury, which we know not, desperate as his situation seemed to be, whether he might have had the fortitude or conscience to resist. — For how many are the follies and crimes mankind are drawn into by opportunity, to gratify a prevailing passion, which, free from the temptation of the moment, they do not even dream of.

Ferdinand walked slowly back the same way that he came; went into the boat, still followed by the lady valet, whom he very uncourteously left, to seat himself as he liked, to the no small amusement of the boatmen, who concluded the gentleman and lady had been falling out.

When he was landed, he began to quicken his pace, and in much less time than when he set off in the morning, he arrived at the Baron's house. Great had been the solicitude of his friends; the dejection that marked his countenance, when he retired for the night, his early rising, and unaccountable long absence, were circumstances that gave rise to the most painful conjectures: Mr. D'Alenberg had attended the breakfast table, an invitation that had escaped Ferdinand's recollection, and seemed to be extremely surprised when he found the other did not appear; nor could any reason be assigned by his friends, for an omission that carried with it an air of rudeness and neglect.

The Count saw the dissatisfaction of Mr. D'Alenberg, and in justice to his friend, at length mentioned the account he had recently received of his wife's death, which he said deeply affected him.

"How!" said Mr. D'Alenberg, "is his wife dead? "

"She is," replied the Count; "and although, for certain family reasons, they were separated, yet Ferdinand dearly loved her, and tenderly regrets her for the present. — When reason and judgment resume their empire over the heart, I hope he will be sensible of the duties he owes to his child and his friends, nor by unavailing grief, hurt his own peace and wound theirs."

"He has a child, then?"

"Yes, a son placed at an academy in Baden."

"He is a very young father," observed the Baron. — "He married very young, a love match — but not a happy one."

"I understand," said Mr. d'Allenberg — "Poor young man; 'tis natural enough that he should feel sorrow on such an event; but I earnestly hope he will not injure his health, nor meet with any accident this morning. — I shall look in upon you again by and bye, after paying a few visits, and shall be glad to see him returned."

He did call in again, and was greatly surprised to see the anxiety of his friend's increased; the Count had intended to pay his devoirs to the two ladies; but he was so extremely uneasy concerning Ferdinand, that he felt no inclination to dress or visit.

Baron Reiberg had just determined to send his servants in quest of Ferdinand, when he appeared, followed, as they thought, by a lady, who stopped short at the door, looking down exceedingly confused. The Count had flown to embrace Ferdinand, reproaching him at the same time for giving them so much concern; but he had hardly spoken, when the lady, standing so awkwardly, struck him; he left his friend, and hastily offered his hand to lead her into the room; an offer which, to his great astonishment, she declined, by a low bow.

Ferdinand, who was about to apologize to the Baron, that moment turned his head, and seeing the surprise of one, and the confusion of the other, with the attitudes of both, tho' he was far from being cheerful, yet the ridiculous situation of the valet, caused him to burst out in a violent laugh, which still more disconcerted the Count, who, bowing to the lady again, came up to Ferdinand.

"For Heaven's sake, what does this mean; who is that—woman?"

"That woman," answered he, "has a long story to tell, and is accountable for great part of the time I have been absent.—Suspend your curiosity, however, for a few minutes, and we will return to satisfy it."

He then withdrew, followed still by the lady; the Count and Baron looked at each other for a minute, when the latter exclaimed, laughing heartily,

"Upon my soul, I believe 'tis a fellow disguised."

"A man!" cried the Count; 'then indeed, I have made myself ridiculous enough; and now that you have started the idea, I own that I thought she was an odd figure."

"Yet how gallant you was," returned the other: "I wish Reiberg had been here, to have shared your politeness."

"Pray be sparing of your jeers," said the Count; "they may be premature.—You are not certain that your conjectures are right."

The Baron, having once entertained the idea, seemed to be every moment more strongly confirmed in his judgment, and rallied the Count most unmercifully on his politeness to the fair sex.

In a short time, Ferdinand returned, having equipped the man with an old suit of clothes, that fitted him tolerably.

"Now," said he, smiling, "allow me to introduce the metamorphosed lady as the late Count Wolfran's valet."

"Is it possible," they both cried; "for Heaven's sake, how have you been so fortunate as to meet with him?"

"I know not," replied Ferdinand very gravely, "whether I can deem it as any piece of good fortune; for the meeting has been productive of strange scenes, and I am in a very perplexing predicament; but I will repeat the circumstances to you, and you will be the more competent to advise me. Mean time, permit this man to retire into your kitchen; when his presence is necessary, I will call him. — "Go," said he to the valet, "keep your own secret, and wait my orders."

The man bowed, and withdrew.

"What!" cried the Baron, "do you permit him to be at liberty?"

"Keep your surprise for my story," answered he, "and then judge according to the circumstances that will appear before you."

He then entered upon all the events of the day; described Fatima's extraordinary assurance and menaces, and the astonishment that overcame him, and impeded him from making any efforts to stop or to pursue her.

"Her wickedness," added he, "is so complete, that I am confident there is nothing she would leave undone, no perjuries she would scruple at, to be revenged on those who interfere to the prejudice of her schemes. Where, or with whom she is gone, I know not, or whether I ought to inform Heli of the particulars I have related to you. Have you heard of him to-day; has the Baron produced the servant who made the discoveries?"

"Yes," replied the Count; 'the man was carried this morning before the magistrate, and, as his story was partly corroborated by Heli, and many particulars confirmed by Louisa, on whom the magistrate waited to take her information, orders were given to discharge the men who kept Heli in custody: Your innocence was declared, and fresh orders sent forth to search for Fatima and the valet, on account of the robbery. — How they have contrived to hide themselves, and yet venture at a place so public as the pleasurable little Island of Pratt, I can't conceive; but I think it very probable Fatima will be discovered."

"Though she justly deserves punishment," returned Ferdinand, "I must hope she will elude the search. — I am sorry, indeed, she is possessed of the jewels; but she is so profligate a creature, that I am persuaded she will derive but little benefit from the possession. — Mean time, what is to be done with this valet of the Count's: If he is discovered, we shall not be able to serve him, because his guilt is clearly proved; yet I think he deserves consideration, for the fellow seems penitent; followed me without reluctance, and certainly proved, by their conversation, that he had some principle — a conscience that resisted the idea, and was proof against the persuasion of committing a murder."

"What you say is very true," said the Count; "and I have other reasons for wishing he may escape punishment; the story of Count Wolfran will not bear an investigation." Ferdinand took the hint: This fellow had been present at the marriage of Louisa; had entered into all his master's schemes against her; the whole would therefore come before the public; himself and his friends exposed; the deceit and indignity put upon the Countess would be brought forward, to the mortification of her and young Reiberg. In short, he saw the most painful consequences would ensue, should this man be taken up; and how to aid his escape now, seemed a very difficult affair, without risque or reflection to themselves.

"I think," said the Baron, after a little pause, "I can manage this matter. — The description of his person, with the particular orders for seizing him, can hardly take place 'till to-morrow; I want to send an express to my steward in Bavaria: If he sets off immediately this night with credentials from me, he will precede the orders for his arrest, which are not likely to extend far beyond the city. I will give orders to my steward to employ him upon my estate, to use him well, but to keep a watchful eye upon him 'till my return; what think you of this scheme?"

"Let us hear him," said Ferdinand, and called for his servant. — He appeared with a confused and mortified air. — Ferdinand told him of the orders given for his apprehension; explained to him the magnitude of his guilt in the bad actions he had been guilty of, and privy to, for his late master; and then repeated the Baron's noble and generous offer to preserve him from shame and death: — "An offer," said he, "so inconsistent with prudence, in trusting to a reformation of your life, that it must appear wonderful to you, and for which you are indebted solely to a few words I heard you say to Fatima, which makes us hope you are not quite abandoned; and if we can save a guilty being to atone for his past offences, and by penitence and good behaviour, to deserve forgiveness from Heaven, we are willing to run the chance in your favour—What say you?"

"My Lords," said the man, throwing himself at their feet, "I humbly thank your goodness: I have been a very wicked wretch; I had a very bad master; and I was too ready to obey him, and join in bad actions; but if your Lordships will please to trust me, in return for a life saved, I will devote it to you, and as faithfully obey a good master, as I too well served a wicked one."

"Rise," said the Baron; "your words please me, and I will trust you; within two hours you shall set off; I am only apprehensive the servants may recollect his person."

"My Lord," said he, "fearful that I might be known, I have had my handkerchief to my face, complaining of a violent tooth-ache, and only two servants have seen me at all."

"That's well," returned the Baron; "retire to the antechamber, until all is ready."—The Baron bid his servants instantly to get a horse at the door, as he was going to send Mr. Ferdinand's new servant off with an express.—Mean time, among them, they contrived a small parcel of linen; got him boots and a great coat, and being furnished with money for the journey, and letters from the Baron, he was soon on horseback, and lost no time in pursuing his journey; doubtless no less anxious to get beyond the environs of Vienna, than they were to have him.

This whole business, from the return of Ferdinand, had been planned and executed in about three hours, and he felt great relief to his mind, and a heavy weight taken from his spirits, when the man was gone.

CHAPTER III

"Now, then," said Ferdinand, "I begin to breathe; and unless Fatima should be apprehended, the preceding circumstances may as well remain untold to Heli."

His friends were of the same opinion, and then mentioned to him the little resentment Mr. d'Allenberg had expressed, and his subsequent uneasiness.

"I expect him every moment," said the Baron; "for I would not send him word of your return, whilst we had so much business in hand; but I am persuaded his anxiety for your safety will bring him here very shortly."

The Baron was right; for in less than a quarter of an hour afterwards, Mr. d'Allenberg was announced. On entering the room, the first object that met his eyes was Ferdinand, who rose to receive him.

"What a truant you are," exclaimed he, embracing him. — "I hope you can well account for your absence, or I know not what punishment you do not deserve, for giving so much uneasiness to your friends."

"A consciousness of that," replied Ferdinand, "would be as severe a one as you can wish, since I never yet gave a pain to the bosom of a friend, that did not tenfold wound my own."

"I believe you" returned the other; — "and therefore, without being impertinently inquisitive, or arrogating to myself the power of punishing you, for depriving us of a comfortable breakfast, I shall only say that I am glad to see you returned in safety."

"Most cordially, Sir, I thank you; but I should ill deserve your indulgence, if I held any reserves to you."

He then briefly recapitulated the events which had happened, down to the conclusion of them, just before Mr. d'Allenberg had entered the house.

"This has indeed been a busy day," said that gentleman; "for the young Baron has had an infinity of perplexities on his hands to procure Heli's freedom, and the grant of an indulgence to the man who made a confession.

"He is under a gentle restraint at present; and if, at the expiration of three weeks, Fatima and the Count's valet cannot be found, he is to have his liberty, when the Baron has promised to provide for him; though, for my own part," continued Mr. d'Allenberg, "I think it is showing too much indulgence to vice, to set them on a footing with honest men."

"Not if they repent, my dear Sir," said Ferdinand; "you will allow it possible, I hope, that a wicked person may, from conviction, repent of his crimes; and if the world is merciless, if no good humane man holds out a hand to help the humble and contrite spirit; if they are shunned, reprobated, and despised, where can they seek for shelter, from the sting of conscience, and the scorn of the world? Desperate, wretched and undone; renounced by the good, they are driven—they are compelled to return to the society of the wicked.—Hopeless, enraged, and disappointed, a hundred to one but they grow more wicked, more abandoned, than in their first career; and are lost, perhaps, body and soul, because the too fastidious, or uncharitable good man, conceives it an abomination to show mercy to the sinner, or stretch forth his hand to drag him from the vortex of vice, into which he is sinking."

"You are right my young monitor," said Mr. d'Allenberg; "I acknowledge my error; your system is consistent with humanity and our duty; and whether our endeavours to reform the wicked succeed or not, the consciousness of having performed that duty, is a sufficient recompense to us, and over-pays all our trouble. You see I am your convert at least, and will remember your short lesson as long as I live.

"But to return to ourselves, I must inform you, two fair ladies think themselves extremely neglected, and I fancy you will find it difficult to exculpate a gallant young man who has proved so very un gallant as not to pay his devoirs to a young lady that has come post here to see her friends."

"If I have been deficient in those duties, I, Sir, am the sufferer; and the circumstances that has impeded my attendance on the ladies, will, I hope, acquit me in your eyes. Doubtless, my friend, the Count has made his peace there, and then my presence or absence can be of little consequence."

The moment these words escaped from the lips of Ferdinand, he would have given the world to have recalled them, apprehensive that he had betrayed the Count's secret, and the confidence of Louisa.

Mr. d'Allenberg looked at him with a keen and penetrating eye; the Count, with much surprise, and was for a moment silent.

"I take shame to myself," said he at last, 'that I have not performed a duty gratitude, respect, and esteem, claimed from me; but in truth, the business of the day, your unexpected elopement this morning, and a variety of perplexing thoughts, totally unqualified me for paying visits. You see, therefore, that you have not only been guilty of omissions yourself, but are the cause of other people's deficiencies."

The Count spoke the last words with a gay air, that a little reconciled Ferdinand to himself for the petulancy of his answer to Mr. D'Alenberg, which he sought to cover by saying, "To-morrow, Sir, I hope we shall have the honour of waiting upon the ladies, and apologizing for our seeming neglect."

"Very well," replied he, "I shall so report it, that you may receive a tolerable welcome; and now that I see you safe, I bid you good evening; remember to come early, as I wish to confer with you respecting Louisa's affairs."

Mr. d'Allenberg having left them, the Baron expressed some surprise at the absence of his son. — He had scarcely spoken before he entered, and was rejoiced to see Ferdinand. — He said that he had been with Heli, who was in a very gloomy way for the loss of his riches: Fortunately they had not stripped his person; he had a snuff-box of value, a watch, and two rings, that were in his pocket; the whole might be worth about eight hundred Louis d'ors; but this, he said, was a trifle; what could he do with a sum like that.

"I then," continued Reiberg, "told him of the generous intentions the Count and Ferdinand had adopted. — I saw he was by no means grateful; and the interpreter told me, that he peremptorily declined all favours from them. — I did not urge the point, from an idea, that when he is in better health, his temper may lose its present ferocity. The women servants had called there, under some apprehensions at having concealed themselves in a small cottage on one side of the wood, and two days being elapsed, they prevailed upon a man and woman to accompany them back.

The poor creatures were rejoiced to find their little property untouched; one of these he discharged; the other, with the interpreter, remains; I have promised to send an honest jeweller to him tomorrow; for he is resolved to dispose of his property, and lodge the money in safe hands; and when he is well, he intends to give up the cottage, and lodge with the interpreter. So much for Heli." The gentlemen retired at an early hour, with a strict injunction to Ferdinand, not to steal away at day-break again.

"The next morning, when they met at breakfast, all seemed to have recovered their spirits, except Ferdinand; his looks denoted a mind ill at ease; he eat little, and soon left them to write letters, previous to their purposed visit to Mr. d'Allenberg.

"He wrote to Mr. Dunloff, to Ernest, and a short epistle to his brother; he mentioned, that he hoped, in a fortnight or three weeks, he should revisit Suabia; that however earnestly he wished to be at Baden, and see his dear children, the painful remembrance of past scenes, made him dread an interview that must renew all his sorrows.

"Having a little relieved his mind by communicating his thoughts, he rejoined his friends, and prepared to accompany them.

"They soon arrived at the Doctor's, who had kindly accommodated them all.—Mr. D'Alenberg was ready to introduce them;—the two Barons, as strangers, were first announced; but when the Count and Ferdinand approached Miss D'Alenberg, the latter observed her emotions; she blushed, turned pale, trembled, and, with difficulty, replied to the compliment the Count made her; he, guessing at the situation of her heart, felt extremely for her and the Count; to relieve both, he advanced, and paid his respects;—congratulated himself on the happiness of seeing her; and then turning to Louisa, "I rejoice, my amiable friend, to see you so perfectly recovered."

"I am, indeed," said she, "much better in health, and cannot be otherwise than happy, when blessed with the society of my friends and benefactors."

"The two Barons were charmed with the ladies, and Mr. D'Alenberg, studious to avoid any retrospection to unpleasant scenes, entered into a spirited conversation on Germanic affairs; the peace concluded with the Turks, the Emperor's schemes in favour of his daughter, Maria Theresa, and such themes as carried them out of their own concerns.

"But on talking more fully about the late war, Louisa cried out, "will you forgive me, gentlemen, for interrupting your politics, I long to hear the story of our friends" captivity, and how they amused themselves in Turkey."

"Our amusements, Madam," said the Count, "were very limited; but Ferdinand had certainly the advantage of me, and therefore is best qualified to gratify your curiosity."

"Will you have the goodness to indulge us," Sir, asked Miss d'Allenberg, in a voice so low and tremulous, that it touched Ferdinand, who passed the momentary thought, "What an amazing alteration between Miss d'Allenberg and Louisa! the ladies seem to have changed characters."

Then addressing himself to her — "There is so little to entertain you, Madam, in the relation, that it is soon made; for no great variety could be thrown into a life of confinement; he very readily obeyed her, however, and gave a brief recital of particulars, which have been already noticed."

When he had concluded, the ladies thanked him; Louisa observed archly, "You were peculiarly unfortunate, in not being noticed by some Turkish beauty, who might have broken your chains, and become a partner in your flight. — What a pretty romantic tale is here spoiled for want of a lady to embellish it."

"You will recollect, Madam," answered he, 'that I never was permitted to walk, but when Heli was with me; and the side where the ladies resided, was far distant from the apartments I inhabited; therefore I cannot, with any plausibility, violate truth, by boasting of ladies favours; indeed I have no obligations of that kind."

"How!" returned she; "are you so vain as to consider our friendship and good opinion so entirely your due, that it confers neither favour nor obligation?" "Pardon me, Madam, to deserve the friendship of two such ladies, would be my highest ambition; and to obtain it, I must consider as an honour that will gratify my vainest wishes."

"You have extorted a compliment, my dear Louisa," said Miss D'Alenberg, "and now I hope are satisfied."

Ferdinand ought to have replied to this "extorted," but he was out of spirits, and gladly availed himself of some trivial observation of young Reiberg's, to change the subject. This evasion passed not unobserved, which, with the melancholy air of his countenance, made them feel great compassion for him.

For his part, he was not sorry when the visit ended; Mr. d'Allenberg was requested by the Baron to accompany them back to dinner, as the ladies were engaged in making preparations for their appearance in public the next day, Louisa's health being much restored, and company and amusement being indeed indispensables towards removing the dejection of Miss d'Allenberg's spirits.

In their walk home, Ferdinand and the Count being together, the former remarked how thin and pale Miss d'Allenberg was grown.

"She is much altered," added he; "yet I think her more captivating than ever: — There is something so interesting in the softness of her looks, and the melody of her voice."

"You are partial to melancholy beauties," said the Count, smiling. — "I remember you admired Louisa much when she was sorrowful, and apparently declining into her grave; now, that the goddess, health, deigns to revisit, she seems to have lost her estimation with you."

"Not so," quickly replied Ferdinand, apprehensive that his friend was jealous of his attention to Miss d'Allenberg; "I am rejoiced to see her so unexpectedly recovered, and admire her as greatly as ever I did; her pleasing vivacity will, I hope, be of service to her friend. — Yet you must allow, the Count's death so recent, a man whom she so passionately loved, 'tis rather extraordinary that she appears to be so little affected."

"Not at all," answered the Count; "she had long ceased to esteem him; his conduct merited her scorn; and his late attempt against her must have eradicated every trait of affection; nor could she think herself safe from his machinations whilst he had existed. Her behaviour, therefore, is very natural; — she is freed from a villain, who had cruelly used her, and relieved from that fear and anxiety which must have embittered every hour in his life time. I applaud her for not pretending to a regret or sorrow, it was impossible she should feel."

"Do you suppose, then," said Ferdinand, "'tis so easy a matter to teach the heart to resign its affections; can the unworthiness of a beloved object so soon eradicate all tenderness from a bosom accustomed to love?"

"I know at least, that it ought to be so," replied the Count; "because love ought to be grafted on esteem; and the loss of one should be the death of the other."

"Should be," repeated Ferdinand with a sigh.—"Alas! how seldom is the refractory heart under the guidance of reason."

Being joined by their friends, the conversation became general, and they walked together to the Baron's house.

They had hardly dined, when a servant entered and said, a man on horseback had a letter for Count Ferdinand, which he refused to deliver to any but himself.—Surprised, he hastily run to the door; the man respectfully gave him the letter "from my master, Count Rhodophil Renaud." Ferdinand, with a trembling hand, broke the seal:—The contents were these:

"My Dear Brother,

"Life is ebbing fast; all hopes are over; if you ever wish to see me more, lose no time; set off directly; I have things of consequence to impart, for your interest; if you ever loved me, hasten to the dying

"Rhodophil."

"Good God!" exclaimed Ferdinand, "how long has my brother been ill?"

"He has been drooping some time," answered the servant; "but 'tis only a week since the doctor told him his danger, and the Countess is half distracted; for I have heard that day and night he wishes to see you."

"Go to the next inn," said Ferdinand; "refresh yourself; order post horses from the post house; I will be ready in two hours to accompany you."

Excessively agitated, he returned to his friends, produced the letter, and announced his intention of quitting Vienna immediately.

This design produced a general concern; every face was clouded.

"I will go with you," said the Count.

"Indeed you will not," replied Ferdinand; "it was your intention to stay some time longer; the business we have been engaged in may require your presence here; I cannot ask you to my brother's castle; a short time may decide how I am at liberty to act; I shall write the moment I get home."

"Indeed," said Mr. d'Allenberg, "this is very unlucky, and will shorten our stay in Vienna."

"Perhaps, then," said the Baron, "we may all soon follow you; for I have business that calls me into Bavaria, though I postponed it until the time for your departure was fixed, and which indeed I concluded would not happen for some time."

"I wish," said the Count, "you would permit me to go with you; I feel as if I ought to go."

"Not a word on the subject," returned Ferdinand; "I leave you here to answer for me to Miss d'Allenberg, to her friend, and all other claims upon me; have the kindness to acquaint the ladies of the necessity which tears me from them for the present, though I hope it will not be long before we meet again."

"I hope the same," said Mr. d'Allenberg; "for you possess my warmest esteem and best wishes."

Ferdinand felt the kindness of his friends, and withdrew, to hide his emotions, and prepare for his journey.

"You will excuse me," said Mr. d'Allenberg, "if I leave you; I like not the parting minute, and have an unpleasant task to perform, in preparing my young folks to receive you in the evening without your friend. I shall expect you, however; we will mingle our regrets."

He left them; the Count repaired to Ferdinand's apartment; again urged his wish to accompany him; but the other as firmly refused it.

"Stay here," said he, "'till you hear from me, and then perhaps I shall solicit, as the first wish of my heart, what I now refuse, the company of my friend."

The Count was silenced, though not satisfied, and assisted very reluctantly in settling things for their separation. The moment arrived; the post horses were at the door, and they parted with equal regret on all sides. Ferdinand determined to take no rest until he arrived at Lintz, but merely changed horses, and proceeded with the greatest expedition. The servant informed him he had business of consequence to do for Madam, the Countess, at Lintz, but which would not detain him many hours.

Here then Ferdinand thought he might rest, and to Lintz they at length arrived, excessively fatigued with long and hard riding. When Ferdinand had ordered some refreshment, the servant left him, and he seized five minutes to write a few lines to Count M — — —; the man was not long absent; they retired for a few hours to sleep, and then rose to pursue their journey with fresh spirits.

They had got near five miles from Lintz, and had ascended a steep hill, which was covered with trees. — On one side, you saw the plain through which the road lay; on the other side was a craggy mountain, at the foot of which run the river: The pathway was narrow; one horse only could with safety proceed at a time: Ferdinand was turning his horse round a clump of trees, when he received a shot, that brought him tumbling on the earth, and in the same moment, before he had recovered any recollection, he was precipitated down the broken mountain, and fell into the river, so bruised and senseless, that when he recovered his reason, he could scarcely recollect what had befallen him, nor the smallest idea from what hand he had received the injury.

Providentially, in rolling into the river, one of his hands got entangled in some low bushes, that grew on the edge of the water, that he was suspended from sinking, as he might otherwise have done, and the chill of the water restored his senses, but he saw the water was coloured with his blood, and felt that he was growing very faint; he therefore made an effort, by clinging fast to the wood and weeds, to drag himself out, and with some difficulty succeeded.

He found the shot had gone through the fleshy part of his right arm, and slightly wounded his side. With no small labour he got his coat off; for he had many bruises which began to grow painful; he tore his shirt, and with that and his handkerchief, bound up the wound as well as pain would enable him to do; but the effort, loss of blood, and the soreness of his limbs, rendered him extremely faint, and he had just time to drag himself farther on the bank, when he again felt his senses leaving him, and supposed death was at hand.

He returned a second time to life, but so enfeebled, and in so much pain, that he found it impossible to rise, and saw no prospect of relief: He looked round to see if the servant was in a similar situation, but no object met his view, and he had much reason to fear that he was killed upon the spot, and thrown into the river, where he sunk; for he had no doubt upon his mind but that he received the wound from some banditti, and even seemed to have an idea of seeing some objects among the trees just as he was wounded; and he supposed, by falling from the horse, he had accidentally rolled down the mountain, as their intention was doubtless to plunder him. Having settled the matter in his own mind, he pitied the fate of the servant, and lamented the distress his brother and friends would feel, when hearing no intelligence of him.

Hopeless of assistance, he thought his struggles for life, had only protracted his fate a few short hours, when he must inevitably perish; his only chance of help was the passing of a boat, and that hope was a very feeble one.

He happened to have two small biscuits, which he had put into his pocket at one of their last stages, but which he found broken in pieces by his fall; for the present he wanted no refreshment; his faintness arose from pain, and the sickness occasioned by rolling down such a tremendous height, which, when he raised his eyes to view it, he considered it as next to a miracle that he had not been dashed to pieces.

For some hours, he remained comfortless and despairing on the bank, when suddenly he saw a figure issue from a cavity in one of the hanging fragments of the rock, that appeared like something human, though bent almost double with age; a blanket wrapped round him, with holes to let out his arms, and tied round the middle with a cord; a long beard, and feeble steps, proclaimed his age and weakness. As this object approached nearer, Ferdinand saw his head was uncovered, exposed to the weather, his venerable silver locks flowing round his shoulders.

He was so struck with wonder and admiration, that he had no power to cry out; and, as he lay, the weeds and wild shrubs almost hid him from being seen. The old man was passing on slowly, and seemingly deeply meditating, when the other exerted himself to say, "Stop! Oh! stop!"

The man started. — "From whence comes that voice?" said he, advancing, and presently discovered Ferdinand.

"Gracious Father!" exclaimed he, "who are you, and how came you here, my son?"

"I fell from the brow of the hill into the river."

"Wonderful Providence! What, unhurt?"

"I cannot say that," replied he; "I am very much bruised, I believe, besides being wounded by a pistol in my arm and side, which occasioned my falling."

"Alas! my son, how shall I help you;—you cannot rise."

"Indeed I cannot; but perhaps I may endeavour to crawl a small distance, if there is any place to receive me."

"Try, then, my child; for I have a comfortable cell, if 'tis possible for you to reach it."

Ferdinand, suddenly inspired with hope, and fresh desires for life, exerted himself with uncommon resolution, and though he felt agonies of pain, he bore it without a groan, so anxious was he to obtain rest and help.

Such is the natural fondness for life implanted in the mind of man, that when sickness and despair has annihilated hope, and taught the suffering wretch to look forward to the close of his existence, as his only refuge from misery, if some unlooked for crisis changes the nature of his disorder, or a dawn of better prospects is presented to his view—he no longer courts death as the end of his troubles, but with new desires, new hopes, he struggles to retain and preserve life, though sure of encountering future ills, and of going through the same sad scene again.

So was it with Ferdinand, to whom an existence for many months, nay, even for years, had been an evil, he thought, he should have felt grateful to be released from, but the near prospect of death had taught him a different lesson; he found he had still some ties on earth that clung to his heart, and whom he shuddered to think of parting with for ever.

Eager, therefore, to profit by the old man's offer, he so successfully laboured, that he got to the part of the rock from whence he saw him emerge; but it was a work of extreme difficulty, and with all the assistance that old age was capable of lending, that he crawled up the broken fragments, and at length crept through the cavity into a spacious cell. The moment he entered, the spirit that had supported him failed, and he fainted.

The venerable man poured water upon him, and when he perceived returning life, forced a little wine down his throat, that revived him.—He next examined his bruises, and anointed them with some oil, the only thing he had that could do good, and having shook up his mattress of straw, he covered it with a blanket, and laid Ferdinand upon it. In a very short time, overcome with fatigue and weakness, he dropped asleep, and enjoyed comfortable rest for more than six hours.

When he awoke, though stiff and sore, yet his spirits and strength seemed much recruited; the good man gave him some bread and wine, and with a few simple herbs and oil, prepared to dress his wound and bruises. — Luckily the ball passed quite through his arm, and wounded his side, without lodging in it; therefore his venerable host gave him hopes no ill consequences would ensue from that; the bruises would be more troublesome than the wound; but as he observed, 'twas a miracle that every bone had not been broken.

Ferdinand mentioned to him the accident as well as he could recollect; for the whole was so momentary, that he was hardly sensible how it happened. The old man paused, and considered.

"Possibly," said he, "there may be banditti in the neighbouring hills and woods, but I never heard of any accident there; 'tis a strange business; but thank Heaven, my son, whatever was their evil intent, you have escaped with life; and if in a few days you are able to walk, there is a castle not far off, where you will be better taken care of than by me."

Ferdinand thanked the venerable man, and was grateful to Heaven, who had so wonderfully preserved him. The simple remedies applied to his hurts, agreed perfectly well with them; and in the course of two days he began to feel considerably better.

CHAPTER IV

During this time he had inquired of his host "how long he had lived in that rock?"

"Many years (replied he;) I had once a place at Court, was esteemed by the late Emperor, and not a small favourite with a Lady he loved. I often attended him when he visited her privately, and I happened to be young and pleased her fancy: I do not pretend to defend my conduct, I ought to have remembered the Emperor was my master and benefactor; but the seductive arts of women it is difficult to withstand, and perhaps I made no efforts for the purpose; be that as it may, the intrigue was discovered, the Lady was disgraced and confined; a criminal accusation, certainly without the least foundation, was set on foot against me; I fled to save my life, for a price was set on my head.

"In a boat I got landed on this side of the river, and strolled to these mountains, resolved to hide myself in a cave till the search was over, and then leave Germany for ever. Climbing the different rocks I at length discovered this cavity, and took courage to enter it: I found it such as you see, whether made by the hand of nature, or the work of some unhappy proscribed man, I know not. This I made my resting place; water and a few herbs, that grew wild here, was all I had for three days, and I found life could not long be supported in that way.

"The fourth day I followed the course of the river a good way, and saw one of the packet-boats, that goes between Ulm and Lintz, with passengers, going by: I called to them, and they drew near; I entreated some provisions; they offered to take me on board; that I declined, telling them peculiar misfortunes had made society hateful to me, and that I had resolved to live in an uninhabited place. The people I believe supposed me to be deranged, but very humanely supplied me. I had not fled without money, which, in the situation I had chosen, was likely to last me a great while; I bargained therefore with the master of the packet-boat regularly to call near that spot, and relieve my necessities, for which I would pay him liberally. This he never failed doing, and though doubtless I ran some risque from the variety of passengers who saw me, yet, whether want of curiosity, indolence, or compassion, saved me I know not; but I suppose the Emperor's wrath abated, and I was totally forgotten.

"I had resided here near two months without venturing to climb the hills, or explore the country beyond the spot I inhabited; but the failure of the regular packet, from what cause I know not, had exhausted my provisions, and gave me a prospect of approaching death if I was not relieved. I saw several boats pass, but at too great a distance to make myself heard. The weather set in cold and dreary, and I was almost in a state of despair, which at length conquered my fears of being discovered, and I resolved to ascend the hills, and penetrate through the woods.

"One morning I set off, but from want of food was too feeble to proceed with any expedition; however I persevered, and with much labour got round the side of these rocky hills to a most beautiful wood of chestnuts, about three miles from hence, and in the midst of the grove saw a Castle. Overcome with fatigue, without hesitation, I advanced and rung at the gate; a man appeared, to whom I mentioned my necessities. I was courteously invited in, had some food given me, and questioned how far I was travelling? Without any disguise I freely told my place of abode, and that hunger had driven me to make application there.

"This story was related to the Lord of the Castle, and I was ordered to attend him. He was a venerable old man, two youths, his sons, were with him. Without telling my name, or assigning my motives, I briefly said, misfortunes had deprived me of my fortune, and driven me from my country.

"The old Lord blamed me for seeking an abode among the mountains, told me that a young and active mind ought not to indulge in solitude and idleness, that there were other countries, and many situations, in which a young man might be useful to society, and creditable to himself. — He was certainly right, but I felt no inclination to seek my fortune, without a name I dared avow, or recommendations to give me consequence.

"I liked the solitary rambling life I had led for some time, an habitual indolence, perhaps an unsocial temper, and I acknowledge, not the smallest inclination for a military life, had altogether received strength from the silence and obscurity of my present dwelling; I therefore declined all his kind advice, and indeed offers, evaded his inquiries, and persisted in my resolution of living among the mountains, woods and glens, so that I could find sufficient sustenance.

"When he found my determination was fixed, I thought he eyed me with contempt: 'A young man to live secluded from society, and from choice lead such an inactive desultory kind of life (said he) can have but a very weak mind, an ignoble soul, or must have deserved to be proscribed by mankind: However, as a fellow creature, you claim relief, therefore I will order for you a few necessaries that may make your cave comfortable, and twice a week my steward shall have orders to relieve your wants. I am going to leave this country in a few days; but will take care you shall not want the means to support your existence.'

"He turned from me and I felt severely humbled. Two servants were sent with me loaded with blankets, a mattress, and several little conveniences. I was something amused by the mixture of curiosity and fear those fellows expressed when they saw my habitation, they assisted me in disposing of the things, and seemed extremely glad when I dismissed them.

"From that hour to this my life has been uniformly the same. My dislike of society gained ground daily, and accustoming myself to live upon little, and finding many palatable herbs round the mountains, I have been no great tax upon the bounty of the Castle.—The old Lord I never saw more; one of his sons married and resided in the Castle, but I have understood, from little hints thrown out by the present steward, that he was unhappy, and now lives at some distant part of the country.

"As my clothes wore out I refused others, determined to appear as I lived, like a hermit detached from the world. I take fish here sometimes, and still have what I please from the Castle, which has been long deserted by the family, and only inhabited by the steward, his wife, and two men, who look after the ground and cattle."

Here the hermit stopped; Ferdinand had been very attentive to him, and had decided in his own mind, that he had glossed over his conduct by only a slight account of his falseness and ingratitude to his Prince: He concluded his errors had been of no common magnitude, and such as deserved the severest punishment, or he would never have given up the world. This conclusion was strengthened as he proceeded in the story, and though he felt himself indebted for his assistance, yet the contempt that naturally arose in his mind for a character so unamiable, lessened his sense of gratitude.

He had continual occasions to observe an unequal and unpleasant temper in the hermit. He had a few books, with which he was supplied from the Castle, pens, ink and paper, neither of which seemed to afford him amusement. He was always rambling about, as if weary of his existence, and though he affected the language, as well as the manners, of a hermit, yet he paid but little attention to the duties of religion; his devotions were by fits and starts, and seemed not to proceed from a regular and habitual course.

From all these observations Ferdinand could not respect his host, and therefore was very impatient to get well enough to leave him; but more than a week passed without having strength to walk, his bruises being infinitely more painful than the wound.

During this time the hermit had not been at the Castle, for he had received his usual supply of bread, meat and wine, the very day that Ferdinand was so wonderfully saved from a dreadful death, and having caught a good deal of fish, they had not felt any want of provisions; but now the stock being exhausted, he signified his intention of going to the Castle. — "I should think (said Ferdinand) that blanket covering must be very troublesome to walk any distance with."

"No (replied the other) it is as commodious as a coat, and, were it otherwise, custom would render it easy."

The hermit set off for his walk; Ferdinand, just able to creep about, came out of the cave to enjoy the sun and fresh air; looking round him, he observed on one side a smaller opening nearer to the ground; curiosity led him to this, and stooping almost to the earth, he saw that it widened, and appeared to have light within. This discovery engaged him to crawl into it; at first he found some difficulty, the passage was dark, and the faint light seemed farther off; still he persisted to crawl on, when on a sudden it opened into a large cave, with a rill of water running through it, and dropping from the sides.

A ray of light, which proceeded from a small chasm at the top, served to discover the most beautiful sight that imagination can form: the waters petrified round looked like so many diamonds, hanging in long spars, and twisted into a variety of shapes, glittering so as to dazzle the eye; several large pieces of rock-work hung over the top; many of those shining spars suspended from them, which, with the rill of water, and the solemn stillness of the place, had a most wonderful effect upon the mind of Ferdinand; he was never tired of admiring the beauties of this enchanting cavern.

"How comes it (said he) that the hermit never mentioned this sweet place? What an insensible blockhead he must be; he is fit indeed to live alone, since neither society, nor the beauties of nature have any charms for him, he merely vegetates: What a horrid life! The wild and foolish scheme of rambling that once possessed me, though I am now convinced of its absurdity, yet was ordered by Providence to prove beneficial to others; but this man can have no opportunity of doing good, unless another is thrown over the mountain, or cast up from the river, and even his assistance is given with an apathy that is disgusting."

These ideas passed in his mind whilst he admired the dazzling petrifactions; but feeling himself very chilly, he wisely crept back to the entrance, and remained on the Beach till the old man appeared tolerably loaded. — "Here (said he) is some provisions, and I have related your accident to the steward; he will come here tomorrow, and you may be taken to the Castle if you like."

"Most certainly I shall like it (said Ferdinand) for many reasons." He then told him where he had been, and expressed his surprise, that he had not mentioned a place so replete with natural curiosities."

"To you indeed (answered he) I might have thought it would be interesting; but after once seeing it, I never went a second time, so it slipped my memory: I dare say there are a hundred such places about, but I never sought for any of them."

"What a lifeless, inanimate lump! — (thought Ferdinand:) Yes, indeed, I shall be mighty glad to quit such a being, who has no more soul than the rock he inhabits."

The next day a well-looking, middle aged man appeared at the opening of the rock, and being invited, entered within it. He congratulated Ferdinand with kindness and respect on his miraculous escape from death, or at least broken limbs, and invited him to come and spend a few days at the Castle until he was able to travel.

Ferdinand accepted the offer, but was fearful he could not get there. "With my assistance, a good firm stick, and a little resting, I do not despair (said the steward) and the sooner you make the trial the better." — Ferdinand wanted but very few persuasions to a thing so agreeable to his inclinations as leaving his insensible companion; therefore, after returning his thanks, they parted with equal indifference, and taking the steward's arm he turned his back on the rock.

The distance to the Castle was about three miles, but it was through the woods on the side of the hills, and not very easy walking, which, with the weakness of Ferdinand, made it full three hours before they arrived at it. A bed was ordered to be got ready, and, as it was a luxury he had not enjoyed for some time, he soon fell asleep, and forgot all his cares. Whilst he enjoys a comfortable repose we will look back on his friends at Vienna.

CHAPTER V

MR. D'Alenberg, after leaving the Baron's, returned to his daughter, whom he found in tears, her head reclining on the shoulder of Louisa. — "My dear Theresa (said this tender father) have some compassion upon me; must the remnant of my days be embittered by seeing my child unhappy. I have already told you there exists a possibility that every wish of your heart may be gratified."

"No, my dear father, No (said she, raising her head) my happiness is beyond the reach of possibilities; but I trust despair will have the same effects of making me composed and resigned, as if I could indulge a visionary hope. These tears will be the last you shall see me shed, not one sigh more shall give you pain; I have given too much indulgence to a fatal weakness which stole upon me insensibly, but now I throw it from my heart for ever. Your daughter never shall live to blush for her attachment to an insensible object; but she will admire the constancy of an unfortunate man, and imitate a character that rises upon her every hour. Yes, his fortitude, his discretion, his strict adherence to honour and rectitude of conduct, shall inspire me with equal courage, to bear the misfortunes of life without sinking under them, and teach me to respect your feelings by suppressing my own."

She rose, and kissing her father's hand. — "Do not look at me (said she) with such tender surprise; this is not a false heroism; you shall see what resolution and a sense of duty will enable me to perform."

Mr. D'Alenberg was charmed with the behaviour of his daughter; but taking an opportunity, on her leaving him, of speaking to Louisa, she followed her friend to another apartment.

In the evening the Count and the two Barons paid a visit to the Ladies; every one expressed their regret at the sudden mandate which had taken their friend from Vienna, and every tongue was lavish in his praise. The Count seemed but half himself without Ferdinand, and could not reconcile it to his own feelings, that he submitted to let him go alone with only his brother's messenger.

Two days after the departure of Ferdinand, a messenger came to the Baron's from Mr. D'Alenberg, acquainting him with the arrival of the Countess Wolfran, and requested to see the Count immediately. He obeyed the summons. On being introduced to an apartment where that Gentleman waited to receive him, after saluting him, "I have been a witness (said he) to one of the most interesting scenes you can possibly conceive, between two amiable and noble minded women. The indiscretion of Louisa, in marrying Count Wolfran without her parent's sanction, she has amply atoned for, not only by her subsequent sufferings, but by a generosity of conduct that highly exalts her.

You know the subject of the letter she wrote to the Countess, and her fixed determination never to avail herself of the Count's last declaration in her favour. The Countess, on the receipt of her letters, without communicating the contents to any one, set off post for Vienna, leaving her child to the care of a friend in the Convent.

She came directly to this house; the meeting was truly affecting, and the self-denying arguments on both sides, such as did honour to the goodness of their hearts. — Louisa held one that I thought was incontrovertible. "In resigning those rights (said she) which you wish me to assume, I forfeit nothing; claims which were never publicly made, nor at any time allowed, from which I could derive but a trifling pecuniary advantage to myself only, which must subject me to the talk of the country, and drag me into public notice as an object of compassion for past injuries, and of curiosity for the claims and circumstances so mortifying, which I must adduce to prove my rights; advantages attained under all these considerations would be to me more humiliating than indigence if unnoticed.

Had the Count acknowledged me in the life time of my father, my duty, and regard for his honour, would certainly have made me act very differently, and then, my dear Countess, I should not have known the superior nobleness of your mind, so different from the jealousy and hatred a narrow and contracted heart would have felt towards an object who had, however innocently, interrupted her happiness.

Never, were I to live a thousand years, shall I forget your kind visit, and subsequent generosity: And will you deny the poor Louisa the heart-felt satisfaction of imitating, as well as she can, so bright an example? — But to do away every idea of any obligation to me, I own to you, my dear friends, that was I a parent, had I a child to inherit from the claims I might bring forward, then, I should feel it a duty to assert them; but to wrong the Countess, married in the face of the world, to disinherit a lawful heir, for such is your son; to throw the estates and titles into a very distant branch of the family, to the prejudice of his own child, merely for a temporary advantage to myself—never, never, can I think of it! And after all, what merit is there in giving up claims which the uncertainty of the law might long with-hold, and, perhaps, deny me at last for want of sufficient proofs."

"Those arguments of Louisa, which I think I have pretty exactly repeated," continued Mr. D'Alenberg, "seemed unanswerable; the Countess had only to oppose what she termed justice and equity; the matter was at length referred to me, and both parties pledged themselves to abide by my determination; without hesitation I pronounced Louisa's conduct both just and proper, and that the Countess ought, without scruple, to act for her son according to the rights allowed her by the world.

"My opinion was decisive, and concluded the debate. Louisa has drawn up a short declaration in these words, to which myself and daughter have signed as witnesses, and to which you also are requested to put your signature.

"Louisa, the daughter of Claude Hautweitzer, thus publicly acknowledges Theodosia—to be the true and lawful wife of Frederic Count Wolfran; and as such entitled to all his estates and effects in right of her son, heir to the late Count Wolfran.—This declaration made before, and witnessed by, &c. &c."

"This paper (pursued Mr. D'Alenberg) she has written herself for the farther satisfaction of the Countess, not that I think there will ever exist any cause that shall make it necessary to produce it, only that there were some persons in the room when Mr. Hautweitzer claimed the Count as his daughter's husband; but as the affair fell to the ground, and that claim has never been renewed, there is no great chance that it will be noticed; if it should, this paper will be conclusive, and, Louisa being almost entirely unknown, has consented to adopt our name, and to reconcile the Countess to herself, agrees to accept a very handsome independent settlement.

"Thus all parties are satisfied at last, and all this business has been begun and ended in little more than three hours."

Mr. D'Alenberg having concluded, introduced the Count to the Ladies. He was much struck with the fine person and noble air of the young Countess, and with admiration gazed on three such women, as it would have been extremely difficult to produce their equals.

He earnestly inquired after Eugenia. — "I have a letter for you, Sir," said the Countess, "from my amiable friend. Thank Heaven, her health is amazingly restored, though the fatigues and fasts she voluntarily inflicts upon herself are great trials to a delicate constitution. I have left my child to her tender care, and shall feel inconceivable regret to part from that Lady, and attend to the necessary cares my friends have heaped upon me for the advantage of my son. All my objections are over-ruled and silenced, Sir, but I shall never feel half satisfied with myself."

The Count joined heartily in the opinion before given, and then mentioned the civilities for which he was indebted to Baron Reiberg and his son. The Countess blushed at the name; but with a noble frankness she said, "I doubt not, Sir, from the expression of your countenance, but that you have heard of the early attachment the young Baron honoured me with. My dear father was pleased to consign both my person and fortune to the care of Baron Nolker, and made his consent absolutely necessary to my marriage with any man, at the same time recommending Count Wolfran for my husband, if he desired my hand.

The Baron, though a good man, availed himself of this authority in favour of his nephew, whom he certainly thought a good character; my preference of the Baron was reprobated, the acquaintance broken off, and in obedience to the will of my father I consented to sacrifice myself rather than wound my character and delicacy, by forfeiting my fortune to indulge what might have been deemed a juvenile attachment in a giddy young woman.

I owe the Baron much respect, and many obligations for his strict adherence to my wishes and entreaties. He respected my peace, and I had too much regard for his, ever to inform him of the cruel duplicity of Count Wolfran; I rather wished him to believe our separation was my own work, and the effects of my own weak and discontented spirit."

"And your secret, Madam," said the Count, "has never transpired; the Baron feared you was unhappy, suspected the Count did not behave well; but he had no grounds to form his opinion from, as upon inquiry he was told the Count opposed your retirement; and grieved at your absence."

"I am glad the Baron was so informed," returned she; "but the hypocrite never regretted me; the possession of my estates easily consoled him for my absence."

As the Countess was now compelled to appear as the widow of the late Count Wolfran, she was obliged to confine herself till after the funeral, which was ordered to be at the burial-place of his family near Ulm, and every preparation was set on foot to forward the procession in a day or two.

It was singular enough to the company to see two widows, both of whom disdained to assume any appearance of sorrow for a man they equally despised, whose interests, one would suppose, must have been incompatible with each other, linked in the firmest bands of friendship, and each feeling the highest admiration for the merits of her friend.

The fortunate escape of Louisa being talked of, naturally led to the situation of Heli, and she avowed much pain that the poor Turk should have been so great a sufferer by affording her an asylum in his house. "I think it a duty upon me," said she, "to reimburse his losses in some degree, and the Countess having made me so handsome a provision, infinitely beyond my wants, I shall certainly appropriate a part of it for his use, since it is through him ultimately that I am indebted for the blessings I at present enjoy."

This generous intention was only opposed in part, the Count insisting both for himself and Ferdinand, that they should participate in the benefits she proposed for Heli. This claim was at length allowed, and he was commissioned to get a settlement drawn up for the advantage of the Turk.

The day following Mr. D'Alenberg and his daughter was to be presented at Court; she would gladly have declined a fatiguing, and to her little pleasing, ceremony; but as her father appeared desirous of it, she submitted to his wishes. The Count, the two Barons, and the Lady of the first Minister, were to be of the party.

The day came, and Miss D'Alenberg went through the ceremony, was graciously received, and very much admired. One Nobleman of high rank and fortune, was particularly charmed with her, fixed himself in her party, and paid her the most marked attention.

In the evening, when all the friends met at Mr. D'Alenberg's lodgings, the Count gave an account of his commission to Heli, which he had executed that morning, and at length prevailed upon him to accept the settlement; but he declared he would not relax in his endeavours to trace Fatima, and should he recover his jewels, or such part of them as would enable him to live, he would throw up his obligations to Christians, and enjoy the pleasure of revenge upon an ungrateful, abandoned woman.

After the Count had repeated his negotiation with Heli, the Gentlemen all rallied Miss D'Alenberg on the conquest she had made that morning at Court. — "I have no doubt," said Baron Reiberg, "but that Mr. D'Alenberg will receive a visit from Count Dusseldoff."

"It will be an unnecessary piece of politeness," said the young Lady, hastily; "for I hope in a few days we shall leave Vienna, and return home. Our appearance this morning I thought a work of supererogation, as our stay here will be so very short."

"Indeed, Madam," returned the Baron, "few young Ladies would think so lightly of such a conquest. Count Dusseldoff is a very worthy young Nobleman, highly in favour with his Royal Master, a very handsome fortune in possession, and his reversionary ones." — — —

"Dear Sir," exclaimed she, "neither his possessions, or reversions, can be any thing to me. I hope and believe you mistake the nature of his attentions, which certainly extended no farther than common politeness. I beg," continued she, very seriously, seeing the Baron smile, and going to speak, "I entreat you, Sir, to choose some other subject for your observations. Your present ideas are very visionary ones."

"I beg your pardon, Madam," said he, "and have done."

The Countess gladly availed herself of the privilege allowed her as a widow to retire from company, and therefore avoided being seen by the young Baron; but he was changed into a new man, life and animation informed his whole person, and the hope, though a distant one, that a day would arrive when he might be permitted to see his adored Theodosia, and resume his former claims upon her heart, made him submit with a tolerable grace to the rules of decorum.

The next morning the Baron's predictions were verified; Count Dusseldoff sent in his name to Mr. D'Alenberg, his daughter was not present, and he received a visit he considered as an honour. After a very little prefatory discourse, the Count frankly avowed his admiration of Miss D'Alenberg, and requested permission to visit her.

Her father most respectfully acknowledged the honour intended to her, told him that he had long since resigned all parental authority to dictate to her choice, having reason to be perfectly satisfied with her prudence, and assured that she would never form an imprudent attachment; that his Lordship being but little acquainted with her person, and not at all with her disposition, or understanding, he hoped he might be excused for saying, "it was rather a premature declaration."

The Count said, "that it became his character to be candid towards Mr. D'Alenberg; but to the young Lady he should be more reserved, and only requested, for the present, permission to pay him and his daughter that attention, which, as strangers, they were entitled to." This politeness could not be refused, and on that footing the Count was permitted to pay his respects to them in the evening.

He had scarcely left the house before Count M— — — was announced, who with great joy produced a few lines he had received from Ferdinand, the same he had written at Lintz. The Ladies were soon informed of the letter, which conveyed his best respects to them, and the whole party seemed rejoiced to hear of his safe arrival there: But this pleasure was short-lived, when Mr. D'Alenberg mentioned the visit he had received, and the permission he had granted.

For a few minutes his daughter seemed in great agitation; she stole several looks at the Count; his countenance said nothing. She soon recovered, and only replied, "her father had a right to see whom he pleased, although she could not see the necessity of adding to their acquaintance for the very short time they should stay in that city." — No answer was made to this observation, and the Count receiving an invitation for himself and his friends, they separated soon after.

As he walked back he recollected the secret attachment which Louisa had hinted at as the cause of her friend's disorder upon her spirits, and revolving every occurrence as they rose to his mind, he began to entertain an idea, that either Ferdinand or himself was the object of it. He was many years older than his friend, and he thought very inferior to him in every personal endowment; yet he had remarked she generally addressed herself to him, and the particular looks she had eyed him with when her father spoke of the Count's visit, had not passed unobserved then, and now, from several corroborating circumstances, seemed to proceed from no common cause.

There is no man, at any time of life, but has some latent spark of vanity, which may be raised by accidental and concurring incidents. Count M— — — had still such advantages of person, as might well warrant more than a bare supposition that he was not deficient in attraction, and from the idea once obtruding on his mind, many little trifling instances were recollected, that fixed it there, and he concluded Miss D'Alenberg had certainly entertained a decided partiality for him.

He was too noble and generous not to lament that he was so distinguished, because he still retained a warm affection for Eugenia, and had that affection been cooled, yet his honour and feelings never would suggest him to pay particular attention to any woman whilst she existed; he therefore concluded it would be most prudent and proper for him to relax in his visits, and, if possible, to avoid being a companion in their journey when they should return into Suabia.

Count Dusseldoff made his visit, and was still more charmed with Miss D'Alenberg than at first. The little she did say, and that was as little as was consistent with politeness, gave him the highest opinion of her understanding and cultivated mind. She was above assuming any consequence from his partiality to her, and being perfectly indifferent to him, she treated him as a Gentleman chance had thrown in her way, and whom possibly she might never see again; for she took an opportunity of saying they should soon leave Vienna, and that she was so devoid of fashion, as to prefer the country to all the amusements a gay and crowded city could hold out to her.

In the course of a week his visits were several times repeated, and at length he took courage to avow his admiration in very explicit terms. Her answer was short, but decided: "I am truly sensible of the honour of your good opinion; but, my Lord, there are insuperable obstacles to any union between us. My father has the goodness to permit me in this important business to decide for myself; therefore I am not accountable to any other person. My Lord, I never can be your's: I respect you, I am grateful, but I can entertain no other sentiments for you, and I beg that I may never more hear a word on this subject."

The Count, mortified and disappointed, appealed to the father, he absolutely declined any interference, though he acknowledged the Count's proposals were highly honourable both to himself and daughter; but he was convinced her resolution was unalterable.—Thus ended the hopes of Count Dusseldoff, and he ceased to importune her farther.

Whilst this affair was pending Count M— — — very seldom called, and when he did his visits were short, his behaviour cool. The Ladies noticed this alteration, but supposed it was occasioned by his uneasiness in not hearing from Ferdinand; indeed all grew impatient at his silence, as they only waited to hear of his arrival and situation to fix on a day for following him.

Baron Reiberg had received a letter from his steward that the valet was safe with him, and appeared to be a very good sort of a man. This indefinite term was not misapplied to him, for he had a few good traits in his character, which, if he had belonged to a better master, might have made him a valuable servant; for he was strictly faithful to him, and made his inclinations and conscience subservient to what he thought was his duty to his employer; unfortunately he had not understanding, or strength of mind, to distinguish between that duty, and what he owed to himself and society, the consequence of that slavery and vassalage, which the German Lords exact from their poor tenantry and servants.

Ferdinand had been gone now ten days, no news was received, and they were extremely uneasy; when one day an express arrived to Baron Reiberg from Count Rhodophil, requesting to know "if any servant of his had appeared at the Baron's house to attend on his brother, he had dispatched a messenger more than a fortnight since to implore Ferdinand's return, as he supposed himself then at the point of death; that although much recovered, he was still in a weak state, and very unhappy from not seeing or hearing of his brother, or whether the messenger had reached Vienna or not."

Never was consternation greater than what the Baron and his friends felt on the receipt of this letter; from the date Ferdinand ought to have been there several days preceding it. This, with his silence to them, gave unspeakable apprehensions to the whole party, and accelerated their resolution to quit Vienna. The messenger was sent back with an account of Ferdinand's arrival at Lintz on his way to Baden, since which they had heard nothing of him.

Mr. D'Allenberg declined acquainting the Ladies of the cause which hastened their journey, and Miss D'Alllenberg was so desirous of returning, that she readily fell in with her father's opinion, that it was unnecessary to wait for letters from Ferdinand, as they were going to him, and letters could be dispatched after them. Louisa had no will but her friends, and the Countess was anxious to see her son, and had much business to go through at Ulm. Thus the whole party made up their mind for the journey, and the second day after the next was fixed upon for their departure. Here then we leave them to follow Ferdinand.

CHAPTER VI

The comforts of a bed, and the prospect of being soon able to pursue his journey, gave him some hours of quiet rest at the castle of Danhaet; he awoke refreshed, and in spirits. — The steward and his wife were worthy people; advanced rather above the middle age, plain in their language and habits, but with excellent hearts, and an honest frankness that engaged confidence.

Ferdinand was extremely desirous to write to his brother and friends; the steward furnished him with materials for writing, and advised his taking a passage in one of the boats that took passengers between Lintz and Ulm. This advice the other readily agreed to follow, as the most easy way of proceeding for a person whose limbs had not yet recovered their strength and pliability. The steward told him they were about seven miles from a post town, but he would get his letters conveyed thither, and also inquire about his passage.

Ferdinand was charmed with the situation of this castle; it was built on the side of a hanging wood, which rose gradually to the top of a high hill, and sheltered it from the keen blasts of the north. — Large plantations of chestnuts seemed to surround it, among which were cut several beautiful walks and narrow vistas, terminated by some picturesque views. In front was a hanging garden of large extent, from whence there was a declivity down to the banks of the river. The castle itself was old and out of repair, but the apartments were noble, and the furniture, though faded and decayed, yet perfectly clean and commodious.

Talking with the steward, he observed the situation was so romantic, and the environs so beautiful, that he was astonished his lord never came to it.

"Why, Sir," answered he, "it is the general opinion of the country, that the left wing of the castle, or rather a detached pavilion, which you see is almost enveloped by the trees, is haunted; and the reason is this; a state prisoner was once confined there, and, as the story goes, was murdered; one of my lord's ancestors had the care of him; 'tis an old and a foolish story, I think—but so it is, our old lord never permitted any one to live in it, and they do say that the present lord was once much frightened, for he and his lady disagreed, and he confined her for a time in that place, only going to her by day himself; how it was, I don't know, but he was frightened, as they say; so he took her away, and put her into a convent, and since that time never returned here."

"A strange story," said Ferdinand; "but did you ever hear or see any thing to terrify you."

"Why, Sir," replied he, "I never go there, because 'tis shut up; but some of the peasants, who have come here of a night, or early in a morning, swear that they have heard strange noises.—For my part, I had no concern in the business, whatever it was; I do no harm to any one, and therefore I live here very quietly; and if there are ghosts there, why I never disturb them, nor they me; I have often wished that strange old man of the rock to live here with us, because the more the merrier; but whether he is afraid of ghosts, or likes his hole in the rock better than a good chamber, I can't tell, but here he won't live, because he says he likes to be alone.

"Here is a fine library—I offer him what books he likes; but two or three will serve him for months; he likes nothing but fishing, and lives upon very little."

"He is a strange worthless being, I think," said Ferdinand, "and altogether such a character as I had no idea of; for he is not a religious man, a man of knowledge, or in any shape desirous of obtaining useful information; a poor pusillanimous idle creature, that crawls upon the earth, insensible to every thing.

"However, if he has no curiosity, I have, and should like of all things, to examine this pavilion."

"You may walk to it, if you can, with all my heart," said the man; 'tis but a little way detached from the building you see;—there is a private communication below stairs, but that has long been nailed up.

"By day, Sir, I am sure you may go, because I often pass it, and never heard any thing in my life."

"Well, then," said Ferdinand, "I will take an opportunity to look at it; you have the keys, I suppose."

"I have, Sir; but the doors have never been opened for more than twelve, aye, more than fourteen years, I believe; therefore I don't suppose the keys will turn now; they hang in the hall, with a ticket to them."

"I shall try them to-morrow," said Ferdinand.

"As you please, Sir," answered he.

But the wife was not quite so easy; she besought him not to go; told several strange stories; declared she had heard odd noises sometimes, when down stairs near the communication passage, and though she trusted in Heaven, and injured no one, yet she would not go into the pavilion for any money.

Ferdinand, who had no fears of supernatural beings, and much curiosity, waited impatiently for the next day; and taking the keys, which the steward had cleaned a little from the rust, he walked to the pavilion;—he was yet but feeble, and when he came to a flight of steps, which led up to the apartments, he seated himself to take breath.

This sequestered spot was surrounded by high trees, at the foot of which were a profusion of shrubs and wild flowers; it seemed formed for retirement and contemplation;—but being long and totally neglected, the outside was decaying; the weeds almost obscured the lower apartments; the glass, in many places, was broken; and in short, the whole bore the marks of desolation.

After having rested for some time, Ferdinand prepared to view the inside of this forlorn place; he tried his keys, but found it impossible to turn them.—Vexed and disconcerted, he descended, and walked round among the weeds, when he discovered another small door with a padlock to it, but he had no key that looked likely to open that; he drew near to it, and taking up the lock in his hand with a sort of quick pull, the staple fell out, and directly he heard the sound of a bell, and saw a string was fastened to the staple.—Surprised, he waited a few moments, to see if any consequence followed the sound of the bell, but all remained still.

This is very singular, thought Ferdinand; and looking round, he observed the weeds seemed to be more broken, as if trodden down; he turned to pull open the door, which resisted his endeavour, and he found must be fastened inside.—He took up the staple, and pulling the string, the bell sounded a second time, and presently a hollow voice was heard, that muttered some inarticulate words, and then groaned.—Though extremely startled at the moment, yet he was convinced the voice was human; that some mystery was attached to the building, and that something more substantial than ghosts or shadowy forms resided there; else why the bell to alarm, and inside fastenings.

Revolving these circumstances in his mind, he made no reply for the present, but determined to watch near that place in the evening. He returned to the steward, repeated the strange account, and his own conjectures; but he found it impossible to encourage him in the idea of its being inhabited by living persons; and instead of deriving any help from him to elucidate the mystery, he had only strengthened the steward's apprehensions, and confirmed the report which he had often been inclined to doubt, and think proceeded from the superstition and credulity of the peasants.

No persuasions, therefore, could induce him to accompany Ferdinand in the evening to hide among the trees and make observations; he then applied to the two men who looked after the grounds and cattle, but they were still more terrified.—One of them declared, that oftentimes he had heard groans, and had seen smoke ascending among the weeds, which, however, were never burnt, and therefore it must come from "the old one's" house under-ground, where he would take good care never to disturb him.

It was in vain to combat against ignorance and cowardice; therefore Ferdinand saw he must make his own discoveries; and his strength not admitting of much exertion to force his way, or even to escape, if such a step should be necessary, he felt extremely perplexed how to proceed.

After several schemes formed and rejected, it suddenly darted into his mind, to wrap himself up in a sheet, outside of which he would throw the steward's great coat, and having a dark lanthorn with him, he could conceal himself among the trees, and if in danger of being discovered, by throwing off the coat, and presenting himself with the light, he had little doubt but that he might frighten those who had endeavoured to terrify others. This plan he prepared to put in execution, heedless and deaf to the prayers and remonstrances of his host and hostess, who gave him up for lost.

Towards the close of the evening, Ferdinand, properly habited with a tinder box and a dark lanthorn, placed himself among the trees, opposite to this small door, where he could see every transaction without being observed.

Night came on; every thing was still and silent; he began to grow weary of his situation; the castle clock had gone eleven, when suddenly he espied the figures of four people coming through the trees; he could not distinguish their persons, there being no moon. It must be observed, that Ferdinand had replaced the staple and padlock; they made towards the door; he saw them stand, and heard a faint sound of the bell, and in a moment he lost sight of them, and was convinced they were let in through the door.

"Now, then," said he, "the whole is discovered; this is a retreat for robbers, and we shall soon clear the haunted pavilion."

He returned to the castle, to the no small joy of his friends, but he found it impossible to convince them that the persons he described were living ones; they grew more strongly assured that they were wicked spirits, but that Mr. Ferdinand being good, they had no power to hurt him. He, provoked at their incredulity, at length asked the steward if it was possible to open the door of communication, which he said led underneath to the pavilion: The other hesitated a long time; but on being urged, said,

"Perhaps it might, as it was nailed up on this side, supposing that the ghosts had not fastened it on the other, as they did the padlock door."

"But," said the woman, "it would be better to go in the day-time, and force open the front door of the pavilion."

Ferdinand hesitated and considered. — "If, as I suppose," said he, "some part of the gang are always in the house, they are doubtless prepared for resistance, and will sell their lives dearly; in forcing the door, some of us may be killed; no, let us discover, if possible, who and what they are, and then we can take measures to surprise them, perhaps without danger."

The woman shook her head.

"Ah!" said she, "they are no living folks, I dare say; and it would be better to go by day, when they do not appear."

"But," replied Ferdinand, "that won't do; I wish to see them appear."

He then went down to the passage, which twas like the colonnade of a cloister, and saw the door: By the help of an instrument, he drew the screws from the hinges, and with very little noise, opened the door, which discovered a similar passage to the one he was in, but quite dark; he procured his dark lantern, and proceeded softly through the passage; lamps were hung on one side, which no doubt were formerly lighted, but all was extremely gloomy and damp.

He came at length to a flight of steps, and hesitated a few minutes whether he should venture to proceed, yet it would be folly to go back so unsatisfied; he had just ascended the first stair, when he heard a loud laughing, as if of two or three persons: He listened—the sound seemed to come from no great distance, and he heard voices as if extremely merry.

He continued to ascend with great caution, and entered a sort of lobby, from whence he heard the voices more distinctly; to go forwards alone, he thought would be madness, as he must expect instant death, if discovered. He was now sufficiently assured of what mind the inhabitants were, and proper steps might be taken to secure them through this passage.

He turned, therefore, to make good his retreat; he heard the noise of feet directly over his head, and stepped forwards as quick and softly as possible, blaming his own rashness for advancing so far; he looked for the stairs, in his confusion he had past them; for this lobby went the whole length of the building. Sensible of his error, he was going back, when he heard some one coming down stairs, and the glimmering of a light approaching, he could not advance, but turned his lanthorn and retreated on one side, giving himself up for lost.

A man appeared with a light, and passed so close to Ferdinand, that it was impossible to avoid seeing him; he just snatched a look at him as he started, and, with a groan, fell on the floor.—Though infinitely surprised, he had no time to lose, as the fall and groan must alarm the others; he therefore quickly trod back through the lobby, found the stairs, and, with all the strength he could exert, run through the passage, which, having gained, he ventured not to close the door, but in a moment got up to the stair-case of the castle apartments, and appeared before the steward and his wife so out of breath and agitated, that they both concluded he had seen the ghosts.

When he could speak, he informed them of what he had heard and seen; and so far, said he, are the persons there from being shadowy beings, that I have no doubt, from the fellow's fright, but that he took me for one; at least I hope he did, as then my progress through the passages will not be discovered.

"And if it is," said the woman, 'then for a certain we shall all be murdered."

Ferdinand was not perfectly free from the same idea; yet still he thought no time should be lost, to get proper persons to secure those men, who were evidently a gang of banditti.

The steward was persuaded to take a horse, and ride immediately to the next post-town, declare what had happened, and bring a party as private as possible, to seize upon them at night—much against the opinion of the wife, who was for letting them rest quiet, whoever they were, alive or dead, rather than bring themselves into trouble; but at length Ferdinand prevailed, by saying what a great reward they would obtain by taking them.—This consideration a little reconciled her to the absence of her husband; therefore, at day-break, he got his horse, and set off with all haste.

He had been gone about three hours, when there was a knocking at the door; Ferdinand was gone to lay down on a sofa in the library; the good woman was alone, the men being about the grounds, and she was afraid to open the door without some one with her; she came to him in the library, and entreated he would have the goodness to come out, and then she would speak from the window, which she did, and asked the person what he wanted; he wished to speak with her husband; he was not at home; could he come in and wait for him, as he had business of consequence to tell him.—Without answering, she drew in her head to ask Ferdinand's opinion; he advanced to the window, and just as he was in view of the man, the fellow started, screamed, attempted to run, but fell on the ground.

Ferdinand hastened out, spoke, and took the man's arm to assist him; he turned, and looking up, discovered the very face of the servant his brother had sent to attend him back to Baden.

Both were thunderstruck, and for a moment speechless.—The man exclaimed,

"Alive! is it possible—alive!"

"Yes, my good friend," replied the other, "most wonderfully preserved from death, and I rejoice to see you; for I have often felt much concern for the uncertainty of your fate."

"Concern for me! Good God! but I see Providence will always bring wicked deeds to light.—Pray, Sir, tell me. Did I see you last night in the lobby of yonder pavilion?"

"I was certainly there," answered Ferdinand, and frightened a man, I believe—could that be you?"

"It was, Sir; and from that fright, you will now know all; for though I find it was no ghost, as I thought, yet, as I said before, Providence discovers all things, and I will make a free confession."

"Come in then," said Ferdinand, "and whatever you have to confess, speak freely, and assure yourself of my pardon, if you have done me any wrong."

He then entered into a long story, which, as the substance of it will be detailed hereafter, it is not necessary to give now; but it concluded with avowing, that he had orders to destroy Ferdinand on the most convenient spot, to avoid a discovery; that he had engaged others to assist him, who were in waiting in the grove at the top of the hill, one of which fired at him, and he being dismounted, as he fell, rolled him over the hill, supposing he must be dead.

That he hastened to his employer, received the sum agreed for, and only yesterday joined his friends; that having among them got a great deal of money and jewels, they proposed to leave off that trade, go over to England, set up for gentlemen, and take to the gaming-table.

This scheme they had intended to execute in about ten days time; there were six of them concerned, two of whom always remained in the pavilion; the other four occasionally dressed as gentlemen; found out when any travellers of consequence were going on the roads, and then came back, disguised themselves, and plundered where they expected a good booty. Some of his comrades had inhabited that pavilion many years, but he had only joined them lately.

Returning yesterday with his money, which he should not have done, but that he knew his share of their stock was considerably greater than what he possessed, and sure between them of making more money when they pleased, of his employer; he said, they had a feast, and were extremely merry last night, and he was sent down to the cellar for some particular fine wine; going through the lobby, he saw something stand against the wall; going nearer, he saw, as he thought, the ghost of Mr. Ferdinand; terror instantly seized him, and he fell into a fit.

The noise he made brought down the others; and when he recovered, so much had conscience overpowered his senses, that he still insisted that he saw him before his eyes, wherever he turned: Some of his friends ridiculed him, but one or two seemed as much terrified as himself.

In short, he went to bed, but could not stay alone; and when he reflected upon all his wickedness, he thought he would go to the castle, and confess the whole; only he did not intend to say he threw the murdered gentleman over the hill, and, as he did not fire at him, he hoped, by impeaching the rest, he should obtain pardon.

Following this resolution, when the other four went out before day-break, and left him and another in bed; he took the advantage of the other, and stole off; came to the castle, but again seeing Ferdinand, concluded the ghost haunted him, and intended to run away, when his fright threw him down.

This story and discovery so shocked Ferdinand, that he could hardly keep himself from fainting, but he assured the man of his protection, if he would repent of his past life. — This he faithfully promised; but his fears of the ghost having subsided, and his terrors of murder being done away, he already regretted the confession which horror and the fright of the moment had drawn from him.

Ferdinand told him by what means he entered the lobby, and the steps they intended to take that night, to surprise the whole gang, when at table. It was fortunate for him, perhaps, that the two men of the house now entered, and were a check upon the villain, who was inwardly cursing his stars for making him such a terrified coward.

He told Ferdinand they assembled together earlier than usual the last evening, to celebrate his return, but would hardly meet 'till one or two in the morning on this night; that he thought it best for himself to return, as he could account for his absence, and then he would take care to put aside all instruments of destruction against their appearing, to prevent any harm to Ferdinand and his party.

The unsuspecting Ferdinand praised the man's humanity, and advised him to depart immediately, and expect him about one o'clock. Away he went, cured of his fears, and like a true rogue, finding it most for his interest, he would make a merit of being true to his accomplices, and establish an opinion of his own courage and integrity.

The steward returned, properly accompanied for their intended expedition, and was astonished when informed of the visitor they had in his absence, and not sorry that they should have a friend to prevent mischief.

At the appointed hour, they silently proceeded through the passages, and ascending the stairs, reached the lobby; all was still;—not a voice heard.—This appeared extraordinary; however, two resolute men went before up the stairs to the apartment where Ferdinand had heard them the preceding evening; the door was open; the room empty; chairs, tables, and trunks, all in disorder.—They looked at each other.

"What can this mean?" cried Ferdinand

They run from room to room, on that floor which was the lower one; then ascended, searched the house through; it was entirely empty, not only of its inhabitants, but of the vast riches the man had boasted of.

"The villain has betrayed us," said Ferdinand; "they are all off."

They descended to the cellars, and there found the little door wide open, and all clear. 'Twas now plain they had all taken their flight; and to have discovered and irritated such a band of ruffians, was a very serious business. The steward lamented his interference; he had no doubt but that they would return, and murder every one at the castle.

Ferdinand was not quite easy, though he seemed to make light of the fears of others, and they returned extremely disconcerted.

That the robbers could not be at any great distance was certain; but there were so many caves and subterranean passages in the hills and rocks adjacent, that it was judged both fruitless and dangerous to trace them, even if they had any clue to guide their search.—They had taken their riches with them; the informer had said, they intended to leave the place, therefore they were now reduced to hope they never might return.

Ferdinand bore all the vexation and mortification of this disappointment, since, had he not been too credulous, he never would have permitted the man to return back, but have retained him as a necessary evidence. He accused his own imprudence, and execrated the wretch whose feigned penitence had deceived him.

CHAPTER VII

That night was past without rest by any part of the family at the Castle. Every breath of wind, the least motion of the trees, was magnified into the sound of feet, and murmuring of voices. Day-light at last came, and their terrors began a little to subside; they met dejected and unrefreshed; Ferdinand, ashamed of his credulity, tortured by the recollection of the man's information, and grieved at the painful situation his imprudence had thrown the family into, who had so kindly attended to him, with many other additional causes of inquietude, appeared with a countenance so truly dejected, an air of such anxious concern for them, that instead of affording them any comfort, he more completely alarmed their fears.

He found it impossible to raise his own spirits, or recall to his friends that cheerfulness his folly had deprived them of. On that day or the next, the passage boat was expected; but could he leave them in such a perilous situation, forsake them in the prospect of danger they incurred by complying with his wishes? Impossible, neither honour nor humanity would permit it.

He had written to his friends at Vienna, he had little doubt but that some of them would come to him, at any rate he must remain where he was a few days, and share the danger, or, if contrary to their apprehensions, the robbers should have fled the country, he would then have the satisfaction of leaving them as happy as he found them.

Waving therefore all considerations of self-interest, and repelling the extreme solicitude he felt for returning into Suabia, he frankly told the steward, "he would not leave them until he saw the event of what they so much dreaded. A day or two (said he) will, I hope, do away all your fears; there is nothing in this Castle to tempt their avarice, and surely they will scarcely neglect their own safety, and hazard a discovery, solely from a desire of revenge." They heard him, and were pleased at the moment; but when fear has taken absolute possession of the mind, hope is but a temporary guest, and is soon clouded with redoubled terrors at the slightest circumstance that justifies their first emotions.

Thus it happened to them, for soon after he had succeeded in raising them from their dismal apprehensions of death and murder, one of the men came in with a small box he had found in the wood just behind the Castle. This box was opened, and, to their infinite surprise, contained a gold watch, three diamond rings, of no very great value, a purse with thirty Louis-d'ors, and two embroidered handkerchiefs.

"This box was certainly dropped by the robbers," exclaimed the steward; "they are hid in the wood, and when they have secured all their property they will come and be revenged on us." His wife instantly caught the alarm; she cried, and wrung her hands, "lamented the day that ever they had indulged people's curiosity to be their own destruction."

Ferdinand was obliged to give way to the torrent, and remained silent till the turbulence of grief and passion had exhausted itself; then he told them, "he had no doubt but that the gang had dropped the box; at the same time he still believed they were gone from that neighbourhood without any intention of returning, and advised sending the two men at the different post towns to gain intelligence.

But their fears would not let them part with the men beyond sight of the house, and they passed that day and the succeeding night under the same horrors, and with as little rest as the former ones. When the second morning came, it brought a return of spirits, and a glimmering of hope, which Ferdinand encouraged, as indeed his own apprehensions were now done away, and therefore the serenity of his aspect gave weight to his words, and had the desired effect of restoring some degree of tranquillity to their minds.

In the course of the day the steward's wife was capable of admiring the contents of the box, and asked, with some little earnestness, what was to be done with them, and to whom they must belong?

"To you, undoubtedly," said Ferdinand; "it is impossible to guess at, or to find the owner, as they may have been years in the robber's possession; nor is the value of that magnitude to make them of any mighty consequence to a person, such as we may suppose the owner to have been. The watch and rings you will keep; should any inquiry be made, you can restore them; but the money you may use without scruple."

This opinion of Ferdinand's so exactly corresponded with her's, that in a moment her countenance cleared, and if she had any fears, the loss of her riches was the most predominant one. A tolerable quiet night succeeded, and the third day restored them all to so much composure, that the good woman now praised Ferdinand for his courage in "routing the robbers, and convincing the neighbourhood that no ghosts had lived there."

She was one of those very prudent persons, who, feeling their own interest concerned, choose always to judge by the event of things in their own favour, without considering the causes of the fit, or the unfit.

Matters being thus returned into the accustomed channel with the steward and his family, Ferdinand was impatient to leave them, particularly as he had no letters from Vienna. He wrote a second time to the Count, declaring his intention of going immediately to Baden, and to remain in the house of Mr. Dunloff, until apprised of the Count's and Mr. D'Allenberg's arrival at their seats. — — —That same evening he had the satisfaction to hear, he might embark the next morning for Ulm. He took leave of his hospitable friends with much kindness, and requested to hear from them, should they gain any information of the robbers.

With an eager desire to return, but with the most tormenting ideas and suspicions, that wrung his very soul with sorrow, he entered that boat which was to convey him to his own country, where he was to investigate such events as must realize those suspicions, or involve him in a cloud of doubt for the remainder of his days.

So many, and so various, were the causes that produced sorrow and misery to Ferdinand, that there existed no possibility of future comfort, or any cure for those wounds severally inflicted by those he had loved.

The weather was favourable, and he was soon landed at Ulm, where, on application to a Gentleman who knew his family, he as furnished with money to pay his passage, and carry him on his journey.

Without meeting any accident on the road, he at length arrived at Baden; but as he drew near to the spot inhabited by his brother, once in the possession of a beloved and revered father, he turned his head from the Castle of Renaud, shrunk with horror from the ideas that crowded on his mind, and, as if blasted by the view, almost flew on to the city, and arrived at the house of Mr. Dunloff sick and breathless.

The good man flew out to receive him: "Heaven be praised!" said he, and seeing his situation he conducted him to a room, making him drink a bumper of wine, which a little restored him.

"Oh! Sir," cried Mr. Dunloff, "Heaven has sent you in a critical minute, Providence often permits the wicked man to triumph for a time, only to make its justice more conspicuous in the punishment of the offender."

"What do you mean?" said Ferdinand:—"Tell me, how are my dear children?"

"Do not grieve to be told, Sir, that your little daughter is in Heaven. Master Charles is well, and every thing the fondest father can wish him to be. Your little girl has been recalled to its native skies about a fortnight since, no care was wanting, but a weak constitution sunk under the malady of the measles, and— she is at rest."

Seeing Ferdinand was affected, he went on to divert his ideas into another source.—"You must prepare your mind, Sir, for a shocking and interesting discovery, my uncle — — —-"

"The good Ernest?" cried Ferdinand.—"I am ungrateful not to have asked for him." "He is wonderfully recovered, Heaven has heard his prayers, and prolonged his life to see the completion of his wishes. Ah! Sir, your brother"—"What of him?" said Ferdinand, starting at the name—"is in a state of distraction; for this week past he raves incessantly; he has deeply injured you, and now all is discovered."

"Has he then confessed, is it possible it can be true, that he hired a villain to murder me? But before I hear more (said he) let me see my poor Charles." Mr. Dunloff, who stood in an attitude of wild amazement, started, and rung the bell. The lovely boy soon appeared, and flew into the arms of his father. His features were too like the deceased Claudina's not to make Ferdinand's heart bleed at the recollection; he pressed him to his bosom, and for a few moments the tender feelings of nature precluded speech.

Dunloff, who was impatient to explain every thing of so much importance, besought him to let Charles retire for the present.—The other consented in silence, when the tutor said, "Your last words, Sir, overpowered me! Is it possible the Count can have proceeded to such terrible lengths as your question seemed to imply?"

"I hope not (said Ferdinand) for gladly would I believe the villain wronged him."—"Before I request a more explicit account of this alarming business, let me send to my uncle, and rejoice him with the news of your safe arrival."

"I understood," said Ferdinand, 'that he had quitted my brother ———."

"Yes, Sir, but the Countess sent for him again when the Count was seized with this dreadful disorder of his senses."

Mr. Dunloff being returned into the room, after he had dispatched a messenger, respectfully entreated Ferdinand to explain those words which had so greatly shocked him. — He very readily took up his story from the arrival of his brother's messenger to the present hour, repeating the particulars which the assassin had told him in his momentary fit of penitence.

During this recital Mr. Dunloff expressed the utmost surprise and horror. — "How true is the observation (exclaimed he) that one crime leads to a thousand others, and that when a man has made his mind familiar with guilt, he proceeds on to the most detestable actions, and plunges headlong into the blackest enormities! Gracious Heaven! that jealousy and avarice should gradually tend to robbery and murder!

"I would prepare you, Sir, for the scenes you must witness, and the shocking discovery that will wound every feeling of your heart; but I know not where or how to begin, the packet must speak for itself."

"What packet?" demanded Ferdinand.

"It was written and delivered by Madam Claudina to my uncle, with a strict charge not to deliver it to you till after her death, and then you was to have it without delay.

"This packet my uncle entrusted, sealed up, to me for you, lest death should suddenly cut him off, and his papers fall under the inspection of his master. When Madam Claudina was seized with her last illness, the consequence of the general report, and belief of your death, for it threw her into fits that at last occasioned the termination of her existence. She wrote a letter to Count Rhodophil, conjuring my uncle to deliver it himself, and at the same time permitted him to open the packet entrusted for you, to read it, and keep the bond enclosed for the benefit of her son.

"She expired in true penitence for her sins, and I humbly hope the Almighty will extend his mercy towards her. My uncle, borne down with sorrow for your supposed death, though he would sometimes indulge a hope against all apparent probability, was so overcome with the sad scene of her last hour, that he fell ill, and could not attend on the Count; I was commissioned to do it, and accordingly waited upon him: I found him in high spirits, the Countess in the room.

"I had only sent in my name: I took the letter from my pocket, which had been superscribed by my uncle, and delivered it. He broke the seal, and opened it; instantly his colour changed, his hands trembled, and his whole frame was agitated."

"Bless me, Sir (said the Countess) what ails you?" The hypocrite struggled to recover himself; he falteringly told her, "it was a letter that announced the death of an old friend, whom he was grieved to lose."

"I thank you, Sir (said he to me;) be so good to tell your uncle I shall call at his apartment, and ask how he does by and bye."

To give you an idea of his confusion and tremulous voice is impossible. The Countess looked extremely surprised: I gave him a penetrating glance, and withdrew.

The next morning he saw my uncle; he first soothed him, and tried to get the packet Claudina had given him; but in vain were persuasions and threats, for he at length told him it was not in his possession. This highly irritated him; many words passed, which ended in his bidding my uncle to leave his house. — Nothing could be more impolitic, knowing how much he was in his power; but he trusted to the honour of a man he treated ill, and soon repented of his behaviour.

That night my uncle was removed to this house; the Count heard of it, and met him as he was carrying out. He pressed him to turn back.

"No, Sir," said he, "an old and faithful servant can be turned out but once. — You fear me, and therefore you hate me; but I never shall disturb the peace of your family." My uncle continued a long time in a fluctuating way, which at last turned to a fit of the gout, and held him many weeks.

During this time your letter came, I could scarcely credit my senses when I saw the address, and prepared my uncle well as I could; but indeed he almost expired with joy when I presented it to him. The next day, Peter, the Count's man, called "to ask after Mr. Ernest," he said; but I believe to observe whether we had received a letter, which was made no secret of. — "This will be bad news to somebody," said he, and withdrew not much pleased I thought.

A few days after he called again; the Count, he said, was very low spirited, eat nothing, and he believed was going fast. 'He talks of sending for his brother to make his peace with him before he dies.'—'Indeed! (said my uncle) well, then I shall think he does repent; my poor master must know all, for I pledged myself to deliver Madam Claudina's letter after her death.—Peter said it would be better not, it would only make Mr. Ferdinand unhappy. Away he went, and a day or two after we heard you were sent for.

About a week ago Peter came again in a violent hurry; his master was desperately ill in a bad fever, seized the day before, just after writing a letter to Vienna to Mr. Ferdinand's friends, to know why he did not come as he expected. That night the fever grew worse, he was light-headed, and talked at random, often called for his brother and Ernest, therefore the Countess begged my uncle would come to the Castle. He was but poorly, yet thought it his duty to go, and has remained there from that time.

Your brother still continues in a deplorable way, sometimes furious, at other times melancholy, and has made such discoveries of his crimes, as though they must prove beneficial to you, yet, will, I am sure, give you infinite deal of pain, I mean with respect to the will he destroyed, and which your father, the late Count Renaud, made a few days before his death.

"Is it possible," cried Ferdinand, "and was I remembered in that will?"

"Yes, Sir, he gave you his blessing, and pardoned all your undutiful conduct, and persevering obstinacy, and left a handsome fortune to your children."

Before Ferdinand could reply, so greatly was he agitated, the messenger returned from Ernest, and Ferdinand was desired to hasten to the Castle. He obeyed the summons, and was first conducted to the Countess; they met with a little confusion on both sides; she was greatly affected.

"Your unhappy brother (said she) has, within the last two hours, been restored to his reason; the physicians say it is the last effort of nature, and bespeaks approaching death: He has been informed of your arrival; much caution was used to break it to him, but he bore it without any great emotion. He said he wished to be private with Ernest, and I withdrew. Now I will inform him you are here."

Ferdinand was so inexpressibly shocked, and so reluctant to see a man in the agonies of death, whose life had been so culpable, that when the Countess returned in tears, and besought him to hasten into the room, his legs trembled under him, and with great difficulty he tottered into the apartment, where a sight met him sufficiently dreadful to appal the stoutest resolution.

Rhodophil was supported by pillows, his face long, pale, and distorted, his eyes wildly rolling then on Ernest, who supported him on one side, as Peter did on the other, and then throwing them upwards with an earnest supplicating stare. Ferdinand stopped a moment irresolute whether to proceed or not. — Rhodophil's eye dropping, fixed on him, "Save me! save me! (he cried) he comes to strike daggers to my soul!"

"Compose yourself, Sir" (said Ernest.) — Ferdinand advanced to the bed, the scene before him, the horrors of his brother's mind penetrated to his heart. He threw himself on his knees, "I beseech you, Rhodophil, to be composed, to forgive yourself; Heaven is my witness, that of whatsoever nature, and however great, are the injuries you have done me, I forgive you, and most earnestly pray that Heaven may extend its mercy towards you."

"You know not what you say (cried he, looking wildly on his brother;) my crimes are beyond pardon, cannot be forgiven, here or hereafter."

"And who shall dare to limit the mercy of Heaven?" said Ferdinand; "the magnitude of your crimes may deserve punishment, but what can exceed the torments you now feel?"

"O, it is horror indeed!" cried the wretched man: "Let the guilty look on me and tremble, foul deeds will come to light; see, see, there is Claudina calling on me, imprecating curses on my head, me, the seducer of innocence, the destroyer of my brother's honour."

"Gracious Heaven!" cried Ferdinand, and sunk on the floor. This sight threw Rhodophil into ravings: "Now, now, I have murdered him again! See! how the blood streams, it covers me, hide, hide me, from his blood!" During this dreadful paroxysm they had recovered Ferdinand, and placed him in a chair by the bedside. He viewed the guilty Rhodophil with averted looks of mingled horror and compassion.

He again recovered a temporary interval of reason on seeing his brother raised from the floor: "Ferdinand (said he) I have been a most atrocious villain—I have ever deceived and betrayed you; my father's spirit, for I have heard his voice more than once, has warned, has upbraided me, for my crimes: Hark! hark! I hear him now. O, pardon! pardon!" Again he fell into ravings, till again exhausted, by the use of cordials, reason weakly returned. At this moment Ernest fell on his knees: "Do you, Sir, pardon me, and compose your spirits—it was my voice that has occasionally alarmed you."

"How!" cried Ferdinand, "was it your voice that addressed itself to me?"

"I confess it, Sir," said Ernest, "I had many suspicions, and some proofs that you were most unfairly dealt with; excluded from my good master's sight long before he died, by misrepresentations, I could gain no access to him either in person or by letter. I had heard much, but not enough to found proofs upon, nor would my single testimony avail. I saw your misery and despair when cut off from all hope of a last forgiveness. I concealed myself in a closet, and in the agony of the moment, the words I pronounced, you thought proceeded from the dead body of your father. Heaven forgive me, if I did wrong; but it tranquillized your mind, and that was my only object.

"Twice afterwards I made use of the same device; the last time, the deceit was surely meritorious, for then I was master of a secret that froze me with horror; but to spare you, I had recourse to that method of warning you from———."

"O, Heavens!" said Ferdinand, "what a black scene of iniquity opens before me! Unhappy man!" cried he, violently agitated; "What indeed must be the torture of your mind!" Rhodophil gasped for breath, every feature seemed convulsed, he struggled for speech.

"Pray for me, pray for the wretch who cannot pray for himself."—More cordials were administered, and a temporary strength returned: "Now, now, I can speak; I always hated you," said he, hastily addressing Ferdinand; "I sought to warp our father's mind against you, and pretended love to wound more deeply.

"I saw and loved Claudina; I tried to buy her of Dupree through an agent; she loved you; my offers were rejected. In revenge I persuaded you to marry, knowing that would ruin you with your father. I informed him of it. He disbelieved it. He sent for you; all was discovered, and drove you from the house.

"I intercepted every letter, and represented you careless of his affection, and deficient both in love and duty, yet I pleaded with him to forgive you when I had worked him to a pitch of fury that made him outrageous.

"I kept Ernest from his confidence, by assuring him he had encouraged you. Under these impressions, one day, in a great fury, he made a will in my favour; but I believe grief, for your supposed neglect of him, preyed upon his mind, he fell into a swift decay.

"I told him you knew of his illness, but never inquired for him; once or twice Ernest petitioned for you, but he disregarded him.

"A week before his death he one day called me to his bed — 'Tell the ungrateful Ferdinand (said he) that on my death-bed I forgive him: I revoke a curse that has preyed upon my spirits; may Heaven forgive his unnatural behaviour, as I do.'

"The next day he sent for his lawyer; I was alarmed; the lawyer was from home, the clerk came; he would make a new will, he did so: I pretended to rejoice at it. He left your children his estate in Bavaria, and you a thousand crowns a year, with the small farm on the skirts of the Forest; also an annuity to Ernest of two hundred crowns.

"Those bequests were not much in comparison to what I became heir to, but it made you independent, and that was death to me.

"I sounded the clerk; I found him fit for my purpose; he was friendless and venal. The will was destroyed. I kept every one from the room till my father expired; the rest you know.

"Then to complete my revenge I had you at the Castle.

"I poisoned the mind of Claudina; I told a thousand falsehoods; you assisted my designs by going to the army; I made her believe you repented of your marriage, which occasioned your melancholy; in short I succeeded, I corrupted her mind, and dishonoured her person.

"Revenge was complete — she was pregnant — you returning — I sought to persuade her to destroy the child — she was taken ill—miscarried—and all we thought was well.

"You returned; the voice, which she thought supernatural, threw her into horrors. She sent for Ernest, confessed she had wronged you, and, having sworn him to secrecy, got him to procure her escape.

"I had reason to fear Ernest, therefore did not dare to discharge him. My mind was always distracted, terror and guilt my constant companions, for I always dreaded a discovery.

"The clerk who had made the will went into Austria—he spent the money in dissipation—joined with a set of gamblers—frequently made demands upon me for money, accompanied with threats.

"At length news arrived of your death; then I thought my misery at an end, and my fears all done away. One only trouble remained: I had married solely that you nor your children should be benefited after my death: My wife seemed not likely to have children; your boy must inherit, that distracted me; I could not come at him, he was too well taken care of, and I was still in the power of Ernest during the life of Claudina.

"Happily, as I thought, she died soon after; but her letter spoke daggers to my soul, and made me fearful of my own shadow.

"Whilst I was struggling with this imbecility of mind, came an account of your being still in existence which rendered me desperate, and resolve on your death as the only chance of escaping shame and punishment, Claudina having informed me that she had left a packet for you, confessing all her crimes.

"I wrote to the man who had before but too well served me, and held out such advantages, promised such a sum as I knew he would not resist, and when he had completed your destruction, he was to meet me at Ulm, and receive his reward.

"I made an excuse of business to go there, and wait the event. He came, assured me that you was murdered, and thrown into the river; and added, that being associated with a set of men, who were both gamblers and robbers, it was their intention on his return to leave the country with their booty, and go into England, and as banditti were known to infest those mountains, it would be generally believed both you and him had been plundered and murdered.

"I hugged myself in security, gave him the promised reward, returned home, and pretended to be uneasy that you did not arrive: I believed myself safe from a discovery, when the avenging hand of Heaven was uplifted to overwhelm me with the punishment due to my crimes.

"Eternal justice preserved you, and the day of retribution is at hand; a life of deceit, crimes and falsehoods, will soon be terminated here, and my soul trembles for its doom hereafter."

CHAPTER VIII

Thus ended the confession of the wretched guilty Rhodophil, which was not made without many breaks, pauses, and frequent refreshments, to enable him to proceed in the dreadful story; but we would not notice them to interrupt the narrative.

Ferdinand sat fixed in the chair; his eyes riveted on his brother, or occasionally thrown up to Heaven; he shuddered with horror, but spoke not a single word.

When the story was concluded, and the miserable object before him lay gasping for breath, he clasped his hands, tears streaming down his cheeks.

"Gracious father!" said he, "extend thy mercy to this unhappy man; may the long torment conscious guilt has inflicted—may the unspeakable terrors of a distracted mind plead in mitigation of his crimes; and may his sufferings obtain the same forgiveness from Heaven, which, with my whole soul, I accord to him here."

To this fervent address, Ernest pronounced an amen.—The wretched man seemed inwardly to join in prayer; he lay exhausted and speechless; the effort he had made during the confession of his crimes, reduced him to the last extremity; nor could he utter a single word for some time.

At length he wished to be alone with Ernest: Ferdinand, with tottering steps, reached the antechamber, and sunk on a sofa, overpowered by the recollection of what he had heard, and hardly believing it possible human nature could be debased by such deliberate malice and unheard of wickedness.

He remained for three hours alone; for he could not see any one, but was at length again summoned to the sick chamber; Rhodophil had again recovered speech, and besought him once more to pronounce him forgiven, and to join Ernest in prayers for him to Heaven.

Poor—poor Rhodophil! On the bed of death, with all the horrors of a guilty conscience, who can describe thy feelings; what lethean draught can silence the inward monitor, than now shrinks trembling from the view of futurity!!!

Most fervent were the prayers they offered to the throne of mercy; he seemed to have a temporary calmness, and at last dropped into a slumber. Ferdinand was persuaded to withdraw; the Countess had ordered a bed for him; he gladly retired to it for a few hours, to recover his spirits.

The night passed without any change;—Rhodophil dozed, started, and often waked in great horror, but his senses were not much deranged. In the morning Ferdinand entered the room just as he had desired to see his Countess; they met at his bedside; he spoke very inwardly, and with much difficulty of respiration, he entreated her pardon for many acts of unkindness and inattention; owned his motives for marrying her were her large fortune, and the hope of an heir to prevent Ferdinand or his son from succeeding him.

He praised and blessed her.—Then taking Ferdinand's hand, he feebly pressed it,

"Be her friend," said he.—"May Heaven bless you, and pardon me.—See the end of guilt and duplicity.—Truth and innocence only can make a death-bed easy.—The virtuous man looks forward with hope; the guilty one with fear and trembling—Heaven have mercy on me!!!"

Those were the last words he spoke.— — —Violent convulsive hiccups soon came on, which drove the Countess and Ferdinand to their respective apartments, unable to support the last struggle of nature; and in less than a quarter of an hour, the latter was informed the dreadful scene had closed!!!

Thus then expired the unhappy Rhodophil, only seven and twenty years of age.—Ferdinand requested Ernest and Mr. Dunloff to take the management of every thing upon themselves, for he was incapable of giving directions; he entreated them to let the confession of the wretched Rhodophil rest in their own bosoms, and, if possible, never to hint a word relative to the story, on any occasion whatever. This they faithfully promised; and at his request, Mr. Dunloff undertook to write for him to Count M— — — and his friends, directing them at the Count's castle; and if he was not arrived, to have them forwarded to Vienna.

We will now look back on the friends of Ferdinand, who were suffering the most painful inquietude on his account. The day preceding the one appointed by them to leave Vienna, the Count called on Heli at the interpreter's, and, to his surprise, found him preparing to leave Germany in a few days.

"I was coming to you," said he; a great revolution has taken place in my affairs; — the Grand Seigneur is dead; his successor was the friend of our family; my uncle is appointed to a place of much eminence, and I shall return to my own country without fear, and sure of preferment.

"Your bounty to me, therefore, I intended to resign, and only request a sufficient sum to carry me safe into Constantinople. — I go with joy, for I like neither your country or customs; and the women I detest.

"The ungrateful Fatima will have cause to repent her desertion of me, now I might have placed her at the head of a hundred women, perhaps; but no matter, I shall soon find others to please and console me."

The Count was not sorry to hear of this change in Heli's hopes and circumstances; — he assured him of their ready concurrence to his wishes, and took leave of him to get the business immediately settled. They also procured the liberty of the man who had been detained as a witness against Fatima, as after a fruitless search, they had given up any farther inquiry.

On the following day, Mr. D'Alenberg, his daughter, Louisa, the Countess of Wolfran, the two Barons, and the Count M— — —, accompanied by their servants, left Vienna, determined to proceed through Lintz, and make some inquiries after Ferdinand. The ladies were entirely unacquainted with their apprehensions for his safety, and supposed him with his brother.

As they stopped at the same inn Ferdinand had rested in, they were quickly informed of his leaving Lintz on the very day he had written to them, and, in their course of inquiries, learnt that a band of robbers sometimes infested the neighbouring hills and woods, which made it extremely hazardous for passengers, and therefore the landlord persuaded the company to go the lower road, as having less woods to travel through.

This account made them excessively apprehensive that Ferdinand had unhappily fallen in with the gang, and had been murdered. The Count accused himself incessantly, and protested, that, should any accident have befallen his friend, he never should enjoy peace more, or forgive himself, for not insisting upon going with him. — The Barons were extremely concerned; Mr. d'Allenberg overpowered with sorrow.

His extreme dejection, and the inquietude not to be concealed, which pervaded the countenance of Count M— — —, alarmed the ladies, and Miss D'Alenberg earnestly inquired of her father the cause of so visible a disorder.—He tried to evade her curiosity, but only augmented it, because perfectly assured he was uneasy, his endeavours to hide it from her, proved it was a matter of some consequence; she therefore caught the infection of her father's looks, and though she ceased to importune him, she saw there was some affliction preparing for her, which he was unwilling to communicate.

The Countess and Louisa were not more composed; each thought the painful secret must concern herself, and were equally unhappy.

A general air of concern pervaded through the whole party, and every one seemed to avoid particular conversation, though the Count, impressed with the idea that Miss d'Allenberg viewed him with some degree of preference, which indeed was justified by her behaviour to him; exerted all his endeavours to assume a tranquillity far distant from his heart, that he might not communicate his uneasiness to her: But the disguise was too flimsy to succeed, and only the more strongly convinced her that something lay hid, that would not bear investigation.

Mr. d'Allenberg had a small estate at Augsburg; he proposed to his friends going there, and sending off an express to Count Rhodophil, also, another to Mr. Dunloff.—This proposal met their approbation; the Barons could not resolve to separate themselves from the party, until some intelligence was gained to remove or confirm their present conjectures.

The ladies made no opposition; they frankly avowed to each other the painful suspense which tortured their imaginations, and anxiously sought for some clue to elucidate the mystery, but it was plain they must wait for the discovery.

They proceeded on to Augsburg, a very unsocial party, and arrived there without any accident: Being unexpected, they were not presently, or comfortably accommodated, but they were not fastidious, and bore inconveniences without repining.

The same night of their arrival, two messengers were procured; letters written and sent off: One of them was ordered to proceed on to the Count's estate, if he obtained no satisfactory answer from Mr. Dunloff.—The gentlemen took a walk in the garden after this business had been expedited. There was a small pavilion of two rooms, each opening into, and fronting different walks, with a communication door between them.

The gentlemen entered one of these rooms and sat down.

"I am convinced," said the Count, as if continuing a conversation — "I am convinced, that if we do not gain satisfactory information from the return of the expresses, it will be impossible to impose longer on the sagacity of the ladies, already so much alarmed; we cannot dissemble our inquietude, and the dreadful certainty of what we fear, if unhappily it proves such, must be known to them at last."

"True," answered Mr. D'Alenberg; — "but whilst there exists a possibility that Ferdinand lives, I would not wound them by our — — —."

He had not time to finish the sentence; — an exclamation of "Help, help," from the adjoining room, caused them to pull open the door, where they beheld Miss D'Alenberg on the floor, the Countess and Louisa endeavouring to raise her.

They flew to her assistance; she was cold and senseless; what a sight for a father! — Poor Mr. D'Alenberg was in agonies: The young Baron, more collected, had hastened to the house, and returned with drops and water, which, on applying, she showed signs of returning life, and was raised and placed on two chairs, Louisa supporting her in her arms.

She opened her eyes, and saw the whole group standing round her, her father holding her hand between his trembling ones.

"Ah!" said she, "Ferdinand is then dead!"

"Not so, I hope, my dear Theresa," replied he tenderly.

"Dying, if not dead," returned she, "the dreadful certainty will soon arrive — A second time to feel this blow — alas! 'tis too, too much to bear."

Mr. d'Allenberg and the ladies besought her to retire into the house; she submitted in silence to their wishes, and was supported through the garden; the Count remained rooted to the spot, inconceivably astonished at a discovery so little expected.

"What an unfortunate adventure," said Baron Reiberg, "that we should be overheard; I had not the smallest idea of Miss D'Alenberg's attachment to our friend."

"Nor I, I promise you," returned the Count, trying to recover from his surprise; "nor I am sure had Ferdinand."

"But if he lives," said the Baron, "as he is now a disengaged man, I hope the young lady will be happy; for she is a most charming young woman."

"Indeed she is," replied the Count;—"Heaven grant my friend may be alive; the rest we must leave to Providence."

They returned to the house, not a little disconcerted that accident had revealed what they had so industriously sought to conceal.

Mean time, Mr. D'Alenberg found it requisite, for the peace of his daughter, to enter into a full explanation of their hopes and fears; disguise would no longer avail to impose upon her, and he candidly laid every thing before her.

When he had concluded, and again mentioned hope,

"My dear Sir," said she, interrupting him, with a solemnity of look and accent, that penetrated to his heart—"my dear Sir, do not attempt to delude me with hope; rather seek to strengthen my mind, and fortify it to expect the worst. I always told you, because I always felt, that the preference I entertained for that unfortunate young man would terminate unhappily.

"It was the soft melancholy of his air, the tuneful accents of his voice, and the effusions of a bright understanding and pleasing vivacity, which now and then broke through the cloud that seemed to overcast his mind: It was those affecting appearances that stole insensibly into my heart, and to see Ferdinand was to pity him; pity soon ripened into esteem and affection, and now there is an end of all."

"Do not decide so peremptorily," said her father; "hope may still exist."

"You once before told me so, Sir," returned she; "but I have never listened to the flatterer; yet I had brought my mind to a comparative degree of content, when he was so unexpectedly restored to us; not that I could ever flatter myself with his esteem, nor circumstanced as he was, ought I to have wished for it."

"Dear Theresa," said Mr. d'Allenberg, 'those circumstances are changed; he has lately lost his wife, from whom he was parted."

"Why would you tell me so, to enhance my distress? Oh! my dear father, my Louisa, assist me to derive courage from the extent of my misfortunes; teach me to submit to the dispensations of Providence, that I may not cloud the last days of a beloved parent with sorrow, by an imprudent attachment."

Her father embraced her with streaming eyes, entreating her not to give way to despair, though he could hardly bid her to indulge hope. He retired and left her with the ladies, and in the evening she appeared at supper with them.

The gentlemen were agreeably surprised; she tried to eat, though she could not swallow three mouthfuls; she endeavoured to speak, to smile, but it was a smile of woe that shocked every one present; but her efforts were astonishing to her father, and convinced him of the dignity of her mind, and what struggles she was capable of, to afford him peace.

Four days of painful suspense they had endured, in which the delicate frame of Miss d'Allenberg seemed to be falling a sacrifice to the strength of her mind, and the assumption of a fortitude her spirits but ill supplied. They were sitting at the dinner table when the return of a messenger was announced; she turned faint and sick.

"I will retire, if you please," said she to her father, and accompanied by her two friends, tottered out of the room.

With difficulty, they preserved her from fainting.

"I shall soon know the worst," said she, "and that is some degree of ease from this dreadful uncertainty. If he lives, I am indifferent as to myself; for where there is no expectation, there can be no disappointment."

Her trembling frame spoke the agitations of her heart, when suddenly the door opened, and Mr. d'Allenberg appeared with an animated countenance.

"He lives," she exclaimed; and leaning her head on the bosom of Louisa, burst into a flood of tears, the first she had shed for three days.

"He does, my dear Theresa; a letter from Mr. Dunloff has restored us all to happiness.

He lives, indeed, wonderfully preserved, and arrived only two days before the messenger.—His brother had expired that day, and therefore both men went to Dunloff's, who quickly sent one back with intelligence so much desired; the other is gone on to Count M———'s, to give notice of his return."

Mr. d'Allenberg might have proceeded for an hour; his beloved daughter heard nothing, thought of nothing, but "Ferdinand is alive; yes, that amiable and unfortunate young man is the care of Heaven; his life is preserved!!!"

"Will you not come down, my Theresa, and hear read, or read yourself, this charming letter? We shall pursue our journey tomorrow, if you are capable of bearing the fatigue."

"Yes," said she, starting up; "let me hear the letter, dear Sir—how good you are."

She descended to the parlour, where Mr. Dunloff's letter was presented to her; she devoured the contents with great avidity, and joined, with astonishing composure, in the mutual congratulations they made each other, for the completion of their wishes.

The next morning they left Augsburg.—The two Barons resolved to attend them to Ulm, as they made that in their route to drop the Countess, who engaged, the moment she had settled her affairs, to bring her son with her, and spend some weeks at Mr. d'Allenberg's. The Barons took leave of her there; but young Reiberg so earnestly importuned his father, that he might be permitted to accompany his friend the Count, that the old gentleman consented, and also engaged to join them very soon.

They all proceeded to the Count's mansion, as being nearest to Ferdinand; arrived there without any accident, and immediately sent a servant, with letters to Castle Renaud.

Those letters reached Ferdinand just as he returned from the funeral of his brother.—What delightful sensations sprung to his heart, when he found his friends were so near to him; he thought his obligations to them superseded the cold forms of decorum in circumstances like his, therefore, sending for his faithful old Ernest, he requested Mr. Dunloff and his son would come to the castle, and remain with him during his absence.

He had entreated the Countess to remain there, and command, as usual; but she declined the offer, and the day preceding the funeral, had removed to the house of a friend, until one of her own was ready to receive her. She had a good estate of her own, and a very handsome settlement from Rhodophil.

Ferdinand detained the messenger, that he might accompany him, and agreeably surprise his friends. — When he was announced, they could hardly credit the information; — all started up, and, in a moment, he received the embraces of his three friends: The ladies were present; Miss d'Allenberg behaved like a heroine; she said little, but that little was extremely proper.

At length he was quietly seated; they asked him a hundred questions in a breath.

"Spare me at present," said he; "I wish not to remember unpleasant scenes now, when I am so perfectly happy."

He certainly thought himself so at that moment; but soon after, when in conversation, he beheld Miss d'Allenberg speaking with some attention to the Count— Ah! thought he, how unfortunate, that such a charming young woman should encourage a hopeless passion. — Then the numberless little incidents in which he had admired her, came to his recollection; he watched her attentively; thought her more beautiful than ever, and again sighed that the Count was precluded from rendering her happy.

He was so lost in thought, and absorbed in attention towards them, that Mr. d'Allenberg was obliged to remind him that he had not once asked for the lovely Countess.

"Forgive me," said he: "I have the highest respect for that estimable woman, but I have my excuse before me. When looking at those ladies, is it possible to recollect any others. — I hope, however, you left that amiable lady well."

"Perfectly so," said Reiberg; "and 'tis only in this company that I can pardon your omission."

Ferdinand had always so carefully avoided saying even a gallant thing to a lady, that the little compliment he uttered caught the attention of Miss d'Allenberg; she looked at him; he withdrew his eyes, and fixed them on Louisa, to whom he addressed some trifling question, that called the blood from the cheeks of the other, and she again turned towards the Count.

He was a minute observer of the scene, and instantly thought he understood the recesses of Ferdinand's heart better than he did himself. Nor was the Count mistaken.

The very first day Ferdinand had seen Miss D'Alenberg, he was charmed with her humanity, and generous compassion for Louisa. The sentiments she uttered were so congenial to his own feelings, that her character was instantly decided in his breast to be a worthy one. He felt exceedingly for the base duplicity of Count Wolfran's conduct, and rejoiced that such a woman had not fallen a victim to it.

When at her father's house, she seemed still more worthy of admiration; the study, the chief pleasure of her life, was to obey and contribute to his amusement.—She was sensible without affectation; cheerful without levity; attentive to every part of domestic management, without the least ostentation: Added to which, her polite kindness to Louisa denoted a mind above the idea of conferring favours, but was herself the obliged person, in being permitted to offer them.

Such was the character of Miss D'Alenberg.—He admired, he revered her; but at that time, the recent unaccountable troubles that hung over him; his affection for Claudina, which, though weakened, was not extinguished, and his peculiar situation, impeded every thought of Miss D'Alenberg, otherwise than as a most estimable young woman.

But when the Count and himself had so fortunately met with Louisa, the story she related of her friend's melancholy and secret attachment, the dormant admiration of her person and mind, again blazed forth; he felt the sincerest concern for her situation, not entirely unmixed with envy, for the man who was the object of her preferable regard.—This object, his sagacity at length discovered to be Count M———, and he also was convinced the unfortunate partiality was a mutual one. Here then he sighed in silence, as he thought in pity to them, and in that pity stifled his own regrets.

When he received an account of Claudina's death, he was greatly affected; her ill conduct, though plainly avowed, had not effaced her image from his heart, or eradicated the tenderness which was once reciprocal.—He lamented her death; he grieved for her depravity; but his sorrow was not of that deep heart-felt kind, which he must have felt in other circumstances, because reason whispered to his mind that she had proved unworthy.

When Mr. d'Allenberg and his daughter arrived at Vienna, and he waited upon them, he saw, as he judged, a confirmation of his suspicions of the unfortunate preference that young lady entertained for the Count, and without being sensible of it himself, he certainly exhibited some little petulance in his conversation, which did not pass unobserved.

He was then sent for to his brother, and his agitations on that account superseded all other ideas. The subsequent events pretty much engrossed his mind; and it was not until his present arrival at the Count's, when he saw Miss d'Allenberg with circumstances so much altered in his own favour, that the sentiments he had long suppressed, and was scarcely conscious of, now burst full upon him, mingled with the painful regret that his friend possessed that invaluable heart he thought above all price; and from his unfortunate situation, was precluded from even a wish to profit by the preference he was honoured with, and of course both must be unhappy.

Thus have we accounted for the workings of Ferdinand's mind, and for those sentiments which now, for the first time, were no longer concealed from himself.

Louisa made her own observations in silence. — Her friend, who saw the direction of Ferdinand's eyes, and felt the little compliment that had escaped him, immediately gave Louisa the credit of it.

"Yes," said she, mentally, "I see the attraction, and now there exists, on either side, no obstacles to impede their union. — Well, then, I will teach my heart to rejoice in their happiness, and henceforth draw only on my dear father for my future tranquillity." Impressed with this idea, she turned her eyes tenderly towards her father, and saw an expression of joy in his, that greatly surprised her, but which she immediately attributed to the pleasure of seeing his friend.

In the evening, the company walked into the gardens, and strolling through the shrubbery, they accidentally fell into small parties. — Louisa designedly led her friend from the company, and seemed to be in very uncommon spirits; Miss d'Allenberg thought it was not quite so decorous; but she allowed for the human heart; and a conquest, such as Ferdinand, justified the little breach of delicacy towards a friend.

"You are more than usually cheerful, my dear Louisa?"

"Indeed I am; the arrival of our friend has gratified my warmest wishes."

"May every wish of your heart be realized; you may suppose I do not feel less pleasure, though his presence is not of that immediate consequence to me, as to my dear Louisa."

"Indeed," cried the other, at once penetrating into the nature of her feelings, "indeed, have you then changed your favourable opinion of Ferdinand, since he is become a widower and a Count?"

"No," said Miss D'Alenberg, a little piqued; "but I hope I have fortitude and generosity sufficient to change the nature of my sentiments in favour of my friends."

"I see," returned Louisa, 'that you suspect the new Count has a partiality for me."

"It was a suspicion," said the other; "but his behaviour this day amounts to a confirmation; and believe me, my dear Louisa, weak as you have seen me in many instances, I have acquired that command over my feelings, now that I see him alive and happy; that I am enabled to partake in your mutual felicity, though, for a time, perhaps I should not choose to be an eye-witness of it."

"Generous friend," exclaimed Louisa, kissing her hand, "I know the sincerity of your heart, and doubt not but that the nobleness of your mind would support you under the most painful disappointment, if productive of happiness to those you love: But undeceive yourself, my beloved Theresa, Ferdinand respects me as the friend of Miss d'Allenberg; but my amiable Theresa is the sole possessor of his heart."

"Impossible," cried she, "impossible, dear Louisa; you must be mistaken."

"Indeed I am not," returned she; "an attentive observer can translate the looks of a lover, and is not often mistaken; at least suspend your conclusion against him for a day or two. — I will be answerable for the events."

"Against him!" repeated Miss d'Allen-" berg; "his supposed preference of you does credit to his judgment."

I shall not dispute that point with you," answered she, smiling, "because it gratifies my self-love; but here they come,

and I only beseech you to open your eyes, and disperse the mist
that clouds your judgment."

The gentlemen, who had joined in different walks, now
approached the ladies, the eyes of Ferdinand meeting those of
Miss d'Allenberg's. She blushed excessively, from thinking of
the preceding conversation; she turned to Louisa, the archness
of whose looks more greatly disconcerted her; her disorder was
very visible, which, when Louisa remarked, she drew the
attention off from her friend by a sprightly sally, that brought
Mr. d'Allenberg upon her: He rallied her upon her gaiety, for
which he was indebted, he said, to the company of their beaus.
This passed off the confusion of his daughter, and she recovered
her spirits.

CHAPTER IX

The ext morning Mr. D'Allenberg and Ferdinand happened to meet in the avenue before the house, where the latter was strolling apparently lost in thought. — "My good friend," said the old Gentleman, "I have scarce had an opportunity to speak my perfect satisfaction at the termination of your troubles: I know not indeed all your story, but I know enough to interest me warmly in your happiness."

"You do me great honour, Sir," replied Ferdinand; "but though the veil is withdrawn from the mystery, which so long rendered me wretched, yet the disclosure has been attended with the knowledge of so many painful circumstances, that at times I feel my spirits sink under the recollection of them."

"Time, and a variety of objects," said Mr. D'Allenberg, "will, I hope, by and bye, have its usual effects, and blunt the remembrance of former sorrows. I thank Heaven, there is much alteration in the disorder that affected my daughter's spirits, from the very remedy I prescribe for you; do you not think her complexion and cheerfulness are returning?"

"I hope so," replied Ferdinand, "most fervently I hope it; every one must feel interested for a young lady so truly excellent, that the beauty of her person is her least perfection."

"I thank you for the warmth of your sentiments," said Mr. D'Allenberg, "which encourages me to speak freely to you; there is only one man in the world that I am desirous of calling son, that man is a friend of your's."

"A friend of mine!" repeated Ferdinand, starting in great confusion, adding, in a tremulous voice, "any man must be highly honoured by such a distinction; but I am at a loss to guess who you mean."

"The Count's unfortunate situation sets him entirely out of the question," interrupted Mr. D'Allenberg. — "Indeed, Sir! the young Baron's predilection in favour of the Countess is not unknown to you."

"No," returned he, 'that's a point settled. The Gentleman I mean has now, I believe, neither a prior engagement or attachment, he is one who engaged my esteem the first day I saw him, from particular traits of humanity and honour that I observed in him, and from the conversations, short as they were, that gave me a perfect good opinion of his head and his heart. Unfortunate circumstances at that time stepped between me and my wishes, which are now, I believe, all done away. Are you at a loss now to know my man?"

During this speech Ferdinand had been violently agitated; at the conclusion he caught the hand of Mr. D'Allenberg: "Ah! Sir, how flattering is your kindness; I will not affect to misunderstand you, but can that happy distinguished man presume to hope Miss D'Allenberg views him with the partial eyes of her father? No, he cannot, he dares not, flatter himself with an idea, his own observation convinces him would be erroneous."

"You would not then decline the connexion, should Theresa be more discerning than you are so ready to suppose?"

"Decline! dear Sir! to call you father; to contribute to the happiness of your lovely daughter, would indeed be to ensure my own, and render me the most enviable of mankind. Your kindness has dragged a secret forth from the inmost recesses of my heart, and by its palpitation convinces me, that heart is entirely engrossed by Miss D'Allenberg."

"Well," said the old Gentleman, infinitely delighted, "you shall not at any rate bear the torture of suspense, you shall speak to her this day, if she sees with her father's eyes, you have nothing to fear. If I am mistaken, and her inclination is not in your favour, I shall be sorry and disappointed; but — you shall ever be the son of my affection."

Ferdinand was so entirely overcome by this kindness, that words were denied to him, and, confused at his emotions, he turned abruptly from him.

The party assembled at breakfast, all seemed gay and happy except the two lovers. After the repast Mr. D'Alenberg asked the Ladies and Ferdinand to view a small pavilion the Count's steward had lately erected in a beautiful shrubbery. — The name of a pavilion caused his daughter to shudder. — She remembered a conversation which had passed in a similar place that had given her the most poignant grief; but no objection being made, they readily accompanied him, and were highly pleased with the steward's taste.

"There is another spot, not far off," said Mr. D'Allenberg, "where a small building may be erected to an advantage. Come hither, Louisa, I will have your opinion first." She started up, took his arm, and they were out of sight in a moment.

Miss D'Alenberg was rooted to her seat in breathless terror; Ferdinand was little less discomposed, but recovering himself—"I know not, Madam, whether you will have the goodness to pardon my temerity in seizing this opportunity of opening to you my whole heart, a heart long tortured by the most painful events.

"Ever since I had the honour of knowing Miss D'Alenberg I have considered her as the most amiable of women, and respected her accordingly. My unhappy situation precluded every selfish wish, and her happiness was my first concern, independent of my own.

"That situation is now changed, and though perhaps I may err against the common rules of decorum, yet I hope Miss D'Allenberg will not condemn me if I am solicitous to know whether my future destiny is to be happy or wretched; if my kind stars ordain the former, then my anxiety is removed; if on the contrary I am to be unfortunate, the sooner I fly from hence the better.

"Need I add, Madam, that you are the arbitress of that destiny, that on you must rest all my hopes of future bliss? If you will deign to admit me a candidate for your favour, if no happier man has superseded me, and rendered all my hopes of felicity successless, if you will permit me to dedicate my future life to the delightful study of rendering your's happy, then indeed I may congratulate myself on being the most fortunate of mankind; the wounds which have been given by the hands of those I loved and trusted, and which yet rankle in my bosom, you only can heal, and from you I would derive that peace which the world has hitherto denied to me."

Whilst Ferdinand was speaking with an earnestness and solemnity in his manner that was truly touching, Miss D'Allenberg had time to recall her fleeting spirits, and compose her mind sufficiently to answer him, tho" not without some emotion.

"This address, Sir, is so unexpected, so opposite to the idea that I had entertained of your sentiments, that surprise has no small share in my too visible emotions; the love of candour, and a strict adherence to truth, were the first lessons I received from the best of mothers: Her precepts and example have governed every action of my life, I will therefore frankly confess."—She stopped.

"Ah! Madam, speak, go on, keep me not in suspense."

"I scarce know what I ought to say, yet I will confess, such is my esteem for your character, that I am persuaded, if I have really the power of contributing to your happiness, I cannot fail of insuring my own."

The moment she had pronounced the last words, Ferdinand threw himself on his knee, and kissed her hand:—"Forgive me," was all he could utter. She raised him, and for a moment both were silent.

"Your generous frankness, my dear Miss D'Allenberg, has overwhelmed me with rapture; my future life must speak my gratitude; joy is not eloquent when so complete as mine."

She arose—"If you please we will seek my father."—He took her hand, and obeyed in silence. They saw Mr. D'Allenberg and Louisa advancing.

"Heyday!" said the latter, "what are you both speechless? Have you exhausted all your stock of ideas, that not a single word is left to ask our opinion of the intended plan for building?"

"You are malicious, Louisa," returned her friend, blushing.

"Sorrow, my dear Madam," answered Ferdinand, "often makes people plaintive, and the overcharged heart sometimes finds relief in complaining; but joy is a miser, and I feel at present too happy to be communicative."

"Extremely well explained, I must own," said Louisa, "a few words has done the business. Come, my silent friend, you shall give me your opinion of our judgment!"—Saying this she drew Miss d'Allenberg away, leaving her father and Ferdinand together. The latter instantly embraced Mr. d'Allenberg. "I am the happiest of men!"

"One only of the happiest," replied he, returning the embrace, "for I share with you."

The party did not meet together till the dinner hour, but Mr. d'Allenberg had seized an opportunity to inform Count M——— and the young Baron of the completion of his wishes, and they very sincerely rejoiced in the promised happiness of Ferdinand.

At table Louisa was the most talkative of the company.—"I cannot help remarking, with an infinity of pleasure," said the

421

Count, "on the agreeable change there is in your health and spirits, Madam."

"I am sure," answered she, "the intention of your remark is friendly, but not at all calculated to increase my cheerfulness, by reminding me of the alteration. Retrospections are not always pleasing, and I owe much of my health and spirits to a resolution henceforth to look forwards."

"I beg your pardon, my dear Madam," returned he, very seriously, "your reproof is very just, and I take shame to myself for the rudeness of my observation, which I entreat you to believe arose entirely from the real delight I felt in the charms of your conversation."

"It must be owned," said she, with a returning smile, "that you know how to extricate yourself from an error extremely well, and my self-love accepts of the apology."

They had scarcely dined when an express came from Ernest with letters to Ferdinand. He retired to read them, and was surprised to find one from the steward of the Castle of Danhaet, with information, that "two days after his departure, the hermit had called there for his customary allowance, and informed him, that he had been alarmed the preceding day by seeing some men come out of one of the caves in the rock; he was not discovered himself, but he supposed they were some proscribed persons, or banditti.

"This intelligence," continued the steward, "I instantly conveyed to the Magistrates, who sent a party of men that same night to the rocks, and they remained concealed in the hermit's cave to make their observations.

"About midnight a boat was seen advancing to the Beach; two men landed, and were presently out of sight, but in less than half an hour returned with four others, all well loaded. As they proceeded towards the boat, the guards silently issued from the cave, and were upon them before they were discerned. They threw down their booty, and attempted to fly; one fired a pistol; the fire was returned; in the same moment two fell, and they were surrounded, taken, and conveyed to Lintz.

"The two wounded were not in much danger. One of them, who was most hurt, proved to be the villain, who had imposed upon Ferdinand.

"Several robberies and frauds were proved against them, and they had property to a great amount. Amongst the rest, a casket of jewels, which they had defrauded a Lady of, and seduced her from Vienna, where they oftentimes went as Gentlemen, to obtain a knowledge of what travellers were going on the road.

"They had formerly dwelt in the caves under the hills; but hearing the foolish story that the pavilion was haunted; they availed themselves of it, to get possession there, and securing all the doors and windows so as to prevent a surprise, fixing a bell at the little area door, that, should any one attempt it, the persons below by groans might frighten, and impose on the credulity of the peasants, as the gang only came there at night, and had a watch word."

This confession was made by the same villain who had before applied at the Castle, and the same cowardly spirit, generally attendant on roguery, had now induced him to make a complete discovery to save his life.

"He was not of the party when they took the jewels from the Lady, but had heard she had brought them from Turkey. What became of her after they had stripped her on the mountains, none of them could tell."

The steward concluded, by saying, that "there was little doubt but that they would all suffer for their crimes; the property remained in the hands of the Magistrates to be claimed."

This letter gave Ferdinand further occasion to admire at the justice of Providence, which sooner or later brings villainy to its deserved punishment; for

"Foul deeds will rise,

"Tho' all the earth o'erwhelms them, to men's eyes."

He had not the smallest doubt but that Fatima was the Lady from whom they had taken the jewels, and the two Gentlemen, with whom she embarked from Pratt's-Grove at Vienna, two of this abandoned gang of ruffians, though he lamented the depravity of her heart, and detested the baseness of her character, he saw a severe retribution had overtaken her, and therefore felt an anxiety, mixed with compassion, for the uncertain fate of one who claimed her being from his, more than ever, revered father.

423

He could not bear to reflect on the conduct of Rhodophil; a regular course of duplicity, instigated by the vilest passions, had pervaded through his whole life, and when he considered how greatly his own senses and reason had been imposed upon by his artful management, when he found that even his father had been the dupe of a profound dissimulation, difficult to be conceived in the heart of man. He sighed for the late unhappy Claudina, who had fallen a victim to the same complicated baseness.

Nursed in vice and dissipation, the seeds of virtue were never nourished in her bosom, and the wretch, to whose care she had fallen at an early age, had doubtless taught her but one lesson, 'to make the most of her beauty," yet it is certain (thought he) that she loved me; that she bore adversity with sweetness and patience, and but for the insidious arts of a cruel spoiler, the dormant passions, which accelerated her ruin, for gaiety and dress, might have been buried in the duties of a wife and mother:

But a weak mind, and the taint of early dissipation, aided the work of a cruel enemy; and the progressive vice that marked his conduct, led him at last to the commission of the most horrid crimes.

From those dreadful objects he turned his eyes to contemplate and admire the exemplary conduct of his amiable friends, and most fervently offered his prayers to Heaven, that they might enjoy the happiness their virtues so well deserved; to those friends he returned, and communicated the contents of the letter he had received.

No one could be sorry that such a nest of villains were on the point of being exterminated; but Ferdinand could never prevail upon himself to charge his brother with the assassination he met with, nor the heinous crime which had led to it; those two particular atrocities he forbore to mention even to his best friends; he left them always to suppose he was only attacked in common with other passengers.

A week was spent at the Count's in all the delights of love and friendship, in which time the Ladies heard from the Countess, that "she had found no difficulty in having her affairs settled, no one had doubted her rights, nor any other claim seemed to be remembered; she hoped therefore, in less than a month, to join them at Mr. d'Allenberg's mansion."

The party now prepared to separate; the Baron to his father's Castle for a short time, having received an invitation to meet his beloved Countess; Mr. D'Alenberg, with his daughter and Louisa, to their own house; and the Count returning with Ferdinand, his affairs requiring his presence at Castle Renaud.

He found it extremely difficult to tear himself from his charming Theresa, but she pleaded delicacy and decorum. The recent death of his wife and brother, though separated from the one, and ill-treated by the other, had some claims to observance.

"I am far," said she, "from being a slave to forms, but the good opinion of the world is always worth preserving, and the sacrifice of one's inclinations for a short time, will be much less painful, than a consciousness of having forfeited that opinion by an appearance of indecorum; therefore, until our friends join us, you must not be offended if you are excluded from being an inmate of our house."

Ferdinand turned to Louisa, "Hasten the journey of your sweet Countess, my dear friend; the Baron will feel the attraction, and my time of probation will be shortened." — She nodded an assenting smile; but the remainder of the day passed not like the former ones; they knew they were to separate, and the idea threw a cloud over every countenance.

The next morning they parted different ways, for Miss D'Alenberg would not permit the Gentlemen to accompany them a step out of their road: — "Why should we prolong the pain we feel in separating?" said she; "Let the moment be short and decided; one adieu conveys the same meaning as a thousand." They submitted reluctantly to her wishes, and left the house immediately.

The Count had not heard from Eugenia since his return; he was uneasy at it, and had written to her the preceding day. Francis, their old attendant at the Solitary Castle, lived happy and contented under the protection of Mr. Duclos, the Count's steward, and blessed the day that brought Ferdinand to that desolate mansion.

The two friends arrived in safety at Castle Renaud, where the good and faithful Ernest was ready to receive them, accompanied by his nephew and little Charles. The Count was charmed with the sweet boy, and when he admired his features, thought Ferdinand perfectly acquitted for his strong attachment to his mother.

They had been three days at the Castle, when one evening Ferdinand was informed that a woman, of a very ordinary appearance, wished to speak with him; the Count would have withdrawn: — "By no means," said Ferdinand, and ordered her admittance. — She entered, wrapped in a long cloak, and her head so covered that no part of her face was visible but her eyes.

"What is your business?" demanded he.

"Justice!" replied she, fiercely, and throwing off her hood, discovered Fatima.

"Fatima!" exclaimed he.

"No longer Fatima," said she, "but Charlotte, daughter to the late Count Renaud, and as such entitled to be provided for by his heir."

Her astonishing assurance for a moment disconcerted both Gentlemen; but Ferdinand recovering, and looking on her with some indignation:

"The provision you so rudely demand was once offered, when I was less able to serve you, myself then supported by the bounty of a friend; but you will remember it was offered to you conditionally. Your birth does not entitle you to make any demands upon me; but the respect I owe to the memory of my father will incline me to do it, if you deserve it."

"I scorn the idea of an obligation," said she, "I come to claim my right, and to tell you, that secure as you think yourself of the title and estates you have taken possession of, I can annihilate your claims in a moment, if you dispute mine."

"Charlotte, since that is your name, do not injure yourself by an insolent asperity that ill becomes you: I am inclined to serve you, but it must be in my own manner, nothing shall be extorted from me."

"And I disdain a favour," said she: — "Know then, your father was married to my mother, consequently neither the late Rhodophil or yourself were entitled to inherit."

"This is so wild a chimera," said Ferdinand, 'that I know not which to admire most, the impudence or the falsehood of the assertion."

"You shall find," returned she, "that it is a decided truth; I have two witnesses to prove the marriage, and shall immediately enter a process against you, unless you consent to give me a moiety of your fortune."

"And pray," asked Ferdinand, with a disdainful smile, "who, and where are your witnesses?"

"They are in Baden, and without you accede quietly to my proposal, to-morrow shall witness the publication of my claims, your father's memory shall be branded as it deserves, and you, you shall be known as the child of disgrace, assuming rank and title, to which you have no pretensions."

Never was astonishment equal to the Count's, or perturbation of spirits like Ferdinand's—that this fabricated story was an impudent forgery he had no doubt, and he was well assured could not be maintained; but then she was capable of promulgating the falsehood through the town, his father's memory would be branded by a hundred malicious tongues that delight in a tale of scandal; if in revenge she instituted a suit, he must appear to controvert her assertions, and in the mean time hold only a doubtful title, and a disputed estate.

Whilst he was silently revolving in his mind those perplexities, the Count was considering how to undermine this plot against the interest of his friend.

"I think," said he, mildly, "if this Lady has the proofs she speaks of, it will be much more for your interest and honour to compromise the affair between you, than to enter into a tedious process, that in the end must injure both; I would advise you, my friend, to deal cautiously, hear the witnesses, and, if you cannot disprove their testimony, then settle the business amicably between you.—The Lady can claim neither the title nor family estate, she may injure you by her claims, and throw both into another branch of the family, but she would be no gainer by that; supposing therefore her story to be just, it is for your mutual interest that it should not transpire beyond ourselves."

Whilst the Count was speaking, Ferdinand looked at him with the utmost surprise, but a turn in his eye undeceived him in a moment; therefore when he ended his observations, the other seemed to be considering, and at length, with an air of reluctance, replied, "Your counsel is difficult to follow, yet you are my only friend, and as such best entitled to advise me."

"Well, then, Madam, bring your witnesses to-morrow morning, I only request that till you have produced your proofs, and have my answer, you will not divulge to any one what you have said here."

"I do promise (said she) and will attend you to-morrow, when you will find it most for your advantage to pay attention to my demands, and the advice of your friend."—She then withdrew.

"This is the most impudent, ill-concerted scheme I ever heard of (said the Count.)—This woman knowing how tenderly you regard the reputation of your late father, has founded her plot upon your weakness: Now let us instantly send to Baden for officers of justice to be here at an early hour, and, my life for it, we shall frighten them into a confession, be the witnesses who they may."

Ferdinand was compelled to adopt this plan, though it did not exactly correspond with his inclination. This woman was the child of his father, as such he could have wished to save her from disgrace, and have made her life comfortable; but she insisted upon rights which his duty to himself and his heirs would not permit him to allow of.

He passed a sleepless night.—"Foolish mortals as we are (said he) when pluming ourselves in a fancied security of happiness! here is a blow, which, if persisted in, must at least interrupt, if not annihilate all my hopes of future felicity with Miss D'Alenberg; for no compromise will I make, or enjoy a doubtful title to which I have no claim.—"Ah! (cried he) the sins of the fathers are multiplied upon their children! What a lesson to parents, what a pharos to the gay and dissipated of both sexes, when their crimes and follies are thus extended to their wretched posterity."

The morning came; he arose languid and unhappy; in vain the Count sought to disperse his gloomy ideas; every way he turned his thoughts, they were pregnant with trouble and vexation.

The officers came; they were placed in a closet adjoining to the room in which Ferdinand prepared to receive Fatima, or rather Charlotte. In a short time two women and a man were announced, one of whom proved to be Dupree, the man was unknown.

"How! (exclaimed Ferdinand) Dupree!"

"Yes (said she) Dupree. "Till lately I knew not that your sister was alive, and therefore, for poor Claudina's sake, I was entirely silent on a subject that must have injured you, without benefiting any one I know; but having accidentally discovered Charlotte, justice now compels me to speak."

"You lived then with Charlotte's mother?" asked the Count; for the sight of Dupree had recalled such a train of unpleasant ideas to Ferdinand, that he could not speak.

"Yes (replied she) before the Count paid his addresses to her. He finding she was virtuous, and above all his offers, at length determined to marry her unknown to his father, exactly (said she, addressing Ferdinand) as you proceeded with respect to Claudina. This Gentleman, Mr. Keilheim and myself, were the witnesses to the marriage, which was private in her own house."

"Who was the priest?" demanded the Count.

"Mr. Reinheim, of Baden, who died soon after Charlotte was born, which gave the Count courage to comply with his father's commands, and marry the mother of Rhodophil. He represented to my poor mistress that a discovery of her marriage would ruin him, as he had no fortune to support her; but that, if she would be content to live as she had done, and permit him to marry, she would always be conscious of her own innocence, always enjoy his love, and he would make ample provision for her children.

"She foolishly consented rather than injure the man she loved. He married a wife he never liked, and was constant in his love to my mistress, 'till unluckily, Ferdinand's mother came a visiting to his house, he then fell in love with her, and basely used both wives.

"My mistress sent for him, and threatened to disclose the marriage. He laughed at her, the priest was dead, she had consented to appear at his mistress, his present wife had powerful friends, and every one would be convinced her claim was only founded on malice and revenge; he therefore defied her power.

"Just at this time a young Nobleman, high in the army, whom I shall name by and bye, who was distractedly in love with my mistress, made her the most liberal proposals of a good settlement. She, in a fit of passion and resentment, accepted his offers, and left Baden with him, though she sent word to the Count she would always hold a rod over him, and some day or other prove the rights of her child.

"With this Nobleman she resided till his death, and Claudina was his daughter. They lived very expensive, and she had no great matter left to support her children, which I believe broke her heart, for she died soon after him, leaving her daughters to the care of Mr. Keilheim and myself.

"We did what we could for them, but found it would be necessary for them to do something to maintain themselves, or that we must apply to their relations.

"We were consulting about coming to Baden, and proving the rights of Charlotte, when she foolishly eloped from us with an officer, and followed him to the camp. A battle followed soon after, he was killed, and we could gain no intelligence of her. Mr. Keilheim went to England with a friend on particular business, and advised me to go to Suabia with Claudina, and make her known to her father's brother, who would doubtless provide for her. I took the journey, and came to the Nobleman's house; to my great vexation he had been gone abroad above three years, and nobody knew if he was alive or dead.

"What was this Nobleman's name?" demanded the Count, much agitated.

"Count M — — — (replied she.) I believe you know him.

"Good God! (exclaimed he) but go on."

"Well (said she) after abundance of inquiries, I could hear of no relation likely to be of service to Claudina; I therefore took a small house in the suburbs of Baden, to wait for the return of her uncle, and in the hope that her beauty might get her provided for: I also expected the return of Mr. Keilheim, when I intended making myself known to Count Renaud, and demand of him some provision for keeping his secret.

"In a short time after the Count's sons both fell in love with Claudina. Rhodophil wanted her as a mistress, Ferdinand courted her for a wife, and I learned he was the favourite son; I therefore made no application to the Count on her account; the marriage took place, and Ferdinand was turned out of doors. This vexed me, but I thought time would reconcile the father to his son, so as to provide for him; but he was obstinate, without considering he had done the same thing, and they were reduced to much distress. About this time I heard from Mr. Keilheim that his friend was dead, and had left him some property; that he was ill at Hamburgh, and desired me to come to him. Glad to be no longer a burden upon Claudina, and willing to save her from the sorrow of parting, I went away without taking leave.

"I contrived, however, to hear of her, and was rejoiced to learn the Count was dead, Ferdinand and she provided for, and living at the Castle, not then believing Charlotte was alive, I thought myself free from the whole business, and troubled my head no more about them. "This, Gentlemen, is the whole story.

CHAPTER X

She had repeated every circumstance with such exactitude, and without the least hesitation, there seemed a degree of probability in the story not easily to be controverted, that both the Count and Ferdinand were staggered and confused.

The Count well remembered, that his elder brother was said to have taken a mistress with him from Baden, and he now was struck with the recollection that when he beheld little Charles, the features seemed familiar to him, his was an exact copy of his mother's face, and he had no doubt but she resembled her father.

Turning to Ferdinand, Claudina then was my brother's child, and I have an interest in your sweet boy.

Ferdinand was deeply engaged in revolving Dupree's story. Quickly recollecting himself, said he, "You say, that you left us suddenly to spare Claudina the pain of parting; but was it necessary to rob us, to carry off the few valuables we had, and leave us in distress? Was it consistent with your love for her, never to write, or give any account of yourself?"

"What (said the Count) was you robbed?"

"Yes (answered Ferdinand) on rising one morning we found the door on the latch, and the drawers emptied."

"I know nothing of that (said Dupree) I cannot answer for any person's getting into the house after I left it."

"But you shall answer for it (cried the Count, with joy dancing in his eyes.) Within there!" The officers entered, and instantly seized all three. Ferdinand then spoke: — "I charge you, Dupree, with robbing me, with entering into a vile conspiracy against me, and these persons as your accomplices."

"You shall instantly go to prison, and remain confined on my charges, till I have discovered the whole of your vile plot, which will not be long first (added the Count.) — There is a Gentleman in Baden, you little think of, who will witness to your frauds."

This last speech threw the man and woman into great confusion, though merely an impromptu of the moment.

"For you (said Ferdinand to Fatima) — whatever is your name, base, unprincipled woman, foolish as wicked; by gentleness and contrition for your errors, I may say crimes, you might have obtained from me a comfortable provision for life; by fabricating this compilation of falsehoods, by joining with this worthless pair, whose abandoned principles early sowed the seeds of corruption in your mind, you have entirely shut my heart against you, and the robbery you committed on Heli will prove the depravity of your mind.

The valet of Count Wolfran now lives with a friend of mine. The villains who robbed you of the diamonds which you plundered from your benefactor, they are now in custody, and soon will your story come before the public, as Heli has instituted a criminal process against you.

That name I have been so solicitous to save from the disgrace of giving birth to a wretch like you, can no longer be injured, for such a mother may be supposed to have given many fathers to her children, and any depositions from such infamous persons can only be treated with contempt. Officers take them to prison.

Fatima stood with a sullen intrepidity that both shocked and surprised them. The man changed colour, and was silent, not a syllable had he spoken; but when the officer led Dupree to the door, that cowardice generally attendant on a conviction of crimes, at once took from her all the courage she had assumed. "Stop, stop," she cried, and falling on her knees, "Save me from a prison, preserve me from punishment, and I will confess all."

That moment Fatima, who stood near her, snatched a dagger from her side, and quick as thought stabbed Dupree, and then plunged it into her own bosom; both fell. The action was so sudden, so unexpected, that no one was in time to prevent her.

Ferdinand was inexpressibly alarmed; he ran to her, as the Count did to Dupree:—"Rash, unhappy Fatima! what have you done? Let some one fly for a surgeon."

"He is at hand," said she, faintly, "death will soon preserve me from the shame of detection and punishment; that abandoned wretch is the cause of this, she suggested the scheme to ruin you. I lived long enough in Turkey to learn the use of a dagger."

"Wretched girl!" said Ferdinand, agonized by this scene, "why did you doubt my mercy, or generosity?"

"Because I scorned to humble myself, or sue for favours.

"Heli, you, and all are revenged, and I am beyond your power."—These were the last words she spoke; in a few minutes all was over!

Ferdinand, agitated in the most dreadful manner, accused himself for rashly irritating such a mind as her's, and was exceedingly shocked at so dreadful a catastrophe to the life of an unprincipled woman.

Dupree's wound did not appear to be so dangerous, the blood was stopped, and she was taken to another room; the man was detained in custody in the house for the present. The surgeon came, and examined the wound; it was a doubtful case, he said, and could not as yet be decided upon. After it was dressed, she desired to see Ferdinand and the Count.

"I may now (said she) confess the truth; the story of the marriage was false. My mistress left a good sum of money behind her. Keilheim is my brother: We lived upon it while it lasted, but he gambled a good deal, and it soon went. I had intended to make a good price of Charlotte, but she disposed of herself, and I had only a trifle; then I determined to apply to Count M———, who really is uncle, by the father, to your late wife; but he was abroad.

"Keilheim went as a valet de chambre to an English Gentleman, and left me what he could. I settled at Baden, and had an intention of applying to Count Renaud, and passing Claudina upon him as his daughter, by saying she was older than she was; but then I feared he might take her from me to provide for her, and I should only get a trifle, as I know he never liked me; therefore I thought the only way was to sell her for a good price. You fell in love with her; I had other offers which I wanted her to accept; but she loved you, thought as you would marry her she might one day have a title, and a fortune; the rest you know.

"I heard from my brother; his master was dead, and he had secured to himself all his effects. He was returned to Ratisbon, and proposed I should come and live with him, as he had opened a gambling-house. I did take from you—all I could, and went to him.

"One day, going through the streets, a short time since, I passed a young woman, who seemed to look earnestly at me, and presently pronounced my name; I turned, it was Charlotte.

"Overjoyed at meeting, I took her home. She there told me her whole story of being carried to Turkey, meeting with you, returning to Vienna, and being carried off from the Turk by a Count, who was killed by Heli; upon which she fled from him with a box of jewels the Count had given to her. — She intended to go to England, but crossing some mountains she was set upon by ruffians, and robbed of all her property, and had travelled on to Ratisbon, by the little trifle left in her pocket. In this city she that day arrived with a design to make the most of her beauty, with an Englishman if possible, and then leave Germany.

"Keilheim had been unlucky at play; we were something distressed; the kindness you had shown to Charlotte made me believe it easy to impose upon you. We set an inquiry on foot about you, heard that Claudina and your brother were dead; we then formed this scheme, which has turned out so fatal to Charlotte, and, I fear, to myself."

This confession was made at intervals, as she had power to speak, and amazed the Gentlemen at such a regular system of vice as those wretches had long pursued; but Providence had at length overtaken them, nor would suffer the innocent to be a victim to such abominable duplicity.

In vain may the wicked hope to deceive the virtuous and unsuspecting mind, unobserved and undiscovered; there is a watchful and unerring eye, to whom all their black and artful schemes are laid open, and who, in its own good time, defeats the machinations of the wicked, and brings the offenders to the punishment they deserve.

The wretched Dupree languished three days, and then expired of a mortification. — Keilheim was taken to prison, and being convicted of entering into a conspiracy to injure Ferdinand, was condemned to perpetual imprisonment, which happily prevented him from extending his crimes in future.

This strange and tumultuous business exceedingly deranged and hurried Ferdinand; the Count had written a detail of it to Mr. D'Alenberg, who was greatly concerned for the anxiety it must have given to his friend; nor was his lovely daughter less affected; she added a postscript to her father's letter that more effectually calmed his spirits, and restored his serenity, than a hundred arguments from the Count on the folly of indulging regret for such a character as Charlotte's.

"I must ever pity her fate (said Ferdinand) deprived by her birth of the precepts and example of a virtuous parent, her mind was contaminated before she was of an age to acquire any fixed principles. No father to own, or support her, left, deserted by every connexion, and consigned to the trust of such depraved wretches: Ah! my friend, who can wonder at the excesses that followed, and the ruin that befell two unfortunate young women!

"Let the seducer of innocence but reflect one moment on the crimes he propagates, the destruction he meditates, and the dreadful consequences of his success; let him but reflect on the accumulated sins which may be multiplied on his head by the unfortunate beings he may give existence to; let him but extend his views beyond his own selfish gratifications, and he will shrink with horror from the seduction of innocence, and be himself the guardian of that honour, on which depends the happiness or misery of those unborn!"

"The Count most readily subscribed to the truth of those observations, but to change the immediate subject that distressed him, he congratulated himself on the connexion he claimed with little Charles.

"When you marry (said he) I claim him as my companion, nor must you deny me; Mr. Dunloff shall reside with him; we shall, I trust, often enjoy each other's society, and you will judge whether I perform my duty or not." — Ferdinand could not, without wounding the feelings of his friend, refuse a request so generous and affectionate; he therefore accepted it in the warmest terms of acknowledgment: "He shall have two fathers (said he) and hold a divided affection that will gratify us both."

"It is time now (added he) that I should perform a duty that both affection and gratitude demand. I know it was the intention of my late dear father to have provided handsomely for my worthy Ernest; that trust happily devolves on me: Souls like his are above pecuniary reward, nor does he want it, farther than to have the power of enlarging his benevolent purposes; therefore I must add other gratifications to prove my sense of his worth." He then rang the bell, and requested to speak with Mr. Ernest. The good old man came in, pleasure dancing in every feature to attend the commands of his loved master.

Ferdinand desired he would be seated. — Ernest looked at the Count. He translated the look: "My good friend, pray be seated." He immediately complied. "My dear Ernest (said Ferdinand) the packet Mr. Dunloff delivered to me, after the

death of my brother, contained little more than he himself
acquainted me with, and when I had perused the contents I
committed it to the flames, and with it all resentment for past
injuries.

"I have forborne from that time to enter on the subject. This
Gentleman you know to be the unfortunate Claudina's uncle, I
therefore speak freely before him; it can be attended with no ill
consequences now, if I ask you where she resided? where she
died?"

"In a small house, Sir, on the skirts of the Forest, with a
worthy man and woman, who had known better days; but were
reduced to be pensioners to your good father, the late Lord; it
was one of the things that gave me a suspicion against that will,
that no mention was made of this worthy pair: I had recollected
the sending for the lawyer, and the clerk's being shut up, and
my heart presaged that a will, dictated by resentment, would be
cancelled or altered.

"The will produced therefore surprised me, because I knew
it was the hasty work of a moment. After the funeral I inquired
for this clerk; he had left his master. This confirmed me in my
suspicions, but they availed nothing. I once or twice dropped a
hint to the late Count, which I saw alarmed him; I believe he
feared and hated me. — Pardon my prolixity, Sir.

"This worthy couple that I was speaking of, were strangers
to every one in the Castle but myself. When Madam Claudina
opened her mind to me, and resolved to quit the house, I went
there, said it was an unfortunate sick Lady and her child, who
wished to remain entirely unknown and unseen. They received
her with pleasure; there she lived repentant, and her health
soon fell a sacrifice to the remembrance of her errors. The news
of your death closed the scene."

"And where is this worthy pair at present?" asked
Ferdinand.

"In the same house, Sir."

"Who supports them?"

"Their wants are very few; their little garden and a cow
supply the chief of them."

"And you the rest, good and respectable man! (cried
Ferdinand) what a heart is yours! Kings might envy your

feelings, for justice and charity preside over them."

At that moment dinner was announced. Ernest arose: "Stop, my friend, (said he) this day ends all other distinctions between us; my heart swells to imitate your's; henceforth be always near me; teach me by your example to be loved in my youth, and revered in my decline of life, like you." Yes, you are the father of my affections, the friend of my friend," putting his hand into the Count's, who pressed it with both of his; "no longer my steward, but my companion and benefactor."

Ernest, overcome by emotions that swelled to his throat, and almost burst his bosom, had just strength to pull open a button or two, and sunk into a chair: — "Too much (said he, sobbing) it is too much, this graciousness!" A friendly shower of tears fell down his venerable face, and relieved the oppressed heart; neither of them had dry eyes for the moment.

"Come (said Ferdinand, trying to recover himself) come, the dinner waits, we dine together," taking Ernest by the arm.

"Excuse me, Sir, good Sir excuse me, not to-day, I cannot; give me time to recover myself; I cannot obey you now."

"Dear Ernest, obedience and command exists no longer between us; I will oblige you now, but from this day we have no separate tables. Within an hour I hope you will join us to drink a health to all our friends."

"I will, I will attend you, Sir (cried he, still sobbing) but spare me for the present." The friends withdrew.

"I honour you, my dear friend (said the Count) for the deserved kindness you have shown that good man. Would to Heaven that such instances were more frequent, that virtue, and goodness of heart, should be the only distinguishing mark to exact respect and attention; hereditary honours, when disgraced by improper and disorderly conduct, ought, in my opinion, to be classed far beneath the poorest upright man, whilst principles, and a mind like Ernest's would grace a diadem."

That evening the Count received a letter from Eugenia, who continued in tolerable health and spirits. She much regretted the loss of her friend, the Countess; but loved her too well not to rejoice in her opening prospects of happiness, though she was the sufferer.

Two days after Mr. D'Alenberg wrote to them that the Countess was arrived, and that the family party wanted their agreeable society, of which due notice had been sent to Baron Reiberg.

The friends wanted no further persuasions to a visit so gratifying to their wishes; Ernest no longer the steward, but friend of Ferdinand, undertook all necessary arrangements for the reception of a Lady, whose society was to constitute the happiness of his beloved master, a name ever dear to his heart.

Ferdinand paid a visit to his sister-in-law, the Countess, entreated her friendship in very sincere terms, saying, "he hoped shortly to bring home a Lady who would feel happy to cultivate her acquaintance." — Her reply was equally affectionate and polite.

He commissioned Ernest to make that family comfortable, who had given an asylum to Claudina. He wrote to the steward of Danfelt Castle, offering him the same situation in his family, if he still was desirous of a change, sending him a handsome present, which, if he preferred remaining at the Castle, he would remit to him annually.

Thus, having settled all the demands of gratitude and civility, with a light heart, and a thousand transporting hopes, he accompanied the Count to Mr. D'Allenberg's.

It is needless to say their arrival was announced to the general satisfaction of the family, and Ferdinand thanked the old Gentleman, with the warmest gratitude, for shortening the time of his probation, and permitting him the happy opportunity of cultivating that esteem his lovely daughter had so generously avowed. In less than a week the young Baron made an addition to their society.

Two months was spent by this agreeable party in all the delights that love and friendship could bestow; and, at the expiration of that time, Mr. D'Allenberg prevailed on his daughter and the Countess to make their lovers happy. — "Enough has been sacrificed to decorum (said he) it is now time to satisfy the demands of a tender attachment; life is short, and I wish to enjoy what remains of it, in the contemplation of my children's felicity."

The plea was unanswerable, and Miss D'Allenberg resigned her hand without the smallest reluctance to the happy Ferdinand. On the same day the Baron and the Countess were

439

also united.

Previous to which, that Lady insisted upon disclosing to him the story of Louisa, and her own situation. — "I could not feel happy (said she) to know there was a transaction of such consequence in my life, a secret to my husband, where mutual confidence must be the basis for mutual happiness; it would also be a treason against Louisa, which I could never forgive myself, not to do justice to a nobleness of mind that has few examples." The Baron was indeed surprised, but having heard the precedent the Countess had set Louisa, when the latter was distressed and unhappy; he said, his admiration was so equally divided between both Ladies, that it was difficult to pronounce where the preference lay."

Ferdinand before his marriage heard from the steward of Danfelt Castle, who gratefully thanked him for his goodness; but said a great alteration had taken place there; his master was reconciled to his Lady after a separation of fifteen years, it being found out by the confession of a servant that the Lady was innocent, and accused only out of revenge; he was therefore now preparing the Castle for their reception. He added, that the robbers, having been convicted by the evidence of several persons, had all suffered death, and the box of jewels was claimed by a Gentleman of Vienna to remit into Turkey. — Thus ended all future concern, either for Heli, or the robbers.

Peter, who had been valet to Rhodophil, who had been privy to most of his bad actions, yet had always felt gratitude to Ernest for preserving his life, and to whose information Ernest was often obliged, him Ferdinand could not retain in his family, but in the hope that a grateful mind could not be ultimately a bad one, he settled on him an annuity sufficient to maintain him with comfort, for so long as his conduct should deserve it.

The Gentlemen and their Ladies resided one month with Mr. D'Allenberg after their marriage, and then separated, with a promise of paying each other an annual visit. Louisa, at her own request, remained with Mr. D'Allenberg to supply the place of his daughter.

The Count accompanied Ferdinand and his Lady to Castle Renaud, where the worthy Ernest was presented to the Countess in such flattering terms, that the good creature almost expired with joy. — "Now (cried he, tears stealing down his face) now I have lived to see my master happy; I have lived long enough for myself; the remainder of my days must be devoted to the service of that Master, whose gracious Providence has defeated the schemes of the wicked, and having punished one error in early youth, which was productive of so many evils, has at length purified him to a fullness of joy!"

Ferdinand, from the day of his marriage with the charming Theresa, had nothing wherewith to reproach himself, or to interrupt their mutual happiness; he found, in the sweets of that union, that perfect felicity, which must result from a connexion formed on the principles of reason and virtue; whilst, generally speaking, those marriages, contracted contrary to the wishes of parents, influenced chiefly by transient personal charms, and hurried on by rash tumultuous passions, seldom fail to be productive of sorrow, regret and reproach—perhaps of punishment and shame.—We have only to add, that in less than three years after the marriage of Ferdinand, the once unfortunate, but then happy Eugenia, was translated from a state of resignation and piety, to a life of blessed immortality:— From her melancholy story may be deduced two observations of equal importance to society; when a parent exercises an undue authority over his child, and compels her to give a reluctant hand without a heart; by giving his sanction in the outset to deception and perjury; he has little to expect but that the consequences will be fatal to her honour and happiness.

A parent has an undoubted right to a negative voice, to persuade, to reason, and direct a young and unexperienced mind; but to force a child to the altar, from motives of ambition, interest, or to gratify any selfish passions, too generally lays the foundation for that indifference, and neglect of the domestic duties, which terminates in folly, vice, and the ruin of all social happiness.

In the conduct of Baron S———, may be traced the fatal effects of indulging that gloomy misanthropy, which feeds a proud spirit and a callosity of heart, insensible to every feeling but its own gratification, which, when opposed, may lead to the most determined cruelty and revenge.

Count M——— was greatly affected at the death of Eugenia; but by their separation he had been long weaned from that excess of passion he had felt in early life, and which had been productive of so much sorrow to both; his grief had less poignancy than he must otherwise have known, and the society of his friends contributed to restore his peace, though he ever preserved a tender remembrance of his first love.

In less than a twelvemonth after her decease, he offered himself to, and was accepted by, the amiable Louisa. They had no children, and Charles, the son of Ferdinand, was the worthy successor to the Count's fortune.

The compulsive marriage of Count Renaud, from which originated all the misfortunes that attended himself and his family, and the very rash and imprudent one which Ferdinand contracted, hold out lessons of equal importance to the consideration of parents and children.

But our hero, having been severely punished for the impetuosity and folly which marked his first attachment, found, in his union with Theresa, that unclouded happiness so seldom the lot of mortals.

Sensible of the blessings he received, it was his unremitting endeavour, by rectitude of conduct, by generosity to the deserving, and by benevolence to the unfortunate, to communicate an equal portion of felicity to all within the circle of his acquaintance.

From the characters of Rhodophil and Fatima, we may trace the progression of vice, and its fatal termination!

"Vice to be hated,

"Needs but to be seen."

The Midnight Bell

By Francis Lathom

CHAPTER I.

I am not mad; this hair I tear is mine;

I am not mad; I would to heaven I were!

For then 'tis like I should forget myself.

Oh, if I could, what grief should I forget!

If I were mad, I should forget my son,

Or madly think a babe of clouts were he;

I am not mad; too well, too well I feel

The diff'rent plague of each calamity.

King John

Count Cohenburg was descended from one of the noblest houses of Saxony; his castle, situated on a branch of the river Elbe, was one of the most magnificent in the German empire; his income was large, and his character celebrated, as one of the first men of his age.

At an early period of his life he espoused the second daughter of the marquis of Brandenburgh, and she blessed her husband with five sons; the eldest and the youngest of whom alone survived their mother.

At the time of count Cohenburg's death, which did not happen till he had some years buried his countess, Alphonsus, his eldest son, was in his twenty-sixth, and Frederic, his youngest, in his nineteenth year.

Alphonsus, now count Cohenburg, in his person was rather pleasing than handsome; his height about the middle stature, his mind well cultivated in every branch of learning, his temper mild and benevolent, but withal addicted to suspicion.

Frederic was a man formed to captivate; his features were regular, his countenance handsome and prepossessing, his figure tall and elegant; the advantages of education had been bestowed on him equally with his brother, but he had not so eagerly drank in instruction, — he was, however, an agreeable and even a fascinating companion, — he was passionate, but his anger was of a moment.

Arrived at his twenty-second year, Frederic became enamoured of a lady of Luxemburg; she was beautiful, but delicate in the extreme; she was an orphan, and possessed of a large fortune: — Frederic purchased a mansion in the vicinity of his brother's castle, and having espoused his beloved Sophia, every earthly happiness seemed to smile on him and his newly-married bride.

Within the year Frederic was blessed by the birth of a son.

Count Alphonsus was a beholder of his brother's happiness: he felt a wish for the same felicity Frederic enjoyed; he accordingly determined to marry, and selected from amongst the beauteous maids who adorned the German court, Anna, the only daughter of the duke of Coblentz. She was a woman in whom every engaging attraction was centred; her form was elegant, her manners affable and polite; there was something in her countenance that outshone regular beauty, and a vivacity in her conversation, that chained the senses of the enraptured listener.

Alphonsus was now as happy as his brother; and in the course of ten months his Anna brought him a son, on the same day on which Sophia gave birth to a second infant, which proved a female.

The name of his father was given to the infant son of count Alphonsus.

The following year Sophia brought her husband a third child, but the period of its entrance into the world was dated by the death of its mother.

The passions of Frederic were strong, and this proved a stroke which went nigh to unman his fortitude; the soothings of his brother however tended greatly to raise his depressed spirits.

Anna proved herself a not less affectionate sister to Frederic, than a mother to his children; she soothed them, consoled their father, performed for them every lenient action; and in short so forcible were her attentions, that she succeeded in lightening the burden of their sorrow.

Count Alphonsus loved his brother tenderly; he looked on his sorrows with a feeling eye; he would have alleviated them at the expense of half his worth; by any means, rather than by the assiduities of his Anna,—he conceived too highly of her to suppose her capable of bestowing on another the minutest particle of that love which she bore him;—he even repeated to himself that it was her love for him, which induced her thus to attend to his brother;—he knew the evil tendency of suspicion, and had always struggled to combat against it; but suspicion was a part of his nature, and would not always be subdued.

He watched his brother, and every turn of the countess's features when in Frederic's presence; he was convinced of his mistake; he was even on the point of apologising to his wife for the wrong he had done her in his thoughts; but he considered that he should, by so doing, only lay open to her an error in his heart, with which she was unacquainted; and therefore contented himself with the resolution of never again admitting a thought to her discredit.

Frederic's youngest child had survived its mother but a few hours, and, in the third year after her death, his eldest fell a victim to the grave: he recovered from this severe shock only to feel a greater,—his daughter died in his arms!—Misfortune seemed to have marked him out for her sport—he resolved to leave the scene of all his woes, and travel:—a hasty farewell was said by him to his brother and sister, and he departed.

In four years he returned; his manners were much altered; he was become dissatisfied, uneasy, absent; in short, no single trace of the former count Frederic was left.

Count Alphonsus was moved by his appearance, but his suspicious temper could not forbear revolving a subject which it had once disclaimed;—he determined however to bear his thoughts in silence,—he did so,—and in the course of eight months, Frederic again left Saxony.

The chief emotion which now swayed the breast of Alphonsus was pity; he fancied he perceived his brother's love for his wife, and his struggle to conceal it. The countess spoke frequently of the change in Frederic's temper,—her language served to convince Alphonsus that his brother was indifferent to her,—this was a point gained that gave him great satisfaction, yet he wished Frederic never to return.

Five years elapsed ere Frederic revisited Germany; he stayed but a short time in Saxony, and was then absent two more years; on his last return, his former disquietude of temper seemed converted into a settled melancholy; he retired to his mansion, and said he had formed a resolution to live a life of seclusion.

Alphonsus now imagined that he had found some means of gaining Anna's love, and that by pretending to keep himself retired in his own mansion, he thought to elude his brother's suspicion; he still, however, determined to keep a seal on his lips, but to open wide his eyes and ears.

The count's only son, Alphonsus, was now in his seventeenth year; his form was manly and well turned, his countenance rendered interesting and handsome by a pair of black eyes, and finely arched eyebrows, his cheeks were ruddy, his lips wore the smile of good-humour, and his short black hair hung curling round his neck; his intellects were strong, his genius discerning, and his mind well informed.

Nearly a year had elapsed since the arrival of Frederic in his native country, when an affair of consequence, relating to the will of his late father, called count Alphonsus to the metropolis of the German empire.

He visited his brother the day prior to his departure;—he bade a tender farewell to his wife and son—"My Anna is now in Frederic's power!" This idea a moment arrested his steps, as he was crossing the hall of the castle to the vehicle that awaited him:—"but is he not bound in honour to protect her?—he is!—and I will not suspect him."—He left the castle and proceeded on his journey, accompanied by an old and faithful servant.

Nearly two months had elapsed since the departure of count Alphonsus, ere the period for his return to the castle of Cohenburg was mentioned by him in his letters to his wife: he had written frequently to her, and every letter was replete with his anxiety again to behold her.

At length the time for his arrival was fixed; and the countess awaited it with every mark of ardent love; when, on the morning of the day which he had stated for his arrival, the servant who had accompanied him came to the castle alone; the anxious looks of the countess demanded a speedy explanation of his business,—"Was he the harbinger of the count?" she asked.

"Alas! no," he answered.

"Oh, he is dead! he is murdered!" she exclaimed, and sunk lifeless on the ground.

Her fears were too well founded; the old servant brought the sorrowing information, that two ruffians, who had burst from a thicket about ten leagues distant from Cohenburg castle, had fallen upon him and stabbed him to the heart.

Tears came to the relief of Alphonsus; and the first words his sorrow permitted him to articulate, were an order to a domestic to convey the sad intelligence to his uncle, and request his immediate presence at the castle.

When recollection again returned to the unhappy Anna, she waved her hand in signal to the surrounding domestics to depart; and, upon being left alone with her son, thus addressed him:

"Alphonsus, thy uncle is the murderer of thy father.—Swear to me thou wilt revenge his death."

Alphonsus looked steadfastly on his mother in silent wonder.

Anna continued: "Thou marvellest at my words,—thou canst not think the smooth-tongued Frederic so great a villain! but he is blacker than thy darkest thoughts can paint him!—Oh! I could tell thee"— —she paused.

"Explain thyself, my dearest mother," cried Alphonsus.

"No! I cannot—I will not let thee think so basely of thy father's brother,—time may come, that thou"—she paused a moment,— —"I cannot prove what I've alleged; therefore bury it in thy breast.—But swear to me, by heaven, whenever the murderer stands confessed, thou wilt revenge thy father's death."

"Oh, my mother! do you then think I would be careless in so great a point of duty?—No! let me but know him, and by all my hopes of heaven, my sword shall pierce his heart."

"Thou art my child indeed! good angels guard thee," cried

447

the countess, and embraced him. — "Oh thou dost not know count Frederic; but time will teach thee him."

In due time count Frederic arrived; his countenance bore the marks of assumed grief; — Alphonsus could ill brook his presence; — he saw his mother's conjecture confirmed; — his tongue laboured to accuse the count of his villainy; — his heart whispered him to await the proof of his guilt; — he bit his tongue in silence; — his sorrow burst into his eyes, and he rushed from the apartment inarticulately exclaiming, "Oh! my father!"

Towards the evening the count departed; the old servant who had brought the sorrowful intelligence was ordered instantly to return to the corpse, and get it conveyed to the castle with all convenient speed.

Count Frederic took upon himself to prepare for the obsequies of his brother.

After the departure of count Frederic, Alphonsus strongly solicited his mother to confide to him her cause for suspecting his uncle; "I must not — cannot, " — she replied: "time will develop and prove my words. Oh Alphonsus! remember what you have sworn."

"Sacredly I will maintain my vow."

On the next day, count Frederic again visited the castle of Cohenburg; Alphonsus shunned his presence, and retired on his arrival, to indulge his grief in solitude. After an interval of some time, thinking his uncle gone, he re-entered the apartment where he had left his mother: but what was his surprise, on his entrance, at seeing her kneeling before the count, and kissing his hand — she rose, and threw herself into a chair. — The count walked to the window: — "How does this conduct agree with the character my mother has given of the count," thought Alphonsus; — his mother perceived his eyes fixed on her; she wrung her hands, and lifted them in silent supplication to heaven.

In a short time Frederic departed.

"You have commanded me," said Alphonsus, after a pause, "not to ask an explanation of your suspicions" — he was proceeding, when the countess rose from her seat, and bursting into tears, left the apartment.

Alphonsus was stretched on the rack of doubt, suspicion,

and perplexity; he traversed the apartment, he threw himself on the ground, he rose again, he walked about the room, he entered the garden; he walked, he sat: it was in vain; the mind cannot fly from itself.

The countess excused herself from appearing at supper; — Alphonsus knew not that the cloth was spread before him, though he leaned the arm on which he rested his head on the table.

At an early hour he retired to his chamber; it was in vain that he attempted to rest; — he read the letters he had received from his father during his absence; his tears ran swiftly down upon them; — he could read no more, — he threw himself upon his bed; — his lamp decayed in the socket, and the obscurity of the scene seemed in unison with his feelings.

The ghostly hour of midnight had just sounded, and all the castle of Cohenburg was wrapped in sleep, save the forlorn Alphonsus; the balm of wounded nature refused to heal his sorrows. Stretched on his restless bed, he lay ruminating on the occurrences of the preceding day, when a piercing shriek caught his ear, and roused him from his meditations, — it seemed to proceed from the chamber of his mother; he listened — it was not repeated — "Again her grief exceeds the bounds of reason!" he cried, — "Oh wretched woman! Kind heaven sooth her sorrows!" He sighed, dropped a tear, and sunk upon his pillow.

After a short interval, he fell into a restless slumber; he had not long enjoyed this first repose, since his father's death, when he was awakened by the opening of his chamber-door; the dawn of day was beginning to break, and served to show Alphonsus, that it was his mother who had entered his apartment; — her mien alarmed him, — her eyes were wildly fixed, her countenance betrayed the most visible signs of an agonized heart; she was wrapped in a loose garment, and her hair hung dishevelled on her shoulders.

"Alphonsus!" she exclaimed, "observe thy mother's words, nor ask their explanation: — instantly fly this castle, nor approach it more, as you value life! — as you value heaven!"

Alphonsus had lain down on the bed without undressing, and now starting from it, — "Why this sudden alarm?" he cried; "is it that you fear my uncle will perpetrate a second deed, horrid as the first? — fear not for me; I shall live to fulfil my oath."

She shrieked, then said, "You have undone yourself and me—your uncle is innocent—one only way can save us both—fly far from hence—fly from me—fly from your uncle—take that purse,—return not to the castle—saddle the fleetest courser in the stables, and depart while yet the earliness of the morn favours your escape unseen—embrace me—Oh! no! no! no!—it would—" a flood of tears prevented for a while her farther utterance; she then added, "Go! and may the blessings I can never hope from heaven fall on thee." She gave him the purse;—the palm of her hand was stained with blood! Alphonsus looked that he saw it; speech was refused him;—the countess met his eye; again she shrieked, "Oh, fly and save me!—I conjure you, fly!"—she cried; and, with a look that seemed to draw blood from her heart, she ran from Alphonsus's chamber, and locked herself within her own.

Thunderstruck by what he had heard and seen, Alphonsus debated some moments how to act; at last he cried,—"Has my unhappy mother lost her reason?—Oh, no! her manner is that of deep sorrow, not of frenzy; she undoubtedly has some strong cause for her commands; but then why conceal it from me?—My uncle, too, declared innocent!—what can she mean?—it is my duty to obey." He left his chamber; as he passed hers, she opened the door, and said,—"Speed thee, my beloved Alphonsus!"—He stopped, but she hastily closed it again. He descended into the hall, unbarred the heavy gates, and proceeded to the stables; having saddled his favourite horse, he mounted, and with a full and sorrowing heart left the castle of Cohenburg.

"Fly me,—fly this castle, as you value life,—as you value heaven." These words he repeated again and again,—he dwelt on them, till conjecture lost itself in a maze of thought;—he proceeded forwards about five leagues without slackening his pace, before he inquired of himself whither he was going,—and he then hesitated how to answer himself. In this dilemma, he perceived a distant village rising above some clustered trees on the brow of an easy hill: thither he directed his steed; the villagers were just risen to their labour as he reached it,—they looked at him with an eye of inquisitiveness:—he perceived that they knew him not, but that idle curiosity had attracted their attention; having refreshed his steed, he again set forward,—he wished, with all possible speed, to leave that part of the country where he was likely to be recognised; he felt that he had no cause for wishing to secrete himself, but he felt also, that he should experience an unconquerable embarrassment, should he encounter any friend, who might ask him whither he was journeying, or make inquiries relative to his family.

Towards noon he had proceeded many leagues into the heart of the country; his strength and spirits were equally exhausted; he dismounted from his horse; and having fastened him to the trunk of a tree, whose branches shaded him from the scorching rays of the mid-day sun, he threw himself down by his side.

Reflection, which clears not the point meditated on, wears away the time sorrowfully, but swiftly:—thus Alphonsus rose not from his bed of grass till the sun was far advanced towards the west; after riding three more weary leagues, a mean inn, where he meant to pass the night, received him; he drank a cup of wine, and was refreshed,—it was the first nourishment, except some water which he had drunk at a brook from the hollow of his hand, that had that day passed his lips; he ate also, but sparingly, and that without relish. At an early hour he saw his steed safely bestowed, and betook himself to his chamber, though not to sleep.

CHAPTER II.

Canst thou not minister to a mind diseas'd,

Pluck from the memory a rooted sorrow,

Raze out the written troubles of the brain,

And, with some sweet oblivious antidote

Cleanse the stuff'd bosom of that perilous stuff,

That weighs upon the heart?

Macbeth

The night was spent by him, as the day had been passed, in vain lamentations and conjectures; towards morning he enjoyed a short slumber.

On waking, he turned his thoughts to find some means by which he might gain a reputable maintenance in life; the army appeared to him the most likely to afford him the asylum he wished, and he trusted to the change of dress and situation, for passing unnoticed in the world.

The German power was at that period engaged in a war against Poland, and he resolved to offer himself as a volunteer in one of the regiments which were then daily raising; for this purpose he determined immediately to proceed to Berlin; accordingly, having settled with the host of the miserable inn, he mounted his horse, and set forward.

His journey of the preceding day had been partly in an opposite angle to the high road leading to Berlin: he accordingly struck into a bye path, which was to conduct him to the high road.

With mournful thoughts he proceeded solitarily along, and gained the desired road about the middle of the day.

Two days served to complete his journey; on the evening of the second he entered the busy city of Berlin; he took up his abode for the night in a small inn, and on the following morning made inquiries for a purchaser for his steed; with this he had determined to part ere he entered into the service of his country, well aware that his pay would ill suffer him to support it.

He walked about the city, he admired the public edifices, he inquired who had been their founders and builders; and for the first two days, found a sufficient stock of amusement to divert his thoughts, in some measure, from the sad subject on which they were too forcibly bent; but as the novelty of the scene began to subside, reflection returned with redoubled perplexities and griefs;—sometimes he resolved to return to the castle:—"My uncle," he said, "my mother avows to be innocent, —why should I fear him?—but still, she conjures me not to see him:—some secret cause doubtless actuates her conduct,—why hide it from me?—Should she have leagued with him to murder my father!—have taken him to her bed, and driven me from the castle, that I might not be a witness of her shame!"—The thought went nigh to madden him. "She is not so base," he cried: "would she, had this been so, have supplicated the count on her knees?—it could not have been done to deceive me, for she expected not my entrance.—What cause could there have been for that mysterious conduct?—for her still more strange appearance on the morning she sent me from the castle?—for the blood that stained her hand?" Imagination could wander no farther:—"Some secret misery wrings her heart,—I cannot alleviate it, or she would call for my assistance,—and I will not aggravate her calamities by disobeying her commands." He prayed fervently for her happiness, and wafted up his prayers to heaven in a heart-felt sigh.

On the third day after his arrival in Berlin, his landlord found him a purchaser for his horse at a fair price; Alphonsus hesitated to strike the bargain; he had no friend left on earth; it had endeared his horse to him, and he felt a reluctance to part from the last remains of his late happy days. He debated in his mind:—what money he possessed would soon be gone, and then— —! He cast a glance at the road before him, the path was gloomy—"He is yours," he cried; "take him, but use him kindly." He rushed into the house, refusing again to behold his favourite steed. The most needful article was then the last in his thoughts, —he recollected not the money, till the landlord awakened him from his reverie by pouring it from his hand upon the table.

His first step was now to offer himself for service; he received the bounty bestowed on a volunteer, and taking the military habit, found it made an alteration in his person which he little expected.

He felt an inexplicable unwillingness to lead to any discourse which might give him information of the general opinion of the world, if any tale relative to his family was current in it, — but of this he was ignorant; he resolved to drive the subject from his thoughts; it only became the more constant attendant on his solitary moments.

He had been about three months in the service of the empire, when the regiment in which he served, was ordered to march to a village about four leagues east of Berlin, till they should be called into action, for which they were commanded to hold themselves in readiness at a short notice.

In the course of another month they were called to the field; Alphonsus was strong, active, and possessed of much natural courage; he acquitted himself in the toils of war with the most becoming spirit and fortitude, insomuch that he gained the favour of his commanding officer, and was by him promoted in the regiment.

The name of the commander was Arieno; the Italian name struck Alphonsus; he was serving in the German army, beloved by his soldiers, had risen to his present rank by the favour of the emperor, fought with peculiar bravery in the German cause, and yet he was palpably an Italian.

Arieno became more and more attached to Alphonsus: he showed him his favour on every occasion. Alphonsus even began to be apprehensive that he was discovered: — but he was deceived.

When the army retired into winter quarters, Arieno invited Alphonsus to pass the winter with him; Alphonsus accepted the offer with gratitude, and retired with Arieno in the quality, as he supposed, of an attendant.

His imagination was pleasurably deceived; Arieno was himself the child of sorrow; — he had perceived by the dejected air, hesitating speech, and pensive mien of Alphonsus, that he was a prey to grief equally with himself: sympathy inclined him to regard the young count, — and the engaging mien of Alphonsus, though his brow was clouded with sorrow, had won Arieno's heart; and he resolved to make him his friend and companion.

The habitation of Arieno was a small retired mansion on the skirts of a village about three leagues east of Frankfort; an old woman, to whom the care of the house had been entrusted during the summer, was the only one of whom the family consisted in addition to the two friends.

Arieno was a man whose person, on first acquaintance, was little prepossessing; but as the virtues of his heart, which was the seat of every good quality, shone forth, he rapidly gained the love and esteem of those who had any knowledge of him: his conversation instructed whilst it pleased the hearer, and Alphonsus hung with delight on his accents, as he spoke of the vicissitudes of life, the fallacy of this world, and the stability of hopes placed in a future state.

Many days passed, ere Arieno touched on the string which tingled to the heart of Alphonsus; he then thus addressed him, —"I think my young friend, there is something in your manner, together with your knowledge of many abstruse subjects, that bespeaks your real rank in life to be far above that in which I first knew you."

Alphonsus was silent; but his reddening countenance betrayed to Arieno the truth of his observations, who thus went on:—"Some secret sorrow preys upon your heart; impart to me your cause of grief; I may have the ability to alleviate your sorrows; if not, I will sooth them."

Alphonsus was still silent.

"Do you not know me sufficiently," Arieno continued, "to be well assured, that the interest I take in your happiness, and not the gratification of an idle curiosity, renders me thus inquisitive?"

"Oh, my friend!" cried Alphonsus, taking Arieno's hand, "I owe you more than my gratitude can ever repay:—you are worthy to be trusted with my inmost concerns; but I would rather forego the comforts which I enjoy from your kindness and conversation, than impart to you the secrets of my heart;—indeed, indeed, they must lie buried in my breast."

"Far be it from me to distress you," returned Arieno; "fear not a repetition of these words from me."

A long silence ensued.

"You are an Italian," said Alphonsus, breaking silence.

"You are right," said Arieno; "and marvel, I doubt not, at my serving under the emperor of these dominions."

"I must confess, it has often excited my wonder."

"You shall conjecture no longer; my story is short, and I will tell it to you."

"I have no right to expect such a communication from you."

"I doubt not but you have good reasons for your secrecy; I wish my story to be known to the world."

Alphonsus bowed, and Arieno thus began.

"My father, count Arieno, was one of the richest noblemen in the state of Venice; his mansion, which was situated nearly a league distant from Venice, was magnificent in the extreme; his gardens were extensive and beautiful, and his gondolas rivalled in elegance any before seen. At an early age he espoused the daughter of a rich senator of Genoa, whom he had accidentally seen at the carnival: she was an only child; and at her father's death, which happened three months after her marriage with my father, she inherited his entire property.

"In the course of six years she brought my father four children, three sons and a daughter; my sister was the first born, I was the second son, my brother Stefano was the eldest. At an early age my youngest brother died; at the period from which I date my story, my brother Stefano was in his nineteenth and I in my eighteenth year. Stefano was in his temper haughty, proud, subtle, and very avaricious; his person was well calculated to hide the deformities of his mind; he was the darling of his mother, whom he much resembled in disposition; and she had entire dominion over her husband.

"In addition to this, when I tell you that from my childhood my brother showed his dislike of me by every means in his power, I have, I think, said enough to convince you, that my life was far from being enviable.

"Not far distant from the mansion of my father, resided a widow lady, Signora Bartini, with her two daughters; their fortunes were small, indeed barely sufficient to support them with any degree of credit; but they possessed a treasure, superior to riches, in their beauty and virtue; the eldest captivated a French chevalier; he married her, and she departed with him into France.

"The youngest, Camilla by name, had given me a wound which it was not in the power of art to heal. Convinced, however, that the inferiority of her condition in life to my own, would prove an unconquerable obstacle to my espousing her in the eyes of my family, I resolved to bury my passion in my own heart;—into my eyes it would, however, sometimes force its way, I even thought Camilla perceived it, and blushed congenial feelings. It was one evening, towards the end of summer, that, as I entered the small garden leading to the house of Signora Bartini (for I sometimes ventured to call, and enjoy the conversation of Camilla), my brother came from the house; as he passed me, he exclaimed, 'My visit is just ended in proper time, I perceive;' and passed on laughing.

"I had been so much accustomed to taunts of this kind from my brother, that I heeded but little what he said, and entered the house: I found Camilla weeping by the window, and her mother standing by her.

"Suspicion, of I know not what, immediately flashed upon my mind in the form of my brother; I tenderly inquired what had disturbed her; her mother gave some trivial and unsatisfactory reason for her tears, and immediately turned the conversation to another subject.

"I could not conceal the emotions of my heart, and in a short time took my leave.

"My father, mother, and brother, were just assembled at supper as I joined them.

"'I knew not whether we were to expect the pleasure of your company this evening,' said my mother.

"'Why, madam?'

"'Nay, perhaps you were not invited with Signora Bartini, and lovers must not be too forward.' She laughed loudly, and my brother did the same.

"I bit my lips with rage, then said, 'I could conceive no impropriety in visiting where my elder brother showed me the example.'

"They were at a loss for an answer, and again laughed.

"My father looked sternly at me, and said, 'You had best beware how you marry contrary to my inclinations;—remember that Camilla Bartini is the last woman I should choose for your wife.'

"I knew my combat was unequal, and remained silent.

"I now found myself more disagreeably situated than ever under my father's roof, and accordingly determined to travel; I asked his permission; he readily granted it, and likewise advanced me a handsome sum of money. His easy consent distressed me, though I wished to obtain it; affection seemed to have no part in so hasty a compliance.

"I went to Camilla's house: but what was my surprise to find that she had left it; she was gone on a visit to her sister in France. — There seemed something mysterious in her conduct; I could not summon resolution to ask signora Bartini to explain it to me. I took my leave of her; and the next morning I departed from my father's mansion.

"Ten months elapsed, and I heard not from any one of my father's family: I wrote to my mother, to inquire the cause of this long silence, instructing her to direct for me in Sicily. In about six weeks after, I received from her a few lines, informing me that my father had paid the debt of nature, and requesting my immediate presence.

"I lost no time in reaching Venice, and arrived at my late father's mansion, on the day of his funeral: the will was then opened; but conceive, if you can, my astonishment, when the following paragraph was read: 'To my second son Philip, in consequence of his disobedience to my commands, I bequeath only five hundred zechins, that he may know I have not forgotten him, but wilfully cut him off from all other share of my property.'

"It was a bolt of ice shot at my heart — it benumbed my vitals. Muttering curses on the villain who had belied me to my father, I left the mansion, darting a look at my brother, which I gloried in perceiving that he felt.

"I flew to the house of Signora Bartini: a female servant was standing by the door; she informed me that her mistress was gone to her daughter's in France.

"'Where does she reside?'

"'At Montpelier.'

"'What is the Chevalier's name, who married her daughter?'

"'The Chevalier D'Albert.'

"I will not trouble you with my reflections during the time

that I was journeying to Montpelier: suffice it to say, that my suspicions were irrevocably fixed on my brother, as the villain who had taken from me the esteem of my father.

"Arrived at Montpelier, Madame D'Albert received me at the house of her husband.

"'You will wonder to see me, Madam,' I exclaimed; 'but' — —

"At this moment Signora Bartini entered the apartment: I saluted her; she made a sign to her daughter to leave us; I sat down by her; I hesitated how to address her. — What I had studied to say during my journey, had now fled from my thoughts, and I could only inquire for Camilla.

"'Ah! Signor,' she cried, 'my child will soon, I hope, be well; the hand of death is heavy on her.'

"Till that moment, I knew not what misery was — my other sufferings had been light.

"I fell from the chair on which I was seated — a dead coldness seized me; and it was with difficulty that Signora Bartini restored me to life.

"When she perceived my senses were returned, she cried, 'Did you then really love my poor girl, Signor?'

"'Love her! oh God, grant me words to prove how tenderly I loved her!'

"'She loved you, but was taught to believe you wedded to another.'

"This was an additional wound to my already lacerated heart.

"She then proceeded to inform me, that, on the evening that I had met my brother coming from her house, and found her daughter weeping, he had been making the basest proposals to my Camilla, and that, fearing her refusal should incense his haughty spirit to any unwarrantable act of revenge, she had removed Camilla to her sister's in France: that Camilla, having heard that I had left Venice, had supposed that I had forgotten her, and given up herself to melancholy; and that, about two months before my arrival at Montpelier, she had received a letter, as from me, informing her that I was married. 'This,' said Signora Bartini, 'has driven her to despair; her faculties are impaired; and we hourly await her death, as the greatest blessing heaven can bestow on her.'

"The letter was shown me:—it was the hand-writing of my villainous brother.

"I informed her of the contents of my father's will, relating to me; I showed her how I conceived myself to have been doubly injured by my brother: she sympathised in my fate, and I in hers; our sorrow flowed from the same source.

"In the course of that day, my beloved Camilla breathed her last. How shall I relate my anguish on receiving the bitter intelligence? you, my friend, must conjecture what I have not words to describe.

"On the following morning, I was permitted to visit her corpse: oh, how altered was her once beautiful countenance! Oh, my God, what did I undergo during the moments I gazed upon her cold form! In an ecstasy of sorrow, I kissed her icy lips.—The scene was too much—it overpowered me;—I was dragged from her, I know not by what means, never again to behold the innocent and unhappy victim of falsehood, my loved Camilla!

"When her funeral obsequies were performed, I returned to Venice; a short time developed to me the perfidy of my brother; I learnt that he had gained the credit of my father to my marriage with Camilla, by showing him a forged certificate of our having been united in a parish church at Montpelier:—how did my heart pant for revenge!—cooler reflection taught me not to spill a brother's blood.—I disdained, however, to ask of him the small legacy portioned out to me by my father, and resolved for ever to leave the Venetian dominions; and having passed over into Germany, I offered myself a volunteer in the service of the emperor.—I have served under him about thirty-two years, and his goodness has raised me to the rank I now hold.—My brother possesses riches; but I enjoy a treasure whose blessings he will never know—an approving conscience."

Alphonsus thanked him for his recital, sympathised with him in his sufferings, and inquired if he had ever heard any tidings of his brother since the period of his leaving Venice.

"By accident I heard, about fourteen years ago, that he had married a woman of fortune immediately on his father's death; that my mother had not long survived her husband, and that his wife died in child-birth of her first infant, which was a female; I heard it by means of an officer who had visited Venice, and mentioned that the discourse of the city, whilst he was there, had turned solely upon the disappearance of the only daughter of one count Arieno. 'He is an avaricious fellow,' said he, 'and was bent on espousing his daughter to a noble as rich as himself, while the poor girl had fallen in love with a German count, whom she had seen at the carnival. Her father forced her to marry the noble; and a short time after she was missed, and no inquiries could discover whither she had fled.'—The name of her lover, I think the officer said, was count Cohenburg, a descendant of a noble family of Saxony:—thus providence punished his avarice by depriving him of his only child."

Alphonsus changed colour at the mention of his name; but Arieno perceived it not; and Alphonsus ventured to inquire, what was conjectured to have been the young lady's fate.

Arieno answered, that she was supposed to have fled with her lover, and eluded the diligence of her father's and husband's search.

Alphonsus's brain was now on the rack to decide on some part of his father's or uncle's conduct, that might tally with this account; his father had never been a sufficient time together absent from his castle to have formed any engagement of the kind; indeed, had opportunity been ever so favourable, he had always loved his mother too tenderly to wrong her in the regard she bore him;—his uncle, he recollected, had been much absent from Saxony about the time mentioned by Arieno; but he had several times at intervals returned to his mansion; and no one had accompanied him;—there were no others of their name in Germany;—he was convinced it was not his father—thus suspicion rested on his uncle;—his next thought was, whether what he had now heard could by any means be made to account for the death of his father, and the conduct of his mother, or in any way be supposed to be connected with either.—Here thought again lost itself in a maze of uncertain conjecture.

CHAPTER III.

Oh, day and night, but this is wond'rous strange!

Hamlet

Before the time of taking the field arrived, Arieno received information from the emperor, that his regiment was to be mounted for the ensuing campaign. Alphonsus wished for his faithful steed: but it was beyond his reach.

In the spring, Alphonsus and his Italian friend set out from the hospitable mansion of the latter; Arieno thanked Alphonsus for the pleasure his society had afforded him, and gave him a warm invitation to renew his visit the following winter.

About the middle of the summer, Arieno lost his life in an engagement on the borders of the empire; the receipt of this intelligence went nigh to cost Alphonsus his life. On the very same day, a fall from his horse had fractured his sword-arm; and he heard not of the tidings of his friend's death, till stretched himself on the bed of sickness.

It was near the end of the campaign, ere Alphonsus recovered from his wound; and in a very short time after the re-establishment of his health, a decisive victory was obtained by the Germans over the Poles. This put an end to a long and vigorously fought war: most of the newly-raised regiments were disbanded, and every incapable soldier also received his discharge. The weakness which still remained in Alphonsus's arm, made him unwilling to sue for his continuance in the army; and he accordingly determined to seek some other means of subsistence, attended with less danger to his already fractured limb.

After much deliberation, he resolved to sue for employment in the least laborious line, which the then lately-discovered silver mine in Bohemia afforded. His regiment had been disbanded at Prague, and thus he had not far to travel, for the purpose of putting his plan into execution. He was readily hired by the contractor for working the mine, and his labour fell short of what he had pictured to himself it would prove; he had felt much bodily weakness, proceeding from what he had suffered when he undertook the employment; and, conscious of his own inability, he had exaggerated in idea the labour of the task he had undertaken.

His fellow-labourers worked hard, and earned their pittance with the sweat of their brow; but it was the more sweetly relished by them at their moments of recreation.

They laughed, they sang, they told tales for each other's diversion; they related anecdotes that had fallen within their knowledge; and thus cheerfulness presided in the midst of labour.

They delighted much to hear Alphonsus recount the course of the battles in which he had fought: some amongst them had served, and to them his narrations were peculiarly interesting; and they ever and anon interrupted him to relate some similar circumstances which had occurred during the campaigns in which they had served.

Alphonsus had belonged to the mines nearly a year, when no new workmen having joined them, and their conversation thus beginning to grow insipid, and anecdotes, from often recounting, becoming stale, they resolved that at evening, when their tasks were ended, each miner should in his turn relate the events of his life.

Alphonsus was amongst the first to whom the lot fell to relate their adventures; he easily fabricated a short and simple tale, which served his purpose, and gained neither the approbation nor the contempt of his hearers: he joyed when the task was ended.

A few days after, the lot fell upon a youth, whose mirth had often drawn forth the loud laughs of his companions. — "Few words will tell my tale," he said, and thus began:

"My father and mother, good souls, rented a farm of count Cohenburg, in Lower Saxony, near the river Elbe."

Alphonsus was all attention.

"Oh, had he lived yet, I should not have been here! but I might have been much worse off: and so I thank the saints that I am here; and may I never fare worse, pray I. — Well, though my father did not come of a great family, a great family came of him; for, boys and girls, he had fifteen of us." — Here a loud laugh applauded the young miner's wit. — He continued — "Well, as I said before, my father rented a farm of count Cohenburg; he

463

was very good to the poor, and promised my father he would do something for all his children;—God rest his soul in heaven!—Let me see, I have now worked in these mines two years and a half; it was about eight months before that time, that the count went out to some foreign part, for aught I know; or it might be only to see our emperor; I can't tell, however, about some such thing"—

The suspense of Alphonsus for the conclusion of this tale, may be easily conceived.

"So, on the day he was expected home, news was brought to his castle by old Robert, who went with him, that his horse had thrown him, and killed him, on his way home; and so Robert went back with orders to have the count buried where he died.—Well, now comes the most extraordinary part of my story; the good dead count had a son about seventeen or eighteen years of age, a fine comely handsome youth, not much unlike me,—only he never worked in a mine."

Again the miners laughed, and Alphonsus heaved an inward sigh.

"Well, two days after, he was missing, and so was the countess; neither of them to be found, high nor low: now the folks say, the good lady killed her son in a mad fit, for the loss of her husband; and was so vexed at what she had done, when she came to herself, that she killed herself too—and directly after, a ghost began to walk; and every night at twelve o'clock, it tolls the great bell in the south turret, because that is the time she killed the young count."

"Well, and did you ever see it?" cried one of the miners.

"Oh no! no body has gone near the castle since; it belonged by right to the count's brother; and he came to it; but he stayed only a day or two; for he saw and heard such things, that he could not bear his own life; and so he discharged all the servants, and locked up the castle gates; and away he went, some folks say, out of the country, and left the ghost to ring away by itself; and I fancy it is pretty safe, for having all the supper the castle walls can give it to itself, for no company will trouble it, I am sure.—Well, so, for want of the count's help, my father went down in the world; and so we most of us left him, to seek our own fortunes; and here am I, a jolly miner:—and though ours is a low calling under ground, I fancy it will bear looking into as well as many great men's upon the surface of the earth."

Here the youth ended his history;—a murmur of applause ran through the assembly, and they parted for the night.

Alphonsus slept not; he had now fresh food for unconfirmed conjecture.—A subject which he had not heard mentioned during two years' intercourse with the busy world, he had at length heard discussed in a mine; this led him to conjecture the story was not in current report.—"The castle deserted!—yet a bell tolled at midnight!"—In spirits he had no faith; and what could it avail any human being to live there, retired from the world? nor did he think it possible they could remain there undiscovered.—That his mother was dead, he did not in the least credit; the youth had said the same of him.—He ruminated again and again on what he had heard, but his meditations ended where they had begun.

Some time elapsed ere Alphonsus ventured to question the youth relative to what he had related of his family; and the only additional intelligence he could gain, was that some people suspected count Frederic to be the murderer of his brother, the countess and her son, for the sake of possessing the castle, which descended by the death of count Alphonsus to his son; —"But then, if this was the case," cried the youth, "what could make him run away, and leave the whole?"

"Conscience!" thought Alphonsus.—But his mother had declared his uncle innocent; and he was determined not to suspect him whom she had exculpated.

It was one day shortly after this time, that a gentleman travelling through Bohemia, came, attracted by curiosity, to visit the mine; Alphonsus and another miner were deputed to conduct him; the gentleman's servant accompanied him: in passing a deep cavity of the mine, over which a narrow plank was laid, the servant's eyes not being directed to the unsteady board over which he was passing, one of his feet slipped, and, unable to recover his balance, he sunk into the space below. The fall was, to any one, inevitable death:—he was dashed to pieces.

The gentleman, whose name was baron Kardsfelt, was much affected by the misfortune that had befallen his servant; he had lived with him many years, and had proved himself a faithful attendant.

The baron immediately returned to the surface of the earth, where the first objects that struck his sight, were his own and his servant's horses, fastened to a post at a short distance from the mouth of the mine: a difficulty immediately arose in his

465

mind, how to get the animal he did not ride himself conveyed to the next town; he accordingly offered Alphonsus a liberal perquisite to ride it thither for him; Alphonsus willingly agreed to his proposal, and they mounted, and rode on.

Alphonsus had for some time considered his situation in the mine as a disagreeable one; he had entered into it from the same motive from which he had so long continued in it, — urgent necessity: he knew no other mode of procuring a subsistence, in which he could pass unknown; and yet he earnestly wished again to mix in the world, in the hope of gaining some light on the mystery which continually occupied his mind; accordingly he determined to offer himself to supply the place of the man whose death he had just witnessed.

The baron asked him many questions as to his abilities for filling the office he wished to undertake, and Alphonsus declared himself capable of every particular: what he had been accustomed formerly to have done for himself, he thought it no difficult matter to perform for another. There was something in his manner of application that interested the baron in his favour; he accepted the offer made to him by Alphonsus, and wrote a few lines to the superintendent of the mine, saying, that he should retain Alphonsus in his service.

The baron Kardsfelt was a man about thirty years of age, and unmarried; his manners were pleasant and his temper mild, unless he conceived himself to be ill-treated or affronted; and then his resentment knew no bounds.

He had at this time been on a visit to his sister, who was married and resided at Prague, and was returning to his own mansion at a short distance from Inspruck, when the accident took place which introduced Alphonsus to his knowledge. — Returned home, Alphonsus was made acquainted with the duties of his station, and executed them much to the satisfaction of his master, who behaved towards him with great kindness.

Alphonsus frequently visited Inspruck, and never missed an opportunity of starting some subject which he hoped might lead to the mention of his family, but he never heard the name. He was often a listener to the tales of spirits and witches, to which the common people in that part of the country give much credit; but the castle of Cohenburg was never spoken of; and he now began to distrust there being any foundation, except the imagination of some weak mind, for the tale the young miner had related.

The baron was fond of play, though he never staked large sums, and passed much of his time at the gaming-table. Having one day engaged a stranger in a game at draughts, his antagonist was accidentally called from the room in the midst of the game. The stranger had been much beaten by the baron: he was chafed by his losses, and, on his return to the room, asserted that the baron had re-drawn his last move. The baron's fiery temper was heated; he rose, drew his sword, and called on his antagonist to defend his assertion: — it proved to the baron a fatal summons, for he received his adversary's weapon in his side.

He was immediately conveyed home, fainting with loss of blood, and the wound pronounced to be mortal: speech was refused him; he beckoned Alphonsus to his bed-side, and gave him his purse; Alphonsus received it, kissed his hand, and retired weeping. The baron pulled the sleeve of his confessor who stood by him, and pointed to Alphonsus; the friar understood that he asked his protection for him, and answered by a significant inclination of the head: about an hour after the baron expired in great agonies.

Alphonsus gazed at him as he closed his eyes for ever.

It was a lesson to the gamester to play no more.

CHAPTER IV.

Ah me! for aught that ever I could read,

Could ever hear by tale or history,

The course of true love never did run smooth;

But either it was different in blood,

Or else misgrafted in respect of years;

Or else it stood upon the choice of friends;

Or if there were a sympathy in choice,

War, death, or sickness did lay siege to it,

Making it momentary as a sound,

Swift as a shadow, short as any dream:

Brief as the lightning in the collied night,

That in a spleen unfolds both heaven and earth;

And, ere a man hath pow'r to say — "Behold!"

The jaws of darkness do devour it up:

So quick, bright things come to confusion.

A Midsummer's Night Dream

When the friar had given the necessary orders, and made the proper arrangements for the funeral of the baron, he thus addressed Alphonsus, — "Young man, you seem greatly interested in the fate of the baron."

Alphonsus wept bitterly. Every added pang of sorrow deeply lacerates a grief-worn heart. "I have lost my only friend!" he cried.

"Do not despair," returned the friar: "the deceased baron has recommended you to my notice: — I will find some means of providing for your future life, be assured."

These words were balm to the wounded breast of Alphonsus.

"farewell," continued the holy man: "place your confidence in the will of heaven to repair your loss, and be comforted; I will be here again to-morrow." —So saying he departed.

On the following day Alphonsus found himself more composed, and at the appointed hour father Matthias arrived.

"Good-morrow to thee, youth."

"The same to thee, good father."

"You have been much in my thoughts since we last parted. To every one the promise made to a dying man should be sacred, particularly to those of our order. I promised the late baron that I would see you provided for,—I have been revolving my mind the means, and I think I have found them: I myself act as a confessor to the convent of Saint Helena, about a league from hence; their sacristan has been dead about a fortnight, and they have not replaced him:—should you like to become his successor?"

Alphonsus readily accepted the offer; and having heaved a farewell sigh over the body of his rash master, the friar undertook to conduct him that evening to the convent, and at the appointed time they set out together.

The convent of Saint Helena was a large and ancient edifice; its ivy-grown towers indicated its antiquity, and the figures carved on its walls bespoke the superstition they enclosed.

The friar opened a small door near the chapel, of which he usually carried the key, and admitted Alphonsus into an enclosed cloister, which led immediately to his apartments; thence a door opened into the hall of the convent: it was spacious,—at the angles were passages leading to the cells of the nuns; and in front, a wide stair-case conducting to the upper range of cells. The apartment in which the lady abbess usually sat, opened into the hall; the friar entered it, and bade Alphonsus follow him: the abbess was alone; father Matthias informed her who the youth was, and she received him graciously. Some conversation then passed between her and the friar in low voices, after which she spoke to Alphonsus, telling him, that, as he was unacquainted with the duties of his office, the porteress should accompany and instruct him in them for the first three or four days and nights; she then, after some farther conversation on the same subject, and exhorting him to be peculiarly diligent in his office, rang her bell; and the porteress attending her summons, she was told that Alphonsus came to succeed the late sacristan, was ordered to show him his apartment, and to give him the necessary instructions. Alphonsus followed her out of the room.

The porteress was about fifty years of age; she was deformed, of a tart humour, and an incessant prattler. "Come, follow me," said she, as soon as the door was closed: "I'll show you your room in a minute; and a good comfortable one it is.—Oh! bow to the cross, young man, bow to the cross." Alphonsus looked up, and perceived one fastened over the arch under which they were passing; he obeyed Perilla's commands, and she continued, "Aye, you'll learn all our ways in time,—you'll have a fine, easy, happy life of it, I'll assure you:—let me see,— vespers are just over; at eight you must ring the bell, and prepare the chapel for prayers before going to bed; then again at twelve, for the midnight prayers; then at six, for matins; and at ten, for mass; and at four, for vespers; and that's all you have to do, except helping me to sweep the chapel, and keeping clean the ornaments; and all the rest of your time is your own."

They had by this time arrived at the apartment appropriated to the use of the sacristan. "There," cried she, throwing open the door, you'll live like a prince; father Matthias's rooms are on that side of you, and there is mine;"—pointing to the other side; —"and this," opening a door facing them, "is your way into the chapel; and you must take care that those tapers on the altar never go out; and when they are nearly done, come to me for some more; and now I think I have told you all, so you may come and sit with me till evening prayers if you like it." She proceeded, and he followed her into her apartment.

Perilla had yet a little taste for the world, though she had been thirty years removed from it, and now expected to hear much news of it, from her new acquaintance; but Alphonsus was the worst subject she could have met with for gratifying her wishes: she thought it might proceed from reserve and modesty, as being with a stranger, and immediately began to set him the example of communication, by relating to him various anecdotes of the nuns; at last, interrupting herself,—"There," said she, "the sand is just out, go, and ring the chapel bell.—Oh, here! but stay, stay, put on your surplice,—it is rather too tight about the neck, but we'll get you a new one;—come."

She proceeded into the chapel, and Alphonsus, according to her directions, tolled a certain number of strokes on the bell. "Now follow me," she again cried, and Alphonsus obeyed:— they crossed the chapel. "Here at this door the nuns come in; now you must take that basin of holy water, and hold it for them to dip their fingers into, to cross their foreheads, and keep them from the influence of the devil while they are at prayers. I'll light the candles at the altar for you, but you must do all yourself another time."

The nuns entered one by one, and throwing up their veils as they approached the hallowed ground, dipped each a finger in the vase which Alphonsus held. As soon as the nuns were all come in, the porteress beckoned Alphonsus to follow her once more; they passed behind the altar, and she instructed him, that he must now assist father Matthias in putting on his sacerdotal robes. Prayers were then chanted by the friar: the nuns joined him, and having sung an evening hymn, received his benediction, and retired to their cells.

Alphonsus then, according to the directions of the porteress, put out all candles, save the two never-to-be extinguished lights; and having locked the chapel doors, again accompanied Perilla to her apartment, where they supped. In a short time, "Come," said she, "father Matthias is in bed: you must go too." So saying, she gave him a lamp, and attended him to his chamber door, saying, "Good night, remember to wake at twelve."

Alphonsus slept not; he feared being found negligent in his office on the first trial, and only threw himself on the bed. Perilla's loud suspiration, however, soon convinced him that she had done otherwise; nevertheless at a few minutes before twelve she awoke, came to his chamber door, and warned him it was time to ring the bell.

The same ceremonies were repeated as before, and Alphonsus on their conclusion ventured to enter his bed; reflection, and the novelty of his situation, however, suffered him not to sleep soundly,—and when he heard Perilla again moving about, he arose and met her at the chamber door. Matins were chanted, and the nuns departed as before. "Now," said Perilla, "we must not go to bed any more; it is our duty to sweep the chapel." She then showed him what was required of him to perform, and afterwards set about her own employments.

Alphonsus was as much pleased with his situation as any line of life could, in his present state of mind, have rendered him; it afforded him shelter from a pitiless world, and he was satisfied. Custom quickly reconciled him to the hours of rising; and he even, in a short time, found little need to consult the hour-glass with which Perilla had provided him. The abbess was pleased with his conduct. Father Matthias paid him much attention; he discovered his mind to be informed above his rank in life: he hinted his suspicions to Alphonsus, who confessed their truth, but instantly declared the silence he wished to maintain. The holy father commiserated his lot; he supplied him with books to sooth his leisure hours, and, when his avocation permitted it, gave him his own society.

In the convent of Saint Helena were twenty-six nuns and ten novices; amongst the latter there was one named Lauretta, whose beautifully pensive countenance never failed to arrest the eyes of Alphonsus, as he held the vase of consecrated water. Had he known what love was, he would have felt that she had inspired him with the soft passion: her appearance gladdened his heart, and her departure from the chapel made him only wish for the hour of her return.

About six months after Alphonsus had become an inmate of the convent, as he was one day conversing familiarly with father Matthias, he ventured to inquire of him, who the young novice was that had so forcibly attracted his regard. "Ah! poor child!" said the holy man, "the lady abbess and myself are alone entrusted with the history of her birth; but as I think, from many instances of your conduct that have fallen under my eye, I may venture to trust you with her story, you shall hear it."

Alphonsus bowed acknowledgment for the compliment paid him by the holy man, who thus began:—

"It is now full seventeen years, since, one wet and stormy evening towards the end of December, a faint knock, twice repeated in a short space of time, called the porteress to the grate of the convent; a soft voice entreated shelter from the storm, and mentioned the name of our lady abbess: the porteress opened the gate; and a slender figure, a youth as she imagined, clad in the habit of a pilgrim, entered, leaning on a staff; the porteress closed the gate, and having conducted the supposed youth into the apartment of the abbess, the stranger had scarcely uttered, 'Oh! protect a suffering woman!' ere she sunk at the feet of the lady abbess.

"Exhausted by fatigue, and benumbed by the keenness of the element, the stranger was with difficulty recovered from the fainting fit into which she had fallen: after some time she drank a cup of balsamic cordial, administered to her by the abbess; and a flood of tears proceeding from the joy she felt, on the assurance given her of experiencing that asylum for which she supplicated, eased her full heart. After eating sparingly of the meal that had been set before her, she begged leave to retire to rest, unable to explain that night the mystery which accompanied her arrival in a male habit.

"On the following day she was much recovered from her fatigue, and her entreaties were earnestly made to the abbess not to deliver her up to any one who might demand her.

"The abbess promised her the full protection of the church and perceiving that she was still weak and ill, forbore to put to her any inquiries.

"In a few days she was much mended; but a deep melancholy, at times approaching to frenzy, clouded her mind; voluntarily, however, she communicated to the lady abbess and myself her afflictions; she afterwards (for she delighted to dwell on her sorrows) wrote down her little history, and presented me with it: there it is, I trust to your discretion not to reveal it out of the convent; peruse it whilst I go and pray by the sick sister, Velina."

Alphonsus promised strict secrecy, and receiving the manuscript from the hand of the friar, retired with it to his own apartment.

Lauretta's Story.

"My name is Lauretta. I am the only daughter of count Arieno, resident near Venice; my mother died on the same day on which I was born; I had a fortune equal to my birth, and many were the suitors for my hand, more of whom I believe were swayed by interest than by any attachment to my person: at length, chance threw in my way count Frederic Cohenburg, a noble Saxon by birth, whom, were I to describe him to you as my burning fancy now paints him to my eyes, you would conceive to have surpassed his sex beyond the limits nature has prescribed; suffice it to say, I thought him all perfection.

"At first, I vainly imagined that the deference I paid him, proceeded only from my consciousness of his merit; and so far from being singular in my attentions to him, I should have been an exception to the females with whom I associated, not to have treated him as I did. But alas! I soon found that my regard proceeded from a softer motive, and I quickly perceived that I adored what others but approved.

"The infancy of love is too sweet to be easily shaken off: — at that delightful period, how little are we aware of the many anxious moments its maturity brings upon us! — fatal enchantment! how severe a scourge hast thou proved to me through life!

"A mutual affection glowed in our congenial breasts; I listened to his vows with rapture, and he heard my promises of constancy with equal delight.

"But an obstacle, to which the eyes of lovers are seldom open, had planted a hedge of thorns across the path which I vainly imagined was conducting me to the summit of earthly happiness.

"The only wealth which true love looks for, is an ardent return of affection: in that no one was more rich than my Frederic; — my father, who weighed merit only by wealth, had destined me for the wife of count Byroff, a nobleman of immense property, at that time on his travels; and he commanded me to check a passion grown too incorporate with my blood to hope a cure; nor did I endeavour to effect it; I would sooner have given up life, than to have lived and ceased to love my Frederic. His visits were now interdicted, on pain of my being immediately sent to a convent, if he was again seen with me. — How feelingly did I then taste that the bitters of love are more poignant than its sweets! Still had I not resolution to shake off my cause of sorrow. — If the idea for a moment entered my harassed brain, it was outweighed by the consideration that the uncertain wheel of fortune might one day turn in my favour, and give me to enjoy my Frederic's love without alloy.

"At length I contrived by stealth to meet him in the garden of my father's sister: — how did the sight of him rekindle the smothered flame! — I again vowed fidelity to him, and imprecated heavy curses on myself, if ever I swerved from the oath I had taken to be his only, and for ever.

"Not long after this, I was one day sitting alone in my chamber, ruminating on my hard fate, and bedewing with my tears a letter I had privately received from count Frederic, replete with vows, which, though often repeated, were still new and dear to me, when my father entered the apartment, and informed me that count Byroff was returned to Venice. — How shall I describe to you the pangs that at that moment rent my heart? — how relate to you the tide of grief which burst its way through my swollen eyes? — But I will leave it to be pictured in your susceptible breast.

"Had not the fullness of my heart sealed my lips, the too certain knowledge of my sentence having proceeded from a mouth whence there was no appeal, would have prevented my giving utterance to ineffectual remonstrances.

"In the evening of that day, my destined spouse waited on my father;—I was summoned to appear;—he rose and took my hand as I entered the apartment; I cast my eyes upon the ground; I could not bear to encounter those of a man whom I considered as the bane of my future peace.—I must, however, in justice to him, say, that, save only one, I never knew a man better calculated to make a woman happy; his address was easy and elegant; his manners conciliating; his person handsome, and his mind well stored with polite and useful learning. He was a man that, had he been my brother, I could have revered him; as it was, in spite of me, I respected him; but with how widely different a passion did he wish to inspire me! and in how mild, how gentle terms did he complain of that coldness with which I treated him! So far did his noble spirit win upon me, that many times I formed the determination of disclosing to him the fatal secret of my heart, and entreating his pity.—Oh, ye powers! why did ye not whisper to my labouring breast the many hours of anguish this confession would have spared me, and the horrid deed that then had never been committed?

"At length the day I long had dreaded was fixed upon; and notice was given me the preceding evening, that I was, on the morning of the following day, to accompany count Byroff to the altar.—I fell at my father's feet, and, clasping his knees, conjured him to have pity on me; I endeavoured by the arguments of reason to convince him of the impropriety and cruelty of his commands: I besought him not to harden his heart against the entreaties of an only child; I represented to him the remorse of conscience my future misery would occasion him, when he considered that he alone had brought it upon me. But his ear was deaf to every voice save that of interest, and casting me from him, he exclaimed, 'Obey my commands, or cease to be my daughter;' and, with a frown that pierced me to the heart, left the apartment.—Exhausted with weeping, I sunk into a fainting fit, which lasted some time; as soon as my strength began to return, I took my woman, and, leaning on her arm, repaired to my aunt's, where I had before met Frederic; I informed her of all that had happened—she sympathised in my distress, but being entirely dependent on my father, durst not exert herself in my behalf; I entreated her to send in search of Frederic: she did so.—After two hours passed in tedious expectation, the messenger returned and informed us that he was not in Venice; he had been absent from it some days on urgent business, but was shortly expected to return.

"My aunt promised to send early in the morning, to inquire whether he was arrived, and if he was, to let me know immediately.

"I returned home like a malefactor, who, knowing his doom to be inevitable, makes no resistance when led to the stake.

"Entering my father's house, I passed quickly to my chamber, and throwing myself upon a couch, I again gave fresh vent to my tears. — My woman was afflicted at my distress; she had been my constant companion since the death of my mother; she loved, and endeavoured to comfort me: but alas! how vain were her counsels! she could only recommend resignation, where it was no virtue, and teach me to hope for that interposition of providence, which it refused to grant me.

"When I became somewhat composed, I began to reason with myself. — 'Shall I,' said I, 'quit my father's house, and fly to Frederic? — surely he will receive me with joy, with rapture!' — I reflected a moment; I had been told that men were false, inconstant, and cruel; that those they professed to love in prosperity, were disregarded by them in adversity. — 'Surely,' cried I, 'Frederic is not one of those! — oh no! what promises has he not made me! — what sacred oaths of fidelity has he not taken! — I will fly to him; he will meet me with transport.' — I sprang from the couch in ecstasy, and walked wildly about the chamber; when, oh cruel reflection! I at that instant remembered somewhere to have read, I know not where, that lovers' vows are made only to be broken. — 'Oh heavens! should Frederic think thus,' I exclaimed; 'for who that has ever loved, but has sighed and sworn as he has done? — And shall I then throw myself upon him, to be accounted a burden by him? perhaps upbraided for my love? — Oh credulity! bane of our sex! why have I so long been thy dupe?' — In a brain harassed as mine then was, any idea, however romantic, is easily admitted; and, half frantic, I loaded the faithful youth with every objurgation my rent heart suggested.

"I fear you will upbraid me with ingratitude, suspicion, and cowardice of nature; I confess to you, I seem to merit the reproach; but the torture of mind I then endured, may well apologise for my strange, and seemingly ungrateful, conduct.

"The thought of my lover's infidelity once admitted, I became more calm; I considered that if the vows of love were disregarded by those who were not compelled to break them, how innocent should I be, whom my relentless fates conspired to force unto it! — I even became in part reconciled to my approaching marriage. — You will marvel at my words: — but put yourself in my situation; conceive but for an instant the distracting thought of being abandoned, if not cursed, by a father; perhaps disregarded by the man to whom you should fly for protection; cast friendless upon an unpitying and prejudiced world: and the idea of giving your hand to a man whom you had already begun to esteem, will not appear in so dark colours as you may perhaps have drawn it.

"I did not retire to rest that night: early in the morning, my aunt sent to inform me that Frederic was not returned. 'It is well!' I cried; 'too sure he has forgotten me. Oh cruel, cruel Frederic! are these thy vows? is this thy boasted constancy?' All the pleasing scenes of future bliss I had once vainly flattered myself I should enjoy with my Frederic, now recurred to my imagination; and, in spite of my efforts to coerce them, a flood of tears again burst from me. I continued weeping till my father entered my chamber, and summoned me to attend count Byroff to the altar. 'To be for ever parted from my Frederic!' returned my heart. All my resolution again failed me, and I should have sunk senseless at my father's feet, had not the voice of count Byroff, inquiring for me in the tenderest accents, met my ear, and roused me from my lethargy of grief. He took my hand within his — it trembled excessively — he mistook the reluctance with which I suffered him to take it, for virgin bashfulness, and encouraged me with the most soothing expressions of affection. — We entered the chapel, and I returned from it a wife.

"My doom once fixed, my heart seemed lightened of a heavy weight of anxiety, and I considered it as vain to afflict myself concerning a sentence which was now irrevocably fixed.

"The day was spent in festivity, and I constrained myself to appear cheerful; the awe in which I stood of my father caused me to wear a smile on my lips, whilst I could not forbear heaving a sigh unheard for Frederic.

"Innumerable were the gifts made me on that day by all my relations: count Byroff presented me with jewels to a vast amount, and many articles of dress not less costly in their kind: even my father's natural parsimony seemed relaxed; for he bestowed on me a valuable string of pearls, the only ornament I now possess, and which, notwithstanding his unrelenting cruelty, I still hold dear and sacred, in memory of him who gave it. Never did woman pass a less joyful bridal day than myself: when the bustle of festivity was subsided, and night again brought opportunity for reflection, I strongly felt that my love for Frederic had lost no ground in my heart.

"In the morning, my kind aunt visited me: I inquired eagerly after count Frederic;—he was not returned.

"In spite of my exertions to appear lively, I was depressed: count Byroff left no means untried to amuse, and render me cheerful. My father, who well knew the cause of my melancholy, let not the first opportunity slip of warning me to beware of raising his anger to a higher pitch than I already had done.

"About a month after my marriage, my most earnest wishes were crowned with success; my aunt informed me, that Frederic was returned, and half frantic at the intelligence she had given him. My father was luckily from home;—I immediately flew to my aunt's, where I once again beheld my only love. But oh! never was the parting of the most faithful lovers, doomed to weep away a sad and solitary life within monastic walls, more truly affecting than our meeting: my ardent lover gazed at me with a look of sorrow, that penetrated to my inmost soul; my heart shed tears of blood, and, in an agony of grief, I fainted in his arms. On recovering my senses, I entreated him to forgive the rash act into which I had been hurried by the threats of a cruel father, and the vain distrust of my own harassed mind: I besought him to pity me; nay, even more, to love me. Yes, I charged him to love me still, as I still loved him. Do not, I beseech you, misconstrue the meaning of these words, nor suppose me now a penitent for a crime which, the Supreme of all is witness, was far from my thoughts: my fates, cruel and relentless as they have been, were however satisfied with the resignation of my peace, and spared me the additional sacrifice of my virtue.

"Oh, Frederic! if some bright star thou reignest on high in yon exalted firmament, look down upon thy faithful Lauretta, faithful to thee, even in death, and witness for me the purity of a heart burnt up by love's devouring fire, yet never swerving from the rules of fairest virtue!

"I continued for some time constantly to meet Frederic at the house of my indulgent aunt, until some circumstances, however trivial in themselves, conspired to inform me that our meetings were discovered. I accordingly forebore to see him; and wrote to him, telling him my reason for absenting myself from my aunt's. A daily correspondence was now commenced between us, which, except that I saw not my Frederic, amounted to the same as if we had met; as, at our interviews, we had only uttered those lamentations, vows, and promises of fidelity, which were now conveyed in our letters. A faithful servant of my aunt's had the care of receiving and delivering them.

"About a fortnight after the commencement of our correspondence, I learned that my father and my husband were going a short journey, and would not return for two days. On the morning of the day on which my husband had told me they intended setting out, I dispatched a letter by our trusty messenger to Frederic, informing him of their intended absence, and that I would that evening meet him at my aunt's.

"In the afternoon my father and count Byroff bade me farewell, mounted their horses, and set out. In about two hours after their departure, I ventured to my aunt's; I informed her how things were circumstanced; she congratulated me on my pleasing prospect of seeing my Frederic, and then inquired for her servant, in order to learn whether he had found Frederic at home; but our messenger was not returned.

"Three hours were passed in anxious expectations and vain surmises: neither Frederic nor the servant appeared: the only conclusion I could draw, was, that Frederic was not in the city, and that our messenger was gone in search of him. But a short interval convinced me of the horrible reverse. Oh! picture to yourself my disappointment, my astonishment, my grief, when, hearing footsteps on the stairs, my aunt opened the door of the apartment, and my father rushed in.—I uttered a violent shriek, and fainted at my aunt's feet; when I recovered, I found myself on my own bed. 'Oh, Frederic! art thou then lost for ever?' I exclaimed; for the first idea which shot across my burning brain on my recovering my senses, was, that the sword of count Byroff had pierced the heart of my Frederic. How I got this intelligence, I am to this moment ignorant: suffice it to say, it was but too true, and I infinitely miserable. My husband was sitting by my bed-side; I upbraided him for his unjust cruelty in the most extravagant terms, suggested by my excessive grief: I laid before him all the history of my love for count Frederic; I wept, I sighed, fainted, and upbraided him by turns.

"He informed me that my father had told him, that he suspected I entertained a connexion with another man; which idea he had at first endeavoured to confute; but my father persisting in it, he had agreed to assist him in making an attempt at the discovery of the truth; that they had pretended to be going on a journey, under the expectation of my then admitting Frederic into my father's house; but that, on the morning of that very day, my father had seized our faithful messenger, and torn from him my letter to Frederic, inviting him to meet me in the evening of that day at my aunt's: that, having confined the servant, they had found means of conveying my letter to him to whom it was addressed; and having waylaid him in an obscure street through which they well knew he must unavoidably pass in his way to my aunt's, count Byroff had stabbed him. God alone knows what were my feelings during this recital; and thanks be to him, that the fullness of my heart sealed my lips, or I, in frantic rage, had cursed the author of my being.

"Count Byroff entreated me to be composed; he represented to me, that my sorrow was now ineffectual, since the deed, which he himself avowed to have been rash, was committed. He set before me the resignation I owed to the will of a father, and endeavoured to work upon me, by the shame I should incur in the opinion of the world, if my conduct became publicly known. But I heeded not what he said; I listened with disdain to words uttered by the murderer of my Frederic. At that moment, I should have scorned the words of an angel, had they been incapable of recalling my Frederic to life.

"I absolutely refused all nourishment and repose: count Byroff became alarmed for my health; he continued with great earnestness to urge me to resignation; made me the most solemn protestations of his love; besought my forgiveness, and prayed me to tell him how he could sooth my anguish.

"I was silent, and count Byroff left my apartment: he had not been long gone, ere I commanded my faithful woman, who had been the companion of my sorrows, to go and inform my father and my husband, that I had fallen into a sound slumber; and warn them against entering my apartment, lest they should disturb me. Against her return, I had thrown on a long cloak and veil; and, having bribed her to keep my secret, I left the house unobserved. It was about nine o'clock in the evening when I set out: I moved towards the suburbs of the city as quickly as I was able: arrived there, I entered a narrow lane, in which I imagined I recollected the shop of a clothier. I walked down in search of it: to my great joy, I soon found it, and entering, I perceived there to be no one in the shop but an old woman. In imperfect language, intermixed with French, I told the woman I was journeying to Loretto, and wanted the habit of a male pilgrim. She immediately produced several: I purchased one, together with a staff and leathern bottle; and, having tied up my bundle, I left the shop, inwardly rejoicing that the old woman had been too busily occupied in praising the quality of her goods, particularly to notice me. I again set forward, and in a few minutes arrived in the great road leading from the city.

"Fortunately for me, the rising moon served to show me my way; and being arrived nearly half a league from the city, and perceiving no one near me, I ventured to exchange my garments for the pilgrim's habit; and having buried the clothes I had taken off under a sod, which I had with difficulty managed to cut up for the purpose of hiding them under it, I once more set forward, intending to journey to this convent, which I had heard my aunt mention, and where I had resolved, if you were so kind as to permit me, to pass the remainder of my days.

"Under favour of my habit, I travelled hither perfectly to my satisfaction, except the inconvenience I suffered from fatigue; but your benevolence and care soon brought me to the happy state in which I now find myself: and I trust I shall never prove ungrateful in my acknowledgments to you, and in prayers to the holy saint in whom you confide, to reward you for the humanity you have shown me."

Here was a part of the mystery, relative to the conduct of the uncle of Alphonsus, cleared up; count Frederic had loved and been beloved by the niece of his much revered friend Arieno; she thought him dead, and lived and died secluded from the world, mourning his loss. "Mistaken woman! oh that some angel," cried he, moved by the affecting narration of Lauretta's hapless lot, "had whispered to thee the falsity of that tale which drove thee forever from thy Frederic and the world!—Her loss was surely the cause of the grief which visibly preyed upon my uncle's heart!—Still this solves not the mystery in which I am concerned."—He sat a few minutes wrapped in melancholy thought; then returned to father Matthias's apartment.

"Well!" cried the holy man—"I perceive you feel what you have read;—you pity the unhappy sufferer?"

"Sincerely I do.—Her Frederic was five years since alive."

"Mysterious heaven!" exclaimed the old man: "explain to me, I beseech you, what you know concerning him."

"Indeed—I cannot now:—the time may come."—He paused.

The father looked disappointed; in a moment he regained his wonted serenity of countenance. "She died," cried he, "as she lived, lamenting the untimely fate of him she loved."

"How long have her cares been ended?"

"Grief wasted her frame to a skeleton, and she has sunk into the grave, now seven years."

"Were any inquiries ever made relative to her?"

"Never."

"But she mentions nothing of her child, nor have you spoken to me of her."

"When she delivered to us the manuscript I put into your hands, she knew not herself that she was about to become a mother.—With tears she some short time after declared her situation to the abbess; and called on heaven to witness that it was the pure offspring of her marriage with count Byroff.—Her sufferings moved the abbess, and she promised to connive at her situation, and protect her child. At the due period of time she gave birth to a female infant, which received its mother's name; this was to her great joy; for had its sex proved other, it must necessarily have been removed from her at an early age."

"And is the young Lauretta destined to a life of seclusion from the world?" asked Alphonsus.

"Her mother," answered the friar, "on her death-bed, ordained, that, should any part of her family by any means gain the knowledge of her having borne a child, and demand it of the abbess, it was to be delivered up to them; but in case of her remaining here unknown unto her eighteenth year, she was at that period to take the veil, as it was not likely that even she herself would then be remembered by them after so many years' absence; and on no account to inform her relations that a child of hers was in existence; dreading, as she said, that they should think it incumbent on them to take home the child, and either doubting the purity of its birth, or, in revenge for its mother's transgression, use it unkindly."

"Of what age is Lauretta?" asked Alphonsus.

"She has about four months attained her seventeenth year," returned the old man; "and I trust both her father, and count Arieno, are ignorant that such an angel is in existence.—She has been made acquainted with her own story by her mother: but the colours in which her parent painted to her her nearest relatives, leave her no wish to enter upon a world which she has never known, and of which she has heard so unprepossessing an account: she declares herself perfectly happy within these walls, and prepared to take the veil."

Alphonsus sighed; his eyes fell on the dropping sand, and it admonished him to ring the evening bell.

CHAPTER V.

— — — — — — — — — —a matchless pair,

With equal virtue form'd, and equal grace;

The same, distinguish'd by the sex alone:

Hers, the mild lustre of the blooming morn,

And his, the radiance of the risen day.

Thomson

The thoughts of Alphonsus were continually fixed on Lauretta; he every day felt a stronger prepossession in her favour; he began to conceive the nature of his regard for her, and wished to snatch her from the eternal gloom of a monastic life: — he longed to impart to her the sentiments with which she had inspired him: all intercourse with the females of the convent, save the lady abbess, and old Perilla, was denied him: — what means could he pursue to communicate to her his affection, or how did he know she would not disregard, nay perhaps despise him for the confession?

He resolved steadfastly to fix his eyes on hers as she entered the chapel: he was practically ignorant that love has a language of the eyes; but he conceived that the eyes might be made to express what passes in the heart.

He fixed on her countenance his black penetrating eyes: the blush of modesty o'ershadowed her cheeks; she cast her eyes on the ground, and proceeded swiftly along.

He was unacquainted with the sex, and knew not yet to distinguish between diffidence and displeasure.

He repeated his experiment frequently: sometimes it was returned in the same manner as on his first trial: mostly she raised not her eyes higher than the vase, and immediately dropped them again.

"No!" — cried he — "Lauretta feels no sentiment congenial with mine; she even meets my looks of love with indifference. — Unhappy Alphonsus!"

The next time she entered the chapel, he resolved not to raise his eyes to hers: a broken sigh burst from his heart. Lauretta sighed also. Alphonsus heard the sound, — it tingled on his heart.

He ventured once more to meet her blue eyes: he imagined a faint blush tinged her cheeks, and a soft smile stole over her countenance.

It was a confirmation of Alphonsus's most exalted hope. "She sees, and is not insensible to my fondest wishes!" he exclaimed. "Oh ecstasy incomparable!"

How light a breath turns the wavering balance of a lover's hopes and fears!

Fearless, he now met her eyes: her diffidence gradually wore off, and she encountered his fond glances with delight.

A method of conversing with her now entered his mind: he wrote to her the fondest declaration of his love, that the desire of its return could dictate: — he held his letter by the side of the vase; and as she extended her finger to touch the water, he slid the paper unobserved into her hand.

Three days elapsed ere he was released from the torture of suspense; on the third, at evening prayers, she put a note into his hand, containing these words, — "Oh, Alphonsus, what a conviction of the state of my own heart has the declaration of yours proved to me! — Oh, let it remain a secret to all besides ourselves! — Be cautious how you write to me again, — we shall be suspected!"

Alphonsus was truly happy for the first time; but ecstasy will cool, and bring time for reflection. It told him that he might never be more closely connected with Lauretta than at that moment.

About five months after this time, the lady abbess was seized with a violent illness. The friar, who was also the administerer of physic in the convent, was an unremitting attendant at her bed-side: in a few days she died, lamented by all the convent, and particularly by Lauretta, to whom she had been a second mother.

Her corpse was placed in its coffin, before the altar of the church; masses were performed three times each day for nine days successively, for the benefit of her soul; and three nuns and a novice alternately watched over her body for the same space of time.

Alphonsus thinking an opportunity might now be given him for presenting Lauretta with a letter, wrote one, informing her that he was the nephew of her deceased mother's beloved Frederic, and entreating her to agree to leave the convent with him on the first opportunity that should offer, — calling on heaven to witness the sanctity of his intentions.

On the evening of the fourth day, Lauretta was returning from her duty of watching the body, as Alphonsus was entering the chapel: she followed the nuns; — they had turned the angle of the chapel door, and Lauretta was in the door-way when Alphonsus met her. He cast a hasty look round, — saw no observing eye, — snatched her hand, — imprinted on it a fervent kiss, and put into it the letter. — The whole was the transaction of a moment.

The funeral obsequies of the abbess were performed at the stated time, with all the pomp of religion and superstition; requiems were chanted the whole night by the friar, and all the nuns and novices. It was morning ere they left the chapel; they were fatigued by their nocturnal worship; they rejoiced when it was ended, and retired hastily from the chapel. Lauretta contrived to be the last; she dropped a piece of paper; Alphonsus flew and hid it in his bosom.

"Explain to me, whither thou wouldst fly."

He read it, — kissed it, — read it again, and tore it.

After much deliberation how to act, whether again to write to his beloved Lauretta, and inform her of the particulars of his unfortunate story, or only urge her to fly with him from the convent, he resolved to impart the whole of his history to father Matthias.

Accordingly he waited with impatience an hour when the old man was alone; and having entered his apartment, he hesitatingly informed him that he had a tale of confidence to impart to him, — which the holy man sacredly promised to bury in his own breast. Alphonsus then related to him every event that had occurred to him since his entrance into life. Having ended the narration, — "Now, good father," he cried, "canst thou solve the mystery that preys upon my breast?"

The holy man sat some minutes wrapped in thought; then, raising his eyes to Alphonsus, and marking his breast with the sign of the cross, he said, "Heaven forbid I should accuse any one unjustly! what I am about to say, is solely conjecture. Thy mother was frantic with grief, and had resolved on suicide."

Alphonsus shuddered at the idea: after a pause, he said, "But, father, her hand was bloody!"

The father paused an instant; then said, "She had grasped, in a moment of frenzy, the instrument she had destined for her destruction."

"Why did she send me from her?"

"Doubtless," returned the friar, "she forcibly felt the shame that would follow the act she was about to commit, and feared it would descend on her innocent son."

"Do you then impute to the same cause her accusation of my uncle, which she afterwards recalled?"

"I do."

"But, father, why has my uncle left the castle of Cohenburg?"

"His mind is open to sensibility; and the remembrance of those who had so lately inhabited it, rendered it unpleasant, and he doubtless retired to his own mansion."

"But why has he never inquired after me?"

"His inquiries may have escaped you."

"Your suppositions," cried Alphonsus, "are good: you consider circumstances; you know the nature of mankind: they may be just; but a heart, harassed as mine has been, pants for certainty."

"It will be difficult to attain it."

"Within these walls, I grant it."

"You do not wish to leave them?"

The hesitating silence of Alphonsus spoke for him in the affirmative.

"Your uncle, and the castle of Cohenburg," continued the friar, "are interdicted to you by your mother."

"But surely," interrupted Alphonsus, "it is not disobedience to act in opposition to the commands of a frantic parent?"

"You just now alleged, Alphonsus, and with reason, that my words could only proceed from conjecture."

Alphonsus felt the force of the friar's remark. The tears started in his eyes, and he exclaimed, "Oh! father! I cannot taste peace of mind till I gain some light on this mystery. — I am an unfit subject for the offices of religion, — my thoughts are too much centred in the world."

"How can you gain information but by visiting the castle? — and then how know you that your pains might not prove futile?"

"No! I would only mix with the world; the possibility of hearing what I so earnestly desire would keep hope alive: here it lies buried, and I have no pleasing thought to cheer me."

"Whither would you go?"

"I have resolved to become a fisher on the banks of the Inn."

"The solitude in which you will there live, will soon cause you to regret the happy station you wish to relinquish."

"I feel I was born for society; not to live with men alone, but to enjoy the soothings of the softer sex."

"Beware of your choice."

"I would have you approve it."

"I am secluded from the world."

"But you intimately know her on whom I dote."

"Oh, shame! shame! Nurtured within our convent walls, art thou the man to wish to break their sacred laws?"

"Lauretta Byroff is not bound by them."

"Have you ever conversed with her?"

"Never."

"How then can you tell her feelings are congenial with yours?"

"Be assured they are."

"I have promised her dying mother, that to no one, but her near relations, I will deliver her."

"And should you then hesitate to deliver her to me?"

"You are not allied to her in blood."

"It is in your power to set all consanguinity a degree below me."

"Explain thyself."

"Make me her nearest relative;—your promise is fulfilled, and I am blessed."

Father Matthias paused awhile; he then said, "What would the world say, should it ever be known that the descendants of your two noble families were living in the obscure and humiliating situation you have mentioned?"

"Oh, father! what have those whom the world has so hardly dealt with, to do with its censure?—I am well convinced that happiness is not confined to an elevated situation in life."

"Nor," returned the old man, "is it always to be found in an humble state, answerable to the expectations of a warm lover." Father Matthias again paused, then added, "Have you explained your fortunes to Lauretta?"

"No."

"Declare them to her."

"But how, good father?—teach me the means."

"This night I will conduct her to my apartment, there thou shalt meet her.—If she consents to share them (and I will pray that heaven guide her tongue for her true felicity), I will not be the means to sunder those whom it has joined.—But mark me, if she refuses thy suit, instantly she takes the veil.—I am hasty in this affair.—I feel an interest in your fates; and what is done must be concluded ere the arrival of our newly-chosen abbess."

Alphonsus kissed the friar's hand, and he made a sign to him to leave him.

When evening prayers were ended, and Perilla was retired to bed, father Matthias stole softly to the cell of Lauretta, and told her to follow him to his apartment. She was reading; but having laid down her book, and taken up her lamp, she drew down her veil and followed him. He stopped at the door of Alphonsus's apartment, and pointed to Lauretta to enter his; she did so, and in a few minutes Alphonsus was at her feet.

Joy and surprise made her hesitate to determine whether what she saw was a vision, or him she really wished it to be.

The first moments, on the part of Alphonsus, were given up to ecstasy; but he considered that the time allotted to him was short, and that he had much to communicate; he accordingly began by imparting to her the indulgence of the good confessor, proceeded to the narration of his own life, and, lastly, recounted the plan he had formed for their mutual happiness, if she deigned to share it with him.

Her eyes spoke the consent that virgin bashfulness prevented her tongue from uttering; — she blushed: — he urged the friar's words — the shortness of the time allowed her for the consideration — the possibility of their being separated for ever. — Her tender heart melted at the idea; — her lips expressed the words her voice scarcely sounded. — the enraptured Alphonsus sealed the sacred bond with an ecstatic kiss.

Quickly after the friar entered, to warn them that the hour of twelve was near at hand; and he read in the eyes of Alphonsus the result of his conversation.

Lauretta returned to her cell, promising to visit the father on the following morning; and Alphonsus entered the chapel to prepare for midnight prayers.

Alphonsus and Lauretta passed the night in sleepless dreams of happiness to come.

At the appointed hour, Lauretta repaired to the apartment of father Matthias; he asked her confession — her heart was spotless, except a chaste and hidden love long entertained for Alphonsus, could be charged on the score of blame: he then represented to her the wayward fortunes that befall alike the good and evil in the world, upon which she was about to enter; he set before her the trials that all who live in it must sustain; he charged her well to consult her heart, that she might not, when too late, blame herself for an act which could not be recalled.

She did consult her heart, and found it firm.

The father had already conversed with Alphonsus to the same purpose; he was steadfastly fixed on again braving those vicissitudes of life to which he had already been exposed.

The old man now rose, and called Alphonsus into his apartment.

Alphonsus quivered with ecstasy.—Lauretta trembled, she knew not why.—She wept.

Father Matthias again exhorted them to reflection ere it was too late.

Their eyes met each other's; Lauretta's tears were dried, and Alphonsus ventured to answer for them both, "that they were resolved."

The indissoluble knot was tied.

"The grace of God shine upon you, my children!" cried the old man.—Alphonsus embraced his bride, while tears of joy sparkled in his eyes.

"To-morrow morning, with the dawn of day, you must leave these walls," said the holy man; "now retire to your respective apartments, and each collect together what little articles you may possess of value."

They followed his directions.

During the course of the day, the friar informed such of the nuns as were acquainted with Lauretta's story, that she had been summoned to leave the convent by her nearest relation; and they bade her tenderly farewell:—"She will depart early in the morning," said the old man; "and we shall, I fear, experience a double loss; for our young sacristan, wishing again to mix with the world, will leave us at the same period."

Perilla expressed much astonishment at his being dissatisfied with his present station,—told him, "he would find it difficult to meet with such another;" gave him "some lessons for his good," as she was pleased to term them, and comforted herself with the hope that his successor would prove more communicative, and thus a companion suited better to her garrulous taste.

On the following morning, after matins had been chanted, and the nuns had again returned to their private devotions in their respective cells, and Perilla was busied in sweeping the chapel, father Matthias went to the cell of Lauretta, and, having directed her to habit herself in the pilgrim's dress in which her mother had arrived at the convent, and which was now in Lauretta's possession, he led her down into the hall. Here she was met by the anxious Alphonsus;—"Accept that small purse of gold," said the good old man: "it may benefit you, my children; with me it lies useless."—They kissed his extended hand:—he gave them his last benediction, and unbarred the heavy gate.—Lauretta dropped a parting tear.—Alphonsus exclaimed, "farewell, my kind friend!"—The old man raised his eyes and hands to heaven; then closed the gates on them for ever.

CHAPTER VI.

Which is the villain? Let me see his eyes;

That, when I note another man like him,

I may avoid him.

Much Ado About Nothing

Supporting herself on the arm of Alphonsus, an hour's journey brought Lauretta to Inspruck; where, wishing to avoid the questions of those who might perceive she was newly entered upon the world, she wisely concealed the surprise which was excited in her breast on beholding scenes to which she had hitherto been totally a stranger.

After a short repast, the travellers again set forward, and arrived about an hour after mid-day at the spot where Alphonsus had determined to fix his residence. — A small inn received them for the night, and in the morning Alphonsus repaired to the owner of the houses on the border of the river. Having bargained for the hire of one of the most commodious dwellings then vacant, and purchased the freedom of exercising his intended trade on the river, he next provided himself with the necessary implements for earning his subsistence; and in a few days entered upon the employment he had chosen for that purpose.

Fortune smiled on his endeavours; his Lauretta was the solace of his unemployed hours; and he enjoyed as great happiness as the mystery which had reduced him to his present humble situation could suffer a thinking mind to enjoy. — Retired from the world, not possessing either those riches or vanities which excite the envy of its inhabitants, Alphonsus and his Lauretta had hoped to live free from its cares and inquietudes; but they were quickly doomed to experience how short is the durability of human felicity, even in its humblest state.

The proprietor of the estate on which Alphonsus rented his humble habitation, was the baron Smaldart: he was a widower, whose wife had died in child-bed together with her infant. He was a man remarkable for his benevolence, hospitality, and mildness of temper.

His only sister had espoused the chevalier D'Aignon, a native of Burgundy, who, having been killed by a fall from his horse a short time after the death of the baroness Smaldart, madame D'Aignon had ever since resided with the baron.

Theodore, the son and only offspring of the deceased chevalier, now in his twentieth year, had for some time been receiving his education in France, and was expected shortly to return to his uncle's. His mother awaited his return with all the ardour of prejudiced fondness; but she was not permitted again to behold her son. She had for some time been slightly indisposed; and one morning, about the time of Theodore's expected arrival in Germany, was found lifeless in her bed.

This was a stroke which severely affected the baron: since the loss of his wife, his sister had been his constant and much-beloved companion: they had been strongly attached to each other; and he had earnestly wished that she might survive him.

At the appointed time Theodore arrived at Smaldart castle: but how great an alteration had taken place in him in the space of five years! When a youth, his every wish had been anticipated by the false indulgence of a kind uncle, and a doting mother; but still his manners had been then unaffected, his deportment unassuming, and his mind untainted with vicious habits. But now he was become haughty, impetuous, confident of his own opinion, and eager to give it unasked. The pecuniary allowance made him by his mother had enabled him to pass the greater part of the time allowed for his education, in a variety of dissipation: thus the acquisition of knowledge had been utterly neglected by him: nor was he himself conscious of his deficiency; having been hitherto connected with a set of men too sensible of their own interest not to pay implicit deference to his opinion on every occasion.

The baron had promised himself a pleasing companion in his nephew: he had expected to reap edification and amusement from the conversation of his well-informed mind; and hoped to find in him a willing partaker of such diversions as the country afforded.

How mistaken were his expectations! Theodore's conversation consisted only in boasting of disgraceful exploits, in which he was careful to hold himself up as the principal actor; and the only amusement he found in the sports of the country, was to make their pursuit a plea for injuring the lands of those who, from their dependence on his uncle, he well knew would not venture to seek redress. In short, had he aimed at making himself the object of general contempt and hatred, he could not have pursued steps that would more satisfactorily have gained him his wish.

He often averred that he despised the good opinion of inferiors; and his actions plainly showed that he would submit to any meanness to gain a smile of approbation from a superior in rank.

At the time of Theodore's arrival in Germany, Lauretta was in an advanced state of pregnancy: but she appeared not the less fascinating in his eyes; and, from the first moment of his beholding her, he marked her out for his lustful prey.

A mode of conduct but too common in life was now adopted by him: he used every means to show himself the friend of the husband, while he was labouring to become his blackest enemy. Often did he, by the most seductive flattery, make in imagination a step towards the heart of Lauretta; and as often did her awful virtue cause him to retrace his visionary path.

The perceptive mind of Alphonsus could not long remain ignorant of the hidden villainy of the young chevalier; but, conscious of the strict chastity of his Lauretta, he determined to appear not to notice the actions of Theodore, whilst he in reality kept the strictest watch over them. His mind recoiled from being daily obliged to increase a debt of gratitude to a man who was studying to wound him in the tenderest part; but policy forbade him to refuse obligations he had once accepted, lest he should open to the chevalier the discovery he had made, and his measures become more determined.

At the expected period Lauretta gave birth to a female infant, whose being was but that of a few hours. Lauretta was much affected by the loss of her first-born: Alphonsus, though he rejoiced at the safety of his wife, dropped a tear in sympathy with her sorrow at the fate of his child.

Theodore appeared daily at the cottage of Alphonsus, making the most solicitous inquiries relative to the health of Lauretta, and offering to her, by means of her husband, the most liberal presents, which Alphonsus was slow to accept, and that sparingly: — of a refusal he saw the bad consequences.

In the summer, Alphonsus was frequently kept out nearly half the night by his occupation; but he dreaded not that his Lauretta would then suffer from the persecutions of Theodore, as he had never visited his cottage in an evening; and more particularly as he well knew the gates of the baron Smaldart's castle to be closed at an early hour.

The conduct of Theodore was, however, becoming daily more alarming to the timid Lauretta; and she obtained a promise from Alphonsus, that, if the chevalier persisted in it, he would appeal to the well-known humanity of the baron.

It was one night, not long after this time, that Lauretta, still weak from her late indisposition, having retired to rest before the return of her husband, was roused by the cries of a girl, whom Alphonsus had procured for her as a nurse and companion in his absence, calling out that the house was on fire; and the girl immediately ran out to procure assistance. — Lauretta, springing from the bed, threw on her clothes as quickly as her alarm would permit her, and was rushing towards the door of the apartment, when Theodore stood before her. She shrieked, and endeavoured to pass him: he seized her hand, and exclaiming "my lucky stars are at length predominant," dragged her into the outer apartment.

Lauretta again raised her feeble voice; but, alas! her cries, had they been heard, would have been thought to proceed from her alarm on hearing the cry of fire. "Oh God of mercy, assist me!" she cried. "Oh my Alphonsus, where art thou?" and, raising her eyes, which had hitherto been averted from the surly smiling Theodore, she perceived, standing near the door, two men, whose scowling mien and haggard looks terrified her more than the villain who held her; and she again uttered a faint cry.

Theodore cast at her a look of mingled triumph and contempt; and, waving his hand to the men, they approached Lauretta. She again struggled to release herself from Theodore; but the effort overpowered her, and she fainted in their arms.

CHAPTER VII.

Eye me, bless'd Providence, and square my trial

To my proportion'd strength.

Milton

Lauretta, on recovering her senses, found herself in total darkness; and, by the motion which she felt, concluded she was in some vehicle, which was drawn swiftly along. It was some time ere she recollected the situation in which she had last seen the light, and she then exclaimed, "Gracious heaven, where am I?" No one answered. She extended her hand; it fell upon the hilt of a sword, and she immediately heard a rough voice, between sleeping and waking, mutter some words which she did not understand.

The image of the men who had so greatly alarmed her, recurred to her, and she shuddered.

The person who sat by her yawned, and turned himself towards her.

The night, although summer was far advanced, was damp: Lauretta was unaccustomed to the night air — she trembled with cold — and her teeth chattered violently.

Her companion again yawned; and then asking her, whether he should throw his woollen wrapper round her, relieved her from the apprehension under which she had at first laboured, that Theodore was the person who wore the sword she had accidentally touched.

That poignant anguish of mind which refuses to relieve the sufferer by an effusion of tears, is seldom more favourable to the utterance. Such was the grief of the unhappy Lauretta: her repeated attempts to articulate were ineffectual, and the pangs of her heart were redoubled by her involuntary silence. The tears, at length, as expressive of the painful efforts which produced them, stole singly down her cold cheeks, and with difficulty she again stammered out, "Where am I?"

"I must answer no questions," returned the man. His voice was hoarse, but by no means so blunt and harsh as Lauretta's fears had led her to expect.

"Whither am I going?" cried Lauretta.

This demand was thrice advanced, but no answer returned.

"Is the chevalier D'Aignon here?" she then asked.

"No," replied the man. "I believe I may venture to tell you, he is at the castle."

To no other question could she obtain the slightest answer: she knew not what to hope or what to fear; the gloominess of the night added greatly to the depression of her spirits, and the predominant idea within her breast was, that her companion was hired by Theodore to be her murderer, in revenge for his slighted love.

Her companion in a short time after addressed her; and, attributing her anxiety in a great measure to the chill, which, by the chattering of her teeth, he found still hung upon her, pressed her to taste some brandy out of a flask which had been almost unremittingly applied to his own lips.

Lauretta was insensible to his attentions. "Oh Alphonsus!" she cried, "shall I never again behold you?" — A flood of tears followed the exclamation, and her sorrow rose almost to frenzy.

After three hours passed in a suspense more poignant than a certainty of suffering the most dreadful calamities that could have befallen her, the vehicle stopped.

Her companion immediately sprang up, and pushing past her, opened the door, and gave her into the arms of his comrade, by whose side stood another figure, holding a lantern.

The man who had received her into his arms, conveyed her into the kitchen of a miserable inn, of which it was difficult to say, whether poverty or dirt was the leading feature: he placed her in a chair, and then returning to the door, saluted the landlord with a volley of oaths, which conveyed the double meaning, that the horses were in want of provender, and his flask void of brandy.

He then approached the fire, and kicking away a dog which lay sleeping in the corner of the chimney, seated himself by Lauretta.

His companion now entered, and placing himself opposite the weeping fair, she imagined she perceived a faint gleam of pity shine in his eye. To avail herself of the moment in which she fancied she saw his heart open to the dictates of humanity, was her immediate resolution; and falling on her knees before him, she entreated him to have pity on her helpless situation, and restore her to her Alphonsus. Ere he could answer, she heard his comrade start from his seat, and turning round her head, she observed that he had drawn his sword nearly out of the scabbard. All her fears now seemed verified; she seized the hand of him before whom she was kneeling, uttered an hysteric shriek, and sunk senseless on the floor.

When she revived, she found herself still on the ground, with her head reclined on the knees of a woman, whose expanded features and brawny limbs seemed to deny her sex.

Whilst Lauretta had continued in a state of insensibility, the hostess had carefully chafed her temples with strong liquors, and now seeing life returned, pressed her to fortify her stomach with a dram of the same cordial, which she had before outwardly administered.

She was now again placed in the chair which she had before occupied, and casting her eyes round, she perceived that several other men had entered the kitchen: amongst them sat the ruffian who had lately given her so much cause for alarm; but she saw not him who had been her companion in the vehicle.

Her fainting fits, together with the extreme agitation of her spirits, had brought on a violent pain in her head; and unable any longer to support her drooping frame, she requested the hostess to conduct her to a bed; but with this petition, Kroonzer, the ruffian of whom Lauretta stood in so great dread, absolutely commanded her not to comply, saying, he must depart in a very short time. The hostess, though of so masculine a figure, seemed not devoid of the feelings of her sex, and now cast a look at Lauretta, which speakingly informed her, she wished to accord in her request, but durst not, from the awe in which she stood of Kroonzer.

After a short interval, Kroonzer ordered the host to bring out the horses and prepare for their departure: his commands were instantly obeyed.

Again lifted into the vehicle, how great were the apprehensions of Lauretta, on perceiving Kroonzer enter after her, together with another man, on whose countenance the light

499

which proceeded from a lantern held by the host, falling, it appeared, if possible, more savage than that of the surly Kroonzer.

They again proceeded swiftly along, and for a length of time a strict silence was observed, not less by the men, than by Lauretta.

The faint taints of saffron hue which now began to streak the clearing sky, afforded extreme delight to the overburdened heart of Lauretta. She considered, that, had these men received orders to destroy her, they would in all probability have executed the deed, whilst the darkness of the night enabled them to evade the eye of man.

The first objects she descried by the rising light, were distant mountains, whose towering summits were rapidly gaining the gilded tinge of advancing day. — The tract of land over which they were journeying, was heathy and barren, save where, at intervals, some small clusters of unpropped vines grew spontaneously on the shelving hillocks.

Her fortitude in some measure returning with the much-wished-for light of day, she ventured to inquire, "whither she was going?" — "Not above a league farther now," cried Kroonzer, "whatever we may do at night." — And from this answer she hesitated not to conclude, that, wherever she was about to be conveyed, Theodore, apprehensive of a rescue, had cautioned her conductors against travelling in the day-time.

The road now turned into a valley: on the left lay high mountains which were speckled with cattle of various kinds; on the right, irregular lines of lofty chestnut and beech trees: it now wound round the mountain, and the sun burst full upon them between the boles of the trees. Never before had its cheering rays so greatly exhilarated the heart of her who now hailed its return from the bosom of the deep.

A few moments brought them to the extremity of the vale, and they entered upon a small but thickly planted forest; the ground was covered with furze, through which, as there was no distinct path, the vehicle found a difficulty in passing: at length turning an angle, Lauretta suddenly perceived a thatched cottage: here the vehicle stopped, and Ralberg, for such was the name of Kroonzer's comrade, having alighted, announced their arrival by a thundering knock with his fist at the door. It was opened by a man half dressed, whose appearance was that of a peasant, and Lauretta was conducted into an apartment which served for the double purpose of kitchen and chamber to the countryman and his wife, who, when they entered, was in the act of dressing behind a ragged curtain, which but ill concealed her from her newly arrived guests.

Lauretta, unable to stand, insensibly seated herself on a bench, which encircled half the fire-place,—unmindful of Kroonzer and his comrade, who had entered into close conversation with the countryman in low voices.

The good woman was no sooner habited, than advancing from behind her flimsy retreat, she began with an apology to Lauretta for not having been up ready to receive her, and ended by requesting her to accompany her to a better apartment. Lauretta, with tottering and uncertain steps, followed her hostess up a few stairs, scarcely superior either in breadth or safety to a ladder, and arrived in a small room, the furniture of which consisted of a mean bed, a disabled chair, and a large box, which served at once for a wardrobe, a seat, and a table.

Having closed the door, and pointed with half a courtesy to the only chair, Bartha again apologised for not having been risen to receive her; but alleged that she had arrived somewhat earlier than her husband had said he expected her.

"Were you then apprised of my coming?" asked Lauretta.

"Oh dear heart, yes," replied Bartha; "and so I got this chamber ready for you; for I said to Ugo,—lack-a-day, said I, she will be sorely tired with journeying all night, and glad to rest her wearied limbs, I warrant me."

"Oh!" cried Lauretta, clasping the hand of old Bartha, as she stood by her side,—"if you are acquainted with the purpose for which I am brought hither, for the love of God, I conjure you to inform me."

"The Holy Virgin wots, I know not," returned the woman.

"But, tell me, whither I am to be conveyed," continued Lauretta; "one of my guards insinuated that I am not to remain here longer than to-day."

"Ah! lack-a-day!" cried Bartha, "I know not indeed! Ugo says, women are tattlers, and should not be trusted with secrets. I pressed him hardly to tell me on what account you were coming hither; but he would not."

"Gave he no reason?"—inquired the disconsolate fair.

"No, by the saints, did he not. He only said, 'Bartha,'—said he, 'ask no questions; no harm is going to be done to any body; so make yourself easy.'"

"In what manner was he informed that I was going to be brought hither?" asked Lauretta.

"By my troth, I know not," answered Bartha. "He told me of it last night, when he came from work in that little forest you see there: he is a wood-cutter."

"Could you find any method of conveying a letter for me to my friends?"

"Not unknown to my husband, if it be far from hence."

"The estate of the baron Smaldart, on the borders of the river Inn, is the place I allude to."

"Lack-a-day, good soul, that is many leagues from hence; and I never go farther than the next village."

Lauretta hung down her head and wept, and Bartha left the apartment.

Unable to taste the refreshments with which Bartha in a short time returned, Lauretta threw herself upon the bed; and although she had never pressed bedding so hard and uncomfortable, the fatigue she had undergone soon closed her eyes, but not to peaceful slumbers: the scenes through which she had so lately passed, returned to her flurried imagination in more terrific colours than the reality had appeared to her,—now exaggerated by sleeping fancy.

CHAPTER VIII.

— — — —Patience and sorrow strove

Which should express her goodliest.

Lear

The day had been close and sultry; towards evening the sky began to lower, and the clouds seemed big with an approaching deluge of rain. Lauretta observed them with sensations of melancholy pleasure; the gloom in which all nature was clad seemed in unison with her feelings: she contemplated the scene before her, till, thought rising successively on thought, she became almost insensible to her own situation. Her reflections were at length interrupted by the entrance of Bartha, who brought her a cup of new milk, some fresh gathered fruit, and a slice of coarse bread, of which she entreated her to partake, as Kroonzer and Ralberg purposed proceeding on their journey in half an hour's time.

Lauretta, in order to please her kind hostess, rather than to satisfy the calls of nature, which were blunted by extreme grief, tasted the fruits, and sipped a small quantity of the milk, whilst Bartha again called forth every argument with which she was acquainted, to persuade Lauretta, that, as her husband had said she had nothing to fear, she was sure she had not. But this reasoning appeared to Lauretta, although she attempted not to confute it, too weak to afford her any solid consolation.

The voice of Kroonzer now called upon her to descend. The feeble resistance she could make, she well knew, would be of no avail; ready compliance might conciliate her guards; she therefore instantly obeyed the summons. Ralberg met her at the foot of the stairs, and taking her in his arms, placed her on a horse before his comrade, and then vaulted upon another himself, which the peasant held till he had mounted it.

A thick darkness blackened the horizon, and a dead silence prevailed, save when, at intervals, short gusts of wind announced a rising storm.

In a short time, vivid flashes of blue lightning momentarily illumined the atmosphere, and shot across the lofty mountains; the combating clouds rolled rapidly towards each other, and jarring, burst in tremendous claps, which, from their loudness, seemed immediately over the heads of Lauretta and her companions.

After an hour and a half, as nearly as Lauretta could guess, passed in journeying amidst this dreadful contention of the elements, and in almost incessant darkness, except when, at intervals, the darting flashes of lightning seemed to clothe the furze-grown earth in flakes of fire, the storm which, fortunately for the unhappy Lauretta, had been attended with but little rain, began gradually to subside, and a misty moon-light succeeded.

Their road, she now perceived, lay through a deep glen. "Oh, God!" she exclaimed, "should this be my destined grave!" and, chilled by the apprehensions her own imagination had raised, she insensibly hung down her head and closed her eyes.

A length of time elapsed ere she again ventured to look around her; and she then saw that they were entering upon a forest of lofty trees, thickly planted with underwood.

Ralberg and his companion had been in conversation together since the cessation of the storm; but she had not been able to gather any thing from their discourse that served either to diminish or increase her terrors.

Lauretta, becoming extremely fatigued and exhausted, again closed her eyes; and, notwithstanding the alarm under which she laboured, she struggled ineffectually against the attacks of sleep, which at length overpowered her fainting frame.

Suddenly starting from her involuntary slumber, she shivered violently, a dizziness seized her head; and although the night was become much clearer, she could not for some time distinguish any object.

A turret, which rose above a distant cluster of trees, now caught her gazing eye; and as she proceeded, she discovered that it formed part of a building towards which her guards were advancing.

Her eyes continued fixed on the object before them; and as she approached it, her alarm became extreme: her conductors spoke not, and she waited her doom in anxious silence.

The light of the moon, reflected on the building, showed her that one wing was entirely in ruins, and the whole edifice in a state of decay.

On being lifted from the horse, she was unable to stand; her knees knocked violently; and, almost insensible of her situation, she sunk upon the supporting arms of Kroonzer.

Ralberg having fastened the horses to a broken pillar of the colonnade, pushed back the heavy gate, which creaked loudly on its hinges; Kroonzer then entered the building with Lauretta in his arms, and as he placed her on a seat seemingly formed by a niche in the stone wall, he called to his companion, telling him instantly to strike a light, and chiding him for having waited his bidding. His words were re-echoed from every part of the building, and in sounds so dismally hollow, as caused Lauretta to shudder violently.

Ralberg made no answer, but began striking his flint: — for some moments Lauretta heard the uninterrupted jarring of the steel and flint; and, with a heart beating high with the anxious desire of seeing the joyful ray of light which was to release her from the horrid gloom in which she now trembled, she fixed her eyes upon the spot where the sound informed her Ralberg was stationed, when a flash of light drew them suddenly to the opposite side of the hall; it appeared to her to have proceeded from a lamp on the side on which she was sitting; she immediately turned round her head, and beheld a man who carried a lamp, with his back towards her, enter a door, which he immediately closed after him.

As the ruinous state of the building had not left Lauretta the least room to doubt that it was uninhabited, she immediately concluded the man she had seen to be Kroonzer, although she knew not whence he had procured the light, and again turned her eyes towards Ralberg; when, to her great astonishment, she saw them both approaching towards her with their lamp lighted. A shriek, which she endeavoured to suppress, burst involuntarily from her lips, and she immediately perceived the same door partly opened, and the arm and visage of a man, whose features she could not distinguish, appear within it. Theodore instantly recurred to her imagination; the recollection of him shot like a bolt of ice across her heart, and she sunk lifeless on the ground.

On the return of her senses, she was lying upon an uncanopied bed, and a dim lamp, which was burning in the apartment, showed her Ralberg standing by her side; she immediately cast her eyes round in search of Theodore; — the apartment was large, and the light thrown out by the lamp insufficient to convince her that he whom she dreaded was not within it; — raising herself upon the bed, she seized the hand of

Ralberg, and, bursting into tears, conjured him "to save her, — to protect her from Theodore." — In as softened accents as his rough voice would permit him to articulate, he bade her be composed, and banish her apprehensions. — With a look of doubt, she again fixed on him her streaming eyes, and grasping more strictly the hand she had before held, she exclaimed, "May heaven reward you as you pity my misfortunes."

The sound of footsteps now called her attention to another part of the chamber. Kroonzer entered: he brought with him a cup of wine, some fruit, and bread; and, having taken the lamp from the ground, he placed them on a table near the bed; he then invited Lauretta to rise and taste them; she answered him only with her tears; he repeated his invitation; she endeavoured to speak, but her sobs prevented her utterance. — Springing from the bed, she threw herself at his feet, and clasped his knees; he pushed her from him, and beckoning to Ralberg to follow him, they left the apartment; and she heard the door locked and bolted after them.

The violent agitation of her spirits being somewhat abated, she took up the lamp, and walked round the apartment, in order to be certified whether any one was secreted within it. — Its form was circular; the roof high and vaulted; the walls of stone; the casements small, and many feet raised from the ground; and the entire appearance led her to conjecture, that she was now in that turret which had attracted her notice while journeying through the forest.

She then set down the lamp, and taking from her bosom a small ivory crucifix, which she placed on the table, she knelt, and, having fervently declared her gratitude for the sufferings of him in memory of whom she wore the sacred remembrancer now before her, she proceeded to implore of him fortitude, to enable her to bear up under the calamities which surrounded her, and his divine aid, against the evil designs of those whom she dreaded more than death; concluding by a declaration of her faith in his beneficence, and her unfeigned submission to his will.

Rising, and replacing in her bosom the crucifix, she felt a composure proceeding from her confidence in that power she had just addressed, which she little imagined she should have experienced; still, however, by no means sufficiently free from alarm to endeavour to compose herself to rest, she placed herself in a chair which stood near the bed, and, as from the stillness of the scene her terrors became gradually abated, she grew more collected, and better able to ruminate on the occurrences of the night.

The figure of the man whom she had seen was unremittingly before her eyes; and the feelings of her mind naturally assigning to him the person of Theodore, her fears began to return as strongly as ever; she sighed deeply, and the tears ran swiftly down her burning cheeks;—she rose, and walked slowly about the apartment, stopping at intervals and fixing her swollen eyes on the ground in mournful reflection on the past, and poignant anticipation of the future.

Faint and exhausted with fatigue of body, and anguish of mind, she again seated herself in the chair.—In a short time, the languor which hung upon her increased almost to inability, her eyes became dim, and big drops of perspiration started from her forehead;—shivering, she extended her trembling arm, and grasped the cup of wine; with difficulty she raised it to her head, and then, for some moments, her quivering lips refused admittance to the reviving cordial;—having twice swallowed a small draught of the liquor contained in the cup, the trembling which had seized her began to subside, the blood began again to circulate in her veins, and life seemed newly warmed within her heart; she again sipped a small quantity of the wine,—a glow succeeded the shivering fit, and a drowsiness, which she endeavoured in vain to shake off, stole gradually upon her, and lulled her into a profound sleep.

CHAPTER IX.

Tho' plung'd in ills, and exercis'd in care,

Yet never let the noble mind despair:

When press'd by dangers, and beset with foes,

The gods their timely succour interpose;

And when our virtue sinks, o'erwhelmed with grief,

By unforeseen expedients bring relief.

Philips

Lauretta, on waking, started from her chair, and cast her eyes wildly about, totally ignorant where she was; and, entirely forgetful of all that had passed the preceding evening. But busy recollection swiftly burst upon her with all its sorrows: she sighed, and raised her eyes to the high casements: the rays of the sun shone hot and full into her apartment; she conjectured it to be noon-day, and marvelled that she had slept so long and soundly; she moved towards the door; it was still fastened; and, from what she remembered of the disposition of the little furniture her prison contained, she saw not the smallest cause for suspecting that any one had visited it during the night. She examined the lamp; it was burnt out in the socket, and the cup of wine stood on the ground where she herself had placed it.

Towards evening, the creaking of the locks announced Kroonzer: he entered with a fresh supply of provisions; which, together with a flask of wine, and another of water, he placed upon the table; and, having trimmed the wick of the lamp, and replenished the wasted oil, he lighted it, and left the apartment, without uttering a single word.

The artificial light produced by the lamp tended swiftly to dispel the declining day; and, with the increasing gloom, the horrors of her situation were greatly accumulated in the imagination of the unhappy Lauretta.

Night had assumed her sablest form; when the fair prisoner, shivering from the inaction in which she had passed the solitary day, and still feeling a reluctance to commit herself to the oblivion of sleep, began slowly to perambulate her chamber:—

languid and feeble she stopped, and, reclining her arm against the flinty wall, her head sunk insensibly upon her hand, and she stood wrapped in painful thought. Suddenly, the trampling of horses struck her ear—she started, and listened—a shrill tucket was shortly after sounded, and she indistinctly heard the sound of voices. Burning with the cheering hope of rescue, her heart beat high within her breast, and her respiration became suspended. "The kind baron," she exclaimed, "has lent his aid to my Alphonsus, and they now come to my relief!"

An interval of dead silence ensued:—she moved towards the door, and, trembling with expectation, doubted whether or not she already heard footsteps. But sad conviction proved her agitated senses had deceived her.

Another interval longer than the first passed away, but no sound met her attentive ear. Delusive hope, however, raised in her harassed brain the flattering possibility, that her friends might be searching for her in some distant part of the building, and would still arrive at her prison.

A confusion of footsteps and voices seemingly approaching towards her apartment, now raised in her panting bosom a tumult of passions, amongst which fear was predominant. Till this instant, the pleasing expectation of enlargement, and restoration to her beloved Alphonsus, had solely occupied her imagination: now the hated Theodore recurred to her, and every footstep seemed to increase the dreadful probability, that she might the next moment be destined to fall a victim to his unruly passion, or breathe her last beneath his injurious arm.

The noise increased, and the persons seemed still to advance. "This way, this way," exclaimed an unknown voice; "follow me, this way." Lauretta breathed with extreme difficulty. A blow against the door thrilled her heart, and the same voice cried out, "The key is not here; ask it of Kroonzer."

Lauretta stood motionless: several voices now spoke at the same time, but so confusedly, that she could not distinguish a word they uttered. Suddenly, all the persons seemed to recede from her prison as swiftly as they had advanced towards it; and the sounds dying gradually away, an awful silence again prevailed.

Trembling lest they should return, Lauretta still continued near the door: she knew not how to account for what she had heard; and the more she ruminated, the more she was bewildered in her conjectures.

A length of time having elapsed, and not the minutest sound met her ear, her alarm began to subside; and the power of reflection returning, she felt in its fullest force the mortifying disappointment she had sustained: at that moment every future prospect of liberty seemed to have vanished in the present; she burst into a flood of tears, and, sinking upon the bed, gave way to the strongest paroxysms of despair.

Oh hope! thou cheering shadow of each desired object! why does the blackening gloom of disappointment so often cloud the sunny path through which thou leadest us, glowing at every anxious step with warmer expectation? while fancy, strengthening with desire, seems the reality, and makes us in imagination blessed; until the dream-dispelling dawn of reason opens our eyes, and shows us the wished-for goal, as distant still, as when we first began the imaginary course!

The mind, harassed beyond its bearing, seeks insensibly the balm designed by nature for its restoration. Thus the fair prisoner, on again opening her eyes to her solitary room, found she had tasted its efficacious sweets, although she had not courted its powers.

During the greatest part of the day, she continued upon the bed, lost in weeping and meditation. The approach of evening again introduced Kroonzer into her apartment: he had brought with him more fruit and another flask of water. He expressed great surprise at her not having tasted what he had set before her the former evening, and asked her to partake of what he had now brought. She paid little attention to his invitation; but besought him to explain to her the occurrences of the preceding night. He did not answer her; but, having prepared the lamp, he lighted it, and left the chamber; repeating the entreaty he had before urged, for her to eat some of the fruit and bread.

Not in compliance with the request of Kroonzer, but the calls of Nature, Lauretta eat of the fruit and bread, and drank a large cup of water: the wine she determined not to taste, concluding, from the effect it had produced on her the first night of her imprisonment, that its nature was somniferous; and, although she wished for an oblivion of her cares, she had not sufficient resolution to act herself towards the production of it; apprehensive of what might befall her in a state of insensibility.

Thus passed on six melancholy days, in a course of sad reflection, perplexed by a variety of conjectures, and cheered only by the idea that Alphonsus was ignorant of her sufferings.

No human being entered her prison save Kroonzer, who never failed at the accustomed hour; but observed an impenetrable silence to every interrogatory made him by Lauretta, relative to her situation.

No sounds similar to those she had heard on the second night of her imprisonment returned: she concluded herself a prisoner for life, and despair began to subside into calm melancholy.

Towards midnight of the seventh day, she was awakened from the soundest sleep she had for some time enjoyed, by a violent crash of thunder, which shook the turret: she sprang from the bed, and stood a moment in wild alarm, scarcely recollecting where she was, or knowing what she had heard; when a flash of lightning struck that side of the turret against which she was leaning; the wall instantaneously fell, and carried along with it the shrieking Lauretta.

CHAPTER X.

Beneath a mountain's brow, the most remote

And inaccessible, by shepherds trod,

In a deep cave, dug by no mortal hand,

A hermit liv'd; a melancholy man.

Home

Stunned by the fall, Lauretta lay a length of time amidst the ruins, insensible of her situation, till reason, beginning again to dawn, brought along with it a recollection of the accident that had befallen her. The tempest was abated, but it still rained violently: her head and right side were much bruised, and her left arm was burnt by the lightning: but, having fortunately dropped upon the wet earth, her body had sustained no other material injury. She lifted up her head, and cast her eyes around; but the twilight, obscured by the thick rain, was insufficient to show her any object but the ruined turret close by which she lay.

Resolved, however, if possible, to profit by an opportunity which seemed providentially given her for effecting her escape, she with difficulty raised herself upon her feet, and, although very weak, she determined to proceed from the castle as quickly as she was able, hoping perchance to arrive at some convent before she was missed—at least could be overtaken—by her guards, who had probably not heard the fall of the turret.

She had proceeded nearly a league without stopping, when the dawn of day, beginning to break, showed her that she was entering upon the precincts of a wood. The ground over which she had passed was heathy and uneven:—heated and panting for breath, she supported herself against the trunk of the first tree; her head ached violently; her arm and side were extremely painful, and her garments, drenched with the continued rain, clung round her, dripping with water. The inaction of a few moments produced a shivering chillness less tolerable than the fatigue of proceeding, and she again endeavoured to walk; but exhausted nature supported her trembling frame only a few paces, ere she sunk upon the rough ground: no prospect but that of a lingering death, or again falling into the hands of

Kroonzer and his companion, now presented itself to her melancholy view: a flood of tears came to the relief of her full heart; she closed her eyes, and sobbed bitterly.

In this situation she had lain a considerable time, when she heard a voice articulate some words which she understood not. She raised her dim eyes, and beheld standing by her side a hermit of a benign aspect and venerable mien, on whose arm hung a flagon, and in whose hand was a staff, on which he supported his aged limbs.

"Praised be the saints!" cried he, as Lauretta opened her eyes, "I am deceived; I thought thee dead." Lauretta extended her feeble hand, which the hermit taking in his, knelt down by her side. "My strength is wasting fast," said Lauretta. After a short pause, she added, "Kind heaven hath sent thee to close my dying eyes."

"Rather do thou hope," returned the hermit, "it has sent me to succour thee from death: thy nature seems exhausted with fatigue; let me conduct thee to my cell hard by, and trust to providence and my endeavours to renovate thy strength."

"Alas, father!" replied Lauretta, "I fear I cannot reach it; I am too faint to walk."

"Let me entreat thee to essay it," cried the hermit. — The old man was feeble, and it required his utmost exertions to assist Lauretta in rising from the ground: he then put the staff into her right hand; and, encircling her waist with his arm, he held the other arm in his, and thus led her tottering steps through a winding path to his rude cell.

Having seated her on a bench covered with moss, the hermit laid a faggot and some dried leaves on the hearth; and, having kindled them, he warmed a small quantity of a restorative cordial he possessed, and gave it to Lauretta to drink. Somewhat revived by the medicine she had swallowed, the old man placed her before the fire, and, having given her a skin mantle, he left her to exchange her wet garments, whilst he went to fill his flagon at a neighbouring spring; which had been his errand abroad when he discovered Lauretta, but which he had left unaccomplished.

On his return, he found his fair guest in some measure refreshed, but still weak and ill. She complained much of the bruises on her head and side, and her arm also was extremely painful: — to this the hermit applied an assuasive balm; and, having given her a healing balsam with which to anoint her head and side, he conducted her into the inner division of his cell; and, having recommended to her to compose herself to sleep on his straw pallet, he left her to repose, whilst he broke his own fast in the outward division of his humble dwelling.

Soft sleep quickly visited the couch of Lauretta, and she embraced it as a friend whose caresses she was unwilling to forego; for she rose not till mid-day had been some hours gone by.

The kind hermit had baked for her some apples on his hearth; and of these, together with some brown bread, she made a sufficient repast, and drank plenteously of the water from the spring.

Lauretta's spirits returning with her strength, she voluntarily gratified the hermit's curiosity in regard to such particulars as led to account for the situation in which he had found her.

"A veil of mystery," cried the old man, as Lauretta ended her account, "has many years clouded that castle. The coward peasantry report it to be the residence of spirits: your words confirm me in the suspicion I have long entertained, that it is infested by a banditti. The castle formerly belonged to the family of Byroff, whose circumstances falling into decay, they have left this country; and their once stately mansion is now mouldering into a pile of ruins."

"Have they ever committed any depredations hereabout?" asked Lauretta.

"Never," answered the hermit. "If they are robbers, as I conjecture, caution would doubtless teach them not to assail the passenger near their haunt, lest it should be detected. But let us hope that the baron Smaldart, whom you represent as your friend, will find some measure for bringing them under the lash of justice."

"But how came Theodore connected with them?" said Lauretta.

"Time will develop that mystery," replied the venerable man: and he added, "However artifice may for a while conceal his guilt, rest assured that providence in its own time will expose the machinations of the wicked, and turn their evil actions on themselves."

"The will of heaven be done," cried Lauretta. "But let me entreat your assistance in devising some method for my returning to my husband."

"We must be cautious in our steps," said the hermit, "lest they lead to the discovery of your retreat, and you again should fall into the power of your malicious enemies."

"By your counsel I will be guided," replied Lauretta.

"Thus then I advise," answered the solitary man. "I will provide thee with implements for writing unto whomsoever it shall best suit thy purpose; and on the morrow I will seek a trusty peasant, residing on the skirts of this forest, who shall convey what thou hast written to the baron Smaldart; and he may then concert some measure for thy safe return to thy husband."

Lauretta gladly adopted this proposal; and, having addressed a brief account of her sufferings and present concealment to her beloved Alphonsus, she enclosed it in a cover directed to the baron; she then drank a second cup of the cordial prepared for her by the hermit, and again retired to his pallet, which he kindly insisted on resigning for her accommodation, having prepared for himself a bed of dried moss and leaves in the outward part of his cell.

Early in the morning Lauretta arose, with a heart lighter than she had for some time felt it; and, having joined her kind host in his accustomed devotions, they sat down to an humble repast, and the hermit then sallied forth in search of the peasant who was to be Lauretta's messenger to the castle of Smaldart.

On his departure, Lauretta again habited herself in her own garments, which a constant fire had now rendered fit for wearing; and, not daring to venture without the cell, she sat ruminating on her happy and unexpected escape from her prison, and anticipating the pleasure of again beholding her Alphonsus.

The hermit, on returning, informed her that the peasant had willingly undertaken the journey; and that, in about five days, she might expect the arrival of her husband, or at least to receive some intelligence of him by the return of the messenger.

Lauretta expressed to him her gratitude for his kindness in the warmest terms; but he silenced her by observing that what he had done was but the debt of man to man, and that it were better not to know than not to perform it. She raised her hands to heaven, in thankfulness for the kind protector she had found; and at the same time dropped a tear for the sorrows of her Alphonsus.

In the course of that day, Lauretta ventured to inquire of her venerable host, what could have induced him, who, from his knowledge of the world, and the exalted sentiments of his heart, seemed to be so well calculated for the offices of society, to have secluded himself from all intercourse with men.

"Canst thou, daughter," he replied, "attend with patience to the tale of a careworn old man?"

Lauretta immediately expressed her anxious wish to be made acquainted with the history of her newly-gained friend.

The hermit heaved a sigh, and thus began.

CHAPTER XI.

When sorrows come, they come not single spies,

But in battalions.

Hamlet

The Hermit's Tale.

"In me you behold the victim of a supposed crime; suffering where I had never erred, and denied the justification which, after years of misery, I was tantalised by having placed fruitlessly in my view.

"My father was a man of some small rank and eminence in the city of Berne, in Switzerland: he had been twice married; my sister was the fruit of his first marriage, myself of his second; and we were his only children.

"My sister was adorned with every beauty and grace that is captivating in a female form: a German count, to whom she by accident became known, grew enamoured of her, asked her hand of my father in marriage, and, as you may readily suppose, was not denied his request.

"About a year after the marriage of my sister, my father died: my mother I never had known; I succeeded to the property of my father, and, in a letter of condolence written me on his death by count Harden (for such was the name of my brother-in-law), he earnestly entreated me to pass over into Germany, and visit my sister.

"The property which had devolved on me by my father's death, being sufficient to maintain me in a comfortable though not in an affluent style of life, I had not turned my thoughts to any vocation, and consequently had no bar to my accepting the kind invitation of the count.

"I accordingly wrote to him, with thanks for his kind remembrance of me, and informing him that I should with pleasure visit my sister at her new abode.

"A few days after, I set out on my intended journey, having resolved to travel on a favourite steed I possessed, for the benefit of the better enjoying the fineness of the country through which I should pass; and, strange as it may seem to you, this resolution was the foundation of a series of misery which has known no abatement.

"You will doubtless think my tale an improbable one; — oft do I myself look back on past occurrences, hardly able to convince myself they could ever be: but I have learnt, from sad experience, that the most trivial accidents may carry in their train a complicated and inexplicable string of misery.

"Let the words which I shall now relate, teach mankind not rashly to fix the stamp of guilt upon that brow on which unproved suspicion hangs, nor to shut the ear of compassion against the voice of him that is accused, because he may seem guilty. — Let my tale be known to all: to the wretched it will teach that he has a brother in affliction; and he on whom fortune has smiled, may gather from the misfortunes of another, a lesson of thankfulness and content.

"My first day's journey was prosperous; on the second, towards evening, when I was within two leagues of the village where I meant to pass the night, having carelessly let my bridle hang upon the horse's neck whilst I eagerly gazed at the delightful prospects which the country afforded, the animal having set his foot on a rolling stone, fell, and so severely wounded his knee, as to render it impossible for him to proceed.

"Perceiving at a short distance from me a neat mansion, I dismounted, and repaired towards it; the door was opened by a man who appeared to be between forty and fifty years of age; I told him the accident that had befallen me, and requested him to direct me to some person who might give assistance to my horse. He immediately called to him a lad of about fourteen years of age, who was working in a garden adjoining to the house, and ordered him to lead the horse to the stable. I was too much in need of assistance, to be very particular in my apologies, and thus willingly accepted his offer.

"It required much persuasion, and even force, to conduct the animal to the stable which had been so kindly offered for his reception.

"Having safely lodged him, my kind inviter himself administered to the wound, and then requested me to follow him into the house. A neatly dressed woman, who, he informed me, was his niece, rose at our entrance, and welcomed me, as did two beautiful little girls, her daughters. — My late accident served to commence our conversation; and the natural questions of whence I came, and whither I was journeying, with their subsequent answers, followed.

"The lad, whom I had left in the stable with my horse, presently entered, and, shaking his head, said, 'Ah, sir! this is a bad job; it will be some time, I doubt, before your beast will be able to set a foot to the ground.'

"I looked melancholy;—my host, whose name was Dulac, observed it, and thus addressed me:—'Nay, sir, don't let this account of your horse distress you; I hope the boy may be mistaken in his conjecture: at all events; if you can pass a few days with comfort to yourself in this humble dwelling, your company will be very acceptable to its inhabitants.'

"I bowed a look of thanks, for an offer by which I felt myself obliged, but hardly thought myself entitled to encroach upon the politeness of a stranger by accepting.

"'Well, well,' continued Dulac, clearly perceiving, I believe, what passed within my breast, 'I must insist on your staying with us to-night; and to-morrow we will talk farther on the subject.—Come, let us step into the stable, and see if our opinion coincides with Peter's.'

"I rose to follow him out, but he stepped back from the door, and, with an inclination of the head, waved his hand for me to precede him; I returned his salutation, and passed on as he directed me: he was then behind, and I heard his niece rise, and call him back. I entered the stable, and found, on examining the condition of my steed's wound, what Peter had said to be but too true. In a few minutes Dulac joined me; smiling, he said, 'My niece, sir, was fearful we should not be able to give you accommodation that you would like; for we have only one unoccupied bed, and my nephew Bertrand is gone to the next town, where he expects to meet his wife's sister and her husband, who are coming back with him to pass a few days here: but I told her not to be uneasy about that, for you were my guest, and if you would condescend to accept half of my pallet, you were heartily welcome to it.'

"I thought this a bad time to apologise for my intrusion; for if I did, it might seem as if I was dissatisfied with my accommodation; and I accordingly accepted his offer with as great warmth as he had made it.

"My frankness seemed to please him; and I could not fail being gratified with his kindness; as his words and actions plainly showed themselves to be such as proceeded from a warm and benevolent heart.

"In about an hour's time, Bertrand and his friends arrived; and Dulac presented me to his nephew, who welcomed me as cordially as his uncle had done. Shortly after, we sat down to supper: good humour presided, and I was happy to see that the party appeared by no means displeased with my society.

"At a late hour we parted; I believe, with mutual regret.

"From their conversation, I learnt that Dulac rented the farm on which he lived, and superintended the management of it himself; while Bertrand and his two sons performed the offices of tillage and husbandry.

"My first business in the morning was to visit my horse; and I was happy to find it in a much more salutary condition than my fears had led me to expect I should.

"Breakfast ended, Dulac invited me to walk with him; an invitation which the beauty of the surrounding country made me eager to accept. Through the most romantic scenery imagination can figure, my host, whose conversation was at once entertaining and instructive, led me to the margin of a small lake, on whose bosom the sun shining in its meridian of splendour, cast the most vivid gilding I had ever beheld; on the other side of the lake, a forest of various trees presented itself to our notice; on our right hand lay the ruins of an ancient monastery, with its decayed bridge, forming a hazardous pass over a bubbling rivulet; on the left, the open country afforded a prospect of many leagues in extent, speckled at intervals with clusters of trees; straggling cottages, easy hills, and browsing cattle; add to this, that the ground on which we rested was the extremity of a gentle declivity of greensward, on whose summit nodded tall and majestic pines, and that, as we reclined on the velvet turf, the falling of a neighbouring cascade met our ears; and you will not wonder that I was entranced by the scene.—At that moment I felt sensations of the most exquisite happiness; or, perhaps, I think them the greatest I ever experienced, because they were the last pleasing moments my heart ever knew.—With the setting of that sun, whose glories I then admired, set my felicity on earth.

"I left the spot of enchantment with regret; on our return home, I expressed in the warmest terms the delight I had experienced in the ravishing scenes I had just been beholding. Bertrand seemed to enjoy the praises I had bestowed on his situation; and promised he would in the evening accompany me to the same place, which he doubted not, he said, that I should view with increased pleasure, as the scene would be in some measure varied by the hour. I gladly accepted his offer, and about sun-set we reached the lake, a short time before the glories of nature in their full perfection had drawn forth my admiration. — A part seemed now to be vanishing, for the ingenious purpose of fixing the attention more strongly on that which was visible. — Bertrand threw himself on the grass; I stood by his side, gazing at the rising moon, who, courting splendour from the departing sun, faintly silvered those waves her rival orb had before deeply gilded, and listened with a melancholy pleasure to the falling of a neighbouring cascade, the view of which I had now so placed myself as to command, till the scene softened me into that ecstasy of sorrow, which must be exquisite if felt at all, and must be felt to be described.

"I had often indulged similar sensations on spots equally inviting, but they had never produced in me feelings so refined as I that evening felt: — how often have I since thought they were too surely the sorrowing omens of my future hapless lot!

"Bertrand made the signal for our departure, and I reluctantly complied with it.

"The exercise I had that day taken had somewhat fatigued me; Dulac observed it, and producing a skin of his old vintage, I drank with pleasure of the cup as it went round, and found myself refreshed and exhilarated.

"The evening passed off with the same harmony and satisfaction that the former one had done: at about the same time as the preceding night, we retired to rest, and sleep quickly overcame me.

"During the day, the heat of the weather had been unusually great; and the warmth of our chamber was oppressive, insomuch that, waking towards the dawn of the morning, I found it had caused me to bleed violently at the nose; I endeavoured in vain for some time to stop the flowing blood; and my restlessness awoke my companion, who, learning my situation, advised me to go and wash at the well, in a small yard adjoining to the garden: I immediately rose, and, having slipped on some of my clothes, was leaving the chamber, for the purpose of following his directions, when he called to me, asking me 'If I had ever opened the door which led out of the house into the garden?' I answered, 'that I did not recollect that I ever had.' — 'Then,' said he, 'take this pocket-knife,' drawing one as he spoke from the pocket of his waistcoat which lay by his bed-side, 'and stick the blade under the latch with one hand, while you lift it up with the other, or you will find a difficulty in getting out.' I thanked him for his attention to me, and taking the knife from his extended hand, ran down stairs, and found it of much service to me in opening the door, the latch of which seemed to have been broken, and not yet mended; I then entered the yard, and, having drawn up a bucket of water, the cold soon produced the desired effect of stopping the blood; and having washed myself, I returned to the chamber. Dulac, who heard me come up, asked me, 'If I had shut the outward door?' I told him I had; and having got into bed, I turned on my side, and was quickly composed to sleep.

"On waking, I found Dulac was risen; I accordingly dressed myself, and went down, where I found the family assembling at breakfast. After the usual salutation of the morning, Bertrand inquired of me for his uncle: I told him, I had not seen him that morning; 'No more have I,' replied Bertrand; 'he has probably strolled down to the lake.'

"'He will return, I dare say, before we have finished our meal,' added Martha; (for so was Bertrand's wife called) 'it is a very usual custom with him to walk early in a morning.'

"Bertrand's two daughters, the one about eleven, and the other about nine years of age, had finished each her cup of milk, before we had completed our meal, and immediately went up stairs, as Martha informed us, to attend to the duties of the house.

"Dulac did not return. — Bertrand began to wonder that he exceeded his accustomed time, and Peter went out to look for him, — as the family now conjectured he had mistaken the hour.

"In a few minutes the girls came running down stairs, with terror painted on their countenances, and the elder of them exclaimed, — 'that her uncle's bed was all over blood!'

"Bertrand and his wife cast a look of surprise at each other — I blushed, and began immediately to apologise for what had happened; informing them also, that I had risen, by the advice of Dulac, 'and gone to the well, where washing had proved the remedy of my complaint.

"'I saw a stain of blood upon the side of the well this morning,' said Bertrand, 'as also in the passage leading to the garden; but I had forgotten to inquire into the cause.'

"'All my uncle's clothes are lying by the bed-side,' said one of the girls.

"'How!' exclaimed Bertrand, and immediately ran up stairs.

"A general silence prevailed till Bertrand returned.

"'What Nicola told us is too true!' said he. 'All his clothes, except his waistcoat, are in the chamber;—in that, he always wore his purse,' added he, at the same time darting at me a look of suspicion and scrutiny.

"Bertrand went on: 'He received thirty louis-d'ors for his trees the day before yesterday: did he give them to you'—looking at Martha—'to lock away?'

"'No,' answered Martha: 'he was counting them to me, when this stranger knocked at the door; and being interrupted, put them all into his pocket again.'

"'This is a strange event!' said Bertrand, again looking at me.

"Astonishment prevented my utterance, and my silence, I believe, strengthened Bertrand in the suspicion of my guilt, which I afterwards found had immediately flashed on his mind.

"Bertrand, his brother-in-law, and the women, now began to converse together, in low voices, throwing, as I observed, at intervals, the most significant glances at me.—I felt confused beyond what I can express, and, had not a false shame prevented me, I should have fallen on my knees to pray for the return of Dulac, and to declare my innocence.

"In a short time, Bertrand's brother-in-law, Laval, left the house, and Bertrand, then turning to me, charged me with being one of a banditti, that had for some time, he said, infested that part of the country, and that having by some means gained intelligence that Dulac was to receive a large sum of money the day before, had planned the stratagem by which I had entered the house, for the purpose of plundering him of it. 'Not satisfied,' added he, 'with robbing him who kindly became your benefactor in an hour of pretended distress, you have endeavoured to shelter one crime by the commission of a blacker enormity: but tremble, young man; for offended justice is diligent in detecting the breakers of her law.'

"The terror I experienced at this open declaration of his sentiments, though I had before read them in his countenance, overpowered me so much, that it was with difficulty I kept myself from sinking on the floor; and my agitation, I am certain, confirmed Bertrand and his wife in thinking me guilty.

"The door was now locked upon me, to prevent my leaving the house, and I was given to understand that Laval was gone to the neighbouring town to fetch the officers of justice.

"In a short time, however, I gained courage from reflecting on my innocence, and I besought Bertrand to hear my vindication; he did not seem to attend to me, nor I believed listened, whilst I laid down at length all the particulars I recollected relative to the preceding night.

"Every sound that met my ear,—every footstep that I heard fall,—made my heart flutter with the hope and expectation of seeing Dulac enter; and oh! how forcibly did every new disappointment add to the load of anxiety that weighed down my heart!

"Presently after, Peter returned from his search of Dulac. 'He had,' he said, 'looked for him in vain.' Bertrand seemed to receive the intelligence he expected.—Martha began in a low voice to communicate to her son what had passed in his absence; and I could not help bursting into tears, as my thoughts continued to dwell on my unhappy situation.

"In about two hours after, the officers of justice arrived, and, on the accusation of Bertrand, Laval, and their wives, bound me their prisoner.—Bertrand then requested that I might be searched: when,—with what words or feelings shall I relate it? —one of them drew from my pocket—open, and bloody—the knife which Dulac had lent me for the purpose of opening the door. In my agitation the circumstance had entirely fled from my mind. Thus I had not related that part of the night's occurrences to Bertrand: no one would now hear me explain it; and it was decided by all, that it had been the instrument of Dulac's death.

"Deaf to my remonstrances, they led me to the next town, and I was thrown into prison, there to lie, till the period at which I was destined to take my trial, should arrive.

"I apprised my brother-in-law of what had happened: he immediately set out for my prison, and having learnt my unhappy story from my own mouth, he, without delay, began to exert such interest as he could command in my favour, against the day of my trial.

"Dulac returned not:—every possible inquiry was made after him by my advocates, but they all proved in vain; and the fatal day arrived, without any one circumstance having occurred which tended in the slightest degree to convince the world of my innocence. The well, it is true, had been searched, and no body found in it; but still that was not reckoned a circumstance sufficiently strong to operate against that of a bloody knife having been found upon my person.

"My trial was short, and I heard myself condemned to die: that sentence was the death-blow to my sister; for, as I have since heard, she never recovered from the shock given her on receiving the tidings of my condemnation. I was taken back to prison, and a confessor was ordered to attend me: my situation moved him; he began, I believe, from my unshaken firmness at the approach of death, to think me innocent, and promised to use his influence in my behalf. His entreaties, joined to what degree of weight my brother count Harden possessed in the city, obtained for me life, on the terms of becoming a galley-slave for the remainder of my days.

"Death would surely on such a condition have been preferable, had I not hoped that something unforeseen might still occur to prove me guiltless, and restore me to my country.

"I pass over the agonising separation from my beloved sister, and my tedious journey, to the moment when I was chained to the oar.

"Ten years' service in the island of Corsica, for to that king had I been sold, inured me to the hardships I experienced, but did not abate the anxiety of my mind. Oh! what a sensation is that of an innocent heart, struggling amidst the most complicated and severe trials, without the means of proving how distant it is from meriting the load it labours under!

"At the end of this period a war broke out between the power to whom I was subject, and the emperor of Morocco. In the course of a year the emperor obtained a great victory over the Corsicans, and I, amongst other prisoners, became the property of the grand vizier: here it became my office to cultivate the gardens belonging to the vizier's palace: my labour was less, but I was still a slave; and the task-master was more severe than he to whom I had before been subservient.

"Thus did I pass on twelve more years, void of comfort either for my mind or my body, when, by an exchange of slaves, with the cause of which I was unacquainted, I was sent to work in a garden belonging to the palace of the emperor.

"On the third day after my removal to my new situation, I observed an old man in a slave's habit, whose countenance I thought was familiar to me. He observed me not at first, but as I passed nearer him, the better to examine his features, he no sooner cast his eyes on me, than he pronounced my name; and his voice instantly convinced me, that it was no other than Dulac who stood before me!

"After our mutual expressions of surprise were ended, I began to inform him of all that had befallen me since our separation,—and with eagerness I then inquired of him, by what means it had been effected.

"'Oh!' said he, 'what hardships have I not suffered since we parted!—what misery have I not undergone!—But I will not murmur; for the decree of heaven is just, and unchangeable till its due time ordains a revocation of it.

"'Not long after you had returned to bed, on the morning on which I last beheld you, I imagined I heard some one enter the house, by the door from the garden; I immediately drew on my waistcoat and slippers, and running down stairs, I beheld in the kitchen, attempting to open the door which led to my private closet, wherein I kept such bonds, papers, and money, as I possessed, two of my nearest neighbours, whom I had long known to be of suspicious characters, from their being connected with a set of smugglers, who resided on the coast of France.

"'Their astonishment at seeing me you may well conceive; they immediately seized and gagged me, and having some moments concerted how they should dispose of me, to prevent my appearing in evidence against them, which by signs I endeavoured to convince them I would not do, if they would depart, and suffer me to remain unmolested, they resolved on carrying me to what they called their cave.

"'Without the house there were two other men, their accomplices, whose countenances I knew not, waiting to assist them in carrying off such booty as they might chance to obtain; they were not a little disappointed at seeing me only brought out to them: but, as I afterwards found that they made a point of securing all who might be liable to act towards their discovery, they dragged me on between two of them, muttering curses on me for having interrupted their plunder, and sourly smiling as they vowed vengeance against me.

"'The cave they had mentioned, was dug out of the earth, some three leagues distant from the spot where I resided, and served for the purpose of concealing their contraband goods. Thither they conducted me; and having searched my pockets, in which was unfortunately a sum of money I had two days before received for some elms, they set by me a pot of water, and some dry crusts of bread, and left me.

"'My prison was shut from the faintest glimmering of light; the air admitted into it was so confined that I found a difficulty in breathing, and its scent was most nauseous; to which, add the agonies my mind was undergoing from the knowledge of my being in the power of these wretches, and torn from those I alone regarded, together with my anxiety for their concern at my unexpected and extraordinary disappearance, and you will easily picture to yourself the agonising feelings of my heart.

"'In the dusk of the evening two other men entered the cave, and having gagged me, led me forth; after some hours' walking, we came up with a body of men, who I soon found were colleagues of those who now conducted me: along with them were fifteen other prisoners, bound and gagged in like manner as myself, and who had been taken in similar caves by these inhuman robbers.

"'After some additional hours' travelling, we arrived at another cave, much resembling that in which I had been confined during the former night; and here the other prisoners, together with myself, were led down, and deposited in an inner division: the outer one, we found, was inhabited by the smugglers themselves.

"'Many were the conjectures we formed with regard to our situation; and though it was impossible we should assign any degree of certainty to any one of them, we could not still forbear drawing them.

"'The next night we were again led forth as before, and after several hours' travelling each night, for six successive nights, and being lodged by day in caverns similar to those I have already mentioned, we found ourselves on the sea coast: we were immediately put on board a vessel lying a short distance out at sea; and we soon understood that its master bargained with these smugglers for slaves, which he sold in Morocco, chiefly to the emperor.

"'There is but one sure friend in misfortune,—resignation to the divine power, and confidence in its will to convert all we suffer here to our glory in a state hereafter: I armed my heart with this cheering thought; and my communication of my feelings had, I believe, much weight on the minds of my fellow-sufferers.

"'After a passage of fatigue and hardship, we arrived where you now find me; here have I dwelt a slave ever since;—and if providence has decreed me here to end my unfortunate days, I bend to its almighty will.'

"With what sorrow did I behold him who had been my kind protector, in the unhappy situation I now saw him, and reduced to it, as I could not help thinking, partly by my means; as, had I not on that fatal night arisen from my bed and broken his repose, he in all probability would never have heard the entrance of those ruffians to whom he had now fallen a prey.

"I imparted to him my thoughts, and the anxiety they occasioned me; but he kindly chid me for forming my judgment from events, and declared that my lot, from the probability of its enduring so many years longer than the natural course of nature threatened him with a painful existence, was his greatest cause of disquietude.

"From the first moment of my finding Dulac, every nerve of thought was unremittingly on the stretch to devise some plan of effecting our escape, fondly anticipating the triumph I should enjoy, were I ever allowed to be the means of restoring him to his country and relatives.

"Whilst my mind was thus employed in forming various stratagems, all of which, however, appeared ineffectual, an occurrence, as unforeseen as unexpected, and which then appeared to me the happiest of my existence, took place: this was no other than intelligence being brought to Morocco, that a French nobleman, lately dead, had left by will, as an expiation of some crime he had committed, a sufficient sum of money for the liberation of fifty European slaves who had been the longest in captivity. And it is, I think, needless for me to relate to you the joy experienced by Dulac and myself, on being informed that we were of the happy number.

"Our slaves' habits were exchanged for European garments; and in a few days we embarked on board a French vessel, which was to transport us to the coast of Languedoc, whence we were each to be conveyed to our respective country.

"Our voyage for the first six days was prosperous: on the seventh, towards sunset, the wind, which had blown freshly through the day, became extremely violent; the angry clouds rolled over each other, producing tremendous claps of thunder, and the flashes of lightning, reflected on the expanse of water, appeared alarmingly vivid. The ship was tossed in an uncertain course by the foaming billows, which at intervals washed over the deck, and then again yielded to the dividing bow of the ship. A general consternation seized every one on board; and, with a silence that increased the awfulness of the scene, each seemed to await the next moment as his last. At length, driven upon the side of a rock obscured by the rolling waves, the vessel split into two equal parts, and an universal cry seemed to announce instantaneous destruction.

"The boat was lashed to that partition of the ship on which Dulac and myself were standing: a sailor instantly ran to it; and, having launched it into the deep, sprang into it. I hesitated not an instant to follow him; and, having gained the boat, I received Dulac from the side of the ship, in my extended arms. Immediately the foaming billows dashed us to a considerable distance from the ship; and in a few moments after we saw her swallowed up in a whirlpool.

"We beheld the sight with horror, and knew not, as yet, whether to be thankful that we had not shared the fate of the unhappy sufferers. In the space of an hour the wind began to abate, but the billows still rolled mountain-high; and it was with extreme difficulty that we could by any means balance our little bark. For some hours we contrived to effect it; till our limbs becoming benumbed by the wet and cold we were enduring, a wave dashed over us, and overset our boat. I could swim; and immediately raising myself in the water, I caught the boat, and exerting strength which was called forth by the urgency of the moment, I managed again to place myself in it. I immediately looked round for Dulac: he had vanished from my sight. An arm was now raised from the water; I seized it, and lifted from the deep the sailor who had been the means of effecting my escape from the ship:—Dulac was gone for ever.

"This was the completion of my misery; but as the preservation of life, when threatened with danger, is always the predominant idea in the breast of man, however his mind may be clouded with sorrow, I did not at that moment feel in its full force the loss I had sustained.

"Towards the break of morning, a small vessel, bound to Villa-Nuova in Spain, perceived our situation; and having sent out to us its boat, we were taken on board, and such accommodation as the vessel would afford kindly bestowed on us: and not till then, when the recollection of the horrors I had lately been exposed to began to subside, did I feel how much more miserable and destitute a being, than I had even before been, the loss of Dulac had rendered me.

"The sailor who had been my companion in the boat, a very short time after our entering the vessel, fell a victim to what he had undergone. Oh! why was I, with so great cause to loathe the world, spared from sharing his fate?

"On the following day the Spanish vessel gained her destined port, and I landed on a country where I was an entire stranger, and possessed neither of the means of purchasing my subsistence, nor of earning it, as I understood not the language of the kingdom.

"Fortunately for me, the captain of the vessel was conversant with the French language; and, being a man of generous disposition, he at my request furnished me with the habit of a seaman; and having given me a piece of gold, I set forward, thinking, in my present disguise, I might reach count Harden's mansion in the vicinity of Ulm, unknown.

"Seven weeks served to complete my journey: when, conceive my disappointment! — on reaching the spot where I had hoped to meet the warm embraces of an affectionate sister, I learned that she had but two months survived my exile; and that count Harden had also some years paid the debt of nature.

"I inquired whether my sister had left any offspring. I was informed, that she had never borne but one child, a daughter, and that she was also dead.

"I believe I had already been wounded so deeply by affliction, that an added pang was imperceptible to my grief-worn heart. I can no other way account for the firm composure with which I heard this defeat of my last and only hope.

"In my way to Ulm I had passed this cell; I had found it was deserted; its late possessor having been some years dead. I had no interest in the world, but rather a wish to secrete myself from it, lest I should be recognized by any of Dulac's relatives; and I possessed nothing in the world, for my property had been confiscated on my receiving sentence of banishment. I accordingly determined to make it my dwelling: and having found that I had sufficient money left, from what I had collected on my journey from the charitable, under the disguise of a shipwrecked sailor, to purchase me a woollen robe, a scrip, staff, and flagon, I immediately repaired hither, and have resided here ever since, indebted for my subsistence to the peasantry round about, in addition to the fruits and berries I collect in the surrounding wood.

"I have now dwelt here fifteen years; and, save the little intercourse I hold with the peasantry, you are the first whose conversation has cheered my solitary dwelling. — I am now fourscore and two years old: may you attain my years, without the sorrows that have numbered mine! and may you await the hour of your death, my now only consolation, with a heart like mine, full of forgiveness towards those who may have injured you."

Here the hermit concluded; and Lauretta, wiping away the tear from her eye, which had been drawn forth by the sufferings of her benefactor, thanked him for the confidence he had reposed in her, and of her own accord promised to be the faithful guardian of his sad tale.

To dwell on the sorrows of others, when the mind is agitated by misfortune, tends only to depress the already sinking spirits. Thus Lauretta now felt a gloom cloud her mind, which she found herself unable to shake off; and her attempts to appear cheerful only added to the depression which in reality weighed down her spirits, while the tears stole insensibly from her downcast eyes.

The old man perceived the melancholy which had seized upon his fair guest, and began to converse on various topics, which he hoped might engage her attention from the gloomy subjects on which he well saw they were dwelling: but finding his endeavours to be in vain, he again heated for her a cup of his balsamic cordial; and having bathed with a mollifying ointment her head and arm, which were now in a healing condition, he prevailed on her, as night was rapidly shutting in, to seek relief for her agitated mind in the composure of sleep.

On the following morning, Lauretta arose at the moment the old man returned from fetching his accustomed measure of water; and he joyed to find that the refreshment of sleep had dispelled the gloom of sorrow which had on the preceding evening clouded her brow.

The hermit had also been to a neighbouring cottage, where he was constantly supplied with bread, and had brought from thence a bunch of fresh-gathered grapes, as a present to Lauretta.

During the course of the day, Lauretta expressed to her host her astonishment at Theodore's never having visited her during her late confinement; as, had he conveyed her thither from the love he bore her person, it was natural to suppose he would have immediately followed her, and by force have rendered her subservient to his base desires. The hermit bade her be contented with the knowledge of having escaped the evil she had dreaded, nor sink her spirits with dwelling on a gloomy retrospect, now a smiling prospect of hope was placed in her view.

"But should it vanish," cried Lauretta, "should the wicked Theodore have by any means cut me off from again beholding my Alphonsus"— —she paused, and the tears started in her eyes.

"Why thus unnecessarily afflict thee, by visionary phantoms of distress?" exclaimed the solitary man. "From the evils experienced in this life of probation no one is exempt: it is a chequered scene, wherein the most submissive to their fate endure the less affliction here, and ensure to themselves the greater reward hereafter: whereas, to anticipate misfortune, is to double our earthly calamities, while we endanger our future felicity, in drawing upon us the displeasure of him who alone can bestow it, by our want of confidence in his will and ability to protect us."

Lauretta felt the force of his words; but she felt also, that it was easier for a man, dead to every connexion with the world, to give philosophic counsel, than for her to cease to be anxious for the fate of him whom alone she loved.

Towards evening, a sprightly fire cheered the hermit's cell, and various discourse wasted the hours pleasantly, till the hermit gave the signal of retiring for the night; and Lauretta having joined him in fervent prayer, they each betook themselves to their respective pallet.

About midnight Lauretta awoke, and Alphonsus immediately becoming the subject of her thoughts, she lay ruminating on what might have befallen him since their separation, when a faint sigh caught her ear; somewhat startled, she raised herself upon her couch and listened; but instantly recollecting the near situation of her host, she smiled at her vain apprehensions, and turning on her pallet, fell insensibly into a second sleep.

On waking in the morning, she called to the hermit, inquiring the hour; and receiving no answer to her demand, she concluded him gone to the spring; she accordingly rose, and entered the outward division of the hermitage, when, what was her astonishment on beholding her venerable benefactor stretched lifeless on his mossy couch!

She uttered a loud shriek, and sunk upon the ground; but there was no one near to hear, or to raise her: at length, with tottering steps she ventured to approach the clay-cold corpse,— she gazed upon it awhile in silent anguish; then, bursting into a flood of tears, she exclaimed—"Hard, when I had found a friend to soothe the loss of those from whom the base designs of villainy have for a while exiled me, that the hand of death should, at that needy moment, have wrested him from me!— Oh! that I had flown to him when I first heard that passing sigh! his last breath, doubtless, then hung lingering on his lips, and my timely aid might have recalled it!—Oh! preserver of my life, pardon my unwilling neglect of thine: and if, after death, exalted saints (for, surely, such thou art) have influence here on earth, unseen by man, Oh! cast a thought on the unhappy wretch thou didst not here disdain to succour."

Weeping, she cast herself upon the bench which had not long before supported the old man and herself in cheerful conversation over the crackling embers;—a dead silence now reigned, broken only by her sighs.—Three tedious days and equal nights were before her, to be passed in solitude, irksome in itself, and which she yet feared to see interrupted by any unwelcome visitant, before the time would elapse, at the expiration of which the hermit had taught her to expect the return of her messenger.

Day was nearly closed ere she awoke from the lethargy of grief and reflection into which she had fallen; and having then eaten a small quantity of bread, and drank a cup of water, she cast a look of sorrow at her deceased friend; and having prayed fervently, she cast herself upon her pallet, relying for protection on that being who, in the trials to which he subjects us in this transient state, consults only our welfare, by fixing our thoughts more forcibly on the blissful scenes of an endless futurity.

CHAPTER XII.

Oh, my wrongs,

My wrongs! they now come rushing o'er my head. —

Again, again, they wake me into madness.

Hartson

We now return to Alphonsus, whom we left on that fatal night on which Lauretta was conveyed from him by the villainy of Theodore.

The night was far advanced, when Alphonsus returned from the water; and, on approaching his little habitation, his surprise was instantly excited by seeing the door open, and no light burning within against his return; — he entered, — all was silent. — He called on Lauretta, and on the girl who attended her; no answer was given him: — he sought her in every part; — again he called on her, it was in vain. — Frantic with surprise and fear, he ran to the habitation nearest to his own: he awoke its inhabitants, and, scarcely knowing what he said, or able to explain his own ideas, he asked for Lauretta; she was not there. — He then flew to the next cottage, and so on to every one in succession: — Lauretta was not to be found, or any information to be gained respecting her. — He again returned to his own dwelling; again he searched it, and again he called on his beloved Lauretta; but Lauretta answered him not. — "She is gone! lost for ever!" he exclaimed — "Theodore, the cursed Theodore, has torn her from me; he triumphs over me, and tortures her!" — In the wildest agitation he threw himself on the ground; then starting from the momentary trance into which he had fallen, and with his net still on his arm, as he had brought it from his boat, he rather flew than ran towards Smaldart castle.

The baron was just risen as Alphonsus reached the castle: — Alphonsus perceived him in the garden, and flying to him, apologised for his abrupt intrusion, and then requested the baron to inform him whether Theodore was absent from the castle.

The baron answered, that he had not seen him since the preceding evening; and immediately asked his reason for the inquiry; and Alphonsus, in as collected a manner as the agitation of his spirits would allow him to speak, related to the baron all that had passed since Theodore's arrival in Germany.

The baron was too well acquainted with the disposition of Theodore, to doubt either what Alphonsus had said of him, or his being the means of Lauretta's being torn from her husband, and immediately dispatched a servant to the chamber of Theodore, to ascertain whether he was in the castle.

The servant quickly returned, with information that Theodore was still in bed.

"I did not suppose he had left the castle," said the baron; "I am well acquainted with his extraordinary temper, and see the motives of his entire conduct;—not love, but pride, first edged him on to supplant you in the affections of an amiable and lovely woman; the triumph he there sought to gain was defeated by your Lauretta's virtue; revenge is now the only passion left open to him, and he seeks its gratification in separating the persons of those whose affections he could not divide:—but rely on my friendship and services; he has doubtless entrusted your wife to the care of some bribed peasant in the neighbourhood till he can find an apt moment for carrying her beyond your reach:—saddle the fleetest horses in my stable, take two of my domestics to accompany you, and visit every habitation in the circle of my estate, commanding them in my name not to retain her.—I will in the mean time be answerable that Theodore shall not pursue her."

With terms of unfeigned gratitude to the baron, Alphonsus ran to the stables, and having announced what the baron had authorised him to perform, in a few minutes' time departed from the castle, together with the two domestics appointed to accompany him.

Theodore, if he had slept at all (and sleep is rarely the portion of even the most secure villainy), had been awakened by the entrance of the servant into his chamber, and had immediately risen, and descended into the hall; he was inquiring of every domestic the cause of his uncle's having asked for him at so early an hour, when the baron entered from the garden; and perceiving Theodore, who was listening with the utmost counterfeited composure to the story of Lauretta's disappearance, as relating by one of the servants to his fellows, he beckoned him to follow him into an apartment.

Theodore obeying his uncle's call, entered the room, and threw himself into a chair; the baron closed the door, and thus addressed him: "Theodore, the unlimited indulgence of a too fond uncle has been your ruin,—boyish errors, left unchastised, have ripened with your years into crimes; those crimes, either from their having been confined within the limits of too lenient laws, or from the inability of those you have wronged, to punish, have escaped with impunity; on this presumption your haughty spirit, triumphing in its imaginary security, seeks revenge for every thwarted inclination; but know, that the forbearance of an uncle may be too far imposed upon, and the laws of your country too highly insulted. I greatly fear you have been tempting the former, and abusing the latter."

Theodore rose in great agitation, and was beginning to speak.—

"Be calm, and hear me," continued the baron; "your passion of revenge has been excited against two amiable persons, sufficiently unhappy in their knowledge of you without the addition of your cruelty: but it was not enough for you that they were not miserable;—this was only to be done by tearing them asunder, and you have effected it: but they shall meet again to your confusion."

Choking with rage at this open declaration of the sentiments of the baron, when he had buoyed himself up with the idea of having so dexterously conducted the villainous act, as to have removed all fear of the slightest suspicion falling upon him, Theodore exclaimed, "Me! accuse me of having carried off the wife of Alphonsus the fisherman! You pay an exalted compliment to my taste, and to my knowledge of my rank in life."—Then, with a satirical smile, he added, "But I beg the female's pardon, 'tis unfair to decide on the merits of her I never saw."

"Never saw!" returned the baron, fixing his eyes steadfastly on his nephew.

Theodore met the baron's eyes;—he read in them his knowledge of the falsehood he had uttered; and a frown of passion succeeding the sneer of contumely which had before sat upon his countenance, he cried, "No, I swear by heaven, that"——

"Hold," interrupted the baron, "violate not heaven by an oath, which, ten times repeated, would not convince me. I cannot suppose that the man whom I suspect to be the perpetrator of a crime, heinous as that of which I now accuse you, will hesitate the commission of a second, whereby he hopes to clear away the imputation of the first."

Perceiving the baron to be firm in the point he was urging, and thinking a patient show of innocence to be most likely to win on the baron in his favour, he said, "If you are determined to think so hardly of me, sir, I must trust alone to the conviction time will give you of my innocence, for my return to your good opinion; in the interval I have, however, my own heart to refer to for consolation."

What villain is not skilled in fair words?—The baron was too well acquainted with the human heart, to ask the confession of Theodore. He knew that guilt is stubborn, and that the urgency of entreaty tends only to harden, not relax, its obstinacy.

He accordingly thus addressed him. "Theodore, you may be innocent with regard to what has occurred; it would greatly delight me to find you so, but I much fear you are not. If you are guilty, the restraint I am about to impose on you, will be only what you merit: if otherwise, the elucidation of this mystery will be to your honour. I am resolute in my determination, that the two apartments at the end of the northern gallery shall be your prison, till Lauretta is restored to her husband. Should it be possible that she has fled from Alphonsus on any other account, or with any other person, you have no business to interfere in what concerns them only: if you have conveyed her hence, it is my duty to prevent your pursuing her, and I will take care to put an effectual bar to your further annoying her peace."

Theodore raised his hands and eyes with a look of astonishment and sorrow, then walked slowly to the window with his handkerchief to his face.

The apartments to which the baron had alluded, were immediately prepared; and Theodore, in sullen silence, entered them; and the lock was turned upon him by the baron's own hand.

The key of the apartments wherein the chevalier was confined, was given, by the baron, to a trusty servant; with orders to visit him frequently, and to supply him with every necessary of life, and any article of amusement he required; but on no account to suffer him to pass the limits of his prison.

Late in the evening, Alphonsus returned much fatigued, and his spirits greatly depressed by the want of success that had attended his numerous inquiries.

Exhausted as he was, he immediately sought the baron, and requested permission of him to exchange his steed, and again set out in search of his beloved Lauretta. The baron informed him of what had passed between him and Theodore since his departure; and besought him, for his health's sake, to await the morning, before he again set out. But no consideration of what he might himself undergo, could restrain Alphonsus from the pursuit of one whose safety was so essential to his happiness; and, having scarcely permitted himself to partake of a hasty repast, he mounted a fresh horse that had been prepared for him, and set out in a different direction from the castle to that he had before taken.

In the course of the following day, the baron visited Theodore. Confinement, to which he was unaccustomed, had already gone far towards curbing his crabbed disposition; and, on seeing his uncle, he burst into a peevish exclamation, which sued for liberty; and during which it was with difficulty that he restrained his tears. The baron having looked round the apartments in order to satisfy himself that they were secure in every part, and the accommodation of his nephew good, left him without speaking a single word.

Midnight brought back Alphonsus to Smaldart castle: the fatigue of body and mind he had undergone, had so far exhausted nature, as to require the most assiduous attention being paid to him; and being lifted off his horse, he was immediately, by the baron's order, conveyed to a bed in the castle.

"She is gone for ever, for ever!" he exclaimed, as the baron approached the side of the bed on which he lay: he endeavoured to say more, but weakness overpowered him.

The baron used every argument he could devise to cheer him, but he was too miserable to be soothed by any consolation, save the presence of his Lauretta.

Early in the morning the baron sent out four horsemen, commanding them to take a more extended circuit than Alphonsus had done, and to omit no possible means that might lead to the discovery of the object they were going in pursuit of.

A fever in the blood had seized upon Alphonsus, and towards evening the wildest delirium possessed him: at intervals, with returning reason, he asked for tidings of

Lauretta; then again raving, in thought, beheld her standing by him; and again, reason returned to prove the pleasing vision a fallacy.

Thus passed on eight days of the most unhappy nature to all parties: to Theodore the most irksome imagination can conceive; the success of his base plan alone affording him a slender satisfaction, which was nearly outweighed by the idea that suspicion fell too heavily upon him to be easily shaken off. A thousand plans had he formed for escaping from his confinement, and as many obstacles arose to render them impracticable: worn out by curbing his violent temper or venting it on empty air, he at length submitted to entreat, where before he had scarcely deigned to command; and in the humblest language, interlarded with the most liberal promises which the hope of obtaining his wish could instigate, he besought the domestic whom the baron had appointed to serve and watch over him, to favour his escape.

The servant, on whom the baron's injunctions had been too forcibly laid, to hesitate a single moment in the discharge of the trust reposed in him, ventured to remonstrate with the chevalier on the impropriety of the request he so strongly urged, and the inadequacy of any reward to the loss of the baron Smaldart's favour.

The baron, who had not visited his nephew since the second day of his inhabiting those apartments, now entered, and thus put a stop to a further conversation. Theodore, on beholding his uncle, burst into a flood of tears, and calling on heaven to witness his innocence, besought a remission of his confinement.

"I had weighed well my reasons for the punishment I have doomed you to," cried the baron, "ere I enforced it; and those tears, the effect of disappointed villainy, shall not impel me to relax its severity. Is every thing here to your satisfaction? I wish you to undergo no farther inconvenience than what you may suffer in being prevented from leaving these walls."

To one subject alone could Theodore attend; he reiterated his declarations of innocence, and in louder accents implored for his accustomed liberty.

The baron had too tenderly loved Theodore, to be entirely unmoved by his protestations and entreaties, and accordingly left the apartment, lest they should exact from him an indulgence he might afterwards repent.

Towards evening of the eighth day Alphonsus' fever began to abate, and the frantic sorrow which had before possessed him began to subside into a silent melancholy.

On the following day the messengers returned; they informed the baron, that they had met with an old woman, who had told them, that a female, answering to the description of Lauretta, and who had talked much of Smaldart castle, had been brought in a vehicle by two men to her cottage, early in the morning of the very day on which Lauretta had been missed, and had remained there during the whole of that day; the woman, they said, had pointed out to them the road along which the men and the female had journeyed, and they had followed the track many leagues, but all their endeavours to discover the object of their search had proved equally fruitless.

Farther conviction of Theodore's guilt beamed upon the baron in this account delivered by the old woman; but conjecture only tended the more to perplex him, and he determined to see her himself, and gain from her such intelligence as she was able to give him: he accordingly commanded two of the horsemen to refresh themselves, and be prepared to set out again with him in an hour's time.

The conduct of Theodore was now exhibiting in striking colours, that villainy will submit to the most humiliating meanness, in the hope of gaining its desired ends. Whenever the domestic visited him, he raved, fawned, and prayed by turns, for the grant of his supplication, till the domestic, sensible how wrongly he should be acting were he to acquiesce, and wishing Theodore not to flatter a hope which he did not mean to realize, gave him a gentle refusal.

Contradiction from a servant Theodore had never yet experienced, and even in his present humiliating state he could not brook it; he therefore seized the domestic by the throat, and throwing him upon the ground, gave a loose to his rage. Stunned by the blow, the man lay in a state of insensibility: Theodore perceived his situation, and determining to avail himself of it, hastily searched his pockets, and having found the key of the outward apartment, he unlocked the door, and sallied cautiously forth, again closing it as he went out.

An hour after mid-day the baron arrived at the cottage; and its hostess, who was no other than Bartha, gave him the same information she had delivered to the horsemen; adding, that the young woman had much wished to write a letter to be conveyed to Smaldart castle, but that she had not been able to furnish her with the requisites; and that her husband had meant to visit the castle on the following day with the message she had then desired her to get conveyed thither, being the first day he could spare from his laborious avocation. The message was only, that she had been conveyed to the cottage by two ruffians, whom she knew to be the instruments of Theodore, and an entreaty that the baron would assist her husband in finding some means to accomplish her rescue.

The wood-cutter, Bartha's husband, then told the baron, that on the afternoon prior to Lauretta's being brought to his cottage, two men had accosted him whilst at his daily labour in the neighbouring wood, and inquired whether he lived near that spot; whether he would give them the use of his dwelling on the following day; and whether money could bribe him to secrecy. "I am very poor," continued the woodman, "and extending my hand to receive a couple of pieces of gold which one of them held in his, I told them I would do any thing but murder to serve them. 'We require nothing but secrecy,' he returned: — 'we shall bring a young woman, for whom you must provide a bed, early in the morning, to your cottage, and stay with you all day.' I agreed to this, and having walked with them a few steps to show them where my cot stood, they wished me good night, and left me."

"Proceed," said the baron.

"Well, sure enough, early in the morning they brought a young woman, and my wife took her up stairs, and then one of the men went away with the vehicle in which they had brought her, and came back with only the horses; and at night one of them took the young woman on a horse before him, and they gave me another piece of gold, and away they went, and we have neither seen them, nor heard of them since."

"Would you had informed me of this sooner!" exclaimed the baron. "But complaints are useless where there is no remedy for the evil." So saying, he presented Bartha with a piece of money, and returned to his castle.

Hoping that this incontrovertible proof of Theodore's guilt might be efficacious in drawing from him a confession of the truth, the baron proceeded towards his apartments, where, to his astonishment, he saw extended on the floor, the servant, just recovering from the blow he had sustained, and unable to give any account of Theodore. As his escape had not been long effected, he could not consequently have proceeded far distant from the castle; accordingly every domestic and even the baron himself, ran out in search of him.

Theodore had, during this interval, concealed himself in his bed-chamber, and now seeing from its window the servants and his uncle issue from the portal, he ventured to descend into the hall of the castle, where having met with no interruption to his progress, he ran hastily out of the postern gate, and having reached the stable, he saddled and mounted his steed: all danger now vanished before him, for he knew his pursuers to be on foot, and he was well acquainted with the fleetness of the horse on which he rode; accordingly he clapped spurs to his beast, and galloped dauntlessly forward.

Thus providence in its all-wise direction allots a certain portion of triumph to the machinations of the wicked, which ultimately shall edge them on to become the instruments of their own conviction and punishment.

Shortly after the baron returned to the castle, and four of his vassals were immediately commanded to mount their horses, and set off, in hope of overtaking Theodore. His horse was now missed, and this information caused the baron the more earnestly to urge their speed.

As the slight information which the baron had received relative to Lauretta, tended only to prove that she was in the power of Theodore's agents—a circumstance which the chevalier's recent escape had rendered the more distressing—he forbore to inform Alphonsus either of what he had heard, or of what had that day occurred at Smaldart castle.

Early on the next morning the baron entered the apartment of Alphonsus, and on meeting his eyes, which the opening of the door had drawn towards the baron, he exclaimed, "Joy! joy, Alphonsus! Lauretta is found! Lauretta is in safety!"

The intelligence was too smiling for Alphonsus instantly to believe that his senses had been true to him; he feared to ask a repetition of the baron's words, lest the pleasing idea should vanish in his reiterated voice. He seized the baron's hand, and pressing it in his own, the tears gushed from his eyes.

The baron now put into his hand the letter of Lauretta's own writing, which he had a few minutes before received from the peasant commissioned by the hermit, who had that morning reached the castle.

Although the fever under which Alphonsus laboured had been much abated by the skill of an able physician whom the baron had procured to attend him, yet while the cause, namely, the violent agitation of his spirits, continued, it was not possible that the effect could have been removed; and he was reduced to so weak a state by what he had undergone during the last ten days, not less in body than in mind, that, on receiving tidings at once so joyful, and yet, from the despondent state of his mind, so little expected, it was with great difficulty for some time that life could be retained within him.

At length an hysteric fit of laughter, accompanied by many tears, relieved his overburdened heart, and he pressed alternately to his lips and to his bosom the paper which contained the account of his Lauretta's safety.

When Alphonsus was sufficiently recovered from the frenzy of joy that had possessed him, to attend to the words of the baron, that kind friend informed him, that he would take upon himself the office of being Lauretta's guardian and conductor to the castle.

Alphonsus sprang from the bed in which he had before been scarcely able to raise himself; and, declaring himself to be now recovered, entreated to accompany the baron: but to this the physician gave a stern denial, declaring that it was absolutely necessary to his health and safety, that he should not yet leave his bed, or have his composure broken by any avoidable means.

Sufficiently secure of the safety of his Lauretta under the protection of the kind baron, Alphonsus reluctantly yielded to the remonstrances of the physician; and the baron departed, accompanied by two of his servants, and the peasant who was to conduct him to the hermit's cell.

The baron had not proceeded far on his journey to the hermitage, ere he was met by his returning vassals, whose pursuit of Theodore had proved ineffectual: and, as he now knew Lauretta to be removed from the reach of the chevalier, he commanded them to discontinue their search.

On the third day after the baron's departure, Alphonsus was so much recovered as to be permitted to leave his chamber:—his fever had quitted him;—his strength was returning, and his spirits were highly elated, as he dwelt on the mortification which Theodore, whom he vainly imagined still to be the sullen inhabitant of the prison his uncle had decreed him, would in his turn experience, on his seeing Lauretta safely restored to the arms of her husband. Theodore's escape the baron had judged it most advisable to conceal from Alphonsus, as the knowledge of it could only increase his fears for Lauretta's sufferings.

On the evening of the fourth day, the baron was expected to return; and Alphonsus awaited on the tiptoe of expectation the hour that should bring him to his castle. Midnight sounded, and the baron did not arrive: Alphonsus endeavoured to console himself with the possibility of the baron's journey having deceived him in the length of a few hours, and sat listening with anxiety for sounds which he might construe into the approach of the expected carriage. Morning dawned, and disappointment still prevailed: day passed on in a state of inexplicable inquietude; and night closed in with increased apprehensions to the trembling Alphonsus.

About the first hour of the morning, as Alphonsus was traversing his chamber, with a mind swelled with the most hideous phantoms of the fate that might have befallen her in whom his every wish and thought were centred, the distant approach of a carriage fell on his ear. He seized his lamp, and the increasing sound of joy accompanied him as he descended into the hall of the castle. Unacquainted with the exact method of opening the door, and his hand being infirm from agitation, it was some time ere he could effect it; and he drew it back on its hinges, at the very moment the carriage stopped.

Alphonsus issued out with the lamp in his hand; and, having scarcely permitted himself to salute the baron as he left the carriage, he sprang forward to meet Lauretta. Vain thought! Lauretta was not within it.

Grief and astonishment petrified Alphonsus.

The baron took his hand in his, and led him into the hall of the castle.

"Tell me the worst at once," cried Alphonsus. When, at length, after many ineffectual efforts, articulation was again granted him, "Tell me she is dead; the sound will be my summons to her grave."

"Afflict thee not so deeply: she is not dead, though gone from us."

"Gone! how? whither? by what means?" exclaimed Alphonsus, his eyes rolling wildly in their sockets. "Has the vile hermit betrayed her to . . . . . . ?"

"Sully not unjustly his venerable name," interrupted the baron. "He has, I fear, suffered much in her cause: when I reached his humble cell, the first object that presented itself to my sight was his lifeless form, stretched on the earth."

"And Lauretta!" cried Alphonsus, waiting to have the sentence filled up by the baron.

"Has baffled my most diligent search of her," added the baron.

"Mysterious heaven!" returned the youth; "who could have learned her retreat? — who have carried her from thence? — Is not the chevalier at this very moment in the castle?"

"Is Theodore then returned?" asked the baron eagerly.

Alphonsus started, and fixed a look of inquiry, surprise, and suspicion, on the baron, that at once convinced him how unguardedly he had spoken, and how fully explicative of Theodore's escape, which he had hitherto so carefully concealed from Alphonsus, the few words he had just uttered had proved. He endeavoured to retract what he had said; but Alphonsus flew to substantial proof; and the deserted apartments, which had been the chevalier's prison, were but a too certain conviction of all his fears.

Ye who have felt, can alone conceive and participate in the poignant feelings of Alphonsus, on this heart-rending discovery: — by turns silent agony and frantic grief possessed him. The plan which one moment suggested, the next taught him to reject; and, from a chaos of ideas, his perturbed mind could fix on no one to adopt in the present moment of despair and madness.

Descending into the hall, he for a short space of time traversed it with hasty and uncertain steps. Suddenly stopping, he exclaimed, "It may not yet be too late to save her! Just heaven, nerve my arm, and guide my steps to the object of my search!" and fled from the hall with hasty steps.

The baron, alarmed by the wild mien of Alphonsus on his discovering the absence of Theodore from Smaldart castle, had ascended to the apartment of the physician, to inform him what had occurred, and summon him to the aid of his patient, at the same moment that Alphonsus had run to investigate the late prison of the chevalier. And, having first sought him in the northern gallery, then in the apartment which had been

assigned to him in the castle, and lastly in the great hall, he saw
not for some minutes the open gate which bespoke his having
left the castle. Immediately on perceiving it, he ran out in search
of him: but it was too late: he had mounted a horse, which he
had taken from the stable, and departed unseen by any one.

CHAPTER XIII.

On her white breast a sparkling cross she wore,

Which Jews might kiss, and infidels adore.

Pope

During the two first days after the death of the hermit, Lauretta's solitude remained unbroken; and the expectation of being quickly restored to the protection of Alphonsus, tended alone to solace her in the gloomy scene she was constrained to contemplate.

On the evening of the day prior to that on which she had been taught to await the return of the peasant, she had about an hour retired to her straw pallet, when whispering voices met her ear: her heart beat high, her breath became suspended, and she listened awhile in that state of silent anxiety which fears to move, lest it lose the sound it wishes to catch. In a few moments she plainly heard footsteps in the outer division of the cave, and immediately after a voice said, "Give me the light." The light was produced, and the first object which it showed to the expecting eyes of Lauretta was the visage of Theodore.

Lauretta shrieked; and immediately the man who had held the lantern, having given it into the hand of Theodore, advanced, and taking her arm in his, led her from the cave. Theodore secreted the light under his garment, and closely followed them.

The moment Lauretta had so much dreaded was now arrived: agony inexplicable filled her heart, and choked her utterance. Her guide continued to walk quickly forward, and she of necessity suited her steps to his:—neither Theodore nor his companion spoke;—and, when the power of speech returned to Lauretta, she well knew how callous the flinty heart of the chevalier would be to any entreaty she could offer up to him; and she judged also, how deaf to the cries of misery must he be, who would hire himself to be Theodore's agent, whether he was acquainted with his base designs, or had blindly sold himself to execute his will.

A few faintly shining stars served to light them on their way; and Lauretta shortly perceived that they had entered the forest through which she had passed on the morning on which she had so miraculously escaped from her confinement in the castle. They still continued to proceed; and, as they advanced, Lauretta began to discern the fatal building rising above a gentle acclivity, which they were ascending.

Presently a tucket, much resembling that Lauretta had heard on the second night of her imprisonment in the castle, sounded at a distance: her heart thrilled at the recollection of the delusive hopes that sound had once raised in her panting breast, and she started as the sound met her ear. Her guard, who probably, from the sudden motion of her body, conjectured she was endeavouring to disengage herself from him, drew her arm more strictly within his, and at the same instant turning round his head to Theodore, said, "There they are." — "Then let us stop a few minutes," returned Theodore. "Oh no!" replied the man; "they will be housed long ere we reach the cavern: besides, were they not, they would not see us." "'Tis well," answered Theodore; "proceed then."

"The cavern!" echoed Lauretta's heart; and busy thought, ever ready to torment the breast it inhabits, pointed out that cavern as her destined grave.

The tears burst from her eyes: — the horrible idea of never again beholding her Alphonsus, at that moment so forcibly impressed on her mind, was too heart-rending a sensation for the tide of grief with which it swelled her aching breast to be suppressed; and she was on the point of falling on her knees, and endeavouring to move the mercy of her guard, when a voice, at some distance from her, exclaimed, "Lauretta Byroff!"

"Oh God!" cried Lauretta, "what is it I hear?"

They were still amongst the trees. Theodore called to the man who conducted Lauretta to stop: he obeyed the summons, and they looked round on all sides: no one was to be seen, and all was still.

"This is astonishing," said Theodore. "These words were addressed to you," turning to Lauretta: "explain them, I charge you."

"I am unable," answered Lauretta.

"Is it not your name?" rejoined Theodore, hastily.

"You know Lauretta is my name."

"You equivocate. I ask, whether Byroff is also your name?"

"No," said Lauretta.

"What is it, then?" asked Theodore. "Beware not to deceive me."

"It is Byroff," replied Lauretta: a moment's thought had reminded her not to utter a name her husband had so cautiously laboured to conceal: and she was too innocent in deceit to substitute a feigned one.

"Your own words have proved upon you one falsehood," cried Theodore. "How am I conscious you have not uttered another? Therefore, unravel the mystery of that voice, or this moment is your last."

"By heaven, I cannot!" answered Lauretta.

"Then I will," exclaimed Theodore, drawing from its scabbard his sword, on which he had laid his hand when he first demanded Lauretta's confession; and, commanding her guard not to leave her, he rushed amongst the trees from whence the voice had proceeded.

Lauretta and her guide followed him with their eyes in silent wonder for some moments, when a sudden blow from an unseen hand levelled her companion with the earth, and, from the firmness with which he had held her arm, he in his fall drew her upon him. Astonishment closed her lips; and in an instant, a man muffled up in a cloak lifted her from the ground, and whispering in her ear "Be silent," he took her arm under his, and led her swiftly along: they continued for some time to approach towards the decayed castle. This was a matter of surprise to Lauretta, for as she could not doubt his being one interested in her safety, it was natural for her to suppose that he would have led her as far distant as possible from the spot that contained Theodore's companions in iniquity. She was now, however, in the power of this stranger; and she was well aware that if he was her enemy, her questions could render her little service; if a friend, that an inquiry would be breaking an injunction on which, perhaps, her safety materially depended. —She suppressed her curiosity: the little portion of thought she could spare from her present mysterious situation, convinced her that the voice of him who now conducted her was familiar to her ear; but she could not recollect where she had heard it.

Being approached within about a furlong of the castle, her guide turned into a narrow glen which lay on their left; they had not proceeded many paces, when he stopped, and disengaging himself from Lauretta, he stooped down, and having drawn aside a bunch of furze and brambles which lay against the side of the glen, he took from an inner pocket of his coat a lantern, which, holding downwards, showed to Lauretta the mouth of a stony rock, which seemed hardly large enough to admit a person on their hands and knees.

Her guide knelt down, and creeping forward, in a low voice called to Lauretta to follow him;—she hesitated a moment: —"This was doubtless the cavern Theodore and the ruffian, who had brought her from the hermit's cave, had alluded to."—She shuddered.—"I conjure you, follow me," said her guide:—his accents seemed mild and persuasive:—Lauretta crossed herself, and followed him.

After having proceeded a few feet, they arrived in an apartment which, by what Lauretta could distinguish of it by the partial and gloomy light thrown out by the lantern of her guide, appeared to her a large vault; they crossed it, and entered a long and narrow passage cut out of the rock;—their footsteps echoed as they traversed it; and Lauretta could not forbear frequently turning her head to assure herself they were not pursued.

Having attained the extremity of the passage, they entered another vaulted chamber, larger than the first.—Her guide opened a door on one side, which presented to their view a flight of stone steps; her guide began to descend them;— Lauretta paused.—"Quick, quick, I entreat you," said he, taking her hand: again the recollection of his voice struck her, and she suffered herself to be led by him down into a passage much resembling that through which they had passed above; on the right hand was a small door, which the guide opened, and presented to her view a small room, in which were a seat, a table, a bed, and a lamp: they entered, and the guide throwing off a long robe and cowl which he had hitherto kept closely round him, discovered to Lauretta the person of Ralberg.

Lauretta was petrified with astonishment;—she knew not what to hope, or what to fear.

"Be not alarmed," he said, "at beholding him you once thought your enemy; he was never willingly so; and be assured that he will now protect you at the hazard of his life: but your safety and my own both depend on my instantly leaving you:—fear not to be interrupted here, and rely on seeing me again very soon."

He lighted the lamp, and was departing.

"Oh! do not leave me," exclaimed Lauretta, catching hold of his garment.

"For heaven's sake, do not detain me to your own destruction.—If you should chance to hear footsteps, extinguish the lamp.—Angels guard you!" So saying, he hastily closed the door, and Lauretta heard him lock it and depart.

For some moments Lauretta remained motionless on the spot where Ralberg had left her.—When before in his power, she had felt no sensation but fear: now, his words had given her room to hope the greatest kindness from him; and yet the air of mystery that had accompanied them, outweighed every consolation they might otherwise have brought her.

Why had this man, who had so lately been an assistant in her misery, so suddenly changed his principles? A man who, when she had before beheld him, had worn on his brow the sullen frown of discontent; yet, she recollected, she had then remarked that the roughness of his voice had appeared assumed, and his whole manner that of restraint.—"May not fond hope again deceive me in this imagination?" she cried; "and yet the softness of voice with which he now addressed me has proved me right in one conjecture; his mien also is varied, the frown on his brow is dispersed, pity and anxiety are mingled in his eye, and a smile of satisfaction sits on his lips.—My name, too! by what means can he have learnt that?"—This was a mystery, to the unravelling of which she had no clue.

Her eyes had hitherto been fixed in deep thought on the ground: she now raised them;—the first object which attracted them was the lamp, and she beheld lying by it on the table—a dagger!

Her blood chilled;—she perfectly recollected that that instrument was not on the table when she entered the apartment; thus no doubt could remain to her of Ralberg having placed it there.—He had declared he would guard her life at the hazard of his own; that very declaration seemed to prove that he knew her life would be attempted: then why had he brought her to a spot over which such imminent danger was impending? — And if he had really meant to protect her, why had he left an instrument of death in her view? — No idea occupied her mind, but that Theodore meant to visit her where she now was, and that the alternative of suicide or dishonour would alone be left to her. — But then, if Ralberg still acted in the interest of the chevalier, how could she account for the occurrences that had so lately taken place on the skirts of the forest? — Perhaps Theodore had doubted the faith of the man whom he had brought with him to the hermit's cell, and had taken those means of freeing himself from him under the cloak of mystery: and this seemed the only conjecture that could in the slightest degree account for her being brought by a man who pretended to be her friend, to the very spot to which her professed enemy had declared his intention of carrying her.

For several hours no sound interrupted the stillness of the scene, and Lauretta with a trembling heart awaited her doom in anxious silence; at length she heard a footstep quickly approaching. — She immediately recollected Ralberg's injunction to blow out the light, but she wanted courage to comply with it: it struck her that her murderer, unable to view her dying agonies, might wish to perpetrate the deed of death in darkness.

The key was now placed in the lock: Lauretta started from the bed on which she had been sitting; the door opened, and Ralberg entered. — Having placed on the table a small basket he had brought with him, he closed the door, and taking Lauretta's hand, thus addressed her: — "Did I understand you rightly this evening in the wood? did you confess yourself to be Lauretta Byroff, when I unseen addressed you by those words?"

"I did," answered Lauretta.

Ralberg now drew from his pocket the ivory crucifix which Lauretta had been accustomed to wear suspended from her neck by the string of pearls, which were presented by her grandfather to her mother on the day of her marriage with count Byroff. "This then is doubtless yours?" said Ralberg, as he produced it.

"It is," replied Lauretta eagerly; "I well remember that I left it in the turret of the castle, and often since have mourned its loss."

" 'Tis then dear to you?" said Ralberg.

"As the dying gift of a lost mother can be!"—Recollection became painful as she uttered these words: she wept;—Ralberg sighed, and for an instant placed his hand before his eyes.

"Where did your mother die?" he asked.

"At the convent of St. Helena."

Again he seized the hand of Lauretta, and, with an energy that seemed to wring his heart, he exclaimed:—"Who was your father?"

"Count Byroff," she answered.

The tears started in Ralberg's eyes. "Deceive me not in this point," he cried, "I conjure you;—I charge you!"

There was something in his manner that awed Lauretta. "On my faith I do not," returned Lauretta. "My mother's dying breath declared him such."

"My child! my child!" uttered Ralberg, in a voice scarcely audible, and fell upon Lauretta's neck.—"I am thy unhappy father! I am he that was count Byroff."

What a blissful sound was this to the grief-worn Lauretta: she had found a friend that would protect her; and, in that friend, a father. She met his embrace with the warmest fervor, and he for some moments held her clasped in silence to his bosom. At length, "that cross," said he, restoring it to Lauretta, "was my first gift to your mother. Oh! tell me! tell me! all that has befallen her.—But no—I must not risk the hearing now; it will too long detain me; I must instantly leave you, or perhaps never see you more."

"Alas!" cried Lauretta, "have I only found a father to be again bereft of him?"

"Oh my child!" said count Byroff, "I blush to confess to you the situation in which you meet that father. Misfortunes had driven me to despair, and that despair tempted me to— —hark! surely I am not discovered?" He paused,—then continued, "No, all is still."

"To what?" asked Lauretta.

"To connect myself with a set of wretches, whose existence disgraces humanity.—Hark! is not that the trampling of horses?" he cried. — "I must fly, or I may lose thee for ever! — farewell; it will be some time ere thou wilt see me again." — He went hastily out, locked the door upon Lauretta as he had before done, and the sound of his footsteps in a few moments dying away, an awful silence prevailed.

It was some time ere Lauretta could convince herself that the transaction of the last minutes was more than a dream, and, when conviction did beam upon her, she wept tears of joy.

When reflection again returned, she began to meditate on the last words her father had uttered, and endeavoured to solve the mystery of his present situation: it baffled her attempts, and his declaration that it would be some time ere she again saw him, raised not less her wonder than her sorrow. "I am in safety," she cried, "but my Alphonsus is ignorant that I am so, and what pangs will not he experience on arriving at the hermit's cave, and finding me gone: — the situation, too, of my deceased benefactor will lead him to credit, that violence has been used against us both. — Oh! why did I not entreat my father to find some means of quieting the apprehensions of my Alphonsus? — When he returns, it may be too late for him to meet the object of my anxiety!"

She slept not that night: a variety of sensations ruffled her mind, and drove off the attacks of sleep: in the morning she examined the basket count Byroff had, on the preceding night, left on the table: it contained provisions which seemed calculated to last her for two or three days; a bottle of wine, another of water, and some oil in a flask to replenish her lamp.

Day passed on, and the solitude of her prison remained uninterrupted: — night arrived, and she still enjoyed little refreshment from sleep; her thoughts were occupied by the disappointed expectations of Alphonsus on not finding her in the hermit's cave. She rose from her bed, and endeavoured to compose her mind by prayer; but the crucifix which she placed before her, only afforded a fresh subject for thought, by recalling to her mind all the mystery dependent on the discovery and conduct of her newly-found parent.

The following day passed on, and count Byroff visited not his daughter. Lauretta's apprehensions were now raised for his safety; she began to fear that the discovery of his last visit to her, which he had seemed so much to dread, had taken place; and the only ray of comfort which shone upon her harassed mind in this fresh cause of alarm, was, that, had this been the case, they who had made the discovery of his visit, would, in all probability, ere this, have made it their business to discover its cause.

Her spirits had become much fatigued by continual watchings, apprehensions, and anxieties; and a few hours before midnight, a sound sleep closed her eyes for a short time; but, on waking, what was her grief to find, that, having too long neglected to feed and trim her lamp, it had burned out. The utter darkness in which she now found herself, appalled her senses; and again throwing herself on the bed, the tears flowed quickly down her burning cheeks.

Fearing, she knew not why, to quit her present situation in the darkness which now surrounded her, she remained upon the bed, till she conjectured it to be nearly midnight. The echoed responses of her own sighs were the only sounds she had heard, till a footstep approaching cautiously towards the door of her apartment, re-illumined a spark of hope and pleasure in her breast: she raised herself on the bed, and a few moments presented to her view count Byroff, habited in the garment of a friar.

Lauretta sprang forward to meet him; he embraced her, and without noticing the darkness in which he found her, and which he might perhaps imagine she had effected in compliance with his instructions, he immediately assisted her to muffle herself in his robe, which he had on the first night left in that apartment, and then told her to follow him with all possible celerity.

The count had reached the door of the apartment, when, stepping back, he took the dagger from the table, and sticking it in his under girdle, again commanded Lauretta to follow him closely, and proceeded swiftly along.

Lauretta followed her father's steps in silence; and by the light of a lamp which he held, she perceived that he was re-conducting her by the path which had led her to the dreary apartment she had just quitted. She remarked that his hand trembled, and on his countenance was depicted the wildest anxiety.

Being arrived in the glen, count Byroff threw down the lamp to extinguish it; and having closed up the mouth of the cavern, he loosened a horse which had been fastened to a stump of a tree near unto it, and having led the animal to the level ground, he mounted it, and taking up Lauretta before him, he clapped spurs to the beast, and they galloped swiftly forwards.

They proceeded nearly a league in silence, except when it was broken by the count addressing himself to his horse to increase his speed: at length Lauretta ventured to inquire, in a low accent, "Whither they were going?" "You must presently direct our road," returned the count;—"but be silent now, I conjure you; some one may be concealed amidst these trees." Lauretta obeyed her father's injunctions; but as suggestion but too often breeds suspicion, she could not forbear turning her eyes by turns on all sides, and watching every shadow as she passed it, fearing it should wear the form of man, and often conjecturing she beheld what she feared.

It was one of those nights when the waning moon sinks to the horizon full and crimson, and casts a tinge of fire upon the objects over which perspective seems to show it impended; and as the travellers turned a sharp angle of a narrow wood through which they had been passing, it suddenly burst upon their view. The scene was mournfully romantic, and Lauretta suffered it to occupy her thoughts;—at intervals a clump of trees intercepted it from her sight, and she then sought its partial light darting momentarily from amidst the breaks of the interwoven branches;—again it darted in full splendour upon her sight, and again an intercepting hillock, whose gilded crown reminded her where it was obscured, shut it from her eyes;—presently its reflected beams played on a crooked lake, along whose bank they were passing, and then again, attracted to the silken leaves of the elm, seemed for a time to clothe its branches with purest snow:—at length its nightly reign being ended, it imperceptibly sunk under the horizon, gradually stealing from the surrounding objects the gilded hue which it had lately sent to beautify them.

After travelling three hours and a half, the count and Lauretta arrived at a mean cottage. In a few minutes its door was opened in compliance with the request of the count; and its inhabitants, a middle-aged man, and a lad his son, shepherds by trade, readily granted admission to the count and his daughter.

The count quickly extorted from them a promise that they would not on any condition suffer any person to enter the cottage whilst he remained in it, or confess that any stranger was concealed within it, should inquiry be made of them. To this petition they agreed not less readily from the temptation of the large reward by which he offered to bribe their secrecy, than from their fear of his resentment falling on them or their flocks, should they betray him; for his habit had immediately led them to believe that he was a brother of some religious order, a circumstance which the count plainly perceived, and in which, from his acquaintance with the natural superstition of the lower ranks of people in that part of the country, he placed his chief dependence for ensuring such secrecy as he should require during the intervals in which he judged it expedient to interrupt his journey.

Having seen his horse safely bestowed, the count questioned Lauretta, whether she wished to compose herself to sleep; but she declared that her mind was too strongly agitated to suffer her to seek repose for her body: the count then hinted to her a wish that she would unfold to him the history of her life; she inwardly lamented that he had not first offered to communicate his own; but considering that his curiosity must be as strongly awakened as hers, in compliance with the obedience due to her father, she immediately acquiesced in his wish; and having retired with him to the only apartment of which the cottage consisted, in addition to that occupied by the shepherd and his son, she informed him of every particular that had occurred to her from the first moment of her entrance into the world, to that on which he had rescued her in the wood from Theodore and his accomplice.

CHAPTER XIV.

This is the state of man; to-day he puts forth

The tender leaves of hope, to-morrow blossoms,

And bears his blushing honours thick upon him:

The third day comes a frost, a killing frost,

And when he thinks, good easy man, full surely

His greatness is a ripening, nips his root,

And then he falls, as I do.

King Henry viii

In relating the occurrences of her own life, Lauretta omitted not to lay before the count such particulars as he was unacquainted with in that of her deceased mother; and the stress which she laid on the declaration of her mother's innocence, with regard to the suspicions which had been raised against her, on account of her continued acquaintance with count Frederic Cohenburg, her first and only love, seemed much to affect him.

"Oh!" exclaimed count Byroff, "had she but explained to me the state of her heart, we might now have both been happy, and I free from guilt."

A short silence ensued: the count then said, "Now, my child, attend to the tale of thy father's fortunes, and learn from thence that the commission of one rash act imperceptibly leads on the human heart to crimes once most distant from its imagination.

"My father and his sister were the only children of my grandfather, count Byroff, a German nobleman, who resided on a small estate about twenty leagues distant from Vienna; for as fortune is not always the sure companion of rank, his narrow circumstances had obliged him to retire from the splendour of the court.

"My aunt had the good fortune to captivate an Italian marchese of immense property; and having received her hand in marriage, he carried her with him into Italy.

"My father married a woman of rank, whose circumstances were but too much in the situation of his own; he did not many years survive his union with the woman of his heart, and dying, left my mother and myself, his only child, to the protection of my grandfather.

"Many unforeseen and cruel misfortunes had occurred to lessen the small property the old count possessed; and by his death, which happened just as I had attained my eighteenth year, I found the fortune which had devolved on me slender indeed. My mother and myself, however, resolved to live retired from the world, and by frugality to increase that little stock which my rank in life forbade me to attempt any other means of increasing.

"How weak are the prejudices by which we suffer ourselves to be ruled!

"A short time after the death of my grandfather a letter arrived in Germany from my aunt, informing us that her husband was lately dead, that the greater part of his property had devolved on her by his will, and inviting my mother and myself to pass over into Italy, and reside with her.

"Being a paternal estate on which we had resided, it would have been deemed a disgrace to a nobleman to sell it; we accordingly left Germany without assigning any reason for our departure.

"My aunt, the marchesa del Parmo, who resided in an elegant mansion in one of the most eligible spots in Venice, received us with the warmest cordiality, and exercised towards us the most friendly attentions; but my mother lived only a short time to be sensible of the marchesa's kindness. On her death my aunt seemed to double her assiduities to me; she told me, that she had resolved never to marry again, and should, with the exception of a few legacies, leave me heir to her entire property; I expressed my gratitude to her in terms suited to the extensive promise she had made me: she then told me, that she had provided for me a tutor, with whom she wished me to travel for a couple of years, before I formed any plan of settling in the world. She at this time was well acquainted with my attachment to your mother, which had begun a very short time after my arrival in Italy; and she as well as myself imagined that my attentions were far from being unfavourably received by her.

"The youthful mind pants for novelty; and the offer made

me by my aunt was too fascinating not to induce me for a short period to forego the society of my Lauretta, flattering myself that from the improvement of travel I should return more worthy of her; for the marchesa having spoken in my favour to count Arieno, he had immediately assented to my proposal of espousing his daughter.

"When I had been absent from Italy about eighteen months I received a letter from the marchesa's steward, informing me that she had died suddenly, and had left me her sole heir.

"I immediately returned to Venice to take possession of my newly-acquired fortune, and had arrived there only a few hours when count Arieno paid me a joint visit of condolence on the loss of my aunt, and congratulation on my acquisition of fortune. Before his departure he reminded me of the verbal contract subsisting between us relative to his daughter, and at the same time entreated me, if I observed a dejectedness in her manner, not to notice it, as I should only renew an acute sorrow which had been preying on her spirits since the sudden death of an intimate friend, and which was now gradually wearing off.

"I readily acquiesced in a proposition which I imagined would conduce to the tranquillity of her I loved; and on visiting my Lauretta I was sensibly touched by the frown of grief which I observed settled on her languid countenance; I endeavoured to sooth her sorrow without reverting to its cause. I could not forbear noticing the striking change in one so tenderly beloved; she wept, and doubtless misconstrued the meaning of my words, as I did the cause of her sorrow.

"Whenever I visited her, I remarked that her father always remained in the apartment with us. I now see the cause of a conduct which then much surprised me; he knew the awe in which his daughter stood of him, and by his presence resolved to prevent an explanation on her side from taking place.

"Curses on the sordidness of a father, who dooms his child to misery, that he may swell his own proud coffers!

"I now never saw count Arieno, that he did not advance arguments to induce me to hasten my marriage, which, from my regard to the recent death of my aunt the marchesa, I had thought it consistent with propriety some time to defer. In a short time, however, his reasonings, from their co-incidence with my real feelings, prevailed over my scruples, and I was united to your mother.

"After the solemnization of our marriage, count Arieno insisted that we should pass at least a couple of months at his mansion; his reason, I then thought, was his averseness to part from his daughter: I now perceive that he wished to keep her under his own eye, in order that he might be the better able to inspect her conduct, which he was well aware his cruelty had given him reason to suspect, and which he hesitated immediately to communicate to me.

"I used every means in my power to restore to your mother that cheerfulness which had once been her never-failing companion; but a settled melancholy, which I found it impossible for me to dissipate, had taken possession of her mind.

"Six weeks after our marriage, I again mentioned to count Arieno, as I had before frequently done, my uneasiness at the unhappy state of my wife; and he then confessed to me, that he had but too much reason to believe I had an unworthy but favoured rival in the heart of his daughter.

"This was a blow which struck at once at the root of my happiness and pride: the whole mystery of count Arieno's interested conduct was in one moment exposed to my view, and I looked with contempt on the wretch who had made a traffic of his child.

"He now declared to me all the particulars of your mother's affection for count Frederic Cohenburg; was lavish in his praises on himself, both for the parental authority he had exerted over his daughter, and for that management which had made me his son-in-law. — He was the wretch who could pride himself on having, by one stroke of keen deceit, stamped the misery of an only child, and inveigled me into a state of eternal suspicion and unhappiness.

"I upbraided him with his base conduct; — he listened to me whilst I spoke, and smiled, as one secure in the completion of his own wish, and regardless of the fate of others: when I stopped speaking,

"'What prevents you to rid yourself of this rival?' he cried.

"'Whither can I fly from him?' I returned — 'No where, but where he can follow.'

"'End him!' — exclaimed Arieno.

"I had never yet drawn my sword against a fellow-creature, and I shuddered at the idea.

"Arieno perceived it; and, pretending to finish a sentence which he had left uncompleted, he said, — 'or suffer patiently that infamy which the world will attach to a man who tamely bears dishonour in the tenderest point.'

"His imputation on my honour pierced my heart.

"'Give me proof of your suspicions,' I returned, 'and I will instantly challenge him.'

"'You shall have proof, rest assured,' he answered, and with these words he left the room.

"To what a state of misery had this intelligence reduced me! — to learn that I was an object of abhorrence to the woman in whom I had placed my hopes of future happiness, and the victim of the joint pride and avarice of her father.

"Still, however, I resolved to bear my feelings in silence till the promised proof was produced to me: at one time doubting the truth of count Arieno's assertion, and at another, fearing I saw it fully confirmed; and alike despising the vile author of my doubts, whichever opinion swayed my mind.

"About a fortnight after my last conversation with count Arieno on the subject of my anxiety, he one day entered the apartment where I was sitting, with an open letter in his hand; he seated himself, and thus addressed me: — 'I yesterday morning gave out that you and myself should this evening set out on a short excursion into the country, from which we should not return in two or three days; the object of my having said this you will clearly perceive, when I tell you, that it has answered my expectation in producing this epistle, which I have contrived to intercept.'

"He gave the letter into my hand; and, to my extreme mortification, I read in it an invitation to count Cohenburg from your mother, written by her own hand, to meet her that evening at her aunt's.

"Count Arieno, when I had concluded reading the letter, which I several times perused ere I could convince myself that my senses were not deceived in what I had read, proceeded to inform me in what manner he had gained it from the servant entrusted by my wife, and what means he had taken to prevent his return to his employer.

"I listened to him without attempting to speak, for my feelings were unutterable; and I was on the point of tearing the fatal letter to atoms, when he hastily sprang from his seat, and snatching it out of my hand,—'Hold!' he exclaimed, 'on this depends our hopes of vengeance.' He again seated himself at the table; and having sealed the note as it had before been, he summoned into the apartment a trusty servant, to whom he confided to carry the epistle to him to whom it was directed.

"Still absorbed in thought, my silence had been broken only by heavy sighs, till, on the servant's quitting the room, the count asked, 'Whether I had perceived what he had done?'

"I told him that I had; and inquired what purpose he meant to answer by it.

"'Count Cohenburg,' he replied, 'will doubtless attend to the invitation given him for this evening; he must necessarily pass through a dark lane in his way to my sister's, which is the place of appointment with your wife; it must therefore be our business to provide those who will there way-lay him: such may easily be found, and such as may be relied on.—We ourselves must leave the city at the hour I had mentioned we should set out; thus suspicion will be hoodwinked, and your rival fall an easy prey into the snare you will have spread for him.'

"I heard him pronounce these words with very different emotions from what I probably should have done had I been an Italian:—when he stopped speaking, I exclaimed, 'If he deserves death, why should I fear to be myself his punisher? If there be a palliation for shedding human blood, 'tis surely in behalf of him whose injuries loudly call for revenge: why then should I tempt another man to become criminal,—and, by paying the price of blood, add to the guilt that would still be mine, by having instigated him to become the instrument of an act whereof I should in reality be the agent?'

"It was some time before I could work upon Arieno, living in a country where the performance of murder is alike venal with other acts of hire, to listen to the arguments I advanced in favour of my being myself the redresser of my wrongs, and before I could prevail on him to promise to accompany me in the evening to the dark lane through which he had informed me count Cohenburg must inevitably pass in his way to the house of appointment with your mother: at length he promised to point it out to me, and we parted till the hour arrived at which

Arieno had given out the preceding day that we should set out on our journey; we then mounted our horses, and rode to a small house about a quarter of a league out of the city, the habitation of a man who had formerly lived in the service of the count, and where we had pre-determined to leave our horses, and in the dusk of the evening return to the city on foot.

"We arrived in the dark lane nearly half an hour before the time mentioned in your mother's letter. — I drew my sword, and we placed ourselves under the shade of a low portico. — In a short time we heard footsteps. — A person muffled up in a cloak advanced rapidly towards us; count Arieno whispered to me, ''Tis he, 'tis the count himself.' — I immediately sprang forward to meet him, and in the name of a villain I called upon him to defend himself against the vengeance of an injured husband! — He made a blow at my sword with a stout cane which he held in his hand, and attempted to rush past me; but I quickly stepped back a few paces, and received his body on the point of my sword: he instantly fell, with a deep groan; and distant voices at the same moment assailing the ears of count Arieno and myself, we fled with all possible speed, I to the count's mansion, and he to the house of his sister, where he expected to find your mother, and from thence to re-conduct her to his own.

"What misery did I that night experience, on entering the apartment to which your mother had been conveyed on her return to her father's house! how did the cries and upbraidings of her agonised heart wound mine, although I conceived myself to have been so deeply injured by her! — She confessed to me all her love for count Frederic, but called on heaven to witness how free she was from the imputation of guilt laid upon her by me and her father. — I hardly dared credit what she affirmed; and yet so forcibly did the recollection of the ardent passion I once bore her plead for her in my heart, that I endeavoured, by every attention and every promise of future regard, to lull her into the oblivion of him she had lost, by fixing her mind on the assiduities of him she retained, fully resolving in my own mind, if she but ceased to upbraid me with the loss of count Frederic, again to take her to my bosom, and use every means of proving to her her loss replaced in an equally tender and affectionate lover.

"She that night altogether refused to listen to me; and I left her chamber with a heart as deeply lacerated as her own.

"Towards evening on the following day, I had again been endeavouring by repeated attentions to win on the heart I had embittered with sorrow, when I was summoned from my painful yet willing task, by count Arieno calling to me hastily to descend to him.

"I immediately went to him, and he in a few words informed me, that count Frederic had escaped; and that the person whom I had killed on the preceding evening proved to be the son of one of the first senators: that five thousand zechins were offered in reward to any one who might apprehend the murderer; and the punishment of exile and confiscation of property denounced by the state of Venice against those who might be acquainted with the perpetrator of the murder, and delay to deliver him into the hands of justice.

"What were my feelings on being informed that I was the murderer of an innocent man! I cannot describe, or you conceive; pain, poverty, sickness, loss of friends, or any other misery in its most aggravated state, and even all these combined, can give no faint idea of the pangs he feels, who has shed blood, which even the effusion of his own cannot re-animate.

"'Now,' said count Arieno, 'what would that friend merit, who would undertake to rescue you from the danger hovering round you?'

"If I were apprehended, death, I well knew, would be my doom; and death I at that moment could have received with ecstasy from any hand but that of the executioner: from dying on a public scaffold my heart, humbled as I felt myself, recoiled, and I eagerly answered, 'Every thing.'

"'Then,' said he, 'I will be that friend.—Now attend to the means: should you be apprehended for this crime, you are well assured your entire property becomes confiscate to the state.'

"I replied, that I was fully convinced it did.

"'Your safety,' he continued, 'depends on your immediately flying from this country; in such case, it is impossible you can collect the value of your possessions in so short a time as it is necessary for you to depart, in order to carry them with you; what you leave behind you in your own name, will be immediately confiscated; thus make over to me your personals, by far the greater division of your property; leave your estate open to confiscation, as some small atonement for your offence; make your escape instantly, while it yet remains in your power to effect it; and depend on my remitting to you what you shall make over to me, as soon as you shall have reached a place of safety.'

"There was a kindness in this offer of count Arieno to assist me in my distress, that made me overlook his past conduct; and with thanks I acquiesced in his proposition, and quickly proceeded to put it in execution.

"I had scarcely put my hand and seal to the deed which transferred to count Arieno my personal property, dispersed through many parts of Italy, when information was brought us by the physician who had attended your mother, that she had fled from her father's house. The count seemed to receive the tidings with indifference; and I was too much occupied by my own safety to give any farther thought to what I had heard, than that she had learned count Cohenburg's existence, and found means of escaping to him.

"A few hours afterwards I set out from the Venetian dominions, and in little more than a week I arrived in Paris, the place where I had determined to seek shelter from the laws of Venice, as I little doubted, from the number of spies I well knew to be employed by that state, I should soon be discovered to be the perpetrator of the deed on which I shuddered to reflect.

"On the day after my arrival, I wrote to count Arieno to inform him of the place of my retreat; I thought it unnecessary to add that an immediate remittance would be welcome to me, as he well knew that I had taken with me only what cash I happened to have in my possession at the time of my departure, and a few trinkets of small value.

"In about three weeks I received from him a letter, the purport of which, to my great consternation, and, I blush to add, astonishment, knowing what I already did of his infamous character, was nearly in the following words: — That the state had gained information of my being the assassin of the senator's son, and had accordingly confiscated such of my property as was publicly known to be mine; that he lamented this discovery having so early taken place, as it would inevitably prevent his being to me the friend he had pledged himself to be; for that, as a Venetian senator, he should incur the fear of death, by being known to assist any man now lying under the penalty of its laws; and could accordingly only send me his thanks for having, by the deed that had passed between us on the evening of my leaving Venice, given him the power of profiting by a sum of money which could never again on any terms be mine, and which would otherwise have fallen to the use of the state.

"'Upright senator!' I exclaimed, on perusing this infernal epistle; 'cautious in observing the outward forms of that state that he hesitates not privately to plunder!'—Oh! my child, how many villains wear the mask of worth like him, and, with the garb of office, cover a heart which knows no interest but its own; and contemplates no crime, of which an accumulation of its private wealth and pride will not seem to authorise the performance!"

The count paused a moment, then continued—"The keen sense of my own feelings, on a revisal of the villainy that had been practised against me, may perhaps have tempted me to draw too harsh a stricture on mankind in general: but surely I cannot be wrong in asserting, that he who will act villainously in the transactions of private life, cannot lay aside his nature when he acts for the public.

"To what a situation was I now reduced! my whole property consisting of only fifteen zechins, and two rings of small value, without the possible means of recovering what had so basely been wrested from me, or of seeking redress from him who had so deeply injured me, without exposing myself to the greatest of dangers;—in a city where I was an entire stranger; without a friend to whom I could apply for assistance; without an acquaintance to whose conversation I could fly for a transitory relief of my painful feelings, and without a cheerful thought that would afford me a momentary consolation within my own breast!

"My first step, however, was to avoid detection; as I knew not what power the state of Venice might have of demanding my person, should my retreat be discovered; and sometimes feared that Arieno, to insure to himself the possession of my property, might give information to the state whither I was fled, and have me apprehended, that, by my death, all doubts of my ever regaining what was lawfully mine, might be done away; but then again I considered, that he would be well aware, that, in case of such an accusation from him, revenge would prompt me to declare the state, rather than him, the possessor of that property I was myself doomed to forego; and this quieted my fears of any farther molestation from him: but, at all events, judging it to my advantage to obscure myself as much as possible, I changed my habit to that of the country I was now in, and called myself Montville, resolving still to remain in Paris, as the place where I was most likely to escape observation, well knowing that I should be most free from observation in the midst of a crowd.

"I had taken a lodging in an obscure part of the city; and my only amusement was the frequenting of a tavern in the neighbourhood, much resorted to by young men, who, though perhaps not in the most exalted stations of life, were however men of fashion and fortune.

"Every evening they met, in a greater or smaller number, at this house, and draughts were their entertainment: as a stranger, I had been generally noticed by them, and solicited to play; I knew myself to be an adept in the game, and thus readily accepted their invitation. The sums they staked were not large, or I could not have hazarded an engagement. I found some my equals in play; and when I engaged with these, good and bad fortune were alternately mine; but as my play was far superior to the generality of those who engaged with me, and as my circumstances, as I was sometimes tempted to think, induced me to place more attention on my game than my adversary usually gave to his, I was commonly, at the hour of retiring, the winner of a trifling sum; a circumstance which in my situation I considered of the most consolatory and promising nature: my precarious situation had taught me, hard as the reverse was, to be an economist; and in the course of six months I had collected nearly fifty louis-d'ors, and I now began to turn my thoughts to a subject to which they had before been directed; namely, whether I should pursue any means of discovering the retreat of your mother, and of revenging myself on the destroyer of my peace.

"After many debates with my own heart, I drew this conclusion: — 'Will the death of count Cohenburg restore my peace? — No! — Will it not add guilt to hands already too deeply imbrued in blood? — It will! — Can I hope that my wife will be to me what she ought to be? — No! — Why then seek after her who shuns me, and add another sting to an already wounded conscience, by the murder of one whose death cannot restore my lost tranquillity?'

"Having resolved that it behoved me to forget an object lately so dear to me, my mind became more calm; for, when an opinion is once firmly adopted, every subsequent thought seems to strengthen the justness of that opinion.

"When my thoughts at times did turn back to your mother, amidst the censures my injuries raised against her in my heart, I still felt a portion of pity for one who had been driven to despair by the cruelty of an unfeeling parent. — For that parent, when my mind reverted to him, and too often, alas! it did, I felt the abhorrence I should have done against a demon. — 'Is it possible,' I would cry, 'the earth can contain a monster capable of his accumulated crimes? — the sacrificer of an only child to his avarice! — the lurer of a youth into a marriage into which he had deceived his senses! — the instigator of that youth, when become his daughter's husband, to murder him who ought to have possessed her hand! — the ravisher of that youth's property, by the abuse of that faith which can alone bind man to man; and by the same act, the plunderer of that state, whose rights he had pledged his most solemn vow and life to defend!'"

CHAPTER XV.

What equal torment to the griefe of minde,

And pyning anguish hid in gentle heart,

That inly feeds itself with thoughts unkinde,

And nourisheth her own consuming smart?

Spencer

Count Byroff was now interrupted by the entrance of the old shepherd, whose son having just returned from milking, the good man had brought the travellers a bowl of warm milk. The count commended his attention, and Lauretta drying those tears which had been drawn into her eyes by her sympathy in the misfortunes of him who had given her being, drank of the milk, and found herself much refreshed by it; the count did the same; and the peasant retiring well pleased at the satisfaction expressed by his guests in their acknowledgments of his kindness, count Byroff thus went on.

"I had resided nearly two years in Paris, when, returning one day from walking in the suburbs of the city, two men, whom I had for some time perceived to be observing me, followed me into the house where I lodged, and introduced themselves into my apartment. On their entrance I raised a look at them which as plainly inquired their business with me, as if I had demanded it in open words. 'You must go with us, Monsieur, if you please:' said one of them. — 'Whither?' I instantly asked. — The man who had before spoken replied to my question, by drawing from his pocket a paper sealed at one corner, which he held out to my view with one hand, whilst he pointed to it with the other. On seeing the paper, it immediately flashed upon my mind that these men were emissaries sent in pursuit of me from the state of Venice; but guess my astonishment when I learnt that the fatal paper was a lettre de cachet to convey me to the Bastile.

"The two men hurried me into a carriage, the blinds of which were drawn up: we rolled rapidly through the streets, and in a short time I felt myself passing over the draw-bridge which leads to the mansion of wanton tyranny and despair.

"When the carriage stopped, I was taken from it by two men whose countenances I had not before beheld, and conducted through a paved court bounded by a lofty wall, into the first hall of that building, the bare glimpse of whose stubborn walls had so lately frozen my blood. Alas! how far was I then from conjecturing I was myself about to pine in solitude within them.

"Through two other halls and many intricate passages, my guards conducted me, till, arrived at an iron door which was nearly at the end of a long gallery terminated by a narrow window, through which the iron bars, fastened across it, suffered but a small portion of light to enter, they stopped; and the door being unlocked by a person who had met us in the second hall, and from thence preceded us, and whom I afterwards found to be the governor, I was commanded to enter, and the door was locked upon me; a small square room presented itself to my sight; a broken table, a stool, a mattress, and a quilt, were its only furniture: the walls, which had been of plaster, were mouldering away in many parts, and in others being covered with a green scurf, confirmed me in the dampness of the place, which the chill that had seized me on entering it, had first caused me to remark.

"The stillness of the scene now gave me room for reflection on my situation; I could form no conjecture for the cause of my present confinement, except that of the state of Venice having found a power of arresting my person for a crime committed within its dominions, even after I had quitted them; but this supposition appeared so repugnant to the idea that I had always been taught to entertain that the authority of every state was bounded by the limits of its territories, that I could not reconcile it to my mind, though still I could discern not even the shadow of any other cause for my present confinement.

"I well knew on how slight and even falsely grounded suspicions of acting against the government, many unhappy men had been condemned to waste away a life of solitude and misery within the dreary and unrelenting walls within which I was now a prisoner; but I was so conscious that the little interest I had felt in the public affairs of a kingdom where I was an entire stranger, had led me still less ever to join in a conversation of which they had been the topic, that I felt too secure in my innocence on that point, to give it a second thought connected with my present confinement.

"For some hours I wandered about my prison in that state of suspense which is perhaps the most acute suffering the mind can undergo; towards evening a small portion of bread and water was brought me by a man who appeared to be an inferior jailer, and who immediately left my apartment on having placed my scanty pittance on the table.

"As night shut in, the horrors of my situation seemed to accumulate: there was only one window in my prison, and it was strongly grated with iron bars; I placed the stool under it, and having got upon it, I perceived that the window looked into a court, similar to the one through which I had passed when conducting to my prison.

"Night passed in intervals of sleeping and waking, and morning brought back my jailer with another scanty portion of the same fare that had been brought me by him the preceding evening.

"Thus passed on three days without any interruption of my sorrows or solitude, save the morning and evening visits of my jailer: for the first two days I had put to him many question relative to my situation; but as his sole answer had been a shake of the head, sometimes accompanied by a sour smile, I desisted from my inquiries.

"On the fourth morning the governor, accompanied by two guards, entered my prison. 'You must take the air to-day,' he said, 'or your health will be injured by your confinement.' The guards took me between them, and followed him out of the apartment into the gallery; he descended the first flight of steps, crossed a short passage, and then ascending a few stone stairs, at the top of which was an iron door, he opened it, and I was led by my guards upon a platform of about twelve feet square, but so closely surrounded by other parts of the building, that no object except the sky was discernible from it.

"The guards stationed themselves one on each side of the door; the governor had gained the middle of the platform: I went up to him, and besought him to inform me of the reasons of my confinement; he refused to answer me, and immediately left the platform. The guards were left with me, and I tried to draw them into conversation, but my efforts were ineffectual. In about half an hour the governor again appeared on the platform, and I was immediately re-conducted to my prison in the same manner as I had been led from it.

"Every fourth day I was led out to take the air and exercise allotted to me; and with this sole interruption of my solitude, crept on seven weary months.

"One morning about this time my prison-door was opened, and the governor and two of his guards entered, not a little to my surprise, as I had visited the platform the day before; the guards took me between them, and following the governor as on other occasions, conducted me into a large hall, where sat at the upper end of the table a man, who, I was given to understand, was the lieutenant de police, and below him sat two other persons. I was placed at the lower end of the table; an oath that I should deliver only the truth was administered to me by the secretary; and the lieutenant then said to me, 'You call yourself, Montville?'

"'I do.'

"'Is it your real name?'

"I hesitated to answer; and he continued, 'Remember you are on oath. Is it your real name? I ask.'

"'It is not.'

"'What is your real name?'

"'I have particular reasons for wishing to conceal it.'

"'Note that accurately,' said the lieutenant, addressing himself to the secretary; and then said to me, 'Are you a Frenchman?'

"'No.'

"'You are an Italian?'

"'No.'

"'Do not attempt to deceive me, or it will be the worse for you. You say you are not an Italian?'

"'I am not.'

"'But you came from Italy to Paris?'

"'I did.'

"'How long have you been in France?'

"'Twenty-two months, exclusive of the seven I have passed here.'

"'What brought you to Paris?'

"'My motive I must decline revealing.'

"'You know it then to be a criminal one?'

"'Why should you draw that inference?'

"'You are to answer, not to question, young man,' said the lieutenant surlily. He whispered to the man who sat by him: they turned over the leaves of a book which lay before them, pointed to different parts of various pages,—again they whispered, and the lieutenant then asked me, 'By what means I was supported?'

"'Does any one accuse me of gaining my means unjustly?' I said.

"'I shall not a third time warn you that you are here to answer, and not to question,' said the lieutenant. 'How are you supported?'

"'I brought money with me from Italy.'

"After many other questions of a similar nature, and which in the aggregate seemed to me to amount to little, though on some of them the lieutenant had laid great stress, I was remanded to my prison, equally ignorant of the charge on which I was arraigned as when I first entered it.

"About two months after I was again summoned to appear in the hall as before; the oath was administered as on the preceding occasion, and the lieutenant began by asking me many questions even more trivial than the former ones had been: at length, starting from the train of questions in which he was advancing, he said, 'On your former examination, you confessed yourself, I think, an Italian.'

"'I did not.'

"'You avowed yourself then to be employed by that state?'

"'I did not.'

"'You alleged that you were lately come from Italy.'

"'I did.'

"'And that your motive for coming hither was a criminal one.'

"'You drew that inference, but I did not subscribe to it.'

"'Why did you not confute it by a declaration of the truth?'

"'May I, before I answer this demand, make one myself?'

"'You cannot oblige us to answer it, though we can force you to reply to ours.'

"'Admirable administration of justice!' hung on my tongue: but I stifled my emotion, and said, 'Am I permitted to ask one question?'

"'Name it.'

"'On what charge am I here a prisoner?'

"The lieutenant de police, and the man on his right hand, whispered together some minutes, and the lieutenant then said, 'You stand here arraigned of being employed by a foreign power as a spy upon this government.'

"'By all my hopes of heaven the accusation is falsely founded,' I cried.

"'Where are your proofs?'

"'You shall have them.'

"The lieutenant smiled contemptuously.

"The innocence of my heart, however, in regard to the accusation now supporting against me, made me view his supercilious countenance with indifference; and knowing myself now not to be retained at the instigation of the state of Venice, I comparatively felt no fear in confessing a crime committed against it, when I hoped by so doing to free myself from my present alarming situation; and I immediately related such parts of my story as tended to show my motive for having taken up my abode in Paris.

"When I had concluded my story — 'We will inquire into the truth of this,' said the lieutenant; and, making a signal to the guards, I was taken back to my prison.

"For some time I felt myself comparatively happy, as I did not doubt that enlargement must be the result of the promised inquiry; but as the mind, in reflecting on any agitated subject, leans alternately to the side of hope and fear, I began to apprehend, that the state of Venice, should it, by means of the lieutenant's inquiries concerning me, learn my present situation, might find means, as I was in prison, of having me retained there for the crime I had really committed, though I might be absolved of that under which I was now lying falsely accused.

"Eight months elapsed in an alternate succession of fear and expectation, before I was again summoned to appear in the hall; and the result of what then passed was, that no satisfactory corroborations of the story I had related having been procured by those employed for that purpose by the lieutenant, the tale I had told was deemed either to have been framed by myself for my own preservation, or an invention delivered to me by the state of Venice when commissioned by it into France, and which I had been commanded to recount in case of my being apprehended, as an excuse for my ambiguous conduct; and that the space of two days only would be allowed me to consider whether I preferred, by confessing my real character, to throw myself on the mercy of my judges, or, by persisting in my deceit, to provoke them to draw from me the truth by torture.

"In answer to this decree, I could only repeat, in the most solemn terms, my innocence of the fact of which they accused me.

"They undoubtedly heard my declarations without interruption, but I could clearly perceive that their opinions were decided, and that either they were not, or would not be, moved by my vows and asseverations.

"On entering my prison I threw myself on my mattress, and amidst the sorrows that seemed to await me, the only idea which induced me to look forward with a degree of calmness and resignation to the fate with which I was threatened, was, that the unjust punishment I was about to suffer, might be accepted by him who alone could read my heart, in expiation of the innocent blood I had shed.

"At length, the day big to me with terror and agony arrived; at an early hour I was once more led into the hall, and the lieutenant again inquired, 'Whether my stubbornness had relaxed, and I was willing to confess my crime?'

"I reiterated my vows and asseverations of innocence; but they and my prayers for mercy were heard with equal indifference, and I was dragged into that earthly hell, where demons, in the shape of men, riot in acts of wanton cruelty.

"Innumerable instruments of torture, of which I knew not the use, but feared too soon to learn it of each I beheld, were suspended against the walls, and scattered on the floor. At one end was an immense fire, which, notwithstanding its size, two men, whose savage countenances were by no means the least terrific features of this soul-harrowing scene, were feeding with every provocative of fierceness.

"Again it was recommended to me to confess ere it was too late, and again I could only repeat, however incredulous were my hearers, that I had nothing to confess.

"I was then placed in a chair, and a circle of about three inches in diameter on the top of my head shaved bare of its hair.

"The soles of my feet and my breast were afterwards bared, and being fastened in the chair, it was drawn near to the fire, to the fierceness of which the naked parts of my body were exposed, whilst large drops of the coldest water were made to fall singly on the crown of my head.

"In a few minutes the pangs produced by the contrast of feelings I was undergoing, became so intense that I shrieked violently. The lieutenant approached me, and asked, 'if I was willing to end my punishment by confession?'

"Had I at the moment been able to have conceived any other means of freeing myself from the sufferings I was enduring, I should without hesitation have adopted it; but I was well aware, that if, to liberate myself at the present moment, I uttered a false confession, I could not afterwards retract it, and that I should in the end probably only suffer the more severely for having allowed their false accusation to be a just one; I therefore only continued to declare my innocence, and in the most moving terms to supplicate for mercy.

"In a quarter of an hour's time the torture inflicted on me became agonising, past all endurance, and I besought my tormentors to give me death: my hands and feet were bound; I had bit my tongue, till the blood streamed from my mouth upon my breast; and my eyes, which the pain I was undergoing had widely extended, from being exposed to the fierceness of the fire, were far from forming the least part of my sufferings.

"Every moment was now so forcibly diminishing the powers of nature, that the physician, who had been brought to announce to my tormentors when I had undergone what my frame could endure, commanded me to be gradually removed from the fire, and the water to cease dropping. I had been drawn back only a few feet, when, exhausted by the agony I had endured, the little strength I had remaining fled from me, and I fainted whilst yet bound in the chair of torture."

CHAPTER XVI.

Each substance of a grief hath twenty shadows,

Which show like grief itself but are not so;

For sorrow's eye, glazed with blinding tears,

Divides one thing entire to many objects;

Like perspectives, which, rightly gaz'd upon,

Shew nothing but confusion; ey'd awry,

Distinguish form.

King Richard ii

"On recovering, I found myself lying on my mattress: a blanket had been added to my quilt; and the physician, on my again opening my eyes, administered to me a cup of wine, the first variation of my daily food of bread and water that had passed my lips since my entrance into the Bastile.

"For several days the physician continued to visit me; and having youth and strength on my side, in a month's time I began to recover the use of my bodily and mental faculties, both of which had been much injured by what I had undergone. The greatest cause of remembrance that remained to me of what was past, was the weakness of my eyes when they met the light.

"Near six months passed ere I was again led out to the platform for air, and I even then found my limbs very inadequate to the task of supporting me more than a few minutes at a time.

"Day rolled on after day, and month after month, but still I received no information whether what I had undergone was deemed a sufficient confirmation of my innocence, or not; and as I was still retained a prisoner, I kept looking forward with increasing apprehension to a trial more severe than the one I had already passed through.

"I must here mention a circumstance which, however trivial it may appear to you, dwells on my mind, and seems to claim my attention.

"Nearly a year had elapsed since my undergoing the torture, when one morning a small part of the window having been left open to air my prison, a red-breast flew into the apartment, and perching on the table, began to peck the bread which had just been brought me as half my day's provision. I approached a few steps towards it, that I might the better observe it; for in my present situation, any object which engaged my attention, afforded me a moment of unexpected happiness. I perceived that it saw me, and I stopped; lest I should drive it away; but the food seemed to be a greater attraction than my presence was a cause of fear, and, to my satisfaction, it went on pecking the bread.

"Its plumage was rough, and raised against the cold, and it bore every mark of having suffered from the inclemency of the season, which was that of a severe frost; a deep snow had some time covered the ground, and the eagerness with which it preyed on its newly-found prize, showed that the weather had proved to it, whose feeble claws were unable to turn up the depth of snow, a season of famine.

"I pitied it for what it had suffered, and participated in its present apparently great satisfaction;—'Yet, poor foolish wanderer!' I cried, 'thy native timidity, when the call of nature is satisfied, will again drive thee to the piercing cold and hunger from which thou hast now found protection!—Thou art not wise enough to insure it to thyself, and mayest perhaps perish for want of that which thou shouldst never lack by living here, could I but teach thee to know my good will towards thee!'—In the energy of what I felt, I drew nearer to the table; and the bird, having either finished its meal, or being terrified by my approach, flew two or three times round the room, in search of the spot by which it had entered, and having found it, vanished in a moment from my sight.

"'Thou art gone!' I exclaimed, 'never to return hither!'—There was a charm in the last words I had uttered, that seemed to render even the biting air and keen famine to which the little animal would be exposed, an enviable situation when compared with my own.—'Many are the hardships thou wilt endure,' I cried; 'but thou hast a balm for all thy sufferings,— thou enjoyest liberty,—the choicest gift and richest blessing heaven pours on its created beings; deprived of it, all other ills in life are light.—Knowing what I have learnt from experience of the bitterness of its loss, I would not be the wretch to inflict it, e'en on the little bird I have just beheld, no! though my own enlargement were the price of its captivity!'

"On the following morning, to my great delight and surprise, the little bird again flew into my prison; I threw it some crumbs; it picked them, hopped about the floor, flew upon the table, fluttered about the room, and again left me.

"Every morning I was now visited by the red-breast; I had nothing else to occupy my attention; and I found a great source of amusement in waiting the arrival of my feathered visitor: I never failed to feed him plenteously, and used every endeavour to divest him of his natural timidity, and dispose him to receive my caresses; and I even flattered myself that he began to view me without fear, as he sometimes remained several hours in my prison; but, alas! when spring began to exhale her inviting sweets, my little companion, wearing too much the complexion of the world he inhabited, forgot his fosterer in the hour of adversity, nor returned to sooth his solitary moments. Spring, summer, and autumn passed, and I began to think that some accident had befallen him, or that he had entirely forgotten the spot where he had been so hospitably received, and gave him up as lost. — On the part of my persecutors also, a strict silence as to my doom had been observed towards me, and I began to fear I was a prisoner for life.

"Winter was now again advancing, when, as I was one morning reclining on my hard bed in mournful meditation, a fluttering in the room called my eyes to the part where I had heard it, and I beheld on the table my long-lamented bird!

"I felt the glow of unexpected pleasure mount into my cheeks; and I immediately rose and crumbled for him a piece of bread: he chirped in thankfulness for my gift, and I even imagined he seemed as pleased as myself at the renewal of our acquaintance.

"During the winter he continued to visit me, as he had done the former one; and having made for him a perch, which I contrived, by means of a crooked nail, to form out of a long splinter which I had shaved from my table, and which I fastened up in one corner of my prison, by supporting it in a small niche I made in either wall, he often remained with me during the night, as well as the day, and sometimes for four or five days successively; and the pleasure which, shut out as I was from all intercourse with my own species, I enjoyed in the unrestrained visits of this little bird, was indescribably great.

"With the spring he again deserted me, and with the winter he again returned to my prison; and thus, till the seventh year after his first visiting me, did he continue to be my companion during the winter season.

"It was one day, about the middle of the seventh winter, that he happened to stand sleeping on his perch, with his head folded in the feathers of his wing, when the jailer entering with my breakfast, and observing him, darted across the prison, and, ere I could stop his cruel arm, seized my unconscious favourite, and wrung his neck.

"Need I blush to own that the tears burst into my eyes?

"I would have remonstrated with the unfeeling wretch on his barbarity, had I not immediately considered that what I could now say would be of no avail, but to gain me the derision of him who had deprived me of my only source of solace and amusement; and I contented myself with requesting him to give me the dead body.

"Without answering me, he aimed to throw it out of the window; but, missing his cast, it fell back into the room; I sprang forward to seize it, but he had snatched it up, and his second aim being more successful, it was gone for ever ere I reached the spot; I followed it with my eyes, and when it disappeared, I still stood gazing on the window.

"The ruthless jailer left the prison in the silence in which he had entered it.

"I immediately placed the stool under the window, and sprang upon it, hoping I might find the body rested on the outward frame of the window: but the hope was vain.

"I descended from the stool, and standing with my arms folded in the middle of my prison, reflection again led me to draw a comparison between the present situation of myself and that of my lamented bird; and the only inference I could draw, from a long train of thought, I expressed in a short exclamation, which I insensibly uttered aloud,—'Thou, little bird, art still the happier.'

CHAPTER XVII.

Seldom, when

The steeled jailer is the friend of men.

Measure for Measure

"Another year passed in solitude like the former ones; and the space of time I had now been imprisoned, in all ten years since my first being brought to the Bastile, began to reconcile me from habit, to that state which seemed to be marked out as the condition of my remaining life.

"No change had taken place in the treatment shown me, but that milk and thin wine were sometimes brought me instead of water with my bread, and that I was not now so frequently led out for air upon the platform as I had formerly been; being now seldom conducted thither above once in eight or nine days.

"About this time a man whom I had never before seen, brought me my morning and evening portion of provision, instead of the jailer who had been accustomed to attend me; he appeared to be about twenty-five years of age, tall, and strongly built, but of a benign aspect, that seemed ill to suit the office in which he served.

"As he visited me for several successive days, and the mildness of his countenance encouraged me to address him, I inquired whether he who had formerly attended me was dead.

"'Oh no!' he answered, and immediately left me, as fearing to say more; whilst his features plainly showed that it was not from want of inclination on his part, that our conversation had been so short.

"I often endeavoured to tempt him into farther conference, but he could never be prevailed by me to utter more than one sentence at a visit. One day, however, when I asked if he knew whether I was a prisoner for life, he cast his eye to the door, as if to be assured no one was watching him, and then putting his face close to mine, he said hastily, and in a low voice, 'Pray don't question me again, but rely on my being your friend,' and again departed as precipitately as he had done on former occasions.

"The first ray of hope, in the course of ten tedious and painful years, now burst upon my afflicted heart, and every nerve was strained to form a conjecture how this youth could be interested in my welfare.

"Five months passed, and this youth still visited me; nor did I once behold him who had before attended me; but still I perceived, from the conduct of my newly-declared friend, that no fit opportunity for conference was given us, for he always hastened from my prison as quickly as possible, seldom however forgetting to cast at me a look of sympathy, which served to keep alive the feeble spark of hope he had lighted in my breast.

"One evening about this time, when he brought in my supper, he said, in the same mysterious way he had always spoken to me in, but apparently with greater signs of fear than he had ever before shown of being overheard, 'Don't go to sleep to-night.' I obeyed his injunctions, and awaited with the greatest impatience the hour that should disclose to me his meaning.

"The clock had just struck two, when a person in an under voice at the grating of my window, which I immediately knew to be that of my new friend, said 'Monsieur, monsieur!'

"I felt for my stool, and placing it under the window, mounted upon it, and our faces then nearly meeting, he said, 'If I should contrive your escape from this place, and this kingdom, will you let me be your servant?'

"'Say rather my friend,' I replied.

"'Only say you won't let me starve, monsieur.'

"'No, by heaven!' I returned, forgetful how destitute I myself was of the means of subsistence.

"'Enough said,' he resumed; 'then don't refuse to drink any thing that is offered you; and leave the rest to me.'

"'Drink!' I repeated, but the young man was gone.

"I remained some minutes at the window, but he did not return, neither did I hear the faintest sound. I then left my station, and throwing myself on my mattress, I began to ruminate on the words which I had just had addressed to me; and the only idea I could suffer myself to connect with the last sentence the young man had uttered, was that I was intended to be poisoned.

"At an early hour in the morning, I heard my prison door unlocked, and a friar entered; he commanded me to kneel by him; and having prayed that I might bear with fortitude the sentence he was about to announce to me, he told me that I was condemned to die on that day.

"A few hours before, I should have thought death the greatest happiness that could have befallen me; but now, with the faint hope of enlargement which my new friend had given me, prepared as I was to receive this sentence, and even tempted to believe that by his means I should escape it, I felt an indescribable shock on its being first announced to me.

"I am inclined to think that the emotions which this intelligence produced in me, were to me of essential service, for I am well convinced, that the sudden change my countenance underwent was so great, as to have baffled the suspicion of the priest, had he entertained any, of what had passed between me and the young jailer.

"He asked my confession. A seclusion of nearly eleven years from the world could have added no sin of magnitude to my account of former misdeeds, and of them I had made a confession on the very morning on which I had first been brought to the Bastile; thus this task was quickly ended. He then again ordered me to kneel, and having prayed by me full two hours, he gave me his blessing, and departed.

"In a few minutes the governor, attended by two guards, and the young man in whom my last and only hope rested, entered.

"Obeying the governor's orders, the young man poured from a phial which he had brought in his hand, a thick black liquor into a small basin, which the governor then took, and holding it out to me, commanded me to drink it, the two guards meanwhile levelling their bayonets at my breast, as a tacit threat in case of my refusing the draught.

"I crossed myself, and drank; the basin fell from my hand, and I raised my eyes in search of my friend: he had left the prison; the governor made a signal to the guards; they went out; he followed them; and I heard him turn the lock upon me.

"What a moment of horror was this! Uncertain whether or not I had swallowed the draught of death: if I had, how near the brink of eternity was I now standing! — if I had not, how dreadful a fate might await both me and the young man, should his stratagem fail!

"Within the course of an hour a faint sickness seized me. I lay down upon my mattress, and pulled the blanket over me; an icy coldness ran through my veins, and big drops of perspiration started on my forehead: in a short time a heaviness, which I could not struggle against, weighed down my eye-lids, and in less than two hours after my swallowing the draught, I sunk into what I then thought the sleep of death!"

Thus far had count Byroff proceeded in his narrative when the shepherd entering the room, informed him, that two men, who had seen his horse in the stable, had declared they knew it, and insisted on coming into the cottage in search of him, and that his son was then endeavouring to prevent their entrance.

The count raised his eyes in silence to Lauretta; they betrayed the wildest agitation and fear; Lauretta rose from her seat, and threw herself upon her father's neck, and at the same instant the voices of Theodore and Kroonzer were heard by them in the adjoining apartment.

Count Byroff started up, and snatching his dagger from his side, prepared himself to meet their entrance into the chamber.

The chevalier was the first that appeared; the count made a dart at him, which he resisting, threw the count upon the floor, and treading on him with his left foot, drew his sword, while he muttered curses on him for a villain and a traitor.

Lauretta, instigated by the scene before her, caught his arm, and falling on her knees by the side of her father's body, she exclaimed, "Here, in this bosom sheath thy sword; but spare, oh spare my father!"

Count Byroff's prayers and struggles confirmed Theodore that Lauretta had truly named him her parent; and a momentary surprise suspended his power of action. This count Byroff perceived, and availing himself of the astonishment of his antagonist, by an instantaneous effort raised himself again on his feet, and dropping his dagger, made himself master of the sword Theodore had just drawn. Kroonzer immediately drew his weapon, and springing forward, presented himself to oppose the count in defence of the chevalier, whilst Lauretta, regardless of herself, her thoughts centred only in her father's safety, and almost made frantic by the danger in which she now beheld him, ran without the cottage, piercing the air with her cries and calls for assistance.

Theodore was in an instant at her heels; and then first recollecting her own danger, on beholding herself so closely pursued by him she most dreaded, she flew to the young cottager who was standing without the cottage door, and clasping his hand, she cried out, "Oh! save me from him, I conjure you!"

The lad, who was still standing with the oaken staff in his hand, with which he had endeavoured to repulse the entrance of the chevalier and his accomplice, and still panting from the unequal combat he had sustained, moved either by the impulse of humanity, or fired by the beauty of his interesting suppliant, flew upon Theodore with the desperation a wolf flies to the combat when attacked by a lion, and conscious that he must either conquer or die.

For some moments the struggle was maintained with equal valour and dexterity; but at length the superior strength of the chevalier prevailing over that of his antagonist, Lauretta beheld her champion levelled with the ground; again she shrieked, and again she attempted to fly, but her trembling limbs could no longer support her, and she sunk on the earth in a swoon.

CHAPTER XVIII.

My soul's delight, my utmost joy, my husband!

I feel once more his panting bosom beat;

Once more I hold him in my eager arms,

Behold his face, and lose my soul in rapture.

Essex. Transporting bliss! my richest, dearest treasure!

My mourning turtle, my long absent peace,

Oh come yet nearer, nearer to my heart!

My raptured soul springs forward to receive thee;

Thou heav'n on earth, thou balm of all my woe.

The Earl of Essex

A fervent kiss, imprinted on her cold lips, recalled Lauretta into existence, and she opened her eyes in the wildest apprehension: but oh! what a glow of mingled ecstasy and delight warmed her frozen blood, when she perceived that it was Alphonsus, her beloved Alphonsus, who had bestowed the kiss that had awakened her from her trance.

In an unbounded transport of joy she embraced him as he stood by her side; then springing from the bed on which she had been laid, she flew to meet the embrace of her father, and then again sunk on the neck of her Alphonsus.

When their mutual effusions of joy gave room for an explanation on the part of count Byroff, Lauretta learnt from the lips of her father, whom it had been her first care to teach Alphonsus to know as such, that she was still in the shepherd's cottage, that Kroonzer had been put to flight by the united efforts of her father and the peasant, and that the chevalier had been killed by a blow from the hand of her husband, with the oaken staff which he had first obtained from the young peasant when he overcame him, and which Alphonsus had wrested from him.

Alphonsus then briefly informed Lauretta of the manner in which he had early that morning left Smaldart castle, and by the most fortunate chance had arrived to her rescue at the moment she was on the point of falling a prey to the villainy of Theodore.

Lauretta shuddered at the idea of the danger she had so unexpectedly escaped, and again clasped to her breast the author of her preservation: he returned her embrace with all the fervor of that warm affection he bore her, and then turning to count Byroff, he said, "Advise me, I beseech you, what course to follow, whither to bend my steps."

"What opposes your now returning to your humble dwelling immediately?" asked the count.

"To meet the baron Smaldart?" rejoined Alphonsus.

"The law is on your side:" resumed count Byroff.

"I should feel less reluctance to behold him if it were against me;" replied Alphonsus. "I cannot bear to meet the man I have so deeply wounded, when I know him void of the means of redress. — He has ever considered Theodore with the partiality of a father, and consequently must have viewed the enormity of his crimes with a softening eye; can he then do otherwise than detest the man who has deprived him of the darling of his heart? — I am convinced I have not acted wrongly: thus I cannot submit to sue for his forgiveness; and the compassion I feel for the grief I shall have excited in the breast of one who has behaved towards me with the kindness I have experienced from the baron Smaldart, commands me not to return to a spot where my presence might seem a triumph over the sorrow I had occasioned: no! I will seek some distant asylum, where, living forgotten, I shall not renew his misery."

"From a selfish motive," said count Byroff, "I warmly subscribe to your idea of leaving this part of the empire; for, having been seen by Kroonzer, it is absolutely necessary for the preservation of my life, that I should fly immediately from hence; thus, should you resolve to return to your late dwelling, I must forego the society of my child: should you remove to some distant spot, I may still be your companion."

The happiness of his Lauretta was at all times the first consideration of Alphonsus; and as he now read speakingly in her blue eyes, her dislike to her separation from her father, he instantly declared that he was resolved on not returning to the vicinity of Smaldart castle, and prepared to travel in any direction the count should dictate as most likely to ensure his safety.

Mutual satisfaction beamed in the eyes of the count and Lauretta, at this declaration of Alphonsus; and the count pressed that they might set out immediately.

In a few minutes the horses were prepared by the peasant, whom count Byroff having liberally rewarded for his exertions, and, at the instigation of Alphonsus, commanded him to send a messenger to Smaldart castle, with a full and exact account of the transactions of the morning, they departed, bending their course, in compliance with the directions of the count, towards the north.

Having stopped during the day no longer than was absolutely necessary for the refreshment of themselves and their horses, they arrived towards night at a little inn, where count Byroff said he trusted himself to be in safety.

Immediately on their being left alone in an apartment of the inn, Lauretta asked of her father the conclusion of his history; eager to learn the mystery of the situation in which she had at first seen him, and the cause of the danger he had so strongly expressed of being overtaken during the course of their day's journey.

"My child," answered count Byroff, "I confess that your curiosity has been strongly excited, but weightier considerations must supersede its gratification; we must look forward to the necessities of the future, ere we allow ourselves leisure to indulge in the remembrance of the past." Then addressing himself to Alphonsus, "Have you formed any plan of future life?" he asked.

Alphonsus answered, not.

After a pause, count Byroff continued, "You have appeared thoughtful during our journey: I conjectured you might have been deliberating on some measures which you were undecided whether or not to adopt."

"You conjectured rightly," replied Alphonsus, "in thinking my mind thus employed."

"What were your thoughts?"

"I fear you will not approve them; however, be assured I will do nothing without the concurrence of yourself and my Lauretta."

Count Byroff besought him to proceed.

"My Lauretta," he continued, "has doubtless related to you the ambiguous and sorrowful event which marks my early life?"

"She has."

"I cannot die happy, unless I solve the mystery by which I am driven a wanderer upon the world; its recollection clouds every moment of my existence, and renders me, in the summer of life, a gloomy and thoughtful companion to her, who, knowing the cause of my melancholy, bears, with an angel-like patience, the sour effects it will at times, in spite of my endeavours to coerce them, produce in me. Were it not better at once to end these agonising doubts, to visit the neighbourhood of Cohenburg castle, and, by discovering if possible the truth, learn at once my future doom?"

"It is a point," returned count Byroff, "whereon I cannot pretend to advise you; your sole guide must be the impulse of your own heart."

"But," said Lauretta, "whence is the intelligence you wish to procure to be gained? — The country round Cohenburg is doubtless unacquainted with the truth, or the young miner, the son of one of your father's vassals, must have known it: — your uncle, he informed you, was gone, no one knew whither, and your mother dead!"

"He said the same of me," returned Alphonsus; "thus his information in this point sways me not. — But he pronounced the castle to be deserted; this was a matter in which he could not be deceived; thus if I visit it secretly, I can offend no one by so doing; and I will guard against wounding my conscience by the relation of any discovery I may there make, should its secrecy seem to be required of me by the injunctions laid on me by my mother: and Oh! I have for some time laboured with an indescribable prepossession that I shall gain knowledge of moment, if I do visit it."

"You are then resolved?" said count Byroff.

"I have nothing wanting to complete my resolution, since you and my Lauretta do not seem to oppose it, but the means of accomplishing my journey."

"I have that in my possession," replied the count, "which, with frugality, will yet support us many weeks."

"Then to-morrow, with the dawn, I will once more turn my steps towards my native soil," said Alphonsus.

The remainder of the evening was spent by them in concerting the route they should travel; and having planned it to their mutual satisfaction, they at an early hour retired to rest.

Reflection on what might be the event of a long-wished, and at length projected, undertaking, suffered Alphonsus to sleep but little, and he rose with the dawn to awake his fellow-traveller: the count instantly obeyed his summons, and at sunrise they set forward on their journey.

As they proceeded, count Byroff lightened the way by again commencing the narrative of his life, in complaisance to the curiosity of Alphonsus; and being arrived at the period to which he had deduced his story, when in the shepherd's cottage he had related it to Lauretta, he thus went on.

"When I had recovered from the influence of the draught I had taken, which had been only a sleeping potion of a very strong nature, the first object on which I opened my eyes, was a black man sitting by my side, in a dry ditch, under the shade of a hedge; the time was twilight in the evening, and being too dusk for me accurately to discern his features, I perceived not, until he spoke, that my companion was the young jailer, with a new countenance: and when I did know him, I was some moments at a loss whether to express my astonishment first, at his change of colour, or my own extraordinary appearance, for I found myself habited in the garments of a French woman of mean rank.

"'Ah, monsieur!' cried he immediately on beholding me open my eyes, 'how glad am I to see you awake again, and out of that vile prison!—Don't you know me, monsieur?' continued he, observing that my eyes were fixed on him in doubt.

"'I think I do now,' I returned, after having been convinced by his voice who he was: 'but I hardly know myself.'

"'I thought how it would be when you awoke,' replied he; 'I contrived these disguises that we might pass unnoticed as beggars;—but here, Monsieur, take a sup of wine, and eat a bit of bread,' said he, pulling a flask and a crust from his pocket, 'and refresh yourself; for you must be faint with so long fasting.'

"I readily accepted his offer; and while the flask was at my mouth, he exclaimed, 'Dieu merci, that we are out of that horrid place!'

"'Why, you were not a prisoner?' I said.

"'Oh no, monsieur; but I felt so much for the poor creatures that were, that I could not bear to see them suffer any longer.—But, however, we are out now, and I hope for ever:—woe be to us if we get in again!'

"'But how did we get out, my good fellow?—How did you contrive our escape?' I asked.

"'I'll tell you another time, monsieur: we must not talk about it any more now, for fear we should be overheard:—Jacques Perlet will tell you all about it another time.—Oh, but, monsieur, you must not call me Jacques now, but some other name, such as blacks go by:—what shall it be, monsieur?'

"'Shall it be Caesar?' I replied.

"'Aye, monsieur,' said he, 'as well as any.—Now, monsieur, please to remember that, for carrying on my plan, you must, if you please, pretend to be my wife; your features are very delicate, and you may easily pass for a woman; and leave the rest to Jac—Caesar I mean, monsieur.'"

"I readily agreed to any plan of security in my present situation; and Jacques then told me we must now walk forwards to a small auberge, which he said he knew stood rather sequestered from the road, and where we were to pass the night.

"In our way, I asked him how far we were from Paris.

"'Oh, nine or ten lieues, monsieur,' answered he.

"'By what means did we perform the journey?'

"'It is so dark, monsieur,' said he, 'that I can't see whether any body is near us or not;—I durst not tell you any thing till by and by.'

"I checked my curiosity, conscious how judiciously my guide was acting; and we arrived within sight of the little inn in silence.

"According to the directions of Jacques, I asked in French for a mean supper and bed, while my companion only occasionally spoke in the vitiated manner in which negroes usually pronounce a language which they have no opportunity of learning but by the ear.

"I was rejoiced to perceive that our stratagem passed unsuspected; and when we retired to bed, which we did in the characters of husband and wife, the better to conceal our real ones, Jacques desired me to sit down, saying he must have a little chat with me before we went to bed, for his tongue was burning to tell me how nicely he had managed our escape.

"I was, as you may suppose, anxious to learn how my salvation from death had been effected during the time of my insensibility; and placing myself on the foot of the bed, I desired him to begin; he seated himself on the ground by my side, and leaning his arm upon the bed, spoke thus:

"'In the first place, monsieur, I must tell you a little about who I am, that you may the better understand my reasons for what I have done. — My father, monsieur, was a very honest savetier in the fauxbourg St. Antoine, and at one time earned a very comfortable living; but misfortunes will happen to the best of people, and one mishap or another had obliged him to borrow small sums of money from several of his neighbours, chiefly to defray the expenses of my mother's illness and funeral, all which he would honestly have repaid, I am sure, if he had lived; but he died, poor man, soon after, and left me without a friend in the world, except my uncle Perlet, the old jailer at the Bastile, and a brother we had none of us heard of for many years.

"'Well, I had been brought up to my father's trade; and if he had not left me heir to his debts as well as to his business, (which God forbid I should blame him for; for how could he have helped it, if even he had known he had been going to die?) I might have gained myself a pretty livelihood: but his creditors threatened to arrest me for the money, and so my uncle Perlet, too avaricious to pay it for me, and too proud to see his nephew confined in a jail, though he lived in a prison himself, took me to serve under him in the Bastile.

"'I did not like going there at all; but what could I do, monsieur? I thought it was better than starving; but by the time I had been there a couple of months, which was about the time I first came to bring you your portion of bread and water, I would almost sooner have died than have staid much longer where I was; for the frightful things I saw, and the groans, and moans, and shrieks I heard in that dismal place, would freeze your blood, and make your hair stand on end, monsieur, if I was to tell you them all.'

"I sighed in the affirmative to Jacques' exclamation; and he continued: 'Ah, monsieur, you have had your share of their devil's works, I dare say?'

"'It is past now, so let us drive away its remembrance,' I replied.

"'I wish I could, monsieur: but I shall dream of it many a night to come, I dare say. — My uncle,' continued he, 'had a room where he and I used to sit by ourselves in an evening: and as my head was continually running upon the poor unhappy wretches I attended in the day-time, I could not forbear questioning him about them; and many a time, when I heard the story of a poor helpless creature condemned to die by the rack, or poison, I could not help thinking of the fate of his persecutors at a future day, that all of us must see.

"'Sometimes I used to remonstrate with my uncle on the cruelty with which he often assisted in using the unhappy prisoners; but his answer always was, 'Jacques, I am a true lover of my king, and I'll never treat those kindly, depend upon it, that it is his pleasure to have otherwise dealt by.' — 'But may not obedience,' I would answer, 'be carried so far as to make conscience troublesome?'

"'Impossible, child,' he once answered me, when I had thus spoken to him; 'the king is the representative of God on earth, chosen by himself; thus we can never be doing wrong, while we implicitly obey his commands.' — 'Then,' returned I, 'how careful ought the king to be, for his own sake, that his conduct is kind, merciful, and forgiving, since, as you say, the consciences of all his subjects, if they have done amiss in compliance with his commands, are cleared from guilt; of course the weight of all their bad actions must lie upon his conscience instead of theirs, and he be punished accordingly hereafter.'

"'You are a foolish boy,' cried he, 'and don't understand these matters.'

"'I made him no answer; for truly, monsieur, I did not wish to know more than I already did of a conduct that seemed to me void of reason and humanity; I had only a mind to ask him whether he prayed to the king instead of le bon Dieu; but I durst not, for fear he should think I was laughing at him, and use me as hardly as he had done others for less offences.'

"I could not help smiling at Jacques's philosophy; he laughed too, and thus went on—

"'Well, monsieur, every day I began to long more and more to quit my situation: but it was a thing I almost despaired to be able to do; for I was well aware that my uncle would never give his consent to my leaving the Bastile for any other employment, for fear I should tell tales out of prison; so I knew the only method must be to run away to a distance from Paris; but then I had not much money, and I did not much like to make such an attempt without a companion.

"'Some how, monsieur, I had taken a liking to you above any of the prisoners I attended; and all I kept wishing for, was some means of setting you at liberty, that we might run away together; I knew, if I could contrive it, you could not dislike it, and there was something in your countenance that told me you would be kind to me afterwards.

"'Oh, monsieur! how often have I wished to sit and talk half an hour or an hour with you, and tell you how much I pitied you, and how I wished to serve you; but I durst not, for all the walls in that Bastile have eyes and ears, I believe; for nothing can be said or done but what is known by my uncle and the governor.—I often inquired of my uncle something about you, and I learnt, a little at a time, that you were, as most of the other prisoners are, a gentleman; and that you were only retained in prison because they were afraid to let you out, for fear you should expose the secrets of their tyranny.

"'And is it owing to the king that the poor gentleman suffers all this for nothing?' said I.

"'Partly,' my uncle answered, 'and partly to those who first represented him to sa majesté, as obnoxious to the state.'

"'Then the king has some good friends, who lighten the burden of his conscience by taking a little of it upon their own,' said I.

"'My uncle answered me with a look which determined me never to hazard a joke again, on what he deemed so sacred a subject.

"'About five weeks ago, my uncle told me, as he had given up the care of half his prisoners to me, I must fill every part of the office myself, and accordingly on the next morning must carry a dose of poison into the apartment of a marquis, who was condemned to die: I was afraid of disobeying my uncle; and I knew besides that if I did not do it, somebody else would, so that my refusal would be of no service to the poor wretch; and thus, at the time appointed, I attended the governor to the cell, just as I came with him into yours, monsieur, on the morning when he thought he was giving you your last dose: but I was too sly for him,—eh, monsieur?

"'When the poor gentleman had swallowed the draught, and the governor had left the apartment, my uncle locked the door upon the dying man, saying, 'nobody must go in any more till he was dead.'

"'What! must we leave him all alone at this terrible moment?' asked I.

"'Why, does he want any body to help him to die?'" returned my uncle.

"'Ah, pauvre diable! I wish it was over with him,' said I.

"'It won't be long, I'll answer for it,' he replied, and then commanded me to leave the door by which I was standing, and could not help trying to listen what was passing within.

"'In the evening, when all the prison doors were double locked for the night, he called me to follow him up stairs, and we went together into the poor marquis's apartment. Oh dear, monsieur, I shall never forget it. There lay the poor gentleman dead and cold, and all his features so dreadfully distorted, and his eyes and mouth wide open, that I should have run out of the room with fright if my uncle had not held me by the collar.

"'Now,' said my uncle, 'we must carry the corpse into the cimetière, and bury it.'

"'I was forced to obey, and we carried down the body to the spot he had named, where stood a coffin ready to receive it.

"'I suppose you think,' said he, 'I am going to bury this man? No! no! I know a better trick than that; I'll never bury a corpse whilst I can get well paid for letting it remain above ground.' He then told me, that a surgeon in La rue de Saint Etienne le grand always bought the bodies of him to dissect; and that as he had the privilege of passing the draw-bridge when he pleased, he had always carried them to him by night; 'but,' said he, 'I'll contrive for you to carry this one, and I'll bury the coffin in the mean time.'

"'Well, monsieur, the body was put into a sack; I pretended it was so heavy I could not carry it; my uncle knew better, and I was forced to set off according to his directions: he went with me to the draw-bridge, and having whispered the guards, they let me pass.

"'Do you know, monsieur, I'd wager my life, the governor and he went shares in selling the dead men; for nobody, I had often heard my uncle say, could go over the draw-bridge without the governor's knowing it, and giving leave.

"'Notwithstanding the weight of my burden, I ran all the way; for not being accustomed to be so near dead people, I thought every moment I could feel him stirring and groaning.

"'When I had got quit of my load, I began to consider whether I should go back or not; I felt in my pocket to see how much money I was worth in case I took the chance of running away, when, pardi, monsieur! if I had not left my purse at home. I did not know what to do now; for having nothing to support myself with, I thought I could not go far without money, so might be heard of by my uncle, taken back to the Bastile, and perhaps roasted alive for what I had done, by the great fire in that room where all the irons are hanging about: I trembled at the very thought of it, and so ran back as fast as my legs could carry me.

"'When I returned back to my uncle, he gave me an écu de six francs out of his profits, as a reward for what I had done, saying, he would double it the next job, for he was determined I should not want for encouragement, and I should soon have another, for monsieur Montville had not much longer to live.

"'I was not a little surprised and disturbed at hearing this, monsieur, as you may suppose; and I was sure that if any thing could be done, it must be done directly. Well, I kept thinking, and thinking, and no way could I contrive to get you out; at last a plan came into my head, and I resolved I would try it whether it succeeded or not. I complained to my uncle that I had got a very bad tooth-ache, and told him that I had frequently been subject to it, and that my father had been used to give me some laudanum to cure it, and begged that he would too.

"'He gave me a small phial about half full, warning me to be very careful how I used it; I immediately ran with it to my own chamber, and having poured it into the phial that had held the poison given to the poor dead marquis, and which I had washed out for that purpose, I let fall the empty phial: it broke with the fall, just as I wished; I ran down to my uncle with the broken pieces in my hand, and telling him my misfortune, begged him to give me some more.

"'The old fox was taken in for once, monsieur, and he brought me about as much as before.

"'I suppose,' said I, as I took it from him, 'if I was to drink all this stuff, it would kill me?'

"'Twice as much would,' he replied: 'that would make you sleep for about two days.'

"'I found by this that my first quantity would have been enough for what I wanted with it, but however I thought it was no bad thing to have two doses by me, in case any accident happened to one of them; and so I put them both carefully by, and by the next night my tooth-ache was gone.

"'Well, monsieur, at last the day was fixed for you to die upon: I found means of coming to your window, as you must recollect, the night before; and when I told you not to refuse to drink any thing that was offered you, I said it because I was afraid you might by some means spill the potion that would be given to you, thinking it to be poison, as you could not know I had contrived to give you laudanum in its stead, and then might be obliged to take the poison indeed, as a second dose would have been brought you, that I should have had no opportunity of changing.

"'When I left the outside of your prison window, I went and got one of my phials half full of laudanum. Now the poison phials are always full; so I knew my false one must be so too, or it would discover the trick. I durst not put in any more laudanum for fear I should kill you, and if I filled it up with water, it would look so much paler than the poison; so at last, what do you think I did, monsieur? — why, I filled it up with treacle and water, and it looked quite black, just like what it should have been.

"'When morning came, I was called to attend the governor: my uncle gave me the phial of poison; and I, to deceive him, said in a low voice, 'to-night I shall earn deux écus.' He nodded significantly, and I followed the governor and his guards. At the turn from the last flight of stairs into the gallery, I stopped an instant, and snatching my phial from my bosom, and slipping the other into its place, I made a noise with my feet as if saving myself from falling; and then running a step or two after the governor, and rubbing my knee as if I had bruised it, 'better so than a broken leg,' I cried: the governor turned round and looked at me; still rubbing my knee, I drew up a face which made him smile at my supposed accident, and he walked on without suspicion.'"

The travellers at this moment arrived within sight of a small house, and Alphonsus interrupted the count's narrative, by proposing, that, if it proved a house of public accommodation, they should make it their abode for the night, as the twilight was already beginning to fall. To this proposal count Byroff agreed; and the habitation proving to be such as they wished it, they here put an end to their day's journey.

CHAPTER XIX.

Wish'd morning's come! And now upon the plains

And distant mountains, where men feed their flocks,

The happy shepherds leave their homely huts,

And with their lusty pipes proclaim the new-born day.

The cheerful birds too, on the tops of trees,

Assemble all in choirs, and with their notes

Salute and welcome up the rising sun.

There's no condition sure so curs'd as mine!

Otway

Refreshed by the salutary balm of sleep, our travellers awoke to one of the most glorious mornings that ever burst from the heavens; the sun was beginning his progress towards his meridian of splendor, without a single cloud to obscure his expanding rays; the pearly drops of dew were still hanging on the dripping leaves, and studding the blades of grass; every bush resounding with the grateful notes of its feathered inhabitants, hailing the return of morn; and every flower exhaling sweets in gratitude to the rising presence of their fostering orb.

Again blessed with her Alphonsus, Lauretta's feelings harmonised in the universal gladness of nature: Alphonsus strove to be cheerful, but his efforts were ineffectual; Lauretta observed his dejectedness, and without remarking upon it, endeavoured to divert it. She was sometimes successful: again Alphonsus sunk into thought; she varied her attentions; he returned a smile of gratitude for her endeavours to please, and she was happy.

Having made a delicious repast of new milk and fruits, they again proceeded on their journey, and after a short conversation on various topics, count Byroff thus pursued his narrative —

"'Well, monsieur,' continued Jacques Perlet, 'all day long I was wishing, I hardly knew why, to come and take a peep at you; however I should not have been allowed if I had asked it, and at all events I thought it was much more prudent not. At night my uncle called me to go up with him about the same time he had done before, and, oh dear, how frightened I was all the way up stairs!—for it had just come into my head you might not be asleep yet; and then, when I found you was asleep, I was as much afraid my uncle's rough handling, or some unlucky blow in lifting you, might awake you.

"'However, Dieu merci, we got you down stairs, and into the cimetière quite safe: I trembled a little when my uncle said he thought you was very warm; but I soon recovered again when he added, that he thought nothing of that, for that he had carried away many a one before they were half cold.

"'In a few minutes I got you put into the sack, taking care to lay you with your head towards the mouth, and away I went, leaving my uncle to bury the coffin, and wait my return.

"'Instead of going to the surgeon's, I made the best of my way for la porte de Saint Jean; and being got out of the city, I looked for the first hedge I could find, and setting down my load on the side farthest from the road, I pulled you out of the sack, terrified to death for fear I should have smothered you; and pleased enough I was, when I put my hand to your side, and felt your heart heave. I directly set about putting on you this gown and petticoat, and hat, and apron, and cloak, that I had taken from the old woman in the Bastile that is kept to make my uncle's and the governor's beds. I did not rob her of them, monsieur, for I put a demi-louis into her box when I took them out; and the manner I contrived to bring them away with me, was by buttoning them in between my coat and waistcoat, and telling my uncle it was a lump of cloth I had put there to keep the weight of my load from hurting my shoulder.

"'When I had dressed you, I set about disguising myself, and having turned all my clothes inside outwards, I dyed my hands and face with some stuff I had brought in my pocket for that purpose; I then threw the clothes I had taken off you, together with the sack, over the opposite hedge, into a deep ditch, and then sat me down by your side, anxiously waiting till some cart might come past that would carry us a little farther from our old abode.

"'About day-break I heard the wheels of some carriage coming from the city; I peeped over the hedge, and saw a wagon full of luggage, in the front of which sat one man, on a bench large enough to hold three or four; I called to him, asking, 'Whither he was going?'—'To Desmartin,' he answered. Then, pretending that I was hardly able to express myself in French, I told him that I had a sick wife almost at the point of death lying behind the hedge, and that I would give him a trifle to carry us some way on our journey, which lay his road; after a short dispute about what I was to pay him, he consented to carry us, and I lifted you into the wagon and placed you upon the seat, carefully holding you, lest you should fall out.

"'We stopped several times during the day; some pitied my poor wife, some laughed at me for a black fourbe, and some were charitable enough to give me a petit sous, and bid me take care of la pauvre ame; and I directly bought the wine and bread in their presence, which I gave you under the hedge, for which they all called me a bon garçon, and one old woman doubled her charity.

"'I had not taken you out of the wagon all day, for fear, if I did, the people should crowd round you out of curiosity, and discover the imposition: evening was coming on, and you did not wake; we were within a lieue of Desmartin, and I did not know what to do; at last I remembered this little cabaret, which stands a few hundred paces from the high road, for I had once in my life travelled as far as Desmartin; and telling the wagoner I meant to pass the night there, as inns in towns were too expensive for me, I desired, when we came in sight of it, to get out. He accordingly stopped, and having taken you out, and paid him his promised fare, we wished one another bon soir, and on he drove.

"'Well, monsieur, I knew it could not be long before you woke; so I determined not to go to the cabaret till you did; so I entered the first field with you in my arms, and having spied the dry ditch where we were when you awoke, I laid you down in it, and seating myself by you, chuckled not a little to myself at the success of my plan,—and when you awoke I was just thinking how you and I should both laugh if we could see ourselves in a miroir.'

"When Jacques had ended his account, having thanked him in the warmest terms for the interest he had so kindly taken in my welfare, and commended the adroitness with which he had effected our escape, I told him that it behoved us immediately to conclude on some plan for leaving the kingdom with all possible expedition; for if my being alive was not discovered, he would doubtless be sent in search of by his uncle, and that if one was taken, the other would in course share his fate, and then both, beyond a doubt, fall sacrifices to the butchers in the Bastile.

"'Why, monsieur,' replied he, 'let us set forward as fast as we can to your home, wherever it is.'

"How astonished was the poor fellow to hear I had neither home nor means of subsistence! He had expected to find me a man of rank and fortune either in Italy or Germany, he knew not which, and who would liberally repay him for his services. He, however, bore his disappointment with the most honourable fortitude, and he drew tears into my eyes by exclaiming, after a short pause of reflection—"Well, monsieur, if you had been un homme de bien, I am sure you would have taken care of pauvre Jacques; as you are not, Jacques will take care of you as well as he is able: as long as that money lasts, half of it is yours;" and so saying, he pulled from his pocket his whole worldly treasure, and threw it upon the bed.

"After much deliberation, we resolved to travel into Germany in our present disguises, for what purpose neither of us knew, except that we must leave France, and that all places were equally indifferent; for to take possession again of the mansion and estate I had once quitted, I knew to be an impossibility for me at the present moment to attempt, encumbered as it was with debts and mortgages.

"Next morning at a very early hour we set forward on our journey, and to our great satisfaction arrived in about ten days' time in Germany, without having suffered more on our journey than what was occasioned by fatigue, and our own fears. During the whole expedition, Jacques' conversation was confined to two subjects—his apprehension of being pursued and overtaken, and his wish of being acquainted in what part of the empire was his brother, who had left Paris about four years ago with a man whom nobody knew, and with whom he had only said, he was going into Germany. 'He was an idle fellow,' continued Jacques, 'and, I dare say, took to some lazy kind of life; and pardi, so was his former one, for he could not have a much easier business than valet de chambre to a marquis: it suited him, for he got fine clothes, and strutted about like a singe poudré: I might have had his place when he went away, but I preferred homeliness and hard work to such frippery; and you see how I am rewarded for my honesty; but hard fare here, better hereafter, says l'évangile; so I am never cast down, monsieur, happen what will.'

"There was something consolatory to me in the reasoning of my humble companion, and I determined to put myself under the guidance of one so cheerful amidst misfortunes, and confident in providence under its painful inflictions, and accordingly told him I was resolved to be entirely directed by him in what course to follow for gaining our future subsistence.

"After some deliberation, Jacques proposed that we should endeavour to push our way to the capital of the empire, where he said he should stand a chance of being better paid for exercising his trade, as the value of his work would there be better estimated, being, as he assured me, an excellent workman.

"On the first day of our arrival in Germany, Jacques took advantage of a pool of water somewhat sequestered from the road, again to change the complexion of his face and hands, but it was some days ere he could accomplish a perfect triumph of the ivory over the ebony; however, having turned his clothes into their proper situation, his appearance became decent; and at the next town, having purchased for me a wrapping coat and a hat, I changed the outward form of my sex behind the first hedge we came to on our again proceeding on our journey.

"The cash Jacques now had left, consisted, in all, of a louis-d'or and deux écus; accordingly, in order to housewife the money we possessed, it not appearing to us so easy a matter to acquire more when it was spent, we resolved to buy a loaf and some cheese, of which we ate, when hungry, under a tree; and, as the season was the middle of summer, we determined to sleep under hedges or in any out-houses we might meet with, thus to avoid the unnecessary expense of entering inns on the road.

"Necessity reconciles measures, which, to those who have never been reduced to adopt them, appear insurmountable; thus we experienced nothing more than accidental inconvenience from pursuing our plan. In the enjoyment of liberty I ever forgot care; and Jacques never failed to declare once every day, that he had rather sleep in a ditch with mud for a feather-bed, than on down in the Bastile.

"Journeying on one night by moonlight, the decayed castle wherein you, Lauretta, was an unfortunate prisoner, attracted our notice: its ruined condition seemed to bespeak it uninhabited; the gate stood open; we entered the hall, and without much farther observation, we determined to make it our abode for the night.

"We lay down together in a corner of the hall, where we had scarcely composed ourselves to sleep, when the sounding of a shrill tucket aroused our attention.—We listened without speaking: — In a couple of minutes a man entered the hall from a distant part of the building, and proceeding to the gate, called out, 'All's safe,' immediately we heard the trampling of horses approaching close to the gate; a number of men, who were talking confusedly, dismounted from them and entered the hall; and the first sentence I distinctly heard, and which opened to me at once the nature of this strange adventure, was, 'curse the barrenness of the road! one can find nobody to plunder,' uttered by one of the men as he vaulted from his horse.

"Presently another man entered the hall from the interior part of the building, carrying a lamp: in an instant Jacques sprung from my side, and running to the man, threw his arms around his neck, exclaiming, 'Ah mon frère, je vous retrouve! Ah mon cher frère! mon cher frère!'

"In his eagerness to embrace his brother, Jacques had knocked the lamp out of his hand, which being extinguished by the fall, the party was left in darkness to exercise their imaginations on what they had heard; and, from what motive I cannot pretend to say, whether from surprise or any supernatural fear, a general silence prevailed till another light was brought into the hall; on the appearance of which, Jacques, regardless of surrounding objects, came running back to me, all the way introducing me to his brother as his 'très bon ami.'

"The banditti, for such, you will have perceived, were the inhabitants of this decayed mansion, immediately came round me; I rose and began to apologise for our intrusion into their dwelling, by stating to them the truth of our circumstances, which Jacques summed up by telling them we were almost penniless, having just escaped from the Bastile.

"Avowed enemies to tyranny, and plainly perceiving there was no deceit in the relationship of the brothers, the banditti invited us to enter that part of the building which they inhabited, and partake of their supper before we retired to rest, when we should be accommodated with a bed.

"I thanked them for their kindness in the warmest terms, and they conducted us into a hall where a repast had been prepared against their return. I ate in complaisance to my entertainers, — and Jacques, because variety, to which he was unaccustomed, whetted his appetite.

"After supper I was requested to relate my adventures, Jacques having awakened their curiosity by repeatedly referring to our late escape; and though I should have preferred retiring to sleep, I felt myself bound to comply with their request.

"When I had concluded my story, the leader rose, and taking my hand,—'We are your brothers in affliction,' he said; 'most of us whom you here behold, have been driven from the haunts of men, by the cruelty of man; but there is not one of us whose heart has been steeled by his misfortunes into inhumanity: never has the traveller whom we have plundered borne the marks of our violence,—never have we left the poor man destitute,—the rich and profligate alone have been our prey,— the unfortunate at all times our care;—you are unfortunate, and we are willing to receive you as a brother; will you then become one of us, and live free from the despotism of tyrants, and the malice of an envious world, enjoying perfect liberty, subject only to laws of our own, and those useless where honour presides?'

"'Well said, noble captain!' cried Jacques, starting up: 'honour amongst thieves is an old proverb of my father's: I'll make one of you with all my heart.'

"During the time I had been reciting my adventures, Jacques had been drinking pretty freely of the palatable wine the table afforded; and having taken somewhat too potent a dose, it was rather the spirit of the wine than that of his own courage which spoke for him in the last sentence. The captain perceived his situation, and commanded his brother to conduct him to bed; but he promised faithfully not to drink another drop, or speak another word, if he might but be permitted to sit up as long as his 'cher maître.'

"During this little altercation between the captain and Jacques, I had a moment of leisure to reflect on the words which had been addressed to me: I thought they appeared rather an apology for a mode of life which the speaker himself knew to be culpable, but was from necessity constrained to follow, than an eulogium which might tempt me to embrace it: I accordingly requested that I might deliberate on his proposal till the morning; a request readily granted me: Jacques and I then retired for the night,—Jacques assuring the captain he had resolved to serve under him.

"A few moments served to change the powers of the deceitful liquor which had produced Jacques's valour; for he was no sooner in bed than his boasted prowess was forgotten in a profound sleep, and I thus left to my own reflections.

"During the greatest part of the night I remained awake, undecided what plan to follow. My mind revolted from becoming a determined robber; but I felt a still greater antipathy to again mixing in the ensnaring scenes of that world from which I had already experienced so much perfidy and sorrow; and I at length resolved to accept the asylum which had been offered me.

"In the morning when Jacques awoke, all the occurrences of the preceding night had entirely fled from his memory, and he awoke me in a great fright, inquiring whether we had got into the Bastile again. Just as I had sufficiently roused myself to begin to rally his recollection, his brother entered to call us to breakfast, and his presence saved me the trouble of farther explanation, as, on sight of him, Jacques immediately recollected where he was.

"On seeing the captain, I immediately declared to him my resolution; and was welcomed by him into my new situation, as also separately by every voice of the community.

"The captain then turned to Jacques, and reminded him of his promise.

"Jacques stared vacantly, and inquired 'what it was?'

"'To become one of the fraternity over which I have the honour to preside,' returned the leader.

"'Did I promise that?'

"'You did.'

"'Well then, I'll keep my word; and if you will but feed me and clothe me, I'll be savetier to you all for nothing: and what more can you desire of me, if you will but consider that a cobbler ought to stick to his last?'

"His brother joined me in interceding for the grant of his petition; and his native mirth, rather than any other qualification, obtained for him the majority of votes in his favour.

CHAPTER XX.

– – – – – – Yes, yes – 'tis she!

This little cross – I know it by sure marks!

Aaron Hill

On the preceding night, the faces of such of the banditti as had been out prowling, had been disguised with some colouring, which was always their custom when going on any expedition; and being now cleared from it, Jacques recognised, in the person of Kroonzer, the man with whom his brother had left France, of which occurrence this was the brief account: Kroonzer was the son of a German man and French woman; his residence had been chiefly in France, and his trade, from his infancy, none of the most creditable; his parents having been people, who, by assuming various disguises and characters in various places, had made these their means of imposing on the credulous, and defrauding the ignorant; thus gaining a fortuitous subsistence, whilst they cautiously kept within the pale of the law, and yet were in reality little better than common thieves.

"This mode of life had initiated Kroonzer into all the intrigues of Paris; and from his first herding with the banditti, to whose knowledge he had been led by accident, he had become extremely useful to them, by going annually into France, and finding means of disposing to advantage of such rings, watches, and other trinkets of value, as had fallen into their hands, and, before their knowledge of Kroonzer, had proved of little worth to them, as no one amongst them had ventured to hazard the experiment of changing them into money.

"It was in one of these expeditions that Kroonzer became acquainted with Jacques's brother; and having found him to be a man whom he believed would be a valuable acquisition to their society, he had enticed him into Germany under false promises, nor made the real truth known to him till he introduced him to his comrades; a measure which he had however been strictly forbidden by the captain ever again to repeat. Guillaume Perlet was, as it fortunately happened for the security of the banditti, an acceptable subject; for, preferring any kind of idleness to work, his new mode of life was pleasing to him the first moment of his being made acquainted with it.

"The captain treated me with great kindness and attention, and indeed my health required it, for the sudden change from eleven years of inactivity, to the great fatigue I had the last twenty days been undergoing, had reduced me to a state of excessive weakness.

"For the first year, I was not required to do any thing more in the various business of our household, of which every one in his turn took a part, than what I chose for my own amusement; nor during the whole of the time I lived amongst the banditti, in all nearly eight years, was any thing more asked of me than to take my turn in the evening and nightly watches.

"The evening watch was to answer the tucket sounded by the banditti, on their return from an excursion, that, in case of the officers of justice having entered their haunt during their absence, they might thus be apprised of it, ere they entered the castle, and, by flying, prevent their being taken with their spoils upon them, which would prove sure evidences of their guilt.

"Of the night watch this was the import; that those who did not go out in the quest of plunder watched for two hours alternately in the hall of the castle, that the fraternity might not be surprised in their sleep.

"During the first six years of my residence amongst the banditti, no circumstance worth relating occurred; and as I was not constrained to act the part of a plunderer, considering myself comparatively free from guilt, I felt myself tolerably happy: at the expiration of that period the captain died.

"A ballot immediately took place for appointing him a successor, and the majority of suffrages fell upon Kroonzer.

"About three months after his becoming leader of the fraternity, was the time at which he had always been accustomed to visit France; and as no one was deemed so fit for the business of that expedition as himself; he again undertook to perform it, notwithstanding his rise to his present situation; and accordingly, having appointed a deputy to guide the helm until his return, he departed as usual.

"The time of his absence was marked with an event of some moment: this was the death of Guillaume Perlet; and for some weeks it required all my most eloquent persuasions and remonstrances to keep Jacques from exceeding the bounds of reasonable sorrow on the loss of his brother; and he declared, that the thought of leaving me alone in my present situation, was his only inducement to struggle against death.

"At the stated time Kroonzer returned, and with him came the chevalier D'Aignon.

"Kroonzer had one fault, —it was that inordinate thirst of money which often leads its possessor to gratify in a heedless moment his ruling passion, and to repent at leisure that he did not subdue it. Conscious that he had acted wrongly, and yet too honourable to attempt a deceit which might endanger the security of those to whom the strongest ties of fellowship connected him, —when Theodore had retired for the night (for no one has a right to question the captain, and thus we knew not yet on what motive Theodore was brought amongst us), he candidly confessed the inconsiderate measure of which he had been guilty, and asked our advice how to act.

"He informed us, that during his visits to Paris, he had been much in the habit of frequenting gaming-tables, at many of which he had for the last three years frequently seen the chevalier, and had at times, he said, won of him sums of money to no small amount. —'He always paid his money without concern, and was so eager to enter into any measure for squandering it,' continued Kroonzer, 'that I soon found him to be a fit subject to exercise my talents upon. No very favourable opportunity offered to forward my plans on him, till a few days ago, happening to meet him at a tavern where he was engaged at dice with a young nobleman, and a dispute arising between them, and swords being called in to adjust their quarrel, the young man fell by the hand of the chevalier: his rage was now lost in fear for his own safety, and he exclaimed madly, that he was lost, ruined, and a dead man. I was the only one in the room with them; and approaching him, I told him if he would sign a draft for five hundred louis-d'ors, which I drew from my pocket, I would insure his safety: he immediately acquiesced, and I gloried in my success, till the reflection of a few moments told me how wrongly I had been acting, since I had no other means of securing him but by bringing him hither; and I could not steel my heart into being the villain to desert him, now he had paid me so liberally for his protection; I accordingly effected his escape, and I have secured my reward: but how shall we secure our own safety?'

"At length it was agreed that Theodore should take an oath, by which he imprecated vengeance on himself if ever he betrayed us, or our haunt; and that we each separately, in his presence, should bind ourselves by a solemn vow, to seek his life, if ever he was known, by the slightest insinuation, to disregard the oath by which he was restricted.

"He willingly agreed to this proposal, probably foreseeing that a refusal would have caused him to have been retained a prisoner amongst us for life; a plan which was first suggested by one of the banditti; but which Kroonzer feared to adopt, knowing that if by any means the haunt should be detected by the officers of justice, the finding a man of rank imprisoned in it, would be an unsurmountable evidence against them on their trial.

"A short time after, on the promise of three hundred louis-d'ors from the chevalier, in addition to the sum Kroonzer had already received, he again set out for Paris, in order to gain intelligence of Theodore's antagonist; and on his return, brought information that the wound had not proved mortal, and that the young nobleman was in a fair way of recovery.

"Theodore immediately left us, and we heard no more of him till three days before your being brought to the decayed castle. It was one night about this time, that the man who held the night watch gave the alarm, having seen, as he said, a man on horseback riding amongst the ruins: the banditti, to whom every unknown person wore the dread appearance of a spy, or officer of justice, immediately prepared themselves for defence; but a few minutes eased their doubts, by their hearing the voice of the chevalier in the hall of the castle.

"Kroonzer then first lamented that he had not interdicted to him their haunt; but still a prey to interest, he again consented to serve him, and Theodore departed before day-break.

"On his departure, Kroonzer informed us that Theodore had bought him, by one thousand louis-d'ors, to secrete in the castle his sister, who, he said, had formed an engagement with a man much her inferior in life, and which he meant to prevent from taking place, by immuring her in a convent, when he had found one suited to his wishes; but should in the mean time leave her with us, judging it expedient immediately to carry her away from her paramour.

"Kroonzer had promised to fetch this supposed sister, whom he had been told to treat with the greatest kindness, and requested me to be his companion in the expedition.

"The story told by Theodore had appeared to me plausible, and his conduct by no means improper: I accordingly consented, and another of the banditti was chosen to attend us;

and at the appointed time, having disguised ourselves, we set out on our journey in an old carriage which had been left in the castle before any of the banditti had known it, and in which we carried provision to supply us on our journey.

"We stopped only twice for a short space of time; the first inn Kroonzer did not like, being in too public a situation: accordingly we proceeded to the cottage where you remained an entire day, and bargained with its owner for our admittance on our return, for he had already been cautioned by Theodore against travelling in the day:—as to the second inn, as he proposed staying at it only a short time on his return, and that in the dead of the night, he paid little attention to its situation.

"We proceeded to the spot where Kroonzer had agreed to meet the chevalier; a tap at the window was the signal to the little girl who attended you to give the alarm of fire, and then open the door to the chevalier under the pretence of running out to call for assistance; we entered, and when you fainted in our arms, we immediately carried you to the vehicle by which our companion was waiting for us at a short distance from your cottage; he entered it with you, and Kroonzer and myself mounted the horses and drove on. Your dress, and the cottage in which we found you, so ill suited to the character of the chevalier's sister, first raised suspicions in us of the truth of what Theodore had told us; but he laughed at our scruples, and explained them away, though I must confess not very satisfactorily either to Kroonzer or myself.

"At the little inn where we first stopped, a plausible story, told by Kroonzer, lulled the curiosity awakened in the host and his guests by our appearance; and at the retired cottage of old Bartha we did not think it necessary to render any account of our actions."

Lauretta could not here forbear interrupting her father to inquire, why Kroonzer, since he had no design upon her life, had drawn his sword, on her supplicating the pity of him who had been her companion in the carriage?

Count Byroff informed her, that it had been drawn by him as a tacit threat to his companion, to prevent his informing her of her destination, which had been particularly forbidden by the chevalier, and which he had not yet had an opportunity of imparting to his comrade.

"After we left this inn," continued the count, "we became your companions; and our comrade, the driver, having fastened our third horse to the back of the vehicle, and being arrived at Bartha's cottage, we sent our companion forward upon it to the castle to prepare for your reception, which had been forgotten by Kroonzer in the hurry of his setting out.

"The vehicle so long disused had been so shattered by the journey, the greatest part of which lay, as you must have remarked, over uneven ground, that we thought it unsafe to proceed farther in it; and accordingly, whilst you were in the cottage, we carried it into the middle of a neighbouring wood, where we left it, and returned with the horses to the cottage: — our journey from thence to the castle I need not repeat."

"It was doubtless, then," said Lauretta, "one of the banditti whom I saw enter a door in the hall of the castle, and whose appearance so much alarmed me, from my conjecturing him to have been Theodore?"

"It was," replied the count; "he knew not that we were returned, and having unguardedly entered the hall, made a precipitate retreat on seeing us; for we had determined, if possible, not to let you suppose the castle inhabited, that in case of your escaping from us, or hereafter, by any means, mixing again with the world, you might have no clue for suspecting those on whom your anger would have fallen to be concealed in a nest of deserted ruins."

"Who were those persons that approached my prison door on the second night of my confinement?" asked Lauretta.

"Some of the banditti," answered count Byroff, "who having been out for nearly three days on an expedition of plunder, knew not where you were lodged, and were proceeding to hide what they had acquired in a secret closet in the apartment where you were confined, but were immediately recalled by Kroonzer."

Thus was the perplexing mystery of Theodore's villainy, and Lauretta's fears, explained away. Lauretta heard it all with wonder and secret satisfaction at the evils she had escaped. Count Byroff paused in silence, while his daughter offered up a short but heart-dictated thanksgiving to the power who had given her fortitude to bear up under her sufferings, and rewarded her confidence in him by his benign interposition: he then proceeded to inform her, how he had discovered her to be his child.

"You must recollect, that on your recovering from the swoon into which you fell in the hall of the castle, and finding yourself on the bed in the prison, you supplicated my protection: it was at that moment that your voice and features struck me, as bearing a strong resemblance to those of your deceased mother, when, on the last night I ever beheld her, she upbraided me with being the supposed murderer of count Frederic Cohenburg; but not knowing that she had ever borne a child, I could only wonder at so strong a resemblance between two persons whom I could not for an instant suppose to be connected by the most distant ties of blood, and I endeavoured to forget it.

"Kroonzer took upon himself the office of attending you; I wished it had been assigned to me; but as I could give no reason that would have appeared satisfactory to the banditti for asking to share it with him, I forebore to express my thoughts.

"On the morning of your escape from the castle, through the chasm in the wall of your prison made by the lightning, I was the first who discovered that you were gone."

Lauretta here interrupted her father, to remark to Alphonsus her providential escape with life in falling from so great a height; but count Byroff, smiling at the miraculous deliverance which she imagined she had experienced, explained to her, "that at that end of the castle which was inhabited by the banditti, stood seven towers, which rose gradually above each other, and that she had been confined in the lowest of these, the floor of which was not above three feet raised from the ground.

"None of the banditti in the retired parts of the building heard the falling of the wall: the one who had the watch in the hall of the castle heard the rumbling of falling stones, but it was so customary a sound amongst those decayed walls, which continually were crumbling on every slight shock of the weather, that he did not attend to it.

"Morning was far advanced, when passing by the turret in a short ramble I was taking for the benefit of the air, I perceived what had occurred; and entering to look whether you were still there, though I was well convinced I could not expect to find you, the cross which is now on your neck, and which from the figures carved upon it, I instantly recollected to be that I had given your mother, caught my eye, and so forcibly did this circumstance strengthen my belief, that I had not been deceived in imagining that I had discovered in you a likeness to my lost Lauretta, that I no longer hesitated to pronounce you her daughter, and count Frederic Cohenburg your father.

"Convinced as I now was that you was the offspring of my lost wife, and conscious that she could not have been a sufficient time from me to have borne a son of Theodore's age, even if his name, and Kroonzer's knowledge of his family, had not baffled the supposition, I immediately again began to doubt the veracity of the tale Theodore had related concerning you, but resolved to conceal my thoughts till Theodore's future conduct should elucidate the truth of this mystery; I accordingly concealed the cross in my bosom, and proceeded to inform Kroonzer of your escape.

"Kroonzer heard my intelligence with sorrow, and alarm for the community, upon whom his temerity in introducing Theodore to a knowledge of their haunt, might bring the worst of consequences, provided you were not regained, and Theodore took measures of vengeance against Kroonzer for his negligence, as he might deem it, in suffering you to escape.

"Horsemen were immediately sent out in pursuit of you, but no success attended their endeavours: the following evening Theodore arrived; disappointment rendered him almost frantic, and he himself went in search of you, still solemnly vowing you were his sister.

"Thus passed on several days, the banditti continually going out by turns in pursuit of you, and again returning unsuccessful to receive fresh orders from Kroonzer or Theodore, one of whom remained constantly at the castle.

"At length one of the banditti, who had been out disguised, brought intelligence, that a peasant whom he had questioned, had told him, that on the very day you had escaped from the castle he had seen the old hermit, who lived on the skirts of the forest, leading a female to his cell.

"Theodore had before this commanded the most secure place about the castle to be prepared for your reception, in case you should be retaken by him; and Kroonzer had prepared what was by the banditti called the cavern, and to which there was a communication from an apartment in the castle; accordingly having learned that it was in readiness to receive you, he took one of the banditti, and as all the horses were out with others of the fraternity on an expedition of plunder, set out on foot towards the hermitage.

"I resolved at once, if practicable, to ease my doubts, by informing myself whether you had any knowledge of my deceased wife; I accordingly followed them, and having stationed myself amidst some trees, close by which I knew they must pass in their return to the castle, provided they found you in the hermitage, I resolved at all risques to pronounce the name of my wife, supposing that if you had any knowledge of her, you must of course be acquainted with her name, and would on thus unexpectedly hearing it, utter some exclamation, from which I might gather what I so earnestly wished to learn; determining, if you were the child of my Lauretta, to befriend you for the sake of the love I had once borne her.

"Your answer thrilled my heart; it recalled to me more forcibly than before the recollection of her I had lost. Whilst Theodore was questioning you, I gained a stand opposite to the spot whence I had spoken to you, and when he rushed to the place from which the sound of my voice had proceeded, I rescued you from his accomplice, and then conducted you to the cavern, which, as having been the place mentioned by Theodore himself, I thought least likely for him to suppose to be your present place of concealment, as he would imagine you taken from him almost by supernatural means.

"Without any suspicion of my having been absent, I arrived at the castle some time before Theodore, who had been delayed by the assistance he had been obliged to give to his companion before he could restore him to his senses: I grieved that I had so hardly used one who had never injured, or even offended me; but it was my only method of rescuing you, undiscovered; and the anxiety of the moment would, I fear, had necessity required it, have tempted me to have done more; I thank heaven that it did not.

"The dagger which you doubtless beheld on the table, I left you as a safeguard against the violence of Theodore, should he by any means have discovered your retreat, and have assailed your person.

"I had the watch that night; trembling I flew to you, and I returned hardly able to contain my joy, that I had preserved, unhoped for, unexpected, my own daughter!

"Again Theodore and the banditti scoured the country in search of you, and horrid was the vengeance Theodore denounced against your protectors.

"I ventured no more to visit you till I again held the watch, against which night I had prepared for our escape, which the eye of providence, regardful of suffering innocence, prospered with its blessing.

"I durst not impart to the banditti the discovery I had made, lest they should refuse their consent to my leaving them; and the alarm I yesterday testified during our day's journey, proceeded from my fear of their overtaking me, and separating me for ever from you; as Kroonzer yesterday morning, when he departed after the death of Theodore, refusing to hear me, bade me beware the vengeance due to a traitor. But," continued the count, "we will seek some retired spot where the secrecy to which my own safety at present enjoins me, will, I trust, be my safeguard against the threatened danger."

Here ended the eventful history of count Byroff, who, with the tear of parental affection starting in his eye, declared his sufferings overpaid by their having led him at last to find an angel he knew not to have been created; to whom he was bound by the most tender ties of nature, and in whose smiles and endearments he might forget to reflect on past calamities.

CHAPTER XXI.

————— — Let me be your servant:

— — — —I will follow thee,

To the last gasp, with truth and loyalty.

As You Like It

During the day our travellers continued to advance on their journey, and when towards evening they again stopped for the night, Alphonsus confessed himself so ill, as to be immediately obliged to retire to bed.

The exertions of body together with the coldness of the air on the night of his leaving Smaldart castle, in conjunction with the precipitate and violent changes from grief to joy which his mind had been lately undergoing, added to his endeavours for the last day and night of concealing that he was otherwise than well, in order to expedite their journey, and the safety of his Lauretta's father, had reduced him to a state of great danger; his fever was returning with increased violence, and with less strength on his part to combat against its attacks.

Such medical assistance as the village afforded, count Byroff made it his immediate business to procure: Lauretta and her father watched over him during the night, and the morning brought with it increased symptoms of danger.

Till the fifth day the violence of his fever had abated only for short intervals, and the physician had given but slender hopes of his recovery: he now pronounced his patient free from danger, at the same time warning the count and Lauretta, against any indulgence which might endanger a relapse.

Lauretta had hitherto been the constant nurse of her husband, insomuch that count Byroff, moved by her entreaties to suffer her to remain with him she most loved, had, with no little alarm for her own safety, now seen her pass five nights without sleep, and an equal number of days without having retired above two hours together from her husband's chamber, which she had always passed rather in prayers for his amendment, than in attempts to enjoy that repose of which she stood so much in need for the preservation of her own health.

On the pleasing change however in the fate of Alphonsus, he had rather commanded than prevailed with her to retire regularly for the night, having promised to be himself the nurse of Alphonsus during her slumbers; and if any material change took place in him, to bring her immediate intelligence of it.

Lauretta had not been long retired, when Alphonsus requiring some drink which was preparing by the hostess, the count went down to fetch it: as he was descending the stairs, he heard a confused noise of talking and laughing, which ceasing at momentary intervals, rendered audible the voice of a person whose lamentations seemed to produce the laughter of the hearers, and the words,"que le diable m'emporte, if I would not give all I am worth to be dead," followed by an ill restrained cry of the speaker, and a laugh, exaggerated beyond their feelings, on the part of the audience, brought him to the door of the kitchen. His attention, excited by what he had heard, was converted into no less astonishment, when, on his entering, a man, whose features the dim lamp hanging over the chimney had not at first suffered him to see distinctly, rising from his seat, and dropping from his hand a pot of wine, which he was just lifting to his mouth, ran up to him, and falling on his knees before him, clasped his arms round him, and exclaimed,"Oh, vous voila! vous voila!" he recognised the person of Jacques Perlet. — "He is crazy, he is mad," called out two or three of the by-standers, and again a loud laugh burst from every mouth.

Joy for some moments suspended the utterance of Jacques, and surprise that of the count; which silence the host misconstruing on the part of the count, advanced to rid him of his troublesome detainer, and for that purpose, seized with both his hands Jacques's left arm; this rough handling first recalled Jacques to his recollection, and immediately springing on his feet, he levelled a blow at the host for attempting to tear him from the count, which, had not the count arrested his arm, and thus prevented its full execution, might have proved of fatal consequences to the unwarranted interferer.

Those who laugh irrationally at trifles, laugh equally whoever is the cause; thus the whole merriment of the kitchen was now turned against the precipitately retreating landlord; but as ridicule has often produced valour in a breast which nature never implanted in it, the landlord, with a countenance which seemed in return for this raillery to wish every one present in his situation, with exactly his feelings (by no means a slender punishment), was advancing to the combat, when the count stepping between the combatants, explained in as few words as he could convey his meaning in, that the offender was

a person in whom he felt interest, and that he wished the
dispute to cease.

A smaller plea would have quieted the fury of the host; and
all Jacques wished for, was a moment for testifying the joy and
triumph he felt at again finding the count, which he did by a
loud huzzah, and exclaiming "that the count was the only good
man ever created, except his own father, who was dead."

The confusion of fists being ended, the confusion of tongues
ensued; Jacques stood on one side of the count, exclaiming
incoherently, "Ah, monsieur, how could you run away and not
take me with you? I am sure I would have been faithful to you:
you know I would.—I would not have staid there without you
for all the world; it was worse than the maudite Bastile:—well,
Dieu merci, I have found you now, and if ever I leave you again,
I wish my uncle and Kroonzer may both catch me the next
minute."—On the other side stood the host, who, regardless of
Jacques's ejaculation, contended to relate, that Jacques had
arrived there on foot about two hours before, that he had
inquired for a person, by whom the host now found him to have
meant the count, whose dress he could not describe, and with
whom he had sometimes said he expected to find a lady;
sometimes a lady and a young man, and sometimes that he was
alone; in short, that he had talked so inconsistently, and so
much in French, that they had not understood above half what
he said, only that he had often mentioned the Bastile; that they
at last conjectured him to be mad, and when the count entered,
he confessed they had been amusing themselves at his expense,
till he had wept for vexation; added to this, the hostess, whose
voice was none of the softest, was continually interlarding her
husband's story with her own emendations and additions, and
no one else in the kitchen desisted from giving their own
opinion, whether it was attended to or not.

The count seized the first moment of silence, which many
attempts to articulate at length gained him from that part of his
audience by which he wished to be heard, to announce to the
host and hostess that Jacques was a person for whom he
entertained a warm friendship, and to desire that he might be
accommodated to his ease, making himself answerable for the
charge: he then turned to Jacques, and having easily convinced
him that he was under the necessity of leaving him to watch
over a sick friend, and with a caution to be careful what he said,
and promising to see him early in the morning, he returned to
the chamber of Alphonsus with the drink he had left it to
procure.

Count Byroff was far from being displeased at so unexpectedly again meeting with Jacques Perlet; he knew him to be faithfully attached to him, and promised himself that he would be a useful companion on their intended journey; that Jacques had contrived to escape from the banditti, after having effected it from the Bastile, could not much excite his wonder; but what chance had fortunately conducted him to the spot where he now was, his curiosity was raised to learn.

At an early hour Lauretta returned to the chamber of her husband; she found him fallen into a soft slumber: the count stole silently out of the room, and left his daughter to the willing task of watching over her Alphonsus.

Early as the hour was, Jacques was risen, and the count descending, found him waiting his arrival, seated on a bench without the door of the little inn, where he was practising his trade on his own shoes, which were a good deal the worse for the journey they had performed.

On seeing the count, he sprang from his seat, and shaking him by the hand with both his, reiterated his joy at their fortunate meeting: the count in return acknowledged the pleasure it gave him, and having told Jacques to resume his seat, and placed himself by his side, he began to inquire what accident had brought him to that spot.

"No accident at all, monsieur," replied Jacques, "but chance; as soon as I had got away from the old castle full of robbers, I resolved to walk all over the empire, and ask every body I met after you, till I found you; and you see, monsieur, what good fortune I have had, graces à Dieu; and I hope you won't send me away from you now, monsieur."

The count immediately eased his doubts on this head, and then proceeded to inform him of the occasion of his having left the banditti, and also gave him the outlines of such occurrences as had befallen him since their last meeting.

"Well, monsieur, and how do you think I got away from them?" cried Jacques, in return to the count's narrative.

"I know you have a ready invention," returned count Byroff, "but cannot possibly presume to guess in what manner you exercised it in effecting your escape."

"Then I'll tell you, monsieur: — when Kroonzer came back at night, and told us of Theodore's death, and that the lady was your daughter, some said one thing of you, and some another; however they all agreed that it was natural enough for you to go with your child, and that they believed you were too much a man of honour to betray them, after they had been so kind to you; so they resolved not to seek after you, or to hurt you, if you again fell into their hands. Well, monsieur, when I heard you were gone, I had a strange inclination to be gone too; but I durst not ask, for I thought perhaps they might not put so much trust in me as a man of honour, as they did in you, and would keep such a tight watch over me, that I might never get away from them at all; so I only pretended to cry, and be very unhappy, because I might never see you again; and I declared, that if you did not come back next day, I would kill myself: they only laughed at me, but, however, I knew what I was doing, and did not mind them a straw; next day I was quite melancholy, and at night they asked me, whether I would keep my word; I did not answer them, but went and threw myself on my bed, dressed as I was: when they were all asleep, I got up, and running past the man who had the watch in the hall, I made for the muddy pond on the west side of the castle, and having thrown in a great stone, a hat, and handkerchief, I climbed up, like a cat, into the top of the old willow that stands on its margin; presently several of the banditti came and dragged for me in the pond; the hat which they saw left them no room to doubt that I had thrown myself in, and not finding my body after some time searching, they concluded me sunk into the mud and smothered, and away they went neither pleased nor sorry at what had happened: when they were gone I came down from the tree, and ever since, monsieur, I have been wandering about, I hardly know where."

The physician arriving to attend his patient put an end to their conversation, as count Byroff rose to accompany him to the chamber of Alphonsus.

In the course of the day Jacques was introduced to the knowledge of Alphonsus and Lauretta, the former of whom received him as graciously as his situation would permit; the latter, in a transport of gratitude, as the sole means of her having ever known a father.

Alphonsus continued rapidly to regain his health and strength, and at the expiration of ten other days the physician pronounced him able to recommence his journey; our travellers accordingly, with the addition of Jacques to their former party, again set forward on their route, and no occurrence worthy of notice happened till their arrival at a solitary inn, which was situated in the road between Cohenburg castle, and the mansion of count Frederic, and about a league distant from each.

CHAPTER XXII.

How many things are there that the fancy makes terrible by
night, which the day turns into ridicule!

Seneca's Morals

Fortunately for Alphonsus, who wished not to be known,
the little inn had changed its inhabitants since he had last
visited it; thus no suspicion of their being any other than
common travellers was entertained by the landlord when they
entered his dwelling.

Shortly after their arrival Alphonsus took occasion to lead to
the subject on which his thoughts were unremittingly bent.

"That's a fine castle that stands about a league from hence,"
said he, addressing his host.

"Yes, sir," was the answer.

"Who inhabits it?"

"Nobody."

"To whom does it belong?"

"To the Cohenburg family."

"And why do they not reside in it?"

"Ah, sir! they are all dead but one poor gentleman, the
brother of him that used to live there, and he can no where find
rest for his guilty mind: folks say he is gone into a monastery to
repent of his sins, and make his peace with heaven."

"Of what crime is he accused?"

"Why, sir, I have not lived here long, but as I have heard
people say, count Frederic, the youngest brother, he that I now
speak of, and who used to live in a handsome mansion about a
league from hence to the left, and which is now inhabited by
one count Radvelt, was so jealous of his brother's castle and
riches, that he had him murdered by assassins in the Wolf's

Wood, in his return home to his castle, from Vienna; and then killed his brother's wife and son with his own hand. The matter was pretty well hushed up at first; it was given out that the countess had died of grief for the loss of her husband, and that her son had killed himself in a fit of madness: nobody much believed it, but as nobody had any proofs to the contrary, nothing durst be said; but the villain soon betrayed himself, for he staid at the castle but two or three days, and then went no one knows whither."

"And did he leave nobody in the castle?"

"No, sir, nobody; people do tell strange stories that it is haunted, and that he was frightened away by the ghost of the murdered count; and some say, that a bell is tolled by it every night at midnight."

"I have a strange curiosity to visit this castle."

"You had better not, sir."

"Why so, friend?"

"Why, sir, people think that the reason of the ghost's ringing the bell is, that it is shut up by priestcraft within the walls of the castle, and prevented from coming out; and that it tolls the bell to call somebody in, that it may reveal the murder of its body to them, and frighten them into promising to revenge its death. Nobody goes near the castle on that account."

Alphonsus pretended to smile at the tale related by his host, but it had an effect on his feelings which he could ill conceal: all his efforts to coerce the wish of immediately gratifying his curiosity he found to be in vain, and he declared to the count and Lauretta, that he felt an impulse he could not resist, to certify himself that night as to the tolling of the bell: in vain did they remonstrate, and endeavour to prevail with him not to leave the inn until the morning; but there was a resolute and anxious wildness in his countenance to follow the impulse he had described, which seemed to bid defiance to every objection.

The tears however of Lauretta, whose alarm was raised, she could hardly express on what account, to a pitch of agony, at the idea of Alphonsus that night approaching the castle, brought him to consent to defer his visit to the following day, on condition that if he could gain no light on the mystery which occupied his mind by traversing the castle, and examining his father's cabinet, she would not object to their there taking up their abode, which he declared would be an alleviation of his sorrows and perplexities.

After a sleepless night, Alphonsus rose to an uneasy morn; every the most minute circumstance attendant on the mystery wherein his happiness was involved, had been turned over in his thoughts during the night; and as heretofore, instead of deriving any clue of elucidation from reflection, the mystery had only thickened upon increased conjecture.

Again he felt scruples arising in his mind against opposing the injunction laid on him by his mother: again his doubts were lulled by the secrecy he had vowed to maintain, relative to any discovery he might make in the castle, which, notwithstanding the strong impulse he felt to visit it, reason seemed to contradict he should do; and then again he felt a momentary fear, for which he shuddered to account, that a snare might be spread for taking his life if he returned to the castle.

Judging it however most consistent with the faith he owed himself to go alone to the castle, he avowed his intention to his Lauretta, and resigning her after a fond embrace to the care of her father till his return, he departed, followed by the eyes of Lauretta till the intervening branches of the trees shut him from her sight.

Alphonsus rode swiftly forward, lost in a maze of fluctuating thought; at length taking a turn of the well-known road, Cohenburg castle burst full upon his sight; he beheld it with mingled sensations of melancholy pleasure, and awful apprehension. Crossing the moat, he proceeded to the stable from whence he had taken his steed on the morning on which he had last departed from the castle: fond remembrance was hasty to contrast the present gloom of desertion with former scenes of happier aspect;—recollection became too painful to be constrained, and burst its way from his eyes in burning drops of sorrow.

Having left his steed in the stable, he proceeded to the castle-gate; it was locked, and bade defiance to his repeated efforts to open it: he next attempted the postern-gate, it in like manner resisted his endeavours. He ran round the castle, gazing upon it in every part, and trying to recollect some window by which he might effect his entrance; he would not trust to recollection for believing them all too high, and too strongly barricaded to favour his attempts, but examined every one separately in the circuit of the castle.

Tortured by having his attempts thus baffled, he threw himself upon the ground in despair; in a few minutes, however, recollecting that inactivity could add little to forward his wishes, he rose from his situation, resolving to return to the inn, and ask advice of count Byroff how to proceed in his present dilemma. Once again he exerted his utmost endeavours to open the two gates, but they proved equally vain with his former efforts; he mounted his steed and returned to the inn.

Alphonsus immediately related his adventure, and opened a consultation with the count, on what steps were the best to be taken by him.

"Much deliberation," the count said, "seemed to be required on a subject of so delicate a nature: the gates of the castle being locked might be construed into an indication either of its being inhabited, or not being inhabited. If it was inhabited, the prevalent idea of its being deserted plainly proved it was the shelter of some person who wished to live in obscurity, and would, from this motive, perhaps, revenge the entrance of any one who dared to trespass on his retirement."

"How can he wish to live unknown?" cried Alphonsus, "who every night publicly announces his dwelling by tolling the castle bell?"

"Have you any proof of this?" said the count.

"The young miner, and now again our landlord, both assert that it is so."

"But they never heard it; nor likely any one who trembles while he relates it, has any authority for it but the dream of some old woman, who having talked all day of the occurrences at the castle, had seen them in her sleep in aggravated colours."

"I will certify myself in this point," returned Alphonsus, "before I proceed to any measures for entering the castle; I will watch the tolling of the bell this night."

After promising Lauretta that he would use no means for entering the castle that night, she consented that he should watch on the outside, in order to learn the truth of the story which had been related of the midnight bell, provided her father accompanied him; but as Alphonsus declared that he could not leave her at the inn with satisfaction to himself, unless the count remained with her, it was at length agreed that Jacques Perlet should be the companion of Alphonsus on his nightly expedition.

As Alphonsus was well aware that his going out in the night could not fail being known by the host, and excite his curiosity, he determined to inform him, that he meant to go and listen for the tolling of the singular bell he had mentioned to be sounded every night at the castle; the host, unsuspicious that Alphonsus meant more than his words conveyed, endeavoured to dissuade him from his purpose by all the arguments of blind superstition, and vulgar fear; and finding him resolute in his purpose, besought him to wear a little cross on his expedition, which, he said, "had belonged to his deceased wife, and which having been kissed by the pope, would secure him from the influence of the devil, and his fiends."

To avoid the imputation of obstinacy and irreligion, Alphonsus accepted the offer of the sacred cross, and placed it within his waistcoat.

At a little after ten Alphonsus and Jacques set out for the castle on foot.

Where flesh and blood were to be contended with by daylight, Jacques was no coward, but a breath of wind, or a shadow in a dark night, were great settlers of his valour. Count Byroff knowing his disposition, had not made him acquainted with any of the particulars which constituted Alphonsus' curiosity in regard to the bell which was sounded at the old castle; and as he fortunately had not heard of any dreadful appearance which had been seen in the vicinity of this building, he endeavoured all the way to keep up his courage by repeating to himself, "that the sound of a bell in the night could be no more than the sound of a bell in the day."

Alphonsus, wrapped in reflection, was not much disposed to converse, and they had proceeded nearly a third of the way without speaking, when Jacques suddenly exclaimed, "Do you hear it, monsieur?"

"What?" asked Alphonsus.

"The bell, monsieur?"

"We are yet too distant from the castle to catch the sound," returned Alphonsus.

"So I thought, monsieur:—that was the reason I asked."

Had Jacques spoken the truth, he would have confessed that he found it very melancholy to proceed so far in silence, and that he despaired of drawing Alphonsus into conversation by any other subject, than the one on which his thoughts were then bent; his stratagem, however, answered but little to his wishes, for Alphonsus again sunk into silent reflection.

"The moon will be up presently, monsieur, it begins to grow a little light already."

Alphonsus raised his eyes for a moment to the atmosphere, and again dropped them to their former situation.

"I wonder how many stars there are, monsieur: — did you ever count them?"

"No."

"Nor I, monsieur; — I wonder whether any body ever did?"

No answer was returned.

"I dare say there are more than a thousand in all; I am sure I can see five hundred to-night, and there are often as many more on a clear night; a'n't there, monsieur?"

"Of what?"

"Stars, monsieur."

Jacques now anxiously waited for a rejoinder, but his hopes were deceived. Alphonsus had spoken to the few words he had accidentally heard, without entering into the subject to which they belonged.

Now the silence had been once broken, its recommencement appeared more unpleasant to Jacques, than whilst it had remained totally uninterrupted; his tongue ached to relieve his eyes and ears, which were unremittingly looking out for shapeless monsters, and listening for uncouth sounds; singing and whistling by night he had heard ridiculed as betraying fear; and he could for some time think on no other expedient to divert the way; at last a lucky thought entered his head: "I think I'll try and count the stars myself, monsieur," he said, and immediately began counting, une, deux, trois, &c. passing them, as he pronounced the number, on his fingers: he chuckled at this happy expedient; it exercised both his eyes and tongue, and amused his hearing; thus passed on another third of the way;

Jacques never the nearer in his knowledge of the numeration of the heavenly bodies, but quite as near in reality as he wished to be. At last wearied by his employment, and not at all satisfied with hearing only his own voice, he desisted from his calculation, and lowered his eyes to the spot where he supposed to find Alphonsus walking by his side; but he was not there; for a few moments he stood motionless, then looking round on all sides, as far as the slender light of the faintly shining stars would permit him to carry his sight, and not beholding his companion, he ran straight forward in the path along which he supposed Alphonsus to have proceeded, as fast as he could move his legs, and attended by all the noise his overstrained voice could make.

Alphonsus, inattentive to every object but what was passing in his own mind, had insensibly passed his companion, whose pace had been retarded by his pretended studies, and had gained some ground upon him ere Jacques perceived his advance; now, however, roused from his reflections by Jacques' exclamations, he stopped for him, and they were quickly again united, to the no small satisfaction of one party; when an explanation of their parting took place on both sides, and Jacques determining not to let the conversation he had now raised, flag, asked Alphonsus "how many ghosts he had ever seen?"

"Not one," replied Alphonsus.

"Then you have seen one less than me, monsieur; and that's what always makes me afraid of being alone in the dark."

"Now I, on the contrary, should have supposed the dark to have been very agreeable to one of your credulous disposition."

"Why so, monsieur?"

"Because I should conceive that in it you could see neither objects to please nor alarm you."

"Oh dear, monsieur, how you talk! why ghosts always light themselves."

Alphonsus had not spirits either to rally Jacques on his false ideas, or to endeavour to correct them by the arguments of reason, and he remained silent.

Jacques had now a clue for conversation, and he chattered on about spirits, ghosts, and witches, to his own joint amusement and terror, till a few minutes brought them within sight of Cohenburg castle, and all his faculties were then absorbed in the use of his eyes.

They advanced within a few yards of the building to a small elevation of the turf, where Alphonsus proposed they should sit down, and wait the expected sound of the bell. The moon was breaking from under a retiring cloud, and, shedding her partial influence on the building, while its shadow fell upon the place which Alphonsus had chosen for his watching post, gave a pleasing yet melancholy aspect to the scene. It produced sensations in the mind of Jacques which he felt at a loss to explain, and after repeated hesitations how to express himself, he exclaimed, "Well, if ever I am to see another ghost, I am sure this is just the place I should expect to meet it in!"

"Folly!" cried Alphonsus: "how should you expect to see what never existed?"

"Mon Dieu, monsieur, how you talk! why all the priests in the world should not make me believe, I did not see one that time I was going to mention to you."

"Well, well, then you did," said Alphonsus, softened by the scene into reflections too dear to be easily shaken off, and wishing to prevent their farther interruption by coalescing in opinion with his companion.

"I thought you would believe me at last, monsieur," said Jacques, who flattered himself he had made a convert of Alphonsus: "I'll tell you the whole story,—may I, monsieur?"

"Oh yes," replied Alphonsus, thoroughly determined not to attend to it, and hoping, by this indulgence of his friend's garrulity, to free himself from the trouble of replying to his questions.

Having cast his eyes around, as a kind of security preparative to his dismal story, and moved a few inches nearer to Alphonsus, Jacques, thus began: "When I was about fifteen years old, monsieur, my father lived in a little village about a lieue from Desmartin, on the road to Paris; ours was a lonely little cottage, for it stood quite at the end of the village, and above a hundred paces distant from the next house; my grandmother was alive then, poor old soul, and she was as much afraid of a ghost as me; so one winter's evening, just before we went to bed, there comes a rap, or indeed it was more like a scratch at the door. 'Come in,' says my father; nobody answered, nor the door did not open; so my father bid me open it, and I did, but nobody was there to be seen; so as I thought it might be somebody that had a mind to frighten us, and had hid themselves behind the wood-stack at the corner of the house, I ran to look, for it was moon-light; and there I saw a man in black, kneeling down, without a head; and when I called out for help, he got up and ran away as fast as ever he could, and when he had got a little way off, his back looked as white as snow.

"Well, monsieur, frightened enough I was, as you may suppose, and so was my father, for he saw it too: and a little while after my grandmother died. 'Now the murder's out,' says my father: 'that was a warning of la bonne's death: we shall see no more ghosts now.' 'I hope not, I am sure,' said I; but he was wrong: for about a month after, one night when the wind was high, there was such a noise in the kitchen after we were gone to bed, that it waked us all, and in a minute or two the door between my father's chamber and mine burst open, as if le diable lui même had kicked it; then again we heard the noise in the kitchen, and in a few minutes came such a crash, as if the very roof had split over our heads; I covered myself with the bed clothes; father said he would go down and see what it was, when, just as he was getting out of bed, there was such a rustling on the stairs; and then it seemed to come into the chamber under the door, and all on a sudden a long, deep, hoarse, frightful . . . ." At this instant the bell in the south turret of the castle tolled several strokes, which sounded on the air hollow and dismal; Alphonsus started from his seat, and Jacques remained sitting on the turf in a state of fear scarcely a degree removed from petrifaction.

CHAPTER XXIII.

O, matter and impertinency mixt!

Reason in madness!

Lear

Count Byroff and Lauretta, eager to learn the result of Alphonsus's watching, had determined not to retire to rest till his return, which they imagined could not be later than an hour after midnight: however, he arrived not with the expected hour, and to add to their consternation, two o'clock brought back Jacques alone, with a countenance distorted by fear and anxiety.

Running up to count Byroff, he exclaimed, "Oh, monsieur, monsieur! the devils have got him; they have shut him up in that cursed old castle; I'd wager my life he never gets out again: pour l'amour de Dieu, let us raise the village here hard by, and pull down the walls."

Count Byroff could not be a moment at a loss to understand to whom he referred; but Lauretta, who had fainted, demanded his care prior to his asking an explanation of Jacques's words.

The landlord brought a glass of water to Lauretta. — "I told the young gentleman how it would be," he said, "if he would but have taken an old man's advice, and not have gone, he had been safe; I said there was no good in the spirits ringing that bell."

"I have seen three of them," returned Jacques, "as tall again as you or me, and all over as black as a crow, face, hands, and all."

"The virgin bless us all!" said the landlord, crossing himself, and raising his eyes to heaven.

In a few minutes Lauretta revived, — she flew to Jacques, — "Where is my Alphonsus? — is he in the castle? — answer me."

"Yes, locked in," replied Jacques; "but don't be afraid, madame: I dare say the ghosts don't mean to hurt him, for they are all gone away, and left him."

"Explain your words: what do you mean to convey by this inconsistent jargon? — Speak plainly, tell us every thing as it happened," said count Byroff.

"Why, monsieur, when the bell tolled —"

"Oh, then you have heard it; — aye, I knew I was right," interrupted the landlord.

"Oh yes, heard it, mon Dieu, I shall never forget it. When the bell tolled, monsieur Alphonsus said, he was sure then there must be somebody within the castle; and so he ran away to watch whether he could see a light in any part of the other side of the castle, and ordered me to keep my eye fixed on that opposite to which I was sitting. I sat still more than half an hour, and he did not come back: sometimes I ventured to look, and sometimes I did not: at last I saw him coming towards me; pleased enough was I, and I ran to meet him; he had seen nothing, no more had I. He said it was very odd, and he would only just try whether the gates were locked yet or not, and come back alone in the morning; and I told him I thought it would be much the best way. The great gate was locked: but when we came to a little gate at one end of the castle, it was partly open. He seemed very much surprised; and without saying any thing more to me, than bidding me wait for him where I was, and on no account to follow him, he ran in."

"In the dark?" said Lauretta.

"Yes, madame."

"He cannot be in any danger on that account," said count Byroff: "he doubtless knows every footstep about the castle."

"Angels guard him!" exclaimed Lauretta; the tears rolled swiftly down her cheeks.

"Go on," said the count to Jacques.

"Well, monsieur, I waited and waited, and he did not come back: I was frightened to stay very near the castle, so I went and sat myself down at a little distance opposite to the little gate, when presently out came the three black things I told you of, and — —"

"What things?" eagerly asked Lauretta, who had not heard Jacques mention them before.

"Why, madame, ghosts I am sure they were, for they stalked past where I was sitting, without speaking, and I could not hear them set a foot; and the last of them locked the gate as he came out, for I heard the key turn in the lock."

"Did you try whether it was locked?" asked the count.

"No, monsieur, I durst not go near it, for fear they should appear again, and take me to task for meddling; so when I had waited a good while longer, and monsieur Alphonsus did not come, I ran home to tell you what had happened; and a fine solitary walk I have had of it, monsieur; graces à Dieu, that I got here at all; — only feel how warm I am with running," continued he, turning to the host.

Count Byroff and Lauretta fixed their eyes on each other in silence, but both their countenances expressively asked the important question of what steps could be taken for the best.

They could ask no foreign assistance without betraying the secret which Alphonsus so strongly wished to remain unknown, and the mystery attendant on which he might at the very moment be solving.

The determination of one moment, the reflection of the next rejected. Lauretta was suffering on the rack of apprehension, and count Byroff was tortured by the agony he perceived his child enduring.

In little more than an hour, a loud knock at the door called out the landlord; Alphonsus rushed in, and threw himself upon a seat, regardless of surrounding objects.

Neither the congratulations of Jacques on his safe return, nor the caresses of his Lauretta, could for some moments obtain even a look in return: a frantic wildness was depicted on his countenance, and his stretched eyes were fixed on vacancy.

Count Byroff requested the landlord and Jacques to retire, they reluctantly complied with his petition.

"Oh, Alphonsus!" said Lauretta, throwing herself on his neck, "what new affliction has happened to you? — what aggravated sorrow is it, that deprives you of the power of teaching me to sympathise in your grief? — Tell me, I beseech you! 'twere mitigation of the agony I now experience, to share with you the most complicated misery."

Alphonsus answered her not.

Sinking on her knees, she clasped his;—"Speak, I conjure you, if you love me: ease these cruel fears: what can I do to serve you?—Name what you wish, and you shall find me ready to obey you."

Springing from her side, "Hate me," he exclaimed with increasing wildness, "hate me! I know you will,—you must hate me."

"Never! witness heaven!—can you suppose so meanly of me, that accumulated misfortune shall win from me the regard of him I once have loved? The hard dealing of the world towards you, shall only strengthen my love for you; and if you still account it as worthy your possession as you once did, your loss shall be your gain."

"Oh that I were worthy of that treasure!" he cried: "but an angel's love like yours must draw down curses on a wretch, whose disobedience to a mother's last command has called her from the silent grave!—Yes, I have seen her!—seen her honoured shade, come to upbraid me for my want of confidence in her commands; to scorch my eyes, and swell with tides of grief my heart-strings till they crack, and end the torture of this maddened brain!"—Again he sunk into the chair.

Lauretta wept, and count Byroff supported her in his arms. —"Oh, my foreboding heart!" she cried, "this danger I foresaw."

" 'Tis here," cried Alphonsus, again starting up; "here, hot and rankling: a parent's curse for disobedience, shot from the glaring eyes of death!"—He turned to Lauretta: his eye regained its wonted calmness.—"Do not you curse me too: I never disobeyed you; say, you will not."

"Have I not this instant conjured you to listen to my vows of love, of truth, of constancy?"

"But you may turn cruel."—The tears stole down his cheek. —"My mother was once kind, as you are now; and for one, one act of disobedience, though my rent heart could no longer exist in uncertainty, she has—Oh, had you seen her!" a sigh, drawn from the bottom of his heart, followed:—falling on his knees, he clasped Lauretta's hand, and pulled her down by him;—"Pray with me; pray to my mother for her forgiveness."—He clasped his hands, and seemed to pray inwardly some moments, whilst his countenance underwent various changes of frantic sorrow and pain: at length he exclaimed, "Oh! revoke, revoke—" The remainder of the sentence died on his tongue, and he fell to the ground.

Count Byroff immediately called in the assistance of Jacques, and Alphonsus was conveyed between them to a bed; and it was, for nearly an hour, a doubt to the count whether he lived or not: at length, when he again raised his eyelids, his eyes which had before betrayed the wildest frenzy, bespoke the most painful sorrow: he looked anxiously round the apartment, and discovering Lauretta, he beckoned eagerly to her; she flew to his side: he grasped her hand in his,—"Do not leave me! promise you will not leave me."

"Indeed I will not," she answered.

"Why are you not in bed?" he rejoined: "I have had so horrid a dream!—Oh!"

Lauretta turned her face aside to conceal her tears.

Alphonsus looked steadfastly on count Byroff:—"You here, my friend? and you too?" observing Jacques—"Did you hear me call out in my dream?"—He then seemed suddenly to observe that he was not undressed, and lying only on the outside of the bed; he looked round in surprise, and tacit inquiry of the cause: then, seeming to recollect himself, he started, a degree of wildness flashed in his eyes, and he exclaimed, "It was reality; it was no dream; would to God it had been!"

The night passed on mournfully: Alphonsus answered rationally, but in slow and despondent accents, to every question that bordered not upon the subject which tingled on his heart. Once count Byroff ventured to touch upon the tender chord; his words then became incoherent, and his gestures indicated a heated brain.

Lauretta became more affected, and count Byroff more alarmed. Jacques wept, prayed, consoled Lauretta, and advised the count by turns, not forgetting to whisper at intervals to the landlord, "that he was sure the black devils had done all the mischief." The host on his part entreated the count, that a friar might be sent for, to pray by Alphonsus, from the monastery of the Holy Spirit, which he said was not above half a league distant.

Alphonsus continued in the same state; and towards noon Lauretta entreated that the landlord's advice might be put in execution. Count Byroff had not much faith in the effect of prayer on a mind disordered by frenzy, but readily consented to the petition of his daughter; and the landlord offered himself to be their messenger to the monastery: some travellers, however, entering at the very moment the host was about to set out, he was obliged to delay going; but Lauretta's anxiety making every lost moment of consequence to the salvation of her husband, a little boy from the neighbouring village, who happened by chance to be passing by, was prevailed on by the promise of a trifling reward to show Jacques the road to the holy mansion.

In little more than an hour Jacques returned, accompanied by a brother of the monastery, who, in addition to his holy office, was skilled in the art of physic.

Count Byroff met him at the door of Alphonsus's apartment, and leading him to the bed, solely informed him, that the senses of the youth, for whom he requested his assistance, had been deranged by some recent and aggravated calamities, which his state of mind had rendered it impossible for him to explain.

The friar requested him to name what he thought to be the cause of his malady; count Byroff declared himself ignorant of it.

The holy man took Alphonsus's hand in one of his, and placed the fingers of the other on his pulse: Alphonsus raised his eyes, and fixing them steadfastly on the countenance of the friar for some moments, he exclaimed, "Who art thou! — Thy garb bespeaks thee a comforter: — dost thou bring me pardon? — Has she pronounced my forgiveness?"

"Compose thyself, my son: confide in heaven, and hope the best," was the answer.

"Shame, shame!" returned Alphonsus: "thou art a deceiver: thy outward garb speaks hope to wretchedness, and thy false tongue belies his expectations. — Away, away! in pity do not torture me."

Alphonsus placed his hand before his eyes, and sunk on his pillow. The friar turned to count Byroff and Lauretta; — "There is some concealed sense even in this seeming madness," he said; "has he been ever thus before?"

"Never," said Lauretta.

"The cause was sudden then?" said the holy man, addressing Lauretta.

"And unknown to us," she returned.

"I will lull awhile his imagination by a draught of a healing and composing nature, and trust its powers will add much to recall his wandering senses."

He then knelt, and prayed devoutly to the divine power to assist his earnest endeavours for the restitution of mental and bodily health to his patient. — Lauretta joined fervently in the prayer.

The friar then departed, and Jacques accompanied him to the monastery, to bring back the medicine he had recommended for Alphonsus.

CHAPTER XXIV.

Now o'er the one-half world

Nature seems dead, and wicked dreams abuse

The curtain'd sleep; now witchcraft celebrates

Pale Hecate's offerings, and wither'd murder,

Alarum'd by his sentinel, the wolf,

Whose howl's his watch, thus with his stealthy pace,

With Tarquin's ravishing strides, towards his design

Moves like a ghost.

Macbeth

When Jacques returned, count Byroff immediately saw by his countenance that he was brimful of some intelligence which he wished to communicate to him; and accordingly, a few minutes after he had left the chamber, he followed him out.

"Ah, monsieur," cried Jacques, on beholding him, "I am glad you are come down, I have got something so unaccountable to tell you, and I did not know whether I might mention it before madame."

"To what does it relate?" asked the count anxiously.

"Why, monsieur, you shall hear. When I got to the monastery, the old friar desired me to wait in the refectoire, in one corner of which was a door a little way open, and behind it I could hear glasses jingling, and people talking and laughing; so, when the friar was gone, I crept a little nearer to the door to listen what they were after, for my curiosity was a good deal raised, I must confess: when I first overheard them, one was telling a story about the pope, I fancy; for it was a man that they said was a good deal like an old woman, and the cardinals wished him dead; so when it was done, says another, 'Come, father Francisco, give us a toast.' 'I will,' says he: — 'Here's the ghost at the castle, and wishing it may ring as long as we all live.' Well, monsieur, they all laughed, and I could hear them pouring out the liquor, and then they repeated what father Francisco had said, and then I could hear them set down the empty glasses. 'I wonder where the young count is,' says another, after a minute or two's silence. 'Why, as to that,' said another—and just then I heard the old man coming back with the draught; so I stepped forward to meet him, and when I had got it he let me out, and so I heard no more."

Count Byroff having told Jacques to wait within Lauretta's call, walked out upon the green before the little inn, to indulge the reflections for which the conversation Jacques had overheard, had given him a subject.

It appeared to him evident beyond a doubt that the midnight bell at the castle was tolled by the friars belonging to the monastery of the Holy Spirit, as a confirmation of the castle's being haunted, which report they had probably been the first to circulate, to promote some private interest: thus he conceived also that the black figures which Jacques had seen issuing from the postern gate of the castle, were three of the fraternity, who had been to the castle for the purpose of raising the nightly alarm by sounding the bell, and were returning to the monastery when Jacques beheld them; that they had gone into the castle at first unseen by Alphonsus and Jacques, and the open gate by which the former had entered the castle had doubtless been left so by them, whilst they were in the castle, unsuspicious of any one having ventured to approach so near a place of such general horror as that building was described to be by all that knew it. But how was he to account for Alphonsus's excessive alarm, which could not have been produced by the appearance of three friars, if even he had seen them, which circumstances seemed to contradict that he had, or they him?—for his getting out of the castle, as Jacques had said that the last figure had locked the gate?—and above all for Alphonsus's assertion that he had seen his mother's shade?— Might it not have been the work of priestcraft? he asked himself; but his knowledge of Alphonsus's manly courage, which, though his eyes might have been a moment deceived by any false appearance, would have led him to have investigated the truth, ere he gave himself up to those feelings which alone could have reduced his faculties to the state he was now in, instantly contradicted the idea. Lengthened conjecture tended but to perplex him, and he determined, if the potion administered by father Nicholas had not the desired effect, at all hazards to himself to attempt the solution of the mystery which clouded the castle equally with the real cause of Alphonsus's present state of mind, by personal investigation.

The draught given by the friar was of a somnific nature, and in a short time after its being swallowed by Alphonsus, produced the intended effect.

Towards midnight count Byroff with much difficulty prevailed on Lauretta, who had not tasted rest the preceding night, to retire to bed.

With the dawn Alphonsus awoke; he raised himself on the bed, and drawing back the curtain, seemed to listen, — "Hark! — was it not she that spoke?"

"Who, my friend?" said count Byroff, advancing to the bed.

"My mother."

A pause ensued. — Count Byroff wished to pursue the discourse, but knew not in what manner to continue it.

"Will you go with me to the castle?" said Alphonsus.

"Why do you wish it? — Is she there?"

"Not now, I fear," replied Alphonsus, raising his eyes to the casement, as indicating that day-light was beginning to appear. "It was in the dead of the night that I saw her; did I not tell you that she had a burning lamp in her hand?"

"No."

"But she was dead: her cheeks were pale and sunk; my disobedience called her from the grave: I would fain see her once more, and kneel for her forgiveness: and would she then but calm her angry looks, I should die happy."

"Did she speak angrily to you?"

"I know not whether she spoke at all, my eyes and heart ached so I could not bear her sight; — feel how my temples beat even now."

Count Byroff raised his hand in compliance with Alphonsus's request; he grasped it. "Do not ask me to go to the castle; indeed I will not, I shall double my crime; I must not go, I dare not see her again. If you should see her, tell her —; but you will not see her; you have not disobeyed her; she will not frown on you; think you no more of it; I must bear with it." He hid his face on the pillow, and the count forebore to interrogate him farther on a subject which he saw was beginning to overpower him.

This short conversation, which tended not to enlighten the subject discussed, strengthened however count Byroff's resolution of visiting the castle on the first opportunity offered to him, and endeavouring to gain some light on this strange mystery.

A few hours after sunrise father Nicholas visited his patient; he pronounced him to have been much benefited by the composing draught, and gave the most encouraging hopes of a speedy amendment. Lauretta was not in the chamber when the holy man arrived, but being informed by Jacques that he was visiting her husband, she immediately entered the apartment, and eagerly inquired of him after the health of her Alphonsus.

The name seemed to produce a momentary surprise in the countenance of the friar, but immediately regaining his former composure, he answered to her inquiry: count Byroff alone perceived the effect which had been produced on father Nicholas, nor was he mistaken in imagining that the friar's a second time approaching the bed under pretence of feeling his patient's pulse, was an excuse for more closely investigating Alphonsus's features than he had yet done. Promising to visit his patient in the afternoon, and to bring with him such medicines as were necessary, the father left the chamber, and count Byroff accompanied him to the door of the inn, in order to prevent his holding any discourse with the landlord; and immediately on the old man's departure, he warned the host against acknowledging to any one that Alphonsus had visited the castle, being as yet uncertain whether benefit or harm to Alphonsus was to be expected from such an avowal.

Towards evening the friar returned. Alphonsus's mind was still in a state that baffled count Byroff's most ingenious attempt to draw from him the cause of his disorder. The friar seated himself by the side of the bed; he again inquired in a more exact manner than he had before done, whether they could form no remote conjecture of the cause of the malady under which his patient was labouring; he received the same answers from the count and Lauretta which had before been given him. He remained for some moments silent, his countenance by no means exhibiting a strong conviction of the veracity of their words. "Have you travelled far?" he then said.

"Many leagues," answered the count.

"And is the place whither you are going far from hence?"

"As soon as my friend is sufficiently recovered to proceed, he will determine our route."

"You are then on an excursion of pleasure!"

A slight inclination of the head on the part of count Byroff, was the answer to this demand.

Many other questions, answered with as little satisfaction to the friar's curiosity, were advanced by him, and he departed for the night.

Lauretta, who was not acquainted with the conversation which Jacques had overheard at the monastery, looked upon what the old man had said to have been dictated by a no more than common curiosity, excited by the situation of her husband; count Byroff, though he did not undeceive his daughter in this point, considered it in a very different light, and he even began to conceive that the solution of the mystery would prove count Frederic Cohenburg to have retired to the monastery of the Holy Spirit, to enjoy, unmolested, possessions criminally acquired. Still, however, as it was certain that if his conjecture was a true one, all the friars were privy to the plot, he saw no means of effecting the discovery but by ascertaining by whom the bell at the castle was nightly rung, and this he determined if possible to learn that very night.

The medicine last administered by the friar to Alphonsus, count Byroff perceived to possess the same quality, only in a less potent degree, as the former one he had taken, and this lessened his anxiety at the idea of leaving Lauretta for so long a space of time as was necessary to his purpose: he determined, however, not to inform her of the plan in agitation, and when she entreated him to retire in his turn for the night, which he well knew she would do, he pretended to comply with her request, on condition that Jacques might be her companion in watching over her husband. The landlord having provided him with a lantern, and implements for striking a light, reluctantly, as he trembled for the safety of the count, conducted him as far on his way as the intricacy of the road made it necessary for a stranger to have a guide; and then, with injunctions to secrecy on the part of the count, and prayers for the count's protection from evil spirits, on the part of the landlord, they parted, — the host returning home, and count Byroff proceeding along the road leading to the castle.

Count Byroff had advanced only a few yards when the distant sound of the bell fell on his ear; he regretted that necessity had obliged him to set out later than he had intended, but still resolving to pursue his enterprise, he proceeded forward with an increased speed.

Arrived at the castle, natural curiosity, which the shining moon favoured, induced him to eye it in every part as he walked round it, in search of the postern-gate: for an instant he thought he caught the glimmering of a light from a window in the second range of apartments; he stopped and looked, but it did not return, and he passed on, believing his imagination had deceived him.

At length he arrived at the postern-gate; it was shut; he pushed against it, and it yielded heavily to the pressure of his arm; he entered a few steps; he looked round; all was silence and darkness.

He stepped back without the gate, and having lighted the wick within his lantern, which he held in such a manner as to be able in an instant to conceal it in the skirts of a mantle which he wore over his shoulders, he again entered, and closed the gate after him as he had found it.

He proceeded along a vaulted passage, at the extremity of which a turn to the left conducted through a door into the great hall of the castle. He stepped forward a few paces, and raising his lantern, the better to view surrounding objects, nothing met his sight but cumbrous pillars of fluted marble, which were ranged on each side of the hall; and at the extremity, the dark iron-gates which seemed to form a blot in the azure-coloured wall. He turned himself round; facing the gates was a spacious flight of stairs, on each side of which was a high and narrow door; by one of them he had entered the hall.

He ascended the stairs; to the right and left lay an extensive gallery; he again held up his lantern, and directed his eyes first to the extremity of that on the right; he perceived doors on either side, and that it ended in a blank wall. He then turned to the left; the extent of the gallery was greater than that on the right, and as he viewed it, a figure seemed to flit quickly through the shade at the extremity.

He advanced swiftly along: at the end of the gallery was a turn to the right, which led, by the descent of a few steps, into another gallery, much resembling that he had just left: at the extremity of this a door, partly open, attracted his notice: hiding his lantern he looked in, and perceived that all was dark: he uncloaked his lantern, and entered a chamber richly furnished: there were no apparent signs of its having been lately inhabited, nor was there a second door in it: he returned to the gallery. The shutting of a door at some distance from him next attracted his attention; he could not determine exactly from what part of the castle the sound had proceeded, but he conjectured it to have issued from the gallery on the right of the flight of stairs which had conducted him from the hall: he followed the sound, and the gallery terminated, as the other had done, by a descent of a few steps into a passage of equal size.

After debating in his mind for some moments what plan to follow, he descended the steps: arrived at the end he found a door as on the other side: he used the same precaution with his lantern as he had before done, and was just grasping the handle of the door, with an intent to open it, when he heard a long groan, which seemed to be uttered by a person not far distant from him: he turned round his head; but nothing was to be seen: he was willing to imagine his senses had been deceived, and was again applying his hand to the door, when his action was arrested by what seemed a stifled shriek in the apartment to which that door led. He listened, the same kind of sound was twice more repeated; he was convinced that it had issued from behind the door, close by which he now stood. For a few moments all was still, and he was a third time on the point of entering, when several voices seemed to break out together into tones of supplication: his astonishment was now wound to a higher pitch than before: suddenly the voices changed their tones into the notes of a solemn chant; in this he immediately recognised the work of priests, and determining at once to unravel the mystery, with his lantern still concealed, he pushed open the door and entered.

Nearly opposite to where he had entered, was a small arched door-way, from which issued a faint light; he proceeded a few steps towards it, and on looking forward, immediately found that he was now in a small vestry behind the altar of a chapel, into which the arched door before him led. He ventured cautiously forward to a spot where he could command a view of the greater part of the chapel; at a short distance from the steps leading to the altar, knelt, by the side of a coffin, a figure of a pale and emaciated countenance, in whose left hand was a cross, and in the right a knotted cord.

On the other side of the coffin knelt three friars, who were singing the chant which count Byroff had heard begun, whilst standing by the outer door: the chant being finished, the friars crossed themselves, and began a prayer, in which they supplicated mercy for the guilty. Upon this the figure, whose sex the sable and loose garments it wore, tended not to declare, rose, and began to lash its shoulders with the cord, the pain occasioned by which caused it to send forth sounds of lamentation, such as the count had before heard: this done, the friars offered up another prayer, in which the penitent figure joined, and they then together left the chapel by a door opposite to the altar, taking with them a lamp which during their devotions had been placed on the coffin round which they had knelt.

All count Byroff's former plans of obstinate perseverance into the mystery in which the castle was enveloped, were put to flight by what he had seen: awe and reverence for the solemnity of the religious worship in which he had seen the friars and the suffering person engaged, whose salvation their prayers seemed meant to effect, had forbade him to interrupt their devotions; and when they were ended he felt an insurmountable objection to introducing himself to those who might have a right to dispute his unlicensed entrance into the castle, and refuse to attend to his excuse.

Some minutes were lost by him in reflection how to proceed, when he heard footsteps at a distance in the gallery; but they were no sooner heard, than they died away, and he doubted not, from what Jacques had told him he had seen on the night of his waiting without the castle for Alphonsus, that the friars were now departing; the shutting of a gate, with the sound of which the castle immediately after rang, confirmed him in his opinion.

He resolved to enter the chapel, and if possible, discover whither was gone the figure whom he had seen; for he strongly conceived, he knew not why, that it had not left the castle: as to who the figure was, his mind wavered between count Frederic, and the countess Anna; the former his own ideas taught him to believe it; but the words uttered by Alphonsus seemed to assign a degree of probability to its being the latter: arrived at the end of the chapel, he found that the door through which the persons he had just beheld had passed, was an iron grating; he pulled at it, but it resisted his efforts, being fastened by a spring, which he was not acquainted how to open. As he stood by it, a glimmering of light, at some distance, caught his eyes; he hid his lantern; the light advanced, and showed him that the iron gate led into a long and narrow passage; at the extremity of which, in a few seconds, appeared, bearing a lamp, the figure he had lately beheld in the chapel: it opened a door facing him, and having entered, immediately closed it, and all was again dark.

He again produced his lantern; but the door through which the figure had passed, was too far removed for him to distinguish it with the aid only of the light in his hand: he determined, however, if possible to find it; and, if he could, to address the person who had so strongly excited his attention and surprise.

After entering many chambers and passages in vain, a suite of rooms brought him to a chamber, from a door in which, a small closet, through which he passed, led him into the passage, at the extremity of which was the grated door from the chapel: he moved hastily to the other end, in search of the door by which the figure had vanished from his sight: the form of the wall was a semicircle, constituting, as he concluded, part of one of the turrets, of which there were four at the angles of the castle; but his most minute investigations could discover in it no door, or even crevice.

He placed his lantern on the ground, and for some time continued to pass his hands over every part of the wall, in the hope of discovering some clue to the object of his search; at length he imagined that he felt through the plaster a small elevation, which appeared to the touch like a flat hinge: he took up his lantern in order to examine the spot where he felt it, when, to his great disappointment, he perceived that his wick was dying out in the socket: he now found it necessary to return to the gallery as quickly as possible, whilst he had light to conduct him, lest from his being delayed a longer time than he wished, by searching his way in the dark, his absence should be learned by Lauretta, and add additional fears on his account, to her already too much afflicted mind: he accordingly precipitately retraced the path which had conducted him to this passage, and arrived in the gallery at the moment the last spark in his lantern became extinguished.

Day was fortunately for him beginning to dawn, and he easily descended into the hall, and gained, by recollecting his way, the postern gate, when, what had never occurred to him till he experienced it, the gate was locked, and thus all means of departing excluded from him.

He upbraided himself for not having forestalled the friars' departure, which, had he but considered the matter, Jacques's narrative of the occurrences of the night before the last had warned him to do; he returned to the hall, and attempted to open the great gates, but they baffled his endeavours; how had

Alphonsus got out after the departure of the friars? was a question he next asked himself, but he found it not less a difficult matter to answer this demand, than at the present moment to effect his escape.

All he now felt was anxiety for what Lauretta would experience, should she discover his absence, and learn whither he was gone.

Nearly two hours were spent by him in vain attempts to leave the castle, and unavailing lamentations; on a sudden he imagined he heard a key turn in the lock of the postern gate; he stopped a few seconds to listen; no sound followed it; and he almost feared his expectations to have been falsely raised; he determined, however, to ascertain the truth, and accordingly proceeded to the postern gate; it was partly open, his heart leaped with joy, and eagerly crossing the threshold, he set forward without stopping to consider by whom, or from what cause, the gate had been opened.

Arrived at the inn panting for breath, count Byroff instantly inquired of the landlord whether Lauretta had asked for him, and with much satisfaction he learned that she had not. The host had, by the count's desire, sat up till his return, and count Byroff having, in recompense for his complacency, satisfied his curiosity in regard to the tolling of the wonderful bell, they both retired to their respective apartments.

Count Byroff threw himself on the bed, and immediately began to re-examine in his mind the occurrences of which he had been a witness in the castle; and severely did he task himself for not having, at all hazards, aimed at a development of the mystery which it seemed so necessary to the welfare of those with whom he was concerned to have explained; and yet he conceived that he had but acted consistently with the respect due to religious offices.

Unable long to bear this contest of opinions within his own breast, on a matter of so great importance, and of so tender a nature, he entered the chamber of Alphonsus, who was still lulled by the soothing influence of the draught he had taken; Lauretta refused to retire to bed that night; Jacques readily accepted the offer of leaving for a few hours his post of watching.

The count determined not to impart to Lauretta his visit to the castle, as he wished to make one more attempt at solving the enigma, now more perplexing to him than ever, and which he feared her entreaties and alarm for his safety, were she acquainted with his intention, or even surmised it, might induce him to abandon.

It was some hours ere Alphonsus spoke, though he had been long awake: he then called Lauretta to him and embraced her; the tears ran down his cheeks. "Is the holy friar here?" he asked.

Lauretta answered, that she every moment expected his arrival.

"Would he were come!" continued Alphonsus. "I would unburden to him my heart: his counsel might relieve me, if his prayers and intercession cannot obtain my pardon."

"Am not I equally worthy the participation of your secret thoughts?" said Lauretta tenderly.

"Oh my Lauretta!" returned Alphonsus, "it is my love for you, that causes me to hide them from you."

"Do you then suppose that I am less moved to see you unhappy, than if you had acquainted me with all the particulars for your present anxiety?—Oh Alphonsus! can you believe my heart less feeling towards you, than yours has been to me?"

"You are too good, too kind," cried Alphonsus, "to one who, choked by melancholy and despair, has never given you a cheerful smile, in gratitude for those endearments, which have been his only comfort."

"Indeed you wrong yourself. I have been happy, very happy—witness heaven, very happy," said Lauretta, stifling her tears.

"I fear I have said too much," replied Alphonsus, looking steadfastly in her face; "I have already told you what afflicts me; have I not?"

"Forget it, I entreat you," answered Lauretta.

"Never! never!" he exclaimed. "My senses have been lately so disordered, that I scarcely know what has passed; did I tell you that I had seen my mother's shade?"

Lauretta was at a loss how to answer for the best: she looked at count Byroff for advice; she saw he was perplexed not less than herself; the door of the chamber opened, and father

Nicholas entered to their relief.

The father passed on to that side of the bed opposite to which Lauretta was standing; "A good and blessed day to thee, my son!" he said.

Alphonsus turned towards him, and said, "Wouldst thou indeed bless me?"

"Thou hast my most fervent prayers to heaven," returned the holy man.

"If thou hast my welfare at heart, thou wilt be secret, if I confess to thee my sorrows," said Alphonsus, with more composure than he had yet spoken.

"Secrecy is a bond of my office; speak freely my son and fear me not."

"Go to the castle of Cohenburg to-night; when the midnight bell has sounded, thou wilt find the postern gate open to thee: enter the chapel, and pray for me forgiveness for my disobedience, of my mother's shade: if thou seest her not, she will hear thee, for she inhabits there; tell her I repent my forbidden visit, though I have learned no secret by it; and if she refuse to pardon me, I will die to prove my penitence."

"Are you indeed the heir of Cohenburg castle?" said father Nicholas, surprise and pleasure mingling in his countenance.

"Oh no! no!" replied Alphonsus, "I am only the lost, abandoned, cursed Alphonsus."

"When did you visit the castle?" asked the friar.

"It was"—said Alphonsus:—he paused: "It was by night; but I cannot recollect whether last night, or not."

"It was two nights ago," said the count.

Lauretta had retired to the window; the friar went to her—"Are you the wife of this young man?"

"I am, father."

"Dry your tears, be comforted; happiness is yet in store for you."

"God grant your words be true."

"Trust to his mercy; through me he compassionates your afflictions."

He again approached the bed: "I will pray for you, my son; rest assured, and place faith in my endeavours;—I shall visit you again to-day; till then peace be with you: farewell."

He departed, and his words for some time occupied, in silent reflection, those he had left.

CHAPTER XXV.

There is but one, one only thing to think on,

My murder'd lord, and his dark gaping grave,

That waits unclos'd, impatient of my coming.

Rowe

Towards evening father Nicholas returned; he found Alphonsus risen: his health was materially restored; but his spirits were still depressed, and a degree of wildness was at times visible in his countenance.

"Didst thou know my mother?" said Alphonsus, first reverting to the subject on which all were thinking, but none had yet touched.

"Full well," returned the holy man. "Is it possible you do not recollect me?" continued he with some hesitation.

"No," replied Alphonsus, "no; and yet methinks that scar above your eye claims place in my remembrance; pardon me, that my harassed brain excludes all thought but on one subject; I pray you tell me your name."

"Father Nicholas, many years your mother's confessor."

"I know you now." He took his hand, pressed it in his, then kissed it. "You saw my mother then before she died?"—The friar hesitated to answer; Alphonsus perceived it not, and continued—"Did she wish again to see her son?"—The friar was still silent; Alphonsus went on, "You doubtless know my sad story?"

"I do."

"Oh! why did she discard me from her affections? wretched forlorn Alphonsus! my mother cruel! my father murdered!—Oh God! grant me to know his assassin!—Father, I have a vow in heaven of vengeance against his murderer, and here again I swear——"

The friar interrupted him, "Calm thy agitation, my son: thou canst not recall him into life by shedding another's blood; why then stain thy hands in murder?"

"Thou sayst true: heaven will avenge the deed better than I can; my hate and curses must fall on him.—Oh, if he must have fallen, would he had fallen by any hand rather than that he did!"

Father Nicholas sighed deeply.

"Who that knew him, could have believed that count Frederic would have murdered his brother?"

"If you believe he did, you wrong his memory."

"Is he too dead?—none left to bear a load of grief but me!—I recollect my mother told me, when she sent me from her, he was innocent; but she had first taught me to believe him guilty: —'twas strange!"

A pause ensued.

Suddenly recollecting himself, Alphonsus exclaimed, "If you can exculpate the innocent, you can arraign the guilty:—confess to me, I conjure you, whom I ought to hate; and guide my vengeance by your own discretion."

"Lay aside all thoughts of revenge; we are enjoined to be charitable to all; and who more strongly claims our pity, than he who suffers from the pangs of a conscience, that reproves him with the commission of murder?"

"It is a sentiment too refined to bias the heart of a son, bleeding at the recollection of a father's untimely death."

"The more severe our trials, the greater will be the reward bestowed on us, if amidst their severity we still do not deviate from the exercise of christian duty."

"If my mother knew the murderer!" Alphonsus exclaimed wildly, without having seemed to attend to father Nicholas's last words; and suddenly he interrupted himself—"Did she know him?" he added.

The holy man was silent.

"Say rather that she killed him,—burst my swelling heart, and end at once my agonies in death, than torture me by this mysterious hesitation."

The old man was affected to tears, by the transports of Alphonsus's feelings.—"Wouldst thou not rather that thy father lived, though thou couldst never see him more, than know him dead?" he asked.

"If he were happy, witness heaven, I would."

"And if thy absence from him constituted but his negative comfort, and even caused thy sorrow, hast thou enough of filial piety in thee to obey him?"

"Oh yes! on any terms, 'twere happiness to know he lived. But to what end avail these questions? I know he lives not, and yet you dazzle my imagination with ideas of what cannot be?"

"You once thought a mother had an equal claim on your obedience."

"Forbear, forbear to rack my heart, by telling me I wanted fortitude to obey her commands."

"Rouse your strength of mind to execute them now."

"What mean you?—explain yourself, I conjure you."

"Know then she lives,—but you must never see her more."

Alphonsus had till this moment been comparatively calm: —"Lives!" he re-echoed, in the most piercing accents; then falling on his knees, and raising his hands to heaven—"Angels of mercy, I thank you!—It was then her living self I saw; my disobedience did not call her from the grave. The eyes she fixed upon me, were not those of death.—Oh God, I thank thee!"—A flood of tears relieved his full heart, swelled with a multiplicity of indescribable sensations.

A general silence prevailed for some moments, when Alphonsus could again articulate, "May I not once more see her, —only once, to implore her forgiveness?" he said.

"You have her pardon; rest satisfied in that assurance," returned the friar.

"Tell me, then," cried Alphonsus, "tell me why she refuses again to behold me?—And hard, very hard as I feel the struggle between duty and inclination, I will not press to see her."

"There is a just cause for her refusal. I have her permission to reveal it to you; and much I think, when you have learnt it, you will no longer press your late entreaty."

"Speak it, I beseech you."

"Have you fortitude to hear a tale of horror, which is nearly related to yourself?"

"Oh yes: my heart has felt too much substantial misery, to sink beneath recited ills."

"I need not warn a wife to secrecy, on a point of tender interest to her husband," said the friar, raising his eyes to Lauretta, and then passing them on to count Byroff.

"Nor her father," said the count, "to act for the welfare of both."

The friar gently inclined his head, in token of his satisfaction, and thus began: — "On the death of your aunt, count Frederic's wife, the kind attentions which the goodness of your mother's heart inclined her to use towards his children, raised in the breast of your deceased father a suspicion that her regards were bestowed on his offspring from the love which she bore their father.

"How this unhappy suspicion ever gained way into his thoughts, I can no otherwise account for, than that the single foible of his nature was an inclination towards distrust; and I am certain that your uncle and mother were both innocent of the false imputation which your father laid on them.

"The three first years after the loss of his wife were sorrowfully marked to count Frederic by the death of his children; and, unable to remain in the midst of scenes which gave him such ample scope for poignant reflection, he resolved to travel. He visited Venice; and here chance introduced him to a lady who seemed to promise a reparation of the loss he had sustained; but a mercenary father doomed her to the arms of a man she disliked, who carried her away from Venice; and his repeated journeys and inquiries could never lead him to discover whither she had been conveyed."

The agitation here expressed by the count and Lauretta, induced the friar to break off his narrative, and inquire the cause of their emotions: count Byroff briefly explained it, to the great surprise of the friar, who in return informed them, that, after the count's departure from Venice, a report had been circulated by Arieno's servants, that count Byroff, having killed the son of a senator in a duel, had fled with his wife into Spain, to which kingdom count Frederic's researches after his Lauretta were then confined.

This, though a new instance of count Arieno's villainy, was but a slight one, and count Byroff requested the friar to proceed.

"Every return of your uncle into Germany refreshed your father's fears, which his absence had lulled: he perceived his brother to be a prey to grief, and as he always refused to explain what afflicted him, your father's suspicion grew stronger on the repeated refusals of your uncle to divulge his cause of sorrow.

"The last time your uncle returned, was with a resolution no longer to pursue a fruitless search after her he loved; and he retired to his own mansion, where he determined to live a recluse from the world, visiting only his brother's castle.

"Every visit continued to increase your father's secret suspicion; and although he was always present when count Frederic saw his wife, he worked himself into a persuasion that a criminal intercourse was actually subsisting between them. At length, no longer able to bear the torture of suspicion, he resolved to clear his doubts, convinced that he could not be more miserable than he now was, be the result of his stratagem what it might.

"He accordingly gave out that an affair of consequence called him to Vienna. It was a probable circumstance, and gained belief; the day prior to his departure, he visited his brother: he told him that he had a matter of the greatest importance to confide to him, and in which he must entreat his assistance, which count Frederic readily promised. Your father then required of him to swear that he would be secret, before he communicated to him the matter in question: to this your uncle at first objected, but after many entreaties on the part of your father, he gave his faith not to reveal to any one what he should impart to him. Your father then told him that he suspected the fidelity of his wife. — Count Frederic, as it is easy to suppose, showed marks of no small surprise at this intelligence. Your father immediately misconstrued his astonishment with secret satisfaction at his own sagacity and penetration. Count Frederic proceeded to inquire whom his brother supposed to be the paramour of your mother? 'Suffice it that I know him,' returned your father; 'what I have to require of you is, that during my absence you will endeavour to win my wife to your love, and inform me of your success on my return.'—Count Frederic remonstrated warmly against measures, from which he could not possibly conceive that any discovery or advantage could be derived; but your father was so earnest in his entreaties, that count Frederic at length yielded to make the experiment.

"On the following day, a fatal day to him, your father left his castle, and taking with him old Robert his faithful servant, they proceeded to the cottage of my sister, about five leagues north of Cohenburg castle. I was in the secret of your father's plan, and had, at his request, there provided for him a reception.

"For nearly two months, your unhappy mother was constrained to bear the blandishments and caresses which count Frederic unwillingly tempted her with; she complained in private to me, and I could only give her such consolation as I taught her to derive from the innocence of her own heart.

"Repeated letters did your uncle write to his brother, assuring him of the fidelity of his wife; and as a proof of her nice sense of honour, added, that no male visitor, except himself and me, had been admitted at the castle since his departure.

"These letters your father read with very opposite sentiments to what they were meant to produce in him.

"The period now arrived which he had determined should stamp his happiness or misery. Robert, as it had been preconcerted, returned to the castle with information of your father's having been assassinated in the Wolf's Wood in his return from Vienna; and the late conduct of your uncle represented him to your mother as the murderer of her husband."

"Oh!" exclaimed Alphonsus, "I remember well the accusation which she then alleged against him; 'twas then I swore to—"

"No more of that now," interrupted the holy man. "Hear the conclusion of thy parent's fate:—when count Frederic arrived at the castle, and you left him with your mother, she accused him with the murder of his brother on the pretensions of his late conduct to her; he denied the charge, again urged his pretended love for her, and departed.

"On the next day, as you doubtless recollect, he returned to the castle; he re-iterated his love; she knelt to him, and implored him to cease adding pangs to the agony he had already inflicted on her. At this instant, as your mother has since told me, you entered the apartment: — this explains to you one mystery which you could not solve.

"Unknown to any one, I that night introduced your father into his own castle; for, as you may well suppose, he had not believed that his brother had written to him true accounts of his wife, and had only acted this farce the more deeply to entrap her, while the close of this hazardous experiment lay with himself.

"In the middle of that night a noise in your mother's chamber alarmed her, — she shrieked; a voice which she immediately concluded to be count Frederic's addressed her in accents of familiar love; she sprang from the bed, as the person advanced towards it; he held her arm; she stretched out her other hand to a table near the bed, and grasping a dagger which she had lately worn to defend herself from count Frederic, should he have attempted force upon her person, and which she now believed him to be doing, she pierced him who held her to the heart.

"Till the dawn arose, she thought herself the murderer of count Frederic; but alas! she beheld her bleeding husband, killed by her own hand! Immediately the vow she had exacted from you recurred to her, and constituted no small part of her agony; for the mad state of her brain taught her to believe you would fulfil it. What followed that morning, you know better than myself."

"Oh, God!" cried Alphonsus, in accents that seemed to proceed from a frame whose every nerve was racked by agony, "'till now I never knew what misery was! Oh, ye pitying angels, bless my unhappy mother! — Forgive my erring father! — Oh, father! thou said'st well that I should no longer press to disobey my mother, when I knew the cause of her commands: — 'twere death to both to meet! — Oh, that vow!" Convulsed by pangs of sorrow he sunk upon count Byroff.

Recovering, he fixed his eyes on the friar: — "Oh, wretch! wretch! doomed to be cursed for parricide or perjury!" He inarticulately whispered, while sighs of agony partially choked his utterance.

"Comfort thee, my son: the church is able, and, I doubt not, will be willing to absolve thee from an oath of such a strange nature."

"Oh, her bloody hand! — methinks I see it now! — I would

have embraced her, but she forbade me." He paused. "Oh, horrible! I swore to murder her who gave me being." He shuddered. "Fool that I was to say that misery had shot at me her keenest shafts, ere I had heard this tale of woe; she has but one other in her quiver that can pierce me. I will not part from thee!" he exclaimed, flying to Lauretta, and clasping her to his bosom. He then turned to the friar:—"Go on, good father: I can hear any thing now; thou shouldst have blunted thus my senses long ago:—go on, I pray thee."

"I will briefly relate the sequel of my tale," returned the friar, with a look to count Byroff, which indicated that he feared to disobey the request of Alphonsus, and yet was apprehensive his senses were again perplexed. "At an early hour I was sent for by your mother; and frantic with grief she confessed to me her involuntary crime, and its consequences. Shortly after count Frederic arrived at the castle, the sad tidings were announced to him by me: never did I behold a man so agonised; he immediately declared to your mother the cause of his pretended love for her, and cursed himself for having been the blind instrument of his brother's jealousy and suspicion.

"The countess entreated me in the most supplicating terms to hide from the world the real means of her husband's death, and to circulate an immediate report of her death: to execute the latter, I was under the necessity of calling in the assistance of some of my brother friars, and we contrived by a pretended funeral to accomplish her wish; after this ceremony, as you was no where to be found, and that count Frederic declared himself determined to pass his future days in seclusion from the world, at the monastery of Saint Paul, the servants were discharged, and the gates of the castle locked.

"Your mother had during this interval been secreted in the apartment to which the secret door in the south turret leads. On the first night of the evacuation of the castle I visited your mother, whom I had constantly supplied with the little provision she had required, and she then told me, that she had formed a resolution of passing the sad remainder of her days in solitude in the castle. I reprobated this idea: but she was firm in her determination, and no arguments could divert her from her purpose.

"An empty coffin had been brought in pomp by means of Robert's adroitness from the Wolf's Wood; in this we contrived to deposit secretly your father's remains, and it was then placed in the vault beneath the chapel; but, by the earnest entreaties of the countess, again removed into the chapel: and by it she has every night since prayed, and inflicted on herself voluntary punishments."

"'Twas there I saw her,—methought she rose from the coffin when I beheld her!" cried Alphonsus.

"But the midnight bell—" said count Byroff.

"Was tolled by her," interrupted the friar, "for the double purpose of keeping idle visitants from the castle, under the idea of its being haunted, and to call to her two holy men of our monastery, who, by turns, together with myself, visited her every night to assist her prayers over the body of her husband."

"But you were not with her," said Alphonsus, "when I beheld her in the chapel."

"No: we had left the castle, but she remained praying by the coffin."

"How know you this?"

"She informed me, that on the night on which I now find you entered the castle, she had seen a man advance a few paces into the chapel, who on beholding her had fled away alarmed."

"Oh! the piercing recollection of that night!" cried Alphonsus. "Oh, what did I not then feel."

"How did you escape from the castle?" asked father Nicholas.

"Frenzy gave me strength to burst the window at the extremity of the hall, and through it I effected my flight."

"Count Frederic," continued the friar, "immediately retired to the monastery of Saint Paul, and did not long survive his brother. Ever since your father's death, the brethren of the Holy Spirit have, by your mother's permission, enjoyed the rents of the estate on which the castle stands, in recompense for their nightly visits, and the assistance of their prayers. I often entreated her to have you sought after, and restore you to your legal possessions: but a wild frenzy of alarm always forbade me to urge my petition, though she unremittingly grieved at the hard lot you were innocently suffering.

"Yesterday morning I visited her alone, for the purpose of informing her of my suspicions, drawn from the name I had heard you called by, and many words I had heard you let fall, of you, her son, being now in the vicinity of the castle."

"Was not your visit to the castle paid between the hours of three and four?" asked count Byroff.

The holy man answered that it was, and this explained to the count the means by which the postern gate had been opened to him.

Father Nicholas continued: — "In return for the information I brought her, she only entreated that you might not see her, scarcely, I believe, crediting what I told her I surmised relative to you; for her faculties have been impaired by her distress of mind. The words you this morning addressed to me confirmed my conjecture, and I again visited her this afternoon; she heard me, contrary to my expectation, with composure; wept when she learnt that you had beheld each other, still however thankful she had not known you; declared her intention of putting you in possession of your natural rights, by immediately departing from the castle; and above all entreated, that when I had related to you her unhappy story, you would confer on her the only proof of affection she could ever desire, or hope to receive from you, namely, your never attempting to see her more."

Alphonsus's spirits were exhausted even to infantile weakness; he seemed no longer to attend to the words of the friar; he urged no farther inquiry into this heart-rending business; but wept, and that without intermission.

The holy man advised that he should retire to rest, and endeavour to compose his spirits; he retired to bed, but without giving any signs that he knew what he did; he sunk on the pillow, and spoke no more that night.

Having addressed some words of comfort to Lauretta, who, except that she respired, existed not, or at least without a thought to bestow on any other object than her Alphonsus and his sorrows; and having told count Byroff that he was called away by an urgent concern, but would return in the morning as early as he was able, father Nicholas left the inn, bestowing a benediction on its inhabitants.

The night passed on in sorrowing silence, broken only by occasional comments on what they had heard from the friar, on the part of count Byroff and his daughter; and heart-drawn sighs on the part of Alphonsus.

The tenth hour of the morning had sounded ere the holy man arrived; he found Alphonsus fallen into a gentle slumber. Count Byroff and the friar had a copious topic for conversation; they indulged themselves in discussing it till Lauretta came to inform them that Alphonsus was awake, and had inquired for the father.

They ascended to his chamber. — "Father," said Alphonsus, on beholding the friar, "you did not tell me whither my unhappy mother was gone."

"When I left you last," replied the holy man, "she was still in Cohenburg castle; I have this night conveyed her to the convent of the Virgin Maria, seven leagues distant from hence, and whose votaries are not permitted, when they have once entered its walls, ever again to hold converse with the world."

"What said she at parting? — nothing which you were to repeat to me from her?"

"She bade me tell you, that her blessing would fall a curse upon you, — thus she forbore to speak it. She entreats your prayers, and that you will sometimes view with pity her resemblance."

The friar here put into Alphonsus's hand a small portrait of his mother.

Alphonsus gazed eagerly upon it, then kissed it. "Forgive her, heaven!" he exclaimed. A small ribbon was fastened to the picture; he tied it round his neck, and turned the face inward to his bosom. "Lie there in peace," he cried: "and, oh! may the shades of my dear father and mother hereafter unite in scenes of bliss, with all the warmth and tenderness their images are now connected in my heart."

CHAPTER XXVI.

But happy they! the happiest of their kind!

Whom gentler stars unite, and in one fate

Their hearts, their fortunes, and their beings blend.

Thomson

In the course of a few days Alphonsus's health and spirits were sufficiently restored to permit him to visit Cohenburg castle; by the care of father Nicholas, the coffin which contained the remains of the late count had been replaced in the vault; but still it required more fortitude than Alphonsus could at that time command, to enter, unmoved, the chapel, and the chamber in which his mother had so mysteriously addressed him on the morning of her sending him away from the castle.

As the castle had required but little preparation to render it fit for the reception of Alphonsus and his Lauretta, count Byroff and the friar had given the necessary orders to that purpose, which had been performed by the daughter of the landlord, and her husband, who resided in the village.

As for Jacques, from the first moment of his receiving the intelligence of Alphonsus's restoration to his rank and possessions, he could find time for nothing but congratulations alternately bestowed on the count, Alphonsus, and Lauretta; and when they would no longer listen to them, he congratulated himself by singing and dancing, every step he moved.

The landlord, on the first arrival of the travellers at his house, had been an attentive and pleasing host; but no sooner did he learn that the heir of Cohenburg castle was an inmate with him, than his attentions became so over-strained, that they lost the very effect of pleasing, they had so strongly possessed, when nothing more than ordinary was meant to be conveyed by them: he was in a bustle all day long, whether he had employment to occasion his being so or not: and, communicative as he had before naturally been, he now seemed to make it a point of politeness, hardly to answer the questions which were asked of him.

Visiting frequently the neighbouring village in his twofold character of priest and physician, father Nicholas was well acquainted with its inhabitants, and readily engaged in it such servants as were immediately necessary to Alphonsus's new establishment; at the same time using his most sedulous endeavours to allay that surprise which would naturally be excited, on the sudden appearance of the heir of the castle.

On the day after Alphonsus became an inhabitant of the castle, he received the congratulations of the brothers of the Holy Spirit in person; how closely their lips and hearts were in unison, deprived as they now were of the rents they had been so long enjoying, it is not perhaps quite fair too accurately to investigate, considering in how handsome a manner they outwardly comported themselves. Jacques stood laughing unobserved in the hall as they went out. "Ah mes amis, " he cried, "you drank the ghost's health just in time; plait à Dieu, you may never have the opportunity again."

Father Nicholas had immediately written to the bishop, stating the peculiarity of Alphonsus's unfortunate situation with regard to his oath, and entreating for him the utmost indulgence of the church; and absolution was readily obtained for him, on the obligation of his bestowing a sum of money on a convent of poor nuns, and undergoing a slight penance.

Alphonsus had resided nearly three months at Cohenburg castle, and the poignancy of reflection was beginning to be softened by scenes of domestic happiness, when Jacques one day abruptly entering the apartment, panting for breath, and hardly able to articulate, addressing himself to count Byroff, exclaimed, "Huzzah, monsieur! huzzah! graces à Dieu, we have not an enemy in the world now, but my uncle Perlet, and the Bastile."

Count Byroff eagerly inquired what occurrence had called forth such extraordinary signs of joy; but it was some time before Jacques could recover breath sufficient to answer: at length he said, "I'll tell you, monsieur: Kroonzer and all the rest of them are sent to the gallies."

"How have you heard this?" asked count Byroff. "Why, monsieur, I have just been as far as the little inn," (a very constant practice with Jacques, who had been in habits of great intimacy with the landlord since the time of his residing at his house) "and whom should I meet there, monsieur, but a man, a stranger; so the landlord asked him what news; and so he told us, that a gang of robbers had been discovered in an old castle, not a day's journey from Inspruck. You may think I knew pretty well where he meant, monsieur. 'How were they found out?' said I; so he told us, that a gentleman that was travelling that way, had been attacked by them, and that his servants had managed to take one of the banditti prisoner, who had confessed all their tricks, and that the gentleman had had them all taken up, and that they had been condemned by the emperor, to be sold for galley slaves, and sent to the Turks. I wish, de toute ma vie, they had been sent to the Bastile."

Count Byroff immediately took measures for inquiring into the truth of this report; and to the excessive delight of Jacques, who, since his escape from the banditti, had stood in great fear, though he had endeavoured to hide it, of being fetched back by them and punished for his desertion,—and to the no small though suppressed satisfaction of count Byroff, who, from the threatened vengeance of Kroonzer, had thought himself in rather an unpleasant predicament,—the report proved to be a true one.

About this time Alphonsus employed a person recommended to his confidence by father Nicholas, to pass over into Italy, and ascertain whether count Arieno was still in existence; intending, if he was alive, to visit Venice himself, together with his Lauretta, whom he looked upon as entitled to become the heiress of count Arieno's property; and that it became him on this account to make her known to her grandfather; but the messenger returned with information, that count Arieno having been proved to be an accomplice with another senator who had embezzled some part of the public revenue, he had died on the scaffold, and his entire property been confiscated to the state.

Thus the wretch whose life had been a disgrace to humanity, was punished by a death equally shocking to the feelings of civilization.

The countess Anna lived but a few months in the seclusion in which she had chosen to end her days, and little doubtful of her forgiveness in a happier state, for the commission of an involuntary crime, Alphonsus could not lament, that her sorrows on earth were ended.

Some years after this, an accident introduced to each other's sight Alphonsus and the baron Smaldart; time had softened the resentment the baron had, immediately on the death of the chevalier D'Aignon, borne to Alphonsus; and Alphonsus had long wished a reconciliation to take place. Thus, though neither party proposed it, both visibly promoted it; and it was effected to their mutual satisfaction.

Shortly after the baron accepted an invitation given him by Alphonsus to visit Cohenburg castle, and beheld a scene that called forth in him the tenderest feelings; Alphonsus and his Lauretta, living in the splendor of rank, yet deriving their comforts from domestic happiness; count Byroff revered by his son and daughter; beloved and caressed by their offspring; that offspring growing up in the sanctioned felicity of innocence, sweetened by the indulgence of a fond grandfather, the endearments of a doting mother, and the instructions of a father, competent to give them. "Learn, above all, my children," Alphonsus would often repeat to them, "to avoid suspicion; for as it is the source of crimes, it is also the worst of crimes, attaching itself with equal mischief to the guilty and the innocent; it is an endless pang to him who harbours it; for it dies only when he dies, and then too often leaves a curse on those that follow him; it is the influence of evil that breeds suspicion, the noble spirit of charity that subdues it!"

The End